THE LOEB CLASSICAL LIBRARY

FOUNDED BY JAMES LOEB

EDITED BY

G. P. GOOLD

LUCIAN

IV

LCL 162

LUCIAN

VOLUME IV

WITH AN ENGLISH TRANSLATION BY

A. M. HARMON

HARVARD UNIVERSITY PRESS
CAMBRIDGE, MASSACHUSETTS
LONDON, ENGLAND

First published 1925
Reprinted 1953, 1961, 1969, 1992, 1999

LOEB CLASSICAL LIBRARY® is a registered trademark
of the President and Fellows of Harvard College

ISBN 0-674-99179-6

Printed in Great Britain by St Edmundsbury Press Ltd,
Bury St Edmunds, Suffolk, on acid-free paper.
Bound by Hunter & Foulis Ltd, Edinburgh, Scotland.

CONTENTS

NOTE

In the constitution of this volume there are two departures from the order in which Lucian's writings are presented in the Codex Vaticanus 90. The *Asinus*, which there follows the *Menippus*, has been left out of this volume and relegated to the last; and *Pro Imaginibus*, which in the MS. is separated by six pieces from *Imagines*, has been brought forward and placed directly after it.

LIST OF LUCIAN'S WORKS

SHOWING THEIR DIVISION INTO VOLUMES IN THIS EDITION

LIST OF LUCIAN'S WORKS

THE WORKS OF LUCIAN

ANACHARSIS, OR ATHLETICS

Taking us back to the early sixth century, Lucian lets us listen to a conversation about Greek athletics between Solon, the Athenian lawgiver, and that legendary figure, the Scythian Anacharsis, who came to Greece in the quest of wisdom just as Solon himself had gone to Egypt and Lycurgus of Sparta to Crete.

K. G. Jacob, who tried to make out that Lucian was an ardent reformer, laid great stress on this dialogue as a tract designed to restore the importance of athletics in Greek education by recalling how much they meant in the good old days But Lucian, who in any case was no *laudator temporis acti*, says nothing of any significance elsewhere to indicate either that he thought athletics especially in need of reform or that he felt any particular interest in them ; and if the *Anacharsis* had been written for any such purpose, surely it would have ended with the conversion of the Scythian to the standpoint of the Greek.

Let us say rather that Lucian, who was especially interested in Anacharsis and Solon, as we see from his *Scythian*, wished, perhaps for the edification of an Athenian audience, to present them in conversation, and shrewdly picks athletics for their theme as that feature of Greek civilization which would be most striking and least intelligible to the foreigner, the ' child of Nature.'

The conversation takes place in the Lyceum at Athens The opening sentence assumes that Anacharsis has just been enquiring about something else, and now turns to a new topic.

ΑΝΑΧΑΡΣΙΣ Η ΠΕΡΙ ΓΥΜΝΑΣΙΩΝ

ΑΝΑΧΑΡΣΙΣ

1   Ταῦτα δὲ ὑμῖν, ὦ Σόλων, τίνος ἕνεκα οἱ νέοι
ποιοῦσιν; οἱ μὲν αὐτῶν περιπλεκόμενοι ἀλλήλους
ὑποσκελίζουσιν, οἱ δὲ ἄγχουσι καὶ λυγίζουσι καὶ
ἐν τῷ πηλῷ συναναφύρονται κυλινδούμενοι ὥσπερ
σύες. καίτοι κατ᾽ ἀρχὰς εὐθὺς ἀποδυσάμενοι—
ἑώρων γάρ—λίπα τε ἠλείψαντο καὶ κατέψησε
μάλα εἰρηνικῶς ἅτερος τὸν ἕτερον ἐν τῷ μέρει. μετὰ
δὲ οὐκ οἶδ᾽ ὅ τι παθόντες ὠθοῦσί τε ἀλλήλους συννενευκότες καὶ τὰ μέτωπα συναράττουσιν ὥσπερ
οἱ κριοί. καὶ ἦν ἰδοὺ ἀράμενος ἐκεινοσὶ τὸν ἕτερον
ἐκ τοῖν σκελοῖν ἀφῆκεν εἰς τὸ ἔδαφος, εἶτ᾽ ἐπικα-
ταπεσὼν ἀνακύπτειν οὐκ ἐᾷ, συνωθῶν κάτω εἰς
τὸν πηλόν· τέλος δὲ ἤδη περιπλέξας αὐτῷ τὰ
σκέλη κατὰ τὴν γαστέρα τὸν πῆχυν ὑποβαλὼν
τῷ λαιμῷ ἄγχει ἄθλιον, ὁ δὲ παρακροτεῖ εἰς
τὸν ὦμον, ἱκετεύων οἶμαι, ὡς μὴ τέλεον ἀποπνι-
γείη. καὶ οὐδὲ τοῦ ἐλαίου ἕνεκα φείδονται μὴ
μολύνεσθαι, ἀλλ᾽ ἀφανίσαντες τὸ χρῖσμα καὶ τοῦ
βορβόρου ἀναπλησθέντες ἐν ἱδρῶτι ἅμα πολλῷ

Available in photographs : ΓΝ.

2

ANACHARSIS, OR ATHLETICS

ANACHARSIS

AND why are your young men doing all this, Solon? Some of them, locked in each other's arms, are tripping one another up, while others are choking and twisting each other and grovelling together in the mud, wallowing like swine. Yet, in the beginning, as soon as they had taken their clothes off, they put oil on themselves and took turns at rubbing each other down very peacefully—I saw it. Since then, I do not know what has got into them that they push one another about with lowered heads and butt their foreheads together like rams. And see there! That man picked the other one up by the legs and threw him to the ground, then fell down upon him and will not let him get up, shoving him all down into the mud; and now, after winding his legs about his middle and putting his forearm underneath his throat, he is choking the poor fellow, who is slapping him sidewise on the shoulder, by way of begging off, I take it, so that he may not be strangled completely.[1] Even out of consideration for the oil, they do not avoid getting dirty; they rub off the ointment, plaster themselves with mud, mixed with streams of

[1] The under man is trying to break his opponent's hold, a "half Nelson," by striking him on the upper arm.

γέλωτα ἐμοὶ γοῦν παρέχουσιν ὥσπερ αἱ[1] ἐγχέλυες ἐκ τῶν χειρῶν διολισθαίνοντες.

2 Ἕτεροι δὲ ἐν τῷ αἰθρίῳ τῆς αὐλῆς τὸ αὐτὸ τοῦτο δρῶσιν, οὐκ ἐν πηλῷ οὗτοί γε, ἀλλὰ ψάμμον ταύτην βαθεῖαν ὑποβαλόμενοι ἐν τῷ ὀρύγματι πάττουσίν τε ἀλλήλους καὶ αὐτοὶ ἑκόντες ἐπαμῶνται τὴν κόνιν ἀλεκτρυόνων δίκην, ὡς ἀφυκτότεροι εἶεν ἐν ταῖς συμπλοκαῖς, οἶμαι, τῆς ψάμμου τὸν ὄλισθον ἀφαιρούσης καὶ βεβαιοτέραν ἐν ξηρῷ παρεχούσης τὴν ἀντίληψιν.

3 Οἱ δὲ ὀρθοστάδην κεκονιμένοι καὶ αὐτοὶ παίουσιν ἀλλήλους προσπεσόντες καὶ λακτίζουσιν. οὑτοσὶ γοῦν καὶ τοὺς ὀδόντας ἔοικεν ἀποπτύσειν ὁ κακοδαίμων, οὕτως αἵματος αὐτῷ καὶ ψάμμου ἀναπέπλησται τὸ στόμα, πύξ, ὡς ὁρᾷς, παταχθέντος εἰς τὴν γνάθον. ἀλλ' οὐδὲ ὁ ἄρχων οὑτοσὶ διίστησιν αὐτοὺς καὶ λύει τὴν μάχην—τεκμαίρομαι γὰρ τῇ πορφυρίδι τῶν ἀρχόντων τινὰ τοῦτον εἶναι—ὁ δὲ καὶ ἐποτρύνει καὶ τὸν πατάξαντα ἐπαινεῖ.

4 Ἄλλοι δὲ ἀλλαχόθι πάντες ἐγκονοῦσι καὶ ἀναπηδῶσιν ὥσπερ θέοντες ἐπὶ τοῦ αὐτοῦ μένοντες καὶ εἰς τὸ ἄνω συναλλόμενοι λακτίζουσιν τὸν ἀέρα.

5 Ταῦτα οὖν ἐθέλω εἰδέναι τίνος ἀγαθοῦ[2] ἂν εἴη ποιεῖν· ὡς ἔμοιγε μανίᾳ μᾶλλον ἐοικέναι δοκεῖ τὸ πρᾶγμα, καὶ οὐκ ἔστιν ὅστις ἂν ῥᾳδίως μεταπείσειέ με ὡς οὐ παραπαίουσιν οἱ ταῦτα δρῶντες.

[1] αἱ Jacobitz : οἱ MSS.
[2] ἀγαθοῦ vulg. : ἀγαθὸν MSS.

[1] "The exercise is that known in the modern gymnasium as 'knees up,' and is apparently the same as that described by Seneca (*Ep.* xv.) as the 'fuller's jump,' from its resemblance

sweat, and make themselves a laughing-stock, to me at least, by slipping through each other's hands like eels.

Another set is doing the same in the uncovered part of the court, though not in mud. They have a layer of deep sand under them in the pit, as you see, and not only besprinkle one another but of their own accord heap the dust on themselves like so many cockerels, in order that it may be harder to break away in the clinches, I suppose, because the sand takes off the slipperiness and affords a firmer grip on a dry surface.

Others, standing upright, themselves covered with dust, are attacking each other with blows and kicks. This one here looks as if he were going to spew out his teeth, unlucky man, his mouth is so full of blood and sand; he has had a blow on the jaw, as you see. But even the official there does not separate them and break up the fight—I assume from his purple cloak that he is one of the officials; on the contrary, he urges them on and praises the one who struck the blow.

Others in other places are all exerting themselves; they jump up and down as if they were running, but stay in the same place; and they spring high up and kick the air.[1]

I want to know, therefore, what good it can be to do all this, because to me at least the thing looks more like insanity than anything else, and nobody can easily convince me that men who act in that way are not out of their minds.

to the action of a fuller jumping up and down on the clothes in his tub." E. N. Gardiner, *Greek Athletic Sports and Festivals*, p. 296.

ΣΟΛΩΝ

6 Καὶ εἰκότως, ὦ Ἀνάχαρσι, τοιαῦτά σοι τὰ
γιγνόμενα φαίνεται, ξένα γε ὄντα καὶ πάμπολυ
τῶν Σκυθικῶν ἐθῶν ἀπάδοντα, καθάπερ καὶ ὑμῖν
πολλὰ εἰκὸς εἶναι μαθήματα καὶ ἐπιτηδεύματα
τοῖς Ἕλλησιν ἡμῖν ἀλλόκοτα εἶναι δόξαντα ἄν,
εἴ τις ἡμῶν ὥσπερ σὺ νῦν ἐπισταίη αὐτοῖς. πλὴν
ἀλλὰ θάρρει, ὦγαθέ· οὐ γὰρ μανία τὰ γιγνόμενά
ἐστιν οὐδ᾽ ἐφ᾽ ὕβρει οὗτοι παίουσιν ἀλλήλους καὶ
κυλίουσιν ἐν τῷ πηλῷ ἢ ἐπιπάττουσιν τὴν κόνιν,
ἀλλ᾽ ἔχει τινὰ χρείαν οὐκ ἀτερπῆ τὸ πρᾶγμα καὶ
ἀκμὴν οὐ μικρὰν ἐπάγει τοῖς σώμασιν· ἢν γοῦν
ἐνδιατρίψῃς, ὥσπερ οἶμαί σε ποιήσειν, τῇ Ἑλλάδι,
οὐκ εἰς μακρὰν εἷς καὶ αὐτὸς ἔσῃ τῶν πεπηλω-
μένων ἢ κεκονιμένων· οὕτω σοι τὸ πρᾶγμα ἡδύ τε
ἅμα καὶ λυσιτελὲς εἶναι δόξει.

ΑΝΑΧΑΡΣΙΣ

Ἄπαγε, ὦ Σόλων, ὑμῖν ταῦτα γένοιτο τὰ ὠφέ-
λιμα καὶ τερπνά, ἐμὲ δὲ εἴ τις ὑμῶν τοιοῦτό τι
διαθείη, εἴσεται ὡς οὐ μάτην παρεζώσμεθα τὸν
7 ἀκινάκην. ἀτὰρ εἰπέ μοι, τί ὄνομα ἔθεσθε τοῖς
γιγνομένοις, ἢ τί φῶμεν ποιεῖν αὐτούς;

ΣΟΛΩΝ

Ὁ μὲν χῶρος αὐτός, ὦ Ἀνάχαρσι, γυμνάσιον
ὑφ᾽ ἡμῶν ὀνομάζεται καὶ ἔστιν ἱερὸν Ἀπόλλωνος
τοῦ Λυκείου. καὶ τὸ ἄγαλμα δὲ αὐτοῦ ὁρᾷς, τὸν
ἐπὶ τῇ στήλῃ κεκλιμένον, τῇ ἀριστερᾷ μὲν τὸ
τόξον ἔχοντα, ἡ δεξιὰ δὲ ὑπὲρ τῆς κεφαλῆς ἀνα-

ANACHARSIS, OR ATHLETICS

SOLON

It is only natural, Anacharsis, that what they are doing should have that appearance to you, since it is unfamiliar and very much in contrast with Scythian customs. In like manner you yourselves probably have much in your education and training which would appear strange to us Greeks if one of us should look in upon it as you are doing now. But have no fear, my dear sir; it is not insanity, and it is not out of brutality that they strike one another and tumble each other in the mud, or sprinkle each other with dust. The thing has a certain usefulness, not unattended by pleasure, and it gives much strength to their bodies. As a matter of fact, if you stop for some time, as I think you will, in Greece, before long you yourself will be one of the muddy or dusty set ; so delightful and at the same time so profitable will the thing seem to you.

ANACHARSIS

Get out with you, Solon! You Greeks may have those benefits and pleasures. For my part, if one of you should treat me like that, he will find out that we do not carry these daggers at our belts for nothing! But tell me, what name do you give to these performances? What are we to say they are doing?

SOLON

The place itself, Anacharsis, we call a gymnasium, and it is consecrated to Lyceian Apollo; you see his statue—the figure leaning against the pillar, with the bow in his left hand; his right arm bent back above

7

κεκλασμένη ὥσπερ ἐκ καμάτου μακροῦ ἀναπαυό-
8   μενον δείκνυσι τὸν θεόν. τῶν γυμνασμάτων δὲ
τούτων τὸ μὲν ἐν τῷ πηλῷ ἐκεῖνο πάλη καλεῖται,
οἱ δ' ἐν τῇ κόνει παλαίουσι καὶ αὐτοί, τὸ δὲ παίειν
ἀλλήλους ὀρθοστάδην παγκρατιάζειν λέγομεν.
καὶ ἄλλα δὲ ἡμῖν ἐστι γυμνάσια τοιαῦτα πυγμῆς
καὶ δίσκου καὶ τοῦ ὑπεράλλεσθαι, ὧν ἁπάντων
ἀγῶνας προτίθεμεν, καὶ ὁ κρατήσας ἄριστος εἶναι
δοκεῖ τῶν καθ' αὑτὸν καὶ ἀναιρεῖται τὰ ἆθλα.

ΑΝΑΧΑΡΣΙΣ

9   Τὰ δὲ ἆθλα τίνα ὑμῖν ταῦτά ἐστιν;

ΣΟΛΩΝ

'Ολυμπίασι μὲν στέφανος ἐκ κοτίνου, 'Ισθμοῖ
δὲ ἐκ πίτυος, ἐν Νεμέᾳ δὲ σελίνων πεπλεγμένος,
Πυθοῖ δὲ μῆλα τῶν ἱερῶν τοῦ θεοῦ, παρ' ἡμῖν δὲ
τοῖς Παναθηναίοις τὸ ἔλαιον τὸ ἐκ τῆς μορίας.
τί ἐγέλασας, ὦ 'Ανάχαρσι; ἢ διότι μικρά σοι
εἶναι ταῦτα δοκεῖ;

ΑΝΑΧΑΡΣΙΣ

Οὔκ, ἀλλὰ πάνσεμνα, ὦ Σόλων, κατέλεξας τὰ
ἆθλα καὶ ἄξια τοῖς τε διαθεῖσιν αὐτὰ φιλοτιμεῖ-
σθαι ἐπὶ τῇ μεγαλοδωρεᾷ καὶ τοῖς ἀγωνισταῖς
αὐτοῖς ὑπερεσπουδακέναι περὶ τὴν ἀναίρεσιν τῶν

---

[1] Solon's statement is not quite full enough. The pancratium included not only boxing, but kicking and wrestling,
and was practised not only upright but on the ground. It
was a rough and tumble affair, in which only gouging and
biting were barred. Some, at least, of the wrestlers in the
mud were engaged, strictly speaking, in the pancratium, as
the choking and striking show.

his head indicates that the god is resting, as if after long exertion. As for these forms of athletics, that one yonder in the mud is called wrestling, and the men in the dust are wrestling too. When they stand upright and strike one another, we call it the pancratium.[1] We have other such athletic exercises, too—boxing, throwing the discus, and jumping— in all of which we hold contests, and the winner is considered best in his class and carries off the prizes.

ANACHARSIS

And these prizes of yours, what are they?

SOLON

At the Olympic games, a wreath made of wild olive, at the Isthmian one of pine, and at the Nemean one of parsley, at the Pythian some of the apples sacred to Apollo, and with us at the Panathenaea, the oil from the holy olive.[2] What made you laugh, Anacharsis? Because you think these prizes trivial?

ANACHARSIS

No, the prizes that you have told off are absolutely imposing, Solon; they may well cause those who have offered them to glory in their munificence and the contestants themselves to be tremendously eager

---

[2] The one planted on the Acropolis by Athena. As to the prize in the Pythia, it may have been apples before the re-organization of the games in 586. But in that year the competition had prizes "in kind," spoils of the Crisaean war (χρηματίτης ἀπὸ λαφύρων : Marmor Parium); and from 582 it was στεφανίτης, like the other three Panhellenic Festivals, with a wreath of laurel.

τηλικούτων, ὥστε μήλων ἕνεκα καὶ σελίνων τοσαῦτα προπονεῖν καὶ κινδυνεύειν ἀγχομένους πρὸς
ἀλλήλων καὶ κατακλωμένους, ὡς οὐκ ἐνὸν ἀπραγ-
μόνως εὐπορῆσαι μήλων ὅτῳ ἐπιθυμία ἢ σελίνῳ
ἐστεφανῶσθαι ἢ πίτυϊ μήτε πηλῷ καταχριόμενον
τὸ πρόσωπον μήτε λακτιζόμενον εἰς τὴν γαστέρα
ὑπὸ τῶν ἀνταγωνιστῶν.

ΣΟΛΩΝ

10 Ἀλλ', ὦ ἄριστε, οὐκ εἰς ψιλὰ τὰ διδόμενα
ἡμεῖς ἀποβλέπομεν. ταῦτα μὲν γάρ ἐστι σημεῖα
τῆς νίκης καὶ γνωρίσματα οἵτινες οἱ κρατήσαντες.
ἡ δὲ παρακολουθοῦσα τούτοις δόξα τοῦ παντὸς
ἀξία τοῖς νενικηκόσιν, ὑπὲρ ἧς καὶ λακτίζεσθαι
καλῶς ἔχει τοῖς θηρωμένοις τὴν εὔκλειαν ἐκ τῶν
πόνων. οὐ γὰρ ἀπονητὶ προσγένοιτο ἂν αὕτη,
ἀλλὰ χρὴ τὸν ὀρεγόμενον αὐτῆς πολλὰ τὰ δυσχερῆ
ἀνασχόμενον ἐν τῇ ἀρχῇ τότ' ἤδη τὸ λυσιτελὲς
καὶ ἡδὺ τέλος ἐκ τῶν καμάτων περιμένειν.

ΑΝΑΧΑΡΣΙΣ

Τοῦτο φῄς, ὦ Σόλων, τὸ τέλος ἡδὺ καὶ λυσι-
τελές, ὅτι πάντες αὐτοὺς ὄψονται ἐστεφανωμένους
καὶ ἐπὶ τῇ νίκῃ ἐπαινέσονται πολὺ πρότερον
οἰκτείραντες ἐπὶ ταῖς πληγαῖς, οἱ δὲ εὐδαιμονή-
σουσιν ἀντὶ τῶν πόνων μῆλα καὶ σέλινα ἔχοντες.

ΣΟΛΩΝ

Ἄπειρος εἶ, φημί, τῶν ἡμετέρων ἔτι· μετὰ
μικρὸν δὲ ἄλλα σοι δόξει περὶ αὐτῶν, ἐπειδὰν

to carry off such guerdons, so that they will go through all these preliminary hardships and risks, getting choked and broken in two by one another, for apples and parsley, as if it were not possible for anyone who wants them to get plenty of apples without any trouble, or to wear a wreath of parsley or of pine without having his face bedaubed with mud or letting himself be kicked in the belly by his opponent!

SOLON

But, my dear fellow, it is not the bare gifts that we have in view! They are merely tokens of the victory and marks to identify the winners. But the reputation that goes with them is worth everything to the victors, and to attain it, even to be kicked is nothing to men who seek to capture fame through hardships. Without hardships it cannot be acquired; the man who covets it must put up with many unpleasantnesses in the beginning before at last he can expect the profitable and delightful outcome of his exertions.

ANACHARSIS

By this delightful and profitable outcome, Solon, you mean that everybody will see them wearing wreaths and will applaud them for their victory after having pitied them a long time beforehand for their hard knocks, and that they will be felicitous to have apples and parsley in compensation for their hardships!

SOLON

You are still unacquainted with our ways, I tell you. After a little you will think differently about

εἰς τὰς πανηγύρεις ἀπιὼν ὁρᾷς τοσοῦτο πλῆθος
ἀνθρώπων συλλεγόμενον ἐπὶ τὴν θέαν τῶν τοιούτων καὶ θέατρα μυρίανδρα συμπληρούμενα καὶ
τοὺς ἀγωνιστὰς ἐπαινουμένους, τὸν δὲ καὶ νική-
σαντα αὐτῶν ἰσόθεον νομιζόμενον.

ΑΝΑΧΑΡΣΙΣ

11 Αὐτὸ τοῦτο, ὦ Σόλων, καὶ τὸ οἴκτιστόν ἐστιν,
εἰ μὴ ἐπ᾽ ὀλίγων ταῦτα πάσχουσιν, ἀλλὰ ἐν
τοσούτοις θεαταῖς καὶ μάρτυσι τῆς ὕβρεως, οἳ
δηλαδὴ εὐδαιμονίζουσιν αὐτοὺς αἵματι ῥαινομένους
ὁρῶντες ἢ ἀγχομένους ὑπὸ τῶν ἀντιπάλων· ταῦτα
γὰρ τὰ εὐδαιμονέστατα πρόσεστι τῇ νίκῃ αὐτῶν.
παρ᾽ ἡμῖν δὲ τοῖς Σκύθαις ἤν τις, ὦ Σόλων, ἢ
πατάξῃ τινὰ τῶν πολιτῶν ἢ ἀνατρέψῃ προσπεσὼν
ἢ θοἰμάτια περιρρήξῃ, μεγάλας οἱ πρεσβῦται τὰς
ζημίας ἐπάγουσι, κἂν ἐπ᾽ ὀλίγων μαρτύρων τοῦτο
πάθῃ τις, οὔτι γε ἐν τηλικούτοις θεάτροις, οἷα σὺ
διηγῇ τὸ Ἰσθμοῖ καὶ τὸ ἐν Ὀλυμπίᾳ. οὐ μὴν
ἀλλὰ τοὺς μὲν ἀγωνιστὰς οἰκτείρειν μοι ἔπεισιν
ὧν πάσχουσιν, τῶν δὲ θεατῶν οὓς φῂς ἀπανταχόθεν τοὺς ἀρίστους παραγίγνεσθαι εἰς τὰς πανηγύρεις καὶ πάνυ θαυμάζω, εἰ τἀναγκαῖα παρέντες
σχολάζουσιν ἐπὶ τοῖς τοιούτοις. οὐδὲ γὰρ ἐκεῖνό
πω δύναμαι κατανοῆσαι ὅ τι τὸ τερπνὸν αὐτοῖς,
ὁρᾶν παιομένους τε καὶ διαπληκτιζομένους ἀνθρώπους καὶ πρὸς τὴν γῆν ἀραττομένους καὶ συντρι-
βομένους ὑπ᾽ ἀλλήλων.

ΣΟΛΩΝ

12 Εἰ καιρὸς ἦν, ὦ Ἀνάχαρσι, Ὀλυμπίων ἢ
Ἰσθμίων ἢ Παναθηναίων, αὐτὸ ἄν σε τὸ γιγνό-

them, when you go to the games and see that great throng of people gathering to look at such spectacles, and amphitheatres filling that will hold thousands, and the contestants applauded, and the one among them who succeeds in winning counted equal to the gods.

ANACHARSIS

That is precisely the most pitiable part of it, Solon, if they undergo this treatment not before just a few but in the presence of so many spectators and witnesses of the brutality, who no doubt felicitate them on seeing them streaming with blood or getting strangled by their opponents; for these are the extreme felicities that go with their victory! With us Scythians, Solon, if anyone strikes a citizen, or assaults him and throws him down, or tears his clothing, the elders impose severe penalties upon him, even if the offence takes place before just a few witnesses, not to speak of such great assemblies as that at the Isthmus and that at Olympia which you describe. I assure you, I cannot help pitying the contestants for what they go through, and I am absolutely amazed at the spectators, the prominent men who come, you say, from all sides to the games, if they neglect their urgent business and fritter their time away in such matters. I cannot yet conceive what pleasure it is to them to see men struck, pummelled, dashed on the ground, and crushed by one another.

SOLON

If it were the time, Anacharsis, for the Olympic or the Isthmian or the Panathenaic games, what

μενον ἐδίδαξεν ὡς οὐ μάτην ἐσπουδάκαμεν ἐπὶ
τούτοις. οὐ γὰρ οὕτω λέγων ἄν τις προσβι-
βάσειέν σε τῇ ἡδονῇ τῶν ἐκεῖ δρωμένων, ὡς εἰ
καθεζόμενος αὐτὸς ἐν μέσοις τοῖς θεαταῖς βλέποις
ἀρετὰς ἀνδρῶν καὶ κάλλη σωμάτων καὶ εὐεξίας
θαυμαστὰς καὶ ἐμπειρίας δεινὰς καὶ ἰσχὺν ἄμαχον
καὶ τόλμαν καὶ φιλοτιμίαν καὶ γνώμας ἀηττήτους
καὶ σπουδὴν ἄλεκτον ὑπὲρ τῆς νίκης. εὖ γὰρ δὴ
οἶδα ὡς οὐκ ἂν ἐπαύσω ἐπαινῶν καὶ ἐπιβοῶν καὶ
ἐπικροτῶν.

ΑΝΑΧΑΡΣΙΣ

13 Νὴ Δί', ὦ Σόλων, καὶ ἐπιγελῶν γε προσέτι καὶ
ἐπιχλευάζων· ἅπαντα γὰρ ὁπόσα κατηριθμήσω
ἐκεῖνα, τὰς ἀρετὰς καὶ τὰς εὐεξίας καὶ τὰ κάλλη
καὶ τόλμαν, ὁρῶ οὐδενὸς μεγάλου ἕνεκα παραπ-
ολλυμένας ὑμῖν, οὔτε πατρίδος κινδυνευούσης
οὔτε χώρας πορθουμένης οὔτε φίλων ἢ οἰκείων
πρὸς ὕβριν ἀπαγομένων. ὥστε τοσούτῳ γελοιό-
τεροι ἂν εἶεν, ἄριστοι μέν, ὡς φής, ὄντες, μάτην
δὲ τοσαῦτα πάσχοντες καὶ ταλαιπωρούμενοι καὶ
αἰσχύνοντες τὰ κάλλη καὶ τὰ μεγέθη τῇ ψάμμῳ
καὶ τοῖς ὑπωπίοις, ὡς μήλου καὶ κοτίνου ἐγκρατεῖς
γένοιντο νικήσαντες. ἡδὺ γάρ μοι ἀεὶ μεμνῆσθαι
τῶν ἄθλων τοιούτων ὄντων. ἀτὰρ εἰπέ μοι, πάντες
αὐτὰ λαμβάνουσιν οἱ ἀγωνισταί;

ΣΟΛΩΝ

Οὐδαμῶς, ἀλλὰ εἷς ἐξ ἁπάντων, ὁ κρατήσας
αὐτῶν.

takes place there would itself have taught you that we had not spent our energy on all this in vain. Just by talking about the delightfulness of the doings there, one cannot convince you of it as thoroughly as if you yourself, sitting in the midst of the spectators, were to see manly perfection, physical beauty, wonderful condition, mighty skill, irresistible strength, daring, rivalry, indomitable resolution, and inexpressible ardour for victory. I am very sure that you would never have stopped praising and cheering and clapping.

ANACHARSIS

No doubt, Solon; and laughing and gibing, into the bargain; for I see that all these things which you have enumerated—the perfection, the condition, the beauty, the daring—are being wasted for you without any great object in view, since your country is not in peril nor your farm-lands being ravaged, nor your friends and kinsmen insolently carried off. So the competitors are all the more ridiculous if they are the flower of the country, as you say, and yet endure so much for nothing, making themselves miserable and defiling their beautiful, great bodies with sand and black eyes to get possession of an apple and an olive-branch when they have won! You see, I like to keep mentioning the prizes, which are so fine! But tell me, do all the contestants get them?

SOLON

Not by any means; only one among them all, the victor.

ΑΝΑΧΑΡΣΙΣ

Εἶτα, ὦ Σόλων, ἐπὶ τῷ ἀδήλῳ καὶ ἀμφιβόλῳ
τῆς νίκης τοσοῦτοι πονοῦσι, καὶ ταῦτ' εἰδότες ὅτι
ὁ μὲν νικῶν εἷς ἔσται πάντως, οἱ δὲ ἡττώμενοι
πάμπολλοι, μάτην ἄθλιοι πληγάς, οἱ δὲ καὶ τραύματα λαβόντες;

ΣΟΛΩΝ

14 Ἔοικας, ὦ Ἀνάχαρσι, μηδέπω ἐννενοηκέναι
πολιτείας ὀρθῆς πέρι μηδέν· οὐ γὰρ ἂν τὰ κάλλιστα τῶν ἐθῶν ἐν ψόγῳ ἐτίθεσο. ἢν δέ σοι
μελήσῃ ποτὲ εἰδέναι ὅπως ἂν τὰ κάλλιστα
οἰκηθείη πόλις καὶ ὅπως ἂν ἄριστοι γένοιντο οἱ
πολῖται αὐτῆς, ἐπαινέσῃ τότε καὶ τὰς ἀσκήσεις
ταύτας καὶ τὴν φιλοτιμίαν ἣν φιλοτιμούμεθα περὶ
αὐτάς, καὶ εἴσῃ ὅτι πολὺ τὸ χρήσιμον ἔχουσιν
ἐγκαταμεμιγμένον τοῖς πόνοις, εἰ καὶ νῦν μάτην
σπουδάζεσθαι δοκοῦσιν.

ΑΝΑΧΑΡΣΙΣ

Καὶ μήν, ὦ Σόλων, κατ' οὐδὲν ἄλλο ἀπὸ τῆς
Σκυθίας ἥκω παρ' ὑμᾶς τοσαύτην μὲν γῆν διο-
δεύσας, μέγαν δὲ τὸν Εὔξεινον καὶ δυσχείμερον
περαιωθείς, ἢ ὅπως νόμους τε τοὺς Ἑλλήνων
ἐκμάθοιμι καὶ ἔθη τὰ παρ' ὑμῖν κατανοήσαιμι καὶ
πολιτείαν τὴν ἀρίστην ἐκμελετήσαιμι. διὸ καὶ σὲ
μάλιστα φίλον ἐξ ἁπάντων Ἀθηναίων καὶ ξένον
προειλόμην κατὰ κλέος, ἐπείπερ ἤκουον νόμων τε
συγγραφέα τινὰ εἶναι σε καὶ ἐθῶν τῶν ἀρίστων
εὑρετὴν καὶ ἐπιτηδευμάτων ὠφελίμων εἰσηγητήν,
καὶ ὅλως πολιτείας τινὸς συναρμοστήν. ὥστε οὐκ

ANACHARSIS, OR ATHLETICS

Then do so many undergo hardships upon the uncertain and precarious chance of winning, Solon, knowing too that there will surely be but one winner and very many losers, who, poor fellows, will have received blows and in some cases even wounds for nothing ?

It seems, Anacharsis, that you have never yet done any thinking about the proper way to direct a state ; otherwise you would not disparage the best of institutions. If ever you make it your object to find out how a state is to be organized in the best way possible, and how its citizens are to reach the highest degree of excellence, you will then praise these exercises and the rivalry which we display in regard to them, and you will know that they have much that is useful intermingled with the hardships, even if you now think our energy is spent on them for nothing.

I assure you, Solon, I had no other object in coming to your country from Scythia, over such a vast stretch of land and across the wide and tempestuous Euxine, than to learn the laws of the Greeks, to observe your institutions, and to acquaint myself with the best form of polity. That is why I selected you in particular out of all the Athenians for my friend and host, in deference to your reputation, for I used to hear that you were a maker of laws, an inventor of excellent institutions, an introducer of advantageous practices, and in a word, the fashioner of a polity. So

ἂν φθάνοις διδάσκων με καὶ μαθητὴν ποιούμενος·
ὡς ἔγωγε ἡδέως ἂν ἄσιτός σοι καὶ ἄποτος παρα-
καθεζόμενος, εἰς ὅσον ἂν αὐτὸς διαρκοίης λέγων,
κεχηνὼς ἐπακούοιμι περὶ πολιτείας τε καὶ νόμων
διεξιόντος.

ΣΟΛΩΝ

15 Τὰ μὲν πάντα οὐ ῥᾴδιον, ὦ ἑταῖρε, διελθεῖν ἐν
βραχεῖ, ἀλλὰ κατὰ μέρη ἐπιὼν εἴσῃ ἕκαστα, οἷα
μὲν περὶ θεῶν, οἷα δὲ περὶ γονέων ἢ περὶ γάμων
ἢ τῶν ἄλλων δοκεῖ ἡμῖν. ἃ δὲ περὶ τῶν νέων
γιγνώσκομεν καὶ ὅπως αὐτοῖς χρώμεθα, ἐπειδὰν
πρῶτον ἄρξωνται συνιέναι τε τοῦ βελτίονος καὶ
τῷ σώματι ἀνδρίζεσθαι καὶ ὑφίστασθαι τοὺς
πόνους, ταῦτα ἤδη σοι διέξειμι, ὡς μάθοις οὗτινος
χάριν τὰς ἀσκήσεις ταύτας προτεθείκαμεν αὐτοῖς
καὶ διαπονεῖν τὸ σῶμα καταναγκάζομεν, οὐ μόνον
ἕνεκα τῶν ἀγώνων, ὅπως τὰ ἆθλα δύναιντο ἀναι-
ρεῖσθαι—ἐπ' ἐκεῖνα μὲν γὰρ ὀλίγοι πάνυ ἐξ ἁπάντων χωροῦσιν—ἀλλὰ μεῖζόν τι ἁπάσῃ τῇ πόλει
ἀγαθὸν ἐκ τούτου καὶ αὐτοῖς ἐκείνοις προσκτώ-
μενοι. κοινὸς γάρ τις ἀγὼν ἄλλος ἅπασι τοῖς
ἀγαθοῖς πολίταις πρόκειται καὶ στέφανος οὐ
πίτυος οὐδὲ κοτίνου ἢ σελίνων, ἀλλ' ὃς ἐν αὐτῷ
συλλαβὼν ἔχει τὴν ἀνθρώπου εὐδαιμονίαν, οἷον
ἐλευθερίαν λέγω αὐτοῦ τε ἑκάστου ἰδίᾳ καὶ κοινῇ
τῆς πατρίδος καὶ πλοῦτον καὶ δόξαν καὶ ἑορτῶν
πατρίων ἀπόλαυσιν καὶ οἰκείων σωτηρίαν, καὶ
συνόλως τὰ κάλλιστα ὧν ἄν τις εὔξαιτο γενέσθαι
οἱ παρὰ τῶν θεῶν. ταῦτα πάντα τῷ στεφάνῳ ὅν
φημι συναναπέπλεκται καὶ ἐκ τοῦ ἀγῶνος ἐκείνου
περιγίγνεται ἐφ' ὃν αἱ ἀσκήσεις αὗται καὶ οἱ πόνοι
ἄγουσιν.

18

do be quick about teaching me and making a disciple of me. For my part I would gladly sit beside you without meat or drink as long as you could endure to talk, and listen to you with avidity while you described government and laws.

SOLON

To describe everything, my friend, in brief compass is not an easy task, but if you take it up a little at a time, you will find out in detail all the opinions we hold about the gods and about parents, marriage, and everything else. And I shall now tell you what we think about our young men, and how we deal with them from the time when they begin to know good from bad, to be physically mature, and to bear hardships, in order that you may learn why we prescribe these exercises for them and compel them to train their bodies. It is not simply on account of the contests, in order that they may be able to take the prizes—very few out of the entire number have the capacity for that—but because we seek a certain greater good from it for the entire state and for the young men themselves. There is another competition which is open to all good citizens in common, and a wreath that is not made of pine or olive or parsley, but contains in itself all human felicity,—that is to say, freedom for each individual singly and for the state in general, wealth, glory, enjoyment of ancestral feast-days, safety for one's family, and in short, the fairest blessings that one could pray to receive from the gods. All these things are interwoven in the wreath that I speak of and accrue from the contest to which these exercises and hardships lead.

ΑΝΑΧΑΡΣΙΣ

16 Εἶτα, ὦ θαυμάσιε Σόλων, τοιαῦτά μοι καὶ
τηλικαῦτα ἔχων ἆθλα διεξιέναι, μῆλα καὶ σέλινα
διηγοῦ καὶ θαλλὸν ἐλαίας ἀγρίας καὶ πίτυν;

ΣΟΛΩΝ

Καὶ μήν, ὦ Ἀνάχαρσι, οὐδ' ἐκεῖνά σοι ἔτι δόξει
μικρὰ εἶναι, ὁπόταν ἃ λέγω καταμάθῃς· ἀπὸ γάρ
τοι τῆς αὐτῆς γνώμης γίγνεται, καὶ μέρη πάντα
ταῦτά ἐστι μικρὰ τοῦ μείζονος ἐκείνου ἀγῶνος καὶ
τοῦ στεφάνου ὃν κατέλεξα τοῦ πανευδαίμονος. ὁ
δὲ λόγος, οὐκ οἶδ' ὅπως ὑπερβὰς τὴν τάξιν, ἐκείνων
πρότερον[1] ἐπεμνήσθη τῶν Ἰσθμοῖ γιγνομένων καὶ
Ὀλυμπίασι καὶ ἐν Νεμέᾳ. πλὴν ἀλλὰ νώ—
σχολὴν γὰρ ἄγομεν καὶ σύ, ὡς φής, προθυμῇ
ἀκούειν—ἀναδραμούμεθα ῥᾳδίως πρὸς τὴν ἀρχὴν
καὶ τὸν κοινὸν ἀγῶνα δι' ὃν φημι πάντα ταῦτα
ἐπιτηδεύεσθαι.

ΑΝΑΧΑΡΣΙΣ

Ἄμεινον, ὦ Σόλων, οὕτως· καθ' ὁδὸν γὰρ ἂν ἡμῖν
ὁ λόγος μᾶλλον προχωροίη, καὶ τάχ' ἂν ἴσως ἀπὸ
τούτων πεισθείην μηδὲ ἐκείνων ἔτι καταγελᾶν,
εἴ τινα ἴδοιμι σεμνυνόμενον κοτίνῳ ἢ σελίνῳ
ἐστεφανωμένον. ἀλλ' εἰ δοκεῖ, εἰς τὸ σύσκιον
ἐκεῖσε ἀπελθόντες καθίσωμεν ἐπὶ τῶν θάκων, ὡς
μὴ ἐνοχλοῖεν ἡμῖν οἱ[2] ἐπικεκραγότες τοῖς παλαίουσιν. ἄλλως τε—εἰρήσεται γάρ—οὐδὲ τὸν
ἥλιον ἔτι ῥᾳδίως ἀνέχομαι ὀξὺν καὶ φλογμώδη
ἐμπίπτοντα γυμνῇ τῇ κεφαλῇ. τὸν γὰρ πῖλόν

---

[1] πρότερον Halm : προτέρων MSS.
[2] οἱ Jacobs : not in MSS.

ANACHARSIS, OR ATHLETICS

Then, Solon, you amazing person, when you had such magnificent prizes to tell of, you spoke of apples and parsley and a sprig of wild olive and a bit of pine?

But really, Anacharsis, even those prizes will no longer appear trivial to you when you understand what I mean. They originate in the same purpose, and are all small parts of that greater contest and of the wreath of complete felicity which I mentioned. Our conversation, departing somehow or other from the natural sequence, touched first upon the doings at the Isthmus and Olympia and Nemea. However, as we are at leisure and you are eager, you say, to hear, it will be an easy matter for us to hark back to the beginning, to the common competition which is, as I say, the object of all these practices.

It would be better, Solon, to do so, for by keeping to the highway our talk would make greater progress, and perhaps knowing these prizes may persuade me never again to laugh at those others, if I should see a man putting on airs because he wears a wreath of wild olive or parsley. But if it is all the same to you, let us go into the shade over yonder and sit on the benches, so as not to be annoyed by the men who are shouting at the wrestlers. Besides—I may as well be frank!—I no longer find it easy to stand the sun, which is fierce and burning as it beats upon my bare head. I thought it best to leave my cap at

μοι ἀφελεῖν οἴκοθεν ἔδοξεν, ὡς μὴ μόνος ἐν ὑμῖν
ξενίζοιμι τῷ σχήματι. ἡ δὲ ὥρα τοῦ ἔτους ὅ τι
περ τὸ πυρωδέστατόν ἐστι, τοῦ ἀστέρος ὃν ὑμεῖς
κύνα φατὲ πάντα καταφλέγοντος καὶ τὸν ἀέρα
ξηρὸν καὶ διακαῆ τιθέντος, ὅ τε ἥλιος κατὰ
μεσημβρίαν ἤδη ὑπὲρ κεφαλῆς ἐπικείμενος φλογ-
μὸν τοῦτον οὐ φορητὸν ἐπάγει τοῖς σώμασιν.
ὥστε καὶ σοῦ θαυμάζω, ὅπως γηραιὸς ἤδη ἄνθρωπος οὔτε ἰδίεις πρὸς τὸ θάλπος ὥσπερ ἐγὼ
οὔτε ὅλως ἐνοχλουμένῳ ἔοικας, οὐδὲ περιβλέπεις
σύσκιόν τι ἔνθα ὑποδύσῃ, ἀλλὰ δέχῃ τὸν ἥλιον
εὐμαρῶς.

ΣΟΛΩΝ

Οἱ μάταιοι γὰρ οὗτοι πόνοι, ὦ Ἀνάχαρσι, καὶ
αἱ συνεχεῖς ἐν τῷ πηλῷ κυβιστήσεις καὶ αἱ
ὕπαιθροι ἐν τῇ ψάμμῳ ταλαιπωρίαι τοῦτο ἡμῖν
τὸ ἀμυντήριον παρέχουσι πρὸς τὰς τοῦ ἡλίου
βολάς, καὶ οὐκέτι πίλου δεόμεθα ὃς τὴν ἀκτῖνα
κωλύσει καθικνεῖσθαι τῆς κεφαλῆς.

17   Ἀπίωμεν δ᾽ οὖν. καὶ ὅπως μὴ καθάπερ νόμοις
προσέξεις οἷς ἂν λέγω πρὸς σέ, ὡς ἐξ ἅπαντος
πιστεύειν αὐτοῖς, ἀλλ᾽ ἔνθα ἄν σοι μὴ ὀρθῶς τι
λέγεσθαι δοκῇ, ἀντιλέγειν εὐθὺς καὶ διευθύνειν
τὸν λόγον. δυοῖν γὰρ θατέρου πάντως οὐκ ἂν
ἁμάρτοιμεν, ἢ σὲ βεβαίως πεισθῆναι ἐκχέαντα
ὁπόσα οἴει ἀντιλεκτέα εἶναι ἢ ἐμὲ ἀναδιδαχθῆναι
ὡς οὐκ ὀρθῶς γιγνώσκω περὶ αὐτῶν. καὶ ἐν
τούτῳ πᾶσα ἄν σοι ἡ πόλις ἡ Ἀθηναίων οὐκ

---

[1] A great pointed cap of felt or skin was part of the
Scythian costume. The Greeks went bare-headed, unless

home, so as not to be the only person among you in a foreign costume.[1]   But the season of the year is the very fieriest, for the star which you call the Dog burns everything up and makes the air dry and parching, and the sun, now hanging overhead at midday, produces this blazing heat, insupportable to the body. I wonder, therefore, how it is that you, an elderly man, do not perspire in the heat as I do, and do not seem to be troubled by it at all; you do not even look about for a shady spot to enter, but stand the sun with ease.

SOLON

These useless exertions, Anacharsis, the continual somersaults in the mud and the open-air struggles in the sand give us our immunity from the shafts of the sun and we have no further need of a cap to keep its rays from striking our heads.

Let us go, however.   And take care not to regard everything that I may say to you as a law, so as to believe it at all hazards.   Whenever you think I am incorrect in anything that I say, contradict me at once and set my reasoning straight.   One thing or the other, certainly, we cannot fail to accomplish : either you will become firmly convinced after you have exhausted all the objections that you think ought to be made, or else I shall be taught that I am not correct in my view of the matter.   In that event the entire city of Athens could not be too quick to

they were ill, or on a journey, or regularly exposed to bad weather, like sailors and farm-labourers, who wore a similar but smaller cap.

23

ἂν φθάνοι χάριν ὁμολογοῦσα· ὅσα γὰρ ἂν ἐμὲ
παιδεύσῃς καὶ μεταπείσῃς πρὸς τὸ βέλτιον,
ἐκείνην τὰ μέγιστα ἔσῃ ὠφεληκώς. οὐδὲν γὰρ
ἂν ἀποκρυψαίμην αὐτήν, ἀλλ' εὐθὺς εἰς τὸ μέσον
καταθήσω φέρων καὶ καταστὰς ἐν τῇ πνυκὶ ἐρῶ
πρὸς ἅπαντας, " Ἄνδρες Ἀθηναῖοι, ἐγὼ μὲν ὑμῖν
ἔγραψα τοὺς νόμους οἵους ᾤμην[1] ὠφελιμωτάτους
ἔσεσθαι τῇ πόλει, ὁ δὲ ξένος οὑτοσί"—δείξας σέ,
ὦ Ἀνάχαρσι—"Σκύθης μέν ἐστι, σοφὸς δὲ ὢν
μετεπαίδευσέ με καὶ ἄλλα βελτίω μαθήματα καὶ
ἐπιτηδεύματα ἐδιδάξατο· ὥστε εὐεργέτης ὑμῶν
ὁ ἀνὴρ ἀναγεγράφθω καὶ χαλκοῦν αὐτὸν ἀναστή-
σατε παρὰ τοὺς ἐπωνύμους ἢ[2] ἐν πόλει παρὰ τὴν
Ἀθηνᾶν." καὶ εὖ ἴσθι ὡς οὐκ αἰσχυνεῖται[3] ἡ
Ἀθηναίων πόλις παρὰ βαρβάρου καὶ ξένου τὰ
συμφέροντα ἐκμανθάνοντες.

ΑΝΑΧΑΡΣΙΣ

18   Τοῦτ' ἐκεῖνο ἦν ἄρα, ὃ ἐγὼ περὶ ὑμῶν ἤκουον
τῶν Ἀθηναίων, ὡς εἴητε εἴρωνες ἐν τοῖς λόγοις.
ἐπεὶ πόθεν ἂν ἐγὼ νομὰς καὶ πλάνης ἄνθρωπος,
ἐφ' ἁμάξης βεβιωκώς, ἄλλοτε ἄλλην γῆν ἀμεί-
βων, πόλιν δὲ οὔτε οἰκήσας πώποτε οὔτε ἄλλοτε
ἢ νῦν ἑωρακώς, περὶ πολιτείας διεξίοιμι καὶ
διδάσκοιμι αὐτόχθονας ἄνδρας πόλιν ταύτην
ἀρχαιοτάτην τοσούτοις ἤδη χρόνοις ἐν εὐνομίᾳ
κατῳκηκότας, καὶ μάλιστα σέ,[4] ὦ Σόλων, ᾧ τοῦτο
ἐξ ἀρχῆς καὶ μάθημα, ὡς φασίν, ἐγένετο, ἐπί-

---

[1] ᾤμην Cobet : ἂν ᾤμην MSS.
[2] ἢ O. Müller : not in MSS.
[3] αἰσχυνεῖται Fritzsche : αἰσχύνηται MSS.
[4] σέ vulg.: not in MSS.

acknowledge its gratitude to you, because in so far as you instruct me and convert me to a better view, you will have conferred the greatest possible benefit upon her. For I could not keep anything from her, but shall at once contribute it all to the public. Taking my stand in the Pnyx, I shall say to everyone: "Men of Athens, I made you the laws which I thought would be most beneficial to the city, but this guest of mine"—and then I shall point to you, Anacharsis,—"a Scythian, indeed, but a man of learning, has converted me and taught me other better forms of education and training. Therefore let him be written down as your benefactor, and set his statue up in bronze beside the Namesakes[1] or on the Acropolis beside Athena." You may be very sure that the city of Athens will not be ashamed to learn what is to her advantage from a foreign guest.

ANACHARSIS

Ah! that is just what I used to hear about you Athenians, that you never really mean what you say. For how could I, a nomad and a rover, who have lived my life on a wagon, visiting different lands at different seasons, and have never dwelt in a city or seen one until now—how could I hold forth upon statecraft and teach men sprung from the soil, who have inhabited this very ancient city for so many years in law and order? Above all, how could I teach you, Solon, who from the first, they say, have made it a special study to know how the government of a state

[1] The ten Athenian tribes were named after legendary heroes whose statues stood in the Potters' Quarter.

στασθαι ὅπως ἂν ἄριστα πόλις οἰκοῖτο καὶ
οἷστισιν νόμοις χρωμένη εὐδαιμονήσειε ; πλὴν
ἀλλὰ καὶ τοῦτο ὡς νομοθέτῃ πειστέον σοι, καὶ
ἀντερῶ ἤν τί μοι δοκῇ μὴ ὀρθῶς λέγεσθαι, ὡς
βεβαιότερον μάθοιμι.

Καὶ ἰδοὺ γὰρ ἤδη ἐκφυγόντες τὸν ἥλιον ἐν τῷ
συνηρεφεῖ ἐσμεν, καὶ καθέδρα μάλα ἡδεῖα καὶ
εὔκαιρος ἐπὶ ψυχροῦ τοῦ λίθου. λέγε οὖν τὸν
λόγον ἐξ ἀρχῆς καθ' ὅ τι τοὺς νέους παραλαβόντες ἐκ παίδων εὐθὺς διαπονεῖτε, καὶ ὅπως
ὑμῖν ἄριστοι ἄνδρες ἀποβαίνουσιν ἐκ τοῦ πηλοῦ
καὶ τῶν ἀσκημάτων τούτων, καὶ τί ἡ κόνις καὶ
τὰ κυβιστήματα συντελεῖ πρὸς ἀρετὴν αὐτοῖς.
τοῦτο γὰρ δὴ μάλιστα ἐξ ἀρχῆς εὐθὺς ἐπόθουν
ἀκοῦσαι· τὰ δ' ἄλλα εἰς ὕστερον διδάξῃ με κατὰ
καιρὸν ἕκαστον ἐν τῷ μέρει. ἐκείνου μέντοι, ὦ
Σόλων, μέμνησό μοι παρὰ τὴν ῥῆσιν, ὅτι πρὸς
ἄνδρα βάρβαρον ἐρεῖς. λέγω δὲ ὡς μὴ περιπλέκῃς
μηδὲ ἀπομηκύνῃς τοὺς λόγους· δέδια γὰρ μὴ
ἐπιλανθάνωμαι τῶν πρώτων, εἰ τὰ μετὰ ταῦτα
πολλὰ ἐπιρρέοι.[1]

ΣΟΛΩΝ

19 Σὺ τοῦτο, ὦ Ἀνάχαρσι, ταμιεύσῃ ἄμεινον,
ἔνθα ἄν σοι δοκῇ μὴ πάνυ σαφὴς ὁ λόγος εἶναι ἢ
πόρρω ποι ἀποπλανᾶσθαι εἰκῆ ῥέων· ἐρήσῃ γὰρ
μεταξὺ ὅ τι ἂν ἐθέλῃς καὶ διακόψεις αὐτοῦ τὸ
μῆκος. ἢν μέντοι μὴ ἐξαγώνια μηδὲ πόρρω τοῦ
σκοποῦ τὰ λεγόμενα ᾖ, κωλύσει οὐδέν, οἶμαι, εἰ
καὶ μακρὰ λέγοιτο, ἐπεὶ καὶ τῇ βουλῇ τῇ ἐξ

---

[1] ἐπιρρέοι Lehmann : ἐπιρρέῃ MSS.

can be conducted best and what laws it should observe to be prosperous? However, in this too, since you are a law-giver, I must obey you; so I shall contradict you if I think that you are incorrect in anything that you say, in order that I may learn my lesson more thoroughly.

See, we have escaped the sun and are now in the shade; here is a very delightful and opportune seat on the cool stone. So begin at the beginning and tell why you take your young men in hand and train them from their very boyhood, how they turn out excellent men as a result of the mud and the exercises, and what the dust and the somersaults contribute to their excellence. That is what I was most eager to hear at the beginning: the rest you shall teach me later, as opportunity offers, each particular in its turn. But bear this in mind, please, Solon, throughout your talk, that you will be speaking to a foreigner. I say this in order that you may not make your explanations too involved or too long, for I am afraid that I may forget the commencement if the sequel should be too profuse in its flow.

SOLON

You yourself, Anacharsis, can regulate that better, wherever you think that my discussion is not fully clear, or that it is meandering far from its channel in a random stream; for you can interpose any question that you will, and cut it short. But if what I say is not foreign to the case and beside the mark, there will be nothing, I suppose, to hinder, even if I should speak at length, since that is the

Ἀρείου πάγου, ἥπερ τὰς φονικὰς ἡμῖν δίκας
δικάζει, πάτριον οὕτω ποιεῖν. ὁπόταν γὰρ ἀνελ-
θοῦσα εἰς τὸν πάγον συγκαθέζηται φόνου ἢ
τραύματος ἐκ προνοίας ἢ πυρκαϊᾶς δικάσοντες,
ἀποδίδοται λόγος ἑκατέρῳ τῶν κρινομένων καὶ
λέγουσιν ἐν τῷ μέρει ὁ μὲν διώκων ὁ δὲ φεύγων,
ἢ αὐτοὶ ἢ ῥήτορας ἀναβιβάζονται τοὺς ἐροῦντας
ὑπὲρ αὐτῶν. οἱ δὲ ἔστ' ἂν μὲν περὶ τοῦ πράγματος λέγωσιν, ἀνέχεται ἡ βουλὴ καθ' ἡσυχίαν
ἀκούουσα· ἢν δέ τις ἢ φροίμιον εἴπῃ πρὸ τοῦ
λόγου, ὡς εὐνουστέρους ἀπεργάσαιτο αὐτούς, ἢ
οἶκτον ἢ δείνωσιν ἔξωθεν ἐπάγῃ [1] τῷ πράγματι—
οἷα πολλὰ ῥητόρων παῖδες ἐπὶ τοὺς δικαστὰς
μηχανῶνται—παρελθὼν ὁ κῆρυξ κατεσιώπησεν
εὐθύς, οὐκ ἐῶν ληρεῖν πρὸς τὴν βουλὴν καὶ περι-
πέττειν τὸ πρᾶγμα ἐν τοῖς λόγοις, ὡς γυμνὰ τὰ
γεγενημένα οἱ Ἀρεοπαγῖται βλέποιεν.

Ὥστε καὶ σέ, ὦ Ἀνάχαρσι, Ἀρεοπαγίτην ἐν
τῷ παρόντι ποιοῦμαι ἔγωγε, καὶ κατὰ τὸν τῆς
βουλῆς μου νόμον ἄκουε, καὶ σιωπᾶν κέλευε, ἢν
αἴσθῃ καταρρητορευόμενος· ἄχρι δ' ἂν οἰκεῖα τῷ
πράγματι λέγηται, ἐξέστω ἀπομηκύνειν. οὐδὲ
γὰρ ὑφ' ἡλίῳ ἔτι ποιησόμεθα τὴν συνουσίαν, ὡς
ἄχθεσθαι εἰ ἀποτείνοιτο ἡ ῥῆσις, ἀλλὰ ἥ τε σκιὰ
πυκνὴ καὶ ἡμεῖς σχολὴν ἄγομεν.

ΑΝΑΧΑΡΣΙΣ

Εὐγνώμονά σου ταῦτα, ὦ Σόλων, καὶ ἔγωγε
ἤδη χάριν οὐ μικρὰν οἶδά σοι καὶ ἐπὶ τούτοις,
ὅτι πάρεργον τοῦ λόγου καὶ τὰ ἐν Ἀρείῳ πάγῳ

---

[1] ἐπάγῃ Fritzsche : ἐπάγοι MSS.

tradition in the court of the Areopagus, which judges our cases of manslaughter. Whenever it goes up to the Areopagus and holds a sitting to judge a case of manslaughter or premeditated wounding or arson, an opportunity to be heard is given to each party to the case, and the plaintiff and defendant plead in turn, either in person or through professional speakers whom they bring to the bar to plead in their behalf. As long as they speak about the case, the court tolerates them and listens in silence ; but if anyone prefaces his speech with an introduction in order to make the court more favourable, or brings emotion or exaggeration into the case— tricks that are often devised by the disciples of rhetoric to influence the judges,—then the crier appears and silences them at once, preventing them from talking nonsense to the court and from tricking the case out in words, in order that the Areopagites may see the facts bare.

So, Anacharsis, I make you an Areopagite for the present. Listen to me according to the custom of the court and tell me to be silent if you perceive that I am plying you with rhetoric. But as long as what I say is germane to the case, let me have the right to speak at length. Besides, we are not going to converse in the sun now, so that you would find it burdensome if my talk were prolonged ; the shade is thick, and we have plenty of time.

ANACHARSIS

What you say is reasonable, Solon, and already I am more than a little grateful to you for incidentally teaching me about what takes place in the Areopagus,

γιγνόμενα ἐδιδάξω με, θαυμάσια ὡς ἀληθῶς καὶ
ἀγαθῶν βουλευτῶν ἔργα πρὸς ἀλήθειαν οἰσόντων
τὴν ψῆφον. ἐπὶ τούτοις οὖν ἤδη λέγε, καὶ ὁ
Ἀρεοπαγίτης ἐγώ—τοῦτο γὰρ ἔθου με—κατὰ
σχῆμα τῆς βουλῆς ἀκούσομαί σου.

ΣΟΛΩΝ

20 Οὐκοῦν διὰ βραχέων προακοῦσαι χρή σε ἃ
περὶ πόλεως καὶ πολιτῶν ἡμῖν δοκεῖ. πόλιν γὰρ
ἡμεῖς οὐ τὰ οἰκοδομήματα ἡγούμεθα εἶναι, οἷον
τείχη καὶ ἱερὰ καὶ νεωσοίκους, ἀλλὰ ταῦτα μὲν
ὥσπερ σῶμά τι ἑδραῖον καὶ ἀκίνητον ὑπάρχειν
εἰς ὑποδοχὴν καὶ ἀσφάλειαν τῶν πολιτευομένων,
τὸ δὲ πᾶν κῦρος ἐν τοῖς πολίταις τιθέμεθα·
τούτους γὰρ εἶναι τοὺς ἀναπληροῦντας καὶ δια-
τάττοντας καὶ ἐπιτελοῦντας ἕκαστα καὶ φυλάττοντας, οἷόν τι ἐν ἡμῖν ἑκάστῳ ἐστὶν ἡ ψυχή.
τοῦτο δὴ τοίνυν κατανοήσαντες ἐπιμελούμεθα
μέν, ὡς ὁρᾷς, καὶ τοῦ σώματος τῆς πόλεως, κατα-
κοσμοῦντες αὐτὸ ὡς κάλλιστον ἡμῖν εἴη, ἔνδοθέν
τε οἰκοδομήμασιν κατεσκευασμένον καὶ ταῖς
ἔκτοσθεν ταύταις περιβολαῖς εἰς τὸ ἀσφαλέ-
στατον πεφραγμένον. μάλιστα δὲ καὶ ἐξ ἅπαντος
τοῦτο προνοοῦμεν, ὅπως οἱ πολῖται ἀγαθοὶ μὲν
τὰς ψυχάς, ἰσχυροὶ δὲ τὰ σώματα γίγνοιντο·
τοὺς γὰρ τοιούτους σφίσι τε αὐτοῖς καλῶς χρή-
σεσθαι ἐν εἰρήνη συμπολιτευομένους καὶ ἐκ πολέμου σώσειν τὴν πόλιν καὶ ἐλευθέραν καὶ εὐδαί-
μονα διαφυλάξειν.

Τὴν μὲν δὴ πρώτην ἀνατροφὴν αὐτῶν μητράσι
καὶ τίτθαις καὶ παιδαγωγοῖς ἐπιτρέπομεν ὑπὸ

which is truly admirable and what good judges would do, who intend to cast their ballot in accordance with the facts. On these conditions, therefore, proceed, and in my capacity of Areopagite, since you have made me that, I shall give you a hearing in the manner of that court.

SOLON

Then you must first let me tell you briefly what our ideas are about a city and its citizens. We consider that a city is not the buildings, such as walls and temples and docks. These constitute a firm-set, immovable body, so to speak, for the shelter and protection of the community, but the whole significance is in the citizens, we hold, for it is they who fill it, plan and carry out everything, and keep it safe; they are something like what the soul is within the individual. So, having noted this, we naturally take care of the city's body, as you see, beautifying it so that it may be as fair as possible, not only well furnished inside with buildings but most securely fenced with these external ramparts. But above all and at all hazards we endeavour to insure that the citizens shall be virtuous in soul and strong in body, thinking that such men, joined together in public life, will make good use of themselves in times of peace, will bring the city safe out of war, and will keep it always free and prosperous.

Their early upbringing we entrust to mothers, nurses, and tutors, to train and rear them with

παιδείαις ἐλευθερίοις ἄγειν τε καὶ τρέφειν αὐτούς,
ἐπειδὰν δὲ συνετοὶ ἤδη γίγνωνται τῶν καλῶς
ἐχόντων, καὶ αἰδὼς καὶ ἐρύθημα καὶ φόβος καὶ
ἐπιθυμία τῶν ἀρίστων ἀναφύηται αὐτοῖς, καὶ
αὐτὰ ἤδη τὰ σώματα ἀξιόχρεα δοκῇ πρὸς τοὺς
πόνους παγιώτερα γιγνόμενα καὶ πρὸς τὸ ἰσχυρότερον συνιστάμενα, τηνικαῦτα ἤδη παραλαβόντες
αὐτοὺς διδάσκομεν, ἄλλα μὲν τῆς ψυχῆς μαθήματα καὶ γυμνάσια προτιθέντες, ἄλλως δὲ πρὸς
τοὺς πόνους καὶ τὰ σώματα ἐθίζοντες. οὐ γὰρ
ἱκανὸν ἡμῖν ἔδοξε τὸ μόνον φῦναι ὡς ἔφυ ἕκαστος
ἤτοι κατὰ τὸ σῶμα ἢ κατὰ τὴν ψυχήν, ἀλλὰ καὶ
παιδεύσεως καὶ μαθημάτων ἐπ᾿ αὐτοὺς δεόμεθα,
ὑφ᾿ ὧν τά τε εὐφυῶς διακείμενα βελτίω παρὰ
πολὺ γίγνοιτο ἂν καὶ τὰ φαύλως ἔχοντα μετα-
κοσμοῖτο πρὸς τὸ βέλτιον. καὶ τὸ παράδειγμα
ἡμῖν παρὰ τῶν γεωργῶν, οἳ τὰ φυτὰ μέχρι μὲν
πρόσγεια καὶ νήπιά ἐστι, σκέπουσιν καὶ περι-
φράττουσιν ὡς μὴ βλάπτοιντο ὑπὸ τῶν πνευ-
μάτων, ἐπειδὰν δὲ ἤδη παχύνηται τὸ ἔρνος,
τηνικαῦτα περιτέμνουσίν τε τὰ περιττὰ καὶ
παραδιδόντες αὐτὰ τοῖς ἀνέμοις δονεῖν καὶ δια-
σαλεύειν καρπιμώτερα ἐξεργάζονται.

21   Τὴν μὲν τοίνυν ψυχὴν μουσικῇ τὸ πρῶτον καὶ
ἀριθμητικῇ ἀναρριπίζομεν, καὶ γράμματα γράψασθαι καὶ τορῶς αὐτὰ ἐπιλέξασθαι διδάσκομεν·
προϊοῦσιν δὲ ἤδη σοφῶν ἀνδρῶν γνώμας καὶ
ἔργα παλαιὰ καὶ λόγους ὠφελίμους ἐν μέτροις
κατακοσμήσαντες, ὡς μᾶλλον μνημονεύοιεν, ῥα-
ψῳδοῦμεν αὐτοῖς. οἱ δὲ καὶ ἀκούοντες ἀριστείας
τινὰς καὶ πράξεις ἀοιδίμους ὀρέγονται κατὰ

liberal teachings; but when at length they become able to understand what is right, when modesty, shame, fear, and ambition spring up in them, and when at length their very bodies seem well fitted for hardships as they get firmer and become more strongly compacted, then we take them in hand and teach them, not only prescribing them certain disciplines and exercises for the soul, but in certain other ways habituating their bodies also to hardships. We have not thought it sufficient for each man to be as he was born, either in body or in soul, but we want education and disciplines for them by which their good traits may be much improved and their bad altered for the better. We take example from the farmers, who shelter and enclose their plants while they are small and young, so that they may not be injured by the breezes: but when the stalk at last begins to thicken, they prune away the excessive growth and expose them to the winds to be shaken and tossed, in that way making them more fruitful.

Their souls we fan into flame with music and arithmetic at first and we teach them to write their letters and to read them trippingly. As they progress, we recite for them sayings of wise men, deeds of olden times, and helpful fictions, which we have adorned with metre that they may remember them better. Hearing of certain feats of arms and famous exploits, little by little they grow covetous

33

μικρὸν καὶ πρὸς μίμησιν ἐπεγείρονται, ὡς καὶ αὐτοὶ
ᾄδοιντο καὶ θαυμάζοιντο ὑπὸ τῶν ὕστερον. οἷα
πολλὰ Ἡσίοδός τε ἡμῖν καὶ Ὅμηρος ἐποίησαν.

Ἐπειδὰν δὲ πλησιάζωσι πρὸς τὴν πολιτείαν
καὶ δέῃ αὐτοὺς ἤδη μεταχειρίζεσθαι τὰ κοινά—
καίτοι ἔξω τοῦ ἀγῶνος ἴσως ταῦτα· οὐ γὰρ ὅπως
τὰς ψυχὰς αὐτῶν ἀσκοῦμεν ἐξ ἀρχῆς προὔκειτο
εἰπεῖν, ἀλλὰ δι' ὅ τι τοῖς τοιούτοις πόνοις κατα-
γυμνάζειν αὐτοὺς ἀξιοῦμεν. ὥστε αὐτὸς ἐμαυτῷ
σιωπᾶν προστάττω, οὐ περιμείνας τὸν κήρυκα
οὐδὲ τὸν Ἀρεοπαγίτην σέ, ὃς ὑπ' αἰδοῦς, οἶμαι,
ἀνέχῃ ληροῦντα ἤδη τοσαῦτα ἔξω τοῦ πράγματος.

ΑΝΑΧΑΡΣΙΣ

Εἰπέ μοι, ὦ Σόλων, πρὸς δὲ δὴ τοὺς τὰ ἀναγ-
καιότατα μὴ λέγοντας ἐν Ἀρείῳ πάγῳ, ἀλλὰ
ἀποσιωπῶντας, οὐδὲν τῇ βουλῇ πρόστιμον ἐπι-
νενόηται;

ΣΟΛΩΝ

Τί τοῦτο ἤρου με; οὐδέπω γὰρ δῆλον.

ΑΝΑΧΑΡΣΙΣ

Ὅτι τὰ κάλλιστα καὶ ἐμοὶ ἀκοῦσαι ἥδιστα
παρείς, τὰ περὶ τῆς ψυχῆς, τὰ ἧττον ἀναγκαῖα
λέγειν διανοῇ, γυμνάσια καὶ διαπονήσεις τῶν
σωμάτων.

ΣΟΛΩΝ

Μέμνημαι γάρ, ὦ γενναῖε, τῶν ἀπ' ἀρχῆς
προρρήσεων καὶ ἀποπλανᾶν οὐ βούλομαι τὸν

and are incited to imitate them, in order that they too may be sung and admired by men of after time. Both Hesiod and Homer have composed much poetry of that sort for us.

When they enter political life and have at length to handle public affairs—but this, no doubt, is foreign to the case, as the subject proposed for discussion at the outset was not how we discipline their souls, but why we think fit to train their bodies with hardships like these. Therefore I order myself to be silent, without waiting for the crier to do it, or for you, the Areopagite; it is out of deference, I suppose, that you tolerate my saying so much that is beside the point.

ANACHARSIS

Tell me, Solon, when people do not say what is most essential in the Areopagus, but keep it to themselves, has the court devised no penalty for them?

SOLON

Why did you ask me that question? I do not understand.

ANACHARSIS

Because you propose to pass over what is best and for me most delightful to hear about, what concerns the soul, and to speak of what is less essential, gymnastics and physical exercises.

SOLON

Why, my worthy friend, I remember your admonitions in the beginning and do not wish the discussion

35

λόγον, μὴ σου ἐπιταράξῃ τὴν μνήμην ἐπιρρέων.
πλὴν ἀλλὰ καὶ ταῦτα ἐρῶ διὰ βραχέων, ὡς οἷόν
τε· τὸ γὰρ ἀκριβὲς τῆς περὶ αὐτῶν διασκέψεως
ἑτέρου ἂν εἴη λόγου.

22 Ῥυθμίζομεν οὖν τὰς γνώμας αὐτῶν νόμους τε
τοὺς κοινοὺς ἐκδιδάσκοντες, οἳ δημοσίᾳ πᾶσι
πρόκεινται ἀναγιγνώσκειν μεγάλοις γράμμασιν
ἀναγεγραμμένοι, κελεύοντες ἅ τε χρὴ ποιεῖν καὶ
ὧν ἀπέχεσθαι, καὶ ἀγαθῶν ἀνδρῶν συνουσίαις,
παρ' ὧν λέγειν τὰ δέοντα ἐκμανθάνουσι καὶ
πράττειν τὰ δίκαια καὶ ἐκ τοῦ ἴσου ἀλλήλοις
συμπολιτεύεσθαι καὶ μὴ ἐφίεσθαι τῶν αἰσχρῶν
καὶ ὀρέγεσθαι τῶν καλῶν, βίαιον δὲ μηδὲν ποιεῖν.
οἱ δὲ ἄνδρες οὗτοι σοφισταὶ καὶ φιλόσοφοι πρὸς
ἡμῶν ὀνομάζονται. καὶ μέντοι καὶ εἰς τὸ θέατρον
συνάγοντες αὐτοὺς δημοσίᾳ παιδεύομεν ὑπὸ κω-
μῳδίαις καὶ τραγῳδίαις ἀρετάς τε ἀνδρῶν παλαιῶν
καὶ κακίας θεωμένους, ὡς τῶν μὲν ἀποτρέποιντο,
ἐπ' ἐκεῖνα δὲ σπεύδοιεν. τοῖς δέ γε κωμῳδοῖς καὶ
λοιδορεῖσθαι καὶ ἀποσκώπτειν ἐφίεμεν εἰς τοὺς
πολίτας οὓς ἂν αἰσχρὰ καὶ ἀνάξια τῆς πόλεως
ἐπιτηδεύοντας αἴσθωνται, αὐτῶν τε ἐκείνων χάριν,
ἀμείνους γὰρ οὕτω γίγνονται ὀνειδιζόμενοι, καὶ
τῶν πολλῶν, ὡς φεύγοιεν τὸν ἐπὶ τοῖς ὁμοίοις
ἔλεγχον.

ΑΝΑΧΑΡΣΙΣ

23 Εἶδον, ὦ Σόλων, οὓς φὴς τοὺς τραγῳδοὺς καὶ
κωμῳδούς, εἴ γε ἐκεῖνοί εἰσιν, ὑποδήματα μὲν
βαρέα καὶ ὑψηλὰ ὑποδεδεμένοι, χρυσαῖς δὲ ται-
νίαις τὴν ἐσθῆτα πεποικιλμένοι, κράνη δὲ ἐπικεί-

to meander out of its channel for fear of confusing your memory with its flow. However, I shall discuss this, too, in brief, as best I can. To consider it carefully would be matter for another conversation.

We harmonize their minds by causing them to learn by heart the laws of the community, which are exposed in public for everyone to read, written in large letters, and tell what one should do and what one should refrain from doing ; also by causing them to hold converse with good men, from whom they learn to say what is fitting and do what is right, to associate with one another on an equal footing, not to aim at what is base, to seek what is noble, and to do no violence. These men we call sophists and philosophers. Furthermore, assembling them in the theatre, we instruct them publicly through comedies and tragedies, in which they behold both the virtues and the vices of the ancients, in order that they may recoil from the vices and emulate the virtues. The comedians, indeed, we allow to abuse and ridicule any citizens whom they perceive to be following practices that are base and unworthy of the city, not only for the sake of those men themselves, since they are made better by chiding, but for the sake of the general public, that they may shun castigation for similar offences.

ANACHARSIS

I have seen the tragedians and comedians **that** you are speaking of, Solon, if I am not mistaken ; they [1] had on heavy, high footgear, clothing that was gay with gold stripes, and very ludicrous head-

---

[1] The tragedians. There may be a lacuna in the text.

μένοι παγγέλοια κεχηνότα παμμέγεθες· αὐτοὶ δὲ
ἔνδοθεν μεγάλα τε ἐκεκράγεσαν καὶ διέβαινον οὐκ
οἶδ' ὅπως ἀσφαλῶς ἐν τοῖς ὑποδήμασιν. Διονύσῳ
δὲ οἶμαι τότε ἡ πόλις ἑώρταζεν. οἱ δὲ κωμῳδοὶ
βραχύτεροι μὲν ἐκείνων καὶ πεζοὶ καὶ ἀνθρωπι-
νώτεροι καὶ ἧττον ἐβόων, κράνη δὲ πολὺ γελοιότερα. καὶ τὸ θέατρον γοῦν ἅπαν ἐγέλα ἐπ' αὐτοῖς·
ἐκείνων δὲ τῶν ὑψηλῶν σκυθρωποὶ ἅπαντες
ἤκουον, οἰκτείροντες, οἶμαι, αὐτοὺς πέδας τηλι-
καύτας ἐπισυρομένους.

ΣΟΛΩΝ

Οὐκ ἐκείνους, ὦγαθέ, ᾤκτειρον, ἀλλὰ ποιητὴς
ἴσως ἀρχαίαν τινὰ συμφορὰν ἐπεδείκνυτο τοῖς
θεαταῖς καὶ ῥήσεις οἰκτρὰς ἐτραγῴδει πρὸς τὸ
θέατρον ὑφ' ὧν εἰς δάκρυα κατεσπῶντο οἱ ἀκούοντες. εἰκὸς δέ σε καὶ αὐλοῦντας ἑωρακέναι τινὰς
τότε καὶ ἄλλους συνᾴδοντας ἐν κύκλῳ συνεστῶτας.
οὐδ' αὐτά, ὦ Ἀνάχαρσι, ἀχρεῖα ᾄσματα καὶ
αὐλήματα.

Τούτοις δ' οὖν ἅπασι καὶ τοῖς τοιούτοις παρα-
θηγόμενοι τὰς ψυχὰς ἀμείνους ἡμῖν γίγνονται.

24 Τὰ δὲ δὴ σώματα, ὅπερ μάλιστα ἐπόθεις ἀκοῦσαι, ὧδε καταγυμνάζομεν. ἀποδύσαντες αὐτά, ὡς
ἔφην, οὐκέτι ἁπαλὰ καὶ τέλεον ἀσυμπαγῆ ὄντα,
πρῶτον μὲν ἐθίζειν ἀξιοῦμεν πρὸς τὸν ἀέρα, συνοι-
κειοῦντες αὐτὰ ταῖς ὥραις ἑκάσταις, ὡς μήτε
θάλπος δυσχεραίνειν μήτε πρὸς κρύος ἀπαγο-
ρεύειν, ἔπειτα δὲ χρίομεν ἐλαίῳ καὶ καταμαλάτ-
τομεν, ὡς εὐτονώτερα γίγνοιτο· ἄτοπον γάρ, εἰ
τὰ μὲν σκύτη νομίζομεν ὑπὸ τῷ ἐλαίῳ μαλαττό-
μενα δυσραγέστερα καὶ πολλῷ διαρκέστερα γίγνε-

pieces with great, gaping mouths; they shouted
loudly from out of these, and strode about in the
footgear, managing somehow or other to do it safely.
The city was then holding a feast, in honour, I think,
of Dionysus. The comedians were shorter, nearer
to the common level, more human, and less given
to shouting, but their headpieces were far more
ludicrous. In fact the whole audience laughed at
them; but they all wore long faces while they
listened to the tall fellows, pitying them, I suppose,
because they were dragging such clogs about!

SOLON

It was not the actors that they pitied, my dear
fellow. No doubt the poet was presenting some
calamity of old to the spectators and declaiming
mournful passages to the audience by which his
hearers were moved to tears. Probably you also saw
flute-players at that time, and others who sang in
concert, standing in a circle. Even singing and
flute-playing is not without value, Anacharsis.

By all these means, then, and others like them,
we whet their souls and make them better.

As to their bodies—for that is what you were
especially eager to hear about—we train them as
follows. When, as I said,[1] they are no longer soft
and wholly strengthless, we strip them, and think it
best to begin by habituating them to the weather,
making them used to the several seasons, so as not
to be distressed by the heat or give in to the cold.
Then we rub them with olive-oil and supple them
in order that they may be more elastic, for since
we believe that leather, when softened by oil, is
harder to break and far more durable, lifeless as it

[1] P. 33

σθαι νεκρά γε ἤδη ὄντα, τὸ δ' ἔτι ζωῆς μετέχον σῶμα μὴ ἂν ἄμεινον ἡγοίμεθα ὑπὸ τοῦ ἐλαίου διατεθήσεσθαι.

Τοὐντεῦθεν ποικίλα τὰ γυμνάσια ἐπινοήσαντες καὶ διδασκάλους ἑκάστων ἐπιστήσαντες τὸν μέν τινα πυκτεύειν, τὸν δὲ παγκρατιάζειν διδάσκομεν, ὡς τούς τε πόνους καρτερεῖν ἐθίζοιντο καὶ ὁμόσε χωρεῖν ταῖς πληγαῖς μηδὲ ἀποτρέποιντο δέει τῶν τραυμάτων. τοῦτο δὲ ἡμῖν δύο τὰ ὠφελιμώτατα ἐξεργάζεται ἐν αὐτοῖς, θυμοειδεῖς τε παρασκευάζον εἰς τοὺς κινδύνους καὶ τῶν σωμάτων ἀφειδεῖν καὶ προσέτι ἐρρῶσθαι καὶ καρτεροὺς εἶναι.

Ὅσοι δὲ αὐτῶν κάτω συννενευκότες παλαίουσιν, καταπίπτειν τε ἀσφαλῶς μανθάνουσι καὶ ἀνίστασθαι εὐμαρῶς καὶ ὠθισμοὺς καὶ περιπλοκὰς καὶ λυγισμοὺς καὶ ἄγχεσθαι δύνασθαι καὶ εἰς ὕψος ἀναβαστάσαι τὸν ἀντίπαλον, οὐκ ἀχρεῖα οὐδὲ οὗτοι ἐκμελετῶντες, ἀλλὰ ἐν μὲν τὸ πρῶτον καὶ μέγιστον ἀναμφιβόλως κτώμενοι· δυσπαθέστερα γὰρ καὶ καρτερώτερα τὰ σώματα γίγνονται αὐτοῖς διαπονούμενα. ἕτερον δὲ οὐδὲ αὐτὸ μικρόν· ἔμπειροι γὰρ δὴ ἐκ τούτου καθίστανται, εἴ ποτε ἀφίκοιντο εἰς χρείαν τῶν μαθημάτων τούτων ἐν ὅπλοις· δῆλον γὰρ ὅτι καὶ πολεμίῳ ἀνδρὶ ὁ τοιοῦτος συμπλακεὶς καταρρίψει τε θᾶττον ὑποσκελίσας καὶ καταπεσὼν εἴσεται ὡς ῥᾷστα ἐξανίστασθαι. πάντα γὰρ ταῦτα, ὦ Ἀνάχαρσι, ἐπ' ἐκεῖνον τὸν ἀγῶνα ποριζόμεθα τὸν ἐν τοῖς ὅπλοις καὶ ἡγούμεθα πολὺ ἀμείνοσι χρήσασθαι τοῖς οὕτως ἀσκηθεῖσιν, ἐπειδὰν πρότερον αὐτῶν γυμνὰ τὰ σώματα καταμαλάξαντες καὶ διαπονήσαντες ἐρρωμενέστερα καὶ ἀλκιμώτερα ἐξεργασώμεθα καὶ

is, it would be extraordinary if we should not think that the living body would be put in better condition by the oil.

After that, having invented many forms of athletics and appointed teachers for each, we teach one, for instance, boxing, and another the pancratium, in order that they may become accustomed to endure hardships and to meet blows, and not recoil for fear of injuries. This helps us by creating in them two effects that are most useful, since it makes them not only spirited in facing dangers and unmindful of their bodies, but healthy and strong into the bargain.

Those of them who put their bent heads together and wrestle learn to fall safely and get up easily, to push, grip and twist in various ways, to stand being choked, and to lift their opponent high in the air. They too are not engaging in useless exercises; on the contrary, they indisputably acquire one thing, which is first and greatest: their bodies become less susceptible and more vigorous through being exercised thoroughly. There is something else, too, which itself is not trivial: they become expert as a result of it, in case they should ever come to need what they have learned in battle. Clearly such a man, when he closes with an enemy, will trip and throw him more quickly, and when he is down, will know how to get up again most easily. For we make all these preparations, Anacharsis, with a view to that contest, the contest under arms, and we expect to find men thus disciplined far superior, after we have suppled and trained their bodies naked, and so have made them healthier and stronger, light and

κοῦφα καὶ εὔτονα καὶ τὰ αὐτὰ βαρέα τοῖς ἀντα-
γωνισταῖς.

25 Ἐννοεῖς γάρ, οἶμαι, τὸ μετὰ τοῦτο, οἵους εἰκὸς
σὺν ὅπλοις ἔσεσθαι τοὺς καὶ γυμνοὺς ἂν φόβον
τοῖς δυσμενέσιν ἐμποιήσαντας, οὐ πολυσαρκίαν
ἀργὸν καὶ λευκὴν ἢ ἀσαρκίαν μετὰ ὠχρότητος
ἐπιδεικνυμένους οἷα γυναικῶν σώματα ὑπὸ σκιᾷ
μεμαρασμένα, τρέμοντα ἱδρῶτί τε πολλῷ εὐθὺς
ῥεόμενα καὶ ἀσθμαίνοντα ὑπὸ τῷ κράνει, καὶ
μάλιστα ἢν καὶ ὁ ἥλιος ὥσπερ νῦν τὸ μεσημβρι-
νὸν ἐπιφλέγῃ. οἷς τί ἄν τις χρήσαιτο διψῶσι
καὶ τὸν κονιορτὸν οὐκ ἀνεχομένοις καὶ εἰ αἷμα
ἴδοιεν, εὐθὺς ταραττομένοις καὶ προαποθνήσκουσι
πρὶν ἐντὸς βέλους γενέσθαι καὶ εἰς χεῖρας ἐλθεῖν
τοῖς πολεμίοις;

Οὗτοι δὲ ἡμῖν ὑπέρυθροι εἰς τὸ μελάντερον ὑπὸ
τοῦ ἡλίου κεχρωσμένοι καὶ ἀρρενωποί, πολὺ τὸ
ἔμψυχον καὶ θερμὸν καὶ ἀνδρῶδες ἐπιφαίνοντες,
τοσαύτης εὐεξίας ἀπολάμποντες,[1] οὔτε ῥικνοὶ καὶ
κατεσκληκότες οὔτε περιπληθεῖς εἰς βάρος, ἀλλὰ
εἰς τὸ σύμμετρον περιγεγραμμένοι, τὸ μὲν ἀχρεῖον
τῶν σαρκῶν καὶ περιττὸν τοῖς ἱδρῶσιν ἐξαναλω-
κότες, ὃ δὲ ἰσχὺν καὶ τόνον παρεῖχεν ἀμιγὲς τοῦ
φαύλου περιλελειμμένον ἐρρωμένως φυλάττοντες.
ὅπερ γὰρ δὴ οἱ λικμῶντες τὸν πυρόν, τοῦτο ἡμῖν
καὶ τὰ γυμνάσια ἐργάζεται ἐν τοῖς σώμασι, τὴν
μὲν ἄχνην καὶ τοὺς ἀθέρας ἀποφυσῶντα, καθαρὸν
δὲ τὸν καρπὸν διευκρινοῦντα καὶ προσωρεύοντα.

26 Καὶ διὰ τοῦτο ὑγιαίνειν τε ἀνάγκη καὶ ἐπὶ
μήκιστον διαρκεῖν ἐν τοῖς καμάτοις· ὀψέ τε ἂν

---

[1] ἀπολάμποντες J. F. Reitz : ἀπολάμπτοντες ΓΕ, ἀπολαύοντες
Ν, vulg.

elastic, and at the same time too heavy for their opponents.

You can imagine, I suppose, the consequence—what they are likely to be with arms in hand when even unarmed they would implant fear in the enemy. They show no white and ineffective corpulence or pallid leanness, as if they were women's bodies bleached out in the shade, quivering and streaming with profuse sweat at once and panting beneath the helmet, especially if the sun, as at present, blazes with the heat of noon. What use could one make of men like that, who get thirsty, who cannot stand dust, who break ranks the moment they catch sight of blood, who lie down and die before they get within a spear's cast and come to grips with the enemy?

But these young men of ours have a ruddy skin, coloured darker by the sun, and manly faces; they reveal great vitality, fire, and courage; they are aglow with such splendid condition; they are neither lean and emaciated nor so full-bodied as to be heavy, but symmetrical in their lines; they have sweated away the useless and superfluous part of their tissues, but what made for strength and elasticity is left upon them uncontaminated by what is worthless, and they maintain it vigorously. In fact, athletics do in our bodies just what winnowers do to wheat: they blow away the husks and the chaff, but separate the grain out cleanly and accumulate it for future use.

Consequently a man like that cannot help keeping well and holding out protractedly under exhausting labours; it would be long before he would begin

43

ἰδίειν ὁ τοιοῦτος ἄρξαιτο καὶ ὀλιγάκις ἂν ἀσθενῶν
φανείη. ὥσπερ ἂν εἰ πῦρ τις φέρων ἅμα ἐμβάλοι
εἰς πυρὸν αὐτὸν καὶ εἰς τὴν καλάμην αὐτοῦ καὶ
εἰς τὴν ἄχνην—αὖθις γὰρ ἐπὶ τὸν λικμῶντα
ἐπάνειμι—θᾶττον ἄν, οἶμαι, παρὰ πολὺ ἡ καλάμη
ἀναφλεγείη, ὁ δὲ πυρὸς κατ᾽ ὀλίγον οὔτε φλογὸς
μεγάλης ἀνισταμένης οὔτε ὑπὸ μιᾷ τῇ ὁρμῇ, ἀλλὰ
κατὰ μικρὸν ὑποτυφόμενος χρόνῳ ὕστερον καὶ
αὐτὸς ἂν κατακαυθείη.

Οὐ τοίνυν οὐδὲ νόσος οὐδὲ κάματος εἰς τοιοῦτο
σῶμα ἐμπεσόντα ῥᾳδίως ἐλέγξειεν ἂν οὐδ᾽ ἐπικρα-
τήσειεν εὐμαρῶς· ἔνδοθέν τε γὰρ εὖ παρεσκεύα-
σται αὐτῷ καὶ τὰ ἔξω μάλα καρτερῶς πέφρακται
πρὸς αὐτά, ὡς μὴ παριέναι εἰς τὸ εἴσω, μηδὲ
παραδέχεσθαι μήτε ἥλιον αὐτὸν μήτε κρύος ἐπὶ
λύμῃ τοῦ σώματος. πρός τε τὸ ἐνδιδὸν ἐν τοῖς
πόνοις πολὺ τὸ θερμὸν τὸ ἔνδοθεν ἐπιρρέον, ἅτε
ἐκ πολλοῦ προπαρεσκευασμένον καὶ εἰς τὴν
ἀναγκαίαν χρείαν ἀποκείμενον, ἀναπληροῖ εὐθὺς
ἐπάρδον τῇ ἀκμῇ καὶ ἀκαμάτους ἐπὶ πλεῖστον
παρέχεται· τὸ γὰρ προπονῆσαι πολλὰ καὶ προ-
καμεῖν οὐκ ἀνάλωσιν τῆς ἰσχύος, ἀλλ᾽ ἐπίδοσιν
ἐργάζεται, καὶ ἀναρριπιζομένη πλείων γίγνεται.

27 Καὶ μὴν καὶ δρομικοὺς εἶναι ἀσκοῦμεν αὐτοὺς
εἰς μῆκός τε διαρκεῖν ἐθίζοντες καὶ εἰς τὸ ἐν βραχεῖ
ὠκύτατον ἐπικουφίζοντες· καὶ ὁ δρόμος οὐ πρὸς
τὸ στερρὸν καὶ ἀντίτυπον, ἀλλὰ ἐν ψάμμῳ βαθείᾳ,
ἔνθα οὔτε βεβαίως ἀπερεῖσαι τὴν βάσιν οὔτε
ἐπιστηρίξαι ῥᾴδιον ὑποσυρομένου πρὸς τὸ ὑπεῖκον
τοῦ ποδός. ἀλλὰ καὶ ὑπεράλλεσθαι τάφρον, εἰ
δέοι, ἢ εἴ τι ἄλλο ἐμπόδιον, καὶ πρὸς τοῦτο
ἀσκοῦνται ἡμῖν, ἔτι καὶ μολυβδίδας χειροπληθεῖς

to sweat, and he would rarely be found ill. It is as if you should take firebrands and throw them simultaneously into the wheat itself and into its straw and chaff—for I am going back again to the winnower. The straw, I take it, would blaze up far more quickly, while the wheat would burn slowly, not with a great blaze springing up nor at a single burst, but smouldering gradually, until in course of time it too was totally consumed.

Neither illness nor fatigue, then, could easily invade and rack such a body, or readily overmaster it; for it has been well stocked within and very strongly fortified against them without, so as not to admit them, nor yet to receive either sun itself or frost to the detriment of the body. To prevent giving way under hardships, abundant energy that gushes up from within, since it has been made ready long beforehand and stored away for the emergency, fills them at once, watering them with vigour, and makes them unwearying for a very long period, for their great preliminary hardships and fatigues do not squander their strength but increase it; the more you fan its flame, the greater it becomes.

Furthermore, we train them to be good runners, habituating them to hold out for a long distance, and also making them light-footed for extreme speed in a short distance. And the running is not done on hard, resisting ground but in deep sand, where it is not easy to plant one's foot solidly or to get a purchase with it, since it slips from under one as the sand gives way beneath it. We also train them to jump a ditch, if need be, or any other obstacle, even carrying lead weights as large as they

ἐν ταῖν χεροῖν ἔχοντες. εἶτα περὶ ἀκοντίου βολῆς
εἰς μῆκος ἀμιλλῶνται. εἶδες δὲ καὶ ἄλλο τι ἐν
τῷ γυμνασίῳ χαλκοῦν περιφερές, ἀσπίδι μικρᾷ
ἐοικὸς ὄχανον οὐκ ἐχούσῃ οὐδὲ τελαμῶνας, καὶ
ἐπειράθης γε αὐτοῦ κειμένου ἐν τῷ μέσῳ καὶ ἐδόκει
σοι βαρὺ καὶ δύσληπτον ὑπὸ λειότητος. ἐκεῖνο
τοίνυν ἄνω τε ἀναρριπτοῦσιν εἰς τὸν ἀέρα καὶ
εἰς τὸ πόρρω, φιλοτιμούμενοι ὅστις ἐπὶ μήκιστον
ἐξέλθοι καὶ τοὺς ἄλλους ὑπερβάλοιτο· καὶ ὁ πόνος
οὗτος ὤμους τε αὐτῶν κρατύνει καὶ τόνον τοῖς
ἄκροις ἐντίθησιν.

28   Ὁ πηλὸς δὲ καὶ ἡ κόνις, ἅπερ σοι γελοιότερα
ἐξ ἀρχῆς ἔδοξεν, ἄκουσον, ὦ θαυμάσιε, ὅτου ἕνεκα
ὑποβέβληται. πρῶτον μέν, ὡς μὴ ἐπὶ τὸ κρα-
ταιὸν ἡ πτῶσις αὐτοῖς γίγνοιτο, ἀλλ' ἐπὶ τὸ
μαλακὸν ἀσφαλῶς πίπτοιεν· ἔπειτα καὶ τὸν ὄλισθον ἀνάγκη πλείω γίγνεσθαι, ἱδρούντων ἐν τῷ
πηλῷ, ὃ σὺ ταῖς ἐγχέλεσιν εἴκαζες, οὐκ ἀχρεῖον
οὐδὲ γελοῖον ὄν, ἀλλὰ καὶ τοῦτο εἰς ἰσχὺν καὶ
τόνον οὐκ ὀλίγα συντελεῖ, ὁπόταν οὕτως ἐχόντων
ἀλλήλων ἀναγκάζωνται ἐγκρατῶς ἀντιλαμβά-
νεσθαι καὶ συνέχειν διολισθάνοντας· αἴρεσθαί τε
ἐν πηλῷ ἱδρωκότα μετ' ἐλαίου, ἐκπεσεῖν καὶ διαρ-
ρυῆναι τῶν χειρῶν σπουδάζοντα, μὴ μικρὸν εἶναι
νόμιζε. καὶ ταῦτα πάντα, ὥσπερ ἔφην ἔμπροσθεν,
εἰς τοὺς πολέμους καὶ χρήσιμα, εἰ δέοι φίλον
τρωθέντα ῥᾳδίως ἀράμενον ὑπεξενεγκεῖν ἢ καὶ
πολέμιον συναρπάσαντα ἥκειν μετέωρον κομί-
ζοντα. καὶ διὰ τοῦτο εἰς ὑπερβολὴν ἀσκοῦμεν,
τὰ χαλεπώτερα προτιθέντες ὡς τὰ μικρότερα
μακρῷ εὐκολώτερον φέροιεν.

can grasp. Then too they compete in throwing the javelin for distance. And you saw another implement in the gymnasium, made of bronze, circular, resembling a little shield without handle or straps; in fact, you tested it as it lay there, and thought it heavy and hard to hold on account of its smoothness. Well, they throw that high into the air and also to a distance, vying to see who can go the farthest and throw beyond the rest. This exercise strengthens their shoulders and puts muscle into their arms and legs.

As for the mud and the dust, which you thought rather ludicrous in the beginning, you amazing person, let me tell you why it is put down. In the first place, so that instead of taking their tumbles on a hard surface they may fall with impunity on a soft one; secondly, their slipperiness is necessarily greater when they are sweaty and muddy. This feature, in which you compared them to eels, is not useless or ludicrous; it contributes not a little to strength and muscle when both are in this condition and each has to grip the other firmly and hold him fast while he tries to slip away. And as for picking up a man who is muddy, sweaty, and oily while he does his best to break away and squirm out of your hands, do not think it a trifle! All this, as I said before, is of use in war, in case one should need to pick up a wounded friend and carry him out of the fight with ease, or to snatch up an enemy and come back with him in one's arms. So we train them beyond measure, setting them hard tasks that they may manage smaller ones with far greater ease.

29 Τὴν μέντοι κόνιν ἐπὶ τὸ ἐναντίον χρησίμην
οἰόμεθα εἶναι, ὡς μὴ διολισθάνοιεν συμπλεκόμενοι.
ἐπειδὰν γὰρ ἐν τῷ πηλῷ ἀσκηθῶσιν συνέχειν τὸ
διαδιδρᾶσκον ὑπὸ γλισχρότητος, ἐθίζονται ἐκφεύ-
γειν αὐτοὶ ληφθέντες ἐκ τῶν χειρῶν, καὶ ταῦτα
ἐν ἀφύκτῳ ἐχόμενοι. καὶ μὴν καὶ τὸν ἱδρῶτα
συνέχειν δοκεῖ ἡ κόνις ἀθρόον ἐκχεόμενον ἐπι-
παττομένη, καὶ ἐπὶ πολὺ διαρκεῖν ποιεῖ τὴν
δύναμιν, καὶ κώλυμα γίγνεται μὴ βλάπτεσθαι
ὑπὸ τῶν ἀνέμων ἀραιοῖς τότε καὶ ἀνεῳγόσιν τοῖς
σώμασιν ἐμπιπτόντων. ἄλλως τε καὶ τὸν ῥύπον
ἀποσμᾷ καὶ στιλπνότερον ποιεῖ τὸν ἄνδρα. καὶ
ἔγωγε ἡδέως ἂν παραστησάμενος πλησίον τῶν τε
λευκῶν τινα ἐκείνων καὶ ὑπὸ σκιᾷ δεδιῃτημένων
καὶ ὃν ἂν ἕλῃ τῶν ἐν τῷ Λυκείῳ γυμναζομένων,
ἀποπλύνας[1] τὴν κόνιν καὶ τὸν πηλόν, ἐροίμην ἄν
σε ποτέρῳ ἂν ὅμοιος εὔξαιο γενέσθαι· οἶδα γὰρ
ὡς αὐτίκα ἕλοιο ἂν ἐκ πρώτης προσόψεως, εἰ καὶ
μὴ ἐπὶ τῶν ἔργων πειραθείης ἑκατέρου, συνε-
στηκὼς καὶ συγκεκροτημένος εἶναι μᾶλλον ἢ
θρύπτεσθαι καὶ διαρρεῖν καὶ λευκὸς[2] εἶναι ἀπορίᾳ
καὶ φυγῇ εἰς τὰ εἴσω τοῦ αἵματος.

30 Ταῦτ' ἔστιν, ὦ Ἀνάχαρσι, ἃ τοὺς νέους ἡμεῖς
ἀσκοῦμεν οἰόμενοι φύλακας ἡμῖν τῆς πόλεως
ἀγαθοὺς γενέσθαι καὶ ἐν ἐλευθερίᾳ βιώσεσθαι δι'
αὑτούς, κρατοῦντες μὲν τῶν δυσμενῶν εἰ ἐπίοιεν,
φοβεροὶ δὲ τοῖς περιοίκοις ὄντες, ὡς ὑποπτήσσειν
τε καὶ ὑποτελεῖν ἡμῖν τοὺς πλείστους αὐτῶν. ἐν
εἰρήνῃ τε αὖ πολὺ ἀμείνοσιν αὐτοῖς χρώμεθα περὶ
μηδὲν τῶν αἰσχρῶν φιλοτιμουμένοις μηδ' ὑπ'

---

[1] ἀποπλύνας Dindorf : ἀποπλῦναι MSS.

ANACHARSIS, OR ATHLETICS

The dust we think to be of use for the opposite purpose, to prevent them from slipping away when they are grasped. After they have been trained in the mud to hold fast what eludes them because of its oiliness, they are given practice in escaping out of their opponent's hands when they themselves are caught, even though they are held in a sure grip. Moreover, the dust, sprinkled on when the sweat is pouring out in profusion, is thought to check it; it makes their strength endure long, and hinders them from being harmed by the wind blowing upon their bodies, which are then unresisting and have the pores open. Besides, it rubs off the dirt and makes the man cleaner. I should like to put side by side one of those white-skinned fellows who have lived in the shade and any one you might select of the athletes in the Lyceum, after I had washed off the mud and the dust, and to ask you which of the two you would pray to be like. I know that even without testing each to see what he could do, you would immediately choose on first sight to be firm and hard rather than delicate and mushy and white because your blood is scanty and withdraws to the interior of the body.

That, Anacharsis, is the training we give our young men, expecting them to become stout guardians of our city, and that we shall live in freedom through them, conquering our foes if they attack us and keeping our neighbours in dread of us, so that most of them will cower at our feet and pay tribute. In peace, too, we find them far better, for nothing that is base appeals to their ambitions

---

¹ λευκὸς C. C. Reitz : λευκὸν MSS.

ἀργίας εἰς ὕβριν τρεπομένοις, ἀλλὰ περὶ τὰ τοιαῦτα
διατρίβουσιν καὶ ἀσχόλοις οὖσιν ἐν αὐτοῖς. καὶ
ὅπερ ἔφην τὸ κοινὸν ἀγαθὸν καὶ τὴν ἄκραν πόλεως
εὐδαιμονίαν, τοῦτ' ἔστιν, ὁπότε[1] εἴς τε εἰρήνην
καὶ εἰς πόλεμον τὰ ἄριστα παρεσκευασμένη φαί-
νοιτο ἡ νεότης περὶ τὰ κάλλιστα ἡμῖν σπουδά-
ζοντες.

ΑΝΑΧΑΡΣΙΣ

31 Οὐκοῦν, ὦ Σόλων, ἤν ποτε ὑμῖν ἐπίωσιν οἱ
πολέμιοι, χρισάμενοι τῷ ἐλαίῳ καὶ κονισάμενοι
πρόιτε καὶ αὐτοὶ πὺξ τὰς χεῖρας ἐπ' αὐτοὺς προ-
βεβλημένοι, κἀκεῖνοι δηλαδὴ ὑποπτήσσουσιν ὑμᾶς
καὶ φεύγουσιν δεδιότες μὴ σφίσι κεχηνόσι πάσητε
τὴν ψάμμον εἰς τὸ στόμα ἢ περιπηδήσαντες, ὡς
κατὰ νώτου γένησθε, περιπλέξητε αὐτοῖς τὰ σκέλη
περὶ τὴν γαστέρα καὶ διάγχητε ὑπὸ τὸ κράνος
ὑποβαλόντες τὸν πῆχυν. καὶ νὴ Δί' οἱ μὲν τοξεύ-
σουσι δῆλον ὅτι καὶ ἀκοντιοῦσιν, ὑμῶν δὲ ὥσπερ
ἀνδριάντων οὐ καθίξεται τὰ βέλη κεχρωσμένων
πρὸς τὸν ἥλιον καὶ πολὺ τὸ αἷμα πεπορισμένων.
οὐ γὰρ καλάμη καὶ ἀθέρες ὑμεῖς ἐστε, ὡς τάχιστα
ἐνδιδόναι πρὸς τὰς πληγάς, ἀλλὰ ὀψέ ποτε ἂν
καὶ μόλις κατατεμνόμενοι βαθέσι τοῖς τραύμασιν
αἷμα ὀλίγον ὑποδείξαιτε.[2] τοιαῦτα γὰρ φής, εἰ
32 μὴ πάνυ παρήκουσα τοῦ παραδείγματος. ἢ τὰς
πανοπλίας ἐκείνας τότε ἀναλήψεσθε τὰς τῶν
κωμῳδῶν τε καὶ τραγῳδῶν, καὶ ἢν προτεθῇ ὑμῖν
ἔξοδος, ἐκεῖνα τὰ κράνη περιθήσεσθε τὰ κεχηνότα,

---

[1] ὁπότε Dindorf : ὁπόταν MSS.
[2] ὑποδείξαιτε Fritzsche : ὑποδείξετε MSS.

and idleness does not incline them to arrogance, but exercises such as these give them diversion and keep them occupied. The chief good of the public and the supreme felicity of the state, which I mentioned before, are attained when our young men, striving at our behest for the fairest objects, have been most efficiently prepared both for peace and for war.

ANACHARSIS

Then if the enemy attack you, Solon, you yourselves will take the field rubbed with oil and covered with dust, shaking your fists at them, and they, of course, will cower at your feet and run away, fearing that while they are agape in stupefaction you may sprinkle sand in their mouths, or that after jumping behind them so as to get on their backs, you may wind your legs about their bellies and strangle them by putting an arm under their helmets. Yes, by Zeus, they will shoot their arrows, naturally, and throw their spears, but the missiles will not affect you any more than as if you were statues, tanned as you are by the sun and supplied in abundance with blood. You are not straw or chaff, so as to give in quickly under their blows; it would be only after long and strenuous effort, when you are all cut up with deep wounds, that you would show a few drops of blood. This is the gist of what you say, unless I have completely misunderstood your comparison. Or else you will then assume those panoplies of the comedians and tragedians, and if a sally is proposed to you, you will put on those wide-mouthed headpieces in order

ὡς φοβερώτεροι εἴητε τοῖς ἐναντίοις μορμολυττό-
μενοι αὐτούς, καὶ ὑποδήσεσθε τὰ ὑψηλὰ ἐκεῖνα
δηλαδή· φεύγουσί τε γάρ, ἢν δέῃ, κοῦφα, καὶ ἢν
διώκητε, ἄφυκτα τοῖς πολεμίοις ἔσται, ὑμῶν οὕτω
μεγάλα διαβαινόντων ἐπ' αὐτούς.

Ἀλλ' ὅρα μὴ ταῦτα μὲν ὑμῖν τὰ κομψὰ
λῆρος ᾖ καὶ παιδιὰ ἄλλως καὶ διατριβαὶ ἀργοῦ-
σι καὶ ῥᾳθυμεῖν ἐθέλουσι τοῖς νεανίσκοις. εἰ δὲ
βούλεσθε πάντως ἐλεύθεροι καὶ εὐδαίμονες εἶναι,
ἄλλων ὑμῖν γυμνασίων δεήσει καὶ ἀσκήσεως
ἀληθινῆς τῆς ἐν τοῖς ὅπλοις, καὶ ἡ ἅμιλλα
οὐ πρὸς ἀλλήλους μετὰ παιδιᾶς, ἀλλὰ πρὸς
τοὺς δυσμενεῖς ἔσται μετὰ κινδύνων μελετῶσι
τὴν ἀρετήν. ὥστε ἀφέντας τὴν κόνιν καὶ τὸ
ἔλαιον δίδασκε αὐτοὺς τοξεύειν καὶ ἀκοντίζειν μὴ
κοῦφα διδοὺς τὰ ἀκόντια καὶ οἷα διαφέρεσθαι
πρὸς τὸν ἄνεμον, ἀλλ' ἔστω λόγχη βαρεῖα μετὰ
συριγμοῦ ἐλιττομένη καὶ λίθος χειροπληθὴς καὶ
σάγαρις καὶ γέρρον ἐν τῇ ἀριστερᾷ καὶ θώραξ καὶ
κράνος.

33 Ὡς δὲ νῦν ἔχετε, θεῶν τινος εὐμενείᾳ σώζεσθαί
μοι δοκεῖτε, οἳ μηδέπω ἀπολώλατε ὑπό τινων
ὀλίγων ψιλῶν ἐπιπεσόντων. ἰδού γέ τοι ἢν σπα-
σάμενος τὸ μικρὸν τοῦτο ξιφίδιον τὸ παρὰ τὴν
ζώνην μόνος ἐπεισπέσω τοῖς νέοις ὑμῶν ἅπασιν,
αὐτοβοεὶ ἂν ἕλοιμι τὸ γυμνάσιον φυγόντων
ἐκείνων καὶ οὐδενὸς ἀντιβλέπειν τῷ σιδήρῳ τολ-
μῶντος, ἀλλὰ περὶ τοὺς ἀνδριάντας ἂν περιστά-
μενοι καὶ περὶ τοὺς κίονας κατακρυπτόμενοι
γέλωτα ἄν μοι παράσχοιεν δακρύοντες οἱ πολλοὶ
καὶ τρέμοντες. καὶ τότ' ἂν ἴδοις οὐκέτι ἐρυθριῶν-
τας αὐτοὺς τὰ σώματα οἷοι νῦν εἰσιν, ἀλλὰ

that you may be more formidable to your opponents by playing bogey-man, and will of course wear those high shoes, for they will be light to run away in, if need be, and hard for the enemy to escape from, if you go in pursuit, when you take such great strides in chase of them.

No, I am afraid that all these clever tricks of yours are silliness, nothing but child's play, amusements for your young men who have nothing to do and want to lead an easy life. If you wish, whatever betides, to be free and happy, you will require other forms of athletics and real training, that is to say, under arms, and you will not compete against each other in sport, but against the enemy, learning courage in perilous conflict. So let them give up the dust and the oil; teach them to draw the bow and throw the spear; and do not give them light javelins that can be deflected by the wind, but let them have a heavy lance that whistles when it is hurled, a stone as large as they can grasp, a double axe, a target in their left hand, a breastplate, and a helmet.

In your present condition, it seems to me that you are being saved by the grace of some god or other, seeing that you have not yet been wiped out by the onfall of a handful of light-armed troops. Look here, if I should draw this little dirk at my belt and fall upon all your young men by myself, I should capture the gymnasium with a mere hurrah, for they would run away and not one would dare to face the steel; no, they would gather about the statues and hide behind the pillars, making me laugh while most of them cried and trembled. Then you would see that they were no longer ruddy-bodied as they

53

ὠχροὶ ἅπαντες αὐτίκα γένοιντ' ἂν ὑπὸ τοῦ δέους
μεταβαφέντες. οὕτως ὑμᾶς ἡ εἰρήνη διατέθεικε
βαθεῖα οὖσα, ὡς μὴ ἂν ῥᾳδίως ἀνασχέσθαι λόφον
ἕνα κράνους πολεμίου ἰδόντας.

ΣΟΛΩΝ

34 Οὐ ταῦτα ἔφασαν, ὦ Ἀνάχαρσι, Θρᾳκῶν τε
ὅσοι μετ' Εὐμόλπου ἐφ' ἡμᾶς ἐστράτευσαν καὶ αἱ
γυναῖκες ὑμῶν αἱ μετὰ Ἱππολύτης ἐλάσασαι ἐπὶ
τὴν πόλιν οὐδὲ οἱ ἄλλοι ὅσοι ἡμῶν ἐν ὅπλοις
ἐπειράθησαν. ἡμεῖς γάρ, ὦ μακάριε, οὐκ ἐπείπερ
οὕτω γυμνὰ τὰ σώματα ἐκπονοῦμεν τῶν νέων, διὰ
τοῦτο καὶ ἄνοπλα ἐξάγομεν ἐπὶ τοὺς κινδύνους,
ἀλλ' ἐπειδὰν καθ' αὑτοὺς ἄριστοι γένωνται,
ἀσκοῦνται τὸ μετὰ τοῦτο σὺν τοῖς ὅπλοις,
καὶ πολὺ ἄμεινον χρήσαιντ' ἂν αὐτοῖς οὕτω
διακείμενοι.

ΑΝΑΧΑΡΣΙΣ

Καὶ ποῦ τοῦτο ὑμῖν ἐστι τὸ γυμνάσιον τὸ ἐν
τοῖς ὅπλοις; οὐ γὰρ εἶδον ἔγωγε ἐν τῇ πόλει τοιοῦτον οὐδέν, ἅπασαν αὐτὴν ἐν κύκλῳ περιελθών.

ΣΟΛΩΝ

Ἀλλὰ ἴδοις ἄν, ὦ Ἀνάχαρσι, ἐπὶ πλέον ἡμῖν
συνδιατρίψας, καὶ ὅπλα ἑκάστῳ μάλα πολλά,
οἷς χρώμεθα ὁπόταν ἀναγκαῖον ᾖ, καὶ λόφους καὶ
φάλαρα καὶ ἵππους, καὶ ἱππέας σχεδὸν τὸ τέταρ-
τον τῶν πολιτῶν. τὸ μέντοι ὁπλοφορεῖν ἀεὶ καὶ
ἀκινάκην παρεζῶσθαι περιττὸν ἐν εἰρήνῃ οἰόμεθα
εἶναι, καὶ πρόστιμόν γ' ἔστιν, ὅστις ἐν ἄστει

are now ; they would all turn pale on the instant, dyed to another hue by fright. Profound peace has brought you to such a pass that you could not easily endure to see a single plume of a hostile helmet.

SOLON

The Thracians who campaigned against us with Eumolpus did not say so, Anacharsis, nor your women who marched against the city with Hippolyta,[1] nor any others who have tested us under arms. It does not follow, my unsophisticated friend, that because our young men's bodies are thus naked while we are developing them, they are therefore undefended by armour when we lead them out into dangers. When they become efficient in themselves, they are then trained with arms and can make far better use of them because they are so well conditioned.

ANACHARSIS

Where do you do this training under arms ? I have not seen anything of the sort in the city, though I have gone all about the whole of it.

SOLON

But you would see it, Anacharsis, if you should stop with us longer, and also arms for every man in great quantity, which we use when it is necessary, and crests and trappings and horses, and cavalrymen amounting to nearly a fourth of our citizens. But to bear arms always and carry a dirk at one's belt is, we think, superfluous in time of peace ; in fact, there is a penalty prescribed for anyone who carries

---

[1] The Amazons.

σιδηροφοροίη μηδὲν δέον ἢ ὅπλα ἐξενέγκοι[1] εἰς τὸ
δημόσιον. ὑμεῖς δὲ συγγνωστοὶ ἐν ὅπλοις ἀεὶ
βιοῦντες· τό τε γὰρ ἐν ἀφράκτῳ οἰκεῖν ῥᾴδιον εἰς
ἐπιβουλήν, καὶ οἱ πόλεμοι[2] μάλα πολλοί, καὶ
ἄδηλον ὁπότε τις ἐπιστὰς κοιμώμενον κατα-
σπάσας ἀπὸ τῆς ἁμάξης φονεύσειεν· ἥ τε πρὸς
ἀλλήλους ἀπιστία, αὐθαιρέτως καὶ μὴ ἐν νόμῳ
συμπολιτευομένων, ἀναγκαῖον ἀεὶ τὸν σίδηρον
ποιεῖ, ὡς πλησίον εἶναι ἀμυνοῦντα, εἴ τις βιάζοιτο.

ΑΝΑΧΑΡΣΙΣ

35 Εἶτα, ὦ Σόλων, σιδηροφορεῖν μὲν οὐδενὸς
ἀναγκαίου ἕνεκα περιττὸν ὑμῖν δοκεῖ, καὶ τῶν
ὅπλων φείδεσθε,[3] ὡς μὴ διὰ χειρὸς ὄντα φθείροιτο,
ἀλλὰ φυλάττετε ἀποκείμενα ὡς χρησόμενοι τότε,
τῆς χρείας ἐπιστάσης· τὰ δὲ σώματα τῶν νέων
οὐδενὸς δεινοῦ ἐπείγοντος καταπονεῖτε παίοντες
καὶ ὑπὸ τῶν ἱδρώτων καταναλίσκοντες, οὐ τα-
μιευόμενοι πρὸς τὸ ἀναγκαῖον τὰς ἀλκὰς αὐτῶν,
ἀλλ᾽ εἰκῆ ἐν τῷ πηλῷ καὶ τῇ κόνει ἐκχέοντες;

ΣΟΛΩΝ

Ἔοικας, ὦ Ἀνάχαρσι, τοιόνδε τι δυνάμεως πέρι
ἐννοεῖν, ὡς οἴνῳ ἢ ὕδατι ἢ ἄλλῳ τῶν ὑγρῶν
ὁμοίαν αὐτὴν οὖσαν. δέδιας οὖν μὴ ὥσπερ ἐξ
ἀγγείου κεραμεοῦ λάθῃ διαρρυεῖσα ἐν τοῖς πόνοις

---

[1] ἐξενέγκοι vulg. : ἐξενέγκῃ MSS.
[2] πολέμιοι du Soul. But the allusion is to the tribal
struggles so familiar to readers of Horace. *Cf.* Herod. 4, 65.

weapons unnecessarily within the city limits or brings armour out into a public place. As for your people, you may be pardoned for always living under arms. Your dwelling in unfortified places makes it easy to attack you, and your wars are very numerous, and nobody knows when someone may come upon him asleep, drag him down from his wagon, and kill him. Besides, your distrust of one another, inasmuch as your relations with each other are adjusted by individual caprice and not by law, makes steel always necessary, so as to be at hand for defence if anyone should use violence.

ANACHARSIS

Then is it possible, Solon, that while you think it superfluous to carry weapons without urgent reason, and are careful of your arms in order that they may not be spoiled by handling, keeping them in store with the intention of using them some day, when need arises; yet when no danger threatens you wear out the bodies of your young men by mauling them and wasting them away in sweat, not husbanding their strength until it is needed but expending it fruitlessly in the mud and dust?

SOLON

Apparently, Anacharsis, you think that strength is like wine or water or some other liquid. Anyhow, you are afraid that during exertions it may leak away unnoticed as if from an earthen jar, and then

---

³ φείδεσθε du Soul : φείδεσθαι MSS.

κᾆτα ἡμῖν κενὸν καὶ ξηρὸν οἴχηται τὸ σῶμα
καταλιποῦσα ὑπὸ μηδενὸς ἔνδοθεν ἀναπληρού-
μενον. τὸ δὲ οὐχ οὕτως ἔχει σοι, ἀλλὰ ὅσῳ τις
ἂν αὐτὴν ἐξαντλῇ τοῖς πόνοις, τοσῷδε μᾶλλον
ἐπιρρεῖ κατὰ τὸν περὶ τῆς Ὕδρας μῦθον, εἴ τινα
ἤκουσας, ὡς ἀντὶ μιᾶς κεφαλῆς τμηθείσης δύ᾽
ἀεὶ ἄλλαι ἀνεφύοντο. ἢν δὲ ἀγύμναστος ἐξ ἀρχῆς
καὶ ἄτονος ᾖ μηδὲ διαρκῆ τὴν ὕλην ἔχῃ ὑπο-
βεβλημένην, τότε ὑπὸ τῶν καμάτων βλάπτοιτο
ἂν καὶ καταμαραίνοιτο, οἷόν τι ἐπὶ πυρὸς καὶ
λύχνου γίγνεται. ὑπὸ γὰρ τῷ αὐτῷ φυσήματι
τὸ μὲν πῦρ ἀνακαύσειας ἂν καὶ μεῖζον ἐν βραχεῖ
ποιήσειας παραθήγων τῷ πνεύματι, καὶ τὸ τοῦ
λύχνου φῶς ἀποσβέσειας οὐκ ἔχον ἀποχρῶσαν
τῆς ὕλης τὴν χορηγίαν, ὡς διαρκῆ εἶναι πρὸς τὸ
ἀντιπνέον· οὐ γὰρ ἀπ᾽ ἰσχυρᾶς, οἶμαι, τῆς ῥίζης
ἀνεφύετο.

ΑΝΑΧΑΡΣΙΣ

36 Ταυτὶ μέν,[1] ὦ Σόλων, οὐ πάνυ συνίημι· λεπτό-
τερα γὰρ ἢ κατ᾽ ἐμὲ εἴρηκας, ἀκριβοῦς τινος
φροντίδος καὶ διανοίας ὀξὺ δεδορκυίας δεόμενα.
ἐκεῖνο δέ μοι πάντως εἰπέ, τίνος ἕνεκα οὐχὶ καὶ
ἐν τοῖς ἀγῶσι τοῖς Ὀλυμπίασι καὶ Ἰσθμοῖ καὶ
Πυθοῖ καὶ τοῖς ἄλλοις, ὁπότε πολλοί, ὡς φής,
συνίασιν ὀψόμενοι τοὺς νέους ἀγωνιζομένους,[2]
οὐδέποτε ἐν ὅπλοις ποιεῖσθε τὴν ἅμιλλαν, ἀλλὰ
γυμνοὺς εἰς τὸ μέσον παραγαγόντες λακτιζο-
μένους καὶ παιομένους ἐπιδείκνυτε καὶ νικήσασι
μῆλα καὶ κότινον δίδοτε; ἄξιον γὰρ εἰδέναι τοῦτό
γε, οὕτινος ἕνεκα οὕτω ποιεῖτε.

be gone, leaving our bodies empty and dry, since they are not filled up again with anything from within. As a matter of fact, this is not the case, my friend: the more one draws it out by exertions, the more it flows in, like the fable of the Hydra, if you have heard it, which says that when one head was cut off, two others always grew up in its place. But if a man is undeveloped from the beginning, and untempered, and has an insufficient substratum of reserve material, then he may be injured and reduced in flesh by exertions. Something similar is the case with a fire and a lamp; for with one and the same breath you can start the fire afresh and speedily make it greater, stimulating it with your blowing, and you can put out the light of the lamp, which has not an adequate supply of fuel to maintain itself against the opposing blast: the root from which it sprang was not strong, I suppose.

ANACHARSIS

I do not understand this at all, Solon; what you have said is too subtle for me, requiring keen intellect and penetrating discernment. But do by all means tell me why it is that in the Olympic and Isthmian and Pythian and the other games, where many, you say, come together to see the young men competing, you never match them under arms but bring them out naked and show them receiving kicks and blows, and when they have won you give them apples and parsley. It is worth while to know why you do so.

---

[1] μὲν Dindorf : γὰρ MSS.
[2] ἀγωνιζομένους Jacobitz : ἀγωνισομένους MSS.

ΣΟΛΩΝ

Ἡγούμεθα γάρ, ὦ Ἀνάχαρσι, τὴν εἰς τὰ
γυμνάσια προθυμίαν οὕτως ἂν πλείω ἐγγενέσθαι
αὐτοῖς, εἰ τοὺς ἀριστεύοντας ἐν τούτοις ἴδοιεν
τιμωμένους καὶ ἀνακηρυττομένους ἐν μέσοις τοῖς
Ἕλλησι. καὶ διὰ τοῦτο ὡς εἰς τοσούτους
ἀποδυσόμενοι εὐεξίας τε ἐπιμελοῦνται, ὡς μὴ
αἰσχύνοιντο γυμνωθέντες, καὶ ἀξιονικότατον
ἕκαστος αὐτὸν ἀπεργάζεται. καὶ τὰ ἆθλα, ὥσπερ
ἔμπροσθεν εἶπον, οὐ μικρά, ὁ ἔπαινος ὁ παρὰ τῶν
θεατῶν καὶ τὸ ἐπισημότατον γενέσθαι καὶ δείκνυσθαι τῷ δακτύλῳ ἄριστον εἶναι τῶν καθ᾽ αὑτὸν
δοκοῦντα. τοιγάρτοι πολλοὶ τῶν θεατῶν, οἷς καθ᾽
ἡλικίαν ἔτι ἄσκησις, ἀπίασιν οὐ μετρίως ἐκ τῶν
τοιούτων ἀρετῆς καὶ πόνων ἐρασθέντες. ὡς εἴ γέ
τις, ὦ Ἀνάχαρσι, τὸν τῆς εὐκλείας ἔρωτα ἐκβά-
λοι ἐκ τοῦ βίου, τί ἂν ἔτι ἀγαθὸν ἡμῖν γένοιτο,
ἢ τίς ἄν τι λαμπρὸν ἐργάσασθαι ἐπιθυμήσειεν;
νῦν δὲ καὶ ἀπὸ τούτων εἰκάζειν παρέχοιεν ἄν σοι,
ὁποῖοι ἐν πολέμοις ὑπὲρ πατρίδος καὶ παίδων καὶ
γυναικῶν καὶ ἱερῶν γένοιντ᾽ ἂν ὅπλα ἔχοντες οἱ
κοτίνου πέρι καὶ μήλων γυμνοὶ τοσαύτην προθυμίαν εἰς τὸ νικᾶν εἰσφερόμενοι.

37 Καίτοι τί ἂν πάθοις, εἰ θεάσαιο καὶ ὀρτύγων
καὶ ἀλεκτρυόνων ἀγῶνας παρ᾽ ἡμῖν καὶ σπουδὴν
ἐπὶ τούτοις οὐ μικράν; ἢ γελάσῃ δῆλον ὅτι, καὶ
μάλιστα ἢν μάθῃς ὡς ὑπὸ νόμῳ αὐτὸ δρῶμεν
καὶ προστέτακται πᾶσι τοῖς ἐν ἡλικίᾳ παρεῖναι
καὶ ὁρᾶν τὰ ὄρνεα διαπυκτεύοντα μέχρι τῆς
ἐσχάτης ἀπαγορεύσεως; ἀλλ᾽ οὐδὲ τοῦτο γελοῖον·
ὑποδύεται γάρ τις ἠρέμα ταῖς ψυχαῖς ὁρμὴ εἰς

ANACHARSIS, OR ATHLETICS

SOLON

We think, Anacharsis, that their zeal for the athletic exercises will be increased if they see those who excel in them receiving honours and having their names proclaimed before the assembled Greeks. For this reason, expecting to appear unclothed before so many people, they try to attain good physical condition so that they may not be ashamed of themselves when they are stripped, and each makes himself as fit to win as he can. Furthermore, the prizes, as I said before, are not trivial—to be praised by the spectators, to become a man of mark, and to be pointed at with the finger as the best of one's class. Therefore many of the spectators, who are still young enough for training, go away immoderately in love with manfulness and hard work as a result of all this. Really, Anacharsis, if the love of fame should be banished out of the world, what new blessing should we ever acquire, or who would want to do any glorious deed? But as things are, even from these contests they give you an opportunity to infer what they would be in war, defending country, children, wives, and fanes with weapons and armour, when contending naked for parsley and apples they bring into it so much zeal for victory.

What would your feelings be if you should see quail-fights and cock-fights here among us, and no little interest taken in them? You would laugh, of course, particularly if you discovered that we do it in compliance with law, and that all those of military age are required to present themselves and watch the birds spar to the uttermost limit of exhaustion. Yet this is not laughable, either: their souls are gradually penetrated by an appetite for dangers, in order that

61

τοὺς κινδύνους, ὡς μὴ ἀγεννέστεροι καὶ ἀτολμό-
τεροι φαίνοιντο τῶν ἀλεκτρυόνων μηδὲ προαπα-
γορεύοιεν ὑπὸ τραυμάτων ἢ καμάτου ἤ του ἄλλου
δυσχεροῦς.

Τὸ δὲ δὴ ἐν ὅπλοις πειρᾶσθαι αὐτῶν καὶ ὁρᾶν
τιτρωσκομένους—ἄπαγε· θηριῶδες γὰρ καὶ δεινῶς
σκαιὸν καὶ προσέτι γε ἀλυσιτελὲς ἀποσφάττειν
τοὺς ἀρίστους καὶ οἷς ἄν τις ἄμεινον χρήσαιτο
κατὰ τῶν δυσμενῶν.

38   Ἐπεὶ δὲ φῄς, ὦ Ἀνάχαρσι, καὶ τὴν ἄλλην Ἑλ-
λάδα ἐπελεύσεσθαι, μέμνησο ἥν ποτε καὶ εἰς Λακε-
δαίμονα ἔλθῃς, μὴ καταγελάσαι μηδὲ ἐκείνων μηδὲ
οἴεσθαι μάτην πονεῖν αὐτούς, ὁπόταν ἢ σφαίρας
πέρι ἐν τῷ θεάτρῳ συμπεσόντες παίωσιν ἀλλήλους
ἢ εἰς χωρίον εἰσελθόντες ὕδατι περιγεγραμμένον,
εἰς φάλαγγα διαστάντες, τὰ πολεμίων ἀλλήλους
ἐργάζωνται γυμνοὶ καὶ αὐτοί, ἄχρις ἂν ἐκβάλωσι
τοῦ περιγράμματος τὸ ἔτερον σύνταγμα οἱ ἔτεροι,
τοὺς κατὰ Λυκοῦργον οἱ καθ' Ἡρακλέα ἢ ἔμπαλιν, συνωθοῦντες εἰς τὸ ὕδωρ· τὸ γὰρ ἀπὸ
τούτου εἰρήνη λοιπὸν καὶ οὐδεὶς ἂν ἔτι παίσειε.
μάλιστα δὲ ἣν ὁρᾷς μαστιγουμένους αὐτοὺς ἐπὶ
τῷ βωμῷ καὶ αἵματι ῥεομένους, πατέρας δὲ καὶ
μητέρας παρεστώσας οὐχ ὅπως ἀνιωμένας ἐπὶ
τοῖς γιγνομένοις ἀλλὰ καὶ ἀπειλούσας, εἰ μὴ
ἀντέχοιεν πρὸς τὰς πληγάς, καὶ ἱκετευούσας ἐπὶ
μήκιστον διαρκέσαι πρὸς τὸν πόνον καὶ ἐγκαρ-
τερῆσαι τοῖς δεινοῖς. πολλοὶ γοῦν καὶ ἐναπέ-
θανον τῷ ἀγῶνι μὴ ἀξιώσαντες ἀπαγορεῦσαι
ζῶντες ἔτι ἐν ὀφθαλμοῖς τῶν οἰκείων μηδὲ εἶξαι
τοῖς σώμασιν· ὧν καὶ τοὺς ἀνδριάντας ὄψει τιμωμένους δημοσίᾳ ὑπὸ τῆς Σπάρτης ἀνασταθέντας.

they may not seem baser and more cowardly than
the cocks, and may not show the white feather early
on account of wounds or weariness or any other
hardship.

As for testing them under arms, and watching
them get wounded—no! It is bestial and terribly
cruel and, more than that, unprofitable to kill off
the most efficient men who can be used to better
advantage against the enemy.

As you say that you intend to visit the rest of
Greece, Anacharsis, bear it in mind if ever you go to
Sparta not to laugh at them, either, and not to suppose that they are exerting themselves for nothing
when they rush together and strike one another in
the theatre over a ball, or when they go into a place
surrounded by water, divide into companies and treat
one another like enemies, naked as with us, until one
company drives the other out of the enclosure,
crowding them into the water—the Heraclids driving
out the Lycurgids, or the reverse—after which there
is peace in future and nobody would think of striking
a blow. Above all, do not laugh if you see them
getting flogged at the altar and dripping blood while
their fathers and mothers stand by and are so far
from being distressed by what is going on that they
actually threaten to punish them if they should not
bear up under the stripes, and beseech them to
endure the pain as long as possible and be staunch
under the torture. As a matter of fact, many have
died in the competition, not deigning to give in before
the eyes of their kinsmen while they still had life in
them, or even to move a muscle of their bodies ; you
will see honours paid to their statues, which have
been set up at public cost by the state of Sparta.

Ὅταν τοίνυν ὁρᾷς κἀκεῖνα, μήτε μαίνεσθαι ὑπολάβῃς αὐτοὺς μήτε εἴπῃς, ὡς οὐδεμιᾶς ἕνεκα αἰτίας ἀναγκαίας ταλαιπωροῦσι, μήτε τυράννου βιαζομένου μήτε πολεμίων διατιθέντων. εἴποι γὰρ ἄν σοι καὶ ὑπὲρ ἐκείνων Λυκοῦργος ὁ νομοθέτης αὐτῶν πολλὰ τὰ εὔλογα καὶ ἃ συνιδὼν κολάζει αὐτούς, οὐκ ἐχθρὸς ὢν οὐδὲ ὑπὸ μίσους αὐτὸ δρῶν οὐδὲ τὴν νεολαίαν τῆς πόλεως εἰκῆ παραναλίσκων, ἀλλὰ καρτερικωτάτους καὶ παντὸς δεινοῦ κρείττονας ἀξιῶν εἶναι τοὺς σώζειν μέλλοντας τὴν πατρίδα. καίτοι κἂν μὴ ὁ Λυκοῦργος εἴπῃ, ἐννοεῖς, οἶμαι, καὶ αὐτὸς ὡς οὐκ ἄν ποτε ληφθεὶς ὁ τοιοῦτος ἐν πολέμῳ ἀπόρρητόν τι ἐξείποι τῆς Σπάρτης αἰκιζομένων τῶν ἐχθρῶν, ἀλλὰ καταγελῶν αὐτῶν μαστιγοῖτο ἂν ἁμιλλώμενος πρὸς τὸν παίοντα, ὁπότερος[1] ἀπαγορεύσειεν.

ΑΝΑΧΑΡΣΙΣ

39 Ὁ Λυκοῦργος δὲ καὶ αὐτός, ὦ Σόλων, ἐμαστιγοῦτο ἐφ᾽ ἡλικίας, ἢ ἐκπρόθεσμος ὢν ἤδη τοῦ ἀγῶνος ἀσφαλῶς τὰ τοιαῦτα ἐνεανιεύσατο;

ΣΟΛΩΝ

Πρεσβύτης ἤδη ὢν ἔγραψε τοὺς νόμους αὐτοῖς Κρήτηθεν ἀφικόμενος. ἀποδεδημήκει δὲ παρὰ τοὺς Κρῆτας, ὅτι ἤκουεν εὐνομωτάτους εἶναι, Μίνωος τοῦ Διὸς νομοθετήσαντος ἐν αὐτοῖς.

---

[1] ὁπότερος A.M.H.: ὡς πρότερος MSS.

ANACHARSIS, OR ATHLETICS

When you see all that, do not suppose them crazy, and do not say that they are undergoing misery without any stringent reason, since it is due neither to a tyrant's violence nor to an enemy's maltreatment. Lycurgus, their law-giver, could defend it by telling you many good reasons which he has discerned for punishing them; he is not unfriendly to them, and does not do it out of hatred, nor is he wantonly wasting the young blood of the city, but he desires that those who are destined to preserve their country should be tremendously staunch and superior to every fear. Yet, even if Lycurgus does not say so, you see for yourself, I suppose, that such a man, on being captured in war, would never betray any Spartan secret under torture inflicted by the enemy, but would laugh at them and take his whipping, matching himself against his flogger to see which would give in.

ANACHARSIS

But how about Lycurgus himself, Solon? Did he get flogged in his youth, or was he then over the age-limit for the competition, so that he could introduce such an innovation with impunity?

SOLON

He was an old man when he made the laws for them on his return from Crete. He had gone to visit the Cretans because he was told that they enjoyed the best laws, since Minos, a son of Zeus, had been their law-giver.

ΑΝΑΧΑΡΣΙΣ

Τί οὖν, ὦ Σόλων, οὐχὶ καὶ σὺ ἐμιμήσω Λυκοῦργον καὶ μαστιγοῖς τοὺς νέους; καλὰ γὰρ καὶ
ταῦτα καὶ ἄξια ὑμῶν ἐστιν.

ΣΟΛΩΝ

Ὅτι ἡμῖν ἱκανά, ὦ Ἀνάχαρσι, ταῦτα τὰ
γυμνάσια οἰκεῖα ὄντα· ζηλοῦν δὲ τὰ ξενικὰ οὐ
πάνυ ἀξιοῦμεν.

ΑΝΑΧΑΡΣΙΣ

Οὔκ; ἀλλὰ συνίης, οἶμαι, οἷόν τί ἐστι μαστι-
γοῦσθαι γυμνὸν ἄνω τὰς χεῖρας ἐπαίροντα μηδενὸς
ἕνεκα ὠφελίμου ἢ αὐτῷ ἑκάστῳ ἢ κοινῇ τῇ πόλει.
ὡς ἔγωγε ἤν ποτε ἐπιδημήσω τῇ Σπάρτῃ καθ᾽
ὃν καιρὸν ταῦτα δρῶσι, δοκῶ μοι τάχιστα κατα-
λευσθήσεσθαι δημοσίᾳ πρὸς αὐτῶν, ἐπιγελῶν
ἑκάστοις, ὁπόταν ὁρῶ τυπτομένους καθάπερ
κλέπτας ἢ λωποδύτας ἤ τι ἄλλο τοιοῦτον ἐργα-
σαμένους. ἀτεχνῶς γὰρ ἐλλεβόρου δεῖσθαί μοι
δοκεῖ ἡ πόλις αὐτῶν καταγέλαστα ὑφ᾽ αὑτῆς
πάσχουσα.

ΣΟΛΩΝ

40 Μὴ ἐρήμην, ὦ γενναῖε, μηδὲ τῶν ἀνδρῶν ἀπόν-
των μόνος αὐτὸς λέγων οἴου κρατεῖν· ἔσται γὰρ
τις ὁ καὶ ὑπὲρ ἐκείνων σοι τὰ εἰκότα ἐν Σπάρτῃ
ἀντερῶν.

Πλὴν ἀλλὰ ἐπείπερ ἐγὼ τὰ ἡμέτερά σοι διεξε-
λήλυθα, σὺ δὲ οὐ πάνυ ἀρεσκομένῳ αὐτοῖς
ἔοικας, οὐκ ἄδικα αἰτήσειν ἔοικα παρὰ σοῦ ὡς
καὶ αὐτὸς ἐν τῷ μέρει διεξέλθῃς πρός με ὃν

ANACHARSIS, OR ATHLETICS

ANACHARSIS

Then why is it, Solon, that you have not imitated Lycurgus and do not flog your young men? It is a splendid practice, and worthy of you Athenians!

SOLON

Because we are content, Anacharsis, with these exercises, which are our own; we do not much care to copy foreign fashions.

ANACHARSIS

No: you understand, I think, what it is like to be flogged naked, holding up one's arms, for no advantage either to the individual himself or to the city in general. Oh, if ever I am at Sparta at the time when they are doing this, I expect I shall very soon be stoned to death by them publicly for laughing at them every time I see them getting beaten like robbers or sneak-thieves or similar malefactors. Really, it seems to me that the city stands in need of hellebore [1] if it mishandles itself so ridiculously.

SOLON

Do not think, my worthy friend, that you are winning your case by default, or in the absence of your adversaries, as the only speaker. There will be someone or other in Sparta who will reply to you properly in defence of this.

However, as I have told you about our ways and you do not seem to be much pleased with them, I do not think it will be unfair to ask you to tell me in

---

[1] The specific for insanity.

τρόπον ὑμεῖς οἱ Σκύθαι διασκεῖτε τοὺς νέους τοὺς
παρ' ὑμῖν καὶ οἷστισι γυμνασίοις ἀνατρέφετε καὶ
ὅπως ὑμῖν ἄνδρες ἀγαθοὶ γίγνονται.

ΑΝΑΧΑΡΣΙΣ

Δικαιότατα μὲν οὖν, ὦ Σόλων, καὶ ἔγωγε
διηγήσομαι τὰ Σκυθῶν νόμιμα, οὐ σεμνὰ ἴσως
οὐδὲ καθ' ὑμᾶς, οἵ γε οὐδὲ κατὰ κόρρης πατα-
χθῆναι τολμήσαιμεν ἂν μίαν πληγήν· δειλοὶ γάρ
ἐσμεν· ἀλλὰ εἰρήσεταί γε ὁποῖα ἂν ᾖ.[1] εἰς αὔριον
μέντοι, εἰ δοκεῖ, ὑπερβαλώμεθα τὴν συνουσίαν,
ὡς ἅ τε αὐτὸς ἔφης ἔτι μᾶλλον ἐννοήσαιμι καθ'
ἡσυχίαν ἅ τε χρὴ εἰπεῖν συναγάγοιμι τῇ μνήμῃ
ἐπελθών. τὸ δὲ νῦν ἔχον ἀπίωμεν ἐπὶ τούτοις·
ἑσπέρα γὰρ ἤδη.

[1] ᾖ Fritzsche ; εἴη MSS.

your turn how you Scythians discipline your young
men, what exercises you use in bringing them up,
and how you make them good men.

ANACHARSIS

It is entirely fair, to be sure, Solon, and I shall tell
you the Scythian customs, which are not imposing,
perhaps, or on the same plane as yours, since we
should not dare to receive a single blow in the face ;
we are cowards ! They shall be told, however, no
matter what they are. But let us put off the
discussion, if you will, till to-morrow, so that I may
quietly ponder a little longer over what you have
said, and get together what I must say, going over
it in my memory. At present, let us go away
with this understanding, for it is now evening.

MENIPPUS
OR THE DESCENT INTO HADES

MENIPPUS, who in the *Icaromenippus* (II. 267) described his ascent to Heaven to discover the truth about the nature of the universe, now tells the story of his descent into Hades to find out the right way to live. Utterly perplexed by the philosophers, who neither agree in their doctrines nor practise what they preach, he goes below to consult Teiresias, who tells him to disregard them; that the ordinary man's way of living is best.

The unity of the dialogue is badly marred because Lucian has given it a double point, aiming it not only at the philosophers but at the rich. Indeed, it is not the philosophers but the rich and powerful who are getting on badly in Hades, and against whom a decree is passed by the assembly of the dead.

This curious defect arises, I believe, from the way in which Lucian adapted his model, the *Necyia* of the real Menippus. Helm argues, to be sure, that the *Menippus* is a mere epitome and revision of the *Necyia*, but in my opinion the *Necyia* must have been a satire against wealth and power, in which Menippus told how he (or someone else) had learned, by his own observation and from the lips of Teiresias, that kings and millionaires fared ill in the hereafter, and that the life of the ordinary man was preferable to theirs. This Cynic sermon Lucian parodies and turns against the philosophers, retaining the response of Teiresias, but twisting its point so that the "ordinary man" is now contrasted, not with kings and plutocrats, but with philosophers. He ought to have carried out this idea by recasting the whole show in Hades; but he wanted to work in a decree of the dead, which could not be directed against the philosophers without stealing the thunder of Teiresias. So he aimed it at the rich, and retained the stage setting of Menippus to lead up to it.

The dialogue probably was written in A.D. 161–162 (p. 90, note). Helm's discussion (*Lucian und Menipp*, 15 ff.) contains much valuable comment, especially upon the magic ritual.

On Menippus, see the *Index*.

ΜΕΝΙΠΠΟΣ Η ΝΕΚΥΟΜΑΝΤΕΙΑ

ΜΕΝΙΠΠΟΣ

1   Ὦ χαῖρε μέλαθρον πρόπυλά θ' ἑστίας ἐμῆς,
   ὡς ἄσμενός σ' ἐσεῖδον ἐς φάος μολών.

ΦΙΛΟΣ

Οὐ Μένιππος οὗτός ἐστιν ὁ κύων; οὐ μὲν οὖν
ἄλλος, εἰ μὴ ἐγὼ παραβλέπω· Μένιππος ὅλος.[1]
τί οὖν αὐτῷ βούλεται τὸ ἀλλόκοτον τοῦ σχήματος,
πῖλος καὶ λύρα καὶ λεοντῆ; πλὴν ἀλλὰ προσιτέον
γε αὐτῷ. χαῖρε, ὦ Μένιππε· πόθεν ἡμῖν ἀφῖξαι;
πολὺς γὰρ χρόνος οὐ πέφηνας ἐν τῇ πόλει.[2]

ΜΕΝΙΠΠΟΣ

Ἥκω νεκρῶν κευθμῶνα καὶ σκότου πύλας
λιπών, ἵν' Ἅιδης χωρὶς ᾤκισται θεῶν.

ΦΙΛΟΣ

Ἡράκλεις, ἐλελήθει Μένιππος ἡμᾶς ἀποθα-
νών, κᾆτα ἐξ ὑπαρχῆς ἀναβεβίωκεν;

Available in photographs Γ, PN.

---

[1] Graevius : Μενίππους ὅλους γβ.
[2] Cf. *Dial. Meretr.* 10. 1. : οὐ γὰρ ἑώρακα πολὺς ἤδη χρόνος
αὐτὸν παρ' ὑμῖν.

MENIPPUS
OR THE DESCENT INTO HADES

MENIPPUS

All hail, ye halls and portals of my home!
What joy you give mine eyes, to light returned![1]

A FRIEND

Isn't this Menippus the Cynic? Assuredly nobody
else, unless I cannot see straight; Menippus all over.
Then what is the meaning of that strange costume—
a felt cap, a lyre, and a lion's skin? Anyhow, I must
go up to him. Good day, Menippus; where under
the sun have you come from? It is a long time since
you have shown yourself in the city.

MENIPPUS

I come from Dead Men's Lair and Darkness Gate
Where Hades dwells, remote from other gods.[2]

FRIEND

Heracles! Did Menippus die without our knowing
it, and has he now come to life all over again?

---

[1] Euripides, *Hercules Furens*, 523–4.
[2] Euripides, *Hecuba*, 1; spoken by Polydorus as prologue.

ΜΕΝΙΠΠΟΣ

Οὔκ, ἀλλ' ἔτ' ἔμπνουν 'Αΐδης μ' ἐδέξατο.

ΦΙΛΟΣ

Τίς δὴ αἰτία σοι τῆς καινῆς καὶ παραδόξου
ταύτης ἀποδημίας;

ΜΕΝΙΠΠΟΣ

Νεότης μ' ἐπῆρε καὶ θράσος τοῦ νοῦ πλέον.

ΦΙΛΟΣ

Παῦσαι, μακάριε, τραγῳδῶν καὶ λέγε οὑτωσί
πως ἁπλῶς καταβὰς ἀπὸ τῶν ἰαμβείων, τίς ἡ
στολή; τί σοι τῆς κάτω πορείας ἐδέησεν; ἄλλως
γὰρ οὐχ ἡδεῖά τις οὐδὲ ἀσπάσιος ἡ ὁδός.

ΜΕΝΙΠΠΟΣ

Ὦ φιλότης, χρειώ με κατήγαγεν εἰς 'Αΐδαο
ψυχῇ χρησόμενον Θηβαίου Τειρεσίαο.

ΦΙΛΟΣ

Οὗτος, ἀλλ' ἦ παραπαίεις· οὐ γὰρ ἂν οὕτως
ἐμμέτρως ἐρραψῴδεις πρὸς ἄνδρας φίλους.

ΜΕΝΙΠΠΟΣ

Μὴ θαυμάσῃς, ὦ ἑταῖρε· νεωστὶ γὰρ Εὐριπίδῃ
καὶ Ὁμήρῳ συγγενόμενος οὐκ οἶδ' ὅπως ἀνεπλή-
σθην τῶν ἐπῶν καὶ αὐτόματά μοι τὰ μέτρα ἐπὶ

---

[1] Attributed to Euripides; play unknown, perhaps the
Peirithous (Nauck, *Trag. Graec. Fragm.*, p. 663).

[2] Perhaps from the lost *Andromeda* of Euripides (Nauck,
p. 403).

[3] *Odyssey*. 11, 164. Lucian substitutes "Friend" for
Homer's "Mother."

MENIPPUS

MENIPPUS

Nay, I was living when I went to Hell.[1]

FRIEND

What reason had you for this novel and surprising trip?

MENIPPUS

Youth spurred me, and I had more pluck than sense.[2]

FRIEND

My dear fellow, do stop your play-acting; come off your blank-verse, and tell me in plain language like mine what your costume is, and why you had to go down below. Certainly it is not a pleasant and attractive journey!

MENIPPUS

Friend, 'twas necessity drew me below to the kingdom of Hades,
There to obtain, from the spirit of Theban Teiresias, counsel.[3]

FRIEND

Man, you are surely out of your mind, or you would not recite verse in that way to your friends!

MENIPPUS

Don't be surprised, my dear fellow. I have just been in the company of Euripides and Homer, so that somehow or other I have become filled with poetry, and verses come unbidden to my lips.[4]

[4] The Greek words form a trimeter, possibly borrowed from some comedy.

THE WORKS OF LUCIAN

2 τὸ στόμα ἔρχεται. ἀτὰρ εἰπέ μοι, πῶς τὰ ὑπὲρ γῆς ἔχει καὶ τί ποιοῦσιν οἱ ἐν τῇ πόλει ;

ΦΙΛΟΣ

Καινὸν οὐδέν, ἀλλ' οἷα καὶ πρὸ τοῦ· ἁρπάζουσιν, ἐπιορκοῦσιν, τοκογλυφοῦσιν, ὀβολοστατοῦσιν.

ΜΕΝΙΠΠΟΣ

Ἄθλιοι καὶ κακοδαίμονες· οὐ γὰρ ἴσασιν οἷα ἔναγχος κεκύρωται παρὰ τοῖς κάτω καὶ οἷα κεχειροτόνηται τὰ ψηφίσματα κατὰ τῶν πλουσίων, ἃ μὰ τὸν Κέρβερον οὐδεμία μηχανὴ τὸ διαφυγεῖν αὐτούς.

ΦΙΛΟΣ

Τί φής ; δέδοκταί τι νεώτερον τοῖς κάτω περὶ τῶν ἐνθάδε ;

ΜΕΝΙΠΠΟΣ

Νὴ Δία, καὶ πολλά γε· ἀλλ' οὐ θέμις ἐκφέρειν αὐτὰ πρὸς ἅπαντας οὐδὲ ἐξαγορεύειν τὰ ἀπόρρητα, μὴ καί τις ἡμᾶς γράψηται γραφὴν ἀσεβείας ἐπὶ τοῦ Ῥαδαμάνθυος.

ΦΙΛΟΣ

Μηδαμῶς, ὦ Μένιππε, πρὸς τοῦ Διός, μὴ φθονήσῃς τῶν λόγων φίλῳ ἀνδρί· πρὸς γὰρ εἰδότα σιωπᾶν ἐρεῖς, τά τ' ἄλλα καὶ πρὸς μεμυημένον.

ΜΕΝΙΠΠΟΣ

Χαλεπὸν μὲν ἐπιτάττεις τὸ ἐπίταγμα καὶ οὐ πάντη εὐσεβές· πλὴν ἀλλὰ σοῦ γε ἕνεκα τολμητέον. ἔδοξε δὴ τοὺς πλουσίους τούτους

But tell me, how are things going on earth, and what are they doing in the city?

FRIEND

Nothing new; just what they did before—stealing, lying under oath, extorting usury, and weighing pennies.

MENIPPUS

Poor wretches! They do not know what decisions have been made of late in the lower world, and what ordinances have been enacted against the rich; by Cerberus, they cannot possibly evade them!

FRIEND

What is that? Has any radical legislation been passed in the lower world affecting the upper?

MENIPPUS

Yes, by Zeus, a great deal; but it is not right to publish it broadcast and expose their secrets. Someone might indict me for impiety in the court of Rhadamanthus.

FRIEND

Oh, no, Menippus! In Heaven's name don't withhold your story from a friend! You will be telling a man who knows how to keep his mouth shut, and who, moreover, has been initiated into the mysteries.

MENIPPUS

It is a perilous demand that you are imposing upon me, and one not wholly consistent with piety. However, for your sake I must be bold. The motion, then, was passed that these rich men with

καὶ πολυχρημάτους καὶ τὸ χρυσίον κατάκλειστον
ὥσπερ τὴν Δανάην φυλάττοντας—

ΦΙΛΟΣ

Μὴ πρότερον εἴπῃς, ὦγαθέ, τὰ δεδογμένα πρὶν
ἐκεῖνα διελθεῖν ἃ μάλιστ᾽ ἂν ἡδέως ἀκούσαιμί
σου, τίς ἡ ἐπίνοιά σοι τῆς καθόδου ἐγένετο, τίς δ᾽
ὁ τῆς πορείας ἡγεμών, εἶθ᾽ ἑξῆς ἅ τε εἶδες ἅ τε
ἤκουσας παρ᾽ αὐτοῖς· εἰκὸς γὰρ δὴ φιλόκαλον
ὄντα σε μηδὲν τῶν ἀξίων θέας ἢ ἀκοῆς παρα-
λιπεῖν.

ΜΕΝΙΠΠΟΣ

3 Ὑπουργητέον καὶ ταῦτά σοι· τί γὰρ ἂν καὶ
πάθοι τις, ὁπότε φίλος ἀνὴρ βιάζοιτο; καὶ δὴ
πρῶτά σοι δίειμι τὰ περὶ τῆς γνώμης τῆς ἐμῆς,
ὅθεν ὡρμήθην πρὸς τὴν κατάβασιν. ἐγὼ γάρ,
ἄχρι μὲν ἐν παισὶν ἦν, ἀκούων Ὁμήρου καὶ
Ἡσιόδου πολέμους καὶ στάσεις διηγουμένων οὐ
μόνον τῶν ἡμιθέων, ἀλλὰ καὶ αὐτῶν ἤδη τῶν θεῶν,
ἔτι δὲ καὶ μοιχείας αὐτῶν καὶ βίας καὶ ἁρπα-
γὰς καὶ δίκας καὶ πατέρων ἐξελάσεις καὶ ἀδελφῶν
γάμους, πάντα ταῦτα ἐνόμιζον εἶναι καλὰ καὶ οὐ
παρέργως ἐκινούμην πρὸς αὐτά. ἐπεὶ δὲ εἰς
ἄνδρας τελεῖν ἠρξάμην, πάλιν αὖ ἐνταῦθα
ἤκουον τῶν νόμων τἀναντία τοῖς ποιηταῖς
κελευόντων, μήτε μοιχεύειν μήτε στασιάζειν μήτε
ἁρπάζειν. ἐν μεγάλῃ οὖν καθειστήκειν ἀμφι-
βολίᾳ, οὐκ εἰδὼς ὅ τι χρησαίμην ἐμαυτῷ· οὔτε
γὰρ ἄν ποτε τοὺς θεοὺς μοιχεῦσαι καὶ στασιάσαι
πρὸς ἀλλήλους ἡγούμην εἰ μὴ ὡς περὶ καλῶν
τούτων ἐγίγνωσκον, οὔτ᾽ ἂν τοὺς νομοθέτας
τἀναντία παραινεῖν εἰ μὴ λυσιτελεῖν ὑπελάμβα-

great fortunes who keep their gold locked up as closely as Danae——

Don't quote the motion, my dear fellow, before telling me what I should be especially glad to hear from you; that is to say, what was the purpose of your going down, who was your guide for the journey, and then, in due order, what you saw and heard there; for it is to be expected, of course, that as a man of taste you did not overlook anything worth seeing or hearing.

I must meet your wishes in that, too, for what is a man to do when a friend constrains him? First, then, I shall tell you about my decision— what impelled me to go down. While I was a boy, when I read in Homer and Hesiod about wars and quarrels, not only of the demigods but of the gods themselves, and besides about their amours and assaults and abductions and lawsuits and banishing fathers and marrying sisters, I thought that all these things were right, and I felt an uncommon impulsion toward them. But when I came of age, I found that the laws contradicted the poets and forbade adultery, quarrelling, and theft. So I was plunged into great uncertainty, not knowing how to deal with my own case; for the gods would never have committed adultery and quarrelled with each other, I thought, unless they deemed these actions right, and the lawgivers would not recommend the opposite course unless they supposed it to be advantageous.

79

4 νον. ἐπεὶ δὲ διηπόρουν, ἔδοξέ μοι ἐλθόντα παρὰ
τοὺς καλουμένους τούτους φιλοσόφους ἐγχειρίσαι
τε ἐμαυτὸν καὶ δεηθῆναι αὐτῶν χρῆσθαί μοι ὅ τι
βούλοιντο καί τινα ὁδὸν ἁπλῆν καὶ βέβαιον ὑπο-
δεῖξαι τοῦ βίου.

Ταῦτα μὲν δὴ φρονῶν προσῄειν αὐτοῖς, ἐλελή-
θειν δ' ἐμαυτὸν εἰς αὐτό, φασί, τὸ πῦρ ἐκ τοῦ
καπνοῦ βιαζόμενος. παρὰ γὰρ δὴ τούτοις
μάλιστα εὕρισκον ἐπισκοπῶν τὴν ἄγνοιαν καὶ
τὴν ἀπορίαν πλείονα, ὥστε μοι τάχιστα χρυσοῦν
ἀπέδειξαν οὗτοι τὸν τῶν ἰδιωτῶν τοῦτον βίον.

Ἀμέλει ὁ μὲν αὐτῶν παρῄνει τὸ πᾶν ἥδεσθαι
καὶ μόνον τοῦτο ἐκ παντὸς μετιέναι· τοῦτο γὰρ
εἶναι τὸ εὔδαιμον. ὁ δέ τις ἔμπαλιν, πονεῖν τὰ
πάντα καὶ μοχθεῖν καὶ τὸ σῶμα καταναγκάζειν
ῥυπῶντα καὶ αὐχμῶντα καὶ πᾶσι δυσαρεστοῦντα
καὶ λοιδορούμενον, συνεχὲς ἐπιρραψῳδῶν τὰ
πάνδημα ἐκεῖνα τοῦ Ἡσιόδου περὶ τῆς ἀρετῆς
ἔπη καὶ τὸν ἱδρῶτα καὶ τὴν ἐπὶ τὸ ἄκρον
ἀνάβασιν. ἄλλος καταφρονεῖν χρημάτων παρ-
εκελεύετο καὶ ἀδιάφορον οἴεσθαι τὴν κτῆσιν
αὐτῶν· ὁ δέ τις ἔμπαλιν ἀγαθὸν εἶναι καὶ τὸν
πλοῦτον ἀπεφαίνετο. περὶ μὲν γὰρ τοῦ κόσμου
τί χρὴ καὶ λέγειν; ὅς γε ἰδέας καὶ ἀσώματα καὶ
ἀτόμους καὶ κενὰ καὶ τοιοῦτόν τινα ὄχλον ὀνομάτων ὁσημέραι παρ' αὐτῶν ἀκούων ἐναντίων. καὶ
τὸ πάντων ἀτοπώτατον, ὅτι περὶ τῶν ἐναντιωτά-
των ἕκαστος αὐτῶν λέγων σφόδρα νικῶντας καὶ
πιθανοὺς λόγους ἐπορίζετο, ὥστε μήτε τῷ θερμὸν
τὸ αὐτὸ πρᾶγμα λέγοντι μήτε τῷ ψυχρὸν ἀντι-

---

[1] *Works and Days*, 287 sq.; Lucian is always making fun
of the philosophers for quoting this.

Since I was in a dilemma, I resolved to go to the men whom they call philosophers and put myself into their hands, begging them to deal with me as they would, and to show me a plain, solid path in life.

That was what I had in mind when I went to them, but I was unconsciously struggling out of the smoke, as the proverb goes, right into the fire! For I found in the course of my investigation that among these men in particular the ignorance and the perplexity was greater than elsewhere, so that they speedily convinced me that the ordinary man's way of living is as good as gold.

For instance, one of them would recommend me to take my pleasure always and to pursue that under all circumstances, because that was happiness; but another, on the contrary, would recommend me to toil and moil always and to subdue my body, going dirty and unkempt, irritating everybody and calling names; and to clinch his argument he was perpetually reciting those trite lines of Hesiod's about virtue, and talking of "sweat," and the "climb to the summit." [1] Another would urge me to despise money and think it a matter of indifference whether one has it or not, while someone else, on the contrary, would demonstrate that even wealth was good. As to the universe, what is the use of talking about that? "Ideas," "incorporealities," "atoms," "voids," and a multitude of such terms were dinned into my ears by them every day until it made me queasy. And the strangest thing was that when they expressed the most contradictory of opinions, each of them would produce very effective and plausible arguments, so that when the selfsame thing was called hot by one and cold by another,

λέγειν ἔχειν, καὶ ταῦτ' εἰδότα σαφῶς ὡς οὐκ ἄν
ποτε θερμὸν εἴη τι καὶ ψυχρὸν ἐν ταὐτῷ χρόνῳ.
ἀτεχνῶς οὖν ἔπασχον τοῖς νυστάζουσι τούτοις
ὅμοιον, ἄρτι μὲν ἐπινεύων, ἄρτι δὲ ἀνανεύων
ἔμπαλιν.

5   Πολλῷ δὲ τούτων ἐκεῖνο ἀλογώτερον· τοὺς γὰρ
αὐτοὺς τούτους εὕρισκον ἐπιτηρῶν ἐναντιώτατα
τοῖς αὐτῶν λόγοις ἐπιτηδεύοντας. τοὺς γοῦν
καταφρονεῖν παραινοῦντας χρημάτων ἑώρων ἀπρὶξ
ἐχομένους αὐτῶν καὶ περὶ τόκων διαφερομένους
καὶ ἐπὶ μισθῷ παιδεύοντας καὶ πάντα ἕνεκα
τούτων ὑπομένοντας, τούς τε τὴν δόξαν ἀπο-
βαλλομένους αὐτῆς ταύτης χάριν τὰ πάντα καὶ
πράττοντας καὶ λέγοντας, ἡδονῆς τε αὖ σχεδὸν
ἅπαντας κατηγοροῦντας, ἰδίᾳ δὲ μόνῃ ταύτῃ
προσηρτημένους.

6   Σφαλεὶς οὖν καὶ τῆσδε τῆς ἐλπίδος ἔτι μᾶλλον
ἐδυσχέραινον, ἠρέμα παραμυθούμενος ἐμαυτὸν
ὅτι μετὰ πολλῶν καὶ σοφῶν καὶ σφόδρα ἐπὶ
συνέσει διαβεβοημένων ἀνόητός τέ εἰμι καὶ
τἀληθὲς ἔτι ἀγνοῶν περιέρχομαι. καί μοί ποτε
διαγρυπνοῦντι τούτων ἕνεκα ἔδοξεν εἰς Βαβυλῶνα
ἐλθόντα δεηθῆναί τινος τῶν μάγων τῶν Ζωροά-
στρου μαθητῶν καὶ διαδόχων· ἤκουον δ' αὐτοὺς
ἐπῳδαῖς τε καὶ τελεταῖς τισιν ἀνοίγειν τοῦ Ἅιδου
τὰς πύλας καὶ κατάγειν ὃν ἂν βούλωνται ἀσφαλῶς
καὶ ὀπίσω αὖθις ἀναπέμπειν. ἄριστον οὖν
ἡγούμην εἶναι παρά τινος τούτων διαπραξάμενον

it was impossible for me to controvert either of
them, though I knew right well that nothing could
ever be hot and cold at the same time. So in good
earnest I acted like a drowsy man, nodding now this
way and now that.[1]

But there was something else, far more unreason-
able than that. I found, upon observing these same
people, that their practice directly opposed their
preaching. For instance, I perceived that those who
recommended scorning money clove to it tooth and
nail, bickered about interest, taught for pay, and
underwent everything for the sake of money; and
that those who were for rejecting public opinion
aimed at that very thing not only in all that they
did, but in all that they said. Also that while
almost all of them inveighed against pleasure, they
privately devoted themselves to that alone.

Disappointed, therefore, in this expectation, I was
still more uncomfortable than before, although I con-
soled myself somewhat with the thought that if I
was still foolish and went about in ignorance of the
truth, at all events I had the company of many wise
men, widely renowned for intelligence. So one time,
while I lay awake over these problems, I resolved to
go to Babylon and address myself to one of the
Magi, the disciples and successors of Zoroaster, as
I had heard that with certain charms and ceremonials
they could open the gates of Hades, taking down in
safety anyone they would and guiding him back again.
Consequently I thought best to arrange with one of

---

[1] More literally, "now inclining my head forward, and
now tossing it backward"; that is, assenting one moment
and dissenting the next. To express disagreement, the head
was (and in Greece is now) thrown back, not shaken.

τὴν κατάβασιν ἐλθόντα παρὰ Τειρεσίαν τὸν
Βοιώτιον μαθεῖν παρ' αὐτοῦ ἅτε μάντεως καὶ
σοφοῦ, τίς ἐστιν ὁ ἄριστος βίος καὶ ὃν ἄν τις
ἕλοιτο εὖ φρονῶν.

Καὶ δὴ ἀναπηδήσας ὡς εἶχον τάχους ἔτεινον
εὐθὺ Βαβυλῶνος· ἐλθὼν δὲ συγγίγνομαί τινι
τῶν Χαλδαίων σοφῷ ἀνδρὶ καὶ θεσπεσίῳ τὴν
τέχνην, πολιῷ μὲν τὴν κόμην, γένειον δὲ μάλα
σεμνὸν καθειμένῳ, τοὔνομα δὲ ἦν αὐτῷ Μιθροβαρζάνης. δεηθεὶς δὲ καὶ καθικετεύσας μόγις
ἐπέτυχον παρ' αὐτοῦ, ἐφ' ὅτῳ βούλοιτο μισθῷ,
7 καθηγήσασθαί μοι τῆς ὁδοῦ. παραλαβὼν δέ με
ὁ ἀνὴρ πρῶτα μὲν ἡμέρας ἐννέα καὶ εἴκοσιν ἅμα
τῇ σελήνῃ ἀρξάμενος ἔλουε κατάγων ἕωθεν ἐπὶ
τὸν Εὐφράτην πρὸς ἀνίσχοντα τὸν ἥλιον, ῥῆσίν
τινα μακρὰν ἐπιλέγων ἧς οὐ σφόδρα κατήκουον·
ὥσπερ γὰρ οἱ φαῦλοι τῶν ἐν τοῖς ἀγῶσι κηρύκων
ἐπίτροχόν τι καὶ ἀσαφὲς ἐφθέγγετο. πλὴν ἐῴκει
γέ τινας ἐπικαλεῖσθαι δαίμονας. μετὰ δ' οὖν
τὴν ἐπῳδὴν τρὶς ἄν μου πρὸς τὸ πρόσωπον
ἀποπτύσας, ἐπανῄει πάλιν οὐδένα τῶν ἀπαντών-
των προσβλέπων. καὶ σιτία μὲν ἦν ἡμῖν τὰ
ἀκρόδρυα, ποτὸν δὲ γάλα καὶ μελίκρατον καὶ τὸ
τοῦ Χοάσπου ὕδωρ, εὐνὴ δὲ ὑπαίθριος ἐπὶ τῆς
πόας.

Ἐπεὶ δ' ἅλις εἶχε τῆς προδιαιτήσεως, περὶ
μέσας νύκτας ἐπὶ τὸν Τίγρητα ποταμὸν ἀγαγὼν
ἐκάθηρέν τέ με καὶ ἀπέμαξε καὶ περιήγνισεν
δᾳδὶ καὶ σκίλλῃ καὶ ἄλλοις πλείοσιν, ἅμα καὶ
τὴν ἐπῳδὴν ἐκείνην ὑποτονθορύσας. εἶτά με
ὅλον καταμαγεύσας καὶ περιελθών, ἵνα μὴ
βλαπτοίμην ὑπὸ τῶν φασμάτων, ἐπανάγει εἰς

these men for my going down, and then to call upon Teiresias of Boeotia and find out from him in his capacity of prophet and sage what the best life was, the life that a man of sense would choose.

Well, springing to my feet, I made straight for Babylon as fast as I could go. On my arrival I conversed with one of the Chaldeans, a wise man of miraculous skill, with grey hair and a very majestic beard; his name was Mithrobarzanes. By dint of supplications and entreaties, I secured his reluctant consent to be my guide on the journey at whatever price he would. So the man took me in charge, and first of all, for twenty-nine days, beginning with the new moon, he took me down to the Euphrates in the early morning, toward sunrise, and bathed me; after which he would make a long address which I could not follow very well, for like an incompetent announcer at the games, he spoke rapidly and indistinctly. It is likely, however, that he was invoking certain spirits. Anyhow, after the incantation he would spit in my face thrice and then go back again without looking at anyone whom he met. We ate nuts, drank milk, mead, and the water of the Choaspes, and slept out of doors on the grass.

When he considered the preliminary course of dieting satisfactory, taking me to the Tigris river at midnight he purged me, cleansed me, and consecrated me with torches and squills and many other things, murmuring his incantation as he did so. Then after he had becharmed me from head to foot and walked all about me, that I might not be harmed by the phantoms, he took me home again, just as

85

τὴν οἰκίαν, ὡς εἶχον, ἀναποδίζοντα, καὶ τὸ λοιπὸν
8 ἀμφὶ πλοῦν εἴχομεν. αὐτὸς μὲν οὖν μαγικήν
τινα ἐνέδυ στολὴν τὰ πολλὰ ἐοικυῖαν τῇ Μηδικῇ,
ἐμὲ δὲ τουτοισὶ φέρων ἐνεσκεύασε, τῷ πίλῳ καὶ
τῇ λεοντῇ καὶ προσέτι τῇ λύρᾳ, καὶ παρεκελεύ-
σατο, ἤν τις ἔρηταί με τοὔνομα, Μένιππον μὴ
λέγειν, Ἡρακλέα δὲ ἢ Ὀδυσσέα ἢ Ὀρφέα.

ΦΙΛΟΣ

Ὡς δὴ τί τοῦτο, ὦ Μένιππε ; οὐ γὰρ συνίημι
τὴν αἰτίαν οὔτε τοῦ σχήματος οὔτε τῶν
ὀνομάτων.

ΜΕΝΙΠΠΟΣ

Καὶ μὴν πρόδηλόν γε τοῦτο καὶ οὐ παντελῶς
ἀπόρρητον· ἐπεὶ γὰρ οὗτοι πρὸ ἡμῶν ζῶντες εἰς
Ἅιδου κατεληλύθεσαν, ἡγεῖτο, εἴ με ἀπεικάσειεν
αὐτοῖς, ῥᾳδίως ἂν τὴν τοῦ Αἰακοῦ φρουρὰν δια-
λαθεῖν καὶ ἀκωλύτως ἂν παρελθεῖν ἅτε συνηθέ-
στερον, τραγικῶς μάλα παραπεμπόμενον ὑπὸ τοῦ
σχήματος.

9 Ἤδη δ᾽ οὖν ὑπέφαινεν ἡμέρα, καὶ κατελθόντες
ἐπὶ τὸν ποταμὸν περὶ ἀναγωγὴν ἐγιγνόμεθα.
παρεσκεύαστο δ᾽ αὐτῷ καὶ σκάφος καὶ ἱερεῖα καὶ
μελίκρατον καὶ ἄλλα ὅσα πρὸς τὴν τελετὴν
χρήσιμα. ἐμβαλόμενοι οὖν ἅπαντα τὰ παρε-
σκευασμένα οὕτω δὴ καὶ αὐτοὶ

βαίνομεν ἀχνύμενοι, θαλερὸν κατὰ δάκρυ
χέοντες.

MENIPPUS

I was, walking backward. After that, we made ready for the journey. He himself put on a magician's gown very like the Median dress, and speedily costumed me in these things which you see—the cap, the lion's skin, and the lyre besides; and he urged me, if anyone should ask my name, not to say Menippus, but Heracles or Odysseus or Orpheus.

FRIEND

What was his object in that, Menippus? I do not understand the reason either for the costume or for the names.

MENIPPUS

Why, that, at any rate, is obvious and not at all shrouded in mystery. Since they had been before us in going down to Hades alive, he thought that if he should make me look like them, I might easily slip by the frontier-guard of Aeacus and go in un-hindered as something of an old acquaintance; for thanks to my costume they would speed me along on my journey just as they do in the plays.[1]

Well, day was just beginning to break when we went down to the river and set about getting under way. He had provided a boat, victims, mead, and everything else that we should need for the ritual. So we shipped all the stores, and at length ourselves

"Gloomily hied us aboard, with great tears falling
    profusely." [2]

[1] There were many comedies with this motive. The only one extant is the *Frogs* of Aristophanes, where Dionysus descends in the costume of Heracles.
[2] *Odyssey*, 11, 5.

Καὶ μέχρι μέν τινος ὑπεφερόμεθα ἐν τῷ ποταμῷ,
εἶτα δὲ εἰσεπλεύσαμεν εἰς τὸ ἕλος καὶ τὴν λίμνην
εἰς ἣν ὁ Εὐφράτης ἀφανίζεται. περαιωθέντες δὲ
καὶ ταύτην ἀφικνούμεθα εἴς τι χωρίον ἔρημον καὶ
ὑλῶδες καὶ ἀνήλιον, εἰς ὃ καὶ δὴ ἀποβάντες—
ἡγεῖτο δὲ ὁ Μιθροβαρζάνης—βόθρον τε ὠρυξάμεθα
καὶ τὰ μῆλα κατεσφάξαμεν καὶ τὸ αἷμα περὶ
αὐτὸν ἐσπείσαμεν. ὁ δὲ μάγος ἐν τοσούτῳ δᾷδα
καιομένην ἔχων οὐκέτ' ἠρεμαίᾳ τῇ φωνῇ, παμμέγεθες δέ, ὡς οἷός τε ἦν, ἀνακραγὼν δαίμονάς τε
ὁμοῦ πάντας ἐπεβοᾶτο καὶ Ποινὰς καὶ Ἐρινύας

καὶ νυχίαν Ἑκάτην καὶ ἐπαινὴν Περσεφόνειαν,

παραμιγνὺς ἅμα βαρβαρικά τινα καὶ ἄσημα
ὀνόματα καὶ πολυσύλλαβα.

10 Εὐθὺς οὖν ἅπαντα ἐκεῖνα ἐσαλεύετο καὶ ὑπὸ
τῆς ἐπῳδῆς τοὔδαφος ἀνερρήγνυτο καὶ ὑλακὴ τοῦ
Κερβέρου πόρρωθεν ἠκούετο καὶ τὸ πρᾶγμα
ὑπερκατηφὲς ἦν καὶ σκυθρωπόν.

ἔδδεισεν δ' ὑπένερθεν ἄναξ ἐνέρων Ἀϊδωνεύς—

κατεφαίνετο γὰρ ἤδη τὰ πλεῖστα, καὶ ἡ λίμνη καὶ
ὁ Πυριφλεγέθων καὶ τοῦ Πλούτωνος τὰ βασίλεια.
κατελθόντες δ' ὅμως διὰ τοῦ χάσματος τὸν μὲν
Ῥαδάμανθυν εὕρομεν τεθνεῶτα μικροῦ δεῖν ὑπὸ
τοῦ δέους· ὁ δὲ Κέρβερος ὑλάκτησε μέν τι καὶ
παρεκίνησε, ταχὺ δέ μου κρούσαντος τὴν λύραν
παραχρῆμα ἐκηλήθη ὑπὸ τοῦ μέλους. ἐπεὶ δὲ
πρὸς τὴν λίμνην ἀφικόμεθα, μικροῦ μὲν οὐδὲ
ἐπεραιώθημεν· ἦν γὰρ πλῆρες ἤδη τὸ πορθμεῖον
καὶ οἰμωγῆς ἀνάπλεων, τραυματίαι δὲ πάντες

---

[1] Source of the verse unknown.   [2] *Iliad*, 20, 61.

For a space we drifted along in the river, and then we sailed into the marsh and the lake in which the Euphrates loses itself. After crossing this, we came to a deserted, woody, sunless place. There at last we landed with Mithrobarzanes leading the way; we dug a pit, we slaughtered the sheep, and we sprinkled their blood about it. Meanwhile the magician held a burning torch and no longer muttered in a low tone but shouted as loudly as he could, invoking the spirits, one and all, at the top of his lungs; also the Tormentors, the Furies,

"Hecate, queen of the night, and eery Perse-
        phoneia." [1]

With these names he intermingled a number of foreign-sounding, meaningless words of many syllables.

In a trice the whole region began to quake, the ground was rent asunder by the incantation, barking of Cerberus was audible afar off, and things took on a monstrously gloomy and sullen look.

"Aye, deep down it affrighted the king of the
        dead, Aïdoneus"—[2]

for by that time we could see almost everything— the Lake, and the River of Burning Fire, and the palace of Pluto. But in spite of it all, we went down through the chasm, finding Rhadamanthus almost dead of fright. Cerberus barked a bit, to be sure, and stirred slightly, but when I hastily touched my lyre he was at once bewitched by the music. When we reached the lake, however, we came near not getting across, for the ferry was already crowded and full of groaning. Only

ἐπέπλεον, ὁ μὲν τὸ σκέλος, ὁ δὲ τὴν κεφαλήν, ὁ
δὲ ἄλλο τι συντετριμμένος, ἐμοὶ δοκεῖν, ἔκ τινος
πολέμου παρόντες.

"Ομως δ' οὖν ὁ βέλτιστος Χάρων ὡς εἶδε τὴν
λεοντῆν, οἰηθείς με τὸν Ἡρακλέα εἶναι, εἰσεδέξατο
καὶ διεπόρθμευσέν τε ἄσμενος καὶ ἀποβᾶσι
11 διεσήμηνε τὴν ἀτραπόν. ἐπεὶ δὲ ἦμεν ἐν τῷ
σκότῳ, προῄει μὲν ὁ Μιθροβαρζάνης, εἱπόμην δὲ
ἐγὼ κατόπιν ἐχόμενος αὐτοῦ, ἕως πρὸς λειμῶνα
μέγιστον ἀφικνούμεθα τῷ ἀσφοδέλῳ κατάφυτον,
ἔνθα δὴ περιεπέτοντο ἡμᾶς τετριγυῖαι τῶν νεκρῶν
αἱ σκιαί. κατ' ὀλίγον δὲ προϊόντες παραγιγνό-
μεθα πρὸς τὸ τοῦ Μίνωος δικαστήριον· ἐτύγχανε
δὲ ὁ μὲν ἐπὶ θρόνου τινὸς ὑψηλοῦ καθήμενος,
παρειστήκεσαν δὲ αὐτῷ Ποιναὶ καὶ Ἐρινύες καὶ
Ἀλάστορες. ἑτέρωθεν δὲ προσήγοντο πολλοί
τινες ἐφεξῆς, ἁλύσει μακρᾷ δεδεμένοι· ἐλέγοντο
δὲ εἶναι μοιχοὶ καὶ πορνοβοσκοὶ καὶ τελῶναι καὶ
κόλακες καὶ συκοφάνται καὶ τοιοῦτος ὅμιλος τῶν
πάντα κυκώντων ἐν τῷ βίῳ. χωρὶς δὲ οἵ τε
πλούσιοι καὶ τοκογλύφοι προσῇεσαν ὠχροὶ καὶ
προγάστορες καὶ ποδαγροί, κλοιὸν ἕκαστος αὐτῶν
καὶ κόρακα διτάλαντον ἐπικείμενος. ἐφεστῶτες
οὖν ἡμεῖς ἑωρῶμέν τε τὰ γιγνόμενα καὶ ἠκούομεν
τῶν ἀπολογουμένων· κατηγόρουν δὲ αὐτῶν καινοί
τινες καὶ παράδοξοι ῥήτορες.

---

[1] Supposed to refer to the disasters of A.D. 161 in the
Parthian war.

wounded men were aboard, one injured in the leg, another in the head, and so on. They were there, in my opinion, through some war or other.[1]

However, when good old Charon saw the lion-skin he thought that I was Heracles, so he took me in, and not only ferried me across gladly but pointed out the path for us when we went ashore. Since we were in the dark, Mithrobarzanes led the way and I followed after, keeping hold of him, until we reached a very large meadow overgrown with asphodel, where the shades of the dead flitted squeaking about us. Going ahead little by little, we came to the court of Minos. As it chanced, he himself was sitting on a lofty throne, while beside him stood the Tormentors, the Furies, and the Avengers. From one side a great number of men were being led up in line, bound together with a long chain; they were said to be adulterers, procurers, tax-collectors, toadies, informers, and all that crowd of people who create such confusion in life. In a separate company the millionaires and the money-lenders came up, pale, pot-bellied, and gouty, each of them with a neck-iron and a hundred-pound "crow" upon him.[2] Standing by, we looked at what was going on, and listened to the pleas of the defendants, who were prosecuted by speakers of a novel and surprising sort.

[2] We are left to conjecture as to the nature of Lucian's "crow," for the word does not seem to be used elsewhere in a similar application. The extreme weight, however, suggests something resembling a ball-and-chain, a weight attached by a hook to a chain which perhaps was fastened to the neck-iron. It would have to be carried in the hand.

THE WORKS OF LUCIAN

ΦΙΛΟΣ

Τίνες οὗτοι, πρὸς Διός; μὴ γὰρ ὀκνήσῃς καὶ τοῦτο εἰπεῖν.

ΜΕΝΙΠΠΟΣ

Οἶσθά που ταυτασὶ τὰς πρὸς τὸν ἥλιον ἀποτελουμένας σκιὰς ὑπὸ τῶν σωμάτων;

ΦΙΛΟΣ

Πάνυ μὲν οὖν.

ΜΕΝΙΠΠΟΣ

Αὗται τοίνυν, ἐπειδὰν ἀποθάνωμεν, κατηγοροῦσί τε καὶ καταμαρτυροῦσι καὶ διελέγχουσι τὰ πεπραγμένα ἡμῖν παρὰ τὸν βίον, καὶ σφόδρα τινὲς ἀξιόπιστοι δοκοῦσιν ἅτε ἀεὶ συνοῦσαι καὶ μηδέποτε ἀφιστάμεναι τῶν σωμάτων.

12 Ὁ δ᾽ οὖν Μίνως ἐπιμελῶς ἐξετάζων ἀπέπεμπεν ἕκαστον εἰς τὸν τῶν ἀσεβῶν χῶρον δίκην ὑφέξοντα κατ᾽ ἀξίαν τῶν τετολμημένων, καὶ μάλιστα ἐκείνων ἥπτετο τῶν ἐπὶ πλούτοις τε καὶ ἀρχαῖς τετυφωμένων καὶ μονονουχὶ καὶ προσκυνεῖσθαι περιμενόντων, τήν τε ὀλιγοχρόνιον ἀλαζονείαν αὐτῶν καὶ τὴν ὑπεροψίαν μυσαττόμενος, καὶ ὅτι μὴ ἐμέμνηντο θνητοί τε ὄντες αὐτοὶ καὶ θνητῶν ἀγαθῶν τετυχηκότες. οἱ δὲ ἀποδυσάμενοι τὰ λαμπρὰ ἐκεῖνα πάντα, πλούτους λέγω καὶ γένη καὶ δυναστείας, γυμνοὶ κάτω νενευκότες παρειστήκεσαν ὥσπερ τινὰ ὄνειρον ἀναπεμπαζόμενοι τὴν παρ᾽ ἡμῖν εὐδαιμονίαν· ὥστ᾽ ἔγωγε ταῦτα ὁρῶν ὑπερέχαιρον καὶ εἴ τινα γνωρίσαιμι αὐτῶν, προσιὼν ἂν ἡσυχῇ πως ὑπεμίμνησκον οἷος ἦν παρὰ τὸν βίον καὶ ἡλίκον ἐφύσα τότε, ἡνίκα

MENIPPUS

Who were they, in Heaven's name? Don't hesitate to tell me that also.

You know these shadows that our bodies cast in the sunshine?

Why, to be sure!

Well, when we die, they prefer charges and give evidence against us, exposing whatever we have done in our lives; and they are considered very trustworthy because they always keep us company and never leave our bodies.

But to resume, Minos would examine each man carefully and send him away to the Place of the Wicked, to be punished in proportion to his crimes; and he dealt most harshly with those who were swollen with pride of wealth and place, and almost expected men to bow down and worship them; for he resented their short-lived vainglory and super-ciliousness, and their failure to remember that they themselves were mortal and had become possessed of mortal goods. So, after stripping off all their quondam splendour—wealth, I mean, and lineage and sovereignty—they stood there naked, with hanging heads, reviewing, point by point, their happy life among us as if it had been a dream. For my part I was highly delighted to see that, and whenever I recognized one of them, I would go up and quietly remind him what he used to be in life and how puffed up he had been then, when many men

93

πολλοὶ μὲν ἔωθεν ἐπὶ τῶν πυλώνων παρειστήκεσαν
τὴν πρόοδον αὐτοῦ περιμένοντες ὠθούμενοί τε καὶ
ἀποκλειόμενοι πρὸς τῶν οἰκετῶν· ὁ δὲ μόλις ἄν
ποτε ἀνατείλας αὐτοῖς πορφυροῦς τις ἢ περίχρυσος
ἢ διαποίκιλος εὐδαίμονας ᾤετο καὶ μακαρίους
ἀποφαίνειν τοὺς προσειπόντας, εἰ[1] τὸ στῆθος ἢ
τὴν δεξιὰν προτείνων δοίη καταφιλεῖν. ἐκεῖνοι
μὲν οὖν ἠνιῶντο ἀκούοντες.

13   Τῷ δὲ Μίνῳ μία τις καὶ πρὸς χάριν ἐδικάσθη·
τὸν γάρ τοι Σικελιώτην Διονύσιον πολλά γε καὶ
δεινὰ καὶ ἀνόσια ὑπό τε Δίωνος κατηγορηθέντα
καὶ ὑπὸ τῆς σκιᾶς καταμαρτυρηθέντα παρελθὼν
Ἀρίστιππος ὁ Κυρηναῖος—ἄγουσι δ᾽ αὐτὸν ἐν
τιμῇ καὶ δύναται μέγιστον ἐν τοῖς κάτω—μικροῦ
δεῖν τῇ Χιμαίρᾳ προσδεθέντα[2] παρέλυσε τῆς
καταδίκης λέγων πολλοῖς αὐτὸν τῶν πεπαιδευμένων πρὸς ἀργύριον γενέσθαι δεξιόν.

14   Ἀποστάντες δὲ ὅμως τοῦ δικαστηρίου πρὸς τὸ
κολαστήριον ἀφικνούμεθα. ἔνθα δή, ὦ φιλότης,
πολλὰ καὶ ἐλεεινὰ ἦν καὶ ἀκοῦσαι καὶ ἰδεῖν·
μαστίγων τε γὰρ ὁμοῦ ψόφος ἠκούετο καὶ οἰμωγὴ
τῶν ἐπὶ τοῦ πυρὸς ὀπτωμένων καὶ στρέβλαι καὶ
κύφωνες καὶ τροχοί, καὶ ἡ Χίμαιρα ἐσπάραττεν
καὶ ὁ Κέρβερος ἐδάρδαπτεν. ἐκολάζοντό τε ἅμα
πάντες, βασιλεῖς, δοῦλοι, σατράπαι, πένητες,
πλούσιοι, πτωχοί, καὶ μετέμελε πᾶσι τῶν τετολμημένων. ἐνίους δὲ αὐτῶν καὶ ἐγνωρίσαμεν

---

[1] εἰ Dindorf : ἢ β, ἢν γ.
[2] προτεθέντα Seager, Fritzsche. But compare Horace,
Carm. i. 27, 23-24:

> Vix illigatum te triformi
> Pegasus expediet Chimaera.

stood at his portals in the early morning awaiting
his advent, hustled about and locked out by his
servants, while he himself, bursting upon their
vision at last in garments of purple or gold or gaudy
stripes, thought that he was conferring happiness
and bliss upon those who greeted him if he
proffered his right hand or his breast, to be covered
with kisses. They chafed, I assure you, as they
listened!

But to return to Minos, he gave one decision by
favour; for Dionysius of Sicily had been charged
with many dreadful and impious crimes by Dion as
prosecutor and the shadow as witness, but Aristippus
of Cyrene appeared—they hold him in honour, and
he has very great influence among the people of
the lower world—and when Dionysius was within
an ace of being chained up to the Chimera, he got
him let off from the punishment by saying that
many men of letters had found him obliging in
the matter of money.[1]

Leaving the court reluctantly, we came to the
place of punishment, where in all truth, my friend,
there were many pitiful things to hear and to see.
The sound of scourges could be heard, and there-
withal the wails of those roasting on the fire; there
were racks and pillories and wheels; Chimera tore
and Cerberus ravened. They were being punished
all together, kings, slaves, satraps, poor, rich, and
beggars, and all were sorry for their excesses. Some
of them we even recognized when we saw them, all

---

[1] Aristippus had lived at the court of Dionysius the
Younger. Among the men of letters there present were
Plato, Xenocrates, Speusippos, and Aeschines the Socratic.

ἰδόντες, ὁπόσοι ἦσαν τῶν ἔναγχος τετελευτηκότων·
οἱ δὲ ἐνεκαλύπτοντό τε καὶ ἀπεστρέφοντο, εἰ δὲ
καὶ προσβλέποιεν, μάλα δουλοπρεπές τι καὶ
κολακευτικόν, καὶ ταῦτα πῶς οἴει βαρεῖς ὄντες
καὶ ὑπερόπται παρὰ τὸν βίον; τοῖς μέντοι
πένησιν ἡμιτέλεια τῶν κακῶν ἐδίδοτο, καὶ
διαναπαυόμενοι πάλιν ἐκολάζοντο.   καὶ μὴν
κἀκεῖνα εἶδον τὰ μυθώδη, τὸν Ἰξίονα καὶ τὸν
Σίσυφον καὶ τὸν Φρύγα Τάνταλον, χαλεπῶς γε
ἔχοντα,[1] καὶ τὸν γηγενῆ Τιτυόν, Ἡράκλεις ὅσος·
ἔκειτο γοῦν τόπον ἐπέχων ἀγροῦ.

15   Διελθόντες δὲ καὶ τούτους εἰς τὸ πεδίον
εἰσβάλλομεν τὸ Ἀχερούσιον, εὑρίσκομέν τε
αὐτόθι τοὺς ἡμιθέους τε καὶ τὰς ἡρωίνας καὶ τὸν
ἄλλον ὅμιλον τῶν νεκρῶν κατὰ ἔθνη καὶ κατὰ
φῦλα διαιτωμένους, τοὺς μὲν παλαιούς τινας καὶ
εὐρωτιῶντας καὶ ὥς φησιν Ὅμηρος, ἀμενηνούς,
τοὺς δ᾽ ἔτι νεαλεῖς καὶ συνεστηκότας, καὶ μάλιστα
τοὺς Αἰγυπτίους αὐτῶν διὰ τὸ πολυαρκὲς τῆς
ταριχείας.   τὸ μέντοι διαγιγνώσκειν ἕκαστον οὐ
πάνυ τι ἦν ῥάδιον· ἅπαντες γὰρ ἀτεχνῶς ἀλλήλοις
γίγνονται ὅμοιοι τῶν ὀστῶν γεγυμνωμένων.   πλὴν
ἀλλὰ μόγις τε καὶ διὰ πολλοῦ ἀναθεωροῦντες
αὐτοὺς ἐγιγνώσκομεν.   ἔκειντο δ᾽ ἐπ᾽ ἀλλήλοις
ἀμαυροὶ καὶ ἄσημοι καὶ οὐδὲν ἔτι τῶν παρ᾽ ἡμῖν
καλῶν φυλάττοντες.   ἀμέλει πολλῶν ἐν ταὐτῷ
σκελετῶν κειμένων καὶ πάντων ὁμοίως φοβερόν τι
καὶ διάκενον δεδορκότων καὶ γυμνοὺς τοὺς ὀδόντας

---

[1] χαλεπῶς γε ἔχοντα A.M.H. : χαλεπῶς τε ἔχοντα Γ.   Not
in PN.   Fritzsche reads χολέπ᾽ ἄλγε᾽ ἔχοντα.

---

[1] A reflection (purposely bald and prosaic, in order to

that were recently dead. But they covered their
faces and turned away, and if they so much as
cast a glance at us, it was thoroughly servile and
obsequious, even though they had been unimaginably
oppressive and haughty in life. Poor people, however, were getting only half as much torture and
resting at intervals before being punished again.
Moreover, I saw all that is told of in the legends—
Ixion, Sisyphus, Tantalus the Phrygian, who was
certainly in a bad way,[1] and earthborn Tityus—
Heracles, how big he was! Indeed, he took up land
enough for a farm as he lay there![2]

After making our way past these people also, we
entered the Acherusian Plain, where we found the
demigods and the fair women and the whole crowd
of the dead, living by nations and by clans, some of
them ancient and mouldy, and, as Homer says,
"impalpable," while others were still well preserved
and substantial, particularly the Egyptians, thanks
to the durability of their embalming process. It
was not at all easy, though, to tell them apart, for
all, without exception, become precisely alike when
their bones are bare. However, with some difficulty
and by dint of long study we made them out. But
they were lying one atop of another, ill-defined,
unidentified, retaining no longer any trace of earthly
beauty. So, with many skeletons lying together,
all alike staring horridly and vacuously and baring

fetch a smile) of Homer's χαλέπ' ἄλγε ἔχοντα (*Odyssey*, 11,
582).

[2] He covered nine pelethra; *Odyssey*, 11, 577; unfortunately
we do not know how much a Homeric pelethron was. But
when Athena took the measure of Ares, who could shout as
loud as nine or ten thousand soldiers, it was but seven
pelethra (*Il.* 5, 860; 21, 407).

προφαινόντων, ἠπόρουν πρὸς ἐμαυτὸν ᾧτινι δια-
κρίναιμι τὸν Θερσίτην ἀπὸ τοῦ καλοῦ Νιρέως ἢ
τὸν μεταίτην Ἴρον ἀπὸ τοῦ Φαιάκων βασιλέως ἢ
Πυρρίαν τὸν μάγειρον ἀπὸ τοῦ Ἀγαμέμνονος.
οὐδὲν γὰρ ἔτι τῶν παλαιῶν γνωρισμάτων αὐτοῖς
παρέμενεν, ἀλλ' ὅμοια τὰ ὀστᾶ ἦν, ἄδηλα καὶ ἀν-
επίγραφα καὶ ὑπ' οὐδενὸς ἔτι διακρίνεσθαι δυνά-
μενα.

16   Τοιγάρτοι ἐκεῖνα ὁρῶντί μοι ἐδόκει ὁ τῶν
ἀνθρώπων βίος πομπῇ τινι μακρᾷ προσεοικέναι,
χορηγεῖν δὲ καὶ διατάττειν ἕκαστα ἡ Τύχη, διά-
φορα καὶ ποικίλα τοῖς πομπευταῖς τὰ σχήματα
προσάπτουσα· τὸν μὲν γὰρ λαβοῦσα, εἰ τύχοι,
βασιλικῶς διεσκεύασεν, τιάραν τε ἐπιθεῖσα καὶ
δορυφόρους παραδοῦσα καὶ τὴν κεφαλὴν στέψασα
τῷ διαδήματι, τῷ δὲ οἰκέτου σχῆμα περιέθηκεν·
τὸν δέ τινα καλὸν εἶναι ἐκόσμησεν, τὸν δὲ ἄμορφον
καὶ γελοῖον παρεσκεύασεν· παντοδαπὴν γάρ,
οἶμαι, δεῖ γενέσθαι τὴν θέαν.   πολλάκις δὲ καὶ
διὰ μέσης τῆς πομπῆς μετέβαλε τὰ ἐνίων σχήματα
οὐκ ἐῶσα εἰς τέλος διαπομπεῦσαι ὡς ἐτάχθησαν,
ἀλλὰ μεταμφιέσασα τὸν μὲν Κροῖσον ἠνάγκασε
τὴν τοῦ οἰκέτου καὶ αἰχμαλώτου σκευὴν ἀναλα-
βεῖν, τὸν δὲ Μαιάνδριον τέως ἐν τοῖς οἰκέταις
πομπεύοντα τὴν τοῦ Πολυκράτους τυραννίδα
μετενέδυσε.   καὶ μέχρι μέν τινος εἴασε χρῆσθαι
τῷ σχήματι· ἐπειδὰν δὲ ὁ τῆς πομπῆς καιρὸς
παρέλθῃ, τηνικαῦτα ἕκαστος ἀποδοὺς τὴν σκευὴν
καὶ ἀποδυσάμενος τὸ σχῆμα μετὰ τοῦ σώματος
ἐγένετο οἷόσπερ ἦν πρὸ τοῦ γενέσθαι, μηδὲν τοῦ
πλησίον διαφέρων.   ἔνιοι δὲ ὑπ' ἀγνωμοσύνης,
ἐπειδὰν ἀπαιτῇ τὸν κόσμον ἐπιστᾶσα ἡ Τύχη,

their teeth, I questioned myself how I could distinguish Thersites from handsome Nireus, or the mendicant Irus from the King of the Phaeacians, or the cook Pyrrhias from Agamemnon; for none of their former means of identification abode with them, but their bones were all alike, undefined, unlabelled, and unable ever again to be distinguished by anyone.

So as I looked at them it seemed to me that human life is like a long pageant, and that all its trappings are supplied and distributed by Fortune, who arrays the participants in various costumes of many colours. Taking one person, it may be, she attires him royally, placing a tiara upon his head, giving him body-guards, and encircling his brow with the diadem; but upon another she puts the costume of a slave. Again, she makes up one person so that he is handsome, but causes another to be ugly and ridiculous. I suppose that the show must needs be diversified. And often, in the very middle of the pageant, she exchanges the costumes of several players; instead of allowing them to finish the pageant in the parts that had been assigned to them, she re-apparels them, forcing Croesus to assume the dress of a slave and a captive, and shifting Maeandrius, who formerly paraded among the servants, into the imperial habit of Polycrates. For a brief space she lets them use their costumes, but when the time of the pageant is over, each gives back the properties and lays off the costume along with his body, becoming what he was before his birth, no different from his neighbour. Some, however, are so ungrateful that when Fortune appears to them and asks her trappings back, they are vexed

ἄχθονταί τε καὶ ἀγανακτοῦσιν ὥσπερ οἰκείων τινῶν στερισκόμενοι καὶ οὐχ ἃ πρὸς ὀλίγον ἐχρήσαντο ἀποδιδόντες.

Οἶμαι δέ σε καὶ τῶν ἐπὶ τῆς σκηνῆς πολλάκις ἑωρακέναι τοὺς τραγικοὺς ὑποκριτὰς τούτους πρὸς τὰς χρείας τῶν δραμάτων ἄρτι μὲν Κρέοντας, ἐνίοτε δὲ Πριάμους γιγνομένους ἢ Ἀγαμέμνονας, καὶ ὁ αὐτός, εἰ τύχοι, μικρὸν ἔμπροσθεν μάλα σεμνῶς τὸ τοῦ Κέκροπος ἢ Ἐρεχθέως σχῆμα μιμησάμενος μετ᾽ ὀλίγον οἰκέτης προῆλθεν ὑπὸ τοῦ ποιητοῦ κεκελευσμένος· ἤδη δὲ πέρας ἔχοντος τοῦ δράματος ἀποδυσάμενος ἕκαστος αὐτῶν τὴν χρυσόπαστον ἐκείνην ἐσθῆτα καὶ τὸ προσωπεῖον ἀποθέμενος καὶ καταβὰς ἀπὸ τῶν ἐμβατῶν πένης καὶ ταπεινὸς περίεισιν, οὐκέτ᾽ Ἀγαμέμνων ὁ Ἀτρέως οὐδὲ Κρέων ὁ Μενοικέως, ἀλλὰ Πῶλος Χαρικλέους Σουνιεὺς ὀνομαζόμενος ἢ Σάτυρος Θεογείτονος Μαραθώνιος. τοιαῦτα καὶ τὰ τῶν ἀνθρώπων πράγματά ἐστιν, ὡς τότε μοι ὁρῶντι ἔδοξεν.

ΦΙΛΟΣ

17 Εἰπέ μοι, ὦ Μένιππε, οἱ δὲ τοὺς πολυτελεῖς τούτους καὶ ὑψηλοὺς τάφους ἔχοντες ὑπὲρ γῆς καὶ στήλας καὶ εἰκόνας καὶ ἐπιγράμματα οὐδὲν τιμιώτεροι παρ᾽ αὑτοῖς εἰσι τῶν ἰδιωτῶν νεκρῶν;

ΜΕΝΙΠΠΟΣ

Ληρεῖς, ὦ οὗτος· εἰ γοῦν ἐθεάσω τὸν Μαύσωλον αὐτόν,—λέγω δὲ τὸν Κᾶρα, τὸν ἐκ τοῦ τάφου περιβόητον—εὖ οἶδα ὅτι οὐκ ἂν ἐπαύσω γελῶν, οὕτω ταπεινὸς ἔρριπτο ἐν παραβύστῳ που

and indignant, as if they were being robbed of their own property, instead of giving back what they had borrowed for a little time.

I suppose you have often seen these stage-folk who act in tragedies, and according to the demands of the plays become at one moment Creons, and again Priams or Agamemnons; the very one, it may be, who a short time ago assumed with great dignity the part of Cecrops or of Erectheus soon appears as a servant at the bidding of the poet. And when at length the play comes to an end, each of them strips off his gold-bespangled robe, lays aside his mask, steps out of his buskins, and goes about in poverty and humility, no longer styled Agamemnon, son of Atreus, or Creon, son of Menoeceus, but Polus, son of Charicles, of Sunium, or Satyrus, son of Theogiton, of Marathon.[1] That is what human affairs are like, it seemed to me as I looked.

FRIEND

But tell me, Menippus; those who have such expensive, high monuments on earth, and tombstones and statues and inscriptions—are they no more highly honoured there than the common dead?

MENIPPUS

Nonsense, man! If you had seen Mausolus himself—I mean the Carian, so famous for his monument—I know right well that you would never have stopped laughing, so humbly did he lie where he

---

[1] Polus and Satyrus were famous actors, both of the fourth century B.C.

λανθάνων ἐν τῷ λοιπῷ δήμῳ τῶν νεκρῶν, ἐμοὶ
δοκεῖν, τοσοῦτον ἀπολαύων τοῦ μνήματος, παρ'
ὅσον ἐβαρύνετο τηλικοῦτον ἄχθος ἐπικείμενος·
ἐπειδὰν γάρ, ὦ ἑταῖρε, ὁ Αἰακὸς ἀπομετρήσῃ
ἑκάστῳ τὸν τόπον,—δίδωσι δὲ τὸ μέγιστον οὐ
πλέον ποδός—ἀνάγκη ἀγαπῶντα κατακεῖσθαι
πρὸς τὸ μέτρον συνεσταλμένον. πολλῷ δ' ἂν
οἶμαι μᾶλλον ἐγέλασας, εἰ ἐθεάσω τοὺς παρ'
ἡμῖν βασιλέας καὶ σατράπας πτωχεύοντας παρ'
αὐτοῖς καὶ ἤτοι ταριχοπωλοῦντας ὑπ' ἀπορίας ἢ
τὰ πρῶτα διδάσκοντας γράμματα καὶ ὑπὸ τοῦ
τυχόντος ὑβριζομένους καὶ κατὰ κόρρης παιομένους ὥσπερ τῶν ἀνδραπόδων τὰ ἀτιμότατα.
Φίλιππον γοῦν τὸν Μακεδόνα ἐγὼ θεασάμενος
οὐδὲ κρατεῖν ἐμαυτοῦ δυνατὸς ἦν· ἐδείχθη δέ μοι
ἐν γωνίᾳ τινὶ μισθοῦ ἀκούμενος τὰ σαθρὰ τῶν
ὑποδημάτων. πολλοὺς δὲ καὶ ἄλλους ἦν ἰδεῖν ἐν
ταῖς τριόδοις μεταιτοῦντας, Ξέρξας λέγω καὶ
Δαρείους καὶ Πολυκράτας.

ΦΙΛΟΣ

18 Ἄτοπα διηγῇ τὰ περὶ τῶν βασιλέων καὶ μικροῦ
δεῖν ἄπιστα. τί δὲ ὁ Σωκράτης ἔπραττεν καὶ
Διογένης καὶ εἴ τις ἄλλος τῶν σοφῶν;

ΜΕΝΙΠΠΟΣ

Ὁ μὲν Σωκράτης κἀκεῖ περίεισιν διελέγχων
ἅπαντας· σύνεστι δ' αὐτῷ Παλαμήδης καὶ Ὀδυσ-
σεὺς καὶ Νέστωρ καὶ εἴ τις ἄλλος λάλος νεκρός.
ἔτι μέντοι ἐπεφύσητο αὐτῷ καὶ διῳδήκει ἐκ τῆς
φαρμακοποσίας τὰ σκέλη. ὁ δὲ βέλτιστος Διογένης παροικεῖ μὲν Σαρδαναπάλλῳ τῷ Ἀσσυρίῳ

was flung, in a cubby-hole, inconspicuous among the rest of the plebeian dead, deriving, in my opinion, only this much satisfaction from his monument, that he was heavy laden with such a great weight resting upon him. When Aeacus measures off the space for each, my friend—and he gives at most not over a foot—one must be content to lie in it, huddled together to fit its compass. But you would have laughed much more heartily, I think, if you had seen our kings and satraps reduced to poverty there, and either selling salt fish on account of their neediness or teaching the alphabet, and getting abused and hit over the head by all comers, like the meanest of slaves. In fact, when I saw Philip of Macedon, I could not control my laughter. He was pointed out to me in a corner, cobbling worn-out sandals for pay! Many others, too, could be seen begging at the cross-roads—your Xerxeses, I mean, and Dariuses and Polycrateses.

FRIEND

What you say about the kings is extraordinary and almost incredible. But what was Socrates doing, and Diogenes, and the rest of the wise men?

MENIPPUS

As to Socrates, there too he goes about cross-questioning everyone. His associates are Palamedes, Odysseus, Nestor, and other talkative corpses. His legs, I may say, were still puffed up and swollen from his draught of poison. And good old Diogenes lives with Sardanapalus the Assyrian, Midas the

καὶ Μίδᾳ τῷ Φρυγὶ καὶ ἄλλοις τισὶ τῶν πολυτε-
λῶν· ἀκούων δὲ οἰμωζόντων αὐτῶν καὶ τὴν
παλαιὰν τύχην ἀναμετρουμένων γελᾷ τε καὶ
τέρπεται, καὶ τὰ πολλὰ ὕπτιος κατακείμενος ᾄδει
μάλα τραχείᾳ καὶ ἀπηνεῖ τῇ φωνῇ τὰς οἰμωγὰς
αὐτῶν ἐπικαλύπτων, ὥστε ἀνιᾶσθαι τοὺς ἄνδρας
καὶ διασκέπτεσθαι μετοικεῖν οὐ φέροντας τὸν
Διογένην.

ΦΙΛΟΣ

19 Ταυτὶ μὲν ἱκανῶς· τί δὲ τὸ ψήφισμα ἦν, ὅπερ
ἐν ἀρχῇ ἔλεγες κεκυρῶσθαι κατὰ τῶν πλουσίων;

ΜΕΝΙΠΠΟΣ

Εὖ γε ὑπέμνησας· οὐ γὰρ οἶδ᾽ ὅπως περὶ τούτου λέγειν προθέμενος πάμπολυ ἀπεπλανήθην
τοῦ λόγου.

Διατρίβοντος γάρ μου παρ᾽ αὐτοῖς προὔθεσαν
οἱ πρυτάνεις ἐκκλησίαν περὶ τῶν κοινῇ συμφερόν-
των· ἰδὼν οὖν πολλοὺς συνθέοντας ἀναμίξας
ἐμαυτὸν τοῖς νεκροῖς εὐθὺς εἷς καὶ αὐτὸς ἦν τῶν
ἐκκλησιαστῶν. διῳκήθη μὲν οὖν καὶ ἄλλα,
τελευταῖον δὲ τὸ περὶ τῶν πλουσίων· ἐπεὶ γὰρ
αὐτῶν κατηγόρητο πολλὰ καὶ δεινά, βία καὶ
ἀλαζονεία καὶ ὑπεροψία καὶ ἀδικία, τέλος
ἀναστάς τις τῶν δημαγωγῶν ἀνέγνω ψήφισμα
τοιοῦτον.

ΨΗΦΙΣΜΑ

20 "Ἐπειδὴ πολλὰ καὶ παράνομα οἱ πλούσιοι
δρῶσι παρὰ τὸν βίον ἁρπάζοντες καὶ βιαζόμενοι
καὶ πάντα τρόπον τῶν πενήτων καταφρονοῦντες,

Phrygian, and several other wealthy men. As he hears them lamenting and reviewing their former good-fortune, he laughs and rejoices; and often he lies on his back and sings in a very harsh and unpleasant voice, drowning out their lamentations, so that the gentlemen are annoyed and think of changing their lodgings because they cannot stand Diogenes.

FRIEND

Well, enough of this, but what was the motion that in the beginning you said had been passed against the rich?

MENIPPUS

Thanks for reminding me. Somehow or other, in spite of my intention to speak about that, I went very much astray in my talk.

During my stay there, the city fathers called a public meeting to discuss matters of general interest; so when I saw many people running in the same direction, I mingled with the dead and speedily became one of the electors myself. Well, various business was transacted, and at last that about the rich. After many dreadful charges of violence and mendacity and superciliousness and injustice had been brought against them, at length one of the demagogues rose and read the following motion.

(MOTION)

"Whereas many lawless deeds are done in life by the rich, who plunder and oppress and in every way humiliate the poor,

"Δεδόχθω τῇ βουλῇ καὶ τῷ δήμῳ, ἐπειδὰν
ἀποθάνωσι, τὰ μὲν σώματα αὐτῶν κολάζεσθαι
καθάπερ καὶ τὰ τῶν ἄλλων πονηρῶν, τὰς δὲ
ψυχὰς ἀναπεμφθείσας ἄνω εἰς τὸν βίον καταδύε-
σθαι εἰς τοὺς ὄνους, ἄχρις ἂν ἐν τῷ τοιούτῳ δια-
γάγωσι μυριάδας ἐτῶν πέντε καὶ εἴκοσιν, ὄνοι ἐξ
ὄνων γιγνόμενοι καὶ ἀχθοφοροῦντες καὶ ὑπὸ τῶν
πενήτων ἐλαυνόμενοι, τοὐντεῦθεν δὲ λοιπὸν ἐξεῖναι
αὐτοῖς ἀποθανεῖν.

"Εἶπε τὴν γνώμην Κρανίων Σκελετίωνος Νεκυ-
σιεὺς φυλῆς Ἀλιβαντίδος."

Τούτου ἀναγνωσθέντος τοῦ ψηφίσματος ἐπε-
ψήφισαν μὲν αἱ ἀρχαί, ἐπεχειροτόνησε δὲ τὸ
πλῆθος καὶ ἐβριμήσατο ἡ Βριμὼ καὶ ὑλάκτησεν
ὁ Κέρβερος· οὕτω γὰρ ἐντελῆ γίγνεται καὶ κύρια
τὰ ἐγνωσμένα.

21   Ταῦτα μὲν δή σοι τὰ ἐν τῇ ἐκκλησίᾳ. ἐγὼ δέ,
οὗπερ ἀφίγμην ἕνεκα, τῷ Τειρεσίᾳ προσελθὼν
ἱκέτευον αὐτὸν τὰ πάντα διηγησάμενος εἰπεῖν
πρός με ποῖόν τινα ἡγεῖται τὸν ἄριστον βίον. ὁ
δὲ γελάσας—ἔστι δὲ τυφλόν τι γερόντιον καὶ
ὠχρὸν καὶ λεπτόφωνον—"Ὦ τέκνον," φησί,
"τὴν μὲν αἰτίαν οἶδά σοι τῆς ἀπορίας ὅτι παρὰ
τῶν σοφῶν ἐγένετο οὐ ταὐτὰ γιγνωσκόντων ἑαυ-
τοῖς· ἀτὰρ οὐ θέμις λέγειν πρὸς σέ· ἀπείρηται γὰρ
ὑπὸ τοῦ Ῥαδαμάνθυος." "Μηδαμῶς," ἔφην, "ὦ
πατέριον, ἀλλ' εἰπὲ καὶ μὴ περιίδῃς με σοῦ
τυφλότερον περιιόντα ἐν τῷ βίῳ." ὁ δὲ δή με
ἀπαγαγὼν καὶ πολὺ τῶν ἄλλων ἀποσπάσας
ἤρεμα προσκύψας πρὸς τὸ οὖς φησίν, "Ὁ τῶν
ἰδιωτῶν ἄριστος βίος, καὶ σωφρονέστερος[1] παυσά-

"Be it resolved by the senate and people, that when they die their bodies be punished like those of the other malefactors, but their souls be sent back up into life and enter into donkeys until they shall have passed two hundred and fifty thousand years in the said condition, transmigrating from donkey to donkey, bearing burdens, and being driven by the poor; and that thereafter it be permitted them to die.

"On motion of Scully Fitzbones of Corpsebury, Cadavershire."

After this motion had been read, the officials put it to the vote, the majority indicated assent by the usual sign, Brimo brayed and Cerberus howled. That is the way in which their motions are enacted and ratified.

Well, there you have what took place at the meeting. For my part, I did what I came to do. Going to Teiresias, I told him the whole story and besought him to tell me what sort of life he considered the best. He laughed (he is a blind little old gentleman, pale, with a piping voice) and said: "My son, I know the reason for your perplexity; it came from the wise men, who are not consistent with themselves. But it is not permissible to tell you, for Rhadamanthus has forbidden it." "Don't say that, gaffer," said I. "Tell me, and don't allow me to go about in life blinder than you are." So he took me aside, and after he had led me a good way apart from the others, he bent his head slightly toward my ear and said: "The life of the common sort is best, and you will act more wisely if you

---

[1] καὶ σωφρονέστερος γ: ὡς τῆς ἀφροσύνης β.

μενος τοῦ μετεωρολογεῖν καὶ τέλη καὶ ἀρχὰς
ἐπισκοπεῖν καὶ καταπτύσας τῶν σοφῶν τούτων
συλλογισμῶν καὶ τὰ τοιαῦτα λῆρον ἡγησάμενος
τοῦτο μόνον ἐξ ἅπαντος θηράσῃ, ὅπως τὸ παρὸν
εὖ θέμενος παραδράμῃς γελῶν τὰ πολλὰ καὶ
περὶ μηδὲν ἐσπουδακώς."

ὡς εἰπὼν πάλιν ὦρτο κατ' ἀσφοδελὸν λειμῶνα.

22 Ἐγὼ δὲ—καὶ γὰρ ἤδη ὀψὲ ἦν—"Ἄγε δή, ὦ
Μιθροβαρζάνη," φημί, " τί διαμέλλομεν καὶ οὐκ
ἄπιμεν αὖθις εἰς τὸν βίον "; ὁ δὲ πρὸς ταῦτα,
" Θάρρει," φησίν, " ὦ Μένιππε· ταχεῖαν γάρ σοι
καὶ ἀπράγμονα ὑποδείξω ἀτραπόν." καὶ δὴ
ἀγαγών με πρός τι χωρίον τοῦ ἄλλου ζοφερώτερον
δείξας τῇ χειρὶ πόρρωθεν ἀμαυρὸν καὶ λεπτὸν
ὥσπερ διὰ κλειθρίας φῶς εἰσρέον, " Ἐκεῖνο," ἔφη,
" ἐστὶν τὸ ἱερὸν τὸ Τροφωνίου, κἀκεῖθεν κατίασιν
οἱ ἀπὸ Βοιωτίας. ταύτην οὖν ἄνιθι καὶ εὐθὺς
ἔσῃ ἐπὶ τῆς Ἑλλάδος." ἡσθεὶς δὲ τοῖς εἰρημένοις
ἐγὼ καὶ τὸν μάγον ἀσπασάμενος χαλεπῶς μάλα
διὰ τοῦ στομίου ἀνερπύσας οὐκ οἶδ' ὅπως ἐν
Λεβαδείᾳ γίγνομαι.

stop speculating about heavenly bodies and discussing final causes and first causes, spit your scorn at those clever syllogisms, and counting all that sort of thing nonsense, make it always your sole object to put the present to good use and to hasten on your way, laughing a great deal and taking nothing seriously."

"So he spoke, and betook him again through the asphodel meadow." [1]

As it was late by then, I said: "Come, Mithrobarzanes, why do we delay? Why not go back to life again?" To this he replied: "Never fear, Menippus; I will show you a quick and easy short cut." And then, taking me to a place murkier than the rest of the region and pointing with his finger to a dim and slender ray of light coming in as if through a keyhole, a long way off, he said: "That is the sanctuary of Trophonius, where the people from Boeotia come down. So go up by that route and you will be in Greece directly." Delighted with his words, I embraced the sorcerer, very laboriously crawled up through the hole somehow, and found myself in Lebadeia.

[1] Apparently a cento from Homer; cf. *Odyssey*, 11, 539.

ON FUNERALS

In the introductory note on *Sacrifices* (III. 153) it has been indicated that *Sacrifices* and *Funerals* are closely related. There is reason, I think, to believe that *Sacrifices* was written later than *Funerals*, to be read in public as a continuation of that piece. After the lecture it was put into circulation as a separate piece because *Funerals* was already in the hands of the public, and because the supplement seemed independent enough to stand alone. Thus, without ignoring the fact that the two pieces have come down to us separate, we may account for the further fact that the first sentence of one takes up the last sentence of the other as if it had been meant to do so (see the note on p. 131).

Though Lucian here follows the Cynic pattern pretty closely, and may indeed be drawing directly upon Bion the Borysthenite (p. 128, note 1), there is a difference. He cannot forget his inborn artistry and his rhetorical training. So, instead of preaching at his hearers, he lectures to them, censuring "the many" for the delectation of "the best." Moreover, his constant desire for novelty in literary form finds characteristic expression. In an inconspicuous way he employs once more a "frame" device, somewhat as in the *Prometheus*. The most usual form of this device, and the oldest, is that in which dialogue "frames" narrative, as in Lucian's *Lover of Lies*, and Plato's *Phaedo*. In the *Prometheus*, dialogue forms a setting for plea and counter-plea—the accusation of Hermes and the defence of Prometheus. Here, in a setting of diatribe, we come upon threnody and para-threnody—the father's lament, and the dead son's reply. It may be remarked also that the source and character of the reply contribute a truly Lucianic fillip of surprise.

ΠΕΡΙ ΠΕΝΘΟΥΣ

1 Ἄξιόν γε παρατηρεῖν τὰ ὑπὸ τῶν πολλῶν ἐν
τοῖς πένθεσι γιγνόμενα καὶ λεγόμενα καὶ τὰ ὑπὸ
τῶν παραμυθουμένων δῆθεν αὐτοὺς αὖθις λεγόμενα, καὶ ὡς ἀφόρητα ἡγοῦνται τὰ συμβαίνοντα
σφίσι τε αὐτοῖς οἱ ὀδυρόμενοι καὶ ἐκείνοις οὓς
ὀδύρονται, οὐ μὰ τὸν Πλούτωνα καὶ Φερσεφόνην
κατ᾽ οὐδὲν ἐπιστάμενοι σαφῶς οὔτε εἰ πονηρὰ
ταῦτα καὶ λύπης ἄξια οὔτε εἰ[1] τοὐναντίον ἡδέα
καὶ βελτίω τοῖς παθοῦσι, νόμῳ δὲ καὶ συνηθείᾳ
τὴν λύπην ἐπιτρέποντες. ἐπειδὰν τοίνυν ἀποθάνῃ τις, οὕτω ποιοῦσιν—μᾶλλον δὲ πρότερον
εἰπεῖν βούλομαι ἅστινας περὶ αὐτοῦ τοῦ θανάτου
δόξας ἔχουσιν· οὕτω γὰρ ἔσται φανερὸν οὗτινος
ἕνεκα τὰ περιττὰ ἐκεῖνα ἐπιτηδεύουσιν.

2 Ὁ μὲν δὴ πολὺς ὅμιλος, οὓς ἰδιώτας οἱ σοφοὶ
καλοῦσιν, Ὁμήρῳ τε καὶ Ἡσιόδῳ καὶ τοῖς ἄλλοις
μυθοποιοῖς περὶ τούτων πειθόμενοι καὶ νόμον
θέμενοι τὴν ποίησιν αὐτῶν, τόπον τινα ὑπὸ τῇ γῇ
βαθὺν Ἅιδην ὑπειλήφασιν, μέγαν δὲ καὶ πολύ-
χωρον τοῦτον εἶναι καὶ ζοφερὸν καὶ ἀνήλιον, οὐκ
οἶδ᾽ ὅπως αὐτοῖς φωτίζεσθαι δοκοῦντα πρὸς τὸ
καὶ καθορᾶν τῶν ἐνόντων ἕκαστον· βασιλεύειν δὲ

Codices available in photographs : Γ, UPN.

---

[1] οὔτε εἰ vulg. : εἴτε εἰ γ ; ἤ β.

ON FUNERALS

TRULY, it is well worth while to observe what most people do and say at funerals, and on the other hand what their would-be comforters say ; to observe also how unbearable the mourners consider what is happening, not only for themselves but for those whom they mourn. Yet, I swear by Pluto and Persephone, they have not one whit of definite knowledge as to whether this experience is unpleasant and worth grieving about, or on the contrary delightful and better for those who undergo it. No, they simply commit their grief into the charge of custom and habit. When someone dies, then, this is what they do—but stay ! First I wish to tell you what beliefs they hold about death itself, for then it will become clear why they engage in these superfluous practices.

The general herd, whom philosophers call the laity, trust Homer and Hesiod and the other myth-makers in these matters, and take their poetry for a law unto themselves. So they suppose that there is a place deep under the earth called Hades, which is large and roomy and murky and sunless; I don't know how they imagine it to be lighted up so that everything in it can be seen. The king of the

τοῦ χάσματος ἀδελφὸν τοῦ Διὸς Πλούτωνα κεκλη-
μένον, ὥς μοι τῶν τὰ τοιαῦτα δεινῶν τις ἔλεγε,
διὰ τὸ πλουτεῖν τοῖς νεκροῖς τῇ προσηγορίᾳ
τετιμημένον. τοῦτον δὲ τὸν Πλούτωνα τὴν παρ᾽
αὑτῷ πολιτείαν καὶ τὸν κάτω βίον καταστήσασθαι
τοιοῦτον· κεκληρῶσθαι μὲν γὰρ αὐτὸν ἄρχειν τῶν
ἀποθανόντων, καταδεξάμενον δὲ αὐτοὺς καὶ παρα-
λαβόντα κατέχειν δεσμοῖς ἀφύκτοις, οὐδενὶ τὸ
παράπαν τῆς ἄνω ὁδοῦ ὑφιέμενον πλὴν ἐξ ἅπαντος
τοῦ αἰῶνος πάνυ ὀλίγων ἐπὶ μεγίσταις αἰτίαις.
3 περιρρεῖσθαι δὲ τὴν χώραν αὐτοῦ ποταμοῖς
μεγάλοις τε καὶ φοβεροῖς καὶ ἐκ μόνων τῶν
ὀνομάτων· Κωκυτοὶ γὰρ καὶ Πυριφλεγέθοντες
καὶ τὰ τοιαῦτα κέκληνται. τὸ δὲ μέγιστον, ἡ
Ἀχερουσία λίμνη πρόκειται πρώτη δεχομένη
τοὺς ἀπαντῶντας, ἣν οὐκ ἔνι διαπλεῦσαι ἢ
παρελθεῖν ἄνευ τοῦ πορθμέως· βαθεῖά τε γὰρ
περᾶσαι τοῖς ποσὶν καὶ διανήξασθαι πολλή, καὶ
ὅλως οὐκ ἂν αὐτὴν διαπταίη οὐδὲ τὰ νεκρὰ τῶν
4 ὀρνέων. πρὸς δὲ αὐτῇ τῇ καθόδῳ καὶ πύλῃ οὔσῃ
ἀδαμαντίνῃ ἀδελφιδοῦς τοῦ βασιλέως Αἰακὸς
ἕστηκε τὴν φρουρὰν ἐπιτετραμμένος καὶ παρ᾽
αὐτῷ κύων τρικέφαλος μάλα κάρχαρος, τοὺς μὲν
ἀφικνουμένους φίλιόν τι καὶ εἰρηνικὸν προσβλέπων, τοὺς δὲ πειρῶντας ἀποδιδράσκειν ὑλακτῶν
5 καὶ τῷ χάσματι δεδιττόμενος. περαιωθέντας δὲ
τὴν λίμνην εἰς τὸ εἴσω λειμὼν ὑποδέχεται μέγας

---

[1] The Greeks derived the name Ploutōn (Pluto) from
plouteîn (to be rich), and generally held that it was given
to Hades because he owned and dispensed the riches that
are in the earth. So Lucian in the *Timon* (21). Here, how-

abyss is a brother of Zeus named Pluto, who has been honoured with that appellative, so I was told by one well versed in such matters, because of his wealth of corpses.[1] This Pluto, they say, has organized his state and the world below as follows. He himself has been allotted the sovereignty of the dead, whom he receives, takes in charge, and retains in close custody, permitting nobody whatsoever to go back up above, except, in all time, a very few for most important reasons. His country is surrounded by great rivers, fearful even in name; for they are called "Wailing," "Burning Fire," and the like. But the principal feature is Lake Acheron, which lies in front and first receives visitors; it cannot be crossed or passed without the ferryman, for it is too deep to ford afoot and too broad to swim across—indeed, even dead birds cannot fly across it![2] Hard by the descent and the portal, which is of adamant, stands the king's nephew, Aeacus, who is commander of the guard; and beside him is a three-headed dog, very long-fanged, who gives a friendly, peaceable glance to those who come in, but howls at those who try to run away and frightens them with his great mouth. After passing the lake on going in, one comes next to a

---

ever, we have in substance the view of Cornutus (5): "He was called Pluto because, of all that is perishable, there is nothing which does not at last go down to him and become his property."

[2] Many places on earth, men thought, exhaled vapours so deadly that birds, attempting to cross them, fell dead; the most famous of these "Plutonia" was the lake near Cumae, called Ἄορνος par excellence, whence Avernus. If live birds could not fly across Avernus, surely the ghost of a bird could not fly across Acheron.

THE WORKS OF LUCIAN

τῷ ἀσφοδέλῳ κατάφυτος καὶ ποτὸν μνήμης πολέ-
μιον· Λήθης γοῦν διὰ τοῦτο ὠνόμασται. ταῦτα
γὰρ ἀμέλει διηγήσαντο τοῖς πάλαι ἐκεῖθεν
ἀφιγμένοι Ἄλκηστίς τε καὶ Πρωτεσίλαος οἱ
Θετταλοὶ καὶ Θησεὺς ὁ τοῦ Αἰγέως καὶ ὁ τοῦ
Ὁμήρου Ὀδυσσεύς, μάλα σεμνοὶ καὶ ἀξιόπιστοι
μάρτυρες, ἐμοὶ δοκεῖν οὐ πιόντες τῆς πηγῆς· οὐ
γὰρ ἂν ἐμέμνηντο αὐτῶν.

6   Ὁ μὲν οὖν Πλούτων, ὡς ἐκεῖνοι ἔφασαν, καὶ ἡ
Φερσεφόνη δυναστεύουσι καὶ τὴν τῶν ὅλων
δεσποτείαν ἔχουσιν, ὑπηρετοῦσι δ᾿ αὐτοῖς καὶ τὴν
ἀρχὴν συνδιαπράττουσιν ὄχλος πολύς, Ἐρινύες
τε καὶ Ποιναὶ καὶ Φόβοι καὶ ὁ Ἑρμῆς, οὗτος μέν
7 γε οὐκ ἀεὶ συμπαρών. ὕπαρχοι δὲ καὶ σατράπαι
καὶ δικασταὶ κάθηνται δύο, Μίνως τε καὶ Ῥαδά-
μανθυς οἱ Κρῆτες, ὄντες υἱοὶ τοῦ Διός. οὗτοι δὲ
τοὺς μὲν ἀγαθοὺς τῶν ἀνδρῶν καὶ δικαίους καὶ
κατ᾿ ἀρετὴν βεβιωκότας, ἐπειδὰν συναλισθῶσι
πολλοί, καθάπερ εἰς ἀποικίαν τινὰ πέμπουσιν εἰς
τὸ Ἠλύσιον πεδίον τῷ ἀρίστῳ βίῳ συνεσομένους.
8 ἂν δέ τινας τῶν πονηρῶν λάβωσι, ταῖς Ἐρινύσι
παραδόντες εἰς τὸν τῶν ἀσεβῶν χῶρον εἰσπέμ-
πουσι κατὰ λόγον τῆς ἀδικίας κολασθησομένους.
ἔνθα δὴ τί κακῶν οὐ πάσχουσι στρεβλούμενοί τε
καὶ καιόμενοι καὶ ὑπὸ γυπῶν ἐσθιόμενοι καὶ
τροχῷ συμπεριφερόμενοι[1] καὶ λίθους ἀνακυ-
λίοντες; ὁ μὲν γὰρ Τάνταλος ἐπ᾿ αὐτῇ τῇ λίμνῃ
αὖος ἕστηκεν κινδυνεύων ὑπὸ δίψους ὁ κακοδαίμων
9 ἀποθανεῖν. οἱ δὲ τοῦ μέσου βίου, πολλοὶ ὄντες
οὗτοι, ἐν τῷ λειμῶνι πλανῶνται ἄνευ τῶν σωμάτων
σκιαὶ γενόμενοι καὶ ὑπὸ τῇ ἀφῇ καθάπερ καπνὸς

[1] συμπεριφερόμενοι Bélin de Ballou : συμφερόμενοι MSS.

great meadow overgrown with asphodel, and to a spring that is inimical to memory; in fact, they call it "Oblivion" for that reason. All this, by the way, was told to the ancients by people who came back from there, Alcestis and Protesilaus of Thessaly, Theseus, son of Aegeus, and Homer's Odysseus, highly respectable and trustworthy witnesses, who, I suppose, did not drink of the spring, or else they would not have remembered it all

Well, Pluto and Persephone, as these people said, are the rulers and have the general over-lordship, with a great throng of understrappers and assistants in administration—Furies, Tormentors, Terrors, and also Hermes, who, however, is not always with them.[1] As prefects, moreover, and satraps and judges, there are two that hold court, Minos and Rhadamanthus of Crete, who are sons of Zeus. These receive the good, just men who have lived virtuously, and when many have been collected, send them off, as if to a colony, to the Elysian Fields to take part in the best life. But if they come upon any rascals, turning them over to the Furies, they send them to the Place of the Wicked, to be punished in proportion to their wickedness. There—ah! what punishment do they not undergo? They are racked, burned, devoured by vultures, turned upon a wheel; they roll stones uphill; and as for Tantalus, he stands on the very brink of the lake with a parched throat, like to die, poor fellow, for thirst! But those of the middle way in life, and they are many, wander about in the meadow without their bodies, in the form of shadows that vanish like smoke in your

---

[1] Hermes had to serve two masters, Zeus and Pluto. See *Downward Journey*, 1–2 (ii, 5).

ἀφανιζόμενοι. τρέφονται δὲ ἄρα ταῖς παρ' ἡμῖν
χοαῖς καὶ τοῖς καθαγιζομένοις ἐπὶ τῶν τάφων· ὡς
εἴ τῳ μὴ εἴη καταλελειμμένος ὑπὲρ γῆς φίλος ἢ
συγγενής, ἄσιτος οὗτος νεκρὸς καὶ λιμώττων ἐν
αὐτοῖς πολιτεύεται.

10 Ταῦτα οὕτως ἰσχυρῶς περιελήλυθε τοὺς
πολλοὺς ὥστε ἐπειδάν τις ἀποθάνῃ τῶν οἰκείων,
πρῶτα μὲν φέροντες ὀβολὸν εἰς τὸ στόμα κατέθη-
καν αὐτῷ, μισθὸν τῷ πορθμεῖ τῆς ναυτιλίας
γενησόμενον, οὐ πρότερον ἐξετάσαντες ὁποῖον
τὸ νόμισμα νομίζεται καὶ διαχωρεῖ παρὰ τοῖς
κάτω, καὶ εἰ δύναται παρ' ἐκείνοις Ἀττικὸς ἢ
Μακεδονικὸς ἢ Αἰγιναῖος ὀβολός, οὐδ' ὅτι πολὺ
κάλλιον ἦν μὴ ἔχειν τὰ πορθμεῖα καταβαλεῖν·
οὕτω γὰρ ἂν οὐ παραδεξαμένου τοῦ πορθμέως
ἀναπόμπιμοι πάλιν εἰς τὸν βίον ἀφικνοῦντο.

11 Μετὰ ταῦτα δὲ λούσαντες αὐτούς, ὡς οὐχ
ἱκανῆς τῆς κάτω λίμνης λουτρὸν εἶναι τοῖς ἐκεῖ,
καὶ μύρῳ τῷ καλλίστῳ χρίσαντες τὸ σῶμα πρὸς
δυσωδίαν ἤδη βιαζόμενον καὶ στεφανώσαντες
τοῖς ὡραίοις ἄνθεσι προτίθενται λαμπρῶς
ἀμφιέσαντες, ἵνα μὴ ῥιγῷεν δῆλον ὅτι παρὰ
τὴν ὁδὸν μηδὲ γυμνοὶ βλέποιντο τῷ Κερβέρῳ.

12 Οἰμωγαὶ δὲ ἐπὶ τούτοις καὶ κωκυτοὶ γυναικῶν
καὶ παρὰ πάντων δάκρυα καὶ στέρνα τυπτόμενα
καὶ σπαραττομένη κόμη καὶ φοινισσόμεναι
παρειαί· καί που καὶ ἐσθὴς καταρρήγνυται καὶ
κόνις ἐπὶ τῇ κεφαλῇ πάσσεται, καὶ οἱ ζῶντες
οἰκτρότεροι τοῦ νεκροῦ· οἱ μὲν γὰρ χαμαὶ
κυλινδοῦνται πολλάκις καὶ τὰς κεφαλὰς ἀράτ-
τουσι πρὸς τὸ ἔδαφος, ὁ δ' εὐσχήμων καὶ καλὸς
καὶ καθ' ὑπερβολὴν ἐστεφανωμένος ὑψηλὸς πρό-

fingers. They get their nourishment, naturally, from the libations that are poured in our world and the burnt-offerings at the tomb; so that if anyone has not left a friend or kinsman behind him on earth, he goes about his business there as an unfed corpse, in a state of famine.

So thoroughly are people taken in by all this that when one of the family dies, immediately they bring an obol and put it into his mouth, to pay the ferryman for setting him over. They do not stop to consider what sort of coinage is customary and current in the lower world, and whether it is the Athenian or the Macedonian or the Aeginetan obol that is legal tender there; nor, indeed, that it would be far better not to be able to pay the fare, since in that case the ferryman would not take them and they would be escorted back to life again.

Then they bathe them (as if the lake down below were not big enough for the people there to bathe in); and after anointing with the finest of perfume that body which is already hasting to corruption, and crowning it with pretty flowers, they lay them in state, clothed in splendid raiment, which, very likely, is intended to keep them from being cold on the way and from being seen undressed by Cerberus.

Next come cries of distress, wailing of women, tears on all sides, beaten breasts, torn hair, and bloody cheeks. Perhaps, too, clothing is rent and dust sprinkled on the head, and the living are in a plight more pitiable than the dead; for they roll on the ground repeatedly and dash their heads against the floor, while he, all serene and handsome and

κειται καὶ μετέωρος ὥσπερ εἰς πομπὴν κεκοσμη-
μένος.

13 Εἶθ' ἡ μήτηρ ἢ καὶ νὴ Δία ὁ πατὴρ ἐκ μέσων
τῶν συγγενῶν προελθὼν καὶ περιχυθεὶς αὐτῷ—
προκείσθω γάρ τις νέος καὶ καλός, ἵνα καὶ
ἀκμαιότερον τὸ ἐπ' αὐτῷ δρᾶμα ᾖ—φωνὰς ἀλλο-
κότους καὶ ματαίας ἀφίησι, πρὸς ἃς ὁ νεκρὸς
αὐτὸς ἀποκρίναιτ' ἄν, εἰ λάβοι φωνήν· φήσει γὰρ
ὁ πατὴρ γοερόν τι φθεγγόμενος καὶ παρατείνων
ἕκαστον τῶν ὀνομάτων, "Τέκνον ἥδιστον, οἴχῃ
μοι καὶ τέθνηκας καὶ πρὸ ὥρας ἀνηρπάσθης,
μόνον ἐμὲ τὸν ἄθλιον καταλιπών, οὐ γαμήσας,
οὐ παιδοποιησάμενος, οὐ στρατευσάμενος, οὐ
γεωργήσας, οὐκ εἰς γῆρας ἐλθών· οὐ κωμάσῃ
πάλιν οὐδὲ ἐρασθήσῃ, τέκνον, οὐδὲ ἐν συμποσίοις
μετὰ τῶν ἡλικιωτῶν μεθυσθήσῃ."

14 Ταῦτα δὲ καὶ τὰ τοιαῦτα φήσει οἰόμενος τὸν
υἱὸν δεῖσθαι μὲν ἔτι τούτων καὶ ἐπιθυμεῖν καὶ
μετὰ τὴν τελευτήν, οὐ δύνασθαι δὲ μετέχειν
αὐτῶν. καίτοι τί ταῦτα φημί; πόσοι γὰρ καὶ
ἵππους καὶ παλλακίδας, οἱ δὲ καὶ οἰνοχόους
ἐπικατέσφαξαν καὶ ἐσθῆτα καὶ τὸν ἄλλον κόσμον
συγκατέφλεξαν ἢ συγκατώρυξαν ὡς χρησομένοις
ἐκεῖ καὶ ἀπολαύσουσιν αὐτῶν κάτω;

15 Ὁ δ' οὖν πρεσβύτης ὁ πενθῶν οὑτωσὶ ταῦτα
πάντα ὁπόσα εἴρηκα καὶ ἔτι τούτων πλείονα
οὔτε τοῦ παιδὸς ἕνεκα τραγῳδεῖν ἔοικεν—οἶδε γὰρ
οὐκ ἀκουσόμενον οὐδ' ἂν μεῖζον ἐμβοήσῃ τοῦ
Στέντορος—οὔτε μὴν αὑτοῦ· φρονεῖν γὰρ οὕτω

elaborately decked with wreaths, lies in lofty, exalted state, bedizened as for a pageant.

Then his mother, or indeed his father comes forward from among the family and throws himself upon him; for let us imagine a handsome young man upon the bier, so that the show that is acted over him may be the more moving. The father utters strange, foolish outcries to which the dead man himself would make answer if he could speak. In a plaintive tone, protracting every word, he will say: "Dearest child, you are gone from me, dead, reft away before your time, leaving me behind all alone, woe is me, before marrying, before having children, before serving in the army, before working on the farm, before coming to old age; never again will you roam the streets at night, or fall in love, my child, or drink deep at wine-parties with your young friends."

He will say all that, and more in the same tenor, thinking that his son still needs and wants this sort of thing even after death, but cannot get it. But that is nothing. Have not many sacrificed horses, concubines, sometimes even cup-bearers, over their dead, and burned or buried with them clothing and other articles of personal adornment, as if they would use them there and get some good of them down below?

But as to the old man who mourns after this fashion, it is not, in all probability, on account of his son that he does all this melodramatic ranting that I have mentioned, and more than I have mentioned; for he knows that his son will not hear him even if he shouts louder than Stentor. Nor yet is it on his own account; for it would have been enough

THE WORKS OF LUCIAN

καὶ γιγνώσκειν ἱκανὸν ἦν καὶ ἄνευ τῆς βοῆς·
οὐδεὶς γὰρ δὴ πρὸς ἑαυτὸν δεῖται βοᾶν. λοιπὸν
οὖν ἐστιν αὐτὸν τῶν παρόντων ἕνεκα ταῦτα
ληρεῖν οὔθ᾽ ὅ τι πέπονθεν αὐτῷ ὁ παῖς εἰδότα
οὔθ᾽ ὅποι κεχώρηκε, μᾶλλον δὲ οὐδὲ τὸν βίον
αὐτὸν ἐξετάσαντα ὁποῖός ἐστιν· οὐ γὰρ ἂν τὴν ἐξ
αὐτοῦ μετάστασιν ὥς τι τῶν δεινῶν ἐδυσχέραινεν.

16 Εἴποι δ᾽ ἂν οὖν πρὸς αὐτὸν ὁ παῖς παραιτησά-
μενος τὸν Αἰακὸν καὶ τὸν Ἀϊδωνέα πρὸς ὀλίγον
τοῦ στομίου ὑπερκῦψαι καὶ τὸν πατέρα παῦσαι
ματαιάζοντα, "Ὦ κακόδαιμον ἄνθρωπε, τί
κέκραγας; τί δέ μοι παρέχεις πράγματα;
παῦσαι τιλλόμενος τὴν κόμην καὶ τὸ πρόσωπον
ἐξ ἐπιπολῆς ἀμύσσων. τί μοι λοιδορῇ καὶ ἄθλιον
ἀποκαλεῖς καὶ δύσμορον πολύ σου βελτίω καὶ
μακαριώτερον γεγενημένον; ἢ τί σοι δεινὸν
πάσχειν δοκῶ; ἢ διότι μὴ τοιουτοσὶ γέρων
ἐγενόμην οἷος εἶ σύ, φαλακρὸς μὲν τὴν κεφαλήν,
τὴν δὲ ὄψιν ἐρρυτιδωμένος, κυφὸς καὶ τὰ γόνατα
νωθής, καὶ ὅλως ὑπὸ τοῦ χρόνου σαθρὸς πολλὰς
τριακάδας καὶ ὀλυμπιάδας ἀναπλήσας, καὶ τὰ
τελευταῖα δὴ ταῦτα παραπαίων ἐπὶ τοσούτων
μαρτύρων; ὦ μάταιε, τί σοι χρηστὸν εἶναι δοκεῖ
παρὰ τὸν βίον οὗ μηκέτι μεθέξομεν; ἢ τοὺς
πότους ἐρεῖς δῆλον ὅτι καὶ τὰ δεῖπνα καὶ ἐσθῆτα
καὶ ἀφροδίσια, καὶ δέδιας μὴ τούτων ἐνδεὴς γενόμενος ἀπόλωμαι. οὐκ ἐννοεῖς δὲ ὅτι τὸ μὴ διψῆν
τοῦ πιεῖν πολὺ κάλλιον καὶ τὸ μὴ πεινῆν τοῦ
φαγεῖν καὶ τὸ μὴ ῥιγοῦν τοῦ ἀμπεχόνης εὐπορεῖν;

17 Φέρε τοίνυν, ἐπειδὴ ἔοικας ἀγνοεῖν, διδάξομαί
σε θρηνεῖν ἀληθέστερον, καὶ δὴ ἀναλαβὼν ἐξ

to think this and have it in mind, without his shouting—nobody needs to shout at himself. Consequently it is on account of the others present that he talks this nonsense, when he does not know what has happened to his son nor where he has gone; in fact he has not even considered what life itself is, or else he would not take on so about the leaving of it, as if that were something dreadful.

If his son should receive permission from Aeacus and Aïdoneus to put his head out of the mouth of the pit for a moment and stop his father's silliness, he would say: " Unfortunate man, why do you shriek? Why do you trouble me? Stop tearing your hair and marring the skin of your face! Why do you call me names and speak of me as wretched and ill-starred when I have become far better off and happier than you? What dreadful misfortune do you think I am undergoing? Is it that I did not get to be an old man like you, with your head bald, your face wrinkled, your back bent, and your knees trembling,—like you, who in short are rotten with age after filling out so many months and so many Olympiads, and who now, at the last, go out of your mind in the presence of so many witnesses? Foolish man, what advantage do you think there is in life that we shall never again partake of? You will say drinking, no doubt, and dinners, and dress, and love, and you are afraid that for the want of all this I shall die! But are you unaware that not to thirst is far better than drinking, not to hunger than eating, and not to be cold than to have quantities of clothing?

" Come now, since you apparently do not know how to mourn, I will teach you to do it more truth-

ὑπαρχῆς βόα, "Τέκνον ἄθλιον, οὐκέτι διψήσεις,
οὐκέτι πεινήσεις οὐδὲ ῥιγώσεις. οἴχῃ μοι κακοδαίμων ἐκφυγὼν τὰς νόσους, οὐ πυρετὸν ἔτι
δεδιώς, οὐ πολέμιον, οὐ τύραννον· οὐκ ἔρως σε
ἀνιάσει οὐδὲ συνουσία διαστρέψει, οὐδὲ σπαθή-
σεις ἐπὶ τούτῳ δὶς ἢ τρὶς τῆς ἡμέρας, ὦ τῆς
συμφορᾶς. οὐ καταφρονηθήσῃ γέρων γενόμενος
18 οὐδὲ ὀχληρὸς ἔσῃ τοῖς νέοις βλεπόμενος." ἂν
ταῦτα λέγῃς, ὦ πάτερ, οὐκ οἴει πολὺ ἀληθέστερα
καὶ γενναιότερα[1] ἐκείνων ἐρεῖν;

'Αλλ' ἆρα μὴ τόδε σε ἀνιᾷ, καὶ διανοῇ τὸν παρ'
ἡμῖν ζόφον καὶ τὸ πολὺ σκότος, κᾆτα δέδιας μή
σοι ἀποπνιγῶ κατακλεισθεὶς ἐν τῷ μνήματι; χρὴ
δὲ πρὸς ταῦτα λογίζεσθαι ὅτι τῶν ὀφθαλμῶν
διασαπέντων ἢ καὶ νὴ Δία καέντων μετ' ὀλίγον,
εἴ γε καῦσαί με διεγνώκατε, οὔτε σκότος οὔτε
φῶς ὁρᾶν δεησόμεθα.

19 Καὶ ταῦτα μὲν ἴσως μέτρια· τί δέ με ὁ κωκυτὸς
ὑμῶν ὀνίνησι καὶ ἡ πρὸς τὸν αὐλὸν αὕτη στερ-
νοτυπία καὶ ἡ τῶν γυναικῶν περὶ τὸν θρῆνον
ἀμετρία; τί δὲ ὁ ὑπὲρ τοῦ τάφου λίθος ἐστεφανωμένος; ἢ τί ὑμῖν δύναται τὸν ἄκρατον
ἐπιχεῖν; ἢ νομίζετε καταστάξειν αὐτὸν πρὸς
ἡμᾶς καὶ μέχρι τοῦ Ἅιδου διίξεσθαι; τὰ μὲν
γὰρ ἐπὶ τῶν καθαγισμῶν καὶ αὐτοὶ ὁρᾶτε, οἶμαι,
ὡς τὸ μὲν νοστιμώτατον τῶν παρεσκευασμένων ὁ
καπνὸς παραλαβὼν ἄνω εἰς τὸν οὐρανὸν οἴχεται
μηδέν τι ἡμᾶς ὀνήσαν τοὺς κάτω, τὸ δὲ κατα-
λειπόμενον, ἡ κόνις, ἀχρεῖον, ἐκτὸς εἰ μὴ τὴν

---

[1] γενναιότερα Jacobs : γελοιότερα MSS.

fully. Begin afresh, and cry, 'Poor child, never again will you be thirsty, never again hungry or cold! You are gone from me, poor boy, escaping diseases, no longer fearing fever or foeman or tyrant. Love shall not vex you nor its pleasures rack you, nor shall you squander your strength in them twice and thrice a day, woe is me! You shall not be scorned in your old age, nor shall the sight of you offend the young!' If you say this, father, don't you think it will be far more true and more manly than what you said before?

"But perhaps it is something else that worries you. You are thinking of the gloom where we are, and the profound darkness, and so you fear that I may be stifled in the close custody of the tomb. On that point you should reflect that as my eyes will very soon be corrupted or even burned, if you have decided to burn me, I shall have no need either for darkness or for light as far as seeing is concerned.

"That fear, however, is perhaps reasonable enough; but what good do you think I get from your wailing, and this beating of breasts to the music of the flute, and the extravagant conduct of the women in lamenting? Or from the wreathed stone above my grave? Or what, pray, is the use of your pouring out the pure wine? You don't think, do you, that it will drip down to where we are and get all the way through to Hades? As to the burnt offerings, you yourselves see, I think, that the most nourishing part of your provender is carried off up to Heaven by the smoke without doing us in the lower world the least bit of good, and that what is left, the ashes, is useless, unless

σποδὸν ἡμᾶς σιτεῖσθαι πεπιστεύκατε. οὐχ οὕτως
ἄσπορος οὐδὲ ἄκαρπος ἡ τοῦ Πλούτωνος ἀρχή,
οὐδὲ ἐπιλέλοιπεν ἡμᾶς ὁ ἀσφόδελος, ἵνα παρ'
ὑμῶν τὰ σιτία μεταστελλώμεθα. ὥστε μοι νὴ
τὴν Τισιφόνην πάλαι δὴ ἐφ' οἷς ἐποιεῖτε καὶ
ἐλέγετε παμμέγεθες ἐπῄει ἀνακαγχάσαι, διε-
κώλυσε δὲ ἡ ὀθόνη καὶ τὰ ἔρια, οἷς μου τὰς
σιαγόνας ἀπεσφίγξατε."

20   ὡς ἄρα μιν εἰπόντα τέλος θανάτοιο κάλυψε.

Πρὸς Διός, ἐὰν λέγῃ ταῦτα ὁ νεκρὸς ἐπιστραφείς,
ἀνακλίνας αὑτὸν ἐπ' ἀγκῶνος, οὐκ ἂν οἰόμεθα
δικαιότατα ἂν αὐτὸν εἰπεῖν ; ἀλλ' ὅμως οἱ μάταιοι
καὶ βοῶσι καὶ μεταστειλάμενοί τινα θρήνων
σοφιστὴν πολλὰς συνειλοχότα παλαιὰς συμφορὰς
τούτῳ συναγωνιστῇ καὶ χορηγῷ τῆς ἀνοίας κατα-
χρῶνται, ὅπῃ ἂν ἐκεῖνος ἐξάρχῃ πρὸς τὸ μέλος
ἐπαιάζοντες.

21   Καὶ μέχρι μὲν θρήνων ὁ αὐτὸς ἅπασι νόμος
τῆς ἀβελτερίας· τὸ δὲ ἀπὸ τούτου διελόμενοι
κατὰ ἔθνη τὰς ταφὰς ὁ μὲν Ἕλλην ἔκαυσεν, ὁ δὲ
Πέρσης ἔθαψεν, ὁ δὲ Ἰνδὸς ὑάλῳ περιχρίει, ὁ δὲ
Σκύθης κατεσθίει, ταριχεύει δὲ ὁ Αἰγύπτιος·
οὗτος μέν γε—λέγω δὲ ἰδών—ξηράνας τὸν νεκρὸν
σύνδειπνον καὶ συμπότην ἐποιήσατο. πολλάκις
δὲ καὶ δεομένῳ χρημάτων ἀνδρὶ Αἰγυπτίῳ ἔλυσε

you believe that we eat dust. Pluto's realm is not so devoid of seed and grain, nor is there any dearth of asphodel among us, so that we must import our food from you. So, by Tisiphone, the inclination seized me long ago to burst out in a tremendous guffaw over what you were doing and saying; but I was prevented by the winding-sheet and by the fillets with which you have bound up my jaws."

"These words spoken, at once the doom of death
    overwhelmed him."[1]

By Heaven, if the dead man should face them, raising himself upon his elbow, and say all this, don't you think he would be quite right? Nevertheless, the dolts not only shriek and scream, but they send for a sort of professor of threnodies, who has gathered a repertory of ancient bereavements, and they use him as fellow-actor and prompter in their silly performance, coming in with their groans at the close of each strain that he strikes up!

Up to that point, the wailing, the same stupid custom prevails everywhere; but in what follows, the burial, they have apportioned out among themselves, nation by nation, the different modes. The Greek burns, the Persian buries, the Indian encases in glass,[2] the Scythian eats, the Egyptian salts. And the latter—I have seen whereof I speak—after drying the dead man makes him his guest at table! Many a time, too, when an Egyptian wants money,

---

[1] *Iliad*, 16, 502.

[2] See Herodotus, 3, 24, regarding this practice among the Ethiopians, also discussed by Ctesias (Diodorus 2, 15). To Lucian, ὕαλος certainly meant glass, and perhaps to Herodotus also. What the substance really was is uncertain.

τὴν ἀπορίαν ἐνέχυρον ἢ ὁ ἀδελφὸς ἢ ὁ πατὴρ ἐν
καιρῷ γενόμενος.

22 Χώματα μὲν γὰρ καὶ πυραμίδες καὶ στῆλαι
καὶ ἐπιγράμματα πρὸς ὀλίγον διαρκοῦντα πῶς οὐ
23 περιττὰ καὶ παιδιαῖς προσεοικότα; καίτοι καὶ
ἀγῶνας ἔνιοι διέθεσαν καὶ λόγους ἐπιταφίους
εἶπον ἐπὶ τῶν μνημάτων ὥσπερ συναγορεύοντες
ἢ μαρτυροῦντες παρὰ τοῖς κάτω δικασταῖς τῷ
νεκρῷ.

24 Ἐπὶ πᾶσι τούτοις τὸ περίδειπνον, καὶ πάρεισιν
οἱ προσήκοντες καὶ τοὺς γονέας παραμυθοῦνται
τοῦ τετελευτηκότος καὶ πείθουσι γεύσασθαι, οὐκ
ἀηδῶς μὰ Δία οὐδ' αὐτοὺς ἀναγκαζομένους, ἀλλὰ
ἤδη ὑπὸ λιμοῦ τριῶν ἑξῆς ἡμερῶν ἀπηυδηκότας.
καί, "Μέχρι μὲν τίνος, ὦ οὗτος, ὀδυρόμεθα;
ἔασον ἀναπαύσασθαι τοὺς τοῦ μακαρίτου δαί-
μονας· εἰ δὲ καὶ τὸ παράπαν κλάειν διέγνωκας,
αὐτοῦ γε τούτου ἕνεκα χρὴ μὴ ἀπόσιτον εἶναι,
ἵνα καὶ διαρκέσῃς πρὸς τοῦ πένθους τὸ μέγεθος."
τότε δὴ τότε ῥαψῳδοῦνται πρὸς ἁπάντων δύο τοῦ
Ὁμήρου στίχοι·

καὶ γάρ τ' ἠΰκομος Νιόβη ἐμνήσατο σίτου·

καὶ

γαστέρι δ' οὔπως ἐστὶ νέκυν πενθῆσαι Ἀχαιούς.

---

[1] Compare Teles (Hense,[2] p. 31, l. 9: a lacuna in the text
precedes): "and we hesitate to look at or to touch (the dead),
but they make mummies of them and keep them in the house
as something handsome, and accept dead men as security.
So opposed is their way to ours." As Teles is almost
certainly quoting this from Bion, it seems likely that Lucian
drew from that source. But he had also read Herodotus,
2, 136.

his brother or his father helps him out of his straits by becoming security at the critical juncture.[1]

Regarding grave-mounds, pyramids, tombstones, and epitaphs, all of which endure but a brief space, are they not superfluous and akin to child's play?[2] Some people, moreover, even hold competitions and deliver funeral orations at the monuments, as if they were pleading or testifying on behalf of the dead man before the judges down below!

As the finishing touch to all this, there is the funeral feast, and the relatives come in, consoling the parents of the departed, and inducing them to taste something. The parents themselves, I must say, do not find it disagreeable to be constrained, but are already done up with three days of continuous fasting. It is: "Man dear, how long are we to lament? Let the spirits[3] of the departed rest! But if you have absolutely decided to keep on weeping, for that very reason you must not abstain from food, in order that you may prove equal to the magnitude of your sorrow." Then, ah! then, two lines of Homer are recited by everyone:

"Verily Niobe also, the fair-tressed, thought of her
        dinner,"[4]

and

"Mourning the dead by fasting is not to be done
        by Achaeans."[5]

[2] Compare Teles (Hense, p. 31, l. 8): "But it seems to me that this (closing the eyes of the dead) is just child's play on our part." [3] The "Di Manes"? [4] *Iliad*, 24, 602.
[5] *Iliad*, 19, 225; it is impossible, argues Odysseus, for the Greek army to fast (for Patroclus) and fight at the same time.

οἱ δε ἅπτονται μέν, αἰσχυνόμενοι δὲ τὰ πρῶτα
καὶ δεδιότες εἰ φανοῦνται μετὰ τὴν τελευτὴν τῶν
φιλτάτων τοῖς ἀνθρωπίνοις πάθεσιν ἐμμένοντες.

Ταῦτα καὶ πολὺ τούτων γελοιότερα εὕροι τις
ἂν ἐπιτηρῶν ἐν τοῖς πένθεσι γιγνόμενα διὰ τὸ
τοὺς πολλοὺς τὸ μέγιστον τῶν κακῶν τὸν θάνατον
οἴεσθαι.

ON FUNERALS

So they break bread, of course, but do it at first in shame, and in fear that they will disclose themselves to be still subject to human appetites after the death of their dearest.

You will find, if you take note, that these things and others still more ridiculous are done at funerals, for the reason that people think death the greatest of misfortunes.[1]

---

[1] The first words of *Sacrifices* seem to take up this sentence. They may be translated : "And as to sacrifices, what the dolts do "—ἃ μὲν γὰρ ἐν ταῖς θυσίαις οἱ μάταιοι πράττουσι.

A PROFESSOR OF PUBLIC SPEAKING

A SATIRE upon the new fashion in oratory, and one of its foremost representatives.

The traditional course of training in rhetoric, fully described by the Latin Quintilian, was too arduous, it seems, to attract the general run of would-be public speakers under the Antonines. They sought a royal road to success, and found it; for as success in those days, especially in the case of Greeks, was far less a matter of persuading juries and swaying deliberative assemblies than of entertaining audiences with oratorical display, it could be attained readily by meretricious methods which, in so far as they were capable of being taught at all (natura enim non docetur, says Quintilian), could be taught quickly.

"Some say," remarks the scholiast, "that Lucian was aiming at Pollux the lexicographer when he wrote this piece." This may be mere conjecture on the part of his authorities, but it cannot be dismissed as baseless. Pollux was Lucian's contemporary, was born in Egypt, and certainly could have been called "a namesake of the sons of Zeus and Leda." That phrase, to be sure, would better fit a Dioscorides, or a Didymus or Geminus, but we do not know of any such rhetorician of that period. Lucian may have been a bit vague on purpose. What little Philostratus says of his oratory indicates that Pollux was a follower of the new school; moreover, he was the pupil of the sophist Hadrian, who was decidedly up to date, and the rival of the old-fashioned Chrestus, over whose head he was appointed by Commodus to the public professorship of rhetoric in Athens. The allusion in this piece to the high fees charged by the representative of the old school leads Ranke (*Pollux et Lucianus*) to conclude that Lucian's butt himself must have taught gratis, and must therefore have been a public professor. And from the silence of Philostratus as to the family history and private life of Pollux, Ranke argues that he was of low birth and doubtful reputation.

If the piece was aimed at Pollux and written after he became professor, it must date after A.D. 179.

133

ΡΗΤΟΡΩΝ ΔΙΔΑΣΚΑΛΟΣ

1   Ἐρωτᾷς, ὦ μειράκιον, ὅπως ἂν ῥήτωρ γένοιο
καὶ τὸ σεμνότατον τοῦτο καὶ πάντιμον ὄνομα
σοφιστὴς εἶναι δόξαις·[1] ἀβίωτα γὰρ εἶναί σοι
φῄς, εἰ μὴ τοιαύτην τινὰ τὴν δύναμιν περιβάλοιο
ἐν τοῖς λόγοις ὡς ἄμαχον εἶναι καὶ ἀνυπόστατον
καὶ θαυμάζεσθαι πρὸς ἁπάντων καὶ ἀπο-
βλέπεσθαι, περισπούδαστον ἄκουσμα τοῖς
Ἕλλησι δοκοῦντα· καὶ δὴ τὰς ἐπὶ τοῦτο ἀγούσας
ὁδοὺς αἵτινές ποτέ εἰσιν ἐθέλεις ἐκμαθεῖν. ἀλλ'
οὐδεὶς φθόνος, ὦ παῖ, καὶ μάλιστα ὁπότε νέος τις
αὐτὸς ὤν, ὀρεγόμενος τῶν ἀρίστων, οὐκ εἰδὼς
ὅθεν ἂν ταῦτα ἐκπορίσαιτο, ἱερόν τι χρῆμα τὴν
συμβουλὴν οὖσαν, καθάπερ νῦν σύ, τοῦτο αἰτοίη
προσελθών. ὥστε ἄκουε, τό γε ἐπ' ἐμοὶ καὶ
πάνυ θαρρῶν ὡς τάχιστα δεινὸς ἀνὴρ ἔσῃ γνῶναί
τε τὰ δέοντα καὶ ἑρμηνεῦσαι αὐτά, ἢν τὸ μετὰ
τοῦτο ἐθελήσῃς αὐτὸς ἐμμένειν οἷς ἂν ἀκούσῃς
παρ' ἡμῶν καὶ φιλοπόνως αὐτὰ μελετᾶν καὶ
προθύμως ἀνύειν τὴν ὁδὸν ἔστ' ἂν ἀφίκῃ πρὸς τὸ
τέρμα.

2   Τὸ μὲν οὖν θήραμα οὐ σμικρὸν οὐδὲ ὀλίγης
τῆς σπουδῆς δεόμενον, ἀλλὰ ἐφ' ὅτῳ καὶ πονῆσαι
πολλὰ καὶ ἀγρυπνῆσαι καὶ πᾶν ὁτιοῦν ὑπομεῖναι

Available in photographs: UPNZ. The piece is now
wanting in Γ.
[1] δόξαις Struve: δόξῃς γ, δόξεις β.

A PROFESSOR OF PUBLIC
SPEAKING

You ask, my boy, how you can get to be a public speaker, and be held to personify the sublime and glorious name of sophist; life, you say, is not worth living, unless when you speak you can clothe yourself in such a mantle of eloquence that you will be irresistible and invincible, that you will be admired and stared at by everyone, counting among the Greeks as a highly desirable treat for their ears. Consequently, you wish to find out what the roads are that lead to this goal. Come, I have no desire to be churlish, lad, especially when a mere youngster who craves what is noblest, not knowing how to come by it, draws near and asks, as you do now, for advice— a sacred matter. So listen; and in so far as it lies in my power, you may have great confidence that soon you will be an able hand at discerning what requires to be said and expressing it in words,[1] if only you on your part are willing henceforth to abide by what I tell you, to practise it industriously, and to follow the road resolutely until you reach your goal.

Certainly the object of your quest is not trivial, nor one that calls for little effort, but rather one for which it is worth while to work hard, to scant your sleep, and to put up with anything whatsoever.

---

[1] Like Pericles (Thuc. 2, 60).

ἄξιον. σκόπει γοῦν ὁπόσοι τέως μηδὲν ὄντες
ἔνδοξοι καὶ πλούσιοι καὶ νὴ Δία εὐγενέστατοι
3 ἔδοξαν ἀπὸ τῶν λόγων. ὅμως δὲ μὴ δέδιθι, μηδὲ
πρὸς τὸ μέγεθος τῶν ἐλπιζομένων ἀποδυσπετήσῃς,
μυρίους τινὰς τοὺς πόνους προπονῆσαι οἰηθείς.
οὐ γάρ σε τραχεῖάν τινα οὐδὲ ὄρθιον[1] καὶ
ἱδρῶτος μεστὴν ἡμεῖς ἄξομεν, ὡς ἐκ μέσης
αὐτῆς ἀναστρέψαι καμόντα, ἐπεὶ οὐδὲν ἂν
διεφέρομεν τῶν ἄλλων ὅσοι τὴν συνήθη ἐκείνην ἡγοῦνται, μακρὰν καὶ ἀνάντη καὶ καματηρὰν
καὶ ὡς τὸ πολὺ ἀπεγνωσμένην. ἀλλὰ παρ᾽
ἡμῶν ἐξαίρετον[2] τῆς συμβουλῆς τοῦτό ἐστιν,
ὅτι ἡδίστην τε ἅμα καὶ ἐπιτομωτάτην καὶ
ἱππήλατον καὶ κατάντη σὺν πολλῇ τῇ θυμηδίᾳ
καὶ τρυφῇ διὰ λειμώνων εὐανθῶν καὶ σκιᾶς
ἀκριβοῦς σχολῇ καὶ βάδην ἀνιὼν ἀνιδρωτὶ
ἐπιστήσῃ τῇ ἄκρᾳ καὶ ἀγρεύσεις[3] οὐ καμὼν καὶ
νὴ Δί᾽ εὐωχήσῃ κατακείμενος, ἐκείνους[4] ὁπόσοι
τὴν ἑτέραν ἐτράποντο ἀπὸ τοῦ ὑψηλοῦ ἐπισκοπῶν
ἐν τῇ ὑπωρείᾳ τῆς ἀνόδου ἔτι, κατὰ δυσβάτων
καὶ ὀλισθηρῶν τῶν κρημνῶν μόλις ἀνέρποντας,
ἀποκυλιομένους ἐπὶ κεφαλὴν ἐνίοτε καὶ πολλὰ
τραύματα λαμβάνοντας περὶ τραχείαις ταῖς
πέτραις· σὺ δὲ πρὸ πολλοῦ ἄνω ἐστεφανωμένος
εὐδαιμονέστατος ἔσῃ, ἅπαντα ἐν βραχεῖ ὅσα
ἐστὶν ἀγαθὰ παρὰ τῆς ῥητορικῆς μονονουχὶ
καθεύδων λαβών.

4   Ἡ μὲν δὴ ὑπόσχεσις οὕτω μεγάλη· σὺ δὲ
πρὸς Φιλίου μὴ ἀπιστήσῃς, εἰ ῥᾷστά τε ἅμα καὶ

---

[1] ὕρειον β.
[2] τό γε παρ᾽ ἡμῶν ἐξαιρετόν σοι β, edd. Cf. Navigium 24.
[3] αἱρήσεις β. Cf. θήραμα, c. 2.   [4] ἔκπνους β.

A PROFESSOR OF PUBLIC SPEAKING

Just see how many who previously were nobodies have come to be accounted men of standing, millionaires, yes, even gentlemen, because of their eloquence. Do not be daunted, however, and do not be dismayed at the greatness of your expectations, thinking to undergo untold labours before you achieve them. I shall not conduct you by a rough road, or a steep and sweaty one, so that you will turn back halfway out of weariness. In that case I should be no better than those other guides who use the customary route—long, steep, toilsome, and, as a rule, hopeless. No, my advice has this to commend it, that ascending in the manner of a leisurely stroll through flowery fields and perfect shade in great comfort and luxury by a sloping bridle-path that is very short as well as very pleasant, you will gain the summit without sweating for it, you will bag your game without any effort, yes, by Heaven, you will banquet at your ease, looking down from the height at those who went the other way as they creep painfully upward over sheer and slippery crags, still in the foot-hills of the ascent, rolling off head-first from time to time, and getting many a wound on the sharp rocks—and you, the while, on the top long before them, with a wreath upon your head, will be fortunate beyond compare, for you will have acquired from Rhetoric in an instant, all but in your sleep, every single blessing that there is!

Yes, my promise goes to that extent in its generosity;[1] but in the name of Friendship[2] do not disbelieve me, when I say that I shall show

---

[1] A quotation from Demosthenes, *Phil.* 1, 44, 15.
[2] More literally, Friendship's patron; *i. e.* Zeus.

ἥδιστά σοι ταῦτα ἐπιδείξειν φαμέν. τί γάρ[1] ;
Ἡσίοδος μὲν ὀλίγα φύλλα ἐκ τοῦ Ἑλικῶνος
λαβὼν αὐτίκα μάλα ποιητὴς ἐκ ποιμένος κατέστη
καὶ ᾖδε θεῶν καὶ ἡρώων γένη κάτοχος ἐκ Μουσῶν
γενόμενος, ῥήτορα δέ, ὃ πολὺ ἔνερθε ποιητικῆς
μεγαληγορίας ἐστίν, ἐν βραχεῖ καταστῆναι ἀδύνατον, εἴ τις ἐκμάθοι τὴν ταχίστην ὁδόν ;

5   Ὡς ἔγωγε καὶ διηγήσασθαι σοι βούλομαι
Σιδωνίου τινὸς ἐμπόρου ἐπίνοιαν δι' ἀπιστίαν
ἀτελῆ γενομένην καὶ τῷ ἀκούσαντι ἀνόνητον.
ἦρχε μὲν γὰρ ἤδη Ἀλέξανδρος Περσῶν, μετὰ τὴν
ἐν Ἀρβήλοις μάχην Δαρεῖον καθῃρηκώς· ἔδει δὲ
πανταχόσε τῆς ἀρχῆς διαθεῖν τοὺς γραμ-
ματοφόρους τὰ ἐπιτάγματα τοῦ Ἀλεξάνδρου
κομίζοντας. ἐκ Περσῶν δὲ πολλὴ εἰς Αἴγυπτον
ἐγίγνετο ἡ ὁδός· ἐκπεριιέναι γὰρ ἔδει τὰ ὄρη,
εἶτα διὰ τῆς Βαβυλωνίας εἰς τὴν Ἀραβίαν
ἐλθεῖν, εἶτα ἐρήμην πολλὴν περάσαντα[2] ἀφικέ-
σθαι ποτὲ μόλις εἰς Αἴγυπτον, εἴκοσι μηκίστους
ἀνδρὶ εὐζώνῳ σταθμοὺς τούτους διανύσαντα.
ἤχθετο οὖν ὁ Ἀλέξανδρος ἐπὶ τούτῳ, διότι
Αἰγυπτίους τι παρακινεῖν ἀκούων οὐκ εἶχε διὰ
ταχέων ἐκπέμπειν τοῖς σατράπαις τὰ δοκοῦντά
οἱ περὶ αὐτῶν. τότε δὴ ὁ Σιδώνιος ἔμπορος,
"Ἐγώ σοι," ἔφη, "ὦ βασιλεῦ, ὑπισχνοῦμαι
δείξειν ὁδὸν οὐ πολλὴν ἐκ Περσῶν εἰς Αἴγυπτον.
εἰ γάρ τις ὑπερβαίη τὰ ὄρη ταῦτα—ὑπερβαίη δ'
ἂν τριταῖος—αὐτίκα μάλα ἐν Αἰγύπτῳ οὗτός

[1] τί γάρ Sauppe : εἰ γὰρ MSS.

you that its attainment is at once easy and pleasant. Why should you? Hesiod was given a leaf or two from Helicon, and at once he became a poet instead of a shepherd and sang the pedigrees of gods and heroes under the inspiration of the Muses.[1] Is it impossible, then, to become a public speaker—something far inferior to the grand style of poetry—in an instant, if one could find out the quickest way?

Just to show you, I should like to tell you the tale of a Sidonian merchant's idea which disbelief made ineffectual and profitless to the man who heard it. Alexander was then ruler of the Persians, having deposed Darius after the battle of Arbela, and postmen had to run to every quarter of the realm carrying Alexander's orders. The journey from Persia to Egypt was long, since one had to make a detour about the mountains, then to go through Babylonia to Arabia, and then to traverse a wide expanse of desert before reaching Egypt at last, after spending in this way, even if one travelled light, twenty very long days on the road. Well, this annoyed Alexander, because he had heard that the Egyptians were showing signs of disaffection, and he was unable to be expeditious in transmitting his decisions concerning them to his governors. At that juncture the Sidonian merchant said: "I give you my word, King Alexander, to show you a short route from Persia to Egypt. If a man went over these mountains—and he could do it in three

---

[1] *Theogony*, 30–34. The Muses plucked a branch of laurel and gave it him as a staff of office ($\sigma\kappa\hat{\eta}\pi\tau\rho\sigma\nu$).

---

[2] $\pi\epsilon\rho\acute{a}\sigma\alpha\nu\tau\alpha$ A. M. H. ($\pi\epsilon\rho\acute{a}\sigma\alpha\nu\tau\alpha\varsigma$ Bekker): $\grave{\epsilon}\pi\epsilon\lambda\acute{a}\sigma\alpha\nu\tau\alpha\varsigma$ β, $\grave{\epsilon}\lambda\acute{a}\sigma\alpha\nu\tau\alpha\varsigma$ γ.

ἐστιν." καὶ εἶχεν οὕτω. πλὴν ὅ γε Ἀλέξανδρος
οὐκ ἐπίστευσεν, ἀλλὰ γόητα ᾤετο εἶναι τὸν ἔμ-
πορον. οὕτω τὸ παράδοξον τῆς ὑποσχέσεως
6 ἄπιστον δοκεῖ τοῖς πολλοῖς. ἀλλὰ μὴ σύ γε
πάθῃς τὸ αὐτό· εἴσῃ γὰρ πειρώμενος ὡς οὐδέν σε
κωλύσει ῥήτορα δοκεῖν μιᾶς οὐδὲ ὅλης ἡμέρας
ὑπερπετασθέντα τὸ ὄρος ἐκ Περσῶν εἰς Αἴγυπτον.

Ἐθέλω δέ σοι πρῶτον ὥσπερ ὁ Κέβης ἐκεῖνος
εἰκόνα γραψάμενος τῷ λόγῳ ἑκατέραν ἐπιδεῖξαι
τὴν ὁδόν· δύο γάρ ἐστον, αἳ πρὸς τὴν Ῥητορικὴν
ἄγετον, ἧς ἐρᾶν οὐ μετρίως μοι δοκεῖς. καὶ δῆτα
ἡ μὲν ἐφ᾽ ὑψηλοῦ καθήσθω πάνυ καλὴ καὶ
εὐπρόσωπος, τὸ τῆς Ἀμαλθείας κέρας ἔχουσα ἐν
τῇ δεξιᾷ παντοίοις καρποῖς ὑπερβρύον· ἐπὶ θατέρα
δέ μοι τὸν πλοῦτον δόκει παρεστῶτα ὁρᾶν, χρυσοῦν
ὅλον καὶ ἐπέραστον. καὶ ἡ δόξα δὲ καὶ ἡ ἰσχὺς
παρέστωσαν, καὶ οἱ ἔπαινοι περὶ πᾶσαν αὐτὴν
Ἔρωσι μικροῖς ἐοικότες πολλοὶ ἀπανταχόθεν
περιπλεκέσθωσαν ἐκπετόμενοι. εἴ που τὸν
Νεῖλον εἶδες γραφῇ μεμιμημένον, αὐτὸν μὲν
κείμενον ἐπὶ κροκοδείλου τινὸς ἢ ἵππου τοῦ
ποταμίου, οἷοι πολλοὶ ἐν αὐτῷ, μικρὰ δέ τινα
παιδία παρ᾽ αὐτὸν παίζοντα—πήχεις δὲ αὐτοὺς
οἱ Αἰγύπτιοι καλοῦσι,—τοιοῦτοι καὶ περὶ τὴν
Ῥητορικὴν οἱ ἔπαινοι.

Πρόσει δὴ σὺ ὁ ἐραστὴς ἐπιθυμῶν δηλαδὴ ὅτι

---

[1] The Sidonian merchant was exaggerating, but there was
truth in his tale. From Persepolis, by crossing the mountains
to the head of the Persian Gulf one could pick up a trade-
route that led from Alexandria on the Tigris (Charax) to
Petra (see Pliny 6, 145), whence one could get to Rhinocolura,
and so to Egypt. This would have been much shorter than

days—he is in Egypt in no time!" And it was so!
Alexander, however, put no faith in it, but thought
that the merchant was a liar.[1] So true is it that
amazing promises seem untrustworthy to most
people. But you must not make the same mistake.
Experience will convince you that nothing can prevent you from arriving as a public speaker, in a single
day, and not a full day at that, by flying across the
mountains from Persia to Egypt!

I wish first of all to paint you a picture in words,
like Cebes of old, and show you both the roads;
for there are two that lead to Lady Rhetoric, of
whom you seem to me exceedingly enamoured. So
let her be sitting upon a high place, very fair of
face and form, holding in her right hand the Horn
of Plenty, which runs over with all manner of fruits.
Beside her imagine, pray, that you see Wealth
standing, all golden and lovely. Let Fame, too,
and Power stand by; and let Compliments, resembling tiny Cupids, swarm all about her on the
wing in great numbers from every side. If you
have ever seen the Nile represented in a painting,
lying on the back of a crocodile or a hippopotamus,
such as are frequent in his stream, while tiny infants
play beside him—the Egyptians call them cubits—
the Compliments that surround Rhetoric are like
these.[2]

Now you, her lover, approach, desiring, of course,

the normal (Susa, Babylon, Damascus) route, but it might not
have been any quicker.

[2] Evidently there were many copies of this picture about,
and they were not all exactly alike. The Vatican has a
treatment of the theme in sculpture, in which Nile rests
upon a sphinx, and has about him sixteen "cubits,"
symbolizing the desired yearly rise of his stream.

τάχιστα γενέσθαι ἐπὶ τῆς ἄκρας, ὡς γαμήσειάς
τε αὐτὴν ἀνελθὼν καὶ πάντα ἐκεῖνα ἔχοις, τὸν
πλοῦτον τὴν δόξαν τοὺς ἐπαίνους· νόμῳ γὰρ

7 ἅπαντα γίγνεται τοῦ γεγαμηκότος. εἶτ᾽ ἐπειδὰν
πλησιάσῃς τῷ ὄρει, τὸ μὲν πρῶτον ἀπογιγνώσκεις
τὴν ἄνοδον, καὶ τὸ πρᾶγμα ὅμοιον εἶναί σοι δοκεῖ
οἷα ἡ Ἄορνος ἐφάνη τοῖς Μακεδόσιν ἀπόξυρον
αὐτὴν ἁπανταχόθεν ἰδοῦσιν, ἀτεχνῶς οὐδὲ ὀρνέοις
ὑπερπτῆναι ῥᾳδίαν, Διονύσου τινὸς ἢ Ἡρακλέους,
εἰ μέλλοι καθαιρεθήσεσθαι, δεομένην.

Ταῦτά σοι δοκεῖ τὸ πρῶτον· εἶτα μετ᾽ ὀλίγον
ὁρᾷς δύο τινὰς ὁδούς. μᾶλλον δὲ ἡ μὲν ἀτραπός
ἐστι στενὴ καὶ ἀκανθώδης καὶ τραχεῖα, πολὺ τὸ
δίψος ἐμφαίνουσα καὶ ἱδρῶτα· καὶ ἔφθη γὰρ ἤδη
Ἡσίοδος εὖ μάλα ὑποδείξας αὐτήν, ὥστε οὐδὲν
ἐμοῦ δεήσει. ἡ ἑτέρα δὲ πλατεῖα καὶ ἀνθηρὰ καὶ
εὔυδρος, τοιαύτη οἵαν μικρῷ πρόσθεν εἶπον, ἵνα
μὴ πολλάκις τὰ αὐτὰ λέγων ἐπέχω σε ἤδη ῥήτορα

8 εἶναι δυνάμενον. πλὴν τό γε τοσοῦτον προσ-
θήσειν μοι δοκῶ, διότι ἡ μὲν τραχεῖα ἐκείνη καὶ
ἀνάντης οὐ πολλὰ ἴχνη τῶν ὁδοιπόρων εἶχεν, εἰ
δέ τινα, πάνυ παλαιά. καὶ ἔγωγε κατ᾽ ἐκείνην
ἄθλιος ἀνῆλθον τοσαῦτα καμὼν οὐδὲν δέον· ἡ
ἑτέρα δὲ ἅτε ὁμαλὴ οὖσα καὶ ἀγκύλον οὐδὲν
ἔχουσα πόρρωθέν μοι ἐφάνη οἵα ἐστὶν οὐχ
ὁδεύσαντι αὐτῷ. οὐ γὰρ ἑώρων νέος ὢν ἔτι τὸ
βέλτιον, ἀλλὰ τὸν ποιητὴν ἐκεῖνον ἀληθεύειν

---

[1] A table-mountain captured by Alexander on his way to
India, 11 stades high at its lowest point, according to
Arrian (*Alex.* 4, 28). Cunningham identifies it as Ranigat.
Tomaschek considers the Greek name derived from Sanscrit

to get upon the summit with all speed in order to marry her when you get there, and to possess all that she has—the Wealth, the Fame, the Compliments; for by law everything accrues to the husband. Then when you draw near the mountain, at first you despair of climbing it, and the thing seems to you just as Aornus[1] looked to the Macedonians when they observed that it was precipitous on every side, truly far from easy even for a bird to fly over, calling for a Dionysus or a Heracles if it were ever going to be taken.

That is how it seems to you at first; and then, after a little, you see two roads. To be more exact, one of them is but a path, narrow, briery, and rough, promising great thirstiness and sweat; Hesiod has been beforehand with us and has already described it very carefully, so that I shall not need to do so.[2] The other, however, is level, flowery, and well-watered, just as I described it a moment ago, not to detain you by saying the same things over and over when you might even now be a speaker. But I must add at least this much, that the rough, steep road used not to have many tracks of wayfarers, and whatever tracks there were, were very old. I myself, unlucky dog, got up by that road and did all that hard work without any need; but as the other was level and had no windings at all, I could see from a distance what it was like without having travelled it myself. You see, being still young, I could not discern what was better, but believed that poet[3] to be telling the truth when he said that

avarana by popular etymology; but compare the Avestan name *Upairi-saena* (above the eagle).

[2] *Works and Days*, 286–292.   [3] Epicharmus.

ᾤμην λέγοντα ἐκ τῶν πόνων φύεσθαι τὰ ἀγαθά. τὸ δ' οὐκ εἶχεν οὕτως· ἀπονητὶ γοῦν ὁρῶ τοὺς πολλοὺς μειζόνων ἀξιουμένους εὐμοιρίᾳ τῆς αἱρέσεως τῶν λόγων καὶ ὁδῶν.

Ἐπὶ δ' οὖν τὴν ἀρχὴν ἀφικόμενος εὖ οἶδ' ὅτι ἀπορήσεις, καὶ ἤδη ἀπορεῖς, ποτέραν τρεπτέον. ὡς οὖν ποιήσας ἤδη ῥᾶστα ἐπὶ τὸ ἀκρότατον ἀναβήσῃ καὶ εὐδαιμονήσεις καὶ γαμήσεις καὶ θαυμαστὸς πᾶσι δόξεις, ἐγώ σοι φράσω· ἱκανὸν γὰρ τὸ αὐτὸν ἐξαπατηθῆναι καὶ πονῆσαι. σοὶ δὲ ἄσπορα καὶ ἀνήροτα πάντα φυέσθω καθάπερ ἐπὶ τοῦ Κρόνου.

9   Εὐθὺς οὖν σοι πρόσεισι καρτερός τις ἀνήρ, ὑπόσκληρος, ἀνδρώδης τὸ βάδισμα, πολὺν τὸν ἥλιον ἐπὶ τῷ σώματι δεικνύων, ἀρρενωπὸς τὸ βλέμμα, ἐγρηγορώς, τῆς τραχείας ὁδοῦ ἐκείνης ἡγεμών, λήρους τινὰς ὁ μάταιος διεξιὼν πρὸς σέ. ἕπεσθαι γάρ οἱ[1] παρακελευόμενος, ὑποδεικνὺς τὰ Δημοσθένους ἴχνη καὶ Πλάτωνος καὶ ἄλλων τινῶν, μεγάλα μὲν καὶ ὑπὲρ τοὺς νῦν, ἀμαυρὰ δὲ ἤδη καὶ ἀσαφῆ τὰ πολλὰ ὑπὸ τοῦ χρόνου, φήσει[2] εὐδαίμονά σε ἔσεσθαι καὶ νόμῳ γαμήσειν τὴν Ῥητορικήν, εἰ κατὰ τούτων ὀδεύσειας ὥσπερ οἱ

---

[1] ἕπεσθαί οἱ β, edd.
[2] φήσει A.M.H.: καὶ φήσει vulg., καί φησιν MSS.

---

[1] The thought is expressed in *Works and Days*, 289: "The immortal gods have put sweat before virtue;" but Lucian's wording is closer to the famous line of Epicharmus quoted (just after the passage from Hesiod) in Xenophon's

blessings were engendered of toil.[1] That was not so, however; at all events, I notice that most people are accorded greater returns without any labour, through their felicitous choice of words and ways.

But, to resume—when you reach the starting-point, I am sure that you will be in doubt, and indeed are even now in doubt, which road to follow. I propose, therefore, to tell you how to do now in order to mount to the highest peak with the greatest ease, to be fortunate, to bring off the marriage, and to be accounted wonderful by every-one. It is quite enough that I should have been duped and should have worked hard. For you, let everything grow "without sowing and without ploughing," as in the time of Cronus.[2]

On the instant, then, you will be approached by a vigorous man with hard muscles and a manly stride, who shows heavy tan on his body, and is bold-eyed and alert. He is the guide of the rough road, and he will talk a lot of nonsense to you, the poor simpleton. In exhorting you to follow him, he will point out the footprints of Demosthenes and of Plato, and one or two more—great prints, I grant you, too great for men of nowadays, but for the most part dim and indistinct through lapse of time; and he will say that you will have good fortune and will contract a lawful marriage with Rhetoric if you

---

Memorabilia, 2, 1, 20: "'Tis at the price of toil that the gods sell us all their blessings."

[2] The quotation is from *Odyssey*, 9, 109, but there is also an allusion to Hesiod's description of the time of Cronus, the golden age, when the "grain-giving earth bore fruit of itself, in plenty and without stint" (*Works and Days*, 117–118).

ἐπὶ τῶν κάλων βαίνοντες· εἰ δὲ κἂν μικρόν τι
παραβαίης ἢ ἔξω πατήσειας ἢ ἐπὶ θάτερα μᾶλλον
κλιθείης τῇ ῥοπῇ, ἐκπεσεῖσθαί σε τῆς ὀρθῆς
ὁδοῦ καὶ ἀγούσης ἐπὶ τὸν γάμον. εἶτά σε κελεύ-
σει ζηλοῦν ἐκείνους τοὺς ἀρχαίους ἄνδρας ἕωλα
παραδείγματα παρατιθεὶς τῶν λόγων οὐ ῥᾴδια
μιμεῖσθαι, οἷα τὰ τῆς παλαιᾶς ἐργασίας ἐστίν,
Ἡγησίου καὶ τῶν ἀμφὶ Κριτίον[1] καὶ Νησιώτην,
ἀπεσφιγμένα καὶ νευρώδη καὶ σκληρὰ καὶ
ἀκριβῶς ἀποτεταμένα ταῖς γραμμαῖς. πόνον δὲ
καὶ ἀγρυπνίαν καὶ ὑδατοποσίαν καὶ τὸ ἀλιπαρὲς[2]
ἀναγκαῖα ταῦτα καὶ ἀπαραίτητα φήσει· ἀδύνατον
γὰρ εἶναι ἄνευ τούτων διανύσαι τὴν ὁδόν. ὃ δὲ
πάντων ἀνιαρότατον, ὅτι σοι καὶ τὸν χρόνον
πάμπολυν ὑπογράψει τῆς ὁδοιπορίας, ἔτη πολλά,
οὐ κατὰ ἡμέρας καὶ τριακάδας, ἀλλὰ κατὰ
ὀλυμπιάδας ὅλας ἀριθμῶν, ὡς καὶ προαποκαμεῖν
ἀκούοντα καὶ ἀπαγορεῦσαι, πολλὰ χαίρειν
φράσαντα τῇ ἐλπιζομένῃ ἐκείνῃ εὐδαιμονίᾳ. πρὸς
δὲ τούτοις οὐδὲ μισθοὺς ὀλίγους ἀπαιτεῖ τῶν
τοσούτων κακῶν, ἀλλὰ οὐκ ἂν ἡγήσαιτό σοι, εἰ
μὴ μεγάλα πρότερον λάβοι.

10   Ὁ μὲν ταῦτα φήσει, ἀλαζὼν καὶ ἀρχαῖος ὡς
ἀληθῶς καὶ Κρονικὸς ἄνθρωπος, νεκροὺς εἰς
μίμησιν παλαιοὺς προτιθεὶς καὶ ἀνορύττειν ἀξιῶν
λόγους πάλαι κατορωρυγμένους ὥς τι μέγιστον
ἀγαθόν, μαχαιροποιοῦ υἱὸν καὶ ἄλλον Ἀτρομήτου

---

[1] Κριτίον Dindorf : Κριτίαν β, Κράτητα γ.
[2] λιπαρὲς β.   But cf. *Hermotimus* 24, Hesychius, and Soph. *Electra*, 451.

A PROFESSOR OF PUBLIC SPEAKING

follow these footprints like a rope-dancer; but if you should make even a slight mis-step, or set your foot out of them, or let your weight sway you somewhat to one side, you will fall from the direct road that leads to the marriage. Then he will tell you to imitate those ancient worthies, and will set you fusty models for your speeches, far from easy to copy, resembling sculptures in the early manner such as those of Hegesias and of Critius and Nesiotes [1] —wasp-waisted, sinewy, hard, meticulously definite in their contours. And he will say that hard work, scant sleep, abstention from wine, and untidiness are necessary and indispensable; it is impossible, says he, to get over the road without them. What is most vexatious of all, even the time which he will prescribe to you for the journey will be very long—many years, for he counts not by days and months, but by whole Olympic cycles,[2] so that you will be foredone in advance as you listen and will forswear your project, bidding a fond farewell to the good fortune that you expected. Besides, he demands no small fee for all these hardships; in fact, he would not guide you unless he should get a huge sum in advance.

That is what this man will say, the impostor, the absolute old fogey, the antediluvian, who displays dead men of a bygone age to serve as patterns, and expects you to dig up long-buried speeches as if they were something tremendously helpful, wanting you to emulate the son of a sword-maker, and some other

---

[1] Pre-Phidian sculptors, Hegesias famous for his *Dioscuri*, Critius and Nesiotes for their joint work, the *Tyrant Slayers* (Harmodius and Aristogeiton).

[2] *I.e.*, of four years.

τινὸς γραμματιστοῦ ζηλοῦν ἀξιῶν, καὶ ταῦτα ἐν
εἰρήνῃ μήτε Φιλίππου ἐπιόντος μήτε Ἀλεξάνδρου
ἐπιτάττοντος, ὅπου τὰ ἐκείνων ἴσως ἐδόκει
χρήσιμα, οὐκ εἰδὼς ὁποία νῦν κεκαινοτόμηται
ταχεῖα καὶ ἀπράγμων καὶ εἰς τὸ εὐθὺ τῆς
ῥητορικῆς ὁδός. σὺ δὲ μήτε πείθεσθαι μήτε
προσέχειν αὐτῷ, μή σε ἐκτραχηλίσῃ που παραλαβὼν ἢ τὸ τελευταῖον προγηρᾶσαι τοῖς πόνοις
παρασκευάσῃ. ἀλλὰ εἰ πάντως ἐρᾷς καὶ τάχιστα
ἐθέλεις τῇ ῥητορικῇ συνεῖναι ἀκμάζων ἔτι, ὡς καὶ
σπουδάζοιο πρὸς αὐτῆς, ἴθι, τῷ μὲν δασεῖ τούτῳ
καὶ πέρα τοῦ μετρίου ἀνδρικῷ μακρὰ χαίρειν λέγε,
ἀναβαίνειν αὐτὸν καὶ ἄλλους ὁπόσους ἂν ἐξαπατᾶν
δύνηται ἀνάγειν καταλιπὼν ἀσθμαίνοντα καὶ
ἱδρῶτι πολλῷ συνόντα.

11   Πρὸς δὲ τὴν ἑτέραν ἐλθὼν εὑρήσεις πολλοὺς
καὶ ἄλλους, ἐν τούτοις δὲ καὶ πάνσοφόν τινα καὶ
πάγκαλον ἄνδρα, διασεσαλευμένον τὸ βάδισμα,
ἐπικεκλασμένον τὸν αὐχένα, γυναικεῖον τὸ
βλέμμα, μελιχρὸν τὸ φώνημα, μύρων ἀποπνέοντα,
τῷ δακτύλῳ ἄκρῳ τὴν κεφαλὴν κνώμενον, ὀλίγας
μὲν ἔτι, οὔλας δὲ καὶ ὑακινθίνας τὰς τρίχας εὐθε-
τίζοντα, πάναβρόν τινα Σαρδανάπαλλον ἢ Κι-
νύραν ἢ αὐτὸν Ἀγάθωνα, τὸν τῆς τραγῳδίας
ἐπέραστον ἐκεῖνον ποιητήν. λέγω δὲ ὡς ἀπὸ
τούτων γνωρίζοις αὐτόν, μηδέ σε οὕτω θεσπέσιον
χρῆμα καὶ φίλον Ἀφροδίτῃ καὶ Χάρισι διαλάθοι.
καίτοι τί φημί; κἂν εἰ μύοντι γάρ σοι προσελθὼν
εἴποι τι, τὸ Ὑμήττιον ἐκεῖνο ἀνοίξας στόμα, καὶ
τὴν συνήθη φωνὴν ἀφείη,[1] μάθοις ἂν ὡς οὐχὶ τῶν

---

[1] ἀφείη Jacobs : ἀφίη γβ.

fellow, the son of a school-master named Atrometus,[1] and that too in times of peace, when no Philip is making raids and no Alexander issuing orders—situations in which their speeches were perhaps considered useful. He does not know what a short, easy road, direct to Rhetoric, has recently been opened. But do not you believe or heed him for fear he may give you a neck-breaking tumble somewhere after he gets you in charge, or may in the end make you prematurely old with your labours. No, if you are unquestionably in love, and wish to marry Rhetoric forthwith, while you are still in your prime, so that she may be fond of you, do bid a long good-bye to that hairy, unduly masculine fellow, leaving him to climb up himself, all blown and dripping with sweat, and lead up what others he can delude.

If you turn to the other road, you will find many people, and among them a wholly clever and wholly handsome gentleman with a mincing gait, a thin neck, a languishing eye, and a honeyed voice, who distils perfume, scratches his head with the tip of his finger,[2] and carefully dresses his hair, which is scanty now, but curly and raven-black—an utterly delicate Sardanapalus, a Cinyras, a very Agathon (that charming writer of tragedies, don't you know?). I am thus explicit that you may recognize him by these tokens, and may not overlook a creature so marvellous, and so dear to Aphrodite and the Graces. But what am I talking about? Even if you had your eyes shut, and he should come and speak to you, unsealing those Hymettus lips and releasing upon the air those wonted intonations, you would

---

[1] The sword-maker's son is Demosthenes, the schoolmaster's Aeschines.   [2] Cf. Plutarch, *Pompey*, 48 fin.

καθ' ἡμᾶς ἐστιν, οἳ ἀρούρης καρπὸν ἔδομεν, ἀλλά
τι ξένον φάσμα δρόσῳ ἢ ἀμβροσίᾳ τρεφόμενον.

Τούτῳ τοίνυν προσελθὼν καὶ παραδοὺς σεαυτὸν
αὐτίκα μάλα ῥήτωρ καὶ περίβλεπτος καί, ὡς
ὀνομάζει αὐτός, βασιλεὺς ἐν τοῖς λόγοις ἀπονητὶ
καταστήσῃ τὰ τέθριππα ἐλαύνων τοῦ λόγου.
διδάξεται γάρ σε παραλαβὼν τὰ πρῶτα μὲν
12 ἐκεῖνα—μᾶλλον δὲ αὐτὸς εἰπάτω πρὸς σέ· γελοῖον
γὰρ ὑπὲρ τοιούτου ῥήτορος ἐμὲ ποιεῖσθαι τοὺς
λόγους, φαῦλον ὑποκριτὴν ἴσως τῶν τοιούτων καὶ
τηλικούτων, μὴ καὶ συντρίψω που πεσὼν τὸν
ἥρωα ὃν ὑποκρίνομαι.

Φαίη τοιγαροῦν ἂν πρὸς σὲ ὡδέ πως ἐπισπασά-
μενος ὁπόσον ἔτι λοιπὸν τῆς κόμης καὶ ὑπο-
μειδιάσας τὸ γλαφυρὸν ἐκεῖνο καὶ ἁπαλὸν οἷον
εἴωθεν, Αὐτοθαΐδα τὴν κωμικὴν ἢ Μαλθάκην ἢ
Γλυκέραν τινὰ μιμησάμενος τῷ προσηνεῖ τοῦ
φθέγματος· ἄγροικον γὰρ τὸ ἀρρενωπὸν καὶ οὐ
13 πρὸς ἁβροῦ καὶ ἐρασμίου ῥήτορος. φήσει δ' οὖν
πάνυ μετριάζων ὑπὲρ αὐτοῦ· "Μῶν σε, ὦγαθέ, ὁ
Πύθιος ἔπεμψε πρός με ῥητόρων τὸν ἄριστον
προσειπών, ὥσπερ ὅτε Χαιρεφῶν ἤρετο αὐτόν,
ἔδειξεν ὅστις ἦν ὁ σοφώτατος ἐν τοῖς τότε; εἰ δὲ
μὴ τοῦτο, ἀλλὰ κατὰ κλέος αὐτὸς ἥκεις ἀκούων
ἁπάντων ὑπερεκπεπληγμένων τὰ ἡμέτερα καὶ
ὑμνούντων καὶ τεθηπότων καὶ ὑπεπτηχότων,
αὐτίκα μάλα εἴσῃ πρὸς οἷόν τινα δαιμόνιον ἄνδρα
ἥκεις. προσδοκήσῃς δὲ μηδὲν τοιοῦτον ὄψεσθαι

---

[1] *Iliad* 6, 142.
[2] Socrates, in the *Apology* of Plato, says that when
Chaerephon in his zeal "asked whether anyone was wiser
than I, the Pythia responded that nobody was wiser" (21 A).

discover that he is not like us "who eat the fruit of the glebe," [1] but some unfamiliar spirit, nurtured on dew or on ambrosia.

If, then, you go to him and put yourself in his hands, you will at once, without effort, become an orator, the observed of all, and, as he himself calls it, king of the platform, driving the horses of eloquence four-in-hand. For on taking you in charge, he will teach you first of all—but let him address you himself. It would be comical for me to do the talking on behalf of such an accomplished speaker, as I should be poorly cast, it may very well be, for parts of that nature and importance; I might fall down and so put out of countenance the hero whom I impersonated.

He would address you, then, somewhat in this fashion, tossing back what hair is still left him, faintly smiling in that sweet and tender way which is his wont, and rivalling Thais herself of comic fame, or Malthace, or Glycera, in the seductiveness of his tone, since masculinity is boorish and not in keeping with a delicate and charming platform-hero —he will address you, I say, using very moderate language about himself: " Prithee, dear fellow, did Pythian Apollo send you to me, entitling me the best of speakers, just as, when Chaerephon questioned him, he told who was the wisest in that generation? [2] If that is not the case, but you have come of your own accord in the wake of rumour, because you hear everybody speak of my achievements with astonishment, praise, admiration, and self-abasement, you shall very soon learn what a superhuman person you have come to. Do not expect to see something that you can compare with

οἷον τῷδε ἢ τῷδε παραβαλεῖν, ἀλλ' εἴ τις ἢ
Τιτυὸς ἢ Ὦτος ἢ Ἐφιάλτης, ὑπὲρ ἐκείνους πολὺ
φανεῖταί σοι τὸ πρᾶγμα ὑπερφυὲς καὶ τεράστιον·
ἐπεὶ τούς γε ἄλλους τοσοῦτον ὑπερφωνοῦντα
εὑρήσεις ὁπόσον ἡ σάλπιγξ τοὺς αὐλοὺς καὶ οἱ
τέττιγες τὰς μελίττας καὶ οἱ χοροὶ τοὺς ἐνδι-
δόντας.

14 "Ἐπεὶ δὲ καὶ ῥήτωρ αὐτὸς ἐθέλεις γενέσθαι
καὶ τοῦτο οὐκ ἂν παρ' ἄλλου ῥᾷον μάθοις, ἕπου
μόνον, ὦ μέλημα, οἷς ἂν εἴπω καὶ ζήλου πάντα,
καὶ τοὺς νόμους οἷς ἂν ἐπιτάξω χρῆσθαι ἀκριβῶς
μοι παραφύλαττε. μᾶλλον δὲ ἤδη προχώρει
μηδὲν ὀκνήσας μηδὲ πτοηθείς, εἰ μὴ προετελέσθης
ἐκεῖνα τὰ πρὸ τῆς ῥητορικῆς, ὁπόσα ἡ ἄλλη
προπαιδεία τοῖς ἀνοήτοις καὶ ματαίοις μετὰ
πολλοῦ καμάτου ὁδοποιεῖ· οὐδὲν γὰρ αὐτῶν
δεήσει. ἀλλ' ἀνίπτοις ποσίν—ἡ παροιμία φησίν
—ἔμβαινε, οὐ μεῖον ἕξων διὰ τοῦτο, οὐδ' ἄν, τὸ
κοινότατον, μηδὲ γράφειν τὰ γράμματα εἰδῇς·
ἄλλο γάρ τι παρὰ ταῦτα ὁ ῥήτωρ.

15 "Λέξω δὲ πρῶτον μὲν ὁπόσα χρὴ αὐτόν σε
οἴκοθεν ἔχοντα ἥκειν ἐφόδια πρὸς τὴν πορείαν
καὶ ὅπως ἐπισιτίσασθαι, ὡς ἂν τάχιστα διανύσαι
δυνηθείης. ἔπειτα καὐτὸς ἃ μὲν προϊόντι ἐπι-
δεικνὺς κατὰ τὴν ὁδόν, ἃ δὲ καὶ παραινῶν, πρὶν
ἥλιον δῦναι ῥήτορά σε ὑπὲρ τοὺς πάντας
ἀποφανῶ, οἷος αὐτός εἰμι, ἀναμφιλέκτως τὰ

---

[1] The saying in full was ἀνίπτοις ποσὶν ἀναβαίνων ἐπὶ τὸ
στέγος (going up to the roof with unwashed feet), and so can

So-and-so, or So-and-so; no, you will consider the achievement far too prodigious and amazing even for Tityus or Otus or Ephialtes. Indeed, as far as the others are concerned, you will find that I drown them out as effectively as trumpets drown flutes, or cicadas bees, or choirs their leaders.

"As you yourself wish to become a speaker, and cannot learn this with greater ease from anyone else, just attend, dear lad, to all that I shall say, copy me in everything, and always keep, I beg you, the rules which I shall bid you to follow. In fact, you may press on at once; you need not feel any hesitation or dismay because you have not gone through all the rites of initiation preliminary to Rhetoric, through which the usual course of elementary instruction guides the steps of the senseless and silly at the cost of great weariness. You will not require them at all. No, go straight in, as the proverb says, with unwashen feet,[1] and you will not fare any the worse for that, even if you are quite in the prevailing fashion and do not know how to write. Orators are beyond all that!

"I shall first tell you what equipment you must yourself bring with you from home for the journey, and how you must provision yourself so that you can finish it soonest. Then giving you my personal instruction along the road, partly by example set for you while you proceed, and partly by precept, before sunset I shall make you a public speaker, superior to them all, just like myself—indubitably

---

hardly contain any reference to ceremonial purification. Perhaps going up on the roof was tantamount to going to bed. Cf. *Song of Solomon*, 5, 3.

πρῶτα καὶ μέσα καὶ τελευταῖα τῶν λέγειν
ἐπιχειρούντων.

" Κόμιζε τοίνυν τὸ μέγιστον μὲν τὴν ἀμαθίαν,
εἶτα θράσος, ἐπὶ τούτοις δὲ τόλμαν καὶ ἀναι-
σχυντίαν. αἰδῶ δὲ ἢ ἐπιείκειαν ἢ μετριότητα ἢ
ἐρύθημα οἴκοι ἀπόλιπε· ἀχρεῖα γὰρ καὶ ὑπεναντία
τῷ πράγματι. ἀλλὰ καὶ βοὴν ὅτι μεγίστην καὶ
μέλος ἀναίσχυντον καὶ βάδισμα οἷον τὸ ἐμόν.
ταῦτα δὲ ἀναγκαῖα πάνυ καὶ μόνα ἔστιν ὅτε
ἱκανά. καὶ ἡ ἐσθὴς δὲ ἔστω εὐανθὴς ἢ[1] λευκή,
ἔργον[2] τῆς Ταραντίνης ἐργασίας, ὡς διαφαίνεσθαι
τὸ σῶμα, καὶ ἢ[3] κρηπὶς Ἀττικὴ γυναικεία, τὸ
πολυσχιδές, ἢ ἐμβὰς Σικυωνία πίλοις τοῖς
λευκοῖς ἐπιπρέπουσα, καὶ ἀκόλουθοι πολλοὶ καὶ
βιβλίον ἀεί.

" Ταῦτα μὲν αὐτὸν χρὴ συντελεῖν· τὰ δ' ἄλλα
16 καθ' ὁδὸν ἤδη προϊὼν ὅρα καὶ ἄκουε. καὶ δή σοι
τοὺς νόμους δίειμι, οἷς χρώμενόν σε ἡ Ῥητορικὴ
γνωριεῖ καὶ προσήσεται, οὐδὲ ἀποστραφήσεται
καὶ σκορακιεῖ καθάπερ ἀτέλεστόν τινα καὶ κατά-
σκοπον τῶν ἀπορρήτων. σχήματος μὲν τὸ
πρῶτον ἐπιμεληθῆναι χρὴ μάλιστα καὶ εὐμόρφου
τῆς ἀναβολῆς, ἔπειτα πεντεκαίδεκα ἢ οὐ πλείω
γε τῶν εἴκοσιν Ἀττικὰ ὀνόματα ἐκλέξας ποθὲν
ἀκριβῶς ἐκμελετήσας, πρόχειρα ἐπ' ἄκρας τῆς

---

[1] ἢ A.M.H. : ἡ β, καὶ γ.
[2] ἔργον vulg. : ἔρνα MSS.
[3] ἢ (twice) A.M.H. : ἡ MSS.

first, midmost and last [1] of all who undertake to make speeches.

"Bring with you, then, as the principal thing, ignorance; secondly, recklessness, and thereto effrontery and shamelessness. Modesty, respectability, self-restraint, and blushes may be left at home, for they are useless and somewhat of a hindrance to the matter in hand. But you need also a very loud voice, a shameless singing delivery, and a gait like mine. They are essential indeed, and sometimes sufficient in themselves. [2] Let your clothing be gaily-coloured, or else white, a fabric of Tarentine manufacture, so that your body will show through; and wear either high Attic sandals of the kind that women wear, with many slits, or else Sicyonian boots, trimmed with strips of white felt. Have also many attendants, and always a book in hand.

"That is what you must contribute yourself. The rest you may now see and hear by the way, as you go forward. And next I shall tell you the rules that you must follow in order that Rhetoric may recognize and welcome you, and not turn you her back and bid you go to, as if you were an outsider prying into her privacies. First of all, you must pay especial attention to outward appearance, and to the graceful set of your cloak. Then cull from some source or other fifteen, or anyhow not more than twenty, Attic words, drill yourself carefully in them, and have them ready at the tip of your tongue

---

[1] *I.e.*, the others are not in it with him. Compare Demosthenes 25, 8: "all such beasts, of whom he is midmost and last and first."

[2] Compare the conversation between Demosthenes and the sausage-seller in Aristophanes, *Knights*, 150–235.

γλώττης ἔχε—τὸ ἄττα καὶ κᾷτα καὶ μῶν καὶ
ἀμηγέπη καὶ λῶστε καὶ τὰ τοιαῦτα,—καὶ ἐν
ἅπαντι λόγῳ καθάπερ τι ἥδυσμα ἐπίπαττε αὐτῶν.
μελέτω δὲ μηδὲν τῶν ἄλλων, εἰ ἀνόμοια τούτοις
καὶ ἀσύμφυλα καὶ ἀπῳδά. ἡ πορφύρα μόνον
ἔστω καλὴ καὶ εὐανθής, κἂν σισύρα τῶν παχειῶν
17 τὸ ἱμάτιον ᾖ. μέτει[1] δὲ ἀπόρρητα καὶ ξένα
ῥήματα, σπανιάκις ὑπὸ τῶν πάλαι εἰρημένα, καὶ
ταῦτα συμφορήσας ἀπότόξευε προχειριζόμενος
εἰς τοὺς προσομιλοῦντας. οὕτω γάρ σε ὁ λεὼς ὁ
πολὺς ἀποβλέψονται καὶ θαυμαστὸν ὑπο-
λήψονται καὶ τὴν παιδείαν ὑπὲρ αὐτούς, εἰ
" ἀποστλεγγίσασθαι" τὸ ἀποξύσασθαι λέγοις,
τὸ δὲ ἡλίῳ θέρεσθαι " εἰληθερεῖσθαι," τὸν
ἀρραβῶνα δὲ " προνόμιον," τὸν ὄρθρον δὲ
" ἀκροκνεφές." ἐνίοτε δὲ καὶ αὐτὸς ποίει καινὰ
καὶ ἀλλόκοτα ὀνόματα καὶ νομοθέτει τὸν μὲν
ἑρμηνεῦσαι δεινὸν " εὔλεξιν" καλεῖν, τὸν συνετὸν
" σοφόνουν," τὸν ὀρχηστὴν δὲ " χειρίσοφον." ἂν
σολοικίσῃς δὲ ἢ βαρβαρίσῃς, ἓν ἔστω φάρμακον
ἡ ἀναισχυντία, καὶ πρόχειρον εὐθὺς ὄνομα οὔτε
ὄντος τινὸς οὔτε γενομένου ποτέ, ἢ ποιητοῦ ἢ
συγγραφέως, ὃς οὕτω λέγειν ἐδοκίμαζε σοφὸς
ἀνὴρ καὶ τὴν φωνὴν εἰς τὸ ἀκρότατον ἀπηκριβω-
μένος. ἀλλὰ καὶ ἀναγίγνωσκε τὰ παλαιὰ μὲν μὴ
σύ γε, μηδὲ εἴ τι ὁ λῆρος Ἰσοκράτης ἢ ὁ χαρίτων
ἄμοιρος Δημοσθένης ἢ ὁ ψυχρὸς Πλάτων, ἀλλὰ
τοὺς τῶν ὀλίγον πρὸ ἡμῶν λόγους καὶ ἅς φασι

---

[1] μέτει Bekker : μετὰ MSS.

---

[1] Two of the terms require a word of comment : κᾷτα
means "and then," not "eftsoons," and the peculiarly Attic

A PROFESSOR OF PUBLIC SPEAKING

—'sundry,' 'eftsoons,' 'prithee,' 'in some wise,' 'fair sir,' and the like.[1] Whenever you speak, sprinkle in some of them as a relish. Never mind if the rest is inconsistent with them, unrelated, and discordant. Only let your purple stripe be handsome and bright, even if your cloak is but a blanket of the thickest sort. Hunt up obscure, unfamiliar words, rarely used by the ancients, and have a heap of these in readiness to launch at your audience. The many-headed crowd will look up to you and think you amazing, and far beyond themselves in education, if you call rubbing down 'destrigillation,' taking a sun-bath 'insolation,' advance payments 'hansel,' and daybreak 'crepuscule.' Sometimes you must yourself make new monstrosities of words and pre-scribe that an able writer be called fine-dictioned, an intelligent man sage-minded, and a dancer handi-wise.[2] If you commit a solecism or a barbarism, let shamelessness be your sole and only remedy, and be ready at once with the name of someone who is not now alive and never was, either a poet or a historian, saying that he, a learned man, extremely precise in his diction, approved the expression. As for reading the classics, don't you do it—either that twaddling Isocrates or that uncouth Demosthenes or that tiresome Plato. No, read the speeches of the men who lived only a little before our own time, and

feature was the crasis (καὶ εἶτα being run together); μῶν was used to introduce a question, like *num* in Latin, and was in Lucian's day obsolete.

[2] According to Lucian himself in the treatise *On Dancing* (69), the word χειρίσοφος (handiwise) was applied to dancers by Lesbonax, a rhetorician, whose son was one of Tiberius' teachers. Its appropriateness lay in the extensive use of gesture in Greek dancing.

ταύτας μελέτας, ὡς ἔχῃς ἀπ' ἐκείνων ἐπισιτισά-
μενος ἐν καιρῷ καταχρῆσθαι καθάπερ ἐκ ταμιείου
προαιρῶν.

18   "'Επειδὰν δὲ καὶ δέῃ λέγειν καὶ οἱ παρόντες
ὑποβάλωσί τινας ὑποθέσεις καὶ ἀφορμὰς τῶν
λόγων, ἅπαντα μὲν ὁπόσα ἂν ᾖ δυσχερῆ, ψεγέσθω[1]
καὶ ἐκφαυλιζέσθω ὡς οὐδὲν ὅλως ἀνδρῶδες αὐτῶν.
ἑλομένων δέ, μὴ μελλήσας λέγε ὅττι κεν ἐπ'
ἀκαιρίμαν[2] γλῶτταν ἔλθῃ, μηδὲν ἐκείνων
ἐπιμεληθείς, ὡς τὸ πρῶτον, ὥσπερ οὖν καὶ ἔστι
πρῶτον, ἐρεῖς ἐν καιρῷ προσήκοντι καὶ τὸ
δεύτερον μετὰ τοῦτο καὶ τὸ τρίτον μετ' ἐκεῖνο,
ἀλλὰ τὸ πρῶτον ἐμπεσὸν πρῶτον λεγέσθω, καὶ
ἢν οὕτω τύχῃ, περὶ τῷ μετώπῳ μὲν ἡ κνημίς,
περὶ τῇ κνήμῃ δὲ ἡ κόρυς. πλὴν ἀλλ' ἔπειγε καὶ
σύνειρε καὶ μὴ σιώπα μόνον. κἂν περὶ ὑβριστοῦ
τινος ἢ μοιχοῦ λέγῃς Ἀθήνησι, τὰ ἐν Ἰνδοῖς καὶ
Ἐκβατάνοις λεγέσθω. ἐπὶ πᾶσι δὲ ὁ Μαραθὼν
καὶ ὁ Κυνέγειρος, ὧν οὐκ ἄν τι ἄνευ γένοιτο.
καὶ ἀεὶ ὁ Ἄθως πλείσθω καὶ ὁ Ἑλλήσποντος
πεζευέσθω καὶ ὁ ἥλιος ὑπὸ τῶν Μηδικῶν βελῶν
σκεπέσθω καὶ Ξέρξης φευγέτω καὶ Λεωνίδας
θαυμαζέσθω καὶ τὰ Ὀθρυάδου γράμματα ἀνα-
γιγνωσκέσθω, καὶ ἡ Σαλαμὶς καὶ τὸ Ἀρτεμίσιον
καὶ αἱ Πλαταιαὶ πολλὰ ταῦτα καὶ πυκνά. καὶ
ἐπὶ πᾶσι τὰ ὀλίγα ἐκεῖνα ὀνόματα ἐπιπολαζέτω
καὶ ἐπανθείτω, καὶ συνεχὲς τὸ ἄττα καὶ τὸ

---

[1] ψεγέσθω Hermann : λεγέσθω MSS.
[2] ἐπ' ἀκαιρίμαν Valckenaer : ἐπὶ καιρήματι Ω, ἐπὶ καὶ ῥῆμα B.

---

[1] I.e., declamations.

these pieces that they call 'exercises,'[1] in order to secure from them a supply of provisions which you can use up as occasion arises, drawing, as it were, on the buttery.

"When you really must speak, and those present suggest themes and texts for your discussion, carp at all the hard ones and make light of them as not fit, any one of them, for a real man. But when they have made their selection,[2] unhesitatingly say 'whatever comes to the tip of your unlucky tongue.'[3] Take no pains at all that the first thing, just because it really is first, shall be said at the appropriate time, and the second directly after it, and the third after that, but say first whatever occurs to you first; and if it so happens, don't hesitate to buckle your leggings on your head and your helmet on your leg.[4] But do make haste and keep it going, and only don't stop talking. If you are speaking of a case of assault or adultery at Athens, mention instances in India or Ecbatana. Cap everything with references to Marathon and Cynegeirus, without which you cannot succeed at all. Unendingly let Athos be crossed in ships and the Hellespont afoot; let the sun be shadowed by the arrows of the Medes, and Xerxes flee the field and Leonidas receive admiration; let the inscription of Othryades be deciphered, and let allusions to Salamis, Artemisium, and Plataea come thick and fast. Over everything let those few words of yours run riot and bloom, and let 'sundry'

[2] That is to say, when the audience had selected, from the different topics suggested by individuals, the one that they preferred.

[3] A quotation from an unknown poet, which had become a proverb (Athenaeus 5, 217 c).

[4] Proverbial for putting the cart before the horse.

δήπουθεν, κἂν μηδὲν αὐτῶν δέῃ· καλὰ γάρ ἐστι
καὶ εἰκῆ λεγόμενα.

19 "῍Ην δέ ποτε καὶ ᾆσαι καιρὸς εἶναι δοκῇ, πάντα
σοι ᾀδέσθω καὶ μέλος γιγνέσθω. κἂν ποτε
ἀπορήσῃς πράγματος ᾠδικοῦ, τοὺς ἄνδρας τοὺς
δικαστὰς ὀνομάσας ἐμμελῶς πεπληρωκέναι οἵου
τὴν ἁρμονίαν. τὸ δὲ οἴμοι τῶν κακῶν πολλάκις,
καὶ ὁ μηρὸς πατασσέσθω, καὶ λαρύγγιζε καὶ
ἐπιχρέμπτου τοῖς λεγομένοις καὶ βάδιζε μετα-
φέρων τὴν πυγήν. καὶ ἢν μέν σε μὴ ἐπαινῶσιν,
ἀγανάκτει καὶ λοιδοροῦ αὐτοῖς· ἢν δὲ ὀρθοὶ
ἑστήκωσιν ὑπὸ τῆς αἰσχύνης ἤδη πρὸς τὴν ἔξοδον
ἕτοιμοι, καθέζεσθαι κέλευε, καὶ ὅλως τυραννὶς
τὸ πρᾶγμα ἔστω.

20 "῍Οπως δὲ καὶ τὸ πλῆθος τῶν λόγων θαυμά-
ζωσιν, ἀπὸ τῶν Ἰλιακῶν ἀρξάμενος ἢ καὶ νὴ Δία
ἀπὸ τῶν Δευκαλίωνος καὶ Πύρρας γάμων, ἢν δοκῇ,
καταβίβαζε τὸν λόγον ἐπὶ τὰ νῦν καθεστῶτα.
οἱ μὲν γὰρ συνιέντες ὀλίγοι, οἳ μάλιστα μὲν
σιωπήσονται ὑπ' εὐγνωμοσύνης· ἢν δὲ καὶ λέγωσί
τι, ὑπὸ φθόνου αὐτὸ δόξουσι δρᾶν. οἱ πολλοὶ δὲ
τὸ σχῆμα καὶ φωνὴν καὶ βάδισμα καὶ περίπατον
καὶ μέλος καὶ κρηπῖδα καὶ τὸ ἄττα σου ἐκεῖνο
τεθήπασι, καὶ τὸν ἱδρῶτα ὁρῶντες καὶ τὸ ἆσθμα
οὐκ ἔχουσιν ὅπως ἀπιστήσουσι μὴ οὐχὶ πάνδει-
νόν τινα ἐν τοῖς λόγοις ἀγωνιστὴν εἶναί σε.
ἄλλως τε καὶ τὸ ταχὺ τοῦτο οὐ μικρὰν ἔχει τὴν
ἀπολογίαν καὶ θαῦμα παρὰ τοῖς πολλοῖς· ὥστε
ὅρα μή ποτε γράψῃς ἢ σκεψάμενος παρέλθῃς,
ἔλεγχος γὰρ σαφὴς ταῦτά γε.

---

[1] That is to say, before the Flood.

and 'forsooth' be incessant, even if there is no need
of them; for they are ornamental even when uttered
at random.

"If ever it seems an opportune time to intone,
intone everything and turn it into song. And if
ever you are at a loss for matter to intone, say
'Gentlemen of the jury' in the proper tempo and
consider the music of your sentence complete. Cry
'Woe is me!' frequently; slap your thigh, bawl,
clear your throat while you are speaking, and stride
about swaying your hips. If they do not cry
'Hear!' be indignant and upbraid them; and if
they stand up, ready to go out in disgust, command
them to sit down: in short, carry the thing with a
high hand.

"That they may marvel at the fulness of your
speeches, begin with the story of Troy, or even with
the marriage of Deucalion and Pyrrha,[1] if you like,
and bring your account gradually down to date.
Few will see through you, and they, as a rule, will
hold their tongues out of good nature; if, however,
they do make any comment, it will be thought that
they are doing it out of spite. The rank and file
are already struck dumb with admiration of your
appearance, your diction, your gait, your pacing
back and forth, your intoning, your sandals, and
that 'sundry' of yours; and when they see your
sweat and your labouring breath they cannot fail to
believe that you are a terrible opponent in debates.
Besides, your extemporary readiness goes a long
way with the crowd to absolve your mistakes and
procure you admiration; so see to it that you never
write anything out or appear in public with a
prepared speech, for that is sure to show you up.

21 "Οἱ φίλοι δὲ ἀναπηδάτωσαν[1] ἀεὶ καὶ μισθὸν
τῶν δείπνων ἀποτινέτωσαν, εἴ ποτε αἴσθοιντό σε
καταπεσούμενον, χεῖρα ὀρέγοντες καὶ παρέχοντες
εὑρεῖν τὸ λεχθησόμενον ἐν τοῖς μεταξὺ τῶν
ἐπαίνων διαλείμμασι· καὶ γὰρ αὖ καὶ τοῦδε
μελέτω σοι τὸν χορὸν ἔχειν οἰκεῖον καὶ συνάδοντα.

"Ταῦτα μέν σοι τὰ ἐν τοῖς λόγοις. μετὰ ταῦτα
δὲ προϊόντα σε δορυφορείτωσαν ἐγκεκαλυμμένον
αὐτὸν καὶ περὶ ὧν ἔφης μεταξὺ διαλαμβάνοντα.
καὶ ἤν τις ἐντύχῃ, θαυμάσια περὶ σαυτοῦ λέγε
καὶ ὑπερεπαίνει καὶ ἐπαχθὴς γίγνου αὐτῷ. "τί
γὰρ ὁ Παιανιεὺς πρὸς ἐμέ"; καί, "Πρὸς ἕνα
ἴσως μοι τῶν παλαιῶν ὁ ἀγών·" καὶ τὰ τοιαῦτα.

22 "'Ὁ δὲ μέγιστον καὶ πρὸς τὸ εὐδοκιμεῖν ἀναγ-
καιότατον ὀλίγου δεῖν παρέλιπον, ἁπάντων κατα-
γέλα τῶν λεγόντων. καὶ ἤν μέν τις καλῶς εἴπῃ,
ἀλλότρια καὶ οὐχ ἑαυτοῦ δεικνύειν δοκείτω· ἤν
δὲ μετρίως ἐλεγχθῇ,[2] πάντα ἔστω ἐπιλήψιμα. καὶ
ἐν ταῖς ἀκροάσεσι μετὰ πάντας εἰσιέναι χρή,
ἐπίσημον γάρ· καὶ σιωπησάντων ἁπάντων ξένον
τινὰ ἔπαινον ἐπειπεῖν τὰς ἀκοὰς τῶν παρόντων
ἐπιστρέψοντα[3] καὶ ἐνοχλήσοντα, ὡς ναυτιᾶν
ἅπαντας ἐπὶ τῷ φορτικῷ τῶν ὀνομάτων καὶ

---

[1] ἀναπηδάτωσαν Sommerbrodt : πηδάτωσαν MSS.
[2] ἐλεγχθῇ A.M.H., ἐνεχθῇ MSS.
[3] ἐπιστρέψοντα Bekker : ἐπιστρέφοντα MSS.

---

[1] The word *chorus* here approaches the sense that it has in
Libanius, where it designates the different bands of scholars
attached to the various professors at Athens. So Aelian
(*Var. Hist.* 3, 19) says of Aristotle that he gathered about
him a chorus of pupils, and set upon Plato. Cf. Plato,
Prot. 315 B.

A PROFESSOR OF PUBLIC SPEAKING

"Let your friends spring to their feet constantly and pay you for their dinners by lending you a hand whenever they perceive that you are about to fall down, and giving you a chance to find what to say next in the intervals afforded by their applause. Of course you must make it your business to have a well-attuned chorus of your own.[1]

"There you have what concerns the speaking. Afterwards let them[2] dance attendance upon you as you go away with your head swathed in your mantle, reviewing what you have said. And if any one accosts you, make marvellous assertions about yourself, be extravagant in your self-praise, and make yourself a nuisance to him.[3] 'What was Demosthenes beside me?' 'Perhaps one of the ancients is in the running with me!' and that sort of thing.

"I almost omitted the thing that is most important and most needful for maintaining your reputation. Laugh at all the speakers. If anyone makes a fine speech, let it appear that he is parading something that belongs to someone else and is not his own; and if he is mildly criticized, let everything that he says be objectionable. At public lectures, go in after everybody else, for that makes you conspicuous; and when everybody is silent, let fall an uncouth expression of praise which will draw the attention of the company and so annoy them that they will all be disgusted at the vulgarity of your

---

[2] Not simply the friends, but the spectators also. See Lucian's *Zeuxis*.

[3] This is not the orator, but Lucian himself, breaking through the veil of irony and saying what he really thinks. See below.

ἐπιφράττεσθαι τὰ ὦτα. καὶ ἐπισείσῃς δὲ μὴ
πολλάκις τὴν χεῖρα, εὐτελὲς γάρ, μηδ᾽ ἀναστῇς,
πλὴν ἅπαξ γε ἢ δὶς τὸ πλεῖστον. ὑπομειδία δὲ
τὰ πολλὰ καὶ δῆλος γίγνου μὴ ἀρεσκόμενος τοῖς
λεγομένοις. ἀμφιλαφεῖς δὲ αἱ ἀφορμαὶ τῶν
μέμψεων τοῖς συκοφαντικοῖς τὰ ὦτα.

"Τὰ δ᾽ ἄλλα χρὴ θαρρεῖν· ἡ τόλμα γὰρ καὶ ἡ
ἀναισχυντία καὶ ψεῦδος πρόχειρον καὶ ὅρκος ἐπ᾽
ἄκροις ἀεὶ τοῖς χείλεσι καὶ φθόνος πρὸς ἅπαντας
καὶ μῖσος καὶ βλασφημία καὶ διαβολαὶ πιθαναί—
ταῦτά σε ἀοίδιμον ἐν βραχεῖ καὶ περίβλεπτον
ἀποφανεῖ.

23 "Τοιαῦτα μὲν τὰ φανερὰ καὶ τὰ ἔξω. ἰδίᾳ δὲ
πάντα πράγματα ποιεῖν σοι δεδόχθω, κυβεύειν
μεθύσκεσθαι λαγνεύειν μοιχεύειν, ἢ αὐχεῖν γε,
κἂν μὴ ποιῇς, καὶ πρὸς ἅπαντας λέγειν καὶ
γραμματεῖα ὑποδεικνύναι ὑπὸ γυναικῶν δῆθεν
γραφέντα. καλὸς γὰρ εἶναι θέλε καὶ σοὶ μελέτω
ὑπὸ τῶν γυναικῶν σπουδάζεσθαι δοκεῖν· εἰς τὴν
ῥητορικὴν γὰρ καὶ τοῦτο ἀνοίσουσιν οἱ πολλοί,
ὡς διὰ τοῦτό σου καὶ ἄχρι τῆς γυναικωνίτιδος
εὐδοκιμοῦντος. καὶ τὸ δεῖνα δέ, μὴ αἰδεσθῇς, εἰ
καὶ πρὸς ἀνδρῶν ἐπὶ τῷ ἑτέρῳ [1] ἐρᾶσθαι δοκοίης,
καὶ ταῦτα γενειήτης ἢ καὶ νὴ Δία φαλακρὸς ἤδη
ὤν. ἀλλ᾽ ἔστωσαν οἱ καὶ ἐπὶ τούτῳ συνόντες·
ἢν δὲ μὴ ὦσιν, οἰκέται ἱκανοί. πολλὰ γὰρ καὶ ἐκ
τοῦ τοιούτου πρὸς τὴν ῥητορικὴν χρήσιμα παρα-
γίγνεται· πλείων ἡ ἀναισχυντία καὶ θράσος.

[1] ἑταιρεῖν Bekker.

language and will stop their ears.[1] Do not make
frequent gestures of assent, for that is common,
and do not rise,[2] except once or at most twice. As
a rule, smile faintly, and make it evident that you
are not satisfied with what is being said. There
are plenty of opportunities for criticism if one has
captious ears.

"For the rest, you need have no fear. Effrontery
and shamelessness, a prompt lie, with an oath to
confirm it always on the edge of your lips, jealousy
and hatred of everyone, abuse and plausible slanders
—all this will make you famous and distinguished in
an instant.

"So much for your life in public and in the open.
In your private life, be resolved to do anything and
everything—to dice, to drink deep, to live high and
to keep mistresses, or at all events to boast of it
even if you do not do it, telling everyone about it
and showing notes that purport to be written by
women. You must aim to be elegant, you know,
and take pains to create the impression that women
are devoted to you. This also will be set down
to the credit of your rhetoric by the public, who
will infer from it that your fame extends even to the
women's quarters. And I say—do not be ashamed
to have the name of being an effeminate, even if you
are bearded or actually bald. There should be some
who hang about you on that account, but if there
are none, your slaves will answer. This helps your
rhetoric in many ways; it increases your shameless-

---

[1] Here again Lucian himself breaks through, and describes
what a fellow of this sort actually does. The man himself
would put it quite differently.

[2] A form of applause; cf. *Essays in Portraiture Defended*,
c. 4, at end.

ὁρᾷς ὡς λαλίστεραι αἱ γυναῖκες καὶ λοιδοροῦνται
περιττῶς καὶ ὑπὲρ τοὺς ἄνδρας ; εἰ δὴ τὰ ὅμοια
πάσχοις, καὶ ταῦτα διοίσεις τῶν ἄλλων. καὶ μὴν
καὶ πιττοῦσθαι χρή, μάλιστα μὲν τὰ πάντα, εἰ δὲ
μή, πάντως ἐκεῖνα. καὶ αὐτὸ δέ σοι τὸ στόμα πρὸς
ἅπαντα ὁμοίως κεχηνέτω, καὶ ἡ γλῶττα ὑπηρε-
τείτω καὶ πρὸς τοὺς λόγους καὶ πρὸς τὰ ἄλλα
ὁπόσα ἂν δύνηται. δύναται δὲ οὐ σολοικίζειν
μόνον καὶ βαρβαρίζειν οὐδὲ ληρεῖν ἢ ἐπιορκεῖν ἢ
λοιδορεῖσθαι ἢ διαβάλλειν καὶ ψεύδεσθαι, ἀλλὰ
καὶ νύκτωρ τι ἄλλο ὑποτελεῖν, καὶ μάλιστα ἢν
πρὸς οὕτω πολλοὺς τοὺς ἔρωτας μὴ διαρκέσῃς.
πάντα αὐτή γε ἐπιστάσθω καὶ γονιμωτέρα
γιγνέσθω καὶ μηδὲν ἀποστρεφέσθω.

24   "Ἢν ταῦτα, ὦ παῖ, καλῶς ἐκμάθῃς—δύνασαι δέ·
οὐδὲν γὰρ ἐν αὐτοῖς βαρύ—θαρρῶν ἐπαγγέλλομαι
οὐκ εἰς μακράν σε ἄριστον ῥήτορα καὶ ἡμῖν ὅμοιον
ἀποτελεσθήσεσθαι. τὸ μετὰ τοῦτο δὲ οὐκ ἐμὲ
χρὴ λέγειν, ὅσα ἐν βραχεῖ παρέσται σοι τὰ ἀγαθὰ
παρὰ τῆς Ῥητορικῆς. ὁρᾷς ἐμέ, ὃς πατρὸς μὲν
ἀφανοῦς καὶ οὐδὲ καθαρῶς ἐλευθέρου ἐγενόμην
ὑπὲρ Ξόϊν καὶ Θμοῦιν δεδουλευκότος, μητρὸς δὲ
ἀκεστρίας ἐπ' ἀμφοδίου τινός. αὐτὸς δὲ τὴν
ὥραν οὐ παντάπασιν ἀδόκιμος εἶναι δόξας τὸ μὲν
πρῶτον ἐπὶ ψιλῷ τῷ τρέφεσθαι συνῆν τινι
κακοδαίμονι καὶ γλίσχρῳ ἐραστῇ. ἐπεὶ δὲ τὴν

ness and effrontery. You observe that women are
more talkative, and that in calling names they are
extravagant and outstrip men. Well, if you imitate
them you will excel your rivals even there. Of
course you must use depilatories, preferably all
over, but if not, at least where most necessary.
And let your mouth be open for everything in-
differently; let your tongue serve you not only
in your speeches, but in any other way it can.
And it can not only solecize and barbarize, not only
twaddle and forswear, call names and slander and
lie—it can perform other services even at night,
especially if your love affairs are too numerous.
Yes, that must know everything, be lively, and balk
at nothing.

"If you thoroughly learn all this, my lad—and
you can, for there is nothing difficult about it—I
promise you confidently that right soon you will
turn out an excellent speaker, just like myself.
And there is no need for me to tell you what will
follow—all the blessings that will instantly accrue
to you from Rhetoric. You see my own case. My
father was an insignificant fellow without even a
clear title to his freedom, who had been a slave
above Xoïs and Thmuis,[1] and my mother was a
seamstress in the slums. For myself, as my personal
attractions were considered not wholly contemptible,
at first I lived with an ill-conditioned, stingy admirer
just for my keep. But then I detected the easi-

---

[1] Xois and Thmuis were towns in the Nile delta, the one
in the Sebennitic nome, the other to the eastward, capital of
the Thmuite nome. Lucian may mean simply "up-country
in the Delta"; but it is better, I think, to take his words
more literally as meaning "up-country in each of those two
nomes."

ὁδὸν ταύτην ῥάστην οὖσαν κατεῖδον καὶ διεκπαί-
σας ἐπὶ τῷ ἄκρῳ ἐγενόμην—ὑπῆρχε γάρ μοι, ὦ
φίλη Ἀδράστεια, πάντα ἐκεῖνα ἃ προεῖπον
ἐφόδια, τὸ θράσος, ἡ ἀμαθία, ἡ ἀναισχυντία—
πρῶτον μὲν οὐκέτι Ποθεινὸς ὀνομάζομαι, ἀλλ' ἤδη
τοῖς Διὸς καὶ Λήδας παισὶν ὁμώνυμος γεγένημαι.
ἔπειτα δὲ γραῒ συνοικήσας τὸ πρῶτον μὲν
ἐγαστριζόμην πρὸς αὐτῆς ἐρᾶν προσποιούμενος
γυναικὸς ἑβδομηκοντούτιδος τέτταρας ἔτι λοιποὺς
ὀδόντας ἐχούσης, χρυσίῳ καὶ τούτους ἐνδεδεμέ-
νους. πλὴν ἀλλά γε διὰ τὴν πενίαν ὑφιστάμην
τὸν ἆθλον καὶ τὰ ψυχρὰ ἐκεῖνα τὰ ἐκ τῆς σοροῦ
φιλήματα ὑπερήδιστά μοι ἐποίει ὁ λιμός. εἶτα
ὀλίγου δεῖν κληρονόμος ὧν εἶχεν ἁπάντων
κατέστην, εἰ μὴ κατάρατός τις οἰκέτης ἐμήνυσεν
25 ὡς φάρμακον εἴην ἐπ' αὐτὴν ἐωνημένος. ἐξωσθεὶς
δὲ ἐπὶ κεφαλὴν ὅμως οὐδὲ τότε ἠπόρησα τῶν
ἀναγκαίων, ἀλλὰ καὶ ῥήτωρ δοκῶ κἀν ταῖς δίκαις
ἐξετάζομαι προδιδοὺς τὰ πολλὰ καὶ τοὺς δικαστὰς
τοῖς ἀνοήτοις καθυπισχνούμενος, καὶ ἡττῶμαι
μὲν τὰ πλεῖστα, οἱ φοίνικες δὲ ἐπὶ τῇ θύρᾳ
χλωροὶ καὶ ἐστεφανωμένοι· τούτοις γὰρ ἐπὶ τοὺς
δυστυχεῖς χρῶμαι τοῖς δελέασιν. ἀλλὰ καὶ τὸ
μισεῖσθαι πρὸς ἁπάντων καὶ ἐπίσημον εἶναί με
ἐπὶ τῇ μοχθηρίᾳ τοῦ τρόπου καὶ πολὺ πρότερον
τῶν λόγων καὶ τὸ δείκνυσθαι τῷ δακτύλῳ τοῦτον ἐκεῖνον τὸν ἀκρότατον ἐν πάσῃ κακίᾳ λεγόμενον, οὐ μικρὸν εἶναι ἐμοί γε δοκεῖ.

---

[1] Desiderius, Désiré.
[2] Castor and Pollux. This passage is the corner-stone of
the argument that Pollux is the person at whom Lucian is
hitting.

ness of this road, galloped over it, and reached the summit; for I possessed (by thy grace, Fortune!) all that equipment which I have already mentioned—recklessness, ignorance, and shamelessness. And now, in the first place, my name is no longer Potheinus,[1] but I have become a namesake of the sons of Zeus and Leda.[2] Moreover, I went to live with an old woman and for a time got my victuals from her by pretending to love a hag of seventy with only four teeth still left, and those four fastened in with gold! However, on account of my poverty I managed to endure the ordeal, and hunger made even those frigid, graveyard kisses exceedingly sweet to me. Then I very nearly became heir to all her property, if only a plaguy slave had not blabbed that I had bought poison for her. I was bundled out neck and crop, yet even then I was not at a loss for the necessaries of life. No, I enjoy the name of a speaker, and prove myself such in the courts, generally playing false to my clients, although I promise the poor fools to deliver their juries to them.[3] To be sure I am generally unsuccessful, but the palm-leaves at my door are green and twined with fillets, for I use them as bait for my victims.[4] But even to be detested by everyone, to be notorious for the badness of my character and the still greater badness of my speeches, to be pointed out with the finger—'There he is, the man who, they say, is foremost in all iniquity!'—seems to me no slight achievement.

[3] He is an accomplished *praevaricator*, not only selling out to the other side, but extracting money from his own clients under pretext of bribing the jury.

[4] For palm-branches as a token of success at the bar, see Juvenal 7, 118, and Mayor's note.

"Ταῦτά σοι παραινῶ, νὴ τὴν πάνδημον, πολὺ
πρότερον ἐμαυτῷ παραινέσας καὶ χάριν ἐμαυτῷ
οὐ μικρὰν ἐπιστάμενος."

26 Εἶεν· ὁ μὲν γεννάδας εἰπὼν ταῦτα πεπαύσεται·
σὺ δὲ ἢν πεισθῇς τοῖς εἰρημένοις, καὶ δὴ παρεῖναι
νόμιζε οἷπερ ἐξ ἀρχῆς ἐπόθεις ἐλθεῖν, καὶ οὐδέν
σε κωλύσει ἑπόμενον τοῖς νόμοις ἔν τε τοῖς
δικαστηρίοις κρατεῖν καὶ ἐν τοῖς πλήθεσιν
εὐδοκιμεῖν καὶ ἐπέραστον εἶναι καὶ γαμεῖν οὐ
γραῦν τινα τῶν κωμικῶν, καθάπερ ὁ νομοθέτης
καὶ διδάσκαλος, ἀλλὰ καλλίστην γυναῖκα τὴν
Ῥητορικήν, ὡς τὸ τοῦ Πλάτωνος ἐκεῖνο πτηνὸν
ἅρμα ἐλαύνοντα φέρεσθαι σοὶ μᾶλλον πρέπειν
περὶ σεαυτοῦ εἰπεῖν ἢ ἐκείνῳ περὶ τοῦ Διός· ἐγὼ
δὲ—ἀγεννὴς γὰρ καὶ δειλός εἰμι—ἐκστήσομαι τῆς
ὁδοῦ ὑμῖν καὶ παύσομαι τῇ Ῥητορικῇ ἐπιπολάζων,
ἀσύμβολος ὢν πρὸς αὐτὴν τὰ ὑμέτερα· μᾶλλον
δὲ ἤδη πέπαυμαι, ὥστε ἀκονιτὶ ἀνακηρύττεσθε
καὶ θαυμάζεσθε, μόνον τοῦτο μεμνημένοι, ὅτι μὴ
τῷ τάχει ἡμῶν κεκρατήκατε ὠκύτεροι φανέντες,
ἀλλὰ τῷ ῥᾴστην καὶ πρανῆ τραπέσθαι τὴν ὁδόν.

---

[1] Plato, *Phaedrus*, 246 E.

A PROFESSOR OF PUBLIC SPEAKING

"This is the advice which I bestow upon you. By Our Lady of the Stews, I bestowed it upon myself long ago, and am deeply grateful to myself for it."

Well, the gentleman will end his remarks with that, and then it is up to you. If you heed what he has said, you may consider that even now you are where in the beginning you yearned to be; and nothing can hinder you, as long as you follow his rules, from holding the mastery in the courts, enjoying high favour with the public, being attractive, and marrying, not an old woman out of a comedy, as did your law-giver and tutor, but Rhetoric, fairest of brides. Consequently, Plato's famous phrase about driving full-tilt in a winged car can be applied by you to yourself with a better grace than by him to Zeus.[1] As for me, I am spiritless and faint-hearted, so I will get out of the road for you, and stop trifling with Rhetoric, being unable to recommend myself to her by qualifications like those of yourself and your friend. Indeed, I have stopped already; so get the herald to proclaim an uncontested victory and take your tribute of admiration, remembering only this, that it is not by your speed that you have defeated us, through proving yourself more swift of foot than we, but because you took the road that was easy and downhill.

ALEXANDER THE FALSE PROPHET

An account of the false priest of Asclepius, Alexander of Abonoteichus. It has been discussed in detail by Cumont in the *Mémoires couronnées de l'académie de Belgique*, vol. xl (1887).

Although Alexander achieved honour not only in his own country, a small city in remote Paphlagonia, but over a large part of the Roman world, almost nothing is known of him except from the pages of Lucian. Gems, coins, and inscriptions corroborate Lucian as far as they go, testifying to Alexander's actual existence and widespread influence, and commemorating the name and even the appearance of Glycon, his human-headed serpent. But were it not for Lucian, we should not understand their full significance.

Alexander's religious activity covered roughly the years A.D. 150–170. The cult which he established outlasted him for at least a century. It was highly unusual in its character, as Cumont observes. Sacred snakes were a regular feature of sanctuaries of Asclepius ; but to give a serpent a human head and style it the god incarnate was a distinct innovation. Moreover, the proper function of Asclepius was to heal the sick, who passed the night in his temple, expecting either to be cured while they slept or to have some form of treatment suggested to them in their dreams. But at Abonoteichus we hear nothing of incubation, and only incidentally of healing ; the "new Asclepius" deals in oracles like Apollo, and gives advice on any subject. This, together with Alexander's extravagant claims of divine descent, confirms Lucian in his appraisal of him as an out-and-out charlatan, aiming to play upon the gross credulity of the times and to secure the greatest gain with the least effort.

Lucian was in a position to know a good deal about Alexander, and clearly believes all that he says. Without doubt his account is essentially accurate, but it need not be credited absolutely to the letter. Lucian was no historian at best, and he was angry. In the account of his relations with Alexander he reveals his own personality more clearly than usual, but not in a pleasant light.

The piece was written at the request of a friend, after A.D. 180, when Alexander had been in his grave for ten years.

ΑΛΕΞΑΝΔΡΟΣ Η ΨΕΥΔΟΜΑΝΤΙΣ

1 Σὺ μὲν ἴσως, ὦ φίλτατε Κέλσε, μικρόν τι καὶ
φαῦλον οἴει τὸ πρόσταγμα, προστάττειν τὸν
᾿Αλεξάνδρου σοι τοῦ ᾿Αβωνοτειχίτου γόητος βίον
καὶ ἐπινοίας αὐτοῦ καὶ τολμήματα καὶ μαγγανείας
εἰς βιβλίον ἐγγράψαντα πέμψαι· τὸ δέ, εἴ τις
ἐθέλοι πρὸς τὸ ἀκριβὲς ἕκαστον ἐπεξιέναι, οὐ
μεῖόν ἐστιν ἢ τὰς ᾿Αλεξάνδρου τοῦ Φιλίππου
πράξεις ἀναγράψαι· τοσοῦτος εἰς κακίαν οὗτος,
ὅσος εἰς ἀρετὴν ἐκεῖνος. ὅμως δὲ εἰ μετὰ
συγγνώμης ἀναγνώσεσθαι μέλλοις καὶ τὰ ἐνδέοντα
τοῖς ἱστορουμένοις προσλογιεῖσθαι, ὑποστήσομαί
σοι τὸν ἆθλον, καὶ τὴν Αὐγέου βουστασίαν, εἰ
καὶ μὴ πᾶσαν, ἀλλ᾿ εἰς δύναμίν γε τὴν ἐμαυτοῦ
ἀνακαθάρασθαι πειράσομαι, ὀλίγους ὅσους τῶν
κοφίνων ἐκφορήσας, ὡς ἀπ᾿ ἐκείνων τεκμαίροιο
πόση πᾶσα καὶ ὡς ἀμύθητος ἦν ἡ κόπρος ἦν

Available in photographs: Γ, UPN. (Γ lost as far as
τινος ἄλλου, c. 18 fin. Beginning supplied by late hand g).

[1] The scholiast thinks this Celsus the writer of the *True
Word*, an attack upon Christianity, to which Origen replied
in his eight books *contra Celsum*. He is certainly identical
with the man whom Origen himself believed to be the author
of that work, who, he says, was an Epicurean living under
Hadrian and the Antonines, author also of a treatise against

ALEXANDER THE FALSE PROPHET

No doubt, my dear Celsus,[1] you think it a slight
and trivial matter to bid me set down in a book and
send you the history of Alexander, the impostor of
Abonoteichus, including all his clever schemes, bold
emprises, and sleights of hand; but in point of fact,
if one should aim to examine each detail closely, it
would be no less a task than to record the exploits
of Philip's son Alexander. The one was as great in
villainy as the other in heroism. Nevertheless, if
it should be your intention to overlook faults as you
read, and to fill out for yourself the gaps in my tale,
I will undertake the task for you and will essay to
clean up that Augean stable, if not wholly, yet to
the extent of my ability, fetching out some few
basketsful, so that from them you may judge how
great, how inexpressible, was the entire quantity

sorcery (*vide* c. 21 and note). And the *True Word* itself, a
large part of which is preserved in Origen, seems to have
been written about A.D. 180. But as Origen is not sure who
wrote it, and as it is considered Platonic rather than Epicurean in character, the prevailing opinion is that its author
is not the Celsus of Lucian, but an otherwise unknown
Platonist of the same name and date.

τρισχίλιοι βόες ἐν πολλοῖς ἔτεσιν ποιῆσαι
ἐδύναντο.

2 Αἰδοῦμαι μὲν οὖν ὑπὲρ ἀμφοῖν, ὑπέρ τε σοῦ
καὶ ἐμαυτοῦ· σοῦ μέν, ἀξιοῦντος μνήμῃ καὶ γραφῇ
παραδοθῆναι ἄνδρα τρισκατάρατον, ἐμαυτοῦ δέ,
σπουδὴν ποιουμένου ἐπὶ τοιαύτῃ ἱστορίᾳ καὶ
πράξεσιν ἀνθρώπου, ὃν οὐκ ἀναγιγνώσκεσθαι
πρὸς τῶν πεπαιδευμένων ἦν ἄξιον, ἀλλ' ἐν
πανδήμῳ τινὶ μεγίστῳ θεάτρῳ ὁρᾶσθαι ὑπὸ
πιθήκων ἢ ἀλωπέκων σπαραττόμενον. ἀλλ' ἤν
τις ἡμῖν ταύτην ἐπιφέρῃ τὴν αἰτίαν, ἕξομεν καὶ
αὐτοὶ εἰς παράδειγμά τι τοιοῦτον ἀνενεγκεῖν. καὶ
Ἀρριανὸς γὰρ ὁ τοῦ Ἐπικτήτου μαθητής, ἀνὴρ
Ῥωμαίων ἐν τοῖς πρώτοις καὶ παιδείᾳ παρ' ὅλον
τὸν βίον συγγενόμενος, ὅμοιόν τι παθὼν ἀπο-
λογήσαιτ' ἂν καὶ ὑπὲρ ἡμῶν· Τιλλορόβου[1] γοῦν
τοῦ λῃστοῦ κἀκεῖνος βίον ἀναγράψαι ἠξίωσεν.
ἡμεῖς δὲ πολὺ ὠμοτέρου λῃστοῦ μνήμην ποιησόμεθα, ὅσῳ μὴ ἐν ὕλαις καὶ ἐν ὄρεσιν, ἀλλ' ἐν
πόλεσιν οὗτος ἐλῄστευεν, οὐ Μυσίαν[2] μόνην
οὐδὲ τὴν Ἴδην κατατρέχων οὐδὲ ὀλίγα τῆς Ἀσίας
μέρη τὰ ἐρημότερα λεηλατῶν, ἀλλὰ πᾶσαν ὡς
εἰπεῖν τὴν Ῥωμαίων ἀρχὴν ἐμπλήσας τῆς
λῃστείας τῆς αὑτοῦ.

3 Πρότερον δέ σοι αὐτὸν ὑπογράψω τῷ λόγῳ
πρὸς τὸ ὁμοιότατον εἰκάσας, ὡς ἂν δύνωμαι,
καίτοι μὴ πάνυ γραφικός τις ὤν. τὸ γὰρ δὴ
σῶμα, ἵνα σοι καὶ τοῦτο δείξω, μέγας τε ἦν καὶ
καλὸς ἰδεῖν καὶ θεοπρεπὴς ὡς ἀληθῶς, λευκὸς
τὴν χρόαν, τὸ γένειον οὐ πάνυ λάσιος, κόμην τὴν

---

[1] Τιλλιβόρου γ.
[2] Μυσίαν Palmerius : Μινύαν MSS.

of filth that three thousand head of cattle were able to create in many years.

I blush for both of us, I confess, both for you and for myself—for you because you want a consummate rascal perpetuated in memory and in writing, and for myself because I am devoting my energy to such an end, to the exploits of a man who does not deserve to have polite people read about him, but rather to have the motley crowd in a vast amphitheatre see him being torn to pieces by foxes or apes. Yet if anyone brings this reproach against us, we shall be able to refer to an apt precedent. Arrian, the disciple of Epictetus, a Roman of the highest distinction, and a life-long devotee of letters, laid himself open to the same charge, and so can plead our cause as well as his own ; he thought fit, you know, to record the life of Tillorobus, the brigand.[1] In our own case, however, we shall commemorate a far more savage brigand, since our hero plied his trade not in forests and mountains, but in cities, and instead of infesting just Mysia and Mount Ida and harrying a few of the more deserted districts of Asia, he filled the whole Roman Empire, I may say, with his brigandage.

First I shall draw you a word-picture of the man himself, making as close a likeness as I can, although I am not particularly good at drawing. As regards his person—in order that I may exhibit this also to you—he was tall and handsome in appearance, and really godlike ; his skin was fair, his beard not very

---

[1] There is no life of Tillorobus among the extant writings of Arrian, and we know nothing of him from any other source. His name is given in the γ group of MSS. as Tilliborus, but compare C.I.L. vi, 15295.

μὲν ἰδίαν, τὴν δὲ καὶ πρόσθετον ἐπικείμενος εὖ
μάλα εἰκασμένην καὶ τοὺς πολλοὺς ὅτι ἦν
ἀλλοτρία λεληθυῖαν· ὀφθαλμοὶ πολὺ τὸ γοργὸν
καὶ ἔνθεον διεμφαίνοντες, φώνημα ἥδιστόν τε ἅμα
καὶ λαμπρότατον· καὶ ὅλως οὐδαμόθεν μεμπτὸς
ἦν ταῦτά γε.

4   Τοιόσδε μὲν τὴν μορφήν· ἡ ψυχὴ δὲ καὶ ἡ
γνώμη—ἀλεξίκακε Ἡράκλεις καὶ Ζεῦ ἀποτρόπαιε
καὶ Διόσκουροι σωτῆρες, πολεμίοις καὶ ἐχθροῖς
ἐντυχεῖν γένοιτο καὶ[1] συγγενέσθαι τοιούτῳ τινί.
συνέσει μὲν γὰρ καὶ ἀγχινοίᾳ καὶ δριμύτητι
πάμπολυ τῶν ἄλλων διέφερεν, καὶ τό τε περίεργον
καὶ εὐμαθὲς καὶ μνημονικὸν καὶ πρὸς τὰ μαθήματα εὐφυές, πάντα ταῦτα εἰς ὑπερβολὴν
ἑκασταχοῦ ὑπῆρχεν αὐτῷ. ἐχρῆτο δὲ αὐτοῖς εἰς
τὸ χείριστον, καὶ ὄργανα ταῦτα γενναῖα ὑπο-
βεβλημένα ἔχων αὐτίκα μάλα τῶν ἐπὶ κακίᾳ
διαβοήτων ἀκρότατος ἀπετελέσθη, ὑπὲρ τοὺς
Κέρκωπας, ὑπὲρ τὸν Εὐρύβατον ἢ Φρυνώνδαν ἢ
Ἀριστόδημον ἢ Σώστρατον. αὐτὸς μὲν γὰρ τῷ
γαμβρῷ Ῥουτιλιανῷ ποτε γράφων καὶ τὰ
μετριώτατα ὑπὲρ αὑτοῦ λέγων Πυθαγόρᾳ ὅμοιος
εἶναι ἠξίου. ἀλλ᾽ ἵλεως μὲν ὁ Πυθαγόρας εἴη,
σοφὸς ἀνὴρ καὶ τὴν γνώμην θεσπέσιος, εἰ δὲ κατὰ
τοῦτον ἐγεγένητο, παῖς ἂν εὖ οἶδ᾽ ὅτι πρὸς αὐτὸν
εἶναι ἔδοξε. καὶ πρὸς Χαρίτων μή με νομίσῃς
ἐφ᾽ ὕβρει ταῦτα τοῦ Πυθαγόρου λέγειν ἢ

---

[1] καὶ Sakkoraphos : καὶ μὴ MSS.

---

[1] The Cercopes were two impish pests who crossed the
path of Heracles to their disadvantage.   For the little that
is known about the other typical rascals, see the Index.

thick; his long hair was in part natural, in part false, but very similar, so that most people did not detect that it was not his own. His eyes shone with a great glow of fervour and enthusiasm; his voice was at once very sweet and very clear; and in a word, no fault could be found with him in any respect as far as all that went.

Such, then, was his outward appearance; but his soul and his mind—O Heracles Forfender! O Zeus, Averter of Mischief! O Twin Brethren, our Saviours! may it be the fortune of our enemies and ill-wishers to encounter and have to do with the like of him! In understanding, quick-wittedness, and penetration he was far beyond everyone else; and activity of mind, readiness to learn, retentiveness, natural apti-tude for studies—all these qualities were his, in every case to the full. But he made the worst possible use of them, and with these noble instruments at his service soon became the most perfect rascal of all those who have been notorious far and wide for villainy, sur-passing the Cercopes, surpassing Eurybatus, or Phry-nondas, or Aristodemus, or Sostratus.[1] He himself, writing to his son-in-law Rutilianus once upon a time and speaking of himself with the greatest reserve, claimed to be like Pythagoras; but—with all due respect to Pythagoras, a wise man of more than human intelligence—if he had been this man's contemporary, he would have seemed a child, I am very sure, beside him![2] In the name of the Graces, do not imagine that I say this to insult Pythagoras, or in the endeavour to bring

---

[2] Yet Pythagoras was no mean thaumaturge; see Plutarch, *Numa*, 65.

συνάπτειν πειρώμενον αὐτοὺς πρὸς ὁμοιότητα
τῶν πράξεων· ἀλλ' εἴ τις τὰ χείριστα καὶ
βλασφημότατα τῶν ἐπὶ διαβολῇ περὶ τοῦ
Πυθαγόρου λεγομένων, οἷς ἔγωγε οὐκ ἂν πεισθείην
ὡς ἀληθέσιν οὖσιν, ὅμως συναγάγοι εἰς τὸ αὐτό,
πολλοστὸν ἂν μέρος ἅπαντα ἐκεῖνα γένοιτο τῆς
Ἀλεξάνδρου δεινότητος. ὅλως γὰρ ἐπινόησόν
μοι καὶ τῷ λογισμῷ διατύπωσον ποικιλωτάτην
τινὰ ψυχῆς κρᾶσιν ἐκ ψεύδους καὶ δόλων καὶ
ἐπιορκιῶν καὶ κακοτεχνιῶν συγκειμένην, ῥᾳδίαν,
τολμηράν, παράβολον, φιλόπονον ἐξεργάσασθαι
τὰ νοηθέντα, καὶ πιθανὴν καὶ ἀξιόπιστον καὶ
ὑποκριτικὴν τοῦ βελτίονος καὶ τῷ ἐναντιωτάτῳ
τῆς βουλήσεως ἐοικυῖαν. οὐδεὶς γοῦν τὸ πρῶτον
ἐντυχὼν οὐκ ἀπῆλθε δόξαν λαβὼν ὑπὲρ αὐτοῦ
ὡς εἴη πάντων ἀνθρώπων χρηστότατος καὶ
ἐπιεικέστατος καὶ προσέτι ἁπλοϊκώτατός τε καὶ
ἀφελέστατος. ἐπὶ πᾶσι δὲ τούτοις τὸ μεγαλουργὸν
προσῆν καὶ τὸ μηδὲν μικρὸν ἐπινοεῖν, ἀλλ' ἀεὶ
τοῖς μεγίστοις ἐπέχειν τὸν νοῦν.

5   Μειράκιον μὲν οὖν ἔτι ὢν πάνυ ὡραῖον, ὡς ἐνῆν
ἀπὸ τῆς καλάμης τεκμαίρεσθαι καὶ ἀκούειν τῶν
διηγουμένων, ἀνέδην ἐπόρνευε καὶ συνῆν ἐπὶ
μισθῷ τοῖς δεομένοις. ἐν δὲ τοῖς ἄλλοις λαμβάνει
τις αὐτὸν ἐραστὴς γόης τῶν μαγείας καὶ ἐπῳδὰς
θεσπεσίους ὑπισχνουμένων καὶ χάριτας ἐπὶ τοῖς
ἐρωτικοῖς καὶ ἐπαγωγὰς τοῖς ἐχθροῖς καὶ θησαυρῶν
ἀναπομπὰς καὶ κλήρων διαδοχάς. οὗτος ἰδὼν
εὐφυᾶ παῖδα καὶ πρὸς ὑπηρεσίαν τῶν ἑαυτοῦ
πράξεων ἑτοιμότατον, οὐ μεῖον ἐρῶντα τῆς κακίας

180

them into connection with one another by likening their doings. On the contrary, if all that is worst and most opprobrious in what is said of Pythagoras to discredit him (which I for my part cannot believe to be true) should nevertheless be brought together for comparison, the whole of it would be but an infinitesimal part of Alexander's knavery. In sum, imagine, please, and mentally configure a highly diversified soul-blend, made up of lying, trickery, perjury, and malice; facile, audacious, venturesome, diligent in the execution of its schemes, plausible, convincing, masking as good, and wearing an appearance absolutely opposite to its purpose. Indeed, there is nobody who, after meeting him for the first time, did not come away with the idea that he was the most honest and upright man in the world—yes, and the most simple and unaffected. And on top of all this, he had the quality of magnificence, of forming no petty designs but always keeping his mind upon the most important objects.

While he was still a mere boy, and a very handsome one, as could be inferred from the sere and yellow leaf of him, and could also be learned by hearsay from those who recounted his story, he trafficked freely in his attractiveness and sold his company to those who sought it. Among others, he had an admirer who was a quack, one of those who advertise enchantments, miraculous incantations, charms for your love-affairs, "sendings"[1] for your enemies, disclosures of buried treasure, and successions to estates. As this man saw that he was an apt lad, more than ready to assist him in his affairs, and

---

[1] The word is borrowed from Kipling. A "sending" is a "visitation," seen from a different point of view.

τῆς αὐτοῦ ἢ αὐτὸς τῆς ὥρας τῆς ἐκείνου,
ἐξεπαίδευσέ τε αὐτὸν καὶ διετέλει ὑπουργῷ καὶ
ὑπηρέτῃ καὶ διακόνῳ χρώμενος. ὁ δ' αὐτὸς
ἐκεῖνος δημοσίᾳ μὲν ἰατρὸς δῆθεν ἦν, ἠπίστατο δὲ
κατὰ τὴν Θῶνος τοῦ Αἰγυπτίου γυναῖκα

φάρμακα πολλὰ μὲν ἐσθλὰ μεμιγμένα, πολλὰ
δὲ λυγρά·

ὧν ἁπάντων κληρονόμος καὶ διάδοχος οὗτος
ἐγένετο. ἦν δὲ ὁ διδάσκαλος ἐκεῖνος καὶ ἐραστὴς
τὸ γένος Τυανεύς, τῶν Ἀπολλωνίῳ τῷ πάνυ[1]
συγγενομένων καὶ τὴν πᾶσαν αὐτοῦ τραγῳδίαν
εἰδότων. ὁρᾷς ἐξ οἵας σοι διατριβῆς ἄνθρωπον
λέγω.

6   Ἤδη δὲ πώγωνος ὁ Ἀλέξανδρος πιμπλάμενος
καὶ τοῦ Τυανέως ἐκείνου ἀποθανόντος ἐν ἀπορίᾳ
καθεστώς, ἀπηνθηκυίας ἅμα τῆς ὥρας, ἀφ' ἧς
τρέφεσθαι ἐδύνατο, οὐκέτι μικρὸν οὐδὲν ἐπενόει,
ἀλλὰ κοινωνήσας Βυζαντίῳ τινὶ χορογράφῳ τῶν
καθιέντων εἰς τοὺς ἀγῶνας, πολὺ καταρατοτέρῳ
τὴν φύσιν—Κοκκωνᾶς δέ, οἶμαι, ἐπεκαλεῖτο—
περιῄεσαν γοητεύοντες καὶ μαγγανεύοντες καὶ
τοὺς παχεῖς τῶν ἀνθρώπων—οὕτως γὰρ αὐτοὶ τῇ
πατρίῳ τῶν μάγων φωνῇ τοὺς πολλοὺς[2] ὀνομά-
ζουσιν—ἀποκείροντες. ἐν δὴ τούτοις καὶ Μακέτιν
γυναῖκα πλουσίαν, ἔξωρον μέν, ἐράσμιον δὲ ἔτι
εἶναι βουλομένην, ἐξευρόντες ἐπεσιτίσαντό τε τὰ
ἀρκοῦντα παρ' αὐτῆς καὶ ἠκολούθησαν ἐκ τῆς
Βιθυνίας εἰς τὴν Μακεδονίαν. Πελλαία δὲ ἦν

---

[1] τῷ πάνυ Fritzsche : τῷ Τυανεῖ πάνυ γ ; τῷ Τυανεῖ β.
[2] τοὺς πλουσίους g, editors since Bekker. But cf. 9
παχέων καὶ ἠλιθίων, 17 παχέσι καὶ ἀπαιδεύτοις.

that the boy was quite as much enamoured with his roguery as he with the boy's beauty, he gave him a thorough education and constantly made use of him as helper, servant, and acolyte. He himself was professedly a public physician, but, as Homer says of the wife of Thon, the Egyptian, he knew

" Many a drug that was good in a compound, and
      many a bad one," [1]

all of which Alexander inherited and took over. This teacher and admirer of his was a man of Tyana by birth, one of those who had been followers of the notorious Apollonius, and who knew his whole bag of tricks. You see what sort of school the man that I am describing comes from !

Alexander was just getting his beard when the death of the Tyanean put him in a bad way, since it coincided with the passing of his beauty, by which he might have supported himself. So he abandoned petty projects for ever. He formed a partnership with a Byzantine writer of choral songs, one of those who enter the public competitions, far more abominable than himself by nature—Cocconas,[2] I think, was his nickname,—and they went about the country practising quackery and sorcery, and " trimming the fatheads "—for so they style the public in the traditional patter of magicians. Well, among these they hit upon a rich Macedonian woman, past her prime but still eager to be charming, and not only lined their purses fairly well at her expense, but went with her from Bithynia to Macedon. She

---

[1] *Odyssey* 4, 230.
[2] Cocconas comes from κόκκων (modern Greek κουκουνάρι), pine-kernel, seed, nut. Cf. *Anth. Pal.* 12, 222.

ἐκείνη, πάλαι μὲν εὐδαίμονος χωρίου κατὰ τοὺς
τῶν Μακεδόνων βασιλέας, νῦν δὲ ταπεινοῦ[1] καὶ
7 ὀλιγίστους οἰκήτορας ἔχοντος. ἐνταῦθα ἰδόντες
δράκοντας παμμεγέθεις, ἡμέρους πάνυ καὶ
τιθασούς, ὡς καὶ ὑπὸ γυναικῶν τρέφεσθαι καὶ
παιδίοις συγκαθεύδειν καὶ πατουμένους ἀνέχεσθαι
καὶ θλιβομένους μὴ ἀγανακτεῖν καὶ γάλα πίνειν
ἀπὸ θηλῆς κατὰ ταὐτὰ τοῖς βρέφεσι—πολλοὶ δὲ
γίγνονται παρ' αὐτοῖς τοιοῦτοι, ὅθεν καὶ τὸν περὶ
τῆς Ὀλυμπιάδος μῦθον διαφοιτῆσαι πάλαι εἰκός,
ὁπότε ἐκύει τὸν Ἀλέξανδρον, δράκοντός τινος,
οἶμαι, τοιούτου συγκαθεύδοντος αὐτῇ—ὠνοῦνται
8 τῶν ἑρπετῶν ἓν κάλλιστον ὀλίγων ὀβολῶν. καὶ
κατὰ τὸν Θουκυδίδην ἄρχεται ὁ πόλεμος ἐνθένδε
ἤδη.

Ὡς γὰρ ἂν δύο κάκιστοι καὶ μεγαλότολμοι καὶ
πρὸς τὸ κακουργεῖν προχειρότατοι εἰς τὸ αὐτὸ
συνελθόντες, ῥᾳδίως κατενόησαν τὸν τῶν ἀνθρώπων
βίον ὑπὸ δυοῖν τούτοιν μεγίστοιν τυραννούμενον,
ἐλπίδος καὶ φόβου, καὶ ὅτι ὁ τούτων ἑκατέρῳ εἰς
δέον χρήσασθαι δυνάμενος τάχιστα πλουτήσειεν
ἄν· ἀμφοτέροις γάρ, τῷ τε δεδιότι καὶ τῷ
ἐλπίζοντι, ἑώρων τὴν πρόγνωσιν ἀναγκαιοτάτην
τε καὶ ποθεινοτάτην οὖσαν, καὶ Δελφοὺς οὕτω
πάλαι πλουτῆσαι καὶ ἀοιδίμους γενέσθαι καὶ
Δῆλον καὶ Κλάρον καὶ Βραγχίδας, τῶν ἀνθρώπων
ἀεὶ δι' οὓς προεῖπον τυράννους, τὴν ἐλπίδα καὶ
τὸν φόβον, φοιτώντων εἰς τὰ ἱερὰ καὶ προμαθεῖν
τὰ μέλλοντα δεομένων, καὶ δι' αὐτὸ ἑκατόμβας
θυόντων καὶ χρυσᾶς πλίνθους ἀνατιθέντων.
ταῦτα πρὸς ἀλλήλους στρέφοντες καὶ κυκῶντες

came from Pella, a place once flourishing in the time of the kings of Macedon but now insignificant, with very few inhabitants. There they saw great serpents, quite tame and gentle, so that they were kept by women, slept with children, let themselves be stepped upon, were not angry when they were stroked, and took milk from the breast just like babies. There are many such in the country, and that, probably, is what gave currency in former days to the story about Olympias; no doubt a serpent of that sort slept with her when she was carrying Alexander.[1] So they bought one of the reptiles, the finest, for a few coppers; and, in the words of Thucydides: "Here beginneth the war!"[2]

As you might have expected of two consummate rascals, greatly daring, fully prepared for mischief, who had put their heads together, they readily discerned that human life is swayed by two great tyrants, hope and fear, and that a man who could use both of these to advantage would speedily enrich himself. For they perceived that both to one who fears and to one who hopes, foreknowledge is very essential and very keenly coveted, and that long ago not only Delphi, but Delos and Clarus and Branchidae, had become rich and famous because, thanks to the tyrants just mentioned, hope and fear, men continually visited their sanctuaries and sought to learn the future in advance, and to that end sacrificed hecatombs and dedicated ingots of gold. By turning all this round and round in conference with one

[1] The story was that Alexander was the son of Zeus, who had visited Olympias in the form of a serpent.
[2] Thucydides ii, 1.

---

[1] ταπεινοῦ Bekker: ταπεινοὺς MSS.

μαντεῖον συστήσασθαι καὶ χρηστήριον ἐβου-
λεύοντο· εἰ γὰρ τοῦτο προχωρήσειεν αὐτοῖς,
αὐτίκα πλούσιοί τε καὶ εὐδαίμονες ἔσεσθαι ἤλπι-
ζον—ὅπερ ἐπὶ μεῖζον ἢ κατὰ τὴν πρώτην
προσδοκίαν ἀπήντησεν αὐτοῖς καὶ κρεῖττον
διεφάνη τῆς ἐλπίδος.

9   Τοὐντεῦθεν τὴν σκέψιν ἐποιοῦντο, πρῶτον μὲν
περὶ τοῦ χωρίου, δεύτερον δὲ ἥτις ἡ ἀρχὴ καὶ ὁ
τρόπος ἂν γένοιτο τῆς ἐπιχειρήσεως. ὁ μὲν οὖν
Κοκκωνᾶς τὴν Καλχηδόνα ἐδοκίμαζεν ἐπιτήδειον
εἶναι καὶ εὔκαιρον χωρίον,[1] τῇ τε Θρᾴκῃ καὶ τῇ
Βιθυνίᾳ πρόσοικον, οὐχ ἑκὰς οὐδὲ τῆς Ἀσίας καὶ
Γαλατίας καὶ τῶν ὑπερκειμένων ἐθνῶν ἁπάντων·
ὁ δὲ Ἀλέξανδρος ἔμπαλιν τὰ οἴκοι προὔκρινεν,
λέγων ὅπερ ἀληθὲς ἦν, πρὸς τὴν τῶν τοιούτων
ἀρχὴν καὶ ἐπιχείρησιν ἀνθρώπων δεῖν παχέων
καὶ ἠλιθίων τῶν ὑποδεξομένων, οἵους τοὺς Παφλα-
γόνας εἶναι ἔφασκεν ὑπεροικοῦντας τὸ τοῦ Ἀβώνου
τεῖχος, δεισιδαίμονας τοὺς πολλοὺς καὶ πλουσίους,
καὶ μόνον εἰ φανείη τις αὐλητὴν ἢ τυμπανιστὴν
ἢ κυμβάλοις κροτοῦντα ἐπαγόμενος, κοσκίνῳ τὸ
τοῦ λόγου μαντευόμενος, αὐτίκα μάλα πάντας

---

[1] καὶ εὔκαιρον χωρίον A.M.H. : καὶ ἐμπόρων χωρίον MSS.
ὡς ἐμπόρων χωρίον Schaefer. Cf. *Jup. Trag.* 14; εὔκαιρον γ,
εὔπορον β ; and for the use of the word in connection with
places, Polybius 1, 18, 4 ; 4, 38, 1 ; 4, 44, 1.

---

[1] Asia here and elsewhere in this piece refers to the Roman
province of Asia—western Asia Minor.
[2] Proverbial for cheap trickery. Artemidorus (*Dream-book*
1, 69) says that " if you dream of Pythagoreans, physiogno-
monics, astragalomants, tyromants, gyromants, *coscinomants*,
morphoscopes, chiroscopes, lecanomants, or necyomants, you
must consider all that they say false and unreliable ; for

another and keeping it astir, they concocted the project of founding a prophetic shrine and oracle, hoping that if they should succeed in it, they would at once be rich and prosperous—which, in fact, befell them in greater measure than they at first expected, and turned out better than they hoped.

Then they began planning, first about the place, and next, what should be the commencement and the character of the venture. Cocconas thought Chalcedon a suitable and convenient place, close to Thrace and Bithynia, and not far, too, from Asia[1] and Galatia and all the peoples of the interior. Alexander, on the other hand, preferred his own home, saying—and it was true—that to commence such a venture they needed "fat-heads" and simpletons to be their victims, and such, he said, were the Paphlagonians who lived up above Abonoteichus, who were for the most part superstitious and rich; whenever a man but turned up with someone at his heels to play the flute or the tambourine or the cymbals, telling fortunes with a sieve, as the phrase goes,[2]

their trades are such. They do not know even a little bit about prophecy, but fleece their patrons by charlatanism and fraud." Oneiromants may of course be trusted !

The few allusions to coscinomancy in the ancients give no clue to the method used. As practised in the sixteenth–seventeenth century, to detect thieves, disclose one's future wife, etc., the sieve was either suspended by a string or more commonly balanced on the top of a pair of tongs set astride the joined middle fingers of the two hands (or of two persons) ; then, after an incantation, a list of names was repeated, and the one upon which the sieve stirred was the one indicated by fate. Or the sieve, when suspended, might be set spinning ; and then the name it stopped on was designated. See, in particular, Johannes Praetorius, *de Coscinomantia, Oder vom Sieb-Lauffe*, etc., Curiae Variscorum, 1677.

κεχηνότας πρὸς αὐτὸν καὶ ὥσπερ τινὰ τῶν
ἐπουρανίων προσβλέποντας.

10 Οὐκ ὀλίγης [1] δὲ τῆς περὶ τοῦτο στάσεως αὐτοῖς
γενομένης τέλος ἐνίκησεν ὁ Ἀλέξανδρος, καὶ
ἀφικόμενοι εἰς τὴν Χαλκηδόνα—χρήσιμον γάρ τι
ὅμως ἡ πόλις αὐτοῖς ἔχειν ἔδοξε—ἐν τῷ Ἀπόλλωνος ἱερῷ, ὅπερ ἀρχαιότατόν ἐστι τοῖς Χαλκη-
δονίοις, κατορύττουσι δέλτους χαλκᾶς, λεγούσας
ὡς αὐτίκα μάλα ὁ Ἀσκληπιὸς σὺν τῷ πατρὶ
Ἀπόλλωνι μέτεισιν εἰς τὸν Πόντον καὶ καθέξει
τὸ τοῦ Ἀβώνου τεῖχος. αὗται αἱ δέλτοι ἐξεπίτηδες εὑρεθεῖσαι διαφοιτῆσαι ῥᾳδίως τὸν λόγον
τοῦτον εἰς πᾶσαν τὴν Βιθυνίαν καὶ τὸν Πόντον
ἐποίησαν, καὶ πολὺ πρὸ τῶν ἄλλων εἰς τὸ τοῦ
Ἀβώνου τεῖχος· κἀκεῖνοι γὰρ καὶ νεὼν αὐτίκα
ἐψηφίσαντο ἐγεῖραι καὶ τοὺς θεμελίους ἤδη
ἔσκαπτον. κἀνταῦθα ὁ μὲν Κοκκωνᾶς ἐν Χαλκη-
δόνι καταλείπεται, διττούς τινας καὶ ἀμφιβόλους
καὶ λοξοὺς χρησμοὺς συγγράφων, καὶ μετ᾽ ὀλίγον
ἐτελεύτησε τὸν βίον, ὑπὸ ἐχίδνης, οἶμαι, δηχθείς.

11 προεισπέμπεται δὲ ὁ Ἀλέξανδρος, κομῶν ἤδη καὶ
πλοκάμους καθειμένος καὶ μεσόλευκον χιτῶνα
πορφυροῦν ἐνδεδυκὼς καὶ ἱμάτιον ὑπὲρ αὐτοῦ
λευκὸν ἀναβεβλημένος, ἅρπην ἔχων κατὰ τὸν
Περσέα, ἀφ᾽ οὗ ἑαυτὸν ἐγενεαλόγει μητρόθεν· καὶ
οἱ ὄλεθροι ἐκεῖνοι Παφλαγόνες, εἰδότες αὐτοῦ
ἄμφω τοὺς γονέας ἀφανεῖς καὶ ταπεινούς,
ἐπίστευον τῷ χρησμῷ λέγοντι

Περσείδης γενεὴν Φοίβῳ φίλος οὗτος ὁρᾶται,
δῖος Ἀλέξανδρος, Ποδαλειρίου αἷμα λελογχώς.

---

[1] οὐκ ὀλίγης G. Hermann : ὀλίγης MSS.

they were all agog over him on the instant and stared at him as if he were a god from heaven.

There was no slight difference of opinion between them on that score, but in the end Alexander won, and going to Chalcedon, since after all that city seemed to them to have some usefulness, in the temple of Apollo, which is the most ancient in Chalcedon, they buried bronze tablets which said that very soon Asclepius, with his father Apollo, would move to Pontus and take up his residence at Abonoteichus. The opportune discovery of these tablets caused this story to spread quickly to all Bithynia and Pontus, and to Abonoteichus sooner than anywhere else. Indeed, the people of that city immediately voted to build a temple and began at once to dig for the foundations. Then Cocconas was left behind in Chalcedon, composing equivocal, ambiguous, obscure oracles, and died before long, bitten, I think, by a viper. It was Alexander who was sent in first; he now wore his hair long, had falling ringlets, dressed in a parti-coloured tunic of white and purple, with a white cloak over it, and carried a falchion like that of Perseus, from whom he claimed descent on his mother's side. And although those miserable Paphlagonians knew that both his parents were obscure, humble folk, they believed the oracle when it said:

" Here in your sight is a scion of Perseus, dear
          unto Phoebus ;
    This is divine Alexander, who shareth the blood of
          the Healer ! "

189

οὕτως ἄρα ὁ Ποδαλείριος μάχλος καὶ γυναι-
κομανὴς τὴν φύσιν, ὡς ἀπὸ Τρίκκης μέχρι
Παφλαγονίας στύεσθαι ἐπὶ τὴν Ἀλεξάνδρου
μητέρα.

Εὕρητο δὲ χρησμὸς ἤδη, ὡς Σιβύλλης προ-
μαντευσαμένης·

Εὐξείνου Πόντοιο παρ᾿ ἤόσιν ἄγχι Σινώπης
ἔσται τις κατὰ Τύρσιν ὑπ᾿ Αὐσονίοισι προφήτης,
ἐκ πρώτης δεικνὺς μονάδος τρισσῶν δεκάδων τε
πένθ᾿ ἑτέρας μονάδας καὶ εἰκοσάδα τρισάριθμον,
ἀνδρὸς ἀλεξητῆρος ὁμωνυμίην τετράκυκλον.

12   Εἰσβαλὼν οὖν ὁ Ἀλέξανδρος μετὰ τοιαύτης
τραγῳδίας διὰ πολλοῦ εἰς τὴν πατρίδα περί-
βλεπτός τε καὶ λαμπρὸς ἦν, μεμηνέναι προσποιούμενος ἐνίοτε καὶ ἀφροῦ ὑποπιμπλάμενος
τὸ στόμα· ῥᾳδίως δὲ τοῦτο ὑπῆρχεν αὐτῷ,
στρουθίου τῆς βαφικῆς βοτάνης τὴν ῥίζαν δια-
μασησαμένῳ· τοῖς δὲ θεῖόν τι καὶ φοβερὸν ἐδόκει
καὶ ὁ ἀφρός. ἐπεποίητο δὲ αὐτοῖς πάλαι καὶ
κατεσκεύαστο κεφαλὴ δράκοντος ὀθονίνη ἀνθρω-

---

[1] Podaleirius and his brother Machaon, the Homeric
healers (*Iliad* 11, 833), were sons of Asclepius and lived
in Tricca (now Trikkala), Thessaly.   According to the
Sack of Ilium (Evelyn-White, *Hesiod*, p. 524) Machaon
specialized in surgery, Podaleirius in diagnosis and general
practice.

ALEXANDER THE FALSE PROPHET

Podaleirius, the Healer, it would appear, was so passionate and amorous that his ardour carried him all the way from Tricca to Paphlagonia in quest of Alexander's mother![1]

An oracle by now had turned up which purported to be a prior prediction by the Sibyl:

"On the shores of the Euxine sea, in the neighbourhood of Sinope,
    There shall be born, by a Tower, in the days of the Romans, a prophet;
After the foremost unit and three times ten, he will shew forth
Five more units besides, and a score told three times over,
Matching, with places four, the name of a valiant defender!"[2]

Well, upon invading his native land with all this pomp and circumstance after a long absence, Alexander was a man of mark and note, affecting as he did to have occasional fits of madness and causing his mouth to fill with foam. This he easily managed by chewing the root of soapwort, the plant that dyers use; but to his fellow-countrymen even the foam seemed supernatural and awe-inspiring. Then, too, they had long ago prepared and fitted up a serpent's head of linen, which had something

---

[2] Since in the Greek notation numbers are designated by letters, this combination (1, 30, 5, 60) is αλεξ (alex). Alexander seems to have been a little afraid that some rival might steal his thunder if he were not more specific: at all events the first two words of the last line give, in the Greek, the entire name (andros-alex).

πόμορφόν τι ἐπιφαίνουσα, κατάγραφος, πάνυ
εἰκασμένη, ὑπὸ θριξὶν ἱππείαις ἀνοίγουσά τε καὶ
αὖθις ἐπικλείουσα τὸ στόμα, καὶ γλῶττα οἷα δράκοντος διττὴ μέλαινα προέκυπτεν, ὑπὸ τριχῶν
καὶ αὐτὴ ἑλκομένη. καὶ ὁ Πελλαῖος δὲ δράκων
προϋπῆρχεν καὶ οἴκοι ἐτρέφετο, κατὰ καιρὸν
ἐπιφανησόμενος αὐτοῖς καὶ συντραγῳδήσων,
μᾶλλον δὲ πρωταγωνιστὴς ἐσόμενος.

13 Ἤδη δὲ ἄρχεσθαι δέον, μηχανᾶται τοιόνδε τι·
νύκτωρ γὰρ ἐλθὼν ἐπὶ τοὺς θεμελίους τοῦ νεὼ
τοὺς ἄρτι ὀρυττομένους—συνειστήκει δὲ ἐν αὐτοῖς
ὕδωρ ἢ αὐτόθεν ποθὲν συλλειβόμενον ἢ ἐξ
οὐρανοῦ πεσόν—ἐνταῦθα κατατίθεται χήνειον
ᾠὸν προκεκενωμένον, ἔνδον φυλάττον ἑρπετόν τι
ἀρτιγέννητον, καὶ βυθίσας τοῦτο ἐν μυχῷ τοῦ
πηλοῦ ὀπίσω αὖθις ἀπηλλάττετο. ἔωθεν δὲ
γυμνὸς εἰς τὴν ἀγορὰν προπηδήσας, διάζωμα περὶ
τὸ αἰδοῖον ἔχων, κατάχρυσον καὶ τοῦτο, καὶ τὴν
ἅρπην ἐκείνην φέρων, σείων ἅμα τὴν κόμην ἄνετον
ὥσπερ οἱ τῇ μητρὶ ἀγείροντές τε καὶ ἐνθεαζόμενοι,
ἐδημηγόρει ἐπὶ βωμόν τινα ὑψηλὸν ἀναβὰς καὶ
τὴν πόλιν ἐμακάριζεν αὐτίκα μάλα δεξομένην
ἐναργῆ τὸν θεόν. οἱ παρόντες δέ—συνδεδραμήκει
γὰρ σχεδὸν ἅπασα ἡ πόλις ἅμα γυναιξὶ καὶ
γέρουσι καὶ παιδίοις—ἐτεθήπεσαν καὶ εὔχοντο
καὶ προσεκύνουν. ὁ δὲ φωνάς τινας ἀσήμους
φθεγγόμενος, οἷαι γένοιντο ἂν Ἑβραίων ἢ
Φοινίκων, ἐξέπληττε τοὺς ἀνθρώπους οὐκ εἰδότας
ὅ τι καὶ λέγοι, πλὴν τοῦτο μόνον, ὅτι πᾶσιν

of a human look, was all painted up, and appeared very lifelike. It would open and close its mouth by means of horsehairs, and a forked black tongue like a snake's, also controlled by horsehairs, would dart out. Besides, the serpent from Pella was ready in advance and was being cared for at home, destined in due time to manifest himself to them and to take a part in their show—in fact, to be cast for the leading rôle.

When at length it was time to begin, he contrived an ingenious ruse. Going at night to the foundations of the temple which were just being excavated, where a pool of water had gathered which either issued from springs somewhere in the foundations themselves or had fallen from the sky, he secreted there a goose-egg, previously blown, which contained a snake just born ; and after burying it deep in the mud, he went back again. In the morning he ran out into the market-place naked, wearing a loin-cloth (this too was gilded),[1] carrying his falchion, and tossing his unconfined mane like a devotee of the Great Mother in the frenzy. Addressing the people from a high altar upon which he had climbed, he congratulated the city because it was at once to receive the god in visible presence. The assembly—for almost the whole city, including women, old men, and boys, had come running— marvelled, prayed and made obeisance. Uttering a few meaningless words like Hebrew or Phoenician, he dazed the creatures, who did not know what he

---

[1] Why "this too"? The hilt of the falchion may have been gilt, but Lucian has not said so. Perhaps Lucian is thinking of Alexander's golden thigh (c. 40), and forgets that he has not yet told us of it.

ἐγκατεμίγνυ τὸν ᾿Απόλλω καὶ τὸν ᾿Ασκληπιόν.
14 εἶτ᾿ ἔθει δρόμῳ ἐπὶ τὸν ἐσόμενον νεών· καὶ ἐπὶ τὸ
ὄρυγμα ἐλθὼν καὶ τὴν προῳκονομημένην[1] τοῦ
χρηστηρίου πηγήν, ἐμβὰς εἰς τὸ ὕδωρ ὕμνους τε
ᾖδεν ᾿Ασκληπιοῦ καὶ ᾿Απόλλωνος μεγάλῃ τῇ
φωνῇ καὶ ἐκάλει τὸν θεὸν ἥκειν τύχῃ τῇ ἀγαθῇ
εἰς τὴν πόλιν. εἶτα φιάλην αἰτήσας, ἀναδόντος
τινός, ῥᾳδίως ὑποβαλὼν ἀνιμᾶται μετὰ τοῦ ὕδατος
καὶ τοῦ πηλοῦ τὸ ᾠὸν ἐκεῖνο ἐν ᾧ ὁ θεὸς αὐτῷ
κατεκέκλειστο, κηρῷ λευκῷ καὶ ψιμυθίῳ τὴν
ἁρμογὴν τοῦ πώματος συγκεκολλημένον· καὶ
λαβὼν αὐτὸ εἰς τὰς χεῖρας ἔχειν ἔφασκεν ἤδη
τὸν ᾿Ασκληπιόν. οἱ δὲ ἀτενὲς ἀπέβλεπον ὅ τι
καὶ γίγνοιτο, πολὺ πρότερον θαυμάσαντες τὸ ᾠὸν
ἐν τῷ ὕδατι εὑρημένον. ἐπεὶ δὲ καὶ κατάξας
αὐτὸ εἰς κοίλην τὴν χεῖρα ὑπεδέξατο τὸ τοῦ
ἑρπετοῦ ἐκείνου ἔμβρυον καὶ οἱ παρόντες εἶδον
κινούμενον καὶ περὶ τοῖς δακτύλοις εἰλούμενον,
ἀνέκραγον εὐθὺς καὶ ἠσπάζοντο τὸν θεὸν καὶ τὴν
πόλιν ἐμακάριζον καὶ χανδὸν ἕκαστος ἐνε-
πίμπλατο τῶν εὐχῶν, θησαυροὺς καὶ πλούτους
καὶ ὑγιείας καὶ τὰ ἄλλα ἀγαθὰ αἰτῶν παρ᾿ αὐτοῦ.
ὁ δὲ δρομαῖος αὖθις ἐπὶ τὴν οἰκίαν ἵετο φέρων
ἅμα καὶ τὸν ἀρτιγέννητον ᾿Ασκληπιόν, “δὶς
τεχθέντα, ὅτε ἄλλοι ἅπαξ τίκτουτ᾿ ἄνθρωποι,”
οὐκ ἐκ Κορωνίδος μὰ Δί᾿ οὐδέ γε κορώνης, ἀλλ᾿
ἐκ χηνὸς γεγεννημένον. ὁ δὲ λεὼς ἅπας ἠκολούθει,
πάντες ἔνθεοι καὶ μεμηνότες ὑπὸ τῶν ἐλπίδων.

---

[1] προῳκοδομημένην β edd. But this is inconsistent with the
previous description. The pool is merely casual water; after
it has served its turn as the prima fons et origo mali, we
hear nothing more of it.

was saying save only that he everywhere brought in Apollo and Asclepius. Then he ran at full speed to the future temple, went to the excavation and the previously improvised fountain-head of the oracle, entered the water, sang hymns in honour of Asclepius and Apollo at the top of his voice, and besought the god, under the blessing of Heaven, to come to the city. Then he asked for a libation-saucer, and when somebody handed him one, deftly slipped it underneath and brought up, along with water and mud, that egg in which he had immured the god; the joint about the plug had been closed with wax and white lead. Taking it in his hands, he asserted that at that moment he held Asclepius! They gazed unwaveringly to see what in the world was going to happen; indeed, they had already marvelled at the discovery of the egg in the water. But when he broke it and received the tiny snake into his hollowed hand, and the crowd saw it moving and twisting about his fingers, they at once raised a shout, welcomed the god, congratulated their city, and began each of them to sate himself greedily with prayers, craving treasures, riches, health, and every other blessing from him. But Alexander went home again at full speed, taking with him the new-born Asclepius, "born twice, when other men are born but once," [1] whose mother was not Coronis, [2] by Zeus, nor yet a crow, but a goose! And the whole population followed, all full of religious fervour and crazed with expectations.

[1] Cf. *Odyssey*, 12, 22: "Men of two deaths, when other men die but once."

[2] "Some say that the mother of Asclepius was not Arsinoe, daughter of Leucippus, but Coronis, daughter of Phlegyas" (Apollodorus, 3, 10, 3).

15 Ἡμέρας μὲν οὖν τινας¹ οἴκοι ἔμεινεν ἐλπίζων
ὅπερ ἦν, ὑπὸ τῆς φήμης αὐτίκα μάλα παμπόλλους
τῶν Παφλαγόνων συνδραμεῖσθαι. ἐπεὶ δὲ
ὑπερεπέπληστο ἀνθρώπων ἡ πόλις, ἁπάντων
τοὺς ἐγκεφάλους καὶ τὰς καρδίας προεξῃρημένων
οὐδὲν ἐοικότων σιτοφάγοις ἀνδράσιν, ἀλλὰ μόνῃ
τῇ μορφῇ μὴ οὐχὶ πρόβατα εἶναι διαφερόντων, ἐν
οἰκίσκῳ τινὶ ἐπὶ κλίνης καθεζόμενος μάλα
θεοπρεπῶς ἐσταλμένος ἐλάμβανεν εἰς τὸν κόλπον
τὸν Πελλαῖον ἐκεῖνον Ἀσκληπιόν, μέγιστόν τε
καὶ κάλλιστον, ὡς ἔφην, ὄντα, καὶ ὅλον τῷ
αὐτοῦ τραχήλῳ περιειλήσας καὶ τὴν οὐρὰν ἔξω
ἀφείς—πολὺς δὲ ἦν—ἐν τῷ προκολπίῳ προ-
κεχύσθαι αὐτοῦ² καὶ χαμαὶ τὸ μέρος ἐπισύρεσθαι,
μόνην τὴν κεφαλὴν ὑπὸ μάλης ἔχων καὶ ἀπο-
κρύπτων, ἀνεχομένου πάντα ἐκείνου, προὔφαινεν
τὴν ὀθονίνην κεφαλὴν κατὰ θάτερον τοῦ
πώγωνος, ὡς δῆθεν ἐκείνου τοῦ φαινομένου
πάντως οὖσαν.

16 Εἶτά μοι ἐπινόησον οἰκίσκον οὐ πάνυ φαιδρὸν
οὐδὲ εἰς κόρον τοῦ φωτὸς δεχόμενον καὶ πλῆθος
ἀνθρώπων συγκλύδων, τεταραγμένων καὶ προεκπε-
πληγμένων καὶ ταῖς ἐλπίσιν ἐπαιωρουμένων, οἷς
εἰσελθοῦσι τεράστιον ὡς εἰκὸς τὸ πρᾶγμα ἐφαίνετο,
ἐκ τοῦ τέως μικροῦ ἑρπετοῦ ἐντὸς ἡμερῶν ὀλίγων
τοσοῦτον δράκοντα πεφηνέναι, ἀνθρωπόμορφον
καὶ ταῦτα καὶ τιθασόν. ἠπείγοντο δὲ αὐτίκα
πρὸς τὴν ἔξοδον, καὶ πρὶν ἀκριβῶς ἰδεῖν,
ἐξηλαύνοντο ὑπὸ τῶν ἀεὶ ἐπεισιόντων· ἐτετρύπητο

---

¹ τινας Fritzsche : not in MSS. Cf. ἐντὸς ἡμερῶν ὀλίγων 16.
² πολὺς δὲ ἦν ὡς καὶ ἐν τοῦ προκολπίου αὐτοῦ κεχύσθαι β.

ALEXANDER THE FALSE PROPHET

For some days he remained at home, expecting what actually happened—that as the news spread, crowds of Paphlagonians would come running in. When the city had become over-full of people, all of them already bereft of their brains and sense, and not in the least like bread-eating humans, but different from beasts of the field only in their looks, he seated himself on a couch in a certain chamber, clothed in apparel well suited to a god, and took into his bosom his Asclepius from Pella, who, as I have said, was of uncommon size and beauty.[1] Coiling him about his neck, and letting the tail, which was long, stream over his lap and drag part of its length on the floor, he concealed only the head by holding it under his arm—the creature would submit to anything—and showed the linen head at one side of his own beard, as if it certainly belonged to the creature that was in view.

Now then, please imagine a little room, not very bright and not admitting any too much daylight; also, a crowd of heterogeneous humanity, excited, wonder-struck in advance, agog with hopes. When they went in, the thing, of course, seemed to them a miracle, that the formerly tiny snake within a few days had turned into so great a serpent, with a human face, moreover, and tame! They were immediately crowded towards the exit, and before they could look closely were forced out by those who kept coming in, for another door

---

[1] There was special significance in this performance. "Anyhow, 'God in the bosom' is a countersign of the mysteries of Sabazius to the adepts. This is a snake, passed through the bosom of the initiates" Clement of Alexandria, *Protrept*, 1, 2, 16).

δὲ κατὰ τὸ ἀντίθυρον ἄλλη ἔξοδος. οἷόν τι καὶ
τοὺς Μακεδόνας ἐν Βαβυλῶνι ποιῆσαι ἐπ'
Ἀλεξάνδρῳ νοσοῦντι λόγος, ὅτε ὁ μὲν ἤδη
πονήρως εἶχεν, οἱ δὲ περιστάντες τὰ βασίλεια
ἐπόθουν ἰδεῖν αὐτὸν καὶ προσειπεῖν τὸ ὕστατον.
τὴν δὲ ἐπίδειξιν ταύτην οὐχ ἅπαξ ὁ μιαρός, ἀλλὰ
πολλάκις ποιῆσαι λέγεται, καὶ μάλιστα εἴ τινες
τῶν πλουσίων ἀφίκοιντο νεαλέστεροι.

17   Ἐνταῦθα, ὦ φίλε Κέλσε, εἰ δεῖ τἀληθῆ λέγειν,
συγγνώμην χρὴ ἀπονέμειν τοῖς Παφλαγόσι καὶ
Ποντικοῖς ἐκείνοις, παχέσι καὶ ἀπαιδεύτοις
ἀνθρώποις, εἰ ἐξηπατήθησαν ἁπτόμενοι τοῦ
δράκοντος—καὶ γὰρ τοῦτο παρεῖχεν τοῖς βουλο-
μένοις ὁ Ἀλέξανδρος—ὁρῶντές τε[1] ἐν ἀμυδρῷ
τῷ φωτὶ τὴν κεφαλὴν δῆθεν αὐτοῦ ἀνοίγουσάν
τε καὶ συγκλείουσαν τὸ στόμα, ὥστε πάνυ τὸ
μηχάνημα ἐδεῖτο Δημοκρίτου τινὸς ἢ καὶ αὐτοῦ
Ἐπικούρου ἢ Μητροδώρου ἤ τινος ἄλλου
ἀδαμαντίνην πρὸς τὰ τοιαῦτα τὴν γνώμην ἔχοντος,
ὡς ἀπιστῆσαι καὶ ὅπερ ἦν εἰκάσαι, καὶ εἰ μὴ
εὑρεῖν τὸν τρόπον ἐδύνατο, ἐκεῖνο γοῦν προ-
πεπεισμένου, ὅτι λέληθεν αὐτὸν ὁ τρόπος τῆς
μαγγανείας, τὸ δ' οὖν πᾶν ψεῦδός ἐστι καὶ
γενέσθαι ἀδύνατον.

18   Κατ' ὀλίγον οὖν καὶ ἡ Βιθυνία καὶ ἡ Γαλατία
καὶ ἡ Θρᾴκη συνέρρει, ἑκάστου τῶν ἀπαγγελλόν-
των κατὰ τὸ εἰκὸς λέγοντος ὡς καὶ γεννώμενον
ἴδοι τὸν θεὸν καὶ ὕστερον ἅψαιτο μετ' ὀλίγον
παμμεγέθους αὐτοῦ γεγενημένου καὶ τὸ πρόσωπον
ἀνθρώπῳ ἐοικότος. γραφαί τε ἐπὶ τούτῳ καὶ
εἰκόνες καὶ ξόανα, τὰ μὲν ἐκ χαλκοῦ, τὰ δὲ ἐξ
ἀργύρου εἰκασμένα, καὶ ὄνομά γε τῷ θεῷ ἐπιτεθέν·

had been opened on the opposite side as an exit. That was the way the Macedonians did, they say, in Babylon during Alexander's illness, when he was in a bad way and they surrounded the palace, craving to see him and say good-bye. This exhibition the scoundrel gave not merely once, they say, but again and again, above all if any rich men were newly arrived.

In that matter, dear Celsus, to tell the truth, we must excuse those men of Paphlagonia and Pontus, thick-witted, uneducated fellows that they were, for being deluded when they touched the serpent—Alexander let anyone do so who wished—and besides saw in a dim light what purported to be its head opening and shutting its mouth. Really the trick stood in need of a Democritus, or even Epicurus himself or Metrodorus, or someone else with a mind as firm as adamant toward such matters, so as to disbelieve and guess the truth—one who, if he could not discover how it went, would at all events be convinced beforehand that though the method of the fraud escaped him, it was nevertheless all sham and could not possibly happen.

Little by little, Bithynia, Galatia, and Thrace came pouring in, for everyone who carried the news very likely said that he not only had seen the god born but had subsequently touched him, after he had grown very great in a short time and had a face that looked like a man's. Next came paintings and statues and cult-images, some made of bronze, some of silver, and naturally a name was bestowed

---

[1] τε A.M.H.: γὰρ γ, not in β.

Γλύκων γὰρ ἐκαλεῖτο ἔκ τινος ἐμμέτρου καὶ
θείου προστάγματος. ἀνεφώνησε γὰρ ὁ
Ἀλέξανδρος

Εἰμὶ Γλύκων, τρίτον αἷμα Διός, φάος ἀνθρώποισιν.

19 Καὶ ἐπειδὴ καιρὸς ἦν, οὗπερ ἕνεκα τὰ πάντα
ἐμεμηχάνητο, καὶ χρᾶν τοῖς δεομένοις καὶ
θεσπίζειν, παρ' Ἀμφιλόχου τοῦ ἐν Κιλικίᾳ τὸ
ἐνδόσιμον λαβών—καὶ γὰρ ἐκεῖνος, μετὰ τὴν τοῦ
πατρὸς τελευτὴν τοῦ Ἀμφιάρεω καὶ τὸν ἐν
Θήβαις ἀφανισμὸν αὐτοῦ ἐκπεσὼν τῆς οἰκείας [1] εἰς
τὴν Κιλικίαν ἀφικόμενος, οὐ πονήρως ἀπήλλαξεν,
προθεσπίζων καὶ αὐτὸς τοῖς Κίλιξι τὰ μέλλοντα
καὶ δύ' ὀβολοὺς ἐφ' ἑκάστῳ χρησμῷ λαμβάνων—
ἐκεῖθεν οὖν τὸ ἐνδόσιμον λαβὼν ὁ Ἀλέξανδρος
προλέγει πᾶσι τοῖς ἀφικομένοις ὡς μαντεύσεται
ὁ θεός, ῥητήν τινα ἡμέραν προειπών. ἐκέλευσεν
δὲ ἕκαστον, οὗ δέοιτο ἂν καὶ ὃ μάλιστα μαθεῖν
ἐθέλοι, εἰς βιβλίον ἐγγράψαντα καταρράψαι τε
καὶ κατασημήνασθαι κηρῷ ἢ πηλῷ ἢ ἄλλῳ
τοιούτῳ. αὐτὸς δὲ λαβὼν τὰ βιβλία καὶ εἰς τὸ
ἄδυτον κατελθών—ἤδη γὰρ ὁ νεὼς ἐγήγερτο καὶ
ἡ σκηνὴ παρεσκεύαστο—καλέσειν ἔμελλε κατὰ
τάξιν τοὺς δεδωκότας ὑπὸ κήρυκι καὶ θεολόγῳ,
καὶ παρὰ τοῦ θεοῦ ἀκούων ἕκαστα τὸ μὲν βιβλίον
ἀποδώσειν σεσημασμένον ὡς εἶχε, τὴν δὲ πρὸς
αὐτὸ ἀπόκρισιν ὑπογεγραμμένην, πρὸς ἔπος
ἀμειβομένου τοῦ θεοῦ περὶ ὅτου τις ἔροιτο.

---

[1] οἰκείας Fritzsche : οἰκίας MSS.

upon the god. He was called Glycon in consequence of a divine behest in metre; for Alexander
proclaimed:

" Glycon am I, the grandson of Zeus, bright beacon
    to mortals ! "

When it was time to carry out the purpose for
which the whole scheme had been concocted—that
is to say, to make predictions and give oracles
to those who sought them—taking his cue from
Amphilochus in Cilicia, who, as you know, after the
death and disappearance of his father Amphiaraus
at Thebes,[1] was exiled from his own country, went
to Cilicia, and got on very well by foretelling the
future, like his father, for the Cilicians and getting
two obols for each prediction—taking, as I say, his
cue from him, Alexander announced to all comers
that the god would make prophecies, and named a
date for it in advance. He directed everyone to
write down in a scroll whatever he wanted and what
he especially wished to learn, to tie it up, and to
seal it with wax or clay or something else of that
sort. Then he himself, after taking the scrolls and
entering the inner sanctuary—for by that time the
temple had been erected and the stage set—proposed to summon in order, with herald and priest,
those who had submitted them, and after the god
told him about each case, to give back the scroll
with the seal upon it, just as it was, and the reply
to it endorsed upon it; for the god would reply
explicitly to any question that anyone should put.

[1] In speaking of the " death and disappearance " of
Amphiaraus, Lucian is rationalizing the myth, according to
which Zeus clove the earth with a thunderbolt and it
swallowed him up alive (Pindar, *Nem.* 9, 57).

THE WORKS OF LUCIAN

20 Ἦν δὲ τὸ μηχάνημα τοῦτο ἀνδρὶ μὲν οἵῳ σοί, εἰ δὲ μὴ φορτικὸν εἰπεῖν, καὶ οἵῳ ἐμοί, πρόδηλον καὶ γνῶναι ῥᾴδιον, τοῖς δὲ ἰδιώταις καὶ κορύζης μεστοῖς τὴν ῥῖνα τεράστιον καὶ πάνυ ἀπίστῳ ὅμοιον. ἐπινοήσας γὰρ ποικίλας τῶν σφραγίδων τὰς λύσεις ἀνεγίγνωσκέν τε τὰς ἐρωτήσεις ἑκάστας καὶ τὰ δοκοῦντα πρὸς αὐτὰς ἀπεκρίνετο, εἶτα κατειλήσας αὖθις καὶ σημηνάμενος ἀπεδίδου μετὰ πολλοῦ θαύματος τοῖς λαμβάνουσιν. καὶ πολὺ ἦν παρ' αὐτοῖς τὸ "πόθεν γὰρ οὗτος ἠπίστατο ἃ ἐγὼ πάνυ ἀσφαλῶς σημηνάμενος αὐτῷ ἔδωκα ὑπὸ σφραγῖσιν δυσμιμήτοις, εἰ μὴ θεός τις ὡς ἀληθῶς ὁ πάντα γιγνώσκων ἦν";

21 Τίνες οὖν αἱ ἐπίνοιαι, ἴσως γὰρ ἐρήσῃ με. ἄκουε τοίνυν, ὡς ἔχοις ἐλέγχειν τὰ τοιαῦτα. ἡ πρώτη μὲν ἐκείνη, ὦ φίλτατε Κέλσε· βελόνην πυρώσας τὸ ὑπὸ τὴν σφραγῖδα μέρος τοῦ κηροῦ διατήκων ἐξῄρει καὶ μετὰ τὴν ἀνάγνωσιν τῇ βελόνῃ αὖθις ἐπιχλιάνας τὸν κηρόν, τόν τε κάτω ὑπὸ τῷ λίνῳ καὶ τὸν αὐτὴν τὴν σφραγῖδα ἔχοντα, ῥᾳδίως συνεκόλλα. ἕτερος δὲ τρόπος ὁ διὰ τοῦ λεγομένου κολλυρίου· σκευαστὸν δὲ τοῦτό ἐστιν ἐκ πίττης Βρεττίας καὶ ἀσφάλτου καὶ λίθου τοῦ διαφανοῦς τετριμμένου καὶ κηροῦ καὶ μαστίχης. ἐκ γὰρ τούτων ἁπάντων ἀναπλάσας τὸ κολλύριον καὶ θερμήνας πυρί, σιάλῳ τὴν σφραγῖδα προχρίσας ἐπετίθει καὶ ἀπέματτε τὸν τύπον. εἶτα αὐτίκα ξηροῦ ἐκείνου γενομένου, λύσας ῥᾳδίως καὶ ἀναγνούς, ἐπιθεὶς τὸν κηρὸν ἀπετύπου ὥσπερ ἐκ λίθου τὴν σφραγῖδα εὖ μάλα τῷ ἀρχετύπῳ ἐοικυῖαν. τρίτον ἄλλο πρὸς τούτοις ἄκουσον·

As a matter of fact, this trick, to a man like you, and if it is not out of place to say so, like myself also, was obvious and easy to see through, but to those drivelling idiots it was miraculous and almost as good as incredible. Having discovered various ways of undoing the seals, he would read all the questions and answer them as he thought best. Then he would roll up the scrolls again, seal them, and give them back, to the great astonishment of the recipients, among whom the comment was frequent: "Why, how did he learn the questions which I gave him very securely sealed with impressions hard to counterfeit, unless there was really some god that knew everything?"

"What were his discoveries, then?" perhaps you will ask. Listen, therefore, in order to be able to show up such impostors. The first, my dear Celsus, was a well-known method; heating a needle, he removed the seal by melting through the wax underneath it, and after reading the contents he warmed the wax once more with the needle, both that which was under the thread and that which contained the seal, and so stuck it together without difficulty. Another method was by using what they call plaster; this is a compound of Bruttian pitch, asphalt, pulverized gypsum, wax, and gum Arabic. Making his plaster out of all these materials and warming it over the fire, he applied it to the seal, which he had previously wetted with saliva, and took a mould of the impression. Then, since the plaster hardened at once, after easily opening and reading the scrolls, he applied the wax and made an impression upon it precisely like the original, just as one would with a gem. Let me tell you a third

τιτάνου γὰρ εἰς κόλλαν ἐμβαλὼν ᾗ κολλῶσι τὰ
βιβλία, καὶ κηρὸν ἐκ τούτου ποιήσας, ἔτι ὑγρὸν
ὄντα ἐπετίθει τῇ σφραγῖδι καὶ ἀφελών—αὐτίκα
δὲ ξηρὸν γίγνεται καὶ κέρατος, μᾶλλον δὲ σιδήρου
παγιώτερον—τούτῳ ἐχρῆτο πρὸς τὸν τύπον. ἔστι
δὲ καὶ ἄλλα πολλὰ πρὸς τοῦτο ἐπινενοημένα,
ὧν οὐκ ἀναγκαῖον μεμνῆσθαι ἁπάντων, ὡς μὴ
ἀπειρόκαλοι εἶναι δοκοίημεν, καὶ μάλιστα σοῦ ἐν
οἷς κατὰ μάγων συνέγραψας, καλλίστοις τε ἅμα
καὶ ὠφελιμωτάτοις συγγράμμασιν καὶ δυναμένοις
σωφρονίζειν τοὺς ἐντυγχάνοντας, ἱκανὰ παραθε-
μένου καὶ πολλῷ τούτων πλείονα.

22   Ἔχρη οὖν καὶ ἐθέσπιζε, πολλῇ τῇ συνέσει
ἐνταῦθα χρώμενος καὶ τὸ εἰκαστικὸν τῇ ἐπινοίᾳ
προσάπτων, τοῖς μὲν λοξὰ καὶ ἀμφίβολα πρὸς
τὰς ἐρωτήσεις ἀποκρινόμενος, τοῖς δὲ καὶ πάνυ
ἀσαφῆ· χρησμῳδικὸν γὰρ ἐδόκει αὐτῷ τοῦτο.
τοὺς δὲ ἀπέτρεπεν ἢ προύτρεπεν, ὡς ἄμεινον
ἔδοξεν αὐτῷ εἰκάζοντι· τοῖς δὲ θεραπείας πρού-
λεγεν καὶ διαίτας, εἰδώς, ὅπερ ἐν ἀρχῇ ἔφην,
πολλὰ καὶ χρήσιμα φάρμακα. μάλιστα δὲ
εὐδοκίμουν παρ᾽ αὐτῷ αἱ κυτμίδες, ἀκόπου τι
ὄνομα πεπλασμένον, ἐκ λίπους ἀρκείου[1] συντεθειμένου.[2] τὰς μέντοι ἐλπίδας καὶ προκοπὰς

---

[1] αἰγείου β.
[2] συντεθειμένου Bekker: συντεθειμένον MSS.

---

[1] S. Hippolytus (*Refut. omn. Haeres.* IV. 28–42) contains
a highly interesting section "against sorcerers," including
(34) a treatment of this subject. It is very evidently not his
own work ; and K. F. Hermann thought it derived from the
treatise by Celsus. Ganschinietz, in Harnack's *Texte und
Untersuchungen* 39, 2, has disputed this, but upon grounds

method, in addition to these. Putting marble-dust into the glue with which they glue books and making a paste of it, he applied that to the seal while it was still soft, and then, as it grows hard at once, more solid than horn or even iron, he removed it and used it for the impression. There are many other devices to this end, but they need not all be mentioned, for fear that we might seem to be wanting in taste, especially in view of the fact that in the book which you wrote against the sorcerers, a very good and useful treatise, capable of preserving common-sense in its readers, you cited instances enough, and indeed a great many more than I have.[1]

Well, as I say, Alexander made predictions and gave oracles, employing great shrewdness in it and combining guesswork with his trickery. He gave responses that were sometimes obscure and ambiguous, sometimes downright unintelligible, for this seemed to him in the oracular manner. Some people he dissuaded or encouraged as seemed best to him at a guess. To others he prescribed medical treatments and diets, knowing, as I said in the beginning, many useful remedies. His " cytmides " were in highest favour with him—a name which he had coined for a restorative ointment compounded of bear's grease.[2] Expectations, however, and

that are not convincing. His commentary, however, is valuable.

[2] It is a nice question whether this reading or that of the other group of MSS., " goat's grease," is to be preferred. Galen in his treatment of these ointments (Kuhn xiii, p. 1008) does not mention bear's grease. But he considers goat's grease only moderately good ; and every Yankee knows that in America bear's grease only gave place to goose grease (also mentioned by Galen) when bears became scarce.

καὶ κλήρων διαδοχὰς εἰσαῦθις ἀεὶ ἀνεβάλλετο,
προστιθεὶς ὅτι "ἔσται πάντα ὁπόταν ἐθελήσω
ἐγὼ καὶ Ἀλέξανδρος ὁ προφήτης μου δεηθῇ καὶ
εὔξηται ὑπὲρ ὑμῶν."

23 Ἐτέτακτο δὲ ὁ μισθὸς ἐφ' ἑκάστῳ χρησμῷ
δραχμὴ καὶ δύ' ὀβολώ. μὴ μικρὸν οἰηθῇς, ὦ
ἑταῖρε, μηδ' ὀλίγον γεγενῆσθαι τὸν πόρον τοῦτον,
ἀλλ' εἰς ἑπτὰ ἢ ὀκτὼ μυριάδας ἑκάστου ἔτους
ἤθροιζεν, ἀνὰ δέκα καὶ πεντεκαίδεκα χρησμοὺς
τῶν ἀνθρώπων ὑπὸ ἀπληστίας ἀναδιδόντων.
λαμβάνων δὲ οὐκ αὐτὸς ἐχρῆτο μόνος οὐδ' εἰς
πλοῦτον ἀπεθησαύριζεν, ἀλλὰ πολλοὺς ἤδη περὶ
αὑτὸν ἔχων συνεργοὺς καὶ ὑπηρέτας καὶ πευθῆνας
καὶ χρησμοποιοὺς καὶ χρησμοφύλακας καὶ ὑπο-
γραφέας καὶ ἐπισφραγιστὰς καὶ ἐξηγητάς, ἅπασιν
ἔνεμεν ἑκάστῳ τὸ κατ' ἀξίαν.

24 Ἤδη δέ τινας καὶ ἐπὶ τὴν ἀλλοδαπὴν ἐξέπεμ-
πεν, φήμας ἐμποιήσοντας τοῖς ἔθνεσιν ὑπὲρ τοῦ
μαντείου καὶ διηγησομένους ὡς προείποι καὶ
ἀνεύροι δραπέτας καὶ κλέπτας καὶ λῃστὰς
ἐξελέγξειε καὶ θησαυροὺς ἀνορύξαι παράσχοι
καὶ νοσοῦντας ἰάσαιτο, ἐνίους δὲ καὶ ἤδη ἀπο-
θανόντας ἀναστήσειεν. δρόμος οὖν καὶ ὠθισμὸς
ἁπανταχόθεν ἐγίγνετο καὶ θυσίαι καὶ ἀναθήματα,
καὶ διπλάσια τῷ προφήτῃ καὶ μαθητῇ τοῦ θεοῦ.
καὶ γὰρ αὖ καὶ οὗτος ἐξέπεσεν ὁ χρησμός·

Τιέμεναι κέλομαι τὸν ἐμὸν θεράποντ' ὑποφήτην·
οὐ γάρ μοι κτεάνων μέλεται ἄγαν, ἀλλ'
ὑποφήτου·

---

[1] Alexander's price was high. Amphilochus got but two
obols (one-fourth as much) at Mallus. According to Lucian

advancements and successions to estates he always put off to another day, adding: "It shall all come about when I will, and when Alexander, my prophet, asks it of me and prays for you."

A price had been fixed for each oracle, a drachma and two obols.[1] Do not think that it was low, my friend, or that the revenue from this source was scanty! He gleaned as much as seventy or eighty thousand[2] a year, since men were so greedy as to send in ten and fifteen questions each. What he received he did not use for himself alone nor treasure up to make himself rich, but since he had many men about him by this time as assistants, servants, collectors of information, writers of oracles, custodians of oracles, clerks, sealers, and expounders, he divided with all, giving each one what was proportionate to his worth.

By now he was even sending men abroad to create rumours in the different nations in regard to the oracle and to say that he made predictions, discovered fugitive slaves, detected thieves and robbers, caused treasures to be dug up, healed the sick, and in some cases had actually raised the dead. So there was a hustling and a bustling from every side, with sacrifices and votive offerings—and twice as much for the prophet and disciple of the god. For this oracle also had come out:

" Honour I bid you to give my faithful servant, the prophet;
No great store do I set upon riches, but much on the prophet."

(*Timon* 6; 12; *Epist. Saturn.* 21) the wage of a day-labourer at this time was but four obols.　　[2] Drachmas.

THE WORKS OF LUCIAN

25 Ἐπεὶ δὲ ἤδη πολλοὶ τῶν νοῦν ἐχόντων ὥσπερ
ἐκ μέθης βαθείας ἀναφέροντες συνίσταντο ἐπ'
αὐτόν, καὶ μάλιστα ὅσοι Ἐπικούρου ἑταῖροι
ἦσαν,[1] καὶ ἐν ταῖς πόλεσιν ἐπεφώρατο ἠρέμα ἡ
πᾶσα μαγγανεία καὶ συσκευὴ τοῦ δράματος,
ἐκφέρει φόβητρόν τι ἐπ' αὐτούς, λέγων ἀθέων
ἐμπεπλῆσθαι καὶ Χριστιανῶν τὸν Πόντον, οἳ
περὶ αὐτοῦ τολμῶσι τὰ κάκιστα βλασφημεῖν·
οὓς ἐκέλευε λίθοις ἐλαύνειν, εἴ γε θέλουσιν ἵλεω
ἔχειν τὸν θεόν. περὶ δὲ Ἐπικούρου καὶ τοιοῦτόν
τινα χρησμὸν ἀπεφθέγξατο· ἐρομένου γάρ τινος
τί πράττει ἐν Ἅιδου ὁ Ἐπίκουρος ;

"Μολυβδίνας ἔχων," ἔφη, "πέδας ἐν βορβόρῳ
    κάθηται."

εἶτα θαυμάζεις εἰ ἐπὶ μέγα ἤρθη τὸ χρηστήριον,
ὁρῶν τὰς ἐρωτήσεις τῶν προσιόντων συνετὰς καὶ
πεπαιδευμένας ;

Ὅλως δὲ ἄσπονδος καὶ ἀκήρυκτος αὐτῷ ὁ
πόλεμος πρὸς Ἐπίκουρον ἦν· μάλα εἰκότως. τίνι
γὰρ ἂν ἄλλῳ δικαιότερον προσεπολέμει γόης
ἄνθρωπος καὶ τερατείᾳ φίλος, ἀληθείᾳ δὲ ἔχθιστος,
ἢ Ἐπικούρῳ ἀνδρὶ τὴν φύσιν τῶν πραγμάτων
καθεωρακότι καὶ μόνῳ τὴν ἐν αὐτοῖς ἀλήθειαν
εἰδότι ; οἱ μὲν γὰρ ἀμφὶ τὸν Πλάτωνα καὶ Χρύ-
σιππον καὶ Πυθαγόραν φίλοι, καὶ εἰρήνη βαθεῖα
πρὸς ἐκείνους ἦν· ὁ δὲ ἄτεγκτος Ἐπίκουρος—
οὕτως γὰρ αὐτὸν ὠνόμαζεν—ἔχθιστος δικαίως,
πάντα ταῦτα ἐν γέλωτι καὶ παιδιᾷ τιθέμενος.
διὸ καὶ τὴν Ἄμαστριν ἐμίσει μάλιστα τῶν
Ποντικῶν πόλεων, ὅτι ἠπίστατο τοὺς περὶ

ALEXANDER THE FALSE PROPHET

When at last many sensible men, recovering, as it were, from profound intoxication, combined against him, especially all the followers of Epicurus, and when in the cities they began gradually to detect all the trickery and buncombe of the show, he issued a promulgation designed to scare them, saying that Pontus was full of atheists and Christians who had the hardihood to utter the vilest abuse of him; these he bade them drive away with stones if they wanted to have the god gracious. About Epicurus, moreover, he delivered himself of an oracle after this sort; when someone asked him how Epicurus was doing in Hades, he replied:

" With leaden fetters on his feet in filthy mire he
    sitteth."

Do you wonder, then, that the shrine waxed great, now that you see that the questions of its visitors were intelligent and refined?

In general, the war that he waged upon Epicurus was without truce or parley, naturally enough. Upon whom else would a quack who loved humbug and bitterly hated truth more fittingly make war than upon Epicurus, who discerned the nature of things and alone knew the truth in them? The followers of Plato and Chrysippus and Pythagoras were his friends, and there was profound peace with them; but "the impervious Epicurus"—for that is what he called him—was rightly his bitter enemy, since he considered all that sort of thing a laughing-matter and a joke. So Alexander hated Amastris most of all the cities in Pontus because he knew that

---

[1] καὶ μάλιστα οἱ Ἐπικούρου ἑταῖροι, πολλοὶ δὲ ἦσαν β.

Λέπιδον καὶ ἄλλους ὁμοίους αὐτοῖς πολλοὺς
ἐνόντας ἐν τῇ πόλει· οὐδὲ ἐχρησμῴδησε πώποτε
'Αμαστριανῷ ἀνδρί. ὁπότε δὲ καὶ ἐτόλμησεν
ἀδελφῷ συγκλητικοῦ χρησμῳδῆσαι, κατα-
γελάστως ἀπήλλαξεν, οὐχ εὑρὼν οὔτε αὐτὸς
πλάσασθαι χρησμὸν δεξιὸν οὔτε τὸν ποιῆσαι
πρὸς καιρὸν αὐτῷ δυνησόμενον. μεμφομένῳ γὰρ
αὐτῷ στομάχου ὀδύνην προστάξαι βουλόμενος
ὕειον πόδα μετὰ μαλάχης ἐσκευασμένον ἐσθίειν
οὕτως ἔφη·

Μάλβακα χοιράων ἱερῇ κυμίνευε σιπύδνῳ.

26   Πολλάκις μὲν οὖν, ὡς προεῖπον, ἔδειξε τὸν δράκοντα τοῖς δεομένοις, οὐχ ὅλον, ἀλλὰ τὴν οὐρὰν
μάλιστα καὶ τὸ ἄλλο σῶμα προβεβληκώς, τὴν
κεφαλὴν δὲ ὑπὸ κόλπου ἀθέατον φυλάττων.
ἐθελήσας δὲ καὶ μειζόνως ἐκπλῆξαι τὸ πλῆθος,
ὑπέσχετο καὶ λαλοῦντα παρέξειν τὸν θεόν, αὐτὸν
ἄνευ ὑποφήτου χρησμῳδοῦντα. εἶτα οὐ χαλεπῶς
γεράνων ἀρτηρίας συνάψας καὶ διὰ τῆς κεφαλῆς
ἐκείνης τῆς μεμηχανημένης πρὸς ὁμοιότητα διεί-
ρας, ἄλλου τινὸς ἔξωθεν ἐμβοῶντος, ἀπεκρίνετο
πρὸς τὰς ἐρωτήσεις, τῆς φωνῆς διὰ τοῦ ὀθονίνου
ἐκείνου 'Ασκληπιοῦ προπιπτούσης.

Ἐκαλοῦντο δὲ οἱ χρησμοὶ οὗτοι αὐτόφωνοι, καὶ
οὐ πᾶσιν ἐδίδοντο οὐδὲ ἀνέδην, ἀλλὰ τοῖς εὐ-

---

[1] An inscription from Amastris (C.I.G. 4149) honours
"Tiberius Claudius Lepidus, Chief Priest of Pontus and
President of the Metropolis of Pontus" (i. e. Amastris).
This can be no other than the Lepidus of Lucian. The
priesthood was that of Augustus. Amastris is almost due
N. of Angora, on the Black Sea, W. of Abonoteichus.

the followers of Lepidus [1] and others like them were numerous in the city; and he would never deliver an oracle to an Amastrian. Once when he did venture to make a prediction for a senator's brother, he acquitted himself ridiculously, since he could neither compose a clever response himself nor find anyone else who could do it in time. The man complained of colic, and Alexander, wishing to direct him to eat a pig's foot cooked with mallow, said:

" Mallow with cummin digest in a sacred pipkin of
    piglets."

Again and again, as I said before, he exhibited the serpent to all who requested it, not in its entirety, but exposing chiefly the tail and the rest of the body and keeping the head out of sight under his arm. But as he wished to astonish the crowd still more, he promised to produce the god talking—delivering oracles in person without a prophet. It was no difficult matter for him to fasten cranes' windpipes together and pass them through the head, which he had so fashioned as to be lifelike. Then he answered the questions through someone else, who spoke into the tube from the outside, so that the voice issued from his canvas Asclepius.[2]

These oracles were called autophones, and were not given to everybody promiscuously, but only to

---

[2] S. Hippolytus (*l.c.*, 28) mentions a tube made of windpipes of cranes, storks, or swans, and used in a similar way. Du Soul has a note in the Hemsterhuys-Reitz Lucian (ii, p. 234), telling of a wooden head constructed by Thomas Irson and exhibited to Charles II, which answered questions in any language and produced a great effect until a confederate was detected using a speaking-tube in the next room. Du Soul had the story from Irson himself.

27 παρύφοις καὶ πλουσίοις καὶ μεγαλοδώροις. ὁ
γοῦν Σευηριανῷ δοθεὶς ὑπὲρ τῆς εἰς Ἀρμενίαν
εἰσόδου τῶν αὐτοφώνων καὶ αὐτὸς ἦν. προτρέπων
γὰρ αὐτὸν ἐπὶ τὴν εἰσβολὴν οὕτως ἔφη·

Πάρθους Ἀρμενίους τε θοῷ ὑπὸ δουρὶ
δαμάσσας
νοστήσεις Ῥώμην καὶ Θύβριδος ἀγλαὸν ὕδωρ
στέμμα φέρων κροτάφοισι μεμιγμένον ἀκτί-
νεσσιν.

εἶτ᾽ ἐπειδὴ πεισθεὶς ὁ ἠλίθιος ἐκεῖνος Κελτὸς
εἰσέβαλε καὶ ἀπήλλαξεν αὐτῇ στρατιᾷ ὑπὸ τοῦ
Ὀσρόου[1] κατακοπείς, τοῦτον μὲν τὸν χρησμὸν
ἐξαιρεῖ ἐκ τῶν ὑπομνημάτων, ἐντίθησιν δ᾽ ἄλλον
ἀντ᾽ αὐτοῦ·

Μὴ σύ γ᾽ ἐπ᾽ Ἀρμενίους ἐλάαν στρατόν, οὐ
γὰρ ἄμεινον,
μή σοι θηλυχίτων τις ἀνὴρ τόξου ἄπο λυγρὸν
πότμον ἐπιπροϊεὶς παύσῃ βιότοιο φάους τε.

28 Καὶ γὰρ αὖ καὶ τοῦτο σοφώτατον ἐπενόησε,
τοὺς μεταχρονίους χρησμοὺς ἐπὶ θεραπείᾳ τῶν
κακῶς προτεθεσπισμένων καὶ ἀποτετευγμένων.
πολλάκις γὰρ πρὸ μὲν τῆς τελευτῆς τοῖς νοσοῦσιν

---

[1] Ὀσρόου Kuhn : Ὀθρύου β, Ὀθρυνάδου γ. Cf. *Hist. Conscrib.*
18 and 21.

---

[1] The *corona radiata*, worn by Augustus, Nero, and the
emperors after Caracalla. This passage seems to point to
its use (in addition to the laurel wreath?) as one of the
triumphal insignia.

those who were noble, rich, and free-handed. For example, the oracle given to Severianus in regard to his invasion of Armenia was one of the autophones. Alexander encouraged him to the invasion by saying :

" Under your charging spear shall fall Armenians
    and Parthi ;
  Then you shall fare to Rome and the glorious
    waters of Tiber
  Wearing upon your brow the chaplet studded
    with sunbeams." [1]

Then when that silly Celt, being convinced, made the invasion and ended by getting himself and his army cut to bits by Osroes, Alexander expunged this oracle from his records and inserted another in its place :

" Better for you that your forces against Armenia
    march not,
  Lest some man, like a woman bedight, despatch
    from his bowstring
  Grim death, cutting you off from life and enjoy-
    ment of sunlight." [2]

That was one of his devices, and a very clever one—belated oracles to make amends for those in which he had made bad predictions and missed the mark. Often he would promise good health to sick

---

[1] The Parthians had been interfering with the succession to the throne in Armenia. Severianus, Roman governor of Cappadocia, entered Armenia with a small force in 161, and was disastrously defeated at Elegeia by Chosroes. According to Dio Cassius (71, 2) the entire force was surrounded and wiped out. See also Lucian, *de Hist. Conscrib.* 21, 24, 25.

ὑγίειαν ἐπηγγέλλετο, ἀποθανόντων δὲ χρησμὸς
ἄλλος ἕτοιμος ἦν παλινῳδῶν·

> Μηκέτι δίζησθαι νούσοιο λυγρῆς ἐπαρωγήν·
> πότμος γὰρ προφανὴς οὐδ᾽ ἐκφυγέειν δυνατόν
> σοι.

29 Εἰδὼς δὲ τοὺς ἐν Κλάρῳ καὶ Διδύμοις καὶ
Μαλλῷ καὶ αὐτοὺς εὐδοκιμοῦντας ἐπὶ τῇ ὁμοίᾳ
μαντικῇ ταύτῃ, φίλους αὐτοὺς ἐποιεῖτο, πολλοὺς
τῶν προσιόντων πέμπων ἐπ᾽ αὐτοὺς λέγων·

> Ἐς Κλάρον ἵεσο νῦν, τοὐμοῦ πατρὸς ὡς ὄπ᾽
> ἀκούσῃς.

καὶ πάλιν·

> Βραγχιδέων ἀδύτοισι πελάζεο καὶ κλύε χρη-
> σμῶν.

καὶ αὖθις·

> Ἐς Μαλλὸν χώρει θεσπίσματά τ᾽ Ἀμφιλόχοιο.

30 Ταῦτα μὲν ἐντὸς τῶν ὅρων μέχρι τῆς Ἰωνίας
καὶ Κιλικίας καὶ Παφλαγονίας καὶ Γαλατίας.
ὡς δὲ καὶ εἰς τὴν Ἰταλίαν διεφοίτησεν τοῦ
μαντείου τὸ κλέος καὶ εἰς τὴν Ῥωμαίων πόλιν
ἐνέπεσεν, οὐδεὶς ὅστις οὐκ ἄλλος πρὸ ἄλλου
ἠπείγετο, οἱ μὲν αὐτοὶ ἰόντες, οἱ δὲ πέμποντες,
καὶ μάλιστα οἱ δυνατώτατοι καὶ μέγιστον ἀξίωμα
ἐν τῇ πόλει ἔχοντες· ὧν πρῶτος καὶ κορυφαιότατος
ἐγένετο Ῥουτιλιανός, ἀνὴρ τὰ μὲν ἄλλα καλὸς

---

[1] Apollo.
[2] P. Mummius Sisenna Rutilianus. What office he then
held (see below) is uncertain. He eventually went through
the whole *cursus honorum*, including the consulship (probably
suffect) and the governorship of Upper Moesia, and ending,

men before their demise, and when they died another oracle would be ready with a recantation:

"Seek no more for assistance against thy bitter affliction;

Death now standeth in view; 'tis beyond thy power to'scape him."

As he was aware that the priests at Clarus and Didymi and Mallus were themselves in high repute for the same sort of divination, he made them his friends by sending many of his visitors to them, saying:

"Now unto Clarus begone, to the voice of my father[1] to hearken."

and at another time,

Visit the fane of the Branchids and hear what the oracle sayeth,"

and again,

"Make thy way unto Mallus and let Amphilochus answer."

So far, we have been concerned with his doings near the frontier, extending over Ionia, Cilicia, Paphlagonia, and Galatia. But when the renown of his prophetic shrine spread to Italy and invaded the city of Rome, everybody without exception, each on the other's heels, made haste, some to go in person, some to send; this was the case particularly with those who had the greatest power and the highest rank in the city. The first and foremost of these was Rutilianus,[2] who, though a man of birth and

about A.D. 170, with the proconsulship of the province of Asia.

καὶ ἀγαθὸς καὶ ἐν πολλαῖς τάξεσι Ῥωμαϊκαῖς
ἐξητασμενος, τὰ δὲ περὶ τοὺς θεοὺς πάνυ νοσῶν
καὶ ἀλλόκοτα περὶ αὐτῶν πεπιστευκώς, εἰ μόνον
ἀληλιμμενον που λίθον ἢ ἐστεφανωμένον θεάσαιτο,
προσπίπτων εὐθὺς καὶ προσκυνῶν καὶ ἐπὶ πολὺ
παρεστὼς καὶ εὐχόμενος καὶ τἀγαθὰ παρ' αὐτοῦ
αἰτῶν.

Οὗτος τοίνυν ἀκούσας τὰ περὶ τοῦ χρηστηρίου
μικροῦ μὲν ἐδέησεν ἀφεὶς τὴν ἐγκεχειρισμένην
τάξιν εἰς τὸ τοῦ Ἀβώνου τεῖχος ἀναπτῆναι.
ἔπεμπε δ' οὖν ἄλλους ἐπ' ἄλλοις· οἱ δὲ πεμπό-
μενοι, ἰδιῶταί τινες οἰκέται, ῥᾳδίως ἐξαπατηθέντες
ἂν ἐπανῄεσαν, τὰ μὲν ἰδόντες, τὰ δὲ ὡς ἰδόντες
καὶ ἀκούσαντες[1] διηγούμενοι καὶ προσεπι-
μετροῦντες ἔτι πλείω τούτων, ὡς ἐντιμότεροι
εἶεν παρὰ τῷ δεσπότῃ. ἐξέκαιον οὖν τὸν ἄθλιον
31 γέροντα καὶ εἰς μανίαν ἐρρωμένην ἐνέβαλον. ὁ
δέ, ὡς ἂν τοῖς πλείστοις καὶ δυνατωτάτοις φίλος
ὤν, περιῄει τὰ μὲν διηγούμενος ὡς ἀκούσειε παρὰ
τῶν πεμφθέντων, τὰ δὲ καὶ παρ' αὐτοῦ προστιθείς.
ἐνέπλησεν οὖν τὴν πόλιν καὶ διεσάλευσεν οὗτος,
καὶ τῶν ἐν τῇ αὐλῇ τοὺς πλείστους διεθορύβησεν,
οἳ αὐτίκα καὶ αὐτοὶ ἠπείγοντο ἀκοῦσαί τι τῶν
καθ' αὑτούς.

Ὁ δὲ τοὺς ἀφικνουμένους πάνυ φιλοφρόνως
ὑποδεχόμενος ξενίοις τε καὶ ταῖς ἄλλαις δωρεαῖς
πολυτελέσιν εὔνους ἐργαζόμενος αὐτῷ ἀπέπεμπεν

---

[1] καὶ ὡς ἀκούσαντες γ, edd. But ὡς was added by someone
who thought that καὶ was the conjunction. Its real force
becomes apparent if one transposes thus : τὰ δὲ καὶ ἀκούσαντες
ὡς ἰδόντες διηγούμενοι.

breeding, put to the proof in many Roman offices, nevertheless in all that concerned the gods was very infirm and held strange beliefs about them. If he but saw anywhere a stone smeared with holy oil or adorned with a wreath,[1] he would fall on his face forthwith, kiss his hand, and stand beside it for a long time making vows and craving blessings from it.

When this man heard the tales about the oracle, he very nearly abandoned the office which had been committed to him and took wing to Abonoteichus. Anyhow, he sent one set of messengers after another, and his emissaries, mere illiterate serving-people, were easily deluded, so when they came back, they told not only what they had seen but what they had heard as if they had seen it, and threw in something more for good measure, so as to gain favour with their master. Consequently, they inflamed the poor old man and made him absolutely crazy. Having many powerful friends, he went about not only telling what he had heard from his messengers but adding still more on his own account. So he flooded and convulsed the city, and agitated most of the court, who themselves at once hastened to go and hear something that concerned them.

To all who came, Alexander gave a very cordial reception, made them think well of him by lavish entertainment and expensive presents, and sent

---

[1] For the Greek worship of stones, see Frazer's Pausanias, vol. iv, 154 sq. ; v, 314 sq., 354. In the note last cited he quotes Arnobius *adv. Nationes* 1, 39 : si quando conspexeram lubricatam lapidem et exolivi unguine sordidatam, tamquam inesset vis praesens adulabar adfabar, beneficia poscebam nihil sentiente de trunco. Add Clement of Alexandria, *Strom.* 7, 4, 26 : πᾶν ξύλον καὶ πάντα λίθον τὸ δὴ λεγόμενον λιπαρὸν προσκυνοῦντες.

οὐκ ἀπαγγελοῦντας μόνον τὰς ἐρωτήσεις, ἀλλὰ
καὶ ὑμνήσοντας τὸν θεὸν καὶ τεράστια ὑπὲρ τοῦ
32 μαντείου καὶ αὐτοὺς ψευσομένους. ἀλλὰ καὶ
μηχανᾶταί τι ὁ τρισκατάρατος οὐκ ἄσοφον οὐδὲ
τοῦ προστυχόντος λῃστοῦ ἄξιον. λύων γὰρ τὰ
πεπεμμένα βιβλία καὶ ἀναγιγνώσκων, εἴ τι εὕροι
ἐπισφαλὲς καὶ παρακεκινδυνευμένον ἐν ταῖς
ἐρωτήσεσιν, κατεῖχεν αὐτὸς καὶ οὐκ ἀπέπεμπεν,
ὡς ὑποχειρίους καὶ μονονουχὶ δούλους διὰ τὸ
δέος ἔχοι τοὺς πεπομφότας, μεμνημένους οἷα ἦν ἃ
ἤροντο. συνίης δὲ οἵας[1] εἰκὸς τοὺς πλουσίους
καὶ μέγα δυναμένους τὰς πύστεις πυνθάνεσθαι.
ἐλάμβανεν οὖν πολλὰ παρ' ἐκείνων, εἰδότων ὅτι
ἐντὸς αὐτοὺς ἔχοι τῶν ἀρκύων.

33 Βούλομαι δέ σοι καὶ τῶν Ῥουτιλιανῷ δοθέντων
χρησμῶν ἐνίους εἰπεῖν. πυνθανομένῳ γὰρ αὐτῷ
ὑπὲρ τοῦ παιδὸς ἐκ προτέρας γυναικός, παιδείας
ὥραν ἔχοντος, ὅντινα προστήσεται διδάσκαλον
τῶν μαθημάτων αὐτοῦ, ἔφη·

Πυθαγόρην πολέμων τε διάκτορον ἐσθλὸν
ἀοιδόν.

εἶτα μετ' ὀλίγας ἡμέρας τοῦ παιδὸς ἀποθανόντος,
ὁ μὲν ἠπόρει καὶ οὐδὲν εἶχεν λέγειν πρὸς τοὺς
αἰτιωμένους, παρὰ πόδας οὕτως ἐληλεγμένου τοῦ
χρησμοῦ· ὁ δὲ Ῥουτιλιανὸς αὐτὸς φθάσας ὁ
βέλτιστος ἀπελογεῖτο ὑπὲρ τοῦ μαντείου λέγων,
τοῦτο αὐτὸ προδεδηλωκέναι τὸν θεὸν καὶ διὰ τοῦτο
ζῶντα μὲν κελεῦσαι μηδένα διδάσκαλον ἑλέσθαι
αὐτῷ, Πυθαγόραν δὲ καὶ Ὅμηρον πάλαι τεθνεῶ-
τας, οἷς εἰκὸς τὸ μειράκιον ἐν Ἅιδου νῦν συνεῖναι.

---

[1] οἵας du Soul : οἷα MSS.

them back not merely to report the answers to their questions, but to sing the praises of the god and to tell portentous lies about the oracle on their own account. At the same time, however, the plaguy scoundrel devised a trick which was really clever and not what one would expect of your ordinary swindler. In opening and reading the forwarded scrolls, if he found anything dangerous and venturesome in the questions, he would keep them himself and not send them back, in order to hold the senders in subjection and all but in slavery because of their fear, since they remembered what it was that they had asked. You understand what questions are likely to be put by men who are rich and very powerful. So he used to derive much gain from those men, who knew that he had them in his net.

I should like to tell you some of the responses that were given to Rutilianus. Asking about his son by a former marriage, who was then in the full bloom of youth, he enquired who should be appointed his tutor in his studies. The reply was:

"Be it Pythagoras; aye, and the good bard, master of warfare."

Then after a few days the boy died, and Alexander was at his wit's end, with nothing to say to his critics, as the oracle had been shown up so obviously. But Rutilianus himself, good soul, made haste to defend the oracle by saying that the god had predicted precisely this outcome, and on account of it had bidden him to select as his tutor nobody then alive, but rather Pythagoras and Homer, who died long ago, with whom, no doubt, the lad was then studying

219

τί τοίνυν μέμφεσθαι ἄξιον Ἀλεξάνδρῳ, εἰ τοιούτοις ἀνθρωπίσκοις ἐνδιατρίβειν ἠξίου ;

34 Αὖθις δὲ πυνθανομένῳ αὐτῷ τὴν τίνος ψυχὴν
αὐτὸς διεδέξατο, ἔφη·

Πρῶτον Πηλείδης ἐγένου, μετὰ ταῦτα Μέ-
νανδρος,
εἶθ' ὃς νῦν φαίνῃ, μετὰ δ' ἔσσεαι ἡλιὰς ἀκτίς,
ζήσεις δ' ὀγδώκοντ' ἐπὶ τοῖς ἑκατὸν λυκά-
βαντας.

ὁ δὲ ἑβδομηκοντούτης ἀπέθανεν μελαγχολήσας,
35 οὐ περιμείνας τὴν τοῦ θεοῦ ὑπόσχεσιν. καὶ οὗτος
ὁ χρησμὸς τῶν αὐτοφώνων ἦν.

Ἐρομένῳ δὲ αὐτῷ ποτε καὶ περὶ γάμου ῥητῶς
ἔφη·

Γῆμον Ἀλεξάνδρου τε Σεληναίης τε θύγατρα.

διεδεδώκει δὲ πάλαι λόγον ὡς τῆς θυγατρός, ἣν
εἶχεν, ἐκ Σελήνης αὐτῷ γενομένης· τὴν γὰρ
Σελήνην ἔρωτι ἁλῶναι αὐτοῦ καθεύδοντά ποτε
ἰδοῦσαν, ὅπερ αὐτῇ ἔθος, κοιμωμένων ἐρᾶν τῶν
καλῶν. ὁ δ' οὐδὲν μελλήσας ὁ συνετώτατος
Ῥουτιλιανὸς ἔπεμπεν εὐθὺς ἐπὶ τὴν κόρην καὶ
τοὺς γάμους συνετέλει ἑξηκοντούτης νυμφίος καὶ
συνῆν, τὴν πενθερὰν Σελήνην ἑκατόμβαις ὅλαις
ἱλασκόμενος καὶ τῶν ἐπουρανίων εἷς καὶ αὐτὸς
οἰόμενος γεγονέναι.

36 Ὁ δ' ὡς ἅπαξ τῶν ἐν Ἰταλίᾳ πραγμάτων ἐλά-
βετο, μείζω ἀεὶ προσεπενόει καὶ πάντοσε τῆς

---

[1] A reference to the story of Endymion.

in Hades. What fault, then, should we find with Alexander if he thought fit to amuse himself at the expense of such homunculi?

At another time, when Rutilianus enquired whose soul he had inherited, the reply was:

"Peleus' son wert thou at the first; thereafter
    Menander,
Then what thou seemest now, and hereafter shalt
    turn to a sunbeam.
Four score seasons of life shall be given thee over
    a hundred."

But as a matter of fact he died insane at seventy without awaiting the fulfilment of the god's promise! This oracle too was one of the autophones.

When one time he enquired about getting married, Alexander said explicitly:

"Take Alexander's daughter to wife, who was born
    of Selene."

He had long before given out a story to the effect that his daughter was by Selene; for Selene had fallen in love with him on seeing him asleep once upon a time—it is a habit of hers, you know, to adore handsome lads in their sleep![1] Without any hesitation that prince of sages Rutilianus sent for the girl at once, celebrated his nuptials as a sexagenarian bridegroom, and took her to wife, propitiating his mother-in-law, the moon, with whole hecatombs and imagining that he himself had become one of the Celestials!

No sooner did Alexander get Italy in hand than he began to devise projects that were ever greater and greater, and sent oracle-mongers everywhere in

Ῥωμαίων ἀρχῆς ἔπεμπε χρησμολόγους, ταῖς
πόλεσι προλέγων λοιμοὺς καὶ πυρκαϊὰς φυλάσ-
σεσθαι καὶ σεισμούς· καὶ ἀσφαλῶς βοηθήσειν,
ὡς μὴ γένοιτό τι τούτων, αὐτὸς ὑπισχνεῖτο αὐτοῖς.
ἕνα δέ τινα χρησμόν, αὐτόφωνον καὶ αὐτόν, εἰς
ἅπαντα τὰ ἔθνη ἐν τῷ λοιμῷ διεπέμψατο· ἦν δὲ
τὸ ἔπος ἕν·

Φοῖβος ἀκειρεκόμης[1] λοιμοῦ νεφέλην ἀπερύκει.

καὶ τοῦτο ἦν ἰδεῖν τὸ ἔπος πανταχοῦ ἐπὶ τῶν
πυλώνων γεγραμμένον ὡς τοῦ λοιμοῦ ἀλεξιφάρ-
μακον. τὸ δ' εἰς τοὐναντίον τοῖς πλείστοις
προυχώρει· κατὰ γάρ τινα τύχην αὗται μάλιστα
αἱ οἰκίαι ἐκενώθησαν αἷς τὸ ἔπος ἐπεγέγραπτο.
καὶ μή με νομίσῃς τοῦτο λέγειν, ὅτι διὰ τὸ ἔπος
ἀπώλλυντο· ἀλλὰ τύχῃ τινὶ οὕτως ἐγένετο. τάχα
δὲ καὶ οἱ πολλοὶ θαρροῦντες τῷ στίχῳ ἠμέλουν
καὶ ῥᾳθυμότερον διῃτῶντο, οὐδὲν τῷ χρησμῷ
πρὸς τὴν νόσον συντελοῦντες, ὡς ἂν ἔχοντες
προμαχομένας αὐτῶν τὰς συλλαβὰς καὶ τὸν
ἀκειρεκόμην[2] Φοῖβον ἀποτοξεύοντα τὸν λοιμόν.

37 Πευθῆνας μέντοι ἐν αὐτῇ Ῥώμῃ κατεστήσατο
πάνυ πολλοὺς τῶν συνωμοτῶν, οἳ τὰς ἑκάστου
γνώμας διήγγελλον αὐτῷ καὶ τὰς ἐρωτήσεις
προεμήνυον καὶ ὧν μάλιστα ἐφίενται, ὡς ἕτοιμον
αὐτὸν πρὸς τὰς ἀποκρίσεις καὶ πρὶν ἥκειν τοὺς
πεμπομένους καταλαμβάνεσθαι.

38 Καὶ πρὸς μὲν τὰ ἐν τῇ Ἰταλίᾳ ταῦτα[3] προε-

---

[1] ἀκερσεκόμης β.
[2] ἀτερσεκόμην β.
[3] ταῦτα καὶ τὰ τοιαῦτα γ.

the Roman Empire, warning the cities to be on their guard against plagues and conflagrations and earthquakes; he promised that he would himself afford them infallible aid so that none of these calamities should befall them. There was one oracle, also an autophone, which he despatched to all the nations during the pestilence [1]; it was but a single verse:

"Phoebus, the god unshorn, keepeth off plague's
　　　nebulous onset."

This verse was to be seen everywhere written over doorways as a charm against the plague; but in most cases it had the contrary result. By some chance it was particularly the houses on which the verse was inscribed that were depopulated! Do not suppose me to mean that they were stricken on account of the verse—by some chance or other it turned out that way, and perhaps, too, people neglected precautions because of their confidence in the line and lived too carelessly, giving the oracle no assistance against the disease because they were going to have the syllables to defend them and "unshorn Phoebus" to drive away the plague with his arrows!

Moreover, Alexander posted a great number of his fellow-conspirators in Rome itself as his agents, who reported everyone's views to him and gave him advance information about the questions and the especial wishes of those who consulted him, so that the messengers might find him ready to answer even before they arrived!

He made these preparations to meet the situation in Italy, and also made notable preparations at home.

---

[1] The terrible plague which swept the whole Empire about A.D. 165.

μηχανᾶτο· <οἴκοι δὲ καὶ τὰ τοιαῦτα.>[1] τελετήν τε
γάρ τινα συνίσταται καὶ δᾳδουχίας καὶ ἱερο-
φαντίας, τριῶν ἑξῆς ἀεὶ τελουμένων ἡμερῶν. καὶ
ἐν μὲν τῇ πρώτῃ πρόρρησις ἦν ὥσπερ Ἀθήνησι
τοιαύτη· " Εἴ τις ἄθεος ἢ Χριστιανὸς ἢ Ἐπικού-
ρειος ἥκει κατάσκοπος τῶν ὀργίων, φευγέτω· οἱ
δὲ πιστεύοντες τῷ θεῷ τελείσθωσαν τύχῃ τῇ
ἀγαθῇ." εἶτ' εὐθὺς ἐν ἀρχῇ ἐξέλασις ἐγίγνετο·
καὶ ὁ μὲν ἡγεῖτο λέγων "Ἔξω Χριστιανούς," τὸ δὲ
πλῆθος ἅπαν ἐπεφθέγγετο "Ἔξω Ἐπικουρείους."
εἶτα Λητοῦς ἐγίγνετο λοχεία καὶ Ἀπόλλωνος
γοναὶ καὶ Κορωνίδος γάμος καὶ Ἀσκληπιὸς
ἐτίκτετο. ἐν δὲ τῇ δευτέρᾳ Γλύκωνος ἐπιφάνεια
39 καὶ γέννησις τοῦ θεοῦ. τρίτῃ δὲ ἡμέρᾳ Ποδαλειρίου ἦν καὶ τῆς μητρὸς Ἀλεξάνδρου γάμος·
Δᾳδὶς δὲ ἐκαλεῖτο καὶ δᾷδες δὲ ἐκαίοντο. καὶ
τελευταῖον Σελήνης καὶ Ἀλεξάνδρου ἔρως καὶ
τικτομένη τοῦ Ῥουτιλιανοῦ ἡ γυνή. ἐδᾳδούχει δὲ
καὶ ἱεροφάντει ὁ Ἐνδυμίων Ἀλέξανδρος. καὶ ὁ
μὲν καθεύδων δῆθεν κατέκειτο ἐν τῷ μέσῳ, κατῄει
δὲ ἐπ' αὐτὸν ἀπὸ τῆς ὀροφῆς ὡς ἐξ οὐρανοῦ ἀντὶ
τῆς Σελήνης Ῥουτιλία τις ὡραιοτάτη, τῶν
Καίσαρος οἰκονόμων τινὸς γυνή, ὡς ἀληθῶς ἐρῶσα
τοῦ Ἀλεξάνδρου καὶ ἀντερωμένη ὑπ' αὐτοῦ, καὶ
ἐν ὀφθαλμοῖς τοῦ ὀλεθρίου ἐκείνου ἀνδρὸς φιλή-
ματά τε ἐγίγνετο ἐν τῷ μέσῳ καὶ περιπλοκαί. εἰ

---

[1] Supplement by A.M.H. (after Fritzsche). The preceding
μὲν and the following γὰρ prove a gap in the text, which one
would expect to be of 17–19 letters—a line in the γ β
archetype.

He established a celebration of mysteries, with torch-light ceremonies and priestly offices, which was to be held annually, for three days in succession, in perpetuity. On the first day, as at Athens,[1] there was a proclamation, worded as follows: "If any atheist or Christian or Epicurean has come to spy upon the rites, let him be off, and let those who believe in the god perform the mysteries, under the blessing of Heaven." Then, at the very outset, there was an "expulsion," in which he took the lead, saying: "Out with the Christians," and the whole multitude chanted in response, "Out with the Epicureans!" Then there was the child-bed of Leto, the birth of Apollo, his marriage to Coronis, and the birth of Asclepius. On the second day came the manifestation of Glycon, including the birth of the god. On the third day there was the union of Podaleirius and the mother of Alexander—it was called the Day of Torches, and torches were burned. In conclusion there was the amour of Selene and Alexander, and the birth of Rutilianus' wife. The torch-bearer and hierophant was our Endymion, Alexander. While he lay in full view, pretending to be asleep, there came down to him from the roof, as if from heaven, not Selene but Rutilia, a very pretty woman, married to one of the Emperor's stewards. She was genuinely in love with Alexander and he with her; and before the eyes of her worthless husband there were kisses and embraces in public. If the torches

[1] The reference is to the proclamation that preceded the Eleusinian mysteries. Its entire content is unknown, but it required that the celebrants be clean of hand, pure of heart, and Greek in speech. Barbarians, homicides, and traitors were excluded; and there was some sort of restriction in regard to previous diet.

δὲ μὴ πολλαὶ ἦσαν αἱ δᾷδες, τάχα ἄν τι καὶ τῶν
ὑπὸ κόλπου ἐπράττετο. μετὰ μικρὸν δὲ εἰσῄει
πάλιν ἱεροφαντικῶς ἐσκευασμένος ἐν πολλῇ τῇ
σιωπῇ, καὶ αὐτὸς μὲν ἔλεγε μεγάλῃ τῇ φωνῇ,
" Ἰὴ Γλύκων " ἐπεφθέγγοντο δὲ αὐτῷ ἐπακολου-
θοῦντες Εὐμολπίδαι δῆθεν καὶ Κήρυκές τινες
Παφλαγόνες, καρβατίνας ὑποδεδεμένοι, πολλὴν
τὴν σκοροδάλμην ἐρυγγάνοντες, " Ἰὴ Ἀλέξανδρε."

40   Πολλάκις δὲ ἐν τῇ δᾳδουχίᾳ καὶ τοῖς μυστικοῖς
σκιρτήμασιν γυμνωθεὶς ὁ μηρὸς αὐτοῦ ἐξεπίτηδες
χρυσοῦς διεφάνη, δέρματος ὡς εἰκὸς ἐπιχρύσου
περιτεθέντος καὶ πρὸς τὴν αὐγὴν τῶν λαμπάδων
ἀποστίλβοντος. ὥστε καὶ γενομένης ποτὲ ζητή-
σεως δύο τισὶ τῶν μωροσόφων ὑπὲρ αὐτοῦ, εἴτε
Πυθαγόρου τὴν ψυχὴν ἔχοι διὰ τὸν χρυσοῦν
μηρὸν εἴτε ἄλλην ὁμοίαν αὐτῇ, καὶ τὴν ζήτησιν
ταύτην αὐτῷ Ἀλεξάνδρῳ ἐπανενεγκόντων, ὁ
βασιλεὺς Γλύκων χρησμῷ ἔλυσεν τὴν ἀπορίαν·

Πυθαγόρου ψυχὴ ποτὲ μὲν φθίνει, ἄλλοτε δ᾽
    αὔξει·
ἡ δὲ προφητείη δίης φρενός ἐστιν ἀπορρώξ.
καί μιν ἔπεμψε πατὴρ ἀγαθῶν ἀνδρῶν
    ἐπαρωγόν·
καὶ πάλιν ἐς Διὸς εἶσι Διὸς βληθεῖσα κεραυνῷ.

41   Προλέγων δὲ πᾶσιν ἀπέχεσθαι παιδίου συνου-
σίας, ὡς ἀσεβὲς ὄν, αὐτὸς τοιόνδε τι ὁ γεννάδας
ἐτεχνήσατο. ταῖς γὰρ πόλεσι ταῖς Ποντικαῖς
καὶ ταῖς Παφλαγονικαῖς ἐπήγγελλε θεηκόλους

---

[1] Hereditary priesthoods in the Eleusinian mysteries.
[2] As Pythagoras had a golden thigh (Plutarch, *Numa*, 65 ;
Aelian, *Var. Hist.*, 2, 26), a believer in metempsychosis might
think that Alexander was a reincarnation of Pythagoras.

had not been numerous, perhaps the thing would have been carried even further. After a short time Alexander entered again, robed as a priest, amid profound silence, and said in a loud voice, over and over again, " Hail, Glycon," while, following in his train, a number of would-be Eumolpids and Ceryces[1] from Paphlagonia, with brogans on their feet and breaths that reeked of garlic, shouted in response, " Hail, Alexander ! "

Often in the course of the torchlight ceremonies and the gambols of the mysteries his thigh was bared purposely and showed golden. No doubt gilded leather had been put about it, which gleamed in the light of the cressets. There was once a discussion between two of our learned idiots in regard to him, whether he had the soul of Pythagoras, on account of the golden thigh, or some other soul akin to it.[2] They referred this question to Alexander himself, and King Glycon resolved their doubt with an oracle :

" Nay, Pythagoras' soul now waneth and other
    times waxeth ;
His, with prophecy gifted, from God's mind taketh
    its issue,
Sent by the Father to aid good men in the stress
    of the conflict ;
Then it to God will return, by God's own thunder-
    bolt smitten."

Although he cautioned all to abstain from intercourse with boys on the ground that it was impious, for his own part this pattern of propriety made a clever arrangement. He commanded the cities in Pontus and Paphlagonia to send choir-boys for three

πέμπειν εἰς τριετίαν, ὑμνήσοντας παρ' αὐτῷ τὸν
θεόν, καὶ ἔδει δοκιμασθέντας καὶ προκριθέντας
τοὺς εὐγενεστάτους καὶ ὡραιοτάτους καὶ κάλλει
διαφέροντας πεμφθῆναι· οὓς ἐγκλεισάμενος ὥσπερ
ἀργυρωνήτοις ἐχρῆτο, συγκαθεύδων καὶ πάντα
τρόπον ἐμπαροινῶν. καὶ νόμον δὲ ἐπεποίητο,
ὑπὲρ τὰ ὀκτωκαίδεκα ἔτη μηδένα τῷ αὐτοῦ
στόματι δεξιοῦσθαι μηδὲ φιλήματι ἀσπάζεσθαι,
ἀλλὰ τοῖς ἄλλοις προτείνων τὴν χεῖρα κύσαι
μόνους τοὺς ὡραίους κατεφίλει, καὶ ἐκαλοῦντο
οἱ ἐντὸς τοῦ φιλήματος.

42 Τοιαῦτα ἐντρυφῶν τοῖς ἀνοήτοις διετέλει,
γυναῖκάς τε ἀνέδην διαφθείρων καὶ παισὶ συνών.
καὶ ἦν μέγα καὶ εὐκτὸν ἑκάστῳ, εἴ τινος γυναικὶ
προσβλέψειεν· εἰ δὲ καὶ φιλήματος ἀξιώσειεν,
ἀθρόαν τὴν ἀγαθὴν τύχην ᾤετο ἕκαστος εἰς τὴν
οἰκίαν αὐτῷ εἰσρυήσεσθαι. πολλαὶ δὲ καὶ ηὔχουν
τετοκέναι παρ' αὐτοῦ, καὶ οἱ ἄνδρες ἐπεμαρτύρουν
ὅτι ἀληθῆ λέγουσιν.

43 Ἐθέλω δέ σοι καὶ διάλογον διηγήσασθαι τοῦ
Γλύκωνος καὶ Σακερδῶτός τινος, Τιανοῦ ἀνθρώ-
που· ὁποίου τινὸς τὴν σύνεσιν, εἴσῃ ἀπὸ τῶν
ἐρωτήσεων. ἀνέγνων δὲ αὐτὸν χρυσοῖς γράμμασιν γεγραμμένον ἐν Τίῳ, ἐν τῇ τοῦ Σακερδῶτος
οἰκίᾳ. "Εἰπὲ γάρ μοι," ἔφη, "ὦ δέσποτα
Γλύκων, τίς εἶ;" "Ἐγώ," ἦ δ' ὅς, "Ἀσκληπιὸς
νέος." "Ἄλλος παρ' ἐκεῖνον τὸν πρότερον; πῶς
λέγεις;" "Οὐ θέμις ἀκοῦσαί σε τοῦτό γε."
"Πόσα δὲ ἡμῖν ἔτη παραμενεῖς χρησμῳδῶν;"
"Τρίτον πρὸς τοῖς χιλίοις." "Εἶτα ποῖ μετα-
στήσῃ;" "Ἐς Βάκτρα καὶ τὴν ἐκεῖ γῆν· δεῖ γὰρ
ἀπολαῦσαι καὶ τοὺς βαρβάρους τῆς ἐπιδημίας

years' service, to sing hymns to the god in his household; they were required to examine, select, and send the noblest, youngest, and most handsome. These he kept under ward and treated like bought slaves, sleeping with them and affronting them in every way. He made it a rule, too, not to greet anyone over eighteen years with his lips, or to embrace and kiss him; he kissed only the young, extending his hand to the others to be kissed by them. They were called "those within the kiss."

He duped the simpletons in this way from first to last, ruining women right and left as well as living with favourites. Indeed, it was a great thing that everyone coveted if he simply cast his eyes upon a man's wife; if, however, he deemed her worthy of a kiss, each husband thought that good fortune would flood his house. Many women even boasted that they had had children by Alexander, and their husbands bore witness that they spoke the truth!

I want to include in my tale a dialogue between Glycon and one Sacerdos, a man of Tius, whose intelligence you will be able to appraise from his questions. I read the conversation in an inscription in letters of gold, at Tius, in the house of Sacerdos. "Tell me, Master Glycon," said he, "who are you?" "I am the latter-day Asclepius," he replied. "A different person from the one of former times? What do you mean?" "It is not permitted you to hear that." "How many years will you tarry among us delivering oracles?" "One thousand and three." "Then where shall you go?" "To Bactra and that region, for the barbarians too must profit by my presence among

τῆς ἐμῆς." "Τὰ δ' ἄλλα χρηστήρια, τὸ ἐν
Διδύμοις καὶ τὸ ἐν Κλάρῳ καὶ τὸ ἐν Δελφοῖς,
ἔχουσι τὸν πατέρα τὸν Ἀπόλλω χρησμῳδοῦντα,
ἢ[1] ψευδεῖς εἰσιν οἱ νῦν ἐκπίπτοντες ἐκεῖ χρησμοί ; "
" Μηδὲ τοῦτο ἐθελήσῃς εἰδέναι· οὐ γὰρ θέμις."
"'Εγὼ δὲ τίς ἔσομαι μετὰ τὸν νῦν βίον ; "
" Κάμηλος, εἶτα ἵππος, εἶτ' ἀνὴρ σοφὸς καὶ
προφήτης οὐ μείων Ἀλεξάνδρου."

Τοιαῦτα μὲν ὁ Γλύκων τῷ Σακερδῶτι διελέχθη.
ἐπὶ τέλει δὲ χρησμὸν ἔμμετρον ἐφθέγξατο, εἰδὼς
αὐτὸν Λεπίδῳ ἑταῖρον ὄντα·

Μὴ πείθου Λεπίδῳ, ἐπεὶ ἦ λυγρὸς οἶτος
ὀπηδεῖ.

πάνυ γὰρ ἐδεδίει τὸν Ἐπίκουρον, ὡς προεῖπον, ὥς
τινα ἀντίτεχνον καὶ ἀντισοφιστὴν τῆς μαγγανείας
αὐτοῦ.

44   "Ἕνα γοῦν τινα τῶν Ἐπικουρείων, τολμήσαντα
καὶ διελέγχειν αὐτὸν ἐπὶ πολλῶν τῶν παρόντων,
εἰς κίνδυνον οὐ μικρὸν κατέστησεν. ὁ μὲν γὰρ
προσελθὼν ἔλεγεν μεγάλῃ τῇ φωνῇ· "Σὺ μέντοι
γε, ὦ Ἀλέξανδρε, τὸν δεῖνα Παφλαγόνα προσ-
αγαγεῖν οἰκέτας αὐτοῦ τῷ ἡγουμένῳ τῆς Γαλατίας τὴν ἐπὶ θανάτῳ ἀνέπεισας ὡς ἀπεκτονότας
τὸν υἱὸν αὐτοῦ ἐν Ἀλεξανδρείᾳ παιδευόμενον, ὁ
δὲ νεανίσκος ζῇ καὶ ἐπανελήλυθε ζῶν μετὰ τὴν
τῶν οἰκετῶν ἀπώλειαν, θηρίοις ὑπὸ σοῦ παρα-
δοθέντων." τοιοῦτον δέ τι ἐγεγένητο· ἀναπλεύσας
ὁ νεανίσκος εἰς Αἴγυπτον ἄχρι τοῦ Κλύσματος,
πλοίου ἀναγομένου ἐπείσθη καὶ αὐτὸς εἰς Ἰνδίαν

---

[1] ἔτι σου τὸν προπάτορα ἔχει τὸν Ἀπόλλω, ἢ β.

---

[1] See p. 211, note 1.

men." "What of the other prophetic shrines, the one in Didymi, the one in Clarus, and the one in Delphi—do they still have your father Apollo as the source of their oracles, or are the predictions now given out there false?" "This too you must not wish to know; it is not permitted." "What about myself—what shall I be after my present life?" "A camel, then a horse, then a wise man and prophet just as great as Alexander."

That was Glycon's conversation with Sacerdos; and in conclusion he uttered an oracle in verse, knowing that Sacerdos was a follower of Lepidus:[1]

"Put not in Lepidus faith, for a pitiful doom is in waiting."

That was because he greatly feared Epicurus, as I have said before, seeing in him an opponent and critic of his trickery.

Indeed, he seriously imperilled one of the Epicureans who ventured to expose him in the presence of a great crowd. The man went up to him and said in a loud voice: "Come now, Alexander! You prevailed upon such-and-such a Paphlagonian to put his servants on trial for their lives before the governor of Galatia on the charge that they had murdered his son, a student at Alexandria. But the young man is living, and has come back alive after the execution of the servants, whom you gave over to the wild beasts." What had happened was this. The young man cruised up the Nile as far as Clysma,[2] and as a vessel was just putting to sea, was induced to join others in a voyage to India. Then because

---

[2] Probably Suez; the ancient canal from the Nile to the Red Sea ended there.

πλεῦσαι, κἀπειδήπερ ἐβράδυνεν, οἱ δυστυχεῖς
ἐκεῖνοι οἰκέται αὐτοῦ, οἰηθέντες ἢ ἐν τῷ Νείλῳ
πλέοντα διεφθάρθαι τὸν νεανίσκον ἢ καὶ ὑπὸ
λῃστῶν—πολλοὶ δὲ ἦσαν τότε—ἀνῃρῆσθαι,
ἐπανῆλθον ἀπαγγέλλοντες αὐτοῦ τὸν ἀφανισμόν.
εἶτα ὁ χρησμὸς καὶ ἡ καταδίκη, μεθ᾽ ἣν ἐπέστη ὁ
νεανίσκος διηγούμενος τὴν ἀποδημίαν.

45 Ὁ μὲν ταῦτα ἔλεγεν. ὁ δὲ Ἀλέξανδρος
ἀγανακτήσας ἐπὶ τῷ ἐλέγχῳ καὶ μὴ φέρων τοῦ
ὀνείδους τὴν ἀλήθειαν ἐκέλευεν τοὺς παρόντας
λίθοις βάλλειν αὐτόν, ἢ καὶ αὐτοὺς ἐναγεῖς ἔσεσθαι
καὶ Ἐπικουρείους κληθήσεσθαι. τῶν δὲ βάλλειν
ἀρξαμένων Δημόστρατός τις ἐπιδημῶν, τοῦ Πόντου πρῶτος, περιχυθεὶς ἐρρύσατο τοῦ θανάτου
τὸν ἄνθρωπον μικροῦ δεῖν καταλευσθέντα, πάνυ
δικαίως. τί γὰρ ἔδει μόνον φρονεῖν ἐν τοσούτοις
μεμηνόσιν καὶ παραπολαῦσαι τῆς Παφλαγόνων
μωρίας;

46 Καὶ τὰ μὲν κατ᾽ ἐκεῖνον τοιαῦτα. εἰ δέ τινι,
προσκαλουμένων κατὰ τάξιν τῶν χρησμῶν—πρὸ
μιᾶς δὲ τοῦτο τοῦ θεσπίζειν ἐγίγνετο—καὶ ἐρομένου
τοῦ κήρυκος εἰ θεσπίζει τῷδε,[1] ἀνεῖπεν ἔνδοθεν·
" Ἐς κόρακας," οὐκέτι τὸν τοιοῦτον οὔτε στέγη
τις ἐδέχετο οὔτε πυρὸς ἢ ὕδατος ἐκοινώνει, ἀλλ᾽
ἔδει γῆν πρὸ γῆς ἐλαύνεσθαι ὡς ἀσεβῆ καὶ ἄθεον
καὶ Ἐπικούρειον, ἥπερ ἦν ἡ μεγίστη λοιδορία.

---

[1] τῷδε ς, Seager : τῷ δὲ MSS.

he was overdue, those ill-starred servants concluded that the young man either had lost his life during his cruise upon the Nile or had been made away with by brigands, who were numerous at the time; and they returned with the report of his disappearance. Then followed the oracle and their condemnation, after which the young man presented himself, telling of his travels.

When he told this tale, Alexander, indignant at the exposure and unable to bear the truth of the reproach, told the bystanders to stone him, or else they themselves would be accurst and would bear the name of Epicureans. They had begun to throw stones when a man named Demostratus who happened to be in the city, one of the most prominent men in Pontus,[1] flung his arms about the fellow and saved him from death. But he had come very near to being overwhelmed with stones, and quite properly! Why did he have to be the only man of sense among all those lunatics and suffer from the idiocy of the Paphlagonians?

That man, then, was thus dealt with. Moreover, if in any case, when men were called up in the order of their applications (which took place the day before the prophecies were given out) and the herald enquired: "Has he a prophecy for So-and-so," the reply came from within: "To the ravens," nobody would ever again receive such a person under his roof or give him fire or water, but he had to be harried from country to country as an impious man, an atheist, and an Epicurean—which, indeed, was their strongest term of abuse.

[1] I suspect that the Greek phrase is really a title, but cannot prove it; the use of πρῶτος without the article seems to make the phrase mean "One of the First Citizens."

47 Ἐν γοῦν καὶ γελοιότατον ἐποίησεν ὁ Ἀλέξαν-
δρος· εὑρὼν γὰρ τὰς Ἐπικούρου κυρίας δόξας, τὸ
κάλλιστον, ὡς οἶσθα, τῶν βιβλίων καὶ κεφαλαιώδη
περιέχον τῆς τἀνδρὸς σοφίας τὰ δόγματα, κομίσας
εἰς τὴν ἀγορὰν μέσην ἔκαυσεν ἐπὶ ξύλων συκίνων
ὡς δῆθεν αὐτὸν καταφλέγων, καὶ τὴν σποδὸν εἰς
τὴν θάλασσαν ἐξέβαλεν, ἔτι καὶ χρησμὸν ἐπι-
φθεγξάμενος·

Πυρπολέειν κέλομαι δόξας ἀλαοῖο γέροντος·

οὐκ εἰδὼς ὁ κατάρατος ὅσων ἀγαθῶν τὸ βιβλίον
ἐκεῖνο τοῖς ἐντυχοῦσιν αἴτιον γίγνεται, καὶ ὅσην
αὐτοῖς εἰρήνην καὶ ἀταραξίαν καὶ ἐλευθερίαν
ἐνεργάζεται, δειμάτων μὲν καὶ φασμάτων καὶ
τεράτων ἀπαλλάττον καὶ ἐλπίδων ματαίων καὶ
περιττῶν ἐπιθυμιῶν, νοῦν δὲ καὶ ἀλήθειαν ἐντιθὲν
καὶ καθαῖρον ὡς ἀληθῶς τὰς γνώμας, οὐχ ὑπὸ
δᾳδὶ καὶ σκίλλῃ καὶ ταῖς τοιαύταις φλυαρίαις,
ἀλλὰ λόγῳ ὀρθῷ καὶ ἀληθείᾳ καὶ παρρησίᾳ.

48 Ἐν δὲ τοῖς ἄλλοις ἕν τι καὶ μέγιστον τόλμημα
τοῦ μιαροῦ ἀνδρὸς ἄκουσον. ἔχων γὰρ οὐ μικρὰν
ἐπίβασιν ἐπὶ τὰ βασίλεια καὶ τὴν αὐλὴν τὸν
Ῥουτιλιανὸν εὐδοκιμοῦντα, διαπέμπεται χρησμὸν
τοῦ ἐν Γερμανίᾳ πολέμου ἀκμάζοντος, ὅτε θεὸς
Μάρκος ἤδη τοῖς Μαρκομάνοις καὶ Κουάδοις
συνεπλέκετο. ἠξίου δὲ ὁ χρησμὸς δύο λέοντας
ἐμβληθῆναι ζῶντας εἰς τὸν Ἴστρον μετὰ πολλῶν

One of Alexander's acts in this connection was most comical. Hitting upon the "Established Beliefs" of Epicurus, which is the finest of his books, as you know, and contains in summary the articles of the man's philosophic creed,[1] he brought it into the middle of the market-place, burned it on fagots of fig-wood just as if he were burning the man in person, and threw the ashes into the sea, even adding an oracle also:

"Burn with fire, I command you, the creed of a
    purblind dotard!"

But the scoundrel had no idea what blessings that book creates for its readers and what peace, tranquillity, and freedom it engenders in them, liberating them as it does from terrors and apparitions and portents, from vain hopes and extravagant cravings, developing in them intelligence and truth, and truly purifying their understanding, not with torches and squills and that sort of foolery, but with straight thinking, truthfulness and frankness.

Of all this blackguard's emprises, however, hear one, the greatest. Since he had no slight influence in the palace and at court through the favour which Rutilianus enjoyed, he published an oracle at the height of the war in Germany, when the late Emperor Marcus himself had at last come to grips with the Marcomanni and Quadi. The oracle recommended that two lions be cast into the Danube alive, together with a quantity of perfumes and

[1] Quis enim vostrum non edidicit Epicuri κυρίας δόξας, id est, quasi maxume ratas, quia gravissumae sint ad beate vivendum breviter enuntiatae sententiae? Cicero, de Fin. Bon. et Mal., ii, 7, 20.

ἀρωμάτων καὶ θυσιῶν μεγαλοπρεπῶν. ἄμεινον
δὲ αὐτὸν εἰπεῖν τὸν χρησμόν·

Ἐς δίνας Ἴστροιο διιπετέος ποταμοῖο
ἐσβαλέειν κέλομαι δοιοὺς Κυβέλης θεράποντας,
θῆρας ὀριτρεφέας, καὶ ὅσα τρέφει Ἰνδικὸς ἀὴρ
ἄνθεα καὶ βοτάνας εὐώδεας· αὐτίκα δ' ἔσται
νίκη καὶ μέγα κῦδος ἅμ' εἰρήνῃ ἐρατεινῇ.

γενομένων δὲ τούτων ὡς προσέταξεν, τοὺς μὲν
λέοντας ἐκνηξαμένους εἰς τὴν πολεμίαν οἱ
βάρβαροι ξύλοις κατειργάσαντο ὥς τινας κύνας
ἢ λύκους ξενικούς· αὐτίκα δὲ τὸ μέγιστον τραῦμα
τοῖς ἡμετέροις ἐγένετο, δισμυρίων που σχεδὸν
ἀθρόων[1] ἀπολομένων. εἶτα ἐπηκολούθησε τὰ
περὶ Ἀκυληΐαν γενόμενα καὶ ἡ παρὰ μικρὸν τῆς
πόλεως ἐκείνης ἅλωσις. ὁ δὲ πρὸς τὸ ἀποβεβηκὸς
τὴν Δελφικὴν ἐκείνην ἀπολογίαν καὶ τὸν τοῦ
Κροίσου χρησμὸν ψυχρῶς παρῆγεν· νίκην μὲν
γὰρ προειπεῖν τὸν θεόν, μὴ μέντοι δηλῶσαι
Ῥωμαίων ἢ τῶν πολεμίων.

49   Ἤδη δὲ πολλῶν ἐπὶ πολλοῖς ἐπεισρεόντων καὶ
τῆς πόλεως αὐτῶν θλιβομένης ὑπὸ τοῦ πλήθους
τῶν ἐπὶ τὸ χρηστήριον ἀφικνουμένων καὶ τὰ
ἐπιτήδεια διαρκῆ μὴ ἐχούσης, ἐπινοεῖ τοὺς

---

[1] ἀθρόων N, vulg. : ἀθρόον γβ.

---

[1] The invading tribes flooded Rhaetia, Noricum, upper
and lower Pannonia, and Dacia, taking a vast number of
Roman settlers prisoner, and even entered Italy, capturing
and destroying Oderzo. Details are uncertain; so is the
exact date, which was probably between 167 and 169. On
the column of Marcus Aurelius in Rome, one of the scenes
depicts two animals swimming across a river, near a boat.
These have been thought to be the lions of the oracle, and

magnificent offerings. But it will be better to
repeat the oracle itself.

" Into the pools of the Ister, the stream that from
 Zeus taketh issue,
 Hurl, I command you, a pair of Cybele's faithful
 attendants,
 Beasts that dwell on the mountains, and all that
 the Indian climate
 Yieldeth of flower and herb that is fragrant ;
 amain there shall follow
 Victory and great glory, and welcome peace in
 their footsteps."

But when all this had been done as he had directed,
the lions swam across to the enemy territory and
the barbarians slaughtered them with clubs, thinking
them some kind of foreign dogs or wolves; and
"amain" that tremendous disaster befel our side, in
which a matter of twenty thousand were wiped out
at a blow. Then came what happened at Aquileia,
and that city's narrow escape from capture. To meet
this issue, Alexander was flat enough to adduce the
Delphian defence in the matter of the oracle given to
Croesus, that the God had indeed foretold victory,
but had not indicated whether it would go to the
Romans or to the enemy.[1]

As by this time throngs upon throngs were pouring in and their city was becoming overcrowded on
account of the multitude of visitors to the shrine,
so that it had not sufficient provisions, he devised

indeed they look like lions in the representation of Bartoli
(Pl. XIII). But Petersen takes them to be bisons. It is
clear, too, from Lucian that Alexander's oracle was given
before the campaign depicted on the column

νυκτερινοὺς καλουμένους χρησμούς. λαμβάνων
γὰρ τὰ βιβλία ἐπεκοιμᾶτο, ὡς ἔφασκεν, αὐτοῖς
καὶ ὡς ὄναρ παρὰ τοῦ θεοῦ ἀκούων ἀπεκρίνετο,
οὐ μέντοι σαφεῖς τοὺς πολλούς, ἀλλ' ἀμφιβόλους
καὶ τεταραγμένους καὶ μάλιστα εἴ ποτε θεάσαιτο
περιεργότερον τὸ βιβλίον κατεσφραγισμένον. οὐ
γὰρ παρακινδυνεύων, τὸ ἐπελθὸν [1] ἄλλως ὑπέ-
γραφε, χρησμοῖς πρέπον καὶ τὸ τοιοῦτον οἰόμενος.
καὶ ἦσάν τινες ἐξηγηταὶ ἐπὶ τοῦτο καθήμενοι καὶ
μισθοὺς οὐκ ὀλίγους ἐκλέγοντες παρὰ τῶν τοὺς
τοιούτους χρησμοὺς λαμβανόντων ἐπὶ τῇ ἐξηγήσει
καὶ διαλύσει αὐτῶν. καὶ τοῦτο αὐτῶν τὸ ἔργον
ὑπόμισθον ἦν· ἐτέλουν γὰρ οἱ ἐξηγηταὶ τῷ
Ἀλεξάνδρῳ τάλαντον Ἀττικὸν ἑκάτερος.

50 Ἐνίοτε δὲ μήτε ἐρομένου τινὸς μήτε πεμφθέντος,
ἀλλ' οὐδὲ ὅλως ὄντος ἐχρησμῴδει πρὸς ἔκπληξιν
τῶν ἀνοήτων, οἷον καὶ τοῦτο·

Δίζεαι ὅστις σὴν ἄλοχον μάλα πάγχυ λεληθὼς
Καλλιγένειαν ὑπὲρ λεχέων σαλαγεῖ κατὰ δῶμα;
δοῦλος Πρωτογένης, τῷ δὴ σύ γε πάντα
    πέποιθας.
ὤπυιες γὰρ ἐκεῖνον, ὁ δ' αὖθις σὴν παράκοιτιν,
ἀντίδοσιν ταύτην ὕβρεως ἄκρην [2] ἀποτίνων.
ἀλλ' ἐπὶ σοὶ δὴ φάρμακ' ἀπ' αὐτῶν λυγρὰ
    τέτυκται,
ὡς μήτ' εἰσαΐοις μήτ' εἰσοράοις ἃ ποιοῦσιν.

[1] ἐπελθὸν vulg.: ὑπελθὼν γ. οὐ γὰρ παρακινῶν τὸ ἔδεθλον β.
[2] ἄκρην A.M.H.: ἀκαρὴν β, ἰδίας γ, edd.

the so-called "nocturnal" responses. Taking the scrolls, he slept on them, so he said, and gave replies that he pretended to have heard from the god in a dream; which, however, were in most cases not clear but ambiguous and confused, particularly when he observed that the scroll had been sealed up with unusual care. Taking no extra chances, he would append at random whatever answer came into his head, thinking that this procedure too was appropriate to oracles; and there were certain expounders who sat by with that in view and garnered large fees from the recipients of such oracles for explaining and unriddling them. Moreover, this task of theirs was subject to a levy; the expounders paid Alexander an Attic talent each.

Sometimes, to amaze dolts, he would deliver an oracle for the benefit of someone who had neither enquired nor sent—who, in fact, did not exist at all. For example:

"Seek thou out that man who in utmost secrecy
        shrouded
    Tumbleth at home on the couch thy helpmeet
        Calligeneia,
    Slave Protogenes, him upon whom thou fully
        reliest.
    He was corrupted by thee, and now thy wife he
        corrupteth,
    Making a bitter return unto thee for his own
        violation.
    Aye more, now against thee a baneful charm they
        have fashioned
    So that thou mayst not hear nor see what deeds
        they are doing;

εὑρήσεις δὲ κάτω ὑπὸ σῷ λέχει ἀγχόθι τοίχου
πρὸς κεφαλῆς. καὶ σὴ θεράπαινα σύνοιδε
Καλυψώ.

τίς οὐκ ἂν Δημόκριτος διεταράχθη ἀκούσας
ὀνόματα καὶ τόπους ἀκριβῶς, εἶτα μετ᾽ ὀλίγον
κατέπτυσεν ἄν, συνεὶς τὴν ἐπίνοιαν αὐτῶν ;

52 [1] Ἄλλῳ [2] πάλιν οὔτε παρόντι οὔτε ὅλως τινὶ
ὄντι ἔφη ἄνευ μέτρου ἀναστρέφειν ὀπίσω· "ὁ γὰρ
πέμψας σε τέθνηκεν ὑπὸ τοῦ γείτονος Διοκλέους
τήμερον, λῃστῶν ἐπαχθέντων Μάγνου καὶ Βου-
βάλου, οἳ καὶ ἤδη δέδενται ληφθέντες."

51 Ἀλλὰ καὶ βαρβάροις πολλάκις ἔχρησεν, εἴ τις
τῇ πατρίῳ ἔροιτο φωνῇ, Συριστὶ ἢ Κελτιστί,
ῥᾳδίως [3] ἐξευρίσκων τινὰς ἐπιδημοῦντας ὁμοεθνεῖς
τοῖς δεδωκόσιν. διὰ τοῦτο καὶ πολὺς ὁ ἐν μέσῳ
χρόνος ἦν τῆς τε δόσεως τῶν βιβλίων καὶ τῆς
χρησμῳδίας, ὡς ἐν τοσούτῳ κατὰ σχολὴν λύοιντό
τε οἱ χρησμοὶ ἀσφαλῶς καὶ εὑρίσκοιντο οἱ
ἑρμηνεῦσαι δυνάμενοι ἕκαστα. οἷος καὶ ὁ τῷ
Σκύθῃ δοθεὶς χρησμὸς ἦν·

Μορφὴν εὐβάργουλις εἰς σκιὰν χνεχικραγη
λείψει φάος.[4]

---

[1] Chapters 51 and 52 transposed by Fritzsche.
[2] ἄλλῳ A.M.H.: ἄλλος βγ. But for οὔτε ὅλως β has οὔτε
ἄλλῳ—the correction introduced in the wrong place.
[3] οὐ ῥᾳδίως β.
[4] Text Γ : μορφεῦ· μάργουλος ἰσχιάγχνε χι φι φάος δα U
(β group). B reads as U, but βάργουλος and δάος.

---

[1] Democritus of Abdera is adduced as a typical hard-
headed sceptic; see above, c. 17, and the *Lover of Lies*, 32
(iii, p. 369).
[2] The oracle seems to contain some Greek, in the two

This shalt thou find on the floor, beneath thy bed,
  by the wall-side,
Close to the head; thy servant Calypso shareth
  the secret."

What Democritus[1] would not have been disturbed
on hearing names and places specified—and would
not have been filled with contempt soon afterward,
when he saw through their stratagem?

Again, to someone else who was not there and
did not exist at all, he said in prose: "Go back;
he who sent you was killed to-day by his neighbour
Diocles, with the help of the bandits Magnus, Celer,
and Bubalus, who already have been caught and
imprisoned."

I may say too that he often gave oracles to
barbarians, when anyone put a question in his native
language, in Syrian or in Celtic; since he readily
found strangers in the city who belonged to the
same nation as his questioners. That is why the
time between the presentation of the scrolls and
the delivery of the oracle was long, so that in the
interval the questions might be unsealed at leisure
without risk and men might be found who would be
able to translate them fully. Of this sort was the
response given to the Scythian:

"Morphen eubargoulis eis skian chnechikrage
  leipsei phaos."[2]

phrases eis skian (into the darkness) and leipsei phaos (thou
shalt leave the light of day); it is uncertain, however,
whether these phrases belong to the original text, or to
someone's interpretation, which has become confused with
the text, or are mere corruptions due to a scribe's effort to
convert "Scythian" into Greek. The "Scythian" part
itself is a complete mystery.

53   Ὀλίγους δὲ καὶ τῶν ἐμοὶ δοθέντων ἄκουσον·
ἐρομένου γάρ μου εἰ φαλακρός ἐστιν Ἀλέξανδρος,
καὶ κατασημηναμένου περιέργως καὶ προφανῶς
ὑπογράφεται χρησμὸς νυκτερήσιος,

Σαβαρδαλαχου μαλαχααττηαλος ἦν.[1]

Καὶ πάλιν ἐμοῦ ἐρομένου ἐν δύο βιβλίοις δια-
φόροις τὴν αὐτὴν ἐρώτησιν, πόθεν ἦν Ὅμηρος ὁ
ποιητής, ἐπ' ἄλλου καὶ ἄλλου ὀνόματος, τῷ
ἑτέρῳ μὲν ὑπέγραψεν ἐξαπατηθεὶς ὑπὸ τοῦ ἐμοῦ
νεανίσκου—ἐρωτηθεὶς γὰρ ἐφ' ὅ τι ἦκεν, " Θεραπείας," ἔφη, " αἰτήσων πρὸς ὀδύνην πλευροῦ"—

Κυτμίδα χρίεσθαι κέλομαι δροσίην τε κέλητος·

τῷ δὲ ἑτέρῳ, ἐπειδὴ καὶ τοῦτο ἠκηκόει ὡς ἐρομένου
τοῦ πέμψαντος, εἴτε οἱ[3] πλεῦσαι ἐπ' Ἰταλίαν
εἴτε πεζοπορῆσαι λῶον, ἀπεκρίνατο οὐδὲν πρὸς
τὸν Ὅμηρον·

Μὴ σύ γε πλωέμεναι, πεζὴν δὲ κατ' οἶμον[4]
ὄδευε.

54   Πολλὰ γὰρ τοιαῦτα καὶ αὐτὸς ἐπεμηχανησάμην
αὐτῷ, οἷον καὶ ἐκεῖνο· μίαν ἐρώτησιν ἐρωτήσας
ἐπέγραψα τῷ βιβλίῳ κατὰ τὸ ἔθος· " τοῦ δεῖνος
χρησμοὶ ὀκτώ," ψευσάμενός τι ὄνομα, καὶ τὰς
ὀκτὼ δραχμὰς καὶ τὸ γιγνόμενον ἔτι πρὸς ταύταις

----

[1] Text Γ: σαυαρδάχου μαλα ἄττης ἀλλοήν U, σαβαρδάχου·
μάλα ἄττης ἄλλο ἦν Β.
[2] κέλητος Seidler : κελητοῦς γ, καὶ λητοῦς β.
[3] εἴτε οἱ Seager : εἰ δέοι β, εἴτε μοι γ.
[4] κατ' οἶμον vulg. : καθ' οἶμον βγ.

ALEXANDER THE FALSE PROPHET

Let me also tell you a few of the responses that were given to me. When I asked whether Alexander was bald, and sealed the question carefully and conspicuously, a "nocturnal" oracle was appended:

"Sabardalachou malachaattealos en."[1]

At another time, I asked a single question in each of two scrolls under a different name, "What was the poet Homer's country?" In one case, misled by my serving-man, who had been asked why he came and had said, "To request a cure for a pain in the side," he replied:

"Cytmis[2] I bid you apply, combined with the spume of a charger."

To the other, since in this case he had been told that the one who sent it enquired whether it would be better for him to go to Italy by sea or by land, he gave an answer which had nothing to do with Homer:

"Make not your journey by sea, but travel afoot by the highway."

Many such traps, in fact, were set for him by me and by others. For example, I put a single question, and wrote upon the outside of the scroll, following the usual form: "Eight questions from So-and-so," using a fictitious name and sending the eight drachmas and whatever it came to besides.[3] Rely-

[1] In failing to submit this to the official interpreters, Lucian lost a priceless opportunity.

[2] Alexander's nostrum; cf c. 22.

[3] Since the price of each oracle was one drachma, two obols, the indefinite plus was sixteen obols, or 2dr. 4 obols.

πέμψας· ὁ δὲ πιστεύσας τῇ ἀποπομπῇ τοῦ
μισθοῦ καὶ τῇ ἐπιγραφῇ τοῦ βιβλίου, πρὸς μίαν
ἐρώτησιν—ἦν δὲ αὕτη· "πότε ἁλώσεται μαγγα-
νεύων ᾿Αλέξανδρος " ;—ὀκτώ μοι χρησμοὺς
ἔπεμψεν, οὔτε γῆς φασιν οὔτε οὐρανοῦ ἁπτο-
μένους, ἀνοήτους δὲ καὶ δυσνοήτους ἅπαντας.

῞Απερ ὕστερον αἰσθόμενος, καὶ ὅτι ῾Ρουτιλιανὸν
ἐγὼ ἀπέτρεπον τοῦ γάμου καὶ τοῦ πάνυ προσ-
κεῖσθαι ταῖς τοῦ χρηστηρίου ἐλπίσιν, ἐμίσει,
ὡς τὸ εἰκός, καὶ ἔχθιστον ἡγεῖτο. καί ποτε περὶ
ἐμοῦ ἐρομένῳ τῷ ῾Ρουτιλιανῷ ἔφη·

Νυκτιπλάνοις ὀάροις χαίρει κοίταις τε δυσ-
άγνοις.

καὶ ὅλως ἔχθιστος εἰκότως ἦν ἐγώ.

55 Κἀπειδὴ εἰσελθόντα με εἰς τὴν πόλιν ᾔσθετο
καὶ ἔμαθεν ὡς ἐκεῖνος εἴην ὁ Λουκιανός—ἐπηγόμην
δὲ καὶ στρατιώτας δύο, λογχοφόρον καὶ κοντο-
φόρον, παρὰ τοῦ ἡγουμένου τῆς Καππαδοκίας,
φίλου τότε ὄντος, λαβών, ὥς με παραπέμψειαν
μέχρι πρὸς τὴν θάλατταν—αὐτίκα μεταστέλλεται
δεξιῶς πάνυ καὶ μετὰ πολλῆς φιλοφροσύνης.
ἐλθὼν δὲ ἐγὼ πολλοὺς καταλαμβάνω περὶ αὐτόν·
συνεπηγόμην δὲ καὶ τοὺς στρατιώτας τύχῃ τινὶ
ἀγαθῇ. καὶ ὁ μὲν προὔτεινέ μοι κύσαι τὴν
δεξιάν, ὥσπερ εἰώθει τοῖς πολλοῖς, ἐγὼ δὲ
προσφὺς ὡς φιλήσων, δήγματι χρηστῷ πάνυ
μικροῦ δεῖν χωλὴν αὐτῷ ἐποίησα τὴν χεῖρα.

Οἱ μὲν οὖν παρόντες ἄγχειν με καὶ παίειν
ἐπειρῶντο ὡς ἱερόσυλον, καὶ πρότερον ἔτι ἀγα-
νακτήσαντες ὅτι ᾿Αλέξανδρον αὐτόν, ἀλλὰ μὴ
προφήτην προσεῖπον· ὁ δὲ πάνυ γεννικῶς

ing upon the fee that had been sent and upon the inscription on the roll, to the single question: "When will Alexander be caught cheating?" he sent me eight responses which, as the saying goes, had no connection with earth or with heaven, but were silly and nonsensical every one.

When he found out about all this afterward, and also that it was I who was attempting to dissuade Rutilianus from the marriage and from his great dependence upon the hopes inspired by the shrine, he began to hate me, as was natural, and to count me a bitter enemy. Once when Rutilianus asked about me, he replied:

"Low-voiced walks in the dusk are his pleasure, and impious matings."

And generally, I was of course the man he most hated.

When he discovered that I had entered the city and ascertained that I was the Lucian of whom he had heard (I had brought, I may add, two soldiers with me, a pikeman and a spearman borrowed from the Governor of Cappadocia, then a friend of mine, to escort me to the sea), he at once sent for me very politely and with great show of friendliness. When I went, I found many about him; but I had brought along my two soldiers, as luck would have it. He extended me his right hand to kiss, as his custom was with the public; I clasped it as if to kiss it, and almost crippled it with a right good bite!

The bystanders tried to choke and beat me for sacrilege; even before that, they had been indignant because I had addressed him as Alexander and not as "Prophet." But he mastered himself very hand-

καρτερήσας κατέπαυέν τε αὐτοὺς καὶ ὑπισχνεῖτο
τιθασόν με ῥᾳδίως ἀποφανεῖν καὶ δείξειν τὴν
Γλύκωνος ἀρετήν, ὅτι καὶ τοὺς πάνυ τραχυνο-
μένους φίλους ἀπεργάζεται. καὶ μεταστησάμενος
ἅπαντας ἐδικαιολογεῖτο πρός με, λέγων πάνυ με
εἰδέναι καὶ τὰ ὑπ᾽ ἐμοῦ Ῥουτιλιανῷ συμβουλευό-
μενα, καὶ "Τί παθὼν ταῦτά με εἰργάσω, δυνάμενος ὑπ᾽ ἐμοῦ ἐπὶ μέγα προαχθῆναι παρ᾽ αὐτῷ";
κἀγὼ ἄσμενος ἤδη ἐδεχόμην τὴν φιλοφροσύνην
ταύτην ὁρῶν οἷ κινδύνου καθειστήκειν, καὶ μετ᾽
ὀλίγον προῆλθον φίλος γεγενημένος. καὶ τοῦτο
οὐ μικρὸν θαῦμα τοῖς ὁρῶσιν ἔδοξεν, οὕτω ῥᾳδία
γενομένη μου ἡ μεταβολή.

56   Εἶτα δή μου ἐκπλεῖν προαιρουμένου ξένια καὶ
δῶρα πολλὰ πέμψας—μόνος δὲ σὺν τῷ Ξενοφῶντι
ἔτυχον ἐπιδημῶν, τὸν πατέρα καὶ τοὺς ἐμοὺς εἰς
Ἄμαστριν προεκπεπομφώς — ὑπισχνεῖται καὶ
πλοῖον αὐτὸς παρέξειν καὶ ἐρέτας τοὺς ἀπάξοντας.
κἀγὼ μὲν ᾤμην ἁπλοῦν τι τοῦτο εἶναι καὶ δεξιόν·
ἐπεὶ δὲ κατὰ μέσον τὸν πόρον ἐγενόμην, δακρύοντα
ὁρῶν τὸν κυβερνήτην καὶ τοῖς ναύταις τι ἀντιλέ-
γοντα οὐκ ἀγαθὰς εἶχον περὶ τῶν μελλόντων
ἐλπίδας. ἦν δὲ αὐτοῖς ἐπεσταλμένον ὑπὸ τοῦ
Ἀλεξάνδρου ἀραμένους ῥῖψαι ἡμᾶς εἰς τὴν
θάλασσαν· ὅπερ εἰ ἐγένετο, ῥᾳδίως ἂν αὐτῷ
διεπεπολέμητο τὰ πρὸς ἐμέ. ἀλλὰ δακρύων
ἐκεῖνος ἔπεισεν καὶ τοὺς συνναύτας μηδὲν ἡμᾶς
δεινὸν ἐργάσασθαι, καὶ πρὸς ἐμὲ ἔφη, "Ἔτη
ἑξήκοντα, ὡς ὁρᾷς, ἀνεπίληπτον βίον καὶ ὅσιον
προβεβηκὼς οὐκ ἂν βουλοίμην, ἐν τούτῳ τῆς
ἡλικίας καὶ γυναῖκα καὶ τέκνα ἔχων, μιᾶναι φόνῳ

somely, held them in check, and promised that he
would easily make me tame and would demonstrate
Glycon's worth by showing that he transformed
even bitter foes into friends. Then he removed
everybody and had it out with me, professing to
know very well who I was and what advice I was
giving Rutilianus, and saying, "What possessed you
to do this to me, when I can advance you tremendously in his favour?" By that time I was glad to
receive this proffer of friendship, since I saw what
a perilous position I had taken up ; so, after a little,
I reappeared as his friend, and it seemed quite a
miracle to the observers that my change of heart
had been so easily effected.

Then, when I decided to sail—it chanced that
I was accompanied only by Xenophon[1] during my
visit, as I had previously sent my father and my
family on to Amastris—he sent me many remem-
brances and presents, and promised too that he
himself would furnish a boat and a crew to transport
me. I considered this a sincere and polite offer ;
but when I was in mid-passage, I saw the master
in tears, disputing with the sailors, and began to be
very doubtful about the prospects. It was a fact
that they had received orders from Alexander to
throw us bodily into the sea. If that had been
done, his quarrel with me would have been settled
without ado ; but by his tears the master prevailed
upon his crew to do us no harm. "For sixty years,
as you see," said he to me, "I have led a blameless
and God-fearing life, and I should not wish, at this
age and with a wife and children, to stain my hands

[1] Probably a slave or a freedman. He is not mentioned
elsewhere in Lucian.

τὰς χεῖρας," δηλῶν ἐφ᾽ ὅπερ ἡμᾶς ἀνειλήφει, καὶ
57 τὰ ὑπὸ τοῦ Ἀλεξάνδρου προστεταγμένα. κατα-
θέμενος δὲ ἡμᾶς ἐν Αἰγιαλοῖς, ὧν καὶ ὁ καλὸς
Ὅμηρος μέμνηται, ὀπίσω ἀπήλαυνον.

Ἔνθα ἐγὼ παραπλέοντας εὑρὼν Βοσποριανούς
τινας, πρέσβεις παρ᾽ Εὐπάτορος τοῦ βασιλέως
εἰς τὴν Βιθυνίαν ἀπιόντας ἐπὶ κομιδῇ τῆς ἐπετείου
συντάξεως, καὶ διηγησάμενος αὐτοῖς τὸν περι-
στάντα ἡμᾶς κίνδυνον, καὶ δεξιῶν αὐτῶν τυχών,
ἀναληφθεὶς ἐπὶ τὸ πλοῖον διασώζομαι εἰς τὴν
Ἄμαστριν, παρὰ τοσοῦτον ἐλθὼν ἀποθανεῖν.

Τοὐντεῦθεν καὶ αὐτὸς ἐπεκορυσσόμην αὐτῷ καὶ
πάντα κάλων ἐκίνουν ἀμύνασθαι βουλόμενος, καὶ
πρὸ τῆς ἐπιβουλῆς ἤδη μισῶν αὐτὸν καὶ ἔχθιστον
ἡγούμενος διὰ τὴν τοῦ τρόπου μιαρίαν, καὶ πρὸς
τὴν κατηγορίαν ὡρμήμην πολλοὺς συναγωνιστὰς
ἔχων καὶ μάλιστα τοὺς ἀπὸ Τιμοκράτους τοῦ
Ἡρακλεώτου φιλοσόφου· ἀλλ᾽ ὁ τότε ἡγούμενος
Βιθυνίας καὶ τοῦ Πόντου Αὔειτος[1] ἐπέσχε,
μονονουχὶ ἱκετεύων καὶ ἀντιβολῶν παύσασθαι·
διὰ γὰρ τὴν πρὸς Ῥουτιλιανὸν εὔνοιαν μὴ ἂν
δύνασθαι, καὶ εἰ φανερῶς λάβοι ἀδικοῦντα,
κολάσαι αὐτόν. οὕτω μὲν ἀνεκόπην τῆς ὁρμῆς
καὶ ἐπαυσάμην οὐκ ἐν δέοντι θρασυνόμενος ἐφ᾽
οὕτω δικαστοῦ διακειμένου.

---

[1] Αὔειτος Burmeister : ἄνεκτος β, αὐτὸς γ.

---

[1] *Iliad*, 2, 855.

[2] Tiberius Julius Eupator succeeded Rhoemetalces as King
of the (Cimmerian) Bosporus, on the Tauric Chersonese; its
capital was Panticapaeum (Kertch). The period of his reign
is about A.D. 154–171. At this time the kingdom seems to
have been paying tribute to the Scythians annually as well
as to the Empire (*Toxaris*, 44).

with murder;" and he explained for what purpose he had taken us aboard, and what orders had been given by Alexander. He set us ashore at Aegiali (which noble Homer mentions[1]), and then they went back again.

There I found some men from the Bosporus who were voyaging along the coast. They were going as ambassadors from King Eupator to Bithynia, to bring the yearly contribution.[2] I told them of the peril in which we had been, found them courteous, was taken aboard their vessel, and won safely through to Amastris, after coming so close to losing my life.

Thereupon I myself began to prepare for battle with him, and to employ every resource in my desire to pay him back. Even before his attempt upon me, I detested him and held him in bitter enmity on account of the vileness of his character. So I undertook to prosecute him, and had many associates, particularly the followers of Timocrates, the philosopher from Heraclea. But the then governor of Bithynia and Pontus, Avitus,[3] checked me, all but beseeching and imploring me to leave off, because out of good will to Rutilianus he could not, he said, punish Alexander even if he should find him clearly guilty of crime. In that way my effort was thwarted, and I left off exhibiting misplaced zeal before a judge who was in that state of mind.[4]

---

[3] L. Lollianus Avitus, consul A.D. 144, proconsul Africae ca. 156, praeses Bithyniae 165.

[4] Of course Lucian's case, as it stood, was weak, as Avitus tactfully hinted. But this does not excuse Avitus. The chances of securing enough evidence to convict Alexander in a Roman court were distinctly good, and fear of Alexander's influence is the only reasonable explanation of the failure to proceed.

58　'Εκεῖνο δὲ πῶς οὐ μέγα ἐν τοῖς ἄλλοις τὸ τόλμημα τοῦ 'Αλεξάνδρου, τὸ αἰτῆσαι παρὰ τοῦ
αὐτοκράτορος μετονομασθῆναι τὸ τοῦ 'Αβώνου
τεῖχος καὶ 'Ιωνόπολιν κληθῆναι, καὶ νόμισμα
καινὸν κόψαι ἐγκεχαραγμένον τῇ μὲν τοῦ Γλύκωνος, κατὰ θάτερα δὲ 'Αλεξάνδρου, στέμματά
τε τοῦ πάππου 'Ασκληπιοῦ καὶ τὴν ἅρπην ἐκείνην
τοῦ πατρομήτορος Περσέως ἔχοντος ;

59　Προειπὼν δὲ διὰ χρησμοῦ περὶ αὑτοῦ ὅτι ζῆσαι
εἵμαρται αὐτῷ ἔτη πεντήκοντα καὶ ἑκατόν, εἶτα
κεραυνῷ βληθέντα ἀποθανεῖν, οἰκτίστῳ τέλει
οὐδὲ ἑβδομήκοντα ἔτη γεγονὼς ἀπέθανεν, ὡς
Ποδαλειρίου υἱὸς διασαπεὶς τὸν πόδα μέχρι τοῦ
βουβῶνος καὶ σκωλήκων ζέσας· ὅτεπερ καὶ
ἐφωράθη φαλακρὸς ὤν, παρέχων τοῖς ἰατροῖς
ἐπιβρέχειν αὐτοῦ τὴν κεφαλὴν διὰ τὴν ὀδύνην,
ὃ οὐκ ἂν ποιῆσαι ἐδύναντο μὴ οὐχὶ τῆς φενάκης
ἀφῃρημένης.

60　Τοιοῦτο τέλος τῆς 'Αλεξάνδρου τραγῳδίας καὶ
αὕτη τοῦ παντὸς δράματος ἡ καταστροφὴ ἐγένετο,
ὡς εἰκάζειν προνοίας τινὸς τὸ τοιοῦτον, εἰ καὶ
κατὰ τύχην συνέβη. ἔδει δὲ καὶ τὸν ἐπιτάφιον
αὐτοῦ ἄξιον γενέσθαι τοῦ βίου, καὶ ἀγῶνά τινα
συστήσασθαι ὑπὲρ τοῦ χρηστηρίου, τῶν συνωμοτῶν ἐκείνων καὶ γοήτων, ὅσοι κορυφαῖοι ἦσαν,
ἀνελθόντων ἐπὶ διαιτητὴν τὸν 'Ρουτιλιανόν, τίνα
χρὴ προκριθῆναι αὐτῶν καὶ διαδέξασθαι τὸ
μαντεῖον καὶ στεφανωθῆναι τῷ ἱεροφαντικῷ καὶ

---

[1] The request was granted, at least in part. Beginning
with the reign of Verus, the legends ΙΩΝΟΠΟΛΕΙΤΩΝ and
ΓΛΥΚΩΝ appear on the coins ; and they continue to bear

ALEXANDER THE FALSE PROPHET

Was it not also a great piece of impudence on the part of Alexander that he should petition the Emperor to change the name of Abonoteichus and call it Ionopolis, and to strike a new coin bearing on one side the likeness of Glycon and on the other that of Alexander, wearing the fillets of his grandfather Asclepius and holding the falchion of his maternal ancestor Perseus?[1]

In spite of his prediction in an oracle that he was fated to live a hundred and fifty years and then die by a stroke of lightning, he met a most wretched end before reaching the age of seventy, in a manner that befitted a son of Podaleirius;[2] for his leg became mortified quite to the groin and was infested with maggots. It was then that his baldness was detected when because of the pain he let the doctors foment his head, which they could not have done unless his wig had been removed.

Such was the conclusion of Alexander's spectacular career, and such the *dénouement* of the whole play; being as it was, it resembled an act of Providence, although it came about by chance. It was inevitable, too, that he should have funeral games worthy of his career—that a contest for the shrine should arise. The foremost of his fellow-conspirators and impostors referred it to Rutilianus to decide which of them should be given the preference, should succeed to the shrine, and should be crowned with

the representation of a snake with human head to the middle of the third century (Head, *Hist. Numm.*, 432, Cumont *l.c.*, p. 42). The modern name Inéboli is a corruption of Ionopolis.

[2] As son of Podaleirius, it was fitting, thinks Lucian, that his leg (*poda-*) should be affected.

προφητικῷ στέμματι. ἦν δὲ ἐν αὐτοῖς καὶ Παῖτος, ἰατρὸς τὴν τέχνην, πολιός τις,[1] οὔτε ἰατρῷ πρέπουτα οὔτε πολιῷ ἀνδρὶ ταῦτα ποιῶν. ἀλλ' ὁ ἀγωνοθέτης Ῥουτιλιανὸς ἀστεφανώτους αὐτοὺς ἀπέπεμψεν αὐτῷ τὴν προφητείαν φυλάττων μετὰ τὴν ἐντεῦθεν ἀπαλλαγήν.

61   Ταῦτα, ὦ φιλότης, ὀλίγα ἐκ πολλῶν δείγματος ἕνεκα γράψαι ἠξίωσα, καὶ σοὶ μὲν χαριζόμενος, ἀνδρὶ ἑταίρῳ καὶ φίλῳ καὶ ὃν ἐγὼ πάντων μάλιστα θαυμάσας ἔχω ἐπί τε σοφίᾳ καὶ τῷ πρὸς ἀλήθειαν ἔρωτι καὶ τρόπου πραότητι καὶ ἐπιεικείᾳ καὶ γαλήνῃ βίου καὶ δεξιότητι πρὸς τοὺς συνόντας, τὸ πλέον δέ,—ὅπερ καὶ σοὶ ἥδιον,—Ἐπικούρῳ τιμωρῶν, ἀνδρὶ ὡς ἀληθῶς ἱερῷ καὶ θεσπεσίῳ τὴν φύσιν καὶ μόνῳ μετ' ἀληθείας τὰ καλὰ ἐγνωκότι καὶ παραδεδωκότι καὶ ἐλευθερωτῇ τῶν ὁμιλησάντων αὐτῷ γενομένῳ. οἶμαι δὲ ὅτι καὶ τοῖς ἐντυχοῦσι χρήσιμόν τι ἔχειν δόξει ἡ γραφή, τὰ μὲν διεξελέγχουσα, τὰ δὲ ἐν ταῖς τῶν εὖ φρονούντων γνώμαις βεβαιοῦσα.

---

[1] πολιός τις A.M.H. : πολίτης ὃς γβ : πολιὸς ὤν Fritzsche.

the fillet of priest and prophet. Paetus was one of them, a physician by profession, a greybeard, who conducted himself in a way that befitted neither a physician nor a greybeard. But Rutilianus, the umpire, sent them off unfilleted, keeping the post of prophet for the master after his departure from this life.

This, my friend, is but a little out of a great deal; I have thought fit to set it down as a specimen, not only to pleasure you as an associate and friend whom above all others I hold in admiration for your wisdom, your love of truth, the gentleness and reasonableness of your ways, the peacefulness of your life, and your courtesy toward all whom you encounter, but mostly—and this will give greater pleasure to you also—to right the wrongs of Epicurus, a man truly saintly and divine in his nature, who alone truly discerned right ideals and handed them down, who proved himself the liberator of all who sought his converse. I think too that to its readers the writing will seem to have some usefulness, refuting as it does certain falsehoods and confirming certain truths in the minds of all men of sense.

ESSAYS IN PORTRAITURE

An elaborate compliment to Panthea, a girl of Smyrna, favourite of the Emperor Verus. It was written in the East, almost certainly at Antioch, before the death of Verus (A.D. 169) and probably during his residence in the East (162–166).

It is ungallant to say with La Croze: "Hic adulatorum derisor Lucianus omnes adulatores vincit!" No doubt it is Panthea of whom Capitolinus speaks so slightingly (7, 10). But that a scribbler who never saw her called her a *vulgaris amica* is less significant, I submit, than that an emperor who knew her "laid aside his beard" to suit her whim. She was not of high rank, it may be, but she was certainly attractive. And in all seriousness she cannot have been wholly unworthy. When Marcus Aurelius says (8, 37): "Does Panthea still sit by the sepulchre of her lord?" it accords with what we are told here of her devotion to him; and in Lucian's praise of her character there is a warmth that ensures its sincerity.

For Lucian's circle the piece was an interesting novelty. Making literary portraits by synthesis, though not un-exampled in poetry, was not hackneyed even there, and in prose quite new. It was original, too, to use dialogue as a vehicle for encomium, which commonly took the form of a poem or a speech.

In this piece and in the next, its sequel, the Greek word *eikon* creates unusual difficulty for the translator. In the first place, it denotes any kind of portrayal, whether painting or statue; but its nearest equivalents—likeness, portrait, sketch—all suggest the flat, not the round. Indeed, for a portrait-statue we have no proper word. Moreover—and this, though perhaps less obviously awkward in its consequences, is even more serious—it also means a comparison, or simile; and as Lucian's likenesses are for the most part nothing but comparisons of one sort or another, his *jeu d'esprit* owes a great measure of its effectiveness to a word-play which cannot be transferred.

ΕΙΚΟΝΕΣ

ΛΥΚΙΝΟΣ

1 Ἀλλ' ἦ τοιοῦτόν τι ἔπασχον οἱ τὴν Γοργὼ
ἰδόντες οἷον ἐγὼ ἔναγχος ἔπαθον, ὦ Πολύστρατε,
παγκάλην τινὰ γυναῖκα ἰδών· αὐτὸ γὰρ τὸ τοῦ
μύθου ἐκεῖνο, μικροῦ δέω λίθος ἐξ ἀνθρώπου σοι
γεγονέναι πεπηγὼς ὑπὸ τοῦ θαύματος.

ΠΟΛΥΣΤΡΑΤΟΣ

Ἡράκλεις, ὑπερφυές τι τὸ θέαμα φῂς καὶ δεινῶς
βίαιον, εἴ γε καὶ Λυκῖνον ἐξέπληξε γυνή τις οὖσα·
σὺ γὰρ ὑπὸ μὲν τῶν μειρακίων καὶ πάνυ ῥᾳδίως
αὐτὸ πάσχεις, ὥστε θᾶττον ἄν τις ὅλον τὸν Σί-
πυλον μετακινήσειεν ἢ σὲ τῶν καλῶν ἀπάγοι μὴ
οὐχὶ παρεστάναι αὐτοῖς κεχηνότα καὶ ἐπιδακρύ-
οντά γε πολλάκις ὥσπερ ἐκείνην αὐτὴν τὴν τοῦ
Ταντάλου. ἀτὰρ εἰπέ μοι, τίς ἡ λιθοποιὸς αὕτη
Μέδουσα ἡμῖν ἐστιν καὶ πόθεν, ὡς καὶ ἡμεῖς
ἴδοιμεν· οὐ γάρ, οἶμαι, φθονήσεις ἡμῖν τῆς θέας
οὐδὲ ζηλοτυπήσεις, εἰ μέλλοιμεν πλησίον που καὶ
αὐτοὶ παραπεπηγέναι σοι ἰδόντες.

Available in photographs: Γ, UN.

---

¹ A double allusion. The Niobe story has already been
introduced by the mention of Mount Sipylus, where Niobe
was turned into stone ; and now, by styling her the daughter

ESSAYS IN PORTRAITURE

LYCINUS

Upon my word, Polystratus, those who saw the Gorgon must have been affected by it very much as I was recently when I saw a perfectly beautiful woman: I was struck stiff with amazement and came within an ace of being turned into stone, my friend, just as it is in the fable!

POLYSTRATUS

Heracles! An extraordinary spectacle, that, and a terribly potent one, to astound Lycinus when it was only a woman. To be sure you are very easily affected in that way by boys, so that it would be a simpler matter to move all Sipylus from its base than to drag you away from your pretties and keep you from standing beside them with parted lips, yes, and not infrequently tears in your eyes, the very image of the daughter of Tantalus.[1] But tell me about this petrifying Medusa, who she is and where she comes from, so that we, too, may have a look at her. You surely will not begrudge us the sight or be jealous, if we ourselves are going to be struck stiff at your elbow on seeing her!

of Tantalus, Polystratus compares the plight of Lycinus to that of Tantalus also.

ΛΥΚΙΝΟΣ

Καὶ μὴν εὖ εἰδέναι χρή σε, ὡς κἂν ἐκ περιωπῆς
μόνον ἀπίδῃς εἰς αὐτήν, ἀχανῆ σε καὶ τῶν ἀνδριάντων ἀκινητότερον ἀποφανεῖ. καίτοι τοῦτο μὲν
ἴσως εἰρηνικώτερόν ἐστιν καὶ τὸ τραῦμα ἧττον
καίριον, εἰ αὐτὸς ἴδοις· εἰ δὲ κἀκείνη προσβλέψειέ
σε, τίς ἔσται μηχανὴ ἀποστῆναι αὐτῆς; ἀπάξει
γάρ σε ἀναδησαμένη ἔνθα ἂν ἐθέλῃ, ὅπερ καὶ ἡ
λίθος ἡ Ἡρακλεία δρᾷ τὸν σίδηρον.

ΠΟΛΥΣΤΡΑΤΟΣ

2 Παῦου, ὦ Λυκῖνε, τεράστιόν τι κάλλος ἀναπλάττων, ἀλλ᾿ εἰπέ, τίς ἡ γυνή ἐστιν.

ΛΥΚΙΝΟΣ

Οἴει γάρ με ὑπερβαλέσθαι τῷ λόγῳ, ὃς δέδια
μή σοι ἰδόντι ἀσθενής τις ἐπαινέσαι δόξω, παρὰ
τοσοῦτον ἀμείνων φανεῖται; πλὴν ἀλλὰ ἥτις μέν,
οὐκ ἂν εἰπεῖν ἔχοιμι, θεραπεία δὲ πολλὴ καὶ ἡ
ἄλλη περὶ αὐτὴν παρασκευὴ λαμπρὰ καὶ εὐνούχων
τι πλῆθος καὶ ἅβραι πάνυ πολλαί, καὶ ὅλως
μεῖζόν γε ἢ κατὰ ἰδιωτικὴν τύχην ἐδόκει τὸ
πρᾶγμα εἶναι.

ΠΟΛΥΣΤΡΑΤΟΣ

Οὐδὲ τοὔνομα ἐπύθου σύ γε ἥτις καλοῖτο;

ΛΥΚΙΝΟΣ

Οὐδαμῶς, ἢ τοῦτο μόνον, τῆς Ἰωνίας ἐστίν·
τῶν θεατῶν γάρ τις ἀπιδὼν εἰς τὸν πλησίον,
ἐπεὶ παρῆλθεν, "Τοιαῦτα μέντοι," ἔφη, "τὰ
Σμυρναϊκὰ κάλλη· καὶ θαυμαστὸν οὐδέν, εἰ ἡ

ESSAYS IN PORTRAITURE

You may be very certain that if you get but a
distant view of her she will strike you dumb, and
more motionless than any statue. Yet the effect,
perhaps, is not so violent and the wound less serious
if it should be you who catch sight of her.   But if
she should look at you as well, how shall you manage
to tear yourself away from her?   She will fetter you
to herself and hale you off wherever she wishes,
doing just what the magnet does to iron.

Don't keep evoking fancies of miraculous loveliness, Lycinus, but tell me who the woman is.

Why, do you suppose that I am exaggerating?
No, I am afraid that when you have seen her you
will take me to be a poor hand at turning compliments, so far superior will she prove to be.
Anyhow, I can't say who she is, but she received
much attention, kept splendid state in every way,
had a number of eunuchs and a great many maids,
and, in general, the thing seemed to be on a greater
scale than accords with private station.

You didn't learn even the name they gave her?

No; only that she comes from Ionia, for one of
the onlookers glanced at his neighbour after she had
passed and said: "Well, that is what Smyrna's
beauties are like, and it is no wonder that the fairest

259

καλλίστη τῶν Ἰωνικῶν πόλεων τὴν καλλίστην
γυναῖκα ἤνεγκεν." ἐδόκει δέ μοι Σμυρναῖος καὶ
αὐτὸς ὁ λέγων εἶναι, οὕτως ἐσεμνύνετο ἐπ' αὐτῇ.

ΠΟΛΥΣΤΡΑΤΟΣ

3 Οὐκοῦν ἐπεὶ λίθου τοῦτό γε ὡς ἀληθῶς ἐποίησας
οὔτε παρακολουθήσας οὔτε τὸν Σμυρναῖον ἐκεῖνον
ἐρόμενος, ὅστις ἦν, κἂν τὸ εἶδος ὡς οἷόν τε
ὑπόδειξον τῷ λόγῳ· τάχα γὰρ ἂν οὕτως
γνωρίσαιμι.

ΛΥΚΙΝΟΣ

Ὁρᾷς ἡλίκον τοῦτο ᾔτησας ; οὐ κατὰ λόγων
δύναμιν, καὶ μάλιστά γε τῶν ἐμῶν, ἐμφανίσαι
θαυμασίαν οὕτως εἰκόνα, πρὸς ἣν μόλις ἂν ἢ
Ἀπελλῆς ἢ Ζεῦξις ἢ Παρράσιος ἱκανοὶ ἔδοξαν,
ἢ εἴ τις Φειδίας ἢ Ἀλκαμένης· ἐγὼ δὲ λυμανοῦμαι
τὸ ἀρχέτυπον ἀσθενείᾳ τῆς τέχνης.

ΠΟΛΥΣΤΡΑΤΟΣ

Ὅμως, ὦ Λυκῖνε, ποία τις τὴν ὄψιν ; οὐ γὰρ
ἐπισφαλὲς τὸ τόλμημα, εἰ φίλῳ ἀνδρὶ ἐπιδείξαις
τὴν εἰκόνα, ὅπως ἂν τῆς γραμμῆς ἔχῃ.

ΛΥΚΙΝΟΣ

Καὶ μὴν ἀσφαλέστερον αὐτὸς ποιήσειν μοι
δοκῶ τῶν παλαιῶν τινας ἐκείνων τεχνιτῶν παρα-
καλέσας ἐπὶ τὸ ἔργον, ὡς ἀναπλάσειάν μοι τὴν
γυναῖκα.

ΠΟΛΥΣΤΡΑΤΟΣ

Πῶς τοῦτο φής ; ἢ πῶς ἂν ἀφίκοιντό σοι πρὸ
τοσούτων ἐτῶν ἀποθανόντες ;

of Ionian cities has produced the fairest of women!"
It seemed to me that the speaker himself was of
Smyrna because he was so set up over her.

POLYSTRATUS

Well, inasmuch as you really and truly behaved
like a stone in one way, at least, since you neither
followed her nor questioned that Smyrniote, whoever
he was, at least sketch her appearance in words as
best you can. Perhaps in that way I might
recognize her.

LYCINUS

Are you aware what you have demanded? It is
not in the power of words, not mine, certainly, to
call into being a portrait so marvellous, to which
hardly Apelles or Zeuxis or Parrhasius would have
seemed equal, or even perhaps a Phidias or an
Alcamenes. As for me, I shall but dim the lustre
of the original by the feebleness of my skill.

POLYSTRATUS

Nevertheless, Lycinus, what did she look like?
It would not be dangerously bold if you should show
your picture to a friend, no matter how well or ill it
may be drawn.

LYCINUS

But I think I shall act in a way that involves less
risk for myself if I call in some of those famous
artists of old for the undertaking, to model me a
statue of the woman.

POLYSTRATUS

What do you mean by that? How can they come
to you when they died so many years ago?

ΛΥΚΙΝΟΣ

Ῥᾳδίως, ἤνπερ σὺ μὴ ὀκνήσῃς ἀποκρίνασθαί τί μοι.

ΠΟΛΥΣΤΡΑΤΟΣ

Ἐρώτα μόνον.

ΛΥΚΙΝΟΣ

4 Ἐπεδήμησάς ποτε, ὦ Πολύστρατε, τῇ Κνιδίων ;

ΠΟΛΥΣΤΡΑΤΟΣ

Καὶ μάλα.

ΛΥΚΙΝΟΣ

Οὐκοῦν καὶ τὴν Ἀφροδίτην εἶδες πάντως αὐτῶν ;

ΠΟΛΥΣΤΡΑΤΟΣ

Νὴ Δία, τῶν Πραξιτέλους ποιημάτων τὸ κάλλιστον.

ΛΥΚΙΝΟΣ

Ἀλλὰ καὶ τὸν μῦθον ἤκουσας, ὃν λέγουσιν οἱ ἐπιχώριοι περὶ αὐτῆς, ὡς ἐρασθείη τις τοῦ ἀγάλματος καὶ λαθὼν ὑπολειφθεὶς ἐν ἱερῷ συγγένοιτο, ὡς δυνατὸν ἀγάλματι. τοῦτο μέντοι[1] ἄλλως ἱστορείσθω. σὺ δέ—ταύτην γάρ, ὡς φής, εἶδες—ἴθι μοὶ καὶ τόδε ἀπόκριναι, εἰ καὶ τὴν ἐν κήποις Ἀθήνησι τὴν Ἀλκαμένους ἑώρακας.

ΠΟΛΥΣΤΡΑΤΟΣ

Ἦ πάντων γ' ἄν, ὦ Λυκῖνε, ὁ ῥᾳθυμότατος

---

[1] μέντοι Lehmann : μέν σοι MSS.

---

[1] Furtwängler, *Greek and Roman Sculpture*, pl. xxv, opposite p. 91.
[2] The story, which can be traced back to Posidonius, is told at greater length in the *Amores*.

ESSAYS IN PORTRAITURE

LYCINUS

Easily, if only you do not refuse to answer me a question or two.

POLYSTRATUS

You have but to ask.

LYCINUS

Were you ever in Cnidus, Polystratus?

POLYSTRATUS

Yes indeed!

LYCINUS

Then you certainly saw the Aphrodite there?

POLYSTRATUS

Yes, by Zeus! The fairest of the creations of Praxiteles.[1]

LYCINUS

Well, have you also heard the story that the natives tell about it—that someone fell in love with the statue, was left behind unnoticed in the temple, and embraced it to the best of his endeavours? But no matter about that.[2] Since you have seen her, as you say, tell me whether you have also seen the Aphrodite in the Gardens, at Athens, by Alcamenes?[3]

POLYSTRATUS

Surely I should be the laziest man in all the world

---

[3] Furtwängler's suggestion that the well-known "Venus Genetrix" is a copy of this work is generally accepted. The head is well reproduced in Mitchell, *History of Ancient Sculpture*, opposite p. 320. The Gardens lay outside the walls, on the bank of the Ilissos, opposite the Stadium.

ἦν, εἰ τὸ κάλλιστον τῶν Ἀλκαμένους πλασμάτων
παρεῖδον.

ΛΥΚΙΝΟΣ

Ἐκεῖνο μέν γε, ὦ Πολύστρατε, οὐκ ἐξερήσομαί
σε, εἰ πολλάκις εἰς τὴν ἀκρόπολιν ἀνελθὼν καὶ
τὴν Καλάμιδος Σωσάνδραν τεθέασαι.

ΠΟΛΥΣΤΡΑΤΟΣ

Εἶδον κἀκείνην πολλάκις.

ΛΥΚΙΝΟΣ

Ἀλλὰ καὶ ταῦτα μὲν ἱκανῶς.   τῶν δὲ Φειδίου
ἔργων τί μάλιστα ἐπήνεσας ;

ΠΟΛΥΣΤΡΑΤΟΣ

Τί δ' ἄλλο ἢ τὴν Λημνίαν, ᾗ καὶ ἐπιγράψαι
τοὔνομα ὁ Φειδίας ἠξίωσε; καὶ νὴ Δία τὴν
Ἀμαζόνα τὴν ἐπερειδομένην τῷ δορατίῳ.

ΛΥΚΙΝΟΣ

5   Τὰ κάλλιστα, ὦ ἑταῖρε, ὥστ' οὐκέτ' ἄλλων
τεχνιτῶν δεήσει.   φέρε δή, ἐξ ἁπασῶν ἤδη
τούτων ὡς οἷόν τε συναρμόσας μίαν σοι εἰκόνα
ἐπιδείξω, τὸ ἐξαίρετον παρ' ἑκάστης ἔχουσαν.

ΠΟΛΥΣΤΡΑΤΟΣ

Καὶ τίνα ἂν τρόπον τουτὶ γένοιτο ;

---

[1] No copy of the Sosandra is known, nor is it clear
whether she was a goddess or a woman.

[2] For the beautiful head in Bologna that is believed to be
copied from this statue (a work in bronze, dedicated on the
Acropolis by certain Lemnians) see Furtwängler, *Masterpieces
of Greek Sculpture*, pl. i–iii, and Fig. 3.

if I had neglected the most beautiful of the sculptures of Alcamenes.

LYCINUS

One question, at all events, I shall not ask you, Polystratus—whether you have often gone up to the Acropolis to look at the Sosandra of Calamis?[1]

POLYSTRATUS

I have often seen that, too.

LYCINUS

So far, so good. But among the works of Phidias what did you praise most highly?

POLYSTRATUS

What could it be but the Lemnian Athena, on which Phidias deigned actually to inscribe his name?[2] Oh, yes! and the Amazon who leans upon her spear.[3]

LYCINUS

These are the most beautiful, my friend, so that we shall not need any other artists. Come now, out of them all I shall make a combination as best I can, and shall display to you a single portrait-statue that comprises whatever is most exquisite in each.

POLYSTRATUS

How can that be done?

---

[3] Copies of the Phidian Amazon have not been identified with any certainty. For the several types of Amazon statue that come into consideration, see Michaelis, *Jahrbuch des k. deutschen Archaeologischen Instituts*, i, p. 14 sqq., and Furtwängler, *Masterpieces*, p. 128 sqq.

THE WORKS OF LUCIAN

ΛΥΚΙΝΟΣ

Οὐ χαλεπόν, ὦ Πολύστρατε, εἰ τὸ ἀπὸ τοῦδε
παραδόντες τὰς εἰκόνας τῷ λόγῳ, ἐπιτρέψαιμεν
αὐτῷ μετακοσμεῖν καὶ συντιθέναι καὶ ἁρμόζειν
ὡς ἂν εὐρυθμότατα δύναιτο, φυλάττων ἅμα τὸ
συμμιγὲς ἐκεῖνο καὶ ποικίλον.

ΠΟΛΥΣΤΡΑΤΟΣ

Εὖ λέγεις· καὶ δὴ παραλαβὼν δεικνύτω· ἐθέλω
γὰρ εἰδέναι ὅ τι καὶ χρήσεται αὐταῖς, ἢ ὅπως
ἐκ τοσούτων μίαν τινὰ συνθεὶς οὐκ ἀπᾴδουσαν
ἀπεργάσεται.

ΛΥΚΙΝΟΣ

6 Καὶ μὴν ἤδη σοι ὁρᾶν παρέχει γιγνομένην τὴν
εἰκόνα, ὧδε συναρμόζων, τῆς ἐκ Κνίδου ἡκούσης
μόνον τὴν κεφαλὴν λαβών· οὐδὲν γὰρ τοῦ ἄλλου
σώματος γυμνοῦ ὄντος δεήσεται· τὰ μὲν ἀμφὶ
τὴν κόμην καὶ μέτωπον ὀφρύων τε τὸ εὔγραμμον
ἐάσει ἔχειν ὥσπερ ὁ Πραξιτέλης ἐποίησεν, καὶ
τῶν ὀφθαλμῶν δὲ τὸ ὑγρὸν ἅμα τῷ φαιδρῷ καὶ
κεχαρισμένῳ, καὶ τοῦτο διαφυλάξει κατὰ τὸ
Πραξιτέλει δοκοῦν· τὰ μῆλα δὲ καὶ ὅσα τῆς
ὄψεως ἀντωπὰ παρ᾽ Ἀλκαμένους καὶ τῆς ἐν
κήποις λήψεται, καὶ προσέτι χειρῶν ἄκρα καὶ
καρπῶν τὸ εὔρυθμον καὶ δακτύλων τὸ εὐάγωγον
εἰς λεπτὸν ἀπολῆγον παρὰ τῆς ἐν κήποις καὶ
ταῦτα. τὴν δὲ τοῦ παντὸς προσώπου περιγραφὴν
καὶ παρειῶν τὸ ἁπαλὸν καὶ ῥῖνα σύμμετρον ἡ
Λημνία παρέξει καὶ Φειδίας· ἔτι καὶ στόματος
ἁρμογὴν αὐτὸς καὶ τὸν αὐχένα, παρὰ τῆς
Ἀμαζόνος λαβών· ἡ Σωσάνδρα δὲ καὶ Κάλαμις

ESSAYS IN PORTRAITURE

Nothing hard about it, Polystratus, if from now on we give Master Eloquence a free hand with those statues and allow him to adapt, combine, and unite them as harmoniously as he can, retaining at the same time that composite effect and the variety.

Very well; by all means let him have a free hand and show us his powers, for I am eager to know what he really can do with the statues and how he can combine so many into one without making it discordant.

Well, he permits you to look upon the statue even now, as it comes into being; and this is the way he makes the blend. From the Cnidian he takes only the head, as the body, which is unclothed, will not meet his needs. He will allow the arrangement of the hair, the forehead, and the fair line of the brows to remain as Praxiteles made them; and in the eyes also, that gaze so liquid, and at the same time so clear and winsome—that too shall be retained as Praxiteles conceived it. But he will take the round of the cheeks and all the fore part of the face from Alcamenes and from Our Lady in the Gardens; so too the hands, the graceful wrists, and the supple, tapering fingers shall come from Our Lady in the Gardens. But the contour of the entire face, the delicate sides of it, and the shapely nose will be supplied by the Lemnian Athena and by Phidias, and the master will also furnish the meeting of the lips, and the neck, taking these from his Amazon. Sosandra and Calamis shall adorn her with

αἰδοῖ κοσμήσουσιν αὐτήν, καὶ τὸ μειδίαμα σεμνὸν καὶ λεληθὸς ὥσπερ τὸ ἐκείνης ἔσται· καὶ τὸ εὐσταλὲς δὲ καὶ κόσμιον τῆς ἀναβολῆς παρὰ τῆς Σωσάνδρας, πλὴν ὅτι ἀκατακάλυπτος αὕτη ἔσται τὴν κεφαλήν. τῆς ἡλικίας δὲ τὸ μέτρον ἡλίκον ἂν γένοιτο, κατὰ τὴν ἐν Κνίδῳ ἐκείνην μάλιστα. καὶ γὰρ καὶ τοῦτο κατὰ τὸν Πραξιτέλη μεμετρήσθω.

Τί σοι, ὦ Πολύστρατε, δοκεῖ; καλὴ γενήσεσθαι ἡ εἰκών;

ΠΟΛΥΣΤΡΑΤΟΣ

Καὶ μάλιστα, ἐπειδὰν εἰς τὸ ἀκριβέστατον 7 ἀποτελεσθῇ· ἔτι γάρ, ὦ πάντων γενναιότατε, καταλέλοιπάς τι κάλλος ἔξω τοῦ ἀγάλματος οὕτως πάντα εἰς τὸ αὐτὸ συμπεφορηκώς.

ΛΥΚΙΝΟΣ

Τί τοῦτο;

ΠΟΛΥΣΤΡΑΤΟΣ

Οὐ τὸ¹ μικρότατον, ὦ φιλότης, εἰ μή σοι δόξει ὀλίγα πρὸς εὐμορφίαν συντελεῖν χρόα καὶ τὸ ἑκάστῳ πρέπον, ὡς μέλανα μὲν εἶναι ἀκριβῶς ὁπόσα μέλανα, λευκὰ δὲ ὅσα τοιαῦτα χρή, καὶ τὸ ἐρύθημα ἐπανθεῖν καὶ τὰ τοιαῦτα· κινδυνεύει τοῦ μεγίστου ἔτι ἡμῖν προσδεῖν.

ΛΥΚΙΝΟΣ

Πόθεν οὖν καὶ ταῦτα πορισαίμεθ᾽ ἄν; ἢ παρακαλέσαιμεν δηλαδὴ τοὺς γραφέας, καὶ μάλιστα ὁπόσοι αὐτῶν ἄριστοι ἐγένοντο κεράσασθαι τὰ χρώματα καὶ εὔκαιρον ποιεῖσθαι τὴν ἐπιβολὴν αὐτῶν; καὶ δὴ παρακεκλήσθω Πολύγνωτος καὶ

modesty, and her smile shall be grave and faint
like that of Sosandra, from whom shall come also the
simplicity and seemliness of her drapery, except that
she shall have her head uncovered. In the measure
of her years, whatever it may be, she shall agree
most closely with the Cnidian Aphrodite; that, too,
Praxiteles may determine.

What do you think, Polystratus? Will the statue
be beautiful?

POLYSTRATUS

Yes, surely, when it has been completed to the
uttermost detail; for there is still, despite your
unexampled zeal, one beauty that you have left out
of your statue in collecting and combining everything
as you did.

LYCINUS

What is that?

POLYSTRATUS

Not the most unimportant, my friend, unless you
will maintain that perfection of form is but little
enhanced by colour and appropriateness in each
detail, so that just those parts will be black which
should be black and those white which should be,
and the flush of life will glow upon the surface, and
so forth. I fear we still stand in need of the most
important feature!

LYCINUS

Where then can we get all that? Or shall
we call in the painters, of course, and particularly
those who excelled in mixing their colours and in
applying them judiciously? Come, then, let us call

---

[1] τί τοῦτο; οὐ τὸ Heusde : τοῦτο MSS.

THE WORKS OF LUCIAN

Εὐφράνωρ ἐκεῖνος καὶ Ἀπελλῆς καὶ Ἀετίων·
οὗτοι δὲ διελόμενοι τὸ ἔργον ὁ μὲν Εὐφράνωρ
χρωσάτω τὴν κόμην οἵαν τῆς Ἥρας ἔγραψεν,
ὁ Πολύγνωτος δὲ ὀφρύων τὸ ἐπιπρεπὲς καὶ
παρειῶν τὸ ἐνερευθὲς οἵαν τὴν Κασάνδραν ἐν
τῇ λέσχῃ ἐποίησεν τοῖς Δελφοῖς, καὶ ἐσθῆτα δὲ
οὗτος ποιησάτω εἰς τὸ λεπτότατον ἐξειργασμένην,
ὡς συνεστάλθαι μὲν ὅσα χρή, διηνεμῶσθαι δὲ τὰ
πολλά· τὸ δὲ ἄλλο σῶμα ὁ Ἀπελλῆς δειξάτω
κατὰ τὴν Πακάτην μάλιστα, μὴ ἄγαν λευκὸν
ἀλλὰ ἔναιμον ἁπλῶς· τὰ χείλη δὲ οἷα Ῥωξάνης
8 ὁ Ἀετίων ποιησάτω. μᾶλλον δὲ τὸν ἄριστον
τῶν γραφέων Ὅμηρον παρόντος Εὐφράνορος καὶ
Ἀπελλοῦ δεδέγμεθα· οἷον γάρ τι τοῖς Μενελάου
μηροῖς τὸ χρῶμα ἐκεῖνος ἐπέβαλεν ἐλέφαντι
εἰκάσας ἠρέμα πεφοινιγμένῳ, τοιόνδε ἔστω τὸ
πᾶν· ὁ δ᾽ αὐτὸς οὗτος καὶ τοὺς ὀφθαλμοὺς
γραψάτω βοῶπίν τινα ποιήσας αὐτήν. συνεπι-
λήψεται δὲ τοῦ ἔργου αὐτῷ καὶ ὁ Θηβαῖος
ποιητής, ὡς ἰοβλέφαρον[1] ἐξεργάσασθαι· καὶ
φιλομειδῆ δὲ Ὅμηρος ποιήσει καὶ λευκώλενον
καὶ ῥοδοδάκτυλον, καὶ ὅλως τῇ χρυσῇ Ἀφροδίτῃ
εἰκάσει πολὺ δικαιότερον ἢ τὴν τοῦ Βρισέως.

---

[1] ἰοβλέφαρον du Soul : τὸ βλέφαρον MSS.

---

[1] Painted as one of the Twelve Gods in the portico of Zeus
Eleutherius at Athens (Pausanias 1, 3, 3 ; Pliny 35, 129).

[2] "Above the Cassotis is a building with paintings by
Polygnotus ; it was dedicated by the Cnidians, and is called
by the Delphians the Club-room (*Lesche*, "place of talk"),
because here they used of old to meet and talk over both
mythological and more serious subjects. . . . Cassandra herself is seated on the ground and is holding the image of

in Polygnotus and Euphranor of old, and Apelles and
Aëtion. Let them divide up the work, and let
Euphranor colour the hair as he painted Hera's:[1]
let Polygnotus do the becomingness of her brows
and the faint flush of her cheeks, just as he did
Cassandra in the Lesche at Delphi,[2] and let him also
do her clothing, which shall be of the most delicate
texture, so that it not only clings close where it
should, but a great deal of it floats in the air. The
body Apelles shall represent after the manner of his
Pacate,[3] not too white but just suffused with red;
and her lips shall be done by Aëtion like Roxana's.[4]
But stay! We have Homer, the best of all painters,
even in the presence of Euphranor and Apelles.
Let her be throughout of a colour like that which
Homer gave to the thighs of Menelaus when he
likened them to ivory tinged with crimson;[5] and
let him also paint the eyes and make her "ox-eyed."
The Theban poet, too, shall lend him a hand in the
work, to give her "violet brows."[6] Yes, and
Homer shall make her "laughter-loving" and
"white-armed ' and "rosy-fingered," and, in a word,
shall liken her to golden Aphrodite far more fittingly
than he did the daughter of Briseus.[7]

Athena, for she overturned the wooden image from its
pedestal when Ajax dragged her out of the sanctuary."
(Pausanias 10, 25, 1 and 26, 3, Frazer's translation.)

[3] Called Pancaste by Aelian (*Var. Hist.*, 12, 34), Pancaspe
by Pliny (35, 86). She was a girl of Larissa, the first sweet-
heart of Alexander the Great.

[4] In the famous "Marriage of Alexander and Roxana,"
described fully in Lucian's *Herodotus*, c. 4–6.

[5] *Iliad* 4, 141 sqq.

[6] Pindar; the poem in which he applied this epithet to
Aphrodite (cf. p. 333) is lost.

[7] *Iliad* 19, 282.

9 Ταῦτα μὲν οὖν πλαστῶν καὶ γραφέων καὶ
ποιητῶν παῖδες ἐργάσονται. ὃ δὲ πᾶσιν ἐπανθεῖ
τούτοις, ἡ χάρις, μᾶλλον δὲ πᾶσαι ἅμα ὁπόσαι
Χάριτες καὶ ὁπόσοι Ἔρωτες περιχορεύοντες, τίς
ἂν μιμήσασθαι δύναιτο ;

ΠΟΛΥΣΤΡΑΤΟΣ

Θεσπέσιόν τι χρῆμα, ὦ Λυκῖνε, φὴς καὶ δι-
ιπετὲς ὡς ἀληθῶς, οἷόν τι τῶν ἐξ οὐρανοῦ γένοιτο.
τί δὲ πράσσουσαν εἶδες αὐτήν ;

ΛΥΚΙΝΟΣ

Βιβλίον ἐν ταῖν χεροῖν εἶχεν εἰς δύο συνει-
λημένον, καὶ ἐῴκει τὸ μέν τι ἀναγιγνώσκεσθαι
αὐτοῦ, τὸ δὲ ἤδη ἀνεγνωκέναι. μεταξὺ δὲ προϊοῦσα
διελέγετο τῶν παρομαρτούντων τινὶ οὐκ οἶδα ὅ τι·
οὐ γὰρ εἰς ἐπήκοον ἐφθέγγετο. πλὴν μειδιάσασά
γε, ὦ Πολύστρατε, ὀδόντας ἐξέφηνε πῶς ἂν
εἴποιμί σοι ὅπως μὲν λευκούς, ὅπως δὲ συμ-
μέτρους καὶ πρὸς ἀλλήλους συνηρμοσμένους ; εἴ
που κάλλιστον ὅρμον εἶδες ἐκ τῶν στιλπνοτάτων
καὶ ἰσομεγεθῶν μαργαριτῶν, οὕτως ἐπὶ στίχου
ἐπεφύκεσαν· ἐκοσμοῦντο δὲ μάλιστα τῷ τῶν
χειλῶν ἐρυθήματι. ὑπεφαίνοντο γοῦν, αὐτὸ δὴ
τὸ τοῦ Ὁμήρου, ἐλέφαντι τῷ πριστῷ ὅμοιοι, οὐχ
οἱ μὲν πλατύτεροι αὐτῶν, οἱ δὲ γυροί,[1] οἱ δὲ προέ-

---

[1] οἱ δὲ γυροὶ added from the margin of Γ.

---

[1] The Trojan Palladium was "dropt from the skies"
according to the myth (Apollodorus 3, 12, 3); so also the
image of Athena Tauropolos at Halae in Attica, that was
thought to have been brought there from the country of the
Taurians where it fell (Euripides, *Iph. in Taur.* 87, 977, 986).

ESSAYS IN PORTRAITURE

This, then, is what sculptors and painters and poets can achieve; but who could counterfeit the fine flower of it all—the grace; nay, all the Graces in company, and all the Loves, too, circling hand in hand about her?

POLYSTRATUS

It is a miraculous creature that you describe, Lycinus; "dropt from the skies"[1] in very truth, quite like something out of Heaven. But what was she doing when you saw her?

LYCINUS

She had a scroll in her hands, with both ends of it rolled up, so that she seemed to be reading the one part and to have already read the other.[2] As she walked along, she was discussing something or other with one of her escorts; I do not know what it was, for she did not speak so that it could be overheard. But when she smiled, Polystratus, she disclosed such teeth! How can I tell you how white they were, how symmetrical and well matched? If you have ever seen a lovely string of very lustrous, equal pearls, that is the way they stood in row; and they were especially set off by the redness of her lips. They shone, just as Homer says, like sawn ivory.[3] Nor could you say that some of them were too broad,

---

[2] Lucian's expression amounts to saying that the book was open at the middle. In reading an ancient book, one generally held the roll in the right hand and took the end of it in the left, rolling up in that hand the part that one was done with.

[3] *Odyssey* 18, 196.

χοντες ἢ διεστηκότες οἷοι ταῖς πλείσταις, ἀλλά
τις πάντων ἰσοτιμία καὶ ὁμόχροια καὶ μέγεθος ἓν
καὶ προσεχεῖς ὁμοίως, καὶ ὅλως μέγα τι θαῦμα
καὶ θέαμα πᾶσαν τὴν ἀνθρωπίνην εὐμορφίαν
ὑπερπεπαικός.

ΠΟΛΥΣΤΡΑΤΟΣ

10 Ἔχ' ἀτρέμας. συνίημι γὰρ ἤδη πάνυ σαφῶς
ἥντινα καὶ λέγεις τὴν γυναῖκα, τούτοις τε αὐτοῖς
γνωρίσας καὶ τῇ πατρίδι. καὶ εὐνούχους δέ τινας
ἕπεσθαι αὐτῇ ἔφης.

ΛΥΚΙΝΟΣ

Νὴ Δία, καὶ στρατιώτας τινάς.

ΠΟΛΥΣΤΡΑΤΟΣ

Τὴν βασιλεῖ συνοῦσαν, ὦ μακάριε, τὴν ἀοίδιμον
ταύτην λέγεις.

ΛΥΚΙΝΟΣ

Τί δέ ἐστιν αὐτῇ τοὔνομα;

ΠΟΛΥΣΤΡΑΤΟΣ

Πάνυ καὶ τοῦτο γλαφυρόν, ὦ Λυκῖνε, καὶ
ἐπέραστον· ὁμώνυμος γάρ ἐστιν τῇ τοῦ Ἀβραδάτα
ἐκείνη τῇ καλῇ· οἶσθα πολλάκις ἀκούσας Ξενο-
φῶντος ἐπαινοῦντός τινα σώφρονα καὶ καλὴν
γυναῖκα.

ΛΥΚΙΝΟΣ

Νὴ Δία, καὶ ὥσπερ γε ὁρῶν αὐτὴν οὕτω δια-
τέθειμαι, ὁπόταν κατ' ἐκεῖνό που ἀναγιγνώσκων

---

[1] Panthea, "the woman of Susa, who is said to have been
the fairest in Asia," whose story is told in the *Cyropaedia* (4, 6,
11 ; 5, 1, 2–18 ; 6, 1, 33–51 ; 6, 4, 2–11 ; 7, 3, 2–16). Polystratus

others misshapen, and others prominent or wide apart, as they are with most women. On the contrary, all were of equal distinction, of the self-same whiteness, of uniform size, and similarly close together. In short, it was a great marvel; a spectacle transcending all human beauty!

POLYSTRATUS

Hold still! I perceive now quite clearly who the woman is that you describe; I recognize her by just these points and also by her country. Besides, you said that there were eunuchs in her following.

LYCINUS

Yes, and several soldiers.

POLYSTRATUS

It is the Emperor's mistress, you simpleton—the woman who is so famous!

LYCINUS

What is her name?

POLYSTRATUS

Like herself, it is very pretty and charming. She has the same name as the beautiful wife of Abradatas. You know whom I mean, for you have often heard Xenophon praise her as a good and beautiful woman.[1]

LYCINUS

Yes, and it makes me feel as if I saw her when I reach that place in my reading; I can almost hear

says "heard" because of the ancient practice of reading aloud, to which the Lessons of the Church bear present testimony.

275

γένωμαι, καὶ μονονουχὶ καὶ ἀκούω λεγούσης
αὐτῆς ἃ πεποίηται λέγουσα, καὶ ὡς ὥπλιζε τὸν
ἄνδρα καὶ οἷα ἦν παραπέμπουσα αὐτὸν ἐπὶ τὴν
μάχην.

ΠΟΛΥΣΤΡΑΤΟΣ

11 Ἀλλ᾽, ὦ ἄριστε, σὺ μὲν ὥσπερ τινὰ ἀστραπὴν
παραδραμοῦσαν ἅπαξ εἶδες αὐτήν, καὶ ἔοικας τὰ
πρόχειρα ταῦτα, λέγω δὲ τὸ σῶμα καὶ τὴν
μορφήν, ἐπαινεῖν· τῶν δὲ τῆς ψυχῆς ἀγαθῶν
ἀθέατος εἶ, οὐδὲ οἶσθα ὅσον τὸ κάλλος ἐκεῖνό
ἐστιν αὐτῆς, μακρῷ τινι ἄμεινον καὶ θεοειδέστερον
τοῦ σώματος. ἐγὼ δὲ συνήθης γάρ εἰμι καὶ
λόγων ἐκοινώνησα πολλάκις ὁμοεθνὴς ὤν. καὶ
γάρ, ὡς οἶσθα καὶ αὐτός, τὸ ἥμερον καὶ φιλάν-
θρωπον καὶ τὸ μεγαλόφρον καὶ σωφροσύνην καὶ
παιδείαν πρὸ τοῦ κάλλους ἐπαινῶ· ἄξια γὰρ
προκεκρίσθαι ταῦτα τοῦ σώματος· ἐπεὶ ἄλογον
ἂν εἴη καὶ γελοῖον, ὥσπερ εἴ τις τὴν ἐσθῆτα πρὸ
τοῦ σώματος θαυμάζοι. τὸ δ᾽ ἐντελὲς κάλλος,
οἶμαι, τοῦτό ἐστιν, ὁπόταν εἰς τὸ αὐτὸ συνδράμῃ
ψυχῆς ἀρετὴ καὶ εὐμορφία σώματος. ἀμέλει
πολλὰς ἄν σοι δείξαιμι μορφῆς μὲν εὖ ἠκούσας,
τὰ δ᾽ ἄλλα αἰσχυνούσας τὸ κάλλος, ὡς καὶ μόνον
φθεγξαμένων ἀπανθεῖν αὐτὸ καὶ ἀπομαραίνεσθαι
ἐλεγχόμενόν τε καὶ ἀσχημονοῦν καὶ παρ᾽ ἀξίαν
συνὸν πονηρᾷ τινι δεσποίνῃ τῇ ψυχῇ. καὶ αἵ
γε τοιαῦται ὅμοιαί μοι δοκοῦσιν τοῖς Αἰγυπτίοις
ἱεροῖς· κἀκεῖ γὰρ αὐτὸς μὲν ὁ νεὼς κάλλιστός τε
καὶ μέγιστος, λίθοις τοῖς πολυτελέσιν ἠσκημένος
καὶ χρυσῷ καὶ γραφαῖς διηνθισμένος, ἔνδον δὲ
ἢν ζητῇς τὸν θεόν, ἢ πίθηκός ἐστιν ἢ ἶβις ἢ τράγος
ἢ αἴλουρος. τοιαύτας πολλὰς ἰδεῖν ἔνεστιν.

276

her say what she is described as saying, and see how she armed her husband and what she was like when she sent him off to the battle.

But, my friend, you caught sight of her just once, flying past like a flash, and naturally have praised only what was obvious—I mean, her person and her physical beauty. The good points of her soul you have not beheld, and you do not know how great that beauty is in her, far more notable and more divine than that of her body. I do, for I am acquainted with her, and have often conversed with her, being of the same nationality. As you yourself know, I commend gentleness, kindliness, high-mindedness, self-control, and culture rather than beauty, for these qualities deserve to be preferred over those of the body. To do otherwise would be illogical and ridiculous, as if one were to admire her clothing rather than her person. Perfect beauty, to my mind, is when there is a union of spiritual excellence and physical loveliness. In truth, I could point you out a great many women who are well endowed with good looks, but in every way discredit their beauty, so that if they merely speak it fades and withers, since it suffers by contrast and cuts a shabby figure, unworthily housing as it does with a soul that is but a sorry mistress. Such women seem to me like the temples of Egypt, where the temple itself is fair and great, built of costly stones and adorned with gold and with paintings, but if you seek out the god within, it is either a monkey or an ibis or a goat or a cat! Women of that sort are to be seen in plenty.

Οὐ τοίνυν ἀποχρῆ τὸ κάλλος, εἰ μὴ κεκόσμη-
ται τοῖς δικαίοις κοσμήμασι, λέγω δὴ οὐκ ἐσθῆτι
ἁλουργεῖ καὶ ὅρμοις, ἀλλ᾽ οἷς προεῖπον ἐκείνοις,
ἀρετῇ καὶ σωφροσύνῃ καὶ ἐπιεικείᾳ καὶ φιλαν-
θρωπίᾳ καὶ τοῖς ἄλλοις ὁπόσα ταύτης ὅρος ἐστίν.

ΛΥΚΙΝΟΣ

12 Οὐκοῦν, ὦ Πολύστρατε, μῦθον ἀντὶ μύθου
ἄμειψαι αὐτῷ τῷ μέτρῳ, φασίν, ἢ καὶ λῷον,
δύνασαι γάρ, καί τινα εἰκόνα γραψάμενος τῆς
ψυχῆς ἐπίδειξον, ὡς μὴ ἐξ ἡμισείας θαυμάζοιμι
αὐτήν.

ΠΟΛΥΣΤΡΑΤΟΣ

Οὐ μικρόν, ὦ ἑταῖρε, τὸ ἀγώνισμα προστάτ-
τεις· οὐ γὰρ ὅμοιον τὸ πᾶσι προφανὲς ἐπαινέσαι
καὶ τὰ ἄδηλα ἐμφανίσαι τῷ λόγῳ. καί μοι δοκῶ
συνεργῶν καὶ αὐτὸς δεήσεσθαι πρὸς τὴν εἰκόνα,
οὐ πλαστῶν οὐδὲ γραφέων μόνον, ἀλλὰ καὶ
φιλοσόφων, ὡς πρὸς τοὺς ἐκείνων κανόνας ἀπευ-
θῦναι τὸ ἄγαλμα καὶ δεῖξαι κατὰ τὴν ἀρχαίαν
πλαστικὴν κατεσκευασμένον.

13 Καὶ δὴ πεποιήσθω. αὐδήεσσα μὲν τὸ πρῶτον
καὶ λίγεια, καὶ τὸ "γλυκίων μέλιτος ἀπὸ τῆς
γλώττης" περὶ αὐτῆς[1] μᾶλλον ἢ περὶ τοῦ Πυλίου
γέροντος ἐκείνου ὁ Ὅμηρος εἴρηκεν. πᾶς[2] δὲ ὁ
τόνος τοῦ φθέγματος οἷος ἁπαλώτατος, οὔτε
βαρὺς ὡς εἰς τὸ ἀνδρεῖον ἡρμόσθαι οὔτε πάνυ
λεπτὸς ὡς θηλύτατός τε εἶναι καὶ κομιδῇ ἔκλυτος,
ἀλλ᾽ οἷος γένοιτ᾽ ἂν παιδὶ μήπω ἡβάσκοντι, ἡδὺς
καὶ προσηνὴς καὶ πράως παραδυόμενος εἰς τὴν

---

[1] περὶ αὐτῆς N : not in γβ.
[2] πᾶς vulg. : πῶς MSS.

Beauty, then, is not enough unless it is set off
with its just enhancements, by which I mean, not
purple raiment and necklaces, but those I have
already mentioned—virtue, self-control, goodness,
kindliness, and everything else that is included in
the definition of virtue.

LYCINUS

Well then, Polystratus, trade me description for
description, giving, as the saying goes, measure for
measure, or even better than that, since you can.
Do a likeness of her soul and display it to me, so
that I need not admire her by halves.

POLYSTRATUS

It is no light task, my friend, that you are setting
me; for it is not the same thing to laud what is
manifest to all, and to reveal in words what is in-
visible. I think that I too shall need fellow-work-
men for the portrait, philosophers as well as sculptors
and painters, so that I can make my work of art
conform to their canons and can exhibit it as
modelled in the style of the ancients.

Come now, imagine it made. It will be "gifted
with speech,"[1] first of all, and "clear-voiced";[2]
and Homer's phrase "sweeter than honey from the
tongue" applies to her rather than to that old man
from Pylos.[3] The whole tone of her voice is as soft
as can be; not deep, so as to resemble a man's, nor
very high, so as to be quite womanish and wholly
strengthless, but like the voice of a boy still imma-
ture, delicious and winning, that gently steals into

[1] Like Circe (*Odyssey* 10, 136).
[2] Like the Muse (*Odyssey* 24, 62).
[3] Applied in Homer to the words of Nestor (*Iliad* 1, 249).

ἀκοήν, ὡς καὶ παυσαμένης ἔναυλον εἶναι τὴν
βοὴν καί τι λείψανον ἐνδιατρίβειν καὶ περι-
βομβεῖν τὰ ὦτα, καθάπερ ἠχώ τινα παρατείνου-
σαν τὴν ἀκρόασιν καὶ ἴχνη τῶν λόγων μελιχρὰ
ἄττα καὶ πειθοῦς μεστὰ ἐπὶ τῆς ψυχῆς ἀπολιμ-
πάνουσαν. ὁπόταν δὲ καὶ τὸ καλὸν ἐκεῖνο ᾄδῃ,
καὶ μάλιστα πρὸς τὴν κιθάραν, τότε δὴ τότε[1]
ὥρα μὲν σιωπᾶν τάχιστα[2] ἀλκυόσι καὶ τέττιξι
καὶ τοῖς κύκνοις· ἄμουσα γὰρ ὡς πρὸς ἐκείνην
ἅπαντα· κἂν τὴν Πανδίονος εἴπῃς, ἰδιῶτις κἀκείνη
καὶ ἄτεχνος, εἰ καὶ πολυηχέα τὴν φωνὴν ἀφίησιν.

14 Ὀρφεὺς δὲ καὶ Ἀμφίων, οἵπερ ἐπαγωγότατοι
ἐγένοντο τῶν ἀκροατῶν, ὡς καὶ τὰ ἄψυχα ἐπικα-
λέσασθαι πρὸς τὸ μέλος, αὐτοὶ ἄν, οἶμαι, εἴ γε
ἤκουσαν, καταλιπόντες ἂν τὰς κιθάρας παρεστή-
κεσαν σιωπῇ ἀκροώμενοι. τὸ γὰρ τῆς τε ἁρμονίας
τὸ ἀκριβέστατον διαφυλάττειν, ὡς μὴ παραβαί-
νειν τι τοῦ ῥυθμοῦ, ἀλλ' εὐκαίρῳ τῇ ἄρσει καὶ
θέσει διαμεμετρῆσθαι τὸ ᾆσμα καὶ συνῳδὸν εἶναι
τὴν κιθάραν καὶ ὁμοχρονεῖν τῇ γλώττῃ τὸ πλῆ-
κτρον, καὶ τὸ εὐαφὲς τῶν δακτύλων καὶ τὸ
εὔκαμπες τῶν μελῶν, πόθεν ἂν ταῦτα ὑπῆρχε τῷ
Θρᾳκὶ ἐκείνῳ καὶ τῷ ἀνὰ τὸν Κιθαιρῶνα μεταξὺ
βουκολοῦντι καὶ κιθαρίζειν μελετῶντι ;

Ὥστε ἤν ποτε, ὦ Λυκῖνε, καὶ ἀδούσης ἀκούσῃς
αὐτῆς, οὐκέτι τὸ τῶν Γοργόνων ἐκεῖνο ἔσῃ μόνον
πεπονθώς, λίθος ἐξ ἀνθρώπου γενόμενος, ἀλλὰ

---

[1] τότε δὴ τότε du Soul : τότε δὴ τίποτε MSS.
[2] τάχιστα Jacobitz : ταῦτα MSS.

---

[1] Pandion's daughter is the nightingale ; the inimitable
πολυηχέα comes from Homer (*Odyssey* 19, 521).

the ear, so that even after she has ceased the sound
abides, some remnant of it lingering and filling the
ears with resonance, like an echo that prolongs
audition and leaves in the soul vague traces of her
words, honey-sweet and full of persuasion. And
when she lifts that glorious voice in song, above
all to the lyre, then—ah, then it is the hour for
halcyons and cicadas and swans to hush forthwith;
for they are one and all unmelodious as against her,
and even Pandion's daughter, should you mention her,
is an inexpert amateur, however "soundful" the
voice that she pours out.[1] And as for Orpheus
and Amphion, who exercised so very potent a spell
upon their auditors that even inanimate things
answered the call of their song, they themselves
in my opinion would have abandoned their lyres,
had they heard her, and would have stood by in
silence, listening. That scrupulous observance of
time, so that she makes no mistakes in the rhythm,
but her singing throughout keeps measure with
a beat that is accurate in its rise and fall,[2] while
her lyre is in full accord, and her plectrum keeps
pace with her tongue; that delicacy of touch; that
flexibility of modulations—how could all this be
attained by your Thracian, or by that other who
studied lyre-playing on the slopes of Cithaeron in
the intervals of tending cattle?[3]

Therefore, if ever you hear her sing, Lycinus, not
only will you have learned by experience, through
being turned into stone, what the Gorgons can do,

[2] Compare Horace, Odes 4, 6, 36: Lesbium servate pedem,
meique pollicis ictum.
[3] Orpheus and Amphion, respectively.

καὶ τὸ τῶν Σειρήνων εἴσῃ ὁποῖόν τι ἦν· παρε-
στήξῃ γὰρ εὖ οἶδα κεκηλημένος, πατρίδος καὶ
οἰκείων ἐπιλαθόμενος. καὶ ἢν κηρῷ ἐπιφράξῃ
τὰ ὦτα, καὶ διὰ τοῦ κηροῦ διαδύσεταί σοι τὸ
μέλος. τοιοῦτόν τι ἄκουσμά ἐστι, Τερψιχόρης
τινὸς ἢ Μελπομένης ἢ Καλλιόπης αὐτῆς παί-
δευμα, μυρία τὰ θέλγητρα καὶ παντοῖα ἐν ἑαυτῷ
ἔχον. ἑνί τε λόγῳ συνελὼν φαίην ἄν, τοιαύτης
μοι τῆς ᾠδῆς ἀκούειν νόμιζε, οἵαν εἰκὸς εἶναι τὴν
διὰ τοιούτων χειλῶν, δι' ἐκείνων δὲ τῶν ὀδόντων
ἐξιοῦσαν. ἑώρακας δὲ καὶ αὐτὸς ἥν φημι, ὥστε
ἀκηκοέναι νόμιζε.

15 Τὸ μὲν γὰρ ἀκριβὲς τοῦτο τῆς φωνῆς καὶ καθαρῶς Ἰωνικὸν καὶ ὅτι ὁμιλῆσαι στωμύλη καὶ
πολὺ τῶν Ἀττικῶν χαρίτων ἔχουσα οὐδὲ θαυμάζειν ἄξιον· πάτριον γὰρ αὐτῇ καὶ προγονικόν,
οὐδὲ ἄλλως ἐχρῆν μετέχουσαν τῶν Ἀθηναίων
κατὰ τὴν ἀποικίαν. οὐδὲ γὰρ οὐδὲ ἐκεῖνο θαυ-
μάσαιμ' ἄν, εἰ καὶ ποιήσει χαίρει καὶ τὰ πολλὰ
ταύτῃ ὁμιλεῖ, τοῦ Ὁμήρου πολῖτις οὖσα.

Μία μὲν δή σοι, ὦ Λυκῖνε, καλλιφωνίας αὕτη
καὶ ᾠδῆς εἰκών, ὡς ἄν τις ἐπὶ τὸ ἔλαττον εἰκά-
σειεν. σκόπει δὲ δὴ καὶ τὰς ἄλλας· οὐ γὰρ μίαν
ὥσπερ σὺ ἐκ πολλῶν συνθεὶς ἐπιδεῖξαι διέγνωκα
—ἧττον γὰρ τοῦτο καὶ γραφικόν, συντελεσθὲν [1]
κάλλη τοσαῦτα καὶ πολυειδές τι ἐκ πολλῶν
ἀποτελεῖν αὐτὸ αὐτῷ ἀνθαμιλλώμενον—ἀλλ' αἱ

---

[1] συντελεσθέν: corrupt. An infinitive is wanted, e.g.
συντιθέναι. The usual reading, γραφικῶς συντελεσθέν, leaves
κάλλη τοσαῦτα floating.

but you will know also what the effect of the Sirens was like; for you will stand there enchanted, I know right well, forgetful of country and of kin; and if you stop your ears with wax, the song, in spite of you, will slip through the very wax! Such music is it, a lesson learned of some Terpsichore or Melpomene, or of Calliope herself, fraught with a thousand witcheries of every sort. I may sum it up by saying: "Imagine that you are listening to such singing as would naturally come from such lips and from those teeth." You yourself have seen the lady in question, so consider that you have heard her.

As to the precision of her language, and its pure Ionic quality, as to the fact that she has a ready tongue in conversation and is full of Attic wit—that is nothing to wonder at. It is an inherited trait in her, and ancestral, and nothing else was to be expected, since she partakes of Athenian blood through the settlement which they planted.[1] Nor indeed am I disposed to wonder at the further fact that a countrywoman of Homer likes poetry and holds much converse with it.

There you have one picture, Lycinus, that of her exquisite speech and her singing, as it might be portrayed in an inadequate sort of way. And now look at the others—for I have decided not to exhibit a single picture made up, like yours, out of many. That is really less artistic, to combine beauties so numerous and create, out of many, a thing of many different aspects, completely at odds with itself.

[1] Athens and Theseus were thought to have had a hand in the foundation of Smyrna. Lucian's contemporary Aristides makes much of this.

πᾶσαι τῆς ψυχῆς ἀρεταὶ καθ᾽ ἑκάστην εἰκὼν μία
γεγράψεται πρὸς τὸ ἀρχέτυπον μεμιμημένη.

ΛΥΚΙΝΟΣ

Ἑορτήν, ὦ Πολύστρατε, καὶ πανδαισίαν ἐπαγ-
γέλλεις. ἔοικας γοῦν λώϊον ὡς ἀληθῶς ἀποδώσειν
μοι τὸ μέτρον. ἐπιμέτρει δ᾽ οὖν· ὡς οὐκ ἔστιν ὅ
τι ἂν ἄλλο ποιήσας μᾶλλον χαρίσαιό μοι.

ΠΟΛΥΣΤΡΑΤΟΣ

16 Οὐκοῦν ἐπειδὴ πάντων καλῶν παιδείαν ἡγεῖ-
σθαι ἀνάγκη, καὶ μάλιστα τούτων ὁπόσα με-
λετητά, φέρε καὶ ταύτην ἤδη συστησώμεθα,
ποικίλην μέντοι καὶ πολύμορφον, ὡς μηδὲ κατὰ
τοῦτο ἀπολιποίμεθα τῆς σῆς πλαστικῆς. καὶ δὴ
γεγράφθω πάντα συλλήβδην τὰ ἐκ τοῦ Ἑλικῶνος
ἀγαθὰ ἔχουσα, οὐχ ὥσπερ ἡ Κλειὼ καὶ ἡ Πολύ-
μνια καὶ ἡ Καλλιόπη καὶ αἱ ἄλλαι ἕν τι ἑκάστη
ἐπισταμένη, ἀλλὰ τὰ[1] πασῶν καὶ προσέτι τὰ
Ἑρμοῦ καὶ Ἀπόλλωνος. ὁπόσα γὰρ ἢ ποιηταὶ
μέτροις διακοσμήσαντες ἢ ῥήτορες δεινότητι
κρατύναντες ἐξενηνόχασιν ἢ συγγραφεῖς ἱστορή-
κασιν ἢ φιλόσοφοι παρηνέκασι,[2] πᾶσι τούτοις
ἡ εἰκὼν κεκοσμήσθω, οὐκ ἄχρι τοῦ ἐπικεχρῶσθαι
μόνον, ἀλλ᾽ εἰς βάθος δευσοποιοῖς τισι φαρμάκοις
εἰς κόρον καταβαφεῖσα. καὶ συγγνώμη, εἰ μηδὲν
ἀρχέτυπον ἐπιδεῖξαι ταύτης δυναίμην τῆς γραφῆς·
οὐ γὰρ ἔσθ᾽ ὅ τι τοιοῦτον ἐν τοῖς πάλαι παιδείας
πέρι μνημονεύεται. πλὴν ἀλλά, εἴ γε δοκεῖ,

---

[1] τὰ Lehmann : not in MSS.

No, all the several virtues of her soul shall be portrayed each by itself in a single picture that is a true copy of the model.

LYCINUS

It is a feast, Polystratus, a full banquet, that you promise! In fact, it appears that you really will give me back better measure. Anyhow, get on with your measuring; there is nothing else that you can do which would please me more.

POLYSTRATUS

Then inasmuch as culture must stand at the head of all that is fair, and particularly all that is acquired by study, let us now create its likeness, rich, however, in colours and in modelling, that even in this point we may not fall short of your achievement in sculpture. So let her be pictured as possessing all the good gifts that come from Helicon. Unlike Clio, Polymnia, Calliope, and the others, each of whom has a single accomplishment, she shall have those of all the Muses, and in addition those of Hermes and Apollo. For all that poets have set forth with the embellishment of metre or orators with the might of eloquence, all that historians have related or philosophers recommended shall give beauty to our picture, not simply to the extent of tinting its surface, but staining it all deeply with indelible colours till it will take no more. And you must pardon me if I can show no ancient model for this picture; for tradition tells us of nothing similar in point of culture among the men of olden times. But in spite of that, if you approve, it too may now

---

[2] παρηνέκασι vulg. : παρηνέγκασι MSS.

ἀνακείσθω καὶ αὕτη· οὐ μεμπτὴ γάρ, ὡς ἐμοὶ
φαίνεται.

ΛΥΚΙΝΟΣ

Καλλίστη μὲν οὖν,[1] ὦ Πολύστρατε, καὶ πά-
σαις ταῖς γραμμαῖς ἀπηκριβωμένη.

ΠΟΛΥΣΤΡΑΤΟΣ

17 Μετὰ δὲ ταύτην ἡ τῆς σοφίας καὶ συνέσεως
εἰκὼν γραπτέα. δεήσει δὲ ἡμῖν ἐνταῦθα πολλῶν
τῶν παραδειγμάτων, ἀρχαίων τῶν πλείστων,
ἑνὸς μὲν καὶ αὐτοῦ Ἰωνικοῦ· γραφεῖς δὲ καὶ δη-
μιουργοὶ αὐτοῦ Αἰσχίνης Σωκράτους ἑταῖρος καὶ
αὐτὸς Σωκράτης, μιμηλότατοι τεχνιτῶν ἁπάντων,
ὅσῳ καὶ μετ' ἔρωτος ἔγραφον. τὴν δὲ ἐκ τῆς
Μιλήτου ἐκείνην Ἀσπασίαν, ᾗ καὶ ὁ Ὀλύμπιος
θαυμασιώτατος αὐτὸς συνῆν, οὐ φαῦλον συνέσεως
παράδειγμα προθέμενοι, ὁπόσον ἐμπειρίας πραγμάτων καὶ ὀξύτητος εἰς τὰ πολιτικὰ καὶ ἀγχι-
νοίας καὶ δριμύτητος ἐκείνῃ προσῆν, τοῦτο πᾶν
ἐπὶ τὴν ἡμετέραν εἰκόνα μεταγάγωμεν ἀκριβεῖ
τῇ στάθμῃ· πλὴν ὅσον ἐκείνη μὲν ἐν μικρῷ
πινακίῳ ἐγέγραπτο, αὕτη δὲ κολοσσιαία τὸ
μέγεθός ἐστιν.

ΛΥΚΙΝΟΣ

Πῶς τοῦτο φής;

ΠΟΛΥΣΤΡΑΤΟΣ

Ὅτι, ὦ Λυκῖνε, οὐκ ἰσομεγέθεις εἶναί φημι τὰς
εἰκόνας ὁμοίας οὔσας· οὐ γὰρ ἴσον οὐδὲ ἐγγὺς
Ἀθηναίων ἡ τότε πολιτεία καὶ ἡ παροῦσα τῶν
Ῥωμαίων δύναμις. ὥστε εἰ καὶ τῇ ὁμοιότητι ἡ

[1] οὖν Fritzsche: not in MSS.

be hung; for no fault can be found with it, from my point of view.

It is very beautiful, to be sure, Polystratus, and every line of it correctly drawn.

Next we must delineate her wisdom and understanding. We shall require many models there, most of them ancient, and one, like herself, Ionic, painted and wrought by Aeschines, the friend of Socrates, and by Socrates himself,[1] of all craftsmen the truest copyists because they painted with love. It is that maid of Miletus, Aspasia, the consort of the Olympian,[2] himself a marvel beyond compare. Putting before us, in her, no mean pattern of understanding, let us take all that she had of experience in affairs, shrewdness in statescraft, quick-wittedness, and penetration, and transfer the whole of it to our own picture by accurate measurement; making allowance, however, for the fact that she was painted on a small canvas, but our figure is colossal in its scale.

What do you mean by that?

I mean, Lycinus, that the pictures are not of equal size, though they look alike; for the Athenian state of those days and the Roman empire of to-day are not equal, nor near it. Consequently, although

[1] In the *Aspasia*, a Socratic dialogue by the philosopher Aeschines, not extant.
[2] Pericles.

αὐτή, ἀλλὰ τῷ μεγέθει γε ἀμείνων αὕτη ὡς ἂν
ἐπὶ πλατυτάτου πίνακος καταγεγραμμένη.

18   Δεύτερον δὲ καὶ τρίτον παράδειγμα Θεανώ τε
ἐκείνη καὶ ἡ Λεσβία μελοποιός, καὶ Διοτίμα ἐπὶ
ταύταις, ἡ μὲν τὸ μεγαλόνουν ἡ Θεανὼ συμβαλλο-
μένη εἰς τὴν γραφήν, ἡ Σαπφὼ δὲ τὸ γλαφυρὸν
τῆς προαιρέσεως· τῇ Διοτίμᾳ δὲ οὐχ ἃ Σωκράτης
ἐπήνεσεν αὐτὴν ἐοικυῖα ἔσται μόνον, ἀλλὰ καὶ
τὴν ἄλλην σύνεσίν τε καὶ συμβουλίαν. τοιαύτη
σοι καὶ αὕτη, Λυκῖνε, ἀνακείσθω ἡ εἰκών.

ΛΥΚΙΝΟΣ

19   Νὴ Δί', ὦ Πολύστρατε, θαυμάσιος οὖσα.   σὺ
δὲ ἄλλας γράφου.

ΠΟΛΥΣΤΡΑΤΟΣ

Τὰς[1] τῆς χρηστότητος, ὦ ἑταῖρε, καὶ φιλαν-
θρωπίας, ἣ τὸ ἥμερον ἐμφανιεῖ τοῦ τρόπου καὶ
πρὸς τοὺς δεομένους προσηνές; εἰκάσθω οὖν καὶ
αὐτὴ Θεανοῖ τε ἐκείνῃ τῇ Ἀντήνορος καὶ Ἀρήτῃ
καὶ τῇ θυγατρὶ αὐτῆς τῇ Ναυσικάᾳ, καὶ εἴ τις
ἄλλη ἐν μεγέθει πραγμάτων ἐσωφρόνησε πρὸς
τὴν τύχην.

20   Ἑξῆς δὲ μετὰ ταύτην ἡ τῆς σωφροσύνης αὐτῆς
γεγράφθω καὶ τῆς πρὸς τὸν συνόντα εὐνοίας, ὡς
κατὰ τὴν τοῦ Ἰκαρίου μάλιστα εἶναι τὴν σαό-

---

[1] τὰς should probably be excised.

---

[1] Wife, or disciple, of Pythagoras, herself a philosophical
writer of note.

[2] Diotima, a priestess of Mantinea, probably fictitious, for
we hear of her only through Plato in the *Symposium* (201 D).
Socrates says there that she was wise in Love, and ascribes

ours resembles the other exactly, yet in size at least it is superior, as being painted on a very broad canvas.

The second model and the third shall be the famous Theano[1] and the Lesbian poetess, and Diotima[2] shall be still another. Theano shall contribute her high-mindedness, Sappho the attractiveness of her way of living, and Diotima shall be copied not only in those qualities for which Socrates commended her, but in her general intelligence and power to give counsel. There you have another picture, Lycinus, which may be hung also.

LYCINUS

Yes, Polystratus, for it is marvellous. But paint more of them.

POLYSTRATUS

That of her goodness and loving-kindness, my friend, which will disclose the gentleness of her nature and its graciousness to all those who make demands upon her? Then let her be compared with that Theano who was wife of Antenor,[3] and with Arete,[4] and Arete's daughter Nausicaa, and with any other who in high station behaved with propriety in the face of her good fortune.

Next in order, let her modesty be portrayed, and her love for her consort, in such a way as to be most like the daughter of Icarius, described by

to her the metaphysical rhapsody on Love in which the dialogue culminates.

[3] Theano, priestess of Athena in Troy (*Iliad* 6, 298), brought up Pedaeus, her husband's illegitimate child, as if he were her own son (*Iliad* 5, 69).

[4] See *Odyssey* 7, 67 sq.

φρονα καὶ τὴν περίφρονα ὑπὸ τοῦ Ὁμήρου
γεγραμμένην—τοιαύτην γὰρ τὴν τῆς Πηνελόπης
εἰκόνα ἐκεῖνος ἔγραψεν—ἢ καὶ νὴ Δία κατὰ τὴν
ὁμώνυμον αὐτῆς τὴν τοῦ Ἀβραδάτα, ἧς μικρὸν
ἔμπροσθεν ἐμνημονεύσαμεν.

ΛΥΚΙΝΟΣ

Παγκάλην καὶ ταύτην, ὦ Πολύστρατε, ἀπειρ-
γάσω, καὶ σχεδὸν ἤδη τέλος σοι ἔχουσιν αἱ
εἰκόνες· ἅπασαν γὰρ ἐπελήλυθας τὴν ψυχὴν
κατὰ μέρη ἐπαινῶν.

ΠΟΛΥΣΤΡΑΤΟΣ

21 Οὐχ ἅπασαν· ἔτι γὰρ τὰ μέγιστα τῶν ἐπαίνων
περιλείπεται. λέγω δὲ τὸ ἐν τηλικούτῳ ὄγκῳ
γενομένην αὐτὴν μήτε τῦφον ἐπὶ τῇ εὐπραξίᾳ
περιβαλέσθαι μήτε ὑπὲρ τὸ ἀνθρώπινον μέτρον
ἐπαρθῆναι πιστεύσασαν τῇ τύχῃ, φυλάττειν δὲ
ἐπὶ τοῦ ἰσοπέδου ἑαυτὴν μηδὲν ἀπειρόκαλον ἢ
φορτικὸν φρονοῦσαν καὶ τοῖς προσιοῦσιν δη-
μοτικῶς τε καὶ ἐκ τοῦ ὁμοίου προσφέρεσθαι καὶ
δεξιώσεις καὶ φιλοφροσύνας φιλοφρονεῖσθαι τοσούτῳ ἡδίους τοῖς προσομιλοῦσιν, ὅσῳ καὶ παρὰ
μείζονος ὅμως γιγνόμεναι οὐδὲν τραγικὸν ἐμφαί-
νουσιν. ὡς ὁπόσοι τῷ μέγα δύνασθαι μὴ πρὸς
ὑπεροψίαν, ἀλλὰ καὶ πρὸς εὐποιίαν ἐχρήσαντο,
οὗτοι καὶ ἄξιοι μάλιστα τῶν παρὰ τῆς τύχης
δοθέντων ἀγαθῶν ὤφθησαν, καὶ μόνοι ἂν οὗτοι
δικαίως τὸ ἐπίφθονον διαφύγοιεν· οὐδεὶς γὰρ ἂν
φθονήσειε τῷ ὑπερέχοντι, ἢν μετριάζοντα ἐπὶ
τοῖς εὐτυχήμασιν αὐτὸν ὁρᾷ καὶ μὴ κατὰ τὴν τοῦ
Ὁμήρου Ἄτην ἐκείνην ἐπ᾽ ἀνδρῶν κράατα βεβη-

Homer as modest and prudent (for that is the way
he drew the picture of Penelope); or like her
own homonym, the wife of Abradatas, whom we
mentioned a little while ago.[1]

Once more you have created a very beautiful
picture, Polystratus; and now, perhaps, your portraits are finished, for you have traversed all of
her soul in praising it part by part.

Not all of it! The very greatest items in her
praise are still unincluded. I mean that in so
elevated a station she has not clothed herself in
pride over her success, and has not been uplifted
above the limit that beseems humanity through
confidence in Fortune, but keeps herself upon the
common plane, with no tasteless or vulgar aspirations,
treats her visitors familiarly and as an equal, and
gives her friends greetings and evidences of affection
that are all the sweeter to them because, although
they come from one who is above them, they make
no display of circumstance. Truly, all those who
employ great power not in superciliousness but in
kindness, are regarded as especially worthy of the
blessings that have been bestowed upon them by
Fortune, and they alone deserve to escape envy.
Nobody will envy the man above him if he sees him
behaving with moderation amid his successes and
not, like Homer's Ate,[2] treading on the heads of

---

[1] See page 275.
[2] *Iliad*, 19, 91–94.

κότα καὶ τὸ ὑποδεέστερον πατοῦντα· ὅπερ οἱ
ταπεινοὶ τὰς γνώμας πάσχουσιν ἀπειροκαλίᾳ τῆς
ψυχῆς·[1] ἐπειδὰν γὰρ αὐτοὺς ἡ τύχη μηδὲν τοιοῦτον ἐλπίσαντας ἄφνω ἀναβιβάσῃ εἰς πτηνόν τι
καὶ μετάρσιον ὄχημα, οὐ μένουσιν ἐπὶ τῶν
ὑπαρχόντων οὐδ' ἀφορῶσιν κάτω, ἀλλὰ ἀεὶ
πρὸς τὸ ἄναντες βιάζονται. τοιγαροῦν ὥσπερ ὁ
Ἴκαρος, τακέντος αὐτοῖς τάχιστα τοῦ κηροῦ καὶ
τῶν πτερῶν περιρρυέντων, γέλωτα ὀφλισκάνουσιν
ἐπὶ κεφαλὴν εἰς πελάγη καὶ κλύδωνα ἐμπίπτον-
τες· ὅσοι δὲ κατὰ τὸν Δαίδαλον ἐχρήσαντο τοῖς
πτεροῖς καὶ μὴ πάνυ ἐπήρθησαν, εἰδότες ὅτι ἐκ
κηροῦ ἦν αὐτοῖς πεποιημένα, ἐταμιεύσαντο δὲ
πρὸς τὸ ἀνθρώπινον τὴν φορὰν καὶ ἠγάπησαν
ὑψηλότεροι μόνον τῶν κυμάτων ἐνεχθέντες, ὥστε
μέντοι νοτίζεσθαι αὐτοῖς ἀεὶ τὰ πτερὰ καὶ μὴ
παρέχειν αὐτὰ μόνῳ τῷ ἡλίῳ, οὗτοι δὲ ἀσφαλῶς
τε ἅμα καὶ σωφρόνως διέπτησαν· ὅπερ καὶ ταύτην ἄν τις μάλιστα ἐπαινέσειε. τοιγαροῦν καὶ
ἄξιον παρὰ πάντων ἀπολαμβάνει τὸν καρπόν,
εὐχομένων ταῦτά τε αὐτῇ παραμεῖναι τὰ πτερὰ
καὶ ἔτι[2] πλείω ἐπιρρεῖν τἀγαθά.

ΛΥΚΙΝΟΣ

22 Καὶ οὕτως, ὦ Πολύστρατε, γιγνέσθω· ἀξία
γὰρ οὐ τὸ σῶμα μόνον ὥσπερ ἡ Ἑλένη καλὴ
οὖσα, καλλίω δὲ καὶ ἐρασμιωτέραν[3] ὑπ' αὐτῷ[4]
τὴν ψυχὴν σκέπουσα. ἔπρεπε δὲ καὶ βασιλεῖ
τῷ μεγάλῳ χρηστῷ καὶ ἡμέρῳ ὄντι καὶ τοῦτο
μετὰ τῶν ἄλλων ἀγαθῶν, ὁπόσα ἐστὶν αὐτῷ,

---

[1] ψυχῆς Seager : τύχης MSS.
[2] ἔτι Lehmann : ἐπὶ MSS.

men and crushing whatever is feebler. That is the way in which the low-minded are affected because of their vulgarity of soul. When, without their expecting anything of the sort, Fortune suddenly sets them in a winged, aerial car, they do not bide contentedly where they are, and do not look beneath them, but force themselves ever upwards. Therefore, as in the case of Icarus, their wax quickly melts, their wings moult, and they bring ridicule upon themselves by falling head-first into deep waters and breaking seas. But those who pattern after Daedalus in the use of their wings and do not rise too high, knowing that their pinions were made of wax, but stint their flight as mere mortals should and are content to be carried above, but only just above, the waves, so that they keep their wings always wet and avoid exposing them to sheer sunshine—they wing their passage at once safely and discreetly. This is what might be most praised in her. Consequently she gets from all the return that she deserves; for all pray that these wings may abide with her and that blessings may accrue to her in still greater fulness.

LYCINUS

So be it, Polystratus. She deserves it, because it is not in body alone, like Helen, that she is fair, but the soul that she harbours therein is still more fair and lovely. It was in keeping, too, that our Emperor, kindly and gentle as he is, along with all the other blessings that he enjoys, should be so

---

[3] καλλίων and ἐρασμιωτέρα MSS., corrected by du Soul.
[4] αὐτῷ vulg.: αὐτῶν MSS.

εὐδαιμονῆσαι, ὡς ἐπ' αὐτοῦ καὶ φῦναι γυναῖκα
τοιαύτην καὶ συνοῦσαν αὐτῷ ποθεῖν αὐτόν· οὐ
γὰρ μικρὸν τοῦτο εὐδαιμόνημα, γυνὴ περὶ ἧς ἄν
τις εὐλόγως τὸ Ὁμηρικὸν ἐκεῖνο εἴποι, χρυσείη
μὲν αὐτὴν Ἀφροδίτη ἐρίζειν τὸ κάλλος, ἔργα δὲ
αὐτῇ Ἀθηναίη ἰσοφαρίζειν. γυναικῶν γὰρ συνόλως οὐκ ἄν τις παραβληθείη αὐτῇ "οὐ δέμας
οὐδὲ φυήν," φησὶν Ὅμηρος, "οὔτ' ἀρ φρένας
οὔτε τι ἔργα."

ΠΟΛΥΣΤΡΑΤΟΣ

23 Ἀληθῆ φής, ὦ Λυκῖνε· ὥστε εἰ δοκεῖ, ἀναμί-
ξαντες ἤδη τὰς εἰκόνας, ἥν τε σὺ ἀνέπλασας τὴν
τοῦ σώματος καὶ ἃς ἐγὼ τῆς ψυχῆς ἐγραψάμην,
μίαν ἐξ ἁπασῶν συνθέντες εἰς[1] βιβλίον κατα-
θέμενοι παρέχωμεν ἅπασι θαυμάζειν τοῖς τε νῦν
οὖσι καὶ τοῖς ἐν ὑστέρῳ ἐσομένοις. μονιμωτέρα
γοῦν τῶν Ἀπελλοῦ καὶ Παρρασίου καὶ Πολυ-
γνώτου γένοιτ' ἄν, καὶ αὐτῇ ἐκείνῃ παρὰ πολὺ
τῶν τοιούτων κεχαρισμένη, ὅσῳ μὴ ξύλου καὶ
κηροῦ καὶ χρωμάτων πεποίηται, ἀλλὰ ταῖς παρὰ
Μουσῶν ἐπιπνοίαις[2] εἴκασται, ἥπερ ἀκριβεστάτη
εἰκὼν γένοιτ' ἂν σώματος κάλλος καὶ ψυχῆς
ἀρετὴν ἅμα ἐμφανίζουσα.

---

[1] εἰς Halm : not in MSS.
[2] ἐπιπνοίαις Jacobs : ἐπινοίαις MSS.

favoured by Fortune as to have such a woman born in his time and consort with him and love him. For that is no trivial favour of Fortune—a woman about whom one can quote with propriety the saying of Homer, that she vies with golden Aphrodite in beauty and equals Athena herself in accomplishments.[1] Among mortal women there is none to compare with her, "neither in stature nor mould" (as Homer says), "nor in mind nor in aught that she doeth." [2]

POLYSTRATUS

You are right, Lycinus. So, if you are willing, let us put our portraits together, the statue that you modelled of her body and the pictures that I painted of her soul; let us blend them all into one, put it down in a book, and give it to all mankind to admire, not only to those now alive, but to those that shall live hereafter. It would at least prove more enduring than the works of Apelles and Parrhasius and Polygnotus, and far more pleasing to the lady herself than anything of that kind, inasmuch as it is not made of wood and wax and colours but portrayed with inspirations from the Muses; and this will be found the most accurate kind of portrait, since it simultaneously discloses beauty of body and nobility of soul.

[1] *Iliad* 9, 389–90.   [2] *Iliad* 1, 115.

ESSAYS IN PORTRAITURE
DEFENDED

Panthea justifies Lucian's commendation of her modesty by finding his praises too high for her and sending the piece back to be revised. Lucian could not comply if he would, for it is already in circulation; so he defends it, and incidentally takes occasion to pay her still higher tribute.

That Panthea really did object may be taken as certain. If she had not done so, to say that she had, and to compliment her upon it, would have been an unpardonable affront.

Nothing could be neater than the casual way in which he alludes to the essential fact that the dialogue is already out (c. 14), and hints that the only alternative to a defence of it is a public recantation (c. 15).

ΥΠΕΡ ΤΩΝ ΕΙΚΟΝΩΝ

ΠΟΛΥΣΤΡΑΤΟΣ

1 " Ἐγώ σοι, ὦ Λυκῖνε," φησὶν ἡ γυνή, " τὰ μὲν
ἄλλα πολλὴν ἐνεῖδον τὴν εὔνοιαν πρὸς ἐμὲ καὶ
τιμὴν ἐκ τοῦ συγγράμματος· οὐ γὰρ ἂν οὕτως
ὑπερεπήνει τις, εἰ μὴ καὶ μετ᾽ εὐνοίας συνέγραφε.[1]
τὸ δὲ ἐμὸν ὡς ἂν εἰδῇς, τοιόνδε ἐστίν. οὐδὲ
ἄλλως μὲν χαίρω τοῖς κολακικοῖς τὸν τρόπον,
ἀλλά μοι δοκοῦσιν οἱ τοιοῦτοι γόητες εἶναι καὶ
ἥκιστα ἐλεύθεροι τὴν φύσιν· ἐν δὲ τοῖς ἐπαίνοις
μάλιστα, ὅταν τις ἐπαινῇ με φορτικὰς καὶ ὑπερ-
μέτρους ποιούμενος τὰς ὑπερβολάς, ἐρυθριῶ τε
καὶ ὀλίγου δεῖν ἐπιφράττομαι τὰ ὦτα καὶ τὸ
πρᾶγμα χλεύη μᾶλλον ἢ ἐπαίνῳ ἐοικέναι μοι
2 δοκεῖ. μέχρι γὰρ τοῦδε οἱ ἔπαινοι ἀνεκτοί εἰσιν
εἰς ὅσον ἂν ὁ ἐπαινούμενος γνωρίζῃ ἕκαστον τῶν
λεγομένων προσὸν ἑαυτῷ· τὸ δὲ ὑπὲρ τοῦτο
ἀλλότριον ἤδη καὶ κολακεία σαφής."

"Καίτοι πολλούς," ἔφη, " οἶδα χαίροντας, εἴ
τις αὐτοὺς ἐπαινῶν καὶ ἃ μὴ ἔχουσιν προσάπτοι
τῷ λόγῳ, οἷον εἰ γέροντας ὄντας εὐδαιμονίζοι
τῆς ἀκμῆς ἢ ἀμόρφοις οὖσι τὸ Νιρέως κάλλος
ἢ τὸ Φάωνος περιθείη· οἴονται γὰρ ὑπὸ τῶν
ἐπαίνων ἀλλαγήσεσθαι σφίσι καὶ τὰς μορφὰς

Available in photographs : Γ, N.

---

[1] συνέγραφε vulg. : συνεγράφετο MSS.

ESSAYS IN PORTRAITURE
DEFENDED

POLYSTRATUS

This is the lady's reply: "Lycinus, I have discerned, to be sure, from what you have written that your friendliness and esteem for me is great, for nobody would bestow such high praise if he were not writing in a friendly spirit. But my own attitude, please understand, is this. In general, I do not care for people whose disposition inclines to flattery, but consider such persons deceivers and not at all generous in their natures. Above all, in the matter of compliments, when anyone in praising me employs vulgar and immoderate extravagances I blush and almost stop my ears, and the thing seems to me more like abuse than praise. For praise is endurable only as long as the person who is being praised recognizes that everything which is said is appropriate to him. Whatever goes beyond that is alien, and outright flattery.

"Yet," said she, "I know many who like it if, in praising them, one bestows upon them qualities which they do not possess; for example, if they are old, congratulates them upon their youthfulness, or if they are ugly, clothes them in the beauty of a Nireus or a Phaon. They think that their appearance will be transformed by these compliments, and

καὶ αὐτοὶ ἀνηβήσειν αὖθις, ὥσπερ ὁ Πελίας
3 ᾤετο. τὸ δὲ οὐχ οὕτως ἔχει· πολλοῦ γὰρ ἂν
ὁ ἔπαινος ἦν τίμιος, εἴ τι καὶ ἔργον αὐτοῦ ἀπολαῦσαι δυνατὸν ἦν ἐκ τῆς τοιαύτης ὑπερβολῆς.
νῦν δὲ ὅμοιόν μοι δοκοῦσιν," ἔφη, "πάσχειν,
ὥσπερ ἂν εἴ τινι ἀμόρφῳ προσωπεῖον εὔμορφον
ἐπιθείη τις φέρων, ὁ δὲ μέγα ἐπὶ τῷ κάλλει
φρονοίη, καὶ ταῦτα περιαιρετῷ ὄντι καὶ ὑπὸ τοῦ
τυχόντος συντριβῆναι δυναμένῳ, ὅτε καὶ γελοιό-
τερος ἂν γένοιτο αὐτοπρόσωπος φανείς, οἷος ὢν
ὑφ' οἵῳ κέκρυπτο· ἢ καὶ νὴ Δί' εἴ τις ὑπο-
δησάμενος κοθόρνους μικρὸς αὐτὸς ὢν ἐρίζοι περὶ
μεγέθους τοῖς ἀπὸ τοῦ ἰσοπέδου ὅλῳ πήχει
ὑπερέχουσιν."

4 Ἐμέμνητο γὰρ καὶ τοιούτου τινός. ἔφη γυναῖκά
τινα τῶν ἐπιφανῶν τὰ μὲν ἄλλα καλὴν καὶ
κόσμιον, μικρὰν δὲ καὶ πολὺ τοῦ συμμέτρου
ἀποδέουσαν, ἐπαινεῖσθαι πρός τινος ποιητοῦ ἐν
ᾄσματι τά τε ἄλλα καὶ ὅτι καλή τε καὶ μεγάλη
ἦν· αἰγείρῳ δ' αὐτῆς εἴκαζεν ἐκεῖνος τὸ εὔμηκές
τε καὶ ὄρθιον. τὴν μὲν δὴ γάνυσθαι τῷ ἐπαίνῳ
καθάπερ αὐξανομένην πρὸς τὸ μέλος καὶ τὴν
χεῖρα ἐπισείειν, τὸν ποιητὴν δὲ πολλάκις τὸ αὐτὸ
ᾄδειν ὁρῶντα ὡς ἥδοιτο ἐπαινουμένη, ἄχρι δὴ
τῶν παρόντων τινὰ προσκύψαντα πρὸς τὸ οὖς
εἰπεῖν αὐτῷ, "Πέπαυσο, ὦ οὗτος, μὴ καὶ ἀνα-
στῆναι ποιήσῃς τὴν γυναῖκα."

5 Παραπλήσιον δὲ καὶ μακρῷ τούτου γελοιότερον

---

¹ Lifting and slightly agitating the hand is mentioned in
the *Double Indictment* 28 (iii, p. 139) as one of the milder
forms of applause. Standing up (see below) was the most
emphatic form.

that they will regain their youth afresh, as Pelias thought to do. That, however, is not the case. Praise would be highly valuable if it were possible to derive any actual profit from it through such extravagant employment. But as it is, those people in my opinion are in the same case that an ugly man would be in if someone should officiously put a handsome mask upon him and he were to pride himself greatly upon his beauty, regardless of the fact that it was detachable and could be destroyed by the first comer, in which event he would look still more ridiculous when he stood revealed in his own proper features and showed what ugliness had been hidden behind that lovely mask. Or it would be as if someone who was small should put on the buskins of an actor and try to compete in height with those who, on an even footing, overtop him by a full cubit."

She mentioned an instance in point. She said that a woman of conspicuous position, who was pretty and attractive in every other way, but small, and far beneath the well-proportioned height, was being lauded in song by a certain poet, not only on all other grounds, but because she was fair and tall; he likened her to a black poplar for goodly stature and straightness! Well, she was delighted with the compliment, just as if she were going to grow to match the song, and lifted her hand in approval.[1] So the poet gave many encores, seeing that she liked to be praised, until at last one of the company leaned over to his ear and said: "Have done with it, man—you might make her stand up!"

Something similar and much more comical was

Στρατονίκην ποιῆσαι τὴν Σελεύκου γυναῖκα.
τοῖς γὰρ ποιηταῖς ἀγῶνα προθεῖναι αὐτὴν περὶ
ταλάντου, ὅστις ἂν ἄμεινον ἐπαινέσαι αὐτῆς τὴν
κόμην, καίτοι φαλακρὰ ἐτύγχανεν οὖσα καὶ οὐδὲ
ὅσας ὀλίγας τὰς ἑαυτῆς τρίχας ἔχουσα. καὶ
ὅμως οὕτω διακειμένη τὴν κεφαλήν, ἁπάντων
εἰδότων ὅτι ἐκ νόσου μακρᾶς τὸ τοιοῦτον ἐπε-
πόνθει, ἤκουε τῶν καταράτων ποιητῶν ὑακινθίνας
τὰς τρίχας αὐτῆς λεγόντων καὶ οὔλους τινὰς
πλοκάμους ἀναπλεκόντων καὶ σελίνοις τοὺς μηδὲ
ὅλως ὄντας εἰκαζόντων.

6 Ἁπάντων οὖν τῶν τοιούτων κατεγέλα τῶν
παρεχόντων αὑτοὺς τοῖς κόλαξιν, καὶ προσετίθει
δὲ ὅτι μὴ ἐν ἐπαίνοις μόνον, ἀλλὰ καὶ ἐν γραφαῖς
τὰ ὅμοια πολλοὶ κολακεύεσθαί τε καὶ ἐξαπα-
τᾶσθαι θέλουσι. "Χαίρουσι γοῦν," ἔφη, "τῶν
γραφέων ἐκείνοις μάλιστα, οἳ ἂν πρὸς τὸ εὐμορφότερον αὑτοὺς εἰκάσωσιν." εἶναι δέ τινας, οἳ καὶ
προστάττουσιν τοῖς τεχνίταις ἢ ἀφελεῖν τι τῆς
ῥινὸς ἢ μελάντερα γράψασθαι τὰ ὄμματα ἢ ὅ
τι ἂν ἄλλο ἐπιθυμήσωσιν αὐτοῖς προσεῖναι,
εἶτα λανθάνειν αὑτοὺς ἀλλοτρίας εἰκόνας στε-
φανοῦντας καὶ οὐδὲν αὑτοῖς ἐοικυίας.

7 Ταῦτα δὲ καὶ τὰ τοιαῦτα ἔλεγεν, τὰ μὲν ἄλλα
ἐπαινοῦσα τοῦ συγγράμματος, ἓν δὲ τοῦτο οὐ
φέρουσα, ὅτι θεαῖς αὐτήν, Ἥρᾳ καὶ Ἀφροδίτῃ,
εἴκασας· "Ὑπὲρ ἐμὲ γάρ," φησίν, "μᾶλλον δὲ
ὑπὲρ ἅπασαν τὴν ἀνθρωπίνην φύσιν τὰ τοιαῦτα.
ἐγὼ δέ σε οὐδ' ἐκεῖνα ἠξίουν, ταῖς ἡρωίναις
παραθεωρεῖν με Πηνελόπῃ καὶ Ἀρήτῃ καὶ Θεανοῖ,
οὐχ ὅπως θεῶν ταῖς ἀρίσταις. καὶ γὰρ αὖ
καὶ τόδε, πάνυ," ἔφη, "τὰ πρὸς τοὺς θεοὺς

done, she said, by Stratonice, the wife of Seleucus, who set a competition for the poets, with a talent as the prize, to see which of them could best praise her hair, in spite of the fact that she was bald and had not even a paltry few hairs of her own. Nevertheless, with her head in that pitiful state, when everybody knew that a long illness had affected her in that way, she listened to those rascally poets while they called her hair hyacinthine, and platted soft braids of it, and compared to wild parsley what did not even exist at all!

She made fun of all such people as these, who surrender themselves to flatterers, and she added, too, that many wish to be similarly flattered and cozened in portraits as well as in complimentary speeches. "In fact," said she, "they delight most of all in those painters who make the prettiest pictures of them. And there are some who even direct the artists to take away a little of the nose, or paint the eyes blacker, or give them any other characteristic that they covet; and then, in their blissful ignorance, they hang wreaths of flowers upon portraits of other people, not in the least like themselves!"

That is about what she had to say; she commended most of the piece, but could not put up with one feature of it, that you compared her to goddesses, to Hera and Aphrodite. "Such praise," she said, "is too high for me; indeed, too high for human kind. For my part I did not want you to compare me even to those great ladies, Penelope and Arete and Theano, let alone the noblest of the goddesses. Besides, I am very superstitious and

δεισιδαιμόνως καὶ ψοφοδεῶς ἔχω. δέδια τοίνυν
μὴ κατὰ τὴν Κασσιέπειαν εἶναι δόξω τὸν τοιοῦτον
ἔπαινον προσιεμένη· καίτοι Νηρηΐσιν ἐκείνη
ἀντεξητάζετο, "Ηραν δὲ καὶ 'Αφροδίτην ἔσεβεν."

8 "Ωστε, ὦ Λυκῖνε, μεταγράψαι σε τὰ τοιαῦτα
ἐκέλευσεν, ἢ αὐτὴ μὲν μαρτύρεσθαι τὰς θεὰς ὡς
ἀκούσης αὐτῆς γέγραφας, σὲ δὲ εἰδέναι ὅτι ἀνιάσει
αὐτὴν τὸ βιβλίον οὕτω περινοστοῦν ὥσπερ νῦν
σοι διάκειται, οὐ μάλα εὐσεβῶς οὐδὲ ὁσίως τὰ
πρὸς τοὺς θεούς. ἐδόκει τε ἀσέβημα ἑαυτῆς καὶ
πλημμέλημα τοῦτο δόξειν, εἰ ὑπομένοι τῇ ἐν
Κνίδῳ καὶ τῇ ἐν κήποις ὁμοία λέγεσθαι· καί σε
ὑπεμίμνησκε τῶν τελευταίων ἐν τῷ βιβλίῳ περὶ
αὐτῆς εἰρημένων, ὅτι μετρίαν καὶ ἄτυφον ἔφης
αὐτὴν οὐκ ἀνατεινομένην ὑπὲρ τὸ ἀνθρώπινον
μέτρον, ἀλλὰ πρόσγειον τὴν πτῆσιν ποιουμένην,
ὁ δὲ ταῦτα εἰπὼν ὑπὲρ αὐτὸν τὸν οὐρανὸν ἀνα-
βιβάζεις τὴν γυναῖκα, ὡς καὶ θεαῖς ἀπεικάζειν.

9 'Ηξίου δέ σε μηδὲ ἀξυνετωτέραν αὐτὴν ἡγεῖ-
σθαι τοῦ 'Αλεξάνδρου, ὃς τοῦ ἀρχιτέκτονος
ὑπισχνουμένου τὸν "Αθω ὅλον μετασχηματίσειν
καὶ μορφώσειν πρὸς αὐτόν, ὡς τὸ ὄρος ἅπαν
εἰκόνα γενέσθαι τοῦ βασιλέως, ἔχοντα δύο πόλεις
ἐν ταῖν χεροῖν, οὐ προσήκατο τὴν τερατείαν τῆς
ὑποσχέσεως, ἀλλ' ὑπὲρ αὐτὸν ἡγησάμενος τὸ
τόλμημα ἔπαυσεν τὸν ἄνθρωπον οὐ πιθανῶς
κολοσσοὺς ἀναπλάττοντα καὶ τὸν "Αθω κατὰ
χώραν ἐᾶν ἐκέλευσεν μηδὲ κατασμικρύνειν ὄρος

---

[1] The boastful mother of Andromeda, who would have had
to surrender her daughter to the sea-monster except for the
timely intervention of Perseus.

timorous in all that concerns the gods. Consequently, I am afraid I may be thought to resemble Cassiopeia[1] if I accept such praise as yours; and yet she, as a matter of fact, compared herself only to the Nereids and was duly reverential toward Hera and Aphrodite."

In view of this, Lycinus, she said that you must rewrite everything of that sort, or else for her part she calls the goddesses to witness that you wrote it without her consent, and says you know that the book will annoy her if it circulates in the form in which you have now couched it, which is not at all reverential or pious in its allusions to the gods. She thought, too, that it would be considered a sacrilege and a sin on her own part if she should allow herself to be said to resemble Cnidian Aphrodite, and Our Lady in the Gardens. Moreover, she wanted to remind you of the remark that you made about her at the end of the book. You said that she was modest and free from vanity; and that she did not try to soar higher than a human being should, but made her flight close to the earth. Yet the man who said that sets the woman above the very stars, even to the point of likening her to goddesses!

She did not want you to think her less intelligent than Alexander. In his case, when the master-builder undertook to remodel the whole of Athos and shape it into his likeness, so that the entire mountain would become the image of the king, holding a city in either hand, Alexander would not agree to the monstrous proposal. Thinking the project over-bold for him, he stopped the man from modelling colossi on a scale that transcended convincingness, bidding him to let Athos alone and not

οὕτω μέγα πρὸς μικροῦ σώματος ὁμοιότητα.
ἐπῄνει δὲ τὸν Ἀλέξανδρον τῆς μεγαλοψυχίας
καὶ ἀνδριάντα μείζω τοῦτον τοῦ Ἄθω ἔλεγεν
αὐτοῦ ἀνεστάναι ἐν ταῖς τῶν ἀεὶ μεμνησομένων
διανοίαις· οὐ γὰρ μικρᾶς εἶναι γνώμης ὑπεριδεῖν
οὕτω παραδόξου τιμῆς.

10 Καὶ ἑαυτὴν οὖν τὸ μὲν πλάσμα σου ἐπαινεῖν
καὶ τὴν ἐπίνοιαν τῶν εἰκόνων, μὴ γνωρίζειν δὲ
τὴν ὁμοιότητα· μὴ γὰρ εἶναι τῶν τηλικούτων
ἀξίαν, μηδὲ ἐγγύς, ὅτι μηδὲ ἄλλην τινά, γυναῖκά
γε οὖσαν· ὥστε ἀφίησί σοι ταύτην τὴν τιμὴν
καὶ προσκυνεῖ σου τὰ ἀρχέτυπα καὶ παραδείγματα. σὺ δὲ τὰ ἀνθρώπινα ταῦτα ἐπαίνει
αὐτήν, μηδὲ ὑπὲρ τὸν πόδα ἔστω τὸ ὑπόδημα,
"μὴ καὶ ἐπιστομίσῃ με," φησίν, "ἐμπεριπατοῦσαν
αὐτῷ."

11 Κἀκεῖνο δὲ εἰπεῖν σοι ἐνετείλατο. "Ἀκούω,"
ἔφη, "πολλῶν λεγόντων—εἰ δὲ ἀληθές, ὑμεῖς
οἱ ἄνδρες ἴστε—μηδ' Ὀλυμπίασιν ἐξεῖναι τοῖς
νικῶσι μείζους τῶν σωμάτων ἀνεστάναι τοὺς
ἀνδριάντας, ἀλλὰ ἐπιμελεῖσθαι τοὺς Ἑλλανο-
δίκας ὅπως μηδὲ εἷς ὑπερβάληται τὴν ἀλήθειαν,
καὶ τὴν ἐξέτασιν τῶν ἀνδριάντων ἀκριβεστέραν
γίγνεσθαι τῆς τῶν ἀθλητῶν ἐγκρίσεως. ὥστε
ὅρα," ἔφη, "μὴ αἰτίαν λάβωμεν ψεύδεσθαι ἐν
τῷ μέτρῳ, κᾆτα ἡμῶν ἀνατρέψωσιν οἱ Ἑλλα-
νοδίκαι τὴν εἰκόνα."

12 Ταῦτα μὲν ἔλεγεν ἐκείνη. σὺ δὲ σκόπει, ὦ
Λυκῖνε, ὅπως μετακοσμήσεις τὸ βιβλίον καὶ

---

[1] The same story is in *How to Write History*, c. 12, where
also the name of the architect is not mentioned. Plutarch
says it was Stasicrates (*Alex.* 72; *Moral.* 335 c). In Strabo

to diminish so great a mountain to similarity with a
tiny body. She praised Alexander for his greatness
of soul, and observed that thereby he had erected a
monument greater than Athos itself in the minds of
those who should think of him ever and anon in
time to come: for it took no little determination
to contemn so marvellous an honour.[1]

So it was with her, said she; while she commended your skill in modelling and the idea of the
portraits, she did not recognize the likeness. She
was not worthy of such compliments, not by a great
deal, nor was any other mere woman. Therefore she
absolves you from honouring her thus, and pays her
homage to your patterns and models. You may
praise her in the ordinary, human way, but do not
let the sandal be too large for her foot; "it might
hamper me," she said, "when I walk about in it."

Furthermore, she enjoined it upon me to tell you
this. "I hear many say (whether it is true or not,
you men know)[2] that even at the Olympic games
the victors are not allowed to set up statues greater
than life-size, but the Hellanodicae take care that
not one of them shall exceed the truth, and the
scrutiny of the statues is more strict than the exam-
ination of the athletes. So be on your guard for
fear we incur the imputation of falsifying in the
matter of height, and then the Hellanodicae over-
turn our statue."

That is what she said; and now it is for you,
Lycinus, to see how you can refurbish the book

14, p. 641, Cheirocrates seems to underlie the various read-
ings. Vitruvius (ii, praef.) tells the tale quite differently
and makes Dinocrates the hero of it.
  [2] Women did not attend the Olympic games.

ἀφαιρήσεις τὰ τοιαῦτα, μηδὲ σφαλῇς πρὸς τὸ
θεῖον· ὡς ἐκείνη πάνυ γε αὐτὰ ἐδυσχέραινεν
καὶ ὑπέφριττεν μεταξὺ ἀναγιγνωσκομένων καὶ
παρῃτεῖτο τὰς θεὰς ἵλεως εἶναι αὐτῇ. καὶ
συγγνώμη, εἰ γυναικεῖόν τι ἔπαθεν. καίτοι εἰ χρὴ
τἀληθὲς εἰπεῖν, καὶ αὐτῷ ἐμοὶ τοιοῦτόν τι ἔδοξε.[1]
τὸ μὲν γὰρ πρῶτον ἀκούων οὐδὲν πλημμέλημα
ἐνεώρων[2] τοῖς γεγραμμένοις, ἐπεὶ δὲ ἐκείνη ἐπε-
σημήνατο, καὶ αὐτὸς ἄρχομαι τὰ ὅμοια γιγνώσκειν
περὶ αὐτῶν, καὶ παραπλήσιόν τι ἔπαθον οἷς ἐπὶ
τῶν ὁρωμένων πάσχομεν· ἢν μὲν πάνυ ἐγγύθεν
σκοπῶμέν τι καὶ ὑπὸ τῶν ὀφθαλμῶν αὐτῶν,
οὐδὲν ἀκριβὲς διαγιγνώσκομεν, ἢν δὲ ἀποστάντες
ἐκ τοῦ συμμέτρου διαστήματος ἴδωμεν, ἅπαντα
σαφῶς καταφαίνεται, τὰ εὖ καὶ τὰ μὴ οὕτως
ἔχοντα.

13   Τὸ δὴ ἄνθρωπον οὖσαν Ἀφροδίτῃ καὶ Ἥρᾳ
εἰκάσαι τί ἄλλο ἢ ἄντικρύς ἐστιν εὐτελίζειν τὰς
θεάς; ἐν γὰρ τοῖς τοιούτοις οὐχ οὕτω τὸ μικρὸν
μεῖζον γίγνεται τῇ παραθέσει, ὡς τὸ μεῖζον ἀπο-
μικρύνεται πρὸς τὸ ταπεινότερον κατασπώμενον·
οἷον εἴ τινες ἅμα βαδίζοιεν, ὁ μὲν μέγιστος, ὁ
δὲ πάνυ τῇ ἡλικίᾳ χαμαίζηλος, εἶτα δεήσειεν
ἀπισῶσαι αὐτοὺς ὡς μὴ ὑπερέχειν θατέρου τὸν
ἕτερον, οὐ τοῦ βραχυτέρου ὑπερανατεινομένου
τοῦτο γένοιτ' ἄν, κἂν ὅτι μάλιστα ἀκροποδητὶ
ἐπεγείρῃ ἑαυτόν· ἀλλ' εἰ μέλλουσιν ὁμήλικες
φανεῖσθαι, ὁ μείζων ἐκεῖνος ἐπικύψει καὶ ταπεινότερον ἀποφανεῖ ἑαυτόν. ὡσαύτως δὲ καὶ ἐν
ταῖς τοιαύταις εἰκόσιν οὐχ οὕτως ἄνθρωπος

[1] ἔδοξε Seager: εἰπεῖν ἔδοξε MSS.

and do away with everything of that sort; do not offend against Heaven! Really, she took it very ill, shuddered as it was read, and besought the goddesses to be merciful to her. It is excusable, too, that she should feel as a woman naturally would. Indeed, if the truth must out, I myself had somewhat the same opinion. To be sure, when I heard it first I did not see a single fault in what you had written, but now that she has pointed them out, I myself begin to think as she does about it. My experience in this matter has been just about like that of us all when we look at things. If we see them too close, under our very eyes, we can distinguish nothing accurately, but if we stand off and look at them from the right distance, all the points come out clearly, those that are good and also those that are not.

Truly, to liken a female human being to Aphrodite and to Hera, what else is it but outright cheapening of the goddesses? In such matters the less is not made greater by the comparison, but rather the greater is lessened by being dragged down to the lower level. If two people were walking together, one of whom was very tall and the other quite humble in stature, and it should be needful to equalize them so that the one would not tower above the other, this could not be accomplished by the shorter through stretching himself, however much he were to raise himself on tiptoe. No, if they are to look alike in size, the latter will stoop and make himself appear shorter. Just so in such comparisons; it is not so true that a man becomes

---

[2] Text Guyet: ἐπλημμέλησα ἐνορῶν MSS.

μείζων γίγνεται, ἤν τις αὐτὸν θεῷ ἀπεικάζῃ, ὡς
τὸ θεῖον ἀνάγκη ἐλαττοῦσθαι πρὸς τὸ ἐνδέον
ἐπικλωμενον. καὶ γὰρ εἰ μὲν ὑπὸ ἀπορίας τῶν
ἐπιγείων ἐπὶ τὰ οὐράνια ἐκτείνοι τις τὸν λόγον,
ἧττον ἂν ὁ τοιοῦτος αἰτίαν ἔχοι ὑπὸ ἀσεβείας
αὐτὸ δρᾶν· σὺ δὲ τοσαῦτα ἔχων κάλλη γυναικῶν
Ἀφροδίτῃ καὶ Ἥρᾳ εἰκάσαι αὐτὴν ἐτόλμησας
οὐδὲν δέον.

14 Ὥστε τὸ ἄγαν τοῦτο καὶ ἐπίφθονον ἀφαίρει,
ὦ Λυκῖνε. οὐ γὰρ πρὸς τοῦ σοῦ τρόπου τὸ
τοιοῦτον, ὃς οὐδὲ ἄλλως ῥάδιος πρὸς τοὺς ἐπαίνους καὶ πρόχειρος ὢν ἐτύγχανες· ἀλλὰ νῦν οὐκ
οἶδ᾽ ὅπως ἀθρόαν πεποίησαι τὴν μεταβολὴν
ἐπιδαψιλευόμενος καὶ ἐκ τοῦ τέως φειδομένου
ἄσωτος ἐν τοῖς ἐπαίνοις ἀναπέφηνας. ἀλλὰ μηδὲ
ἐκεῖνο αἰσχυνθῇς, εἰ μεταρρυθμιεῖς τὸν λόγον
ἤδη διαδεδομένον· ἐπεὶ καὶ Φειδίαν φασὶν οὕτω
ποιῆσαι, ὁπότε ἐξειργάσατο τοῖς Ἠλείοις τὸν
Δία. στάντα γὰρ αὐτὸν κατόπιν τῶν θυρῶν,
ὁπότε τὸ πρῶτον ἀναπετάσας ἐπεδείκνυεν τὸ
ἔργον, ἐπακούειν τῶν αἰτιωμένων τι ἢ ἐπαι-
νούντων· ᾐτιᾶτο δὲ ὁ μὲν τὴν ῥῖνα ὡς παχεῖαν,
ὁ δὲ ὡς ἐπιμηκέστερον τὸ πρόσωπον, ὁ δὲ ἄλλος
ἄλλο τι. εἶτ᾽ ἐπειδὴ ἀπηλλάγησαν οἱ θεαταί,
αὖθις τὸν Φειδίαν ἐγκλεισάμενον ἑαυτὸν ἐπα-
νορθοῦν καὶ ῥυθμίζειν τὸ ἄγαλμα πρὸς τὸ τοῖς
πλείστοις δοκοῦν· οὐ γὰρ ἡγεῖτο μικρὰν εἶναι
συμβουλὴν δήμου τοσούτου, ἀλλ᾽ ἀεὶ ἀναγκαῖον
ὑπάρχειν[1] τοὺς πολλοὺς περιττότερον ὁρᾶν τοῦ
ἑνός, κἂν Φειδίας ᾖ.[2]

[1] ὑπάρχειν vulg.: ὑπάρχει MSS.
[2] ᾖ Jacobs: ἦν MSS.

greater if he is likened to a god, as that the divine is inevitably minimized by being forced down to match what is defective. If it were for lack of earthly objects of comparison that one let one's speech range to those in Heaven, one would be less open to the charge of acting impiously therein. But in your case, though you had so many examples of fair women at command, you made bold to liken her to Aphrodite and Hera without any need.

Do away, then, with all this that is excessive and invidious, Lycinus—that sort of thing is not in keeping with your character, for you have not as a rule been ready and quick to praise. Now, however, you have somehow changed all at once and are lavish with it; you who were so niggardly before have become a spendthrift in compliments! Do not be ashamed, either, to reshape the essay after it has been put into circulation. Even Phidias, they say, did that when he made the Zeus for the people of Elis![1] He stood behind the door when he first unveiled and exhibited his work, and listened to those who criticized or commended any part. One would criticize the nose as too thick, another the face as too long, and so it went. Then, when the spectators had left, Phidias locked himself up once more, and corrected and reshaped the statue to suit the opinion of the majority; for he did not think that the advice of so many folk was trivial, but that always of necessity the many could see better than the one, even if that one were Phidias.[2]

---

[1] The chryselephantine statue at Olympia.

[2] The story, which is patently apocryphal, occurs nowhere else. Lucian may have heard it from a guide at Olympia. For a similar story regarding Apelles, see Pliny, *Nat. Hist.* 35, 84–85.

Ταῦτά σοι παρ' ἐκείνης κομίζω καὶ αὐτὸς
παραινῶ ἑταῖρός τε καὶ εὔνους ὤν.

ΛΥΚΙΝΟΣ

15 Πολύστρατε, οἷος ὢν ῥήτωρ ἐλελήθεις με.
ῥῆσιν γοῦν οὕτω μακρὰν καὶ κατηγορίαν τοσαύτην[1] ἐξενήνοχας κατὰ τοῦ συγγράμματος,
ὥστε μηδὲ ἐλπίδα μοι ἀπολογίας ἔτι κατα-
λείπεσθαι. πλὴν ἀλλὰ ἐκεῖνό γε οὐ δικαστικὸν
ἐποιήσατε, καὶ μάλιστα σύ, ἐρήμην καταδιαιτήσας
τοῦ βιβλίου μὴ παρόντος αὐτῷ τοῦ συνηγόρου.
ῥᾷστον δέ, οἶμαι, τοῦτό ἐστιν κατὰ τὴν παροι-
μίαν, μόνον θέοντα κρατεῖν. ὥστε οὐδὲν θαυ-
μαστόν, εἰ καὶ ἡμεῖς ἑάλωμεν οὔτε ὕδατος ἡμῖν
ἐκχυθέντος οὔτε ἀπολογίας ἀποδοθείσης. μᾶλλον
δὲ τοῦτο πάντων ἀτοπώτατον, οἱ αὐτοὶ κατήγοροι
καὶ δικασταὶ ἦτε.

Πότερα δ' οὖν ἐθέλεις; ἀγαπήσας τοῖς ἐγνω-
σμένοις ἡσυχίαν ἄγω, ἢ κατὰ τὸν Ἱμεραῖον
ποιητὴν παλινῳδίαν τινὰ συγγράφω, ἢ δώσετέ
μοι ἐφέσιμον ἀγωνίσασθαι τὴν δίκην;

ΠΟΛΥΣΤΡΑΤΟΣ

Νὴ Δί', ἤνπερ ἔχῃς τι δίκαιον εἰπεῖν· οὐ γὰρ
ἐν ἀντιδίκοις, ὡς σὺ φής, ἀλλ' ἐν φίλοις ποιήσῃ
τὴν ἀπολογίαν. ἐγὼ δὲ καὶ συνεξετάζεσθαί σοι
ἕτοιμος ἐπὶ τῆς δίκης.

---

[1] τοσαύτην vulg. : ταύτην MSS.

---

[1] Stesichorus, who after having maligned Helen, recanted
in a palinode (the first), saying that Helen never went to

That is what she told me to tell you, and what I myself recommend as your friend and well-wisher.

LYCINUS

Polystratus, what an orator you have been all along without my knowing it! You have delivered such a long speech and such a weighty indictment of my essay that you have not left me even a hope of defence now. But see here! you have not dealt fairly, the two of you, and especially you, in that you have condemned the book without a hearing, since its counsel was not in court. It is easy, I take it, to win if you run alone, as the saying goes. So it is no wonder that I was defeated when no water was measured out for me and no chance to defend myself offered. Indeed—and this is the most extraordinary part of it all—you were judges as well as plaintiffs!

Well, what is your wish? Shall I rest content with the decision and hold my peace? Or, like the poet of Himera,[1] shall I compose a palinode? Or will you give me an opportunity to plead my case on appeal?

POLYSTRATUS

Yes, indeed, if you have any just plea to offer; for it is not among opponents in court, as you say, but among friends that you will make your defence. For my part, I am even ready to associate myself with you as joint defendant in the case.

Troy: it was but a wraith! Fable said that he recanted because Helen had struck him blind, and that afterwards he recovered his eyesight.

313

THE WORKS OF LUCIAN

ΛΥΚΙΝΟΣ

16 Ἀλλὰ ἐκεῖνο ἀνιαρόν, ὦ Πολύστρατε, ὅτι μὴ ἐκείνης παρούσης ποιήσομαι τοὺς λόγους· μακρῷ γὰρ ἂν οὕτως ἄμεινον ἦν. νῦν δὲ ἀνάγκη ἀπ᾽ ἐντολῆς ἀπολογήσασθαι. ἀλλ᾽ εἴ μοι τοιοῦτος ἀγγελιαφόρος γένοιο πρὸς αὐτὴν οἷος παρ᾽ ἐκείνης πρὸς μὲ γεγένησαι, τολμήσω ἀναρρῖψαι τὸν κύβον.

ΠΟΛΥΣΤΡΑΤΟΣ

Θάρρει, ὦ Λυκῖνε, τούτου γε ἕνεκα, ὡς οὐ φαῦλόν με ὑποκριτὴν ἕξων τῆς ἀπολογίας, πειρώμενος διὰ βραχέων εἰπεῖν, ὡς ἂν μᾶλλον μνημονεύσαιμι.

ΛΥΚΙΝΟΣ

Καὶ μὴν πάνυ μὲν ἔδει μοι μακρῶν τῶν λόγων πρὸς οὕτω σφοδρὰν τὴν κατηγορίαν. ὅμως δὲ σοῦ ἕνεκα ἐπιτεμοῦμαι τὴν ἀπολογίαν. καὶ παρ᾽ ἐμοῦ τοίνυν τάδε αὐτῇ ἀπάγγελλε.

ΠΟΛΥΣΤΡΑΤΟΣ

Μηδαμῶς, ὦ Λυκῖνε, ἀλλ᾽ ὥσπερ αὐτῆς ἐκείνης παρούσης λέγε τὸν λόγον, εἶτ᾽ ἐγὼ μιμήσομαί σε πρὸς αὐτήν.

ΛΥΚΙΝΟΣ

Οὐκοῦν ἐπειδήπερ οὕτω σοι δοκεῖ, ὦ Πολύστρατε, ἡ μὲν πάρεστι καὶ προείρηκε δηλαδὴ ἐκεῖνα ὁπόσα σὺ παρ᾽ αὐτῆς ἀπήγγειλας, ἡμᾶς δὲ χρὴ τῶν δευτέρων λόγων ἐνάρχεσθαι. καίτοι— οὐ γὰρ ὀκνήσω πρὸς σὲ εἰπεῖν ὃ πέπονθα—οὐκ

The phrase ἀπ᾽ ἐντολῆς means "by direction." Strictly speaking, it is appropriate only to the action of an agent,

ESSAYS IN PORTRAITURE DEFENDED

LYCINUS

But it is annoying, Polystratus, that she will not be present when I make my speech. It would be far better if she were. As it stands, I must plead by proxy.[1] But if you are going to be as faithful in carrying my message to her as you have been in carrying hers to me, I shall make bold to cast the die.

POLYSTRATUS

Never fear, Lycinus, as far as that goes! I shan't be at all bad, you will find, at delivering your plea, if only you try to speak briefly, so that I may be better able to fix it all in memory.

LYCINUS

But I really needed to speak at length in answering so forcible an accusation. Nevertheless, for your sake I shall cut my plea short. Take, then, this message from me to her—

POLYSTRATUS

No, no, Lycinus! Make your speech just as if she herself were present, and then I will do her an imitation of you.

LYCINUS

Well then, since that is the way you want it, Polystratus, she is here and as the first speaker, of course, has said all that you reported as her messenger; and now it is for me to begin my answer. However—for I shall not hesitate to tell you the state of my feelings—somehow or other

but here it is transferred to that of the principal. Compare Aristides, vol. ii, p. 224–5 Dindorf, τὰ δὲ πλεῖστα ἐξ ἐντολῆς τῷ βασιλεῖ κατειργάζετο.

οἶδ' ὅπως φοβερώτερόν μοι τὸ πρᾶγμα πεποίηκας,
καὶ ὡς ὁρᾷς ἱδρῶ τε ἤδη καὶ δέδοικα καὶ μονονουχὶ
καὶ ὁρᾶν αὐτὴν οἴομαι, καὶ τὸ πρᾶγμα πολλήν
μοι τὴν ταραχὴν ἐμπεποίηκεν. ἄρξομαι δ' ὅμως·
οὐ γὰρ οἶόν τε ἀναδῦναι ἤδη παρούσης.

Καὶ νὴ Δία πολλὴν τὴν εὐμένειαν ἐπιφαίνει
τῷ προσώπῳ· φαιδρὰ γὰρ ὡς ὁρᾷς καὶ προσηνής.
ὥστε θαρρῶν λέγε τὸν λόγον.

17 Ἐγώ σε, ὦ γυναικῶν ἀρίστη, μεγάλα, ὡς φής,
καὶ πέρα τοῦ μέτρου ἐπαινέσας οὐχ ὁρῶ ὅ τι
τηλικοῦτον ἐπήνεσα, ἡλίκον αὐτὴ σὺ τοῦτο
ἐγκώμιον ὑπὲρ σεαυτῆς ἐξενήνοχας τὴν πρὸς τὸ
θεῖον τιμὴν ἐν μεγάλῳ τιθεμένη. σχεδὸν γὰρ
ἁπάντων τοῦτο μεῖζον ὧν εἴρηκα περὶ σοῦ, καὶ
συγγνώμη, εἰ μὴ καὶ ταύτην σοι προσέγραψα
τὴν εἰκόνα ὑπ' ἀγνοίας με διαλαθοῦσαν· οὐ γὰρ
ἂν ἄλλην πρὸ αὐτῆς ἐγραψάμην. ὥστε ταύτῃ γε
οὐχ ὅπως ὑπερβάλλεσθαι τοὺς ἐπαίνους, ἀλλὰ
πολὺ καταδεέστερόν μοι δοκῶ τῆς ἀξίας εἰρη-
κέναι. σκόπει γοῦν ἡλίκον τοῦτο παρέλιπον,
ὡς παμμέγεθες εἰς ἐπίδειξιν τρόπου χρηστοῦ καὶ
γνώμης ὀρθῆς· ὡς ὅσοι τὸ θεῖον μὴ ἐν παρέργῳ
σέβουσιν, οὗτοι καὶ τὰ πρὸς ἀνθρώπους ἄριστοι
ἂν εἶεν. ὥστε εἰ πάντως μετακοσμῆσαι δέοι τὸν
λόγον καὶ τὸ ἄγαλμα ἐπανορθώσασθαι, ἀφελεῖν
μὲν οὐκ ἄν τι τολμήσαιμι αὐτοῦ, προσθήσω δὲ
καὶ τοῦτο ὥς τινα κεφαλὴν τοῦ παντὸς ἔργου καὶ
κορυφήν.

you have made the thing more terrifying to me. As you see, I am even now in a sweat and a tremble and almost think I really see her, and the affair has begotten great turmoil within me. But I will begin, anyhow, for it isn't possible to withdraw, with her already here.

POLYSTRATUS

Yes, and she shows great friendliness in her expression, for she is radiant, as you see, and gracious. So get on with your speech boldly.

LYCINUS

Noblest of women, it is true I praised you, as you say, highly and immoderately; but I do not see what commendation I bestowed as great as the encomium which you have pronounced upon yourself in extolling your reverence for the gods. Really, this is more than all that I said about you, and you must forgive me that I did not add this trait to your likeness; it escaped me because I did not know about it, for there is no other which I should have preferred to represent. So in that particular at least I not only did not go beyond bounds, it seems to me, with my praises, but actually said far less than I should. Think what an important point I omitted there—how very significant as evidence of sterling character and sound judgement! For those who assiduously reverence what pertains to the gods will surely be above reproach in their relations with mankind. So if the speech absolutely must be revised and the portrait corrected, I should not venture to take a single thing away from it, but will add this detail to cap, as it were, and crown the complete work.

317

Ἐπ' ἐκείνῳ[1] μέντοι καὶ πάνυ πολλήν σοι εἰδέναι
τὴν χάριν ὁμολογῶ· ἐμοῦ γὰρ ἐπαινέσαντος τὸ
μέτριον τοῦ σοῦ τρόπου καὶ ὅτι μηδὲν ὑπερπετὲς
μηδὲ τύφου μεστὸν ἐνεποίησέ σοι ὁ παρὼν ὄγκος
τῶν πραγμάτων, σὺ τὰ τοιαῦτα αἰτιασαμένη τοῦ
λόγου ἐπιστώσω τοῦ ἐπαίνου τὴν ἀλήθειαν· τὸ
γὰρ μὴ προαρπάζειν τὰ τοιαῦτα τῶν ἐγκωμίων,
ἀλλ' αἰδεῖσθαι ἐπ' αὐτοῖς καὶ μείζω ἢ κατὰ σὲ
εἶναι λέγειν, μετρίας καὶ δημοτικῆς τινος διανοίας
δεῖγμά ἐστι. πλὴν ἀλλὰ ὅσῳπερ ἂν πρὸς τὸ
ἐπαινεῖσθαι αὐτὸ οὕτω διακειμένη τυγχάνῃς, τοσούτῳ ἀξιωτέραν ὑπερεπαινεῖσθαι ἀποφαίνεις
σεαυτήν, καὶ σχεδὸν εἰς τὸν τοῦ Διογένους λόγον
περιελήλυθέν σοι τὸ πρᾶγμα, ὃς ἐρομένου τινὸς
ὅπως ἂν τις ἔνδοξος γένοιτο, " Εἰ δόξης," ἔφη,
" καταφρονήσειε." φαίην γὰρ ἂν καὶ αὐτός,
εἴ τις ἔροιτό με, " Τίνες εἰσὶν μάλιστα ἐπαίνου
ἄξιοι ; " "'Οπόσοι ἐπαινεῖσθαι μὴ θέλουσιν."

18 Ἀλλὰ ταῦτα μὲν ἴσως ἐξαγώνια καὶ πόρρω
τοῦ πράγματος. ὑπὲρ δὲ οὗ χρὴ ἀπολογήσασθαι,
τοῦτό ἐστιν, ὅτι τῇ ἐν Κνίδῳ καὶ τῇ ἐν κήποις
καὶ Ἥρᾳ καὶ Ἀθηνᾷ τὴν μορφὴν ἀναπλάττων
εἴκασα. ταῦτά σοι ἔκμετρα ἔδοξεν καὶ ὑπὲρ τὸν
πόδα. περὶ αὐτῶν δὴ τούτων ἐρῶ.

Καίτοι παλαιὸς οὗτος ὁ λόγος, ἀνευθύνους εἶναι
ποιητὰς καὶ γραφέας, τοὺς δὲ ἐπαινοῦντας καὶ
μᾶλλον, οἶμαι, εἰ καὶ χαμαὶ καὶ βάδην, ὥσπερ
ἡμεῖς, ἀλλὰ μὴ ἐπὶ μέτρων φέροιντο. ἐλεύθερον
γάρ τι ὁ ἔπαινος, οὐδ' ἔστιν αὐτοῦ μέτρον εἰς

___
[1] ἐκείνῳ Fritzsche : ἐκείνων MSS.

ESSAYS IN PORTRAITURE DEFENDED

There is one thing, however, for which I admit that I am very grateful to you. After I had praised the reasonableness of your character and the fact that the present exalted state of your fortunes has not engendered in you any arrogance or pride, you confirmed the truth of my praise by censuring what you did censure in my speech. Not to catch greedily at such praise, but to blush for it and say that it is too high for you betokens a reasonable and unassuming disposition. But the more you manifest that attitude toward praise itself, the more worthy of extravagant praise you prove yourself! Really the thing, despite you, has come to a pass where the remark of Diogenes applies. When he was asked how one could become famous, he answered: "If he were to scorn fame!" If I myself should be asked: "Who are most worthy of praise?" I should answer: "Those who are unwilling to be praised!"

But all this, no doubt, is apart from the issue and has nothing to do with the case; and the charge to which I must answer is that in making my sketch of you I likened you in beauty to Cnidian Aphrodite and Our Lady in the Gardens and Hera and Athena. That seemed to you extravagant and presumptuous. I shall address myself precisely to that point.

It is an ancient saying, however, that poets and painters are not to be held accountable;[1] still less, I think, eulogists, even if they fare humbly afoot like me, instead of being borne on the wings of song. For praise is an unshackled thing, and has

[1]   Pictoribus atque poetis
Quidlibet audendi semper fuit aequa potestas.
                              HORACE, *Ars Poet.* 9 sq.

μέγεθος ἢ βραχύτητα νενομοθετημένον, ἀλλὰ
τοῦτο μόνον ἐξ ἅπαντος ὁρᾷ ὅπως ὑπερθαυμά-
σεται καὶ ζηλωτὸν ἀποφανεῖ τὸν ἐπαινούμενον.
οὐ μὴν ταύτην ἐγὼ βαδιοῦμαι, μὴ καὶ σοὶ δόξω
ὑπ' ἀπορίας αὐτὸ δρᾶν.

19 Ἐκεῖνο δέ γέ[1] φημι, τοιαύτας ἡμῖν τὰς ἀφορμὰς
τῶν ἐπαινετικῶν τούτων λόγων εἶναι,[2] ὡς χρὴ τὸν
ἐπαινοῦντα καὶ εἰκόσι καὶ ὁμοιώσεσι προσχρῆ-
σθαι, καὶ σχεδὸν ἐν τούτῳ τὸ μέγιστόν ἐστιν εὖ
εἰκάσαι· τὸ δὲ εὖ ὧδε μάλιστ' ἂν[3] κρίνοιτο, οὐκ
ἤν τις τοῖς ὁμοίοις παραβάλλῃ οὐδ' ἢν πρὸς τὸ
ὑποδεέστερον ποιῆται τὴν παράθεσιν, ἀλλ' ἢν
πρὸς τὸ ὑπερέχον ὡς οἷόν τε προσβιβάζῃ τὸ
ἐπαινούμενον.

Οἷον εἴ τις κύνα ἐπαινῶν εἴποι ἀλώπεκος εἶναι
μείζω αὐτὸν ἢ αἰλούρου, ἆρά σοι δοκεῖ ὁ τοιοῦτος
ἐπαινεῖν εἰδέναι; οὐκ ἂν εἴποις. ἀλλὰ μὴν οὐδ'
εἰ λύκῳ φαίη ἴσον αὐτὸν ὑπάρχειν, οὐδὲ οὕτως
μεγαλωστὶ ἐπήνεσεν. ἀλλὰ ποῦ τὸ ἴδιον τοῦ
ἐπαίνου ἀποτελεῖται; ἢν ὁ κύων τῷ λέοντι ἐοικέναι λέγηται καὶ μέγεθος καὶ ἀλκήν. ὡς ὁ τὸν
Ὠρίωνος κύνα ἐπαινῶν ἔφη ποιητὴς λεοντοδάμαν
αὐτόν· οὗτος γὰρ δὴ κυνὸς ἐντελὴς ἔπαινος.

Καὶ πάλιν εἴ τις Μίλωνα τὸν ἐκ Κρότωνος ἢ
Γλαῦκον τὸν ἐκ Καρύστου ἢ Πολυδάμαντα ἐπαινέσαι θέλων ἔπειτα λέγοι ἰσχυρότερον ἕκαστον
αὐτῶν γυναικὸς γενέσθαι, οὐκ ἂν οἴει γελασθῆναι
αὐτὸν ἐπὶ τῇ ἀνοίᾳ τοῦ ἐπαίνου; ὅπου γε καὶ εἰ

---

[1] γέ Gesner : σέ MSS., σοί vulg.
[2] εἶναι ς, edd. : not in MSS.
[3] μάλιστ' ἂν Jacobs : μάλιστα MSS.

no limit, whether upper or lower, prescribed for it. The only object that it ever has in view is to excite high admiration and to make its subject enviable. Nevertheless, I shall not take this course, for fear you may think that I do so for want of a better.

This, however, I do say; the conditions that govern us in these laudatory writings are such that the eulogist must employ comparisons and similes, and really the most important part of it is to make successful comparisons. And success would be most likely to be held attained, not if a man compares like to like, or if he makes his comparison with something that is inferior, but if he approximates, in so far as he may, what he is praising to something that surpasses it.

For example, if in praising a dog someone were to say that it was larger than a fox or a cat, does it seem to you that he knows how to praise? You will not say so! But even if he should say it was as large as a wolf, he has not praised it generously. Well, at what point will the special end of praise be achieved? When the dog is said to resemble a lion in size and in strength. So the poet who praised Orion's dog[1] called him "lion-daunting." That, of course, in the case of a dog is perfect praise.

Again, if someone who wished to praise Milo of Croton or Glaucus of Carystus or Polydamas[2] should say of any one of them that he was stronger than a woman, do not you suppose that he would be laughed at for the senselessness of his praise?

---

[1] Pindar, frag. 74 a (Schroeder).
[2] Famous boxers; see the Index.

321

ἑνὸς ἀνδρὸς ἔλεγεν ἀμείνω εἶναι αὐτόν, οὐδὲ τοῦτο
ἀπέχρησεν ἂν εἰς ἔπαινον. ἀλλὰ πῶς ἐπήνεσε
ποιητὴς εὐδόκιμος τὸν Γλαῦκον, 'οὐδὲ Πολυδεύ-
κεος βίαν' φήσας ἀνατείνασθαι ἂν αὐτῷ ἐναντίας
τὰς χεῖρας 'οὐδὲ σιδάρεον Ἀλκμάνας τέκος'[1];
ὁρᾷς ὁποίοις αὐτὸν θεοῖς εἴκασε· μᾶλλον δὲ καὶ
αὐτῶν ἐκείνων ἀμείνω ἀπέφαινεν. καὶ οὔτε αὐτὸς
ὁ Γλαῦκος ἠγανάκτησεν τοῖς ἐφόροις τῶν ἀθλητῶν
θεοῖς ἀντεπαινούμενος, οὔτε ἐκεῖνοι ἠμύναντο ἢ
τὸν Γλαῦκον ἢ τὸν ποιητὴν ὡς ἀσεβοῦντα περὶ
τὸν ἔπαινον, ἀλλὰ εὐδοκίμουν ἄμφω καὶ ἐτιμῶντο
ὑπὸ τῶν Ἑλλήνων, ὁ μὲν ἐπὶ τῇ ἀλκῇ, ὁ Γλαῦκος,
ὁ δὲ ποιητὴς ἐπί τε τοῖς ἄλλοις καὶ ἐπ' αὐτῷ
τούτῳ μάλιστα τῷ ᾄσματι.

Μὴ δὴ θαυμάσῃς εἰ καὶ αὐτὸς εἰκάσαι βουλόμενος, ὅπερ ἦν τῷ ἐπαινοῦντι ἀναγκαῖον,
ὑψηλοτέρῳ ἐχρησάμην τῷ παραδείγματι, τοῦτο
ὑποβαλόντος τοῦ λόγου.

20 Ἐπεὶ δὲ καὶ κολακείας ἐπεμνήσθης, ὅτι μὲν
καὶ σὺ μισεῖς τοὺς κολακικούς, ἐπαινῶ μέν σε,
καὶ οὐκ ἐχρῆν ἄλλως. ἐθέλω δέ σοι διακρῖναι
καὶ διορίσαι τό τε τοῦ ἐπαινοῦντος ἔργον καὶ τὴν
τοῦ κόλακος ὑπερβολήν.

Ὁ μὲν οὖν κόλαξ ἅτε τῆς χρείας ἕνεκα τῆς ἑαυτοῦ ἐπαινῶν, ἀληθείας δὲ ὀλίγην ποιούμενος τὴν
πρόνοιαν, ἅπαντα ὑπερεπαινεῖν οἴεται δεῖν, ἐπι-
ψευδόμενος καὶ προστιθεὶς παρ' αὑτοῦ τὰ πλείω,
ὡς μὴ ἂν ὀκνῆσαι καὶ τὸν Θερσίτην εὐμορφότερον
ἀποφῆναι τοῦ Ἀχιλλέως καὶ τὸν Νέστορα φάναι
τῶν ἐπὶ Ἴλιον στρατευσάντων τὸν νεώτατον εἶναι.

---

[1] Simonides : Bergk, frag. 8.

Indeed, if it had been said that he was better than any single man, that would not have sufficed for praise. Come, how did a famous poet[1] praise Glaucus when he said : " Not even mighty Polydeuces " could have held up his hands against that man, "nor yet the iron-hard son of Alcmene !" You see what gods he likened him to—nay, actually avouched him better than those gods themselves ! And it cannot be said either that Glaucus became indignant when he was praised in opposition to the gods who are the overseers of athletes, or that they punished either Glaucus or the poet as guilty of sacrilege in the matter of that praise. On the contrary, both enjoyed good fame and were honoured by the Greeks, Glaucus for his strength and the poet especially for this very song !

Do not wonder then, that I myself, desiring to make comparisons, as one who sought to praise was bound to do, used an exalted counterfoil, since my theme demanded it.

Since you mentioned flattery, let me say that I praise you for hating flatterers ; I would not have it otherwise. But I wish to make a distinction and a difference for you between the achievement of one who praises, and its exaggeration on the part of one who flatters.

The flatterer, since he praises for a selfish reason and has little regard for truth, thinks that he must praise everything to excess, telling falsehoods and contributing a great deal on his own account, so that he would not hesitate to declare Thersites had a better figure than Achilles, and that of all who took part in the expedition against Troy, Nestor was the youngest ; he would take his oath upon

διομόσαιτο δ' ἂν καὶ τὸν Κροίσου υἱὸν ὀξυηκο-
ώτερον εἶναι τοῦ Μελάμποδος καὶ τὸν Φινέα
ὀξύτερον δεδορκέναι τοῦ Λυγκέως, ἥνπερ μόνον
κερδᾶναί τι ἐλπίσῃ ἐπὶ τῷ ψεύσματι. ὁ δέ γε
αὐτὸ τοῦτο ἐπαινῶν οὐχ ὅπως οὐδ' ἂν ψεύσαιτό
τι ἢ προσθείη τῶν μηδὲ ὅλως προσόντων, τὰ δ'
ὑπάρχοντα αὐτῷ φύσει ἀγαθά, κἂν μὴ πάνυ
μεγάλα ᾖ, παραλαβὼν ἐπηύξησε καὶ μείζω ἀπέ-
φηνε· καὶ τολμήσειεν ἂν εἰπεῖν, ἵππον ἐπαινέσαι
θέλων, φύσει κοῦφον ὢν ἴσμεν ζῴων καὶ δρομικόν,
ὅτι

Ἄκρον ἐπ' ἀνθερίκων καρπὸν θέεν οὐδὲ κατέκλα.

καὶ πάλιν οὐκ ἂν ὀκνήσειεν φάναι " ἀελλοπόδων
δρόμον ἵππων." καὶ ἢν οἰκίαν ἐπαινῇ καλὴν
καὶ ἄριστα κατεσκευασμένην, εἴποι ἄν

Ζηνός που τοιήδε γ' Ὀλυμπίου ἔνδοθεν αὐλή.

ὁ δὲ κόλαξ τοῦτο τὸ ἔπος κἂν περὶ τῆς συβώτου
καλύβης εἴποι, εἰ μόνον τι παρὰ τοῦ συβώτου
λαβεῖν ἐλπίσειεν· ὅπου Κύναιθος ὁ Δημητρίου
τοῦ Πολιορκητοῦ κόλαξ ἁπάντων αὐτῷ τῶν
πρὸς τὴν κολακείαν καταναλωμένων ἐπῄνει ὑπὸ
βηχὸς ἐνοχλούμενον τὸν Δημήτριον, ὅτι ἐμμελῶς
ἐχρέμπτετο.

---

[1] The son of Croesus was a deaf-mute (Herod. 1, 34 and
85) ; Melampus the seer could hear worms in the roof talking
to each other (Apollodorus 1, 9, 12).

[2] Phineus was blind ; Lynceus could see what was under-
ground (Apoll. 3, 10, 3).

[3] *Iliad* 20, 227, of the horses of Erichthonius, sired by
Boreas.

it that the son of Croesus had sharper ears than Melampus,[1] and Phineus sharper sight than Lynceus,[2] if only he hoped to gain something by the lie. But the other, in praising the selfsame object, instead of telling any lie or adding any quality that did not belong to it, would take the good points that it had by nature, even if they were not very great, and would amplify them and make them greater. He would venture to say, when he wished to praise a horse, which is the lightest of foot and the best runner of all the animals that we know.

"Over the top of the flowers he ran without bending them downward."[3]

And again he would not hesitate to speak of "the swiftness of wind-footed horses."[4] And if he were to praise a house that was beautiful and handsomely furnished, he would say:

"Surely like this, inside, is the palace of Zeus on Olympus."[5]

The flatterer, however, would express himself in that way even about the swineherd's hut, if only he hoped to get something from the swineherd! Take Cynaethus, the toady of Demetrius Poliorcetes; when he had used up all his means of flattery, he praised Demetrius, who was troubled with a cough, because he cleared his throat melodiously!

[4] Source unknown, if δρόμον is part of the quotation. But for "wind-footed horses," see *Hymn to Venus* 217, Pindar, frag. 221.

[5] *Odyssey* 4, 74, said by Telemachus to his friend, admiring the palace of Menelaus.

21 Οὐ μόνον δὲ τοῦτο ἑκατέρου αὐτῶν γνώρισμά
ἐστιν, τὸ τοὺς μὲν κόλακας οὐκ ὀκνεῖν καὶ ψεύδεσθαι τοῦ χαρίσασθαι ἕνεκα τοῖς ἐπαινουμένοις,
ἐξαίρειν δὲ τοὺς ἐπαινοῦντας τὰ ὑπάρχοντα πει-
ρᾶσθαι· ἀλλὰ κἀκείνῳ οὐ μικρῷ διαλλάττουσιν,
ὅτι οἱ μὲν κόλακες, ἐφ᾽ ὅσον οἷόν τε αὐτοῖς,
χρῶνται ταῖς ὑπερβολαῖς, οἱ ἐπαινοῦντες δὲ καὶ
ἐν αὐταῖς ταύταις σωφρονοῦσιν καὶ ἐντὸς τῶν
ὅρων μένουσιν.

Ταῦτά σοι ἀπὸ πολλῶν ὀλίγα κολακείας καὶ
ἐπαίνου ἀληθοῦς δείγματα, ὡς μὴ πάντας ὑπο-
πτεύσῃς τοὺς ἐπαινοῦντας, ἀλλὰ διακρίνῃς καὶ
παραμετρῇς τῷ οἰκείῳ μέτρῳ ἑκάτερον.

22 Φέρ᾽ οὖν, εἰ δοκεῖ, πρόσαγε τοῖς ὑπ᾽ ἐμοῦ
εἰρημένοις τοὺς κανόνας ἀμφοτέρους, ὡς μάθῃς
εἴτε τούτῳ εἴτ᾽ ἐκείνῳ ἐοίκασιν. ἐγὼ γὰρ εἰ μέν
τινα ἄμορφον οὖσαν ἔφην τῷ ἐν Κνίδῳ ἀγάλματι
ὁμοίαν, γόης ἂν καὶ τοῦ Κυναίθου κολακικώτερος
ὄντως νομιζοίμην· εἰ δὲ τοιαύτην ὑπάρχουσαν
οἵαν πάντες ἴσασιν, οὐ πάνυ ἐκ πολλοῦ διαστήματος ἦν τὸ τόλμημα.

23 Τάχ᾽ ἂν οὖν[1] φαίης, μᾶλλον δὲ ἤδη εὕρηκας,
"ἐπαινεῖν μέν σοι εἰς τὸ κάλλος ἐφεῖσθο· ἀνεπί-
φθονον μέντοι ποιήσασθαι τὸν ἔπαινον ἐχρῆν,
ἀλλὰ μὴ θεαῖς ἀπεικάζειν ἄνθρωπον οὖσαν."
ἐγὼ δὲ—ἤδη γάρ με προάξεται τἀληθὲς εἰπεῖν—
οὐ θεαῖς σε,[2] ὦ βελτίστη, εἴκασα, τεχνιτῶν δὲ
ἀγαθῶν δημιουργήμασιν λίθου καὶ χαλκοῦ ἢ
ἐλέφαντος πεποιημένοις· τὰ δὲ ὑπ᾽ ἀνθρώπων
γεγενημένα οὐκ ἀσεβές, οἶμαι, ἀνθρώποις εἰκά-

---

[1] Text Fritzsche : τάχα δ νῦν MSS.

That flatterers do not hesitate to lie for the sake of pleasing the objects of their praise, whereas those who really praise try to magnify what actually exists, is not the only distinguishing mark of each. They differ in a further point, and not a trivial one, that flatterers use hyperbole to the full extent of their powers, while those who really praise are discreet in precisely that particular and remain within their bounds.

These are a few out of many earmarks of flattery and of genuine praise which I give you so that you may not suspect all who praise you, but may distinguish between them and gauge each by his proper standard.

Come then, apply, if you will, both canons to my words, that you may discover whether they conform to this one or the other. If it had been some ugly woman whom I likened to the statue in Cnidos, I might indeed be accounted a liar, and a worse flatterer than Cynaethus. But since it was one whose beauty is known to all, the venture was not a *salto mortale*.

Perhaps, then, you may say—indeed, you have already said—that you concede my right to praise you for your beauty, but that I should have made my praise unexceptionable and should not have compared a mortal woman with goddesses. As a matter of fact (now she is going to make me speak the truth!) it was not with goddesses I compared you, my dear woman, but with masterpieces of good craftsmen, made of stone or bronze or ivory; and what man has made, it is not impious, I take it,

---

² σε Jensius : γε MSS.

ζειν. ἐκτὸς εἰ μὴ σὺ τοῦτο εἶναι τὴν Ἀθηνᾶν
ὑπείληφας τὸ ὑπὸ Φειδίου πεπλασμένον ἢ τοῦτο
τὴν οὐρανίαν Ἀφροδίτην ὃ ἐποίησεν Πραξιτέλης
ἐν Κνίδῳ οὐ πάνυ πολλῶν ἐτῶν. ἀλλ᾽ ὅρα μὴ
ἄσεμνον ᾖ τὰ τοιαῦτα περὶ τῶν θεῶν δοξάζειν,
ὧν τάς γε[1] ἀληθεῖς εἰκόνας ἀνεφίκτους εἶναι
ἀνθρωπίνῃ μιμήσει ἔγωγε ὑπολαμβάνω.

24 Εἰ δὲ καὶ ὅτι μάλιστά σε αὐταῖς ἐκείναις εἴκασα,
οὐκ ἐμὸν τοῦτο, οὐδὲ ἐγὼ πρῶτος ταύτην ἐτεμόμην
τὴν ὁδόν, ἀλλὰ πολλοὶ καὶ ἀγαθοὶ ποιηταί, καὶ
μάλιστα ὁ πολίτης ὁ σὸς Ὅμηρος, ὃν καὶ νῦν
ἀναβιβάσομαι συναγορεύσοντά μοι, ἢ οὐδεμία
μηχανὴ μὴ οὐχὶ καὶ αὐτὸν σὺν ἐμοὶ ἁλῶναι.

Ἐρήσομαι τοίνυν αὐτόν, μᾶλλον δὲ σὲ ὑπὲρ
αὐτοῦ—καὶ γὰρ διαμνημονεύεις εὖ ποιοῦσα τὰ
χαριέστατα τῶν ἐρραψῳδημένων αὐτῷ—τί σοι
ἐκεῖνος[2] δοκεῖ, ὁπόταν περὶ τῆς αἰχμαλώτου
λέγῃ τῆς Βρισηΐδος ὅτι χρυσῇ Ἀφροδίτῃ ἰκέλη
ἐπένθει τὸν Πάτροκλον; εἶτα μετὰ μικρόν, ὡς
οὐχ ἱκανὸν εἰ μόνῃ τῇ Ἀφροδίτῃ ἐοικυῖα ἔσται,

Εἶπε δ᾽ ἄρα—φησίν—κλαίουσα γυνὴ εἰκυῖα
θεῇσιν.

Ὁπόταν οὖν τὰ τοιαῦτα λέγῃ, μισεῖς κἀκεῖνον
καὶ ἀπορρίπτεις τὸ βιβλίον, ἢ δίδως αὐτῷ ἐλευ-
θεριάζειν ἐν τῷ ἐπαίνῳ; ἀλλὰ κἂν σὺ μὴ δῷς, ὅ
γε τοσοῦτος αἰὼν δέδωκεν, οὐδ᾽ ἔστιν ὅστις αὐτὸν
ἐπὶ τούτῳ ᾐτιάσατο, οὐδὲ ὁ μαστίξαι τολμήσας

---

[1] γε Fritzsche : τε MSS.
[2] ἐκεῖνος Fritzsche : ἐκεῖνο MSS.

---

[1] Iliad 19, 282.

to compare with man. But perhaps you have assumed that what Phidias fashioned is Athena, and that what Praxiteles made in Cnidus not many years ago is Heavenly Aphrodite? Come now, would it not be unworthy to hold such beliefs about the gods, whose real images I for my part assume to be unattainable by human mimicry?

But if I had actually compared you, as much as you will, with the very goddesses themselves, I should not have been doing it on my own responsibility and should not have been the first to open this road. No, there have been many good poets ahead of me, and above all your fellow-citizen Homer, whom I shall now call up to plead for me, or else there is nothing for it but that he himself will be convicted along with me!

I shall therefore ask him, or, better, ask you in his stead, since you know by heart—and it is greatly to your credit—all the prettiest of the verses that he composed, what you think of him when he says of Briseis, the captive, that as she mourned for Patroclus she resembled golden Aphrodite?[1] Then after a bit, as if it were not enough that she should be like Aphrodite only, he says:

"Then made answer, in tears, the maid as fair as a goddess."[2]

When he says that sort of thing, do you loathe him and fling away the book, or do you permit him to enjoy full freedom in his praise? Well, even if you refuse permission, at all events Time in his long flight has given it, and nobody has found fault with Homer on that score, neither the man who made

[2] *Iliad* 19, 286.

αὐτοῦ τὴν εἰκόνα οὐδ' ὁ τὰ νόθα ἐπισημηνάμενος
τῶν ἐπῶν ἐν τῇ παραγραφῇ τῶν ὀβελῶν.

Εἶτα ἐκείνῳ μὲν ἐφεθήσεται βάρβαρον γυναῖκα,
καὶ ταῦτα κλαίουσαν, τῇ χρυσῇ Ἀφροδίτῃ εἰκάσαι, ἐγὼ δ', ἵνα μὴ τὸ κάλλος εἴπω, διότι μὴ
ἀνέχῃ ἀκούσασα, οὐκ ἂν παραβάλλοιμι θεῶν
εἰκόσι γυναῖκα φαιδρὰν καὶ μειδιῶσαν τὰ πολλά,
ὅπερ θεοῖς ὅμοιον ἄνθρωποι ἔχουσιν;

25   Ἐπὶ μέν γε τοῦ Ἀγαμέμνονος ὅρα ὅσην αὐτὸς
φειδὼ ἐποιήσατο τῶν θεῶν καὶ ὡς ἐταμιεύσατο
τὰς εἰκόνας εἰς τὸ σύμμετρον· ὡς ὄμματα μέν
φησιν καὶ κεφαλὴν ἴκελον αὐτὸν εἶναι τῷ Διί,
τῷ Ἄρεϊ δὲ τὴν ζώνην, στέρνον δὲ τῷ Ποσειδῶνι,
διαιρῶν τὸν ἄνθρωπον κατὰ μέλη πρὸς τοσούτων
θεῶν εἰκόνας· καὶ αὖ πάλιν βροτολοιγῷ Ἄρεΐ
φησίν τιν'[1] ὅμοιον εἶναι καὶ ἄλλον ἄλλῳ, θεοειδῆ
τὸν Φρύγα τὸν τοῦ Πριάμου, καὶ θεοείκελον
πολλάκις τὸν Πηλέως.

Ἀλλὰ ἐπάνειμι αὖθις ἐπὶ τὰ γυναικεῖα τῶν
παραδειγμάτων· ἀκούεις γὰρ δή που αὐτοῦ
λέγοντος

          Ἀρτέμιδι ἰκέλη ἠὲ χρυσέῃ Ἀφροδίτῃ.
καὶ

          οἵη δ' Ἄρτεμις εἶσι κατ' οὔρεος.

26   Οὐ μόνον δὲ τοὺς ἀνθρώπους αὐτοὺς θεοῖς
ἀπεικάζει, ἀλλὰ καὶ τὴν[2] Εὐφόρβου κόμην ταῖς

---

[1] τιν' inserted by A.M.H., following du Soul's hint that
the name Hector had fallen out.

[2] θεοῖς—τὴν N: not in ΕΓΩ.   Probably a conjecture;
ἀπεικάζει is certainly false (Mras).

---

[1] Respectively Zoilus the Homeromastix and Aristarchus
of Alexandria, the grammarian.

bold to flog his statue nor the man who marked the spurious lines by setting daggers beside them.[1]

Then if he is to be permitted to compare a foreign woman, and in tears at that, with golden Aphrodite, for my part, not to speak of your beauty because you will not listen, may not I compare with images of the gods a radiant woman, usually smiling, a trait which men have in common with the gods?

In the case of Agamemnon, moreover, see how parsimonious Homer was with the gods, and with what propriety he doled out his comparisons! He says that in eyes and head he was like to Zeus, in waist to Ares, and in chest to Poseidon,[2] dismembering the man for the sake of comparing him with all those gods. Again, he says that someone is a match for devastating Ares;[3] and just so with the rest of them—the Phrygian, the son of Priam, is beautiful as a god,[4] and the son of Peleus is often godlike.[5]

But I will return to the parallels that concern women. You know, naturally, that he says:

"Artemis she resembleth, or else Aphrodite the golden," [6]

also,

"Just so Artemis runneth adown the slope of a mountain." [7]

Moreover, he not only compares human beings with gods, but likens the long hair of Euphorbus to

---

[2] *Iliad* 2, 478–479.
[3] Notably Hector, *Iliad* 11, 295 ; 13, 802.
[4] Paris, *Iliad* 3, 16.   [5] Achilles, *Iliad* 1, 131.
[6] *Odyssey* 17, 37 (19, 54), of Penelope.
[7] *Odyssey* 6, 102, of Nausicaa.

Χάρισιν ἀπείκασε, καὶ ταῦτα αἵματι δεδευμένην.
καὶ ὅλως τοσαῦτά ἐστι τὰ τοιαῦτα ὡς μηδὲν
εἶναι μέρος τῆς ποιήσεως ὃ μὴ ταῖς θείαις εἰκόσιν
διακεκόσμηται. ὥστε ἢ κἀκεῖνα ἐξαληλίφθω, ἢ
καὶ ἡμῖν τὰ ὅμοια τολμᾶν ἐφείσθω. οὕτω δὲ τὸ
κατὰ τὰς εἰκόνας καὶ τὰς ὁμοιώσεις ἀνεύθυνόν
ἐστιν ὥστε Ὅμηρος καὶ τὰς θεὰς αὐτὰς οὐκ
ὤκνησεν ἀπὸ τῶν ἐλαττόνων ἐπαινέσαι· τοὺς
γοῦν τῆς Ἥρας ὀφθαλμοὺς τοῖς τῶν βοῶν εἴ-
κασεν· ἕτερος δέ τις ἰοβλέφαρον τὴν Ἀφροδίτην
ἔφη. τὴν μὲν γὰρ ῥοδοδάκτυλον τίς ἀγνοεῖ τῶν
κἂν ἐπ' ἐλάχιστον τῇ Ὁμήρου ποιήσει ὡμιλη-
κότων;

27 Καίτοι τὰ μὲν τῆς μορφῆς ἔτι μετριώτερα, εἰ
τις θεῷ ἐοικέναι λέγεται· ἀλλὰ τὰς προσηγορίας
αὐτὰς πόσοι ἐμιμήσαντο τὰς τῶν θεῶν, Διονύσιοι
καὶ Ἡφαιστίωνες καὶ Ζήνωνες καὶ Ποσειδώνιοι
καὶ Ἑρμαῖ προσαγορευόμενοι; Λητὼ δὲ γυνή τις
ἐγένετο Εὐαγόρου τοῦ Κυπρίων βασιλέως, καὶ
ὅμως οὐκ ἠγανάκτησεν ἡ θεὸς δυναμένη λίθον
αὐτὴν ὥσπερ τὴν Νιόβην ἀπεργάσασθαι. ἐῶ
γὰρ τοὺς Αἰγυπτίους, οἵπερ καὶ δεισιδαιμονέ-
στατοί εἰσιν πάντων, ὅμως τοῖς θείοις ὀνόμασιν
εἰς κόρον ἐπιχρωμένους· σχεδὸν γοῦν τὰ πλεῖστα
αὐτοῖς ἐξ οὐρανοῦ ἐστιν.

28 Ὥστε οὐ πρός γε σοῦ τὸ τοιοῦτον, ψοφοδεῶς
διακεῖσθαι πρὸς τὸν ἔπαινον· εἰ γάρ τι ἐν τῷ
συγγράμματι πεπλημμέληται εἰς τὸ θεῖον, σὺ
μὲν ἀνεύθυνος αὐτοῦ, ἐκτὸς εἰ μή τινα νομίζεις
ἀκροάσεως εὔθυναν εἶναι, ἐμὲ δὲ ἀμυνοῦνται οἱ

the Graces, and that too when it was soaked with blood! In short, this sort of thing is so frequent that there is no part of his poetry which is not well adorned with comparisons of gods. Therefore you must either expunge all that, or permit us to be equally venturesome. So exempt from all accountability is the use of comparisons and similes that Homer actually did not hesitate to derive praise for the goddesses from things of lower degree. For instance, he likened Hera's eyes to those of kine. And someone else called Aphrodite violet-browed.[1] As for "rosy-fingered," who that has even the slightest acquaintance with Homer's poetry does not know it?

As far as personal appearance is concerned, it signifies comparatively little if one is said to be like a god. But how many there are who have copied the very names of the gods, calling themselves Dionysius, Hephaestion, Zeno, Poseidonius, Hermes! And there was a Leto, the wife of Evagoras, king of Cyprus; yet the goddess did not take on about it, though she might have turned her into stone as she did Niobe. The Egyptians I forbear to mention, who, though the most superstitious people in the world, yet use the names of the gods to their hearts' content; in fact, most of their names are derived from Heaven.

It is not incumbent upon you, then, to be thus timorous in respect of praise. If any offence at all has been perpetrated against divinity in that essay, you are not accountable for it—unless you think that to listen makes one accountable; it is I whom

The " Theban poet " of the preceding piece (p.271); *i.e.* Pindar.

333

θεοί, ἐπειδὰν πρὸ ἐμοῦ τὸν Ὅμηρον καὶ τοὺς
ἄλλους ποιητὰς ἀμύνωνται. ἀλλ᾽ οὐδέπω οὐδὲ
τὸν ἄριστον τῶν φιλοσόφων ἠμύναντο εἰκόνα θεοῦ
τὸν ἄνθρωπον εἰπόντα εἶναι.

Πολλὰ ἔτι ἔχων πρὸς σὲ εἰπεῖν Πολυστράτου
ἕνεκα τούτου παύσομαι, ἵνα καὶ ἀπομνημονεῦσαι
δυνηθῇ τὰ εἰρημένα.

ΠΟΛΥΣΤΡΑΤΟΣ

29 Οὐκ οἶδα εἴ μοι τοῦτο δυνατὸν ἔτι, ὦ Λυκῖνε·
μακρὰ γὰρ εἴρηταί σοι καὶ ταῦτα, καὶ ὑπὲρ τὸ
ὕδωρ τὸ ἐκκεχυμένον. πειράσομαι δ᾽ ὅμως ἐπι-
μνησθῆναι αὐτῶν. καὶ ὡς ὁρᾷς, ἤδη ἀποσοβῶ
παρ᾽ αὐτὴν ἐπιβυσάμενος τὰ ὦτα, ὡς μή τι
παρεμπεσὸν ἄλλο συγχέῃ τὴν τάξιν αὐτῶν, εἶτά
μοι συρίττεσθαι συμβῇ πρὸς τῶν θεατῶν.

ΛΥΚΙΝΟΣ

Αὐτῷ σοι μελήσει, ὦ Πολύστρατε, ὅπως ἄριστα
ὑποκρίνῃ. ἐγὼ δὲ ἐπείπερ ἅπαξ σοι τὸ δρᾶμα
παραδέδωκα, νῦν μὲν ἐκποδὼν ἀποστήσομαι·
ὁπόταν δὲ τὰς ψήφους ἀνακηρύττωσι τῶν κριτῶν,
τότε ἤδη καὶ αὐτὸς παρέσομαι ὀψόμενος ὁποῖόν
τι τὸ τέλος τοῦ ἀγῶνος ἔσται.

---

[1] Hardly Plato, though he has something similar in the
Republic, 501. But to him the universe is God's image ; see

the gods will punish, after first punishing Homer
and the other poets! But to this day they have
not punished the best of the philosophers for saying
that man was God's image![1]

Although I might say much more to you, I shall
stop for the sake of Polystratus here, so that he may
be able to repeat from memory what has been said.

POLYSTRATUS

I don't know if that is any longer possible for me,
Lycinus. Even as it is, you have made a long
speech, far beyond your allowance of water. But
I shall try to remember it all the same; and, as you
see, I am already making off to her with my ears
stopped for fear that something else may pop in
to confuse its outline, and then I may have the bad
luck to be hissed by my hearers!

LYCINUS

That is your concern, Polystratus, to act your part
to the best advantage. As for me, now that I have
once for all put the play into your hands, I shall
withdraw for the present; but when they announce
the votes of the judges, I shall be there in person to
see what will be the outcome of the contest.

the end of the Timaeus. Perhaps Lucian means Diogenes,
who said that *good* men were images of gods (Diog. Laert. 6,
51).

THE GODDESSE OF SURRYE

An account of the worship of "Juno" (Atargatis) at
Hieropolis in Syria, done, not in Lucian's customary Attic
Greek, but in the Ionic dialect, after the manner of Herodotus, which Lucian counterfeits so cleverly and parodies so
slyly that many have been unwilling to recognize him as the
author.

It would be most unfair to Lucian to turn this tale into
contemporary English. In order to have the same effect
that it had in his own day, and to be really intelligible, it
must seem to come from the lips of an ancient traveller.
The version here offered seeks to secure that effect through
mimicry of Sir John Mandeville. It is true that Herodotus
was better known in Lucian's time than Mandeville is
known now, and his language seemed less remote. In every
other respect, however—in his limited vocabulary, in his
simple style, and in his point of view—Mandeville provides
a mask uniquely adapted to the part—if only its wearer
does not fall down in it and break it.

In the notes, which are more extensive than usual because
Lucian's topic here is outside the ordinary classical range,
several books which have been of particular service are cited
by abbreviated titles: E.Schrader, *Die Keilinschriften und
das Alte Testament*, pt. ii, *Religion und Sprache*, 3rd ed.,
1903, by H. Zimmern (Schrader-Zimmern); Stanley A. Cook,
Religion of Ancient Palestine, etc., London, 1908 (Cook); W. W.
Graf Baudissin, *Adonis und Esmun*, Leipzig, 1911 (Baudissin),
and his *Studien zur Semitischen Religionsgeschichte*, 1878
(*Studien*); Sir J. G. Frazer, *Adonis, Attis, Osiris*, in *Golden
Bough*[3], pt iv, London, 1919 (Frazer), and his *Folklore in the
Old Testament*, London, 1919 (*Folklore*); Albert T. Clay,
A Hebrew Deluge Story, etc, New Haven 1921 (Clay).

Those who wish to see the piece in modern English may be
referred to the version by H. A. Strong (London, 1913).
This is supplied with an introduction and notes by J. E.
Garstang, whose commentary will be found to supplement
this in many points, especially in the matter of Hittite
parallels.

ΠΕΡΙ ΤΗΣ ΣΥΡΙΗΣ ΘΕΟΥ

1 Ἔστιν ἐν Συρίη πόλις οὐ πολλὸν ἀπὸ τοῦ
Εὐφρήτεω ποταμοῦ, καλέεται δὲ Ἱρή, καὶ ἔστιν
ἱρὴ τῆς Ἥρης τῆς Ἀσσυρίης. δοκέει δέ μοι, τόδε
τὸ οὔνομα οὐκ ἅμα τῇ πόλει οἰκεομένῃ ἐγένετο,
ἀλλὰ τὸ μὲν ἀρχαῖον ἄλλο ἦν, μετὰ δὲ σφίσι τῶν
ἱρῶν μεγάλων γιγνομένων ἐς τόδε ἡ ἐπωνυμίη
ἀπίκετο. περὶ ταύτης ὦν τῆς πόλιος ἔρχομαι
ἐρέων ὁκόσα ἐν αὐτῇ ἐστιν· ἐρέω δὲ καὶ νόμους
τοῖσιν ἐς τὰ ἱρὰ χρέωνται, καὶ πανηγύριας τὰς
ἄγουσιν καὶ θυσίας τὰς ἐπιτελέουσιν. ἐρέω δὲ
καὶ ὁκόσα καὶ περὶ τῶν τὸ ἱρὸν εἰσαμένων μυθολογέουσι, καὶ τὸν νηὸν ὅκως ἐγένετο. γράφω δὲ
Ἀσσύριος ἐών, καὶ τῶν ἀπηγέομαι τὰ μὲν αὐτο-
ψίῃ μαθών, τὰ δὲ παρὰ τῶν ἱρέων ἐδάην, ὁκόσα
ἐόντα ἐμεῦ πρεσβύτερα ἐγὼ ἱστορέω.

2 Πρῶτοι μὲν ὦν ἀνθρώπων τῶν ἡμεῖς ἴδμεν
Αἰγύπτιοι λέγονται θεῶν τε ἐννοίην λαβεῖν καὶ

Available in photographs, ΓΝ.

---

[1] Hierapolis, or better, in accordance with the coins,
Hieropolis. It is N.W. of Aleppo, on the main road into
Mesopotamia, 15 Roman miles from the crossing of the
Euphrates, and by road about 116 Roman miles from Lucian's
birthplace, Samosata. Its Syrian name was Mabog, (properly
Manbog, *i.e.* "spring," according to Baudissin, *Studien*, ii,
159), in Greek, Bambyce. It was dubbed Hieropolis in the
time of Seleucus Nicator (Ael. *N.H.* 12, 2), but the old name
persisted (Manbij; le Strange, *Palestine under the Moslems*,

THE GODDESSE OF SURRYE

IN Surrye, not fer fro the Ryvere Eufrate, is a Cytee that Holy highte and holy is in sothe, for it is of Iuno Assurien.[1] Yit I wene that the cyteene hadde not this name atte firste, whan that it was founded, but of olden tyme it was other, and after, whan here servys of the Goddesse wex gret, it was *their* chaunged to this. Touching this cytee I purpos me to seyn alle that is in it, and I schalle speke of the customes that thei folwen in here rytes, and the feste dayes that thei kepen, and the sacrifises that thei perfourmen. And I schalle reherce alle the tales that men tellen of hem that establisschede the holy place, and how that the temple was bylded. And I that write am Assurien,[2] and of that that I devyse you, some partie saughe I with mine owne eyen, and some partie I lerned be informacioun fro the prestes, that is to seyn, tho thynges that I descryve that weren beforn min owne tyme.

Of alle peples whereof wee knowen, Egyptyens weren firste, as men seyn, for to taken conceyte of

---

p. 500) and still attaches to the ruins, on which see Hogarth, *Annual of the British School at Athens*, 1907–8, p. 186 *sqq* ; Cumont, *Études Syriennes*, p. 22 *sqq.*, p. 35 *sqq.* Lucian does not identify the city with "ancient Ninus," as do Philostratus and Ammianus.

[2] Confusion between Assyrian and Syrian is not peculiar to this piece nor to Lucian. It goes back to Herodotus, who says that "Syrian" is the Greek equivalent of the barbarian "Assyrian" (7, 63 ; see Macan's note, and cf. 140).

ἱρὰ εἴσασθαι καὶ τεμένεα καὶ πανηγύριας ἀπο-
δεῖξαι. πρῶτοι δὲ καὶ οὐνόματα ἱρὰ ἔγνωσαν καὶ
λόγους ἱροὺς ἔλεξαν. μετὰ δὲ οὐ πολλοστῷ
χρόνῳ παρ' Αἰγυπτίων λόγον Ἀσσύριοι ἐς θεοὺς
ἤκουσαν, καὶ ἱρὰ καὶ νηοὺς ἤγειραν, ἐν τοῖς καὶ
3 ἀγάλματα ἔθεντο καὶ ξόανα ἐστήσαντο. τὸ δὲ
παλαιὸν καὶ παρ' Αἰγυπτίοισιν ἀξόανοι νηοὶ
ἔσαν. καὶ ἔστιν ἱρὰ καὶ ἐν Συρίῃ οὐ παρὰ πολὺ
τοῖς Αἰγυπτίοισιν ἰσοχρονέοντα, τῶν ἐγὼ πλεῖστα
ὄπωπα, τό γε τοῦ Ἡρακλέος τὸ ἐν Τύρῳ, οὐ
τούτου τοῦ Ἡρακλέος τὸν Ἕλληνες ἀείδουσιν,
ἀλλὰ τὸν ἐγὼ λέγω πολλὸν ἀρχαιότερος καὶ
Τύριος ἥρως ἐστίν.

4 Ἔνι δὲ καὶ ἄλλο ἱρὸν ἐν Φοινίκῃ μέγα, τὸ
Σιδόνιοι ἔχουσιν. ὡς μὲν αὐτοὶ λέγουσιν, Ἀστάρ-
της ἐστίν· Ἀστάρτην δ' ἐγὼ δοκέω Σεληναίην
ἔμμεναι. ὡς δέ μοί τις τῶν ἱρέων ἀπηγέετο,
Εὐρώπης ἐστὶν τῆς Κάδμου ἀδελφεῆς· ταύτην δὲ
ἐοῦσαν Ἀγήνορος τοῦ βασιλέως θυγατέρα, ἐπειδή
τε ἀφανὴς ἐγεγόνεεν, οἱ Φοίνικες τῷ νηῷ ἐτιμήσαντο
καὶ λόγον ἱρὸν ἐπ' αὐτῇ ἔλεξαν, ὅτι ἐοῦσαν καλὴν
Ζεὺς ἐπόθεεν καὶ τὸ εἶδος ἐς ταῦρον ἀμειψάμενος
ἥρπασεν καί μιν ἐς Κρήτην φέρων ἀπίκετο.
τάδε μὲν καὶ τῶν ἄλλων Φοινίκων ἤκουον, καὶ

---

[1] In *Astrology*, Lucian similarly credits the Egyptians with
priority over the Chaldaeans in the study of the stars. In
both cases his view, surprising in a Syrian, was the common
one of his time, to be found, for instance, in Diodorus
(1, 9, 6).

[2] The god was Melkart. Herodotus was told by the
priests there that the cult was established when the city

Goddes, and to stablisschen holy places and closes,
and to apoynten feste dayes. And thei firste knewen
holy names and maden holy tales. But no long
tyme after, Assuryens herden rumour and speche
of Egyptyens as touching to goddes, and rereden
seyntuaryes and temples, in the whiche thei lette
putten ymages and setten symulacres.[1] But aun-
cientlye amonges Egyptyens weren temples without-
en symulacres. And in Surrye ben temples almost
als olde as tho in Egypte, of the whiche I have seen
the moste, and namely the temple of Hercules in
Tyre, not that Hercules that Grekes preysen in here
songes, but that oon wherof I speke is moche elder,
and is Tyres patroun.[2]

In Phenicye is another grete temple that men of
Sidon kepen. Thei seyn, it is of Astarte, and
Astarte, I trowe, is Luna the Mone.[3] But oon of
the prestes tolde me, it belongeth to Europe, Cadmus
suster. Sche was Agenor the Kinges daughter;
and after that sche vanisched, Phenicyens yafen
hir that temple for worschipe and maden a storie
of hir, that sithe sche was fair, Iove coveytede hir,
and transformed his lyknesse in to a bole, and than
ravissched hir awey and bar hir on his bac to Crete.
That same storie I herde of othere Phenicyens also;

was founded, and was then (ca. 430 B.C.) 2,300 years old
(Herod. 2, 44).

[3] The Emperor Elagabalus, being the Sun, brought
Astarte the Moon from Phoenicia and wedded her (Herodian
5, 6, 3–5). But she was not originally or at any time
primarily the moon; and in Babylonia, as Ishtar, she had
for her emblem a star, the planet Venus (Baudissin, 19).
Clay (p. 47) believes that the name Ashera, Ashirta, Ishtar,
is that of a mortal woman, an early queen of Hallab
(Aleppo).

τὸ νόμισμα τῷ Σιδόνιοι χρέωνται τὴν Εὐρώπην
ἐφεζομένην ἔχει τῷ ταύρῳ τῷ Διί· τὸν δὲ νηὸν οὐκ
ὁμολογέουσιν Εὐρώπης ἔμμεναι.

5 Ἔχουσι δὲ καὶ ἄλλο Φοίνικες ἱρόν, οὐκ
Ἀσσύριον ἀλλ' Αἰγύπτιον, τὸ ἐξ Ἡλίου πόλιος
ἐς τὴν Φοινίκην ἀπίκετο. ἐγὼ μέν μιν οὐκ ὄπωπα,
μέγα δὲ καὶ τόδε καὶ ἀρχαῖόν ἐστιν.

6 Εἶδον δὲ καὶ ἐν Βύβλῳ μέγα ἱρὸν Ἀφροδίτης
Βυβλίης, ἐν τῷ καὶ τὰ ὄργια ἐς Ἄδωνιν ἐπιτελέ-
ουσιν· ἐδάην δὲ καὶ τὰ ὄργια. λέγουσι γὰρ δὴ
ὧν τὸ ἔργον τὸ ἐς Ἄδωνιν ὑπὸ τοῦ συὸς ἐν τῇ
χώρῃ τῇ σφετέρῃ γενέσθαι, καὶ μνήμην τοῦ
πάθεος τύπτονταί τε ἑκάστου ἔτεος καὶ θρηνέουσι
καὶ τὰ ὄργια ἐπιτελέουσι καὶ σφίσι μεγάλα
πένθεα ἀνὰ τὴν χώρην ἵσταται. ἐπεὰν δὲ ἀπο-
τύψωνταί τε καὶ ἀποκλαύσωνται, πρῶτα μὲν
καταγίζουσι τῷ Ἀδώνιδι ὅκως ἐόντι νέκυι, μετὰ
δὲ τῇ ἑτέρῃ ἡμέρῃ ζώειν τέ μιν μυθολογέουσι καὶ
ἐς τὸν ἠέρα πέμπουσι καὶ τὰς κεφαλὰς ξύρονται

---

[1] The coins are described in Head, *Historia Nummorum*,
2nd ed., pp. 797 *sq.* The temple itself contained, in later
days at least, a painting of the Europa episode (Achilles
Tatius 1, 1). The story was also localized at Tyre, where
the house of Agenor and the bower of Europa were shown
(Arrian, *Anab.* 2, 24, 2; Nonnus, *Dionys.* 40, 353 *sqq.*) and
where in the eighth century (Malalas, p. 31) the people still
mourned the abduction in a feast called the κακὴ ὀψινή. The
name Europa is considered Greek ; whether this particular
myth is Cretan or Phoenician in origin the evidence does not
seem sufficient to determine.

[2] This cult was at Heliopolis (Baalbek). The god, who
appears to have been originally Hadad but to have undergone
syncrisis with the sun-god and with the Syrian "Apollo,"
was worshipped far and wide as Jupiter Heliopolitanus.

and the moneye that Sidonyes usen hath Europe sittynge on the bole that is Iove.[1] Natheles wille thei not avowen that the temple is of Europe.

And Phenicyens han an other maner servys, not Assuryen but Egyptyen, that cam from Elyople into Phenicye. I have not seen it, but it also is gret and auncien.[2]

But I saughe in Byblos a gret temple of Venus of Byblos, wherin thei performen cerimonyes in mynde of Adoon; and I lernede tho cerimonyes.[3] Thei seyn that the dede that was don to Adoon be the bore befell in here londe, and for memorie of that myschaunce everyche yeer thei beten here brestes and sorwen and perfourmen tho cerimonyes, makynge gret doel thorgh that contree. And whan *mourning* the betynge and the wepynge is atte ende, first thei maken offringes to Adoon, as though he were ded; and than, on the morwe, thei fablen that he is quick, and fecchen him forth in to the eyr, and lette *air*

The cult image, says Macrobius (*Saturn.* 1, 23, 10) came from Heliopolis in Egypt by way of Assyria. The ambiguity of Lucian's Greek (for ἱερὸν suggests "holy place") seems meant to convey the jocose implication that the magnificent new temple, built by Antoninus Pius, had been transported thither without human hands.

[3] To natives of Byblos their goddess was just Baalat (Mistress), and to other Semites Baalat Gebal (Mistress of Byblos); in Syriac and Greek Baltis or Beltis is used as if it were her name. So too Adonis to them was simply Adon (Lord); an early name, or perhaps epithet, was Eliun (Philo of Byblos; cf. Baudissin, p. 76, Meyer, *Gesch.*, p. 395). It was only late, if at all, that he was there identified with Tammuz, upon whom, as fourth king of Erech, see Clay, pp. 44 *sqq* The temple, which contained a baetylic stone, is represented on coins (Babelon, *Perses Achéménides*, p. 200, and pl. xxvii, 11 and 12).

343

ὅκως Αἰγύπτιοι ἀποθανόντος Ἄπιος. γυναικῶν
δὲ ὁκόσαι οὐκ ἐθέλουσι ξύρεσθαι, τοιήνδε ζημίην
ἐκτελέουσιν· ἐν μιῇ ἡμέρῃ ἐπὶ πρήσει τῆς ὥρης
ἵστανται· ἡ δὲ ἀγορὴ μούνοισι ξείνοισι παρα-
κέαται, καὶ ὁ μισθὸς ἐς τὴν Ἀφροδίτην θυσίη
γίγνεται.

7   Εἰσὶ δὲ ἔνιοι Βυβλίων οἳ λέγουσι παρὰ σφίσι
τεθάφθαι τὸν Ὄσιριν τὸν Αἰγύπτιον, καὶ τὰ
πένθεα καὶ τὰ ὄργια οὐκ ἐς τὸν Ἄδωνιν ἀλλ' ἐς
τὸν Ὄσιριν πάντα πρήσσεσθαι. ἐρέω δὲ καὶ
ὁκόθεν καὶ τάδε πιστὰ δοκέουσι. κεφαλὴ ἑκάστου ἔτεος ἐξ Αἰγύπτου ἐς τὴν Βύβλον ἀπικνέεται
πλώουσα τὸν μεταξὺ πλόον ἑπτὰ ἡμερέων, καί
μιν οἱ ἄνεμοι φέρουσι θείῃ ναυτιλίῃ· τρέπεται δὲ
οὐδαμά, ἀλλ' ἐς μούνην τὴν Βύβλον ἀπικνέεται.
καὶ ἔστι τὸ σύμπαν θῶυμα. καὶ τοῦτο ἑκάστου
ἔτεος γίγνεται, τὸ καὶ [1] ἐμεῦ παρεόντος ἐν Βύβλῳ
ἐγένετο· καὶ τὴν κεφαλὴν ἐθεησάμην Βυβλίνην.

[1] καὶ τοῦτο——τὸ καὶ N : not in ΓΕ. In both old MSS. the
first hand left a space in which these words were entered
long afterward.

---

[1] Lucian abridges his account of the rites because they
were familiar. I see no reason to suppose that they differed
essentially from the Alexandrian rites as described by
Theocritus (15 end). From him we learn that Adonis
comes to life for but a day, during which he is couched with
the goddess in the temple. Next morning the women carry
him to the sea-shore, and (cf. scholion) commit him to the
waves. Lucian's phrase ἐς τὸν ἠέρα πέμπουσι, which has
been curiously interpreted, is to my mind equivalent to
ἔξω οἰσεῦμες in Theocritus, and the usual ἐκκομίζουσι.

[2] See Frazer i, 36 sqq., and the comment of How and
Wells on Herodotus 1, 199. Note also the apocryphal
Epistle of Jeremiah, 42 ; and on the "hire," Deuteronomy
23, 18.

schaven here hedes as don Egyptyens whan that
Apis is ded.[1] And alle wommen that wole not lette
schaven hem, thei payen this penance, that upon
o day thei profren hem for achat of here beautee;
but the merkat is open to straungers alle only, and
the huyr becometh an offring to Venus.[2]

Natheles, ther ben somme men of Byblos that
seyn Osiris of Egypte lyeth enterred amonges hem,
and the doel and the cerimonyes ben alle made in
mynde of Osiris in stede of Adoon.[3] And I schalle
seye you the cause whi this semeth hem trewe.
Eech yeer an heed cometh from Egypte to Byblos, *head*
that passeth the see betwene in 7 iorneyes, and the
windes dryven it, be governaunce of the Goddes,
and it torneth not asyde in no wyse but cometh all
only to Byblos. And this is hoolyche merveylle. *wholly*
It befalleth everyche yere, and befel that tyme that
I was in Byblos, and I saughe the heed, that is of
Byblos.[4]

[3] Byblos was known to the Egyptians from the time of the
Old Kingdom, and her goddess impressed them deeply. She
was identified with Hathor at least as early as the Middle
Kingdom. and her story contributed to the shaping of the
Isis-Osiris myth. When the coffin of Osiris was thrown into
the Nile by Typhon, it drifted out to sea, and so to Byblos,
where Isis sought and found it (Plutarch, *Isis and Osiris*,
c. 13 *sqq.*; cf. Frazer, ii. 9 *sqq.*, 12, 127; Baudissin, pp.
193 *sqq.*).

[4] The pun signifies that the head was of papyrus, made, no
doubt, of a sort of papier mâché, as in a mummy-case. In
the commentary of Cyril on Isaiah 18 (Migne 70, 441) we
learn, instead, of an earthen pot that contained a letter from
the women of Alexandria to those of Byblos, saying that
Aphrodite had found Adonis. There may be something in
the tale of its drift, for the Nile current sets over to the
Phoenician shore, and it is Nile mud that silts up Phoenician
harbours (cf. H. Guthe, *Palästina*, p. 27).

8 Ἔνι δὲ καὶ ἄλλο θωῦμα ἐν τῇ χώρῃ τῇ Βυβλίῃ.
ποταμὸς ἐκ τοῦ Λιβάνου τοῦ οὔρεος ἐς τὴν ἅλα
ἐκδιδοῖ· οὔνομα τῷ ποταμῷ Ἄδωνις ἐπικέαται.
ὁ δὲ ποταμὸς ἑκάστου ἔτεος αἱμάσσεται καὶ τὴν
χροιὴν ὀλέσας ἐσπίπτει ἐς τὴν θάλασσαν καὶ
φοινίσσει τὸ πολλὸν τοῦ πελάγεος καὶ σημαίνει
τοῖς Βυβλίοις τὰ πένθεα. μυθέονται δὲ ὅτι
ταύτῃσι τῇσι ἡμέρῃσιν ὁ Ἄδωνις ἀνὰ τὸν Λίβανον
τιτρώσκεται, καὶ τὸ αἷμα ἐς τὸ ὕδωρ ἐρχόμενον
ἀλλάσσει τὸν ποταμὸν καὶ τῷ ῥόῳ τὴν ἐπωνυμίην
διδοῖ. ταῦτα μὲν οἱ πολλοὶ λέγουσιν. ἐμοὶ δέ
τις ἀνὴρ Βύβλιος ἀληθέα δοκέων λέγειν ἑτέρην
ἀπηγέετο τοῦ πάθεος αἰτίην. ἔλεγεν δὲ ὧδε· "ὁ
Ἄδωνις ὁ ποταμός, ὦ ξεῖνε, διὰ τοῦ Λιβάνου
ἔρχεται· ὁ δὲ Λίβανος κάρτα ξανθόγεώς ἐστιν.
ἄνεμοι ὦν τρηχέες ἐκείνῃσι τῇσι ἡμέρῃσι ἱστά-
μενοι τὴν γῆν τῷ ποταμῷ ἐπιφέρουσιν ἐοῦσαν ἐς
τὰ μάλιστα μιλτώδεα, ἡ δὲ γῆ μιν αἱμώδεα
τίθησιν· καὶ τοῦδε τοῦ πάθεος οὐ τὸ αἷμα, τὸ
λέγουσιν, ἀλλ' ἡ χώρη αἰτίη." ὁ μέν μοι Βύβλιος
τοσάδε ἀπηγέετο· εἰ δὲ ἀτρεκέως ταῦτα ἔλεγεν,
ἐμοὶ μὲν δοκέει κάρτα θείη καὶ τοῦ ἀνέμου ἡ
συντυχίη.

9 Ἀνέβην δὲ καὶ ἐς τὸν Λίβανον ἐκ Βύβλου,
ὁδὸν ἡμέρης, πυθόμενος αὐτόθι ἀρχαῖον ἱρὸν

---

[1] The Adonis is the present Nahr Ibrahim, a short distance
S. of Byblos. "I have crossed it on Easter day when it was
turbid and ruddy with the rich red sandstone soil from
Lebanon" (C. R. Conder, *Palestine*, p. 206; cf. Frazer i,
225). A similar discoloration of certain unnamed rivers and
springs is implied in the tale of Philo of Byblos that Uranus

And in the londe of Byblos is an other merveylle, a Ryvere goynge out of the Mount Libanon in to the See, the which is cleped Adoon. Everyche yeer it is bebledde and leseth his kyndely hewe, and whan *natural* it falleth in to the See, it maketh mochel therof rede; and so it betokneth the doel to hem of Byblos.[1] For they seyn that in tho dayes Adoon is ywounded up Libanon, and his blod that cometh into the water chaungeth the ryvere and yeveth the streme his name. Thus seyn lewed folk. But I trowe that a man of Byblos spak sothe that devysed me an other cause of the chaunge, seyinge: "The Flom Adoon, o straunger, renneth thorgh Libanon, and erthe of Libanon is right broun. Therfore whan roughe windes that arysen in tho dayes beren the erthe to the ryvere, the erthe, that is ful rody, maketh him blody. So of this chaunge nys not the blod, as they seyn, the resoun, but the lond." He of Byblos devysed me thus; but and al it so be that he spak trewely, yit to me it semeth passing merveyllous that the wind aryseth at the righte tyme.

Also, I went up on Libanon fro Byblos, oon iorneye, be cause I lernede that ther was an old

was mutilated by Cronus at a certain place in the interior near springs and rivers, that his blood flowed into them, and that the place was still pointed out (Müller, *Fr. Hist. Gruec.*, iii, p. 568). Epiphanius (*adv. Haeres.* 51, 30) bears personal witness that at the exact day and hour of the miracle of Cana the water of a spring at Cibyra in Caria used to turn into wine, and on the word of his brothers that the same was true of the river of Gerasa in Arabia. He does not tell us who is his warrant in the case of the Nile, but observes that that is why the natives bottle and set away Nile-water on a certain date. See also Pausanias 4, 35, 9, and Frazer's note.

Ἀφροδίτης ἔμμεναι, τὸ Κινύρης εἴσατο, καὶ εἶδον
τὸ ἱρόν, καὶ ἀρχαῖον ἦν.

Τάδε μέν ἐστι τὰ ἐν τῇ Συρίῃ ἀρχαῖα καὶ
10 μεγάλα ἱρά. τοσούτων δὲ ἐόντων ἐμοὶ δοκέει
οὐδὲν τῶν ἐν τῇ ἱρῇ πόλει μέζον ἔμμεναι οὐδὲ
νηὸς ἄλλος ἁγιώτερος οὐδὲ χώρη ἄλλη ἱροτέρη.
ἔνι δὲ ἐν αὐτῷ καὶ ἔργα πολυτελέα καὶ ἀρχαῖα
ἀναθήματα καὶ πολλὰ θωύματα καὶ ξόανα θεο-
πρεπέα. καὶ θεοὶ δὲ κάρτα αὐτοῖσιν ἐμφανέες·
ἱδρώει γὰρ δὴ ὦν παρὰ σφίσι τὰ ξόανα καὶ
κινέεται καὶ χρησμηγορέει, καὶ βοὴ δὲ πολλάκις
ἐγένετο ἐν τῷ νηῷ κλεισθέντος τοῦ ἱροῦ, καὶ
πολλοὶ ἤκουσαν. ναὶ μὴν καὶ ὄλβου πέρι ἐν
τοῖσιν ἐγὼ οἶδα πρῶτόν ἐστιν· πολλὰ γὰρ
αὐτοῖσιν ἀπικνέεται χρήματα ἔκ τε Ἀραβίης καὶ
Φοινίκων καὶ Βαβυλωνίων καὶ ἄλλα ἐκ Καππα-
δοκίης, τὰ δὲ καὶ Κίλικες φέρουσι, τὰ δὲ καὶ
Ἀσσύριοι. εἶδον δὲ ἐγὼ καὶ τὰ ἐν τῷ νηῷ λάθρῃ
ἀποκέαται, ἐσθῆτα πολλὴν καὶ ἄλλα ὁκόσα ἐς
ἄργυρον ἢ ἐς χρυσὸν ἀποκέκριται. ὁρταὶ μὲν
γὰρ καὶ πανηγύριες οὐδαμοῖσιν ἄλλοισιν ἀνθρώπων
τοσαίδε ἀποδεδέχαται.

11   Ἱστορέοντι δέ μοι ἐτέων πέρι, ὁκόσα τῷ ἱρῷ
ἐστιν, καὶ τὴν θεὸν αὐτοὶ ἥντινα δοκέουσιν,
πολλοὶ λόγοι ἐλέγοντο, τῶν οἱ μὲν ἱροί, οἱ δὲ

---

[1] At Aphaca, between Byblos and Baalbek, at the head
of the Adonis, where Adon was buried and Baalat died of
grief. Down to the fifth century a bright light appearing in
the sky near the temple summoned the worshippers at set
times, and an artificial pond gave omens; offerings were
thrown into it, which sank if the goddess was favourable or
floated if she was adverse (Zosimus i, 58; cf. Socrates 1, 18).
The site is eloquently described by Frazer, i, 28, and pictured

seyntuarye of Venus that Cinyras founded; and I
saughe the temple, and it was old.[1]

Thise ben the olde and grete seyntuaryes in
Surrye. But of hem alle, as I wene, is non gretter
than tho in the Holy Cytee, ne non other temple
mo blessed, ne non other lond holier. Costevouse *costly*
werkes ben therinne, and aunciene offringes, and
manye merveylles, and symulacres in lyknesse of
goddes. Also, the goddes ben apertely reveled unto
hem; for here symulacres sweten and meven and
prophecyen, and ofte tymes hath ben schowtynge
in the temple whan the holy place was under lokke,
and many han herde. Certes, in richesse it is first
amonges alle that I knowe; for thider cometh moche
tresor from Arabye and Phenicye and Babiloyne,
and moche fro Cappadocye, and som Cilicyens
bryngen, and som Assuryens. And I saughe what
hath ben prively put up in the temple, many robes
and other thinges that have ben chosen out as
silver outher gold. And of festes and solempnytees
noon other folk in the world hath apoynted so
many.

Whan I asked how many yeres the seyntuarye
hadde dured, and who thei wenden that here *supposed*
Goddesse were, manye stories weren tolde, both

---

in Perrot-Chipiez, *Hist. de l'Art* iii, fig. 18, opposite p. 56;
for the rock-sculptures in the neighbourhood, to one of which
the description of the goddess in Macrobius (*Saturn.* 1, 21, 5)
refers, see Baudissin, p. 78 and pls. i–iii, and for the ruins of
the temple, destroyed under Constantine but possibly rebuilt
under Julian, Rouvier, *Bulletin Archéologique*, 1900, 169 *sqq.*
Lucian's amusing reticence is by way of parody on Herodotus,
and derives its point from the fact that his reader, knowing
the reputation of the place (Euseb. *Vit. Constant.* 3, 55), is
all agog to hear about it.

ἐμφανέες, οἱ δὲ κάρτα μυθώδεες, καὶ ἄλλοι
βάρβαροι, οἱ μὲν τοῖσιν Ἕλλησιν ὁμολογέοντες·
τοὺς ἐγὼ πάντας μὲν ἐρέω, δέκομαι δὲ οὐδαμά.

12 Οἱ μὲν ὦν πολλοὶ Δευκαλίωνα τὸν Σκύθεα[1] τὸ
ἱρὸν εἵσασθαι λέγουσιν, τοῦτον Δευκαλίωνα ἐπὶ
τοῦ τὸ πολλὸν ὕδωρ ἐγένετο. Δευκαλίωνος δὲ
πέρι λόγον ἐν Ἕλλησιν ἤκουσα, τὸν Ἕλληνες ἐπ'
αὐτῷ λέγουσιν. ὁ δὲ μῦθος ὧδε ἔχει.

Ἥδε ἡ γενεή, οἱ νῦν ἄνθρωποι, οὐ πρῶτοι
ἐγένοντο, ἀλλ' ἐκείνη μὲν ἡ γενεὴ πάντες ὤλοντο,
οὗτοι δὲ γένεος τοῦ δευτέρου εἰσί, τὸ αὖτις ἐκ
Δευκαλίωνος ἐς πληθὺν ἀπίκετο. ἐκείνων δὲ
πέρι τῶν ἀνθρώπων τάδε μυθέονται· ὑβρισταὶ
κάρτα ἐόντες ἀθέμιστα ἔργα ἔπρησσον, οὔτε γὰρ
ὅρκια ἐφύλασσον οὔτε ξείνους ἐδέκοντο οὔτε ἱκε-
τέων ἠνείχοντο, ἀνθ' ὧν σφίσιν ἡ μεγάλη συμφορὴ
ἀπίκετο. αὐτίκα ἡ γῆ πολλὸν ὕδωρ ἐκδιδοῖ καὶ
ὄμβροι μεγάλοι ἐγένοντο καὶ οἱ ποταμοὶ κατέ-
βησαν μέζονες καὶ ἡ θάλασσα ἐπὶ πολλὸν ἀνέβη,
ἐς ὃ πάντα ὕδωρ ἐγένοντο καὶ πάντες ὤλοντο,
Δευκαλίων δὲ μοῦνος ἀνθρώπων ἐλίπετο ἐς
γενεὴν δευτέρην εὐβουλίης τε καὶ τοῦ εὐσεβέος
εἵνεκα. ἡ δέ οἱ σωτηρίη ἥδε ἐγένετο· λάρνακα
μεγάλην, τὴν αὐτὸς εἶχεν, ἐς ταύτην ἐσβιβάσας
παῖδάς τε καὶ γυναῖκας ἑωυτοῦ ἐσέβη· ἐσβαίνοντι
δέ οἱ ἀπίκοντο σύες καὶ ἵπποι καὶ λεόντων γένεα
καὶ ὄφιες καὶ ἄλλα ὁκόσα ἐν γῇ νέμονται, πάντα

---

[1] Σισύθεα Buttmann.

---

[1] Deucalion in the rôle of a Scythian is odd. Hence
Buttmann, rightly recognising that the tale is close akin to

prestes lore and lewede folkes, and verraye fables;
and some weren outlandissche, but othere somme
acordeden to hem of Grece. Alle thise seyinges I
schalle reherce, but I beleve hem not in no kynde.

The more partie seyn, Deucalioun, the Scythe,[1]
founded the seyntuarye—that Deucalioun in the
tyme thereof the grete Flode befel. Of Deucalioun
I have herd a tale amonges Grekes, that thei tellen
in mynde of him; and the storie is of this maner
kynde.

This generacioun, the men of now a dayes, nas not
the firste, but that firste generacioun al perissched,
and thise ben of the seconde generacioun that cam
of Deucalioun and multiplyed eftsones. Of tho
firste men, thei seyn that thei were right felonouse
and didde wikkede dedis, for thei ne kepten not non
othes, ne herberweden no straungers, ne receyveden *harboured*
no fugityves; and for that skylle the grete tribu- *cause*
lacioun cam upon hem. Anon the erthe sent forthe
moche water and grete reynes were made and the
ryveres flowede gretli and the see wex wondur high,
in to tyme that alle thinges weren chaunged to water
and alle men weren dede, outtaken Deucalioun that
was laft unto the seconde generacioun for his gode
conseil and his gode werkes. And his deliveraunce
cam in this wyse. In to a gret arke that he hadde he
putte his children and his wyves, and thanne entrede,
and at entrynge ther camen to him swyn and hors
and lyouns kynd and serpentes and alle bestes that

the Babylonian flood-story, proposed the reading Σισύθεα,
considering Sisythes a possible variant of the name that in
Berossus is Xisouthros. This is tempting, and has been
widely accepted; but the mistake, if there be one, is quite as
likely to be due to Lucian or to his informant as to a scribe.

ἐς ζεύγεα. ὁ δὲ πάντα ἐδέκετο, καί μιν οὐκ
ἐσίνοντο, ἀλλά σφι μεγάλη διόθεν φιλίη ἐγένετο.
καὶ ἐν μιῇ λάρνακι πάντες ἔπλευσαν ἔστε τὸ
ὕδωρ ἐπεκράτεεν. τὰ μὲν Δευκαλίωνος πέρι
Ἕλληνες ἱστορέουσι.

13 Τὸ δὲ ἀπὸ τούτου λέγεται λόγος ὑπὸ τῶν ἐν
τῇ ἱρῇ πόλει μεγάλως ἄξιος θωυμάσαι, ὅτι ἐν
τῇ σφετέρῃ χώρῃ χάσμα μέγα ἐγένετο καὶ τὸ
σύμπαν ὕδωρ κατεδέξατο· Δευκαλίων δέ, ἐπεὶ
τάδε ἐγένετο, βωμούς τε ἔθετο καὶ νηὸν ἐπὶ τῷ
χάσματι Ἥρης ἅγιον ἐστήσατο. ἐγὼ δὲ καὶ τὸ
χάσμα εἶδον, καὶ ἔστιν ὑπὸ τῷ νηῷ κάρτα μικρόν.
εἰ μὲν ὦν πάλαι καὶ μέγα ἐὸν νῦν τοιόνδε ἐγένετο,
οὐκ οἶδα· τὸ δὲ ἐγὼ εἶδον, μικρόν ἐστιν.

Σῆμα δὲ τῆς ἱστορίης τόδε πρήσσουσιν. δὶς
ἑκάστου ἔτεος ἐκ θαλάσσης ὕδωρ ἐς τὸν νηὸν
ἀπικνέεται. φέρουσι δὲ οὐκ ἱρέες μοῦνον, ἀλλὰ
πᾶσα Συρίη καὶ Ἀραβίη, καὶ πέρηθεν τοῦ
Εὐφρήτεω πολλοὶ ἄνθρωποι ἐς θάλασσαν ἔρχονται καὶ πάντες ὕδωρ φέρουσιν, τὸ πρῶτα μὲν ἐν
τῷ νηῷ ἐκχέουσι, μετὰ δὲ ἐς τὸ χάσμα κατέρ-
χεται, καὶ δέκεται τὸ χάσμα μικρὸν ἐὸν ὕδατος
χρῆμα πολλόν. τὰ δὲ ποιέοντες Δευκαλίωνα ἐν
τῷ ἱρῷ τόνδε νόμον θέσθαι λέγουσι συμφορῆς τε
καὶ εὐεργεσίης μνῆμα ἔμμεναι.

---

[1] In spite of Lucian's repeated assurance, the story is more
Semitic than Greek. On the West Semitic origin of the
flood-story, see Clay, where also a translation of the Babylonian tale according to Berossus may be found (p. 82 *sq.*).

[2] At Gezer, not far from Jerusalem, "there is a living
tradition that the waters of the flood burst forth in the
neighbourhood" (Cook, p. 107). Likewise at Athens, within
the enclosure of Olympian Zeus, in the precinct of Olympian

lyven on erthe, two and two. And he resceyvede
hem alle, and thei diden him non harm, but betwene
hem was great charitee fro the goddes, and in oon
arke thei alle seyleden whyl the water prevayled.
So seyn Grekes of Deucalioun.[1]

But of that that sewede, men of the Holy Cytee *followed*
tellen a tale that is worthy of gret merveyle, how
that in here londe opnede a huge hole and resceyvede
alle the water; and whan this happed, Deucalioun
leet maken awteres and leet bylden over the hole a *altars*
temple halowed to Iuno.[2] I saughe the hole, that is
benethe the temple, a right lityl oon. If whilom it
was gret and now is become suche as it is, I wot
neer, but that I saughe is smal.

In tokene of that storie thei don thus. Twyes
eech yeer water cometh fro the See in to the temple.
And not prestes only bryngen it, but al Surrye and
Arabye; and fro beyonden Eufrate gon manye men
to the See and bryngen alle watre, that anon thei
scheden out in the temple, and thanne it goth
adoun in to that hole; and al be it that the hole is
smal, natheles it taketh inne gret plentee of water.
And in doynge thus thei seyn that Deucalioun made
suche ordeynaunce for the seyntuarye in memorie of
that tribulacioun and that benefice.[3]

Earth: "here the ground is cloven to a cubit's width; and
they say that after the deluge which happened in Deucalion's
time the water ran away down this cleft. Every year they
throw into it wheaten meal kneaded with honey" (Pausanias
1, 18, 7, Frazer's translation).

[3] Further details of this rite are given in c. 48. Frazer's
note on Pausanias *l.c.* compares an Athenian Hydrophoria
connected with the memory of the flood; also the annual
water-pouring in the Temple at Jerusalem on the Feast of
Tabernacles. The performance was not simply commemor-
ative; the offering at Athens of meal and honey was

Ὁ μὲν ὦν ἀρχαῖος αὐτοῖσι λόγος ἀμφὶ τοῦ
14 ἱροῦ τοιόσδε ἐστίν. ἄλλοι δὲ Σεμίραμιν τὴν
Βαβυλωνίην, τῆς δὴ πολλὰ ἔργα ἐν τῇ Ἀσίῃ
ἐστίν, ταύτην καὶ τόδε τὸ ἕδος εἵσασθαι νομίζουσιν, οὐκ Ἥρῃ δὲ εἵσασθαι ἀλλὰ μητρὶ ἑωυτῆς,
τῆς Δερκετὼ οὔνομα. Δερκετοῦς δὲ εἶδος ἐν
Φοινίκῃ ἐθεησάμην, θέημα ξένον· ἡμισέη μὲν
γυνή, τὸ δὲ ὁκόσον ἐκ μηρῶν ἐς ἄκρους πόδας
ἰχθύος οὐρὴ ἀποτείνεται. ἡ δὲ ἐν τῇ ἱρῇ πόλει
πᾶσα γυνή ἐστιν, πίστιες δὲ τοῦ λόγου αὐτοῖσιν
οὐ κάρτα ἐμφανέες. ἰχθύας χρῆμα ἱρὸν νομίζουσιν καὶ οὔκοτε ἰχθύων ψαύουσι· καὶ ὄρνιθας

---

chthonic, and so was the water-pouring there (Cleidemus in
Athenaeus 5, p. 410A). At Hieropolis the object was to quell
evil spirits, according to Melito. "But touching Nebo
which is in Mabug, why should I write to you; for lo! all
the priests which are in Mabug know that it is the image of
Orpheus, a Thracian Magus. And Hadran (*i.e.* Hadaranes,
a double of Hadad) is the image of Zaradusht, a Persian
Magus, because both of these Magi practised Magism to a
well which is in a wood in Mabug, in which was an unclean
spirit, and it committed violence and attacked the passage
of every one who was passing by in all that place in which
now the fortress of Mabug is located; and these same Magi
charged Simi, the daughter of Hadad (cf. c. 33), that she
should draw water from the sea, and cast it into the well, in
order that the spirits should not come up," etc. (Cureton,
Spicil. Syr. 44 *sq.*) Early modern travellers have seen sea-
water poured into a brook (Baudissin, *Studien*, ii, p. 181), and
it is perhaps significant that nowadays the Jâns are angry if
water is spilled on the hearth (Baldensperger, *Immovable
East*, p. 85). Cf. Baudissin, p. 437, 3.

[1] A legend of Ascalon made Semiramis the daughter of
Derceto by a Syrian youth with whom Aphrodite (*i.e.*
Astarte) made Derceto fall in love. In her grief and shame,

THE GODDESSE OF SURRYE

Now that is the olde aunciene storie amonges
hem touching to the temple. But othere men
trowen that Semiramys of Babyloyne, of the which
sothely ben manye werkes in Asye, sche made this
foundacioun, and not for Iuno but for hir owne
Moder, that hadde to name Derketoun.[1] And I
beheld the schap of Derketoun in Phenicye, a
straunge merveylle, halfundel womman, but the
tothere half, wel fro thighes to feet, streccheth out
in a fissches tayl.[2] But the ymage in the Holy
Cytee is hoolyche woman, and the tokenes of here
seyinge ben not right certeyn. Thei leven fissches
holy thynge, and thei ne touchen fissche never; and

Derceto destroyed the youth, exposed the daughter, and herself leaped into a pool and was turned into a fish. Semiramis
was miraculously attended by doves until she was discovered
and handed over to Simmas, a royal overseer ; eventually
she married Ninus (Ctesias, quoted by Diodorus Siculus 2, 4).
She was intimately connected with temple traditions at
Hieropolis : two statues of her stood near the temple, with
one of which the story was connected that she had once
tried to usurp the place of the goddess (cc. 39, 40), and some
thought that the "token" of c. 33 represented her.

[2] Cook, p. 30 *sq.* speaks of "various rude and almost
shapeless objects of bronze which have been interpreted,
thanks to a more realistic specimen from the Judaean Tell
Zakariya, as models of an amphibious creature with human
head and the tail of a fish;" and he adds: "a splendid
Carthaginian sarcophagus of a priestess (M. Moore, *Carthage
of the Phoenicians,* frontispiece) represents a woman of strange
beauty with the lower part of the body so draped as to give
it a close resemblance to a fish's tail." But in Hellenistic
times the goddess was almost always represented in human
form. For other stories of her transformation, see W.
Robertson Smith, *Eng. Hist. Rev.*, ii (1887), 303 *sq.* ; Gruppe,
Gr. Mythol. p. 1345 ; for the survival of the belief into
modern times, Nöldeke, *Zeitschr. der Deutsch. Morgenländ.
Gesellsch.* 35, 220.

τοὺς μὲν ἄλλους σιτέονται, περιστερὴν δὲ μούνην
οὐ σιτέονται, ἀλλὰ σφίσιν ἥδε ἱρή. τὰ δὲ γιγνόμενα δοκέει αὐτοῖς ποιέεσθαι Δερκετοῦς καὶ
Σεμιράμιος εἵνεκα, τὸ μὲν ὅτι Δερκετὼ μορφὴν
ἰχθύος ἔχει, τὸ δὲ ὅτι τὸ Σεμιράμιος τέλος ἐς
περιστερὴν ἀπίκετο. ἀλλ' ἐγὼ τὸν μὲν νηὸν ὅτι
Σεμιράμιος ἔργον ἐστὶν τάχα κου δέξομαι· Δερκετοῦς δὲ τὸ ἱρὸν ἔμμεναι οὐδαμὰ πείθομαι, ἐπεὶ
καὶ παρ' Αἰγυπτίων ἐνίοισιν ἰχθύας οὐ σιτέονται,
καὶ τάδε οὐ Δερκετοῖ χαρίζονται.

15   Ἔστιν δὲ καὶ ἄλλος λόγος ἱρός, τὸν ἐγὼ σοφοῦ
ἀνδρὸς ἤκουσα, ὅτι ἡ μὲν θεὴ Ῥέη ἐστίν, τὸ δὲ
ἱρὸν Ἄττεω ποίημα. Ἄττης δὲ γένος μὲν Λυδὸς
ἦν, πρῶτος δὲ τὰ ὄργια τὰ ἐς Ῥέην ἐδιδάξατο. καὶ
τὰ Φρύγες καὶ Λυδοὶ καὶ Σαμόθρακες ἐπιτελέουσιν, Ἄττεω πάντα ἔμαθον. ὡς γάρ μιν ἡ
Ῥέη ἔτεμεν, βίου μὲν ἀνδρηίου ἀπεπαύσατο, μορφὴν δὲ θηλέην ἡμείψατο καὶ ἐσθῆτα γυναικηίην
ἐνεδύσατο καὶ ἐς πᾶσαν γῆν φοιτέων ὄργιά τε
ἐπετέλεεν καὶ τὰ ἔπαθεν ἀπηγέετο καὶ Ῥέην
ἤειδεν. ἐν τοῖσιν καὶ ἐς Συρίην ἀπίκετο. ὡς δὲ
οἱ πέρην Εὐφρήτεω ἄνθρωποι οὔτε αὐτὸν οὔτε

---

[1] See cc. 45, 54, with the notes thereon.

[2] On the transformation of Semiramis into a dove, see
Athenagoras, *Legat. pro Christ.* 76 (Ctesiae Fragmenta ed.
Müller, p. 17); Diodorus 2, 20, 2. Diodorus (2, 4, 6; cf.
Hesychius) says that the name Semiramis is derived from
the word for dove in the Syrian dialect. At all events the
similarity of the Assyrian word summatu (dove) helps to
account for her introduction into these stories (Lehmann-
Haupt, Roscher's *Lexikon*, s.v. *Semiramis*, p. 694).

[3] Lucian's scepticism is unjustified. Pliny (5, 81) and
Strabo (16, p. 785) were better informed. Atargatis is the
Greek version of 'Atar-'ata; Derceto is the Greek version

though of othere foules thei eten alle, the dowve thei ne eten not, but sche is holy, as thei wenen.[1] And thise thinges ben don, thei trowen, be cause of Derketoun and Semiramys, the oon for that Derketoun hath schap of a fissche, and the tother because that atte laste Semiramys tornede to a dowve.[2] But to me, that the temple was bylded of Semiramys peraventure may I graunte; but that it longeth to Derketoun I ne leve not in no kynde.[3] For amonges somme peples of Egypte thei ne eten not fissche, and that is not don for no favour to Derketoun.[4]

Ther is also an other holy storie that I herde from a wys man, how that the goddesse is Cibella and the servys founded of Attis. Attis was a Lydien of kynde, that first leet teche the ceremonyes that longen to Cibella. And alle rytes that Phrygiens and Lydiens and Samothracyens perfourmen, tho rytes lerneden thei of Attis. For whan Cibella gelt him, he cessed to lede the lyf of a man, but chaunged to femele schappe, and did on wommenes clothynge, and goynge to every londe perfourmed ceremonyes and reherced what betyd him and preysed Cibella in songes. Ther with alle cam he to Surrye, and for als moche as the peple beyonden Eufrate resceyvede

of the abbreviated form Tar-'ata. See Cumont in Pauly-Wissowa, *Realencycl.*, under *Atargatis* and *Dea Syria.*

[4] In *Astrology*, c. 7, Lucian tells why these Egyptians do it; it is because they were especially devoted to the sign Pisces. This may be more than a mere jest; Cumont says: "Old totems of Semitic tribes or of Egyptian nomes survived in the form of constellations" (*Astrology and Religion*, p. 116; cf. p. 81). But for the abstaining in Egypt other reasons were given, from Herodotus on (2, 37; cf. Plutarch, *Isis and Osiris*, cc. 7, 32, 72, and for other references, Frazer, *Pausanias* iv, p. 154). See also page 398, note 1.

ὄργια ἐδέκοντο, ἐν τῷδε τῷ χώρῳ τὸ ἱρὸν ἐποιήσατο. σημήια δέ· ἡ θεὸς τὰ πολλὰ ἐς Ῥέην
ἐπικνέεται.[1] λέοντες γάρ μιν φέρουσι καὶ τύμ-
πανον ἔχει καὶ ἐπὶ τῇ κεφαλῇ πυργοφορέει,
ὁκοίην Ῥέην Λυδοὶ ποιέουσιν. ἔλεγεν δὲ καὶ
Γάλλων πέρι, οἵ εἰσιν ἐν τῷ ἱρῷ, ὅτι Γάλλοι
Ἥρῃ μὲν οὐδαμά, Ῥέῃ δὲ τέμνονται καὶ Ἄττεα
μιμέονται.

Τὰ δέ μοι εὐπρεπέα μὲν δοκέει ἔμμεναι, ἀληθέα
δὲ οὔ· ἐπεὶ καὶ τῆς τομῆς ἄλλην αἰτίην ἤκουσα
16 πολλὸν πιστοτέρην. ἁνδάνει δέ μοι ἃ λέγουσιν
τοῦ ἱροῦ πέρι τοῖς Ἕλλησι τὰ πολλὰ ὁμολογέοντες, τὴν μὲν θεὸν Ἥρην δοκέοντες, τὸ δ' ἔργον
Διονύσου τοῦ Σεμέλης ποίημα· καὶ γὰρ δὴ Διόνυσος ἐς Συρίην ἀπίκετο κείνην ὁδὸν τὴν ἦλθεν
ἐς Αἰθιοπίην. καὶ ἔστι πολλὰ ἐν τῷ ἱρῷ Διονύσου ποιητέω σήματα, ἐν τοῖσι καὶ ἐσθῆτες
βάρβαροι καὶ λίθοι Ἰνδοὶ καὶ ἐλεφάντων κέρεα,
τὰ Διόνυσος ἐξ Αἰθιόπων ἤνεικεν, καὶ φαλλοὶ
δὲ ἑστᾶσι ἐν τοῖσι προπυλαίοισι δύο κάρτα μεγάλοι, ἐπὶ τῶν ἐπίγραμμα τοιόνδε ἐπιγέγραπται,
"τούσδε φαλλοὺς Διόνυσος Ἥρῃ μητρυιῇ ἀνέ-

---

[1] ἐπικνέεται Lehmann : ἐπικέεται ΓΕ : ἀπικέεται Ν.

him not, ne his cerimonyes nouther, he founded the
seyntuarye in this place. And for a signe thereof,
the goddesse for the most partie ressembleth Cibella,
for lyouns drawen hir and sche holt a timbre and
bereth tours on hir hede, right as Lydiens formen
Cibella. Also he spak of Galles that ben in the
temple, seyinge that Galles gelden hem and counter-
feten Attis not at alle for no worschipe of Iuno but
for worschipe of Cibella.[1]

But after myn avis, al be it that this is wel
semynge, it is not trewe, for I have herde an other
cause whi thei gelden hem that is a gret dele mo to
beleven. Me liketh what men seyn of the seyntuarye
that acorden fulle wel to hem of Grece, that demen the
goddesse Iuno and the seyntuarye mad of Bachus,
Semeles sone. For withouten doubte Bachus cam
to Surrye in that passage in the whiche he wente to
Ethiope. And in the temple ben manye tokenes of
Bachus foundour, as namely foreyne garnements and
precious stones of Ynde and olifauntes hornes, that
Bachus broght from Ethiope. And two yerdes, or
pileres, stont in the entree, passynge highe, on the
whiche is writen this scripture : " I Bachus presentede

---

[1] This identification of the Dea Syria with Rhea has been
spoken of as a temple-legend. Is it not rather a simple
deduction of Lucian's "wise man," based upon general
resemblance and upon the presence of Galli in both cults?
The resemblance, however, was real, and the identification
was not unusual ; a striking instance is in Bardesanes, where
the Syriac version (Cureton, 31) has Tharatha, the Greek, as
quoted by Eusebius, Rhea. It has been revived by modern
scholars, notably Meyer, and with good reason ; but whether
the "Mother-goddess" is Semitic in origin, as he formerly
held, or non-Semitic (Hittite), as he now argues, is still, it
seems to me, an open question. See note below on Combabus.

θηκα." τὸ ἐμοὶ μέν νυν καὶ τόδε[1] ἀρκέει, ἐρέω
δὲ καὶ ἄλλ' ὅ τι ἐστὶν ἐν τῷ νηῷ Διονύσου ὄργιον.
φαλλοὺς Ἕλληνες Διονύσῳ ἐγείρουσιν, ἐπὶ τῶν
καὶ τοιόνδε τι φέρουσιν, ἄνδρας μικροὺς ἐκ ξύλου
πεποιημένους, μεγάλα αἰδοῖα ἔχοντας· καλέεται
δὲ τάδε νευρόσπαστα. ἔστι δὲ καὶ τόδε ἐν τῷ
ἱρῷ· ἐν δεξιῇ τοῦ νηοῦ κάθηται μικρὸς ἀνὴρ
χάλκεος ἔχων αἰδοῖον μέγα.

17   Τοσάδε μὲν[2] ἀμφὶ τῶν οἰκιστέων τοῦ ἱροῦ
μυθολογέουσιν. ἤδη δὲ ἐρέω καὶ τοῦ νηοῦ πέρι
θέσιός τε ὅκως ἐγένετο καὶ ὅστις μιν ἐποίησατο.
λέγουσι τὸν νηὸν τὸν νῦν ἐόντα μὴ ἔμμεναι τὸν
τὴν ἀρχὴν γεγενημένον,[3] ἀλλ' ἐκεῖνον μὲν κατενε-
χθῆναι χρόνῳ ὕστερον, τὸν δὲ νῦν ἐόντα Στρατονίκης ἔμμεναι ποίημα, γυναικὸς τοῦ Ἀσσυρίων
βασιλέως.

Δοκέει δέ μοι ἡ Στρατονίκη ἐκείνη ἔμμεναι, τῆς
ὁ πρόγονος ἠρήσατο, τὸν ἤλεγξεν τοῦ ἰητροῦ
ἐπινοίη· ὡς γάρ μιν ἡ συμφορὴ κατέλαβεν, ἀμη-

---

[1] τόδε *A.M.H.* : τάδε MSS.
[2] μὲν Fritzsche: μιν MSS.
[3] μὴ—γεγενημένον: first Aldine ; not in MSS. ΓΕ show
lacunae ; the space in Γ is about 31 letters.

---

[1] Phallic pillars, further described below, cc. 28–29. The
inscription is much too pointed to be genuine ; it is a hoax
like that in the *True Story* 1, 7 (vol. i, p. 255). Pillars were
an ordinary feature of Semitic "high places," both of wood
(asherim) and of stone (masseboth) ; see Frazer, *Folklore*, iii,
62 *sqq.* In the case of the asherim I know of no direct
evidence that they were phallic, but the masseboth, many of
which still survive, are sometimes clearly of that nature
(Cook, 14, 28 ; see also le Strange, *Palestine under the Moslems*,
p. 294, for a curious survival of this significance). The
pillars at Hieropolis were made of wood, since cleats were

thise yerdes to Iuno my step moder." [1] Now to
me this sufficeth, natheles I schalle seye you another
thing that is in the temple, that longeth to ceremonyes of Bachus. Men of Grece formen yerdes
for worschipe of Bachus that beren on hem litylle
men made of wode that han grete membres, the
whiche men thei nempnen Popets. [2] And in the
temple ther is this same thing; on the righte syde
sitt a lityl man of brasse that hath a gret membre.

So seyn thei of the foundours of the holy place.
And now I schalle speke of the temple, wher that it
was sett and who that leet bylden it. Men seyn,
the temple that stont now is not that oon the
whiche was bylded atte firste, but that was beten
doun sithen som tyme, and the temple that stont
now is the werk of Stratonice, wyf to the Kyng
of Assurye. [3]

I trowe, this is thilke Stratonice that hir step
sone lovede, that was betraysed by the phisicyens [4]
invencioun. For whan the infortune oppressed him,

nailed to them; they were therefore asherim, and form a
further bond between Ashera (Astarte) and Atargatis
Whether originally phallic or not, they were in Lucian's day
themselves used as "high places"; see below.

[2] See Herodotus 2, 48, on Egyptian puppets (ἀγάλματα
νευρόσπαστα).

[3] Stratonice was daughter of Demetrius Poliorcetes and
wife of Seleucus Nicator; she was subsequently surrendered
by him to his son Antiochus I, Soter, by a former wife,
Apama. The famous tale which follows (in Lucian a pure
digression, but quite in the Herodotean manner) is rehearsed
at length by Plutarch also (*Demetrius* 38). Rohde has made
it pretty clear that, though possible enough (Galen claimed
to have detected hidden love in the same way), as far as
Antiochus is concerned it is fiction (*Griech. Roman*, p. 52.)

[4] Erasistratus (Plutarch, *l.c.*).

χανέων τῷ κακῷ αἰσχρῷ δοκέοντι κατ' ἡσυχίην
ἐνόσεεν, ἔκειτο δὲ ἀλγέων οὐδέν, καὶ οἱ ἥ τε χροιὴ
πάμπαν ἐτρέπετο καὶ τὸ σῶμα δι' ἡμέρης ἐμα-
ραίνετο. ὁ δὲ ἰητρὸς ὡς εἶδέ μιν ἐς οὐδὲν ἐμφανὲς
ἀρρωστέοντα, ἔγνω τὴν νοῦσον ἔρωτα ἔμμεναι.
ἔρωτος δὲ ἀφανέος πολλὰ σημήια, ὀφθαλμοί τε
ἀσθενέες καὶ φωνὴ καὶ χροιὴ καὶ δάκρυα. μαθὼν
δὲ ταῦτα ἐποίεε· χειρὶ μὲν τῇ δεξιῇ εἶχε τοῦ
νεηνίσκου τὴν καρδίην, ἐκάλεε δὲ τοὺς ἀνὰ τὴν
οἰκίην πάντας· ὁ δὲ τῶν μὲν ἄλλων ἐσιόντων
πάντων ἐν ἠρεμίῃ μεγάλῃ ἦν, ὡς δὲ ἡ μητρυιὴ
ἀπίκετο, τήν τε χροιὴν ἠλλάξατο καὶ ἱδρώειν
ἄρξατο καὶ τρόμῳ εἴχετο καὶ ἡ καρδίη ἀνεπάλ-
λετο. τὰ δὲ γιγνόμενα ἐμφανέα τῷ ἰητρῷ τὸν
18 ἔρωτα ἐποίεεν, καί μιν ὧδε ἰήσατο. καλέσας τοῦ
νεηνίσκου τὸν πατέρα κάρτα ὀρρωδέοντα, " Ἥδε
ἡ νοῦσος," ἔφη, " ἣν ὁ παῖς ὅδε ἀρρωστέει, οὐ
νοῦσός ἐστιν, ἀλλὰ ἀδικίη· ὅδε γάρ τοι ἀλγέει
μὲν οὐδέν, ἔρως δέ μιν καὶ φρενοβλαβείη ἔχει.
ἐπιθυμέει δὲ τῶν οὐδαμὰ τεύξεται, φιλέων γυναῖκα ἐμήν, τὴν ἐγὼ οὔτι μετήσομαι." ὁ μὲν
ὦν τοιάδε σοφίῃ ἐψεύδετο. ὁ δὲ αὐτίκα ἐλίσσετο,
" Πρός τε σοφίης καὶ ἰητρικῆς, μή μοι παῖδα
ὀλέσῃς· οὐ γὰρ ἐθέλων ταύτῃ συμφορῇ ἔσχετο,
ἀλλὰ οἱ ἡ νοῦσος ἀεκουσίη. τῷ σὺ μηδαμὰ
ζηλοτυπέων πένθος ἐγείραι πάσῃ βασιληίῃ μηδὲ
ἰητρὸς ἐὼν φόνον προξενέειν[1] ἰητρικῇ." ὁ μὲν
ὧδε ἀγνὼς ἐὼν ἐδέετο. ὁ δέ μιν αὖτις ἀμείβετο,
" Ἀνόσια σπεύδεις γάμον ἐμὸν ἀπαιρεόμενος ἠδὲ
ἰητρὸν ἄνδρα βιώμενος. σὺ δὲ κῶς ἂν αὐτὸς
ἔπρηξας, εἴ τοι σὴν γυναῖκα ἐπόθεεν, ἐμεῦ τάδε

---

[1] προξενέειν Koene, Schaefer: προξενέεις N: lacuna in ΓΕ.

he mighte not susteyne the mysese that semede
him schamful, and so he stille felle into syknesse, *quietly*
and lay withouten ony peyne; and his hewe
chaunged outerly, and his bodye feblede eech
day. But whan the phisicyen saughe that he
was wayk withouten pleyne cause, he iugged that
the syknesse was love. For of derne love ther *secret*
ben manye signes, as waike eyen, voyce, hewe,
teeres. And whan that he perceyved it, he did
thus. With his righte honde he kepte the yonge
mannes herte, and thanne he sent after all tho that
weren in the house. And whan everyche of the
othere entrede, this was in gret ese, but whan his
step moder cam, he chaunged his hewe and swatte
and schoke and his herte stirte. Thise thinges *leaped*
scheweden his love to the phisicyen, that helede
him thus. After that he hadde clepede the yonge
mannes fader, that was sor adrad, "This syknesse,"
quod he, "wherof thy child is wayk nis not syknesse
but synne, for verrayly he soffreth of no peyn, but
of love and wodenesse. And he coveyteth that *frenzy*
he may not have in no wyse, lovynge my wyf
that I wil not forgon." So that oon lyde in gyle.
And anon that other besoghte him: "Be thy
conynge and thy phisik, destroie me not my sone;
for he is not in this cas of his owne wille but hath
the syknesse mawgree himself. Therfore do thou not
thorghe despyt make sorwe in alle the rewme, ne
thou that art phisicyen brynge manslaughtre in to
phisik." Thus preyde he, al unwar. And that
oon answerde: "Thou forthrest wykked dedis,
revynge me from my mariage and destreyninge a
pore leche. What woldestow thiself have don and
he coveytede thy wyf, thou that axest suche bones *boons*

δεόμενος ; " ὁ δὲ πρὸς τάδε ἔλεγεν ὡς οὐδ' αὐτὸς
ἄν κοτε γυναικὸς ἐφείσατο οὐδὲ παιδὶ σωτηρίης
ἐφθόνεεν, εἰ καί τι μητρυιῆς ἐπεθύμεεν· οὐ γὰρ
ὁμοίην συμφορὴν ἔμμεναι γαμετὴν ἢ παῖδα ὀλέσαι.
ὡς δὲ τάδε ὁ ἰητρὸς ἤκουσεν, " Τί τοι," ἔφη, " ἐμὲ
λίσσεαι ; καὶ γάρ τοι σὴν γυναῖκα ποθέει· τὰ δὲ
ἐγὼ ἔλεγον πάντα ἔην ψεύδεα." πείθεται μὲν
τουτέοισι, καὶ τῷ μὲν παιδὶ λείπει καὶ γυναῖκα καὶ
βασιληίην, αὐτὸς δὲ ἐς τὴν Βαβυλωνίην χώρην
ἀπίκετο καὶ πόλιν ἐπὶ τῷ Εὐφρήτῃ ἐπώνυμον
ἑωυτοῦ ἐποιήσατο, ἔνθα οἱ καὶ ἡ τελευτὴ ἐγένετο.
ὧδε μὲν ὁ ἰητρὸς ἔρωτα ἔγνω τε καὶ ἰήσατο.

19   Ἥδε δὴ ὦν ἡ Στρατονίκη ἔτι τῷ προτέρῳ
ἀνδρὶ συνοικέουσα ὄναρ τοιόνδε ἐθεήσατο, ὡς
μιν ἡ Ἥρη ἐκέλευεν ἐγεῖραί οἱ τὸν ἐν τῇ ἱρῇ
πόλει νηόν, εἰ δὲ ἀπειθέοι, πολλά οἱ καὶ κακὰ
ἀπείλεεν. ἡ δὲ τὰ μὲν πρῶτα οὐδεμίαν ὥρην
ἐποιέετο· μετὰ δέ, ὥς μιν μεγάλη νοῦσος ἔλαβεν,
τῷ τε ἀνδρὶ τὴν ὄψιν ἀπηγήσατο καὶ τὴν Ἥρην
ἱλάσκετο καὶ στήσειν τὸν νηὸν ὑπεδέξατο. καὶ
αὐτίκα ὑγιέα γενομένην ὁ ἀνὴρ ἐς τὴν ἱρὴν πόλιν
ἔπεμπε, σὺν δὲ οἱ καὶ χρήματα καὶ στρατιὴν πολλήν, τοὺς μὲν οἰκοδομέειν, τοὺς δὲ καὶ τοῦ ἀσφαλέος
εἵνεκα. καλέσας δέ τινα τῶν ἑωυτοῦ φίλων, νεηνίην

---

[1] Compare the famous story in Herodotus (3, 119) of the
wife of Intaphrenes, who preferred brother to husband and
sons.

[2] The known facts are that Seleucus made Antiochus
joint-ruler in 293 B.C. ; that the marriage of Stratonice to
Antiochus may have taken place at that time, but the date
is not known ; and that in 281, on becoming master of the
whole realm of Alexander through the defeat of Lysimachus,
he planned to entrust, and perhaps actually did entrust, all

of me?" Therwith he replyede that he him self
wolde never have ben ialous over his wyf ne grucched *be-*
his sone deliveraunce, if so be he hadde coveyted his *grudged*
step moder; for it was not the lyke infortune to
lese a wyf as a sone.[1]   And whan the phisicien herde
that, "Wherfore than," quod he, "dostow beseche
me? Parfey, he loveth thy wyf, and alle that I
seyde was fausse!"   Than was the fader over-
comen, and yold bothe wyf and rewme to his sone, *realm*
and goyinge himself to the contree of Babyloyne leet
make a cytee nyghe Eufrate that was cleped after
his owne name, ther as his dethe befel.[2]   Thus did
the phisicien bothe knowe and hele love.

Now, I seye you, whyl yit that Stratonice duellede
with her formere housbond, hir mette a dreme how
that Iuno bade hir to bylde the temple for hir in the
Holy Cytee, and if sche sholde not obeye, sche
manaced hir with manye harmes. Atte first, sche *note*
ne took no fors of it; but after, whan a grete sykness
hent hir, sche told the dreme to hir housbond and
enforced hir to apayen Iuno, and behight to bylde *appease*
the temple.   Anon sche becam hool, and thanne hir *promised*
housbond wolde sende hir to the Holy Cytee, and
with hir a gret tresor and a gret hoost, some for to
bylden and other some for here seurtee. Therfore
he sompned oon of his frendes, a right fayr yong man

Asia to his son, intending himself to assume the throne
of Macedonia. But within a few months he was assassinated
by Ptolemy Ceraunus near Lysimachia in Thrace. He built
many cities named after him; this Seleucia, 15 miles below
Baghdad, is generally called "on the Tigris," but it lay
between the two rivers, which at that point are only 25
miles apart, and the canal Naarmalcha, connecting the
Euphrates with the Tigris, flowed by it.

κάρτα καλόν, τῷ οὔνομα ἦν Κομβάβος, "Ἐγώ
τοι," ἔφη, "ὦ Κομβάβε, ἐσθλὸν ἐόντα φιλέω
τε μάλιστα φίλων ἐμῶν καὶ πάμπαν ἐπαινέω
σοφίης τε καὶ εὐνοίης τῆς ἐς ἡμέας, ἣν δὴ
ἐπεδέξαο. νῦν δέ μοι χρειὼ μεγάλης πίστιος,
τῷ σε θέλω γυναικὶ ἐμῇ ἑσπόμενον ἔργον τέ
μοι ἐπιτελέσαι καὶ ἱρὰ τελέσαι καὶ στρατιῆς
ἐπικρατέειν· σοὶ δὲ ἀπικομένῳ ἐξ ἡμέων τιμὴ
μεγάλη ἔσσεται."

Πρὸς τάδε ὁ Κομβάβος αὐτίκα λίσσετο πολλὰ
λιπαρέων μή μιν ἐκπέμπειν μηδὲ πιστεύειν οἱ
τὰ πολλὸν ἑωυτοῦ μέζονα χρήματα καὶ γυναῖκα
καὶ ἔργον ἱρόν. τὰ δὲ ὀρρώδεεν μή κοτέ οἱ ζηλο-
τυπίη χρόνῳ ὑστέρῳ ἐς τὴν Στρατονίκην γένοιτο,
20 τὴν μοῦνος ἀπάξειν ἔμελλεν. ὡς δὲ οὐδαμὰ ἐπεί-
θετο, ὁ δὲ ἱκεσίης δευτέρης ἅπτεται δοῦναί οἱ χρόνον
ἑπτὰ ἡμερέων, μετὰ δὲ ἀποστεῖλαί μιν τελέσαντά
τι τῶν μάλιστα ἐδέετο. τυχὼν δὲ ῥηιδίως, ἐς
τὸν ἑωυτοῦ οἶκον ἀπικνέεται καὶ πεσὼν χαμᾶζε
τοιάδε ὠδύρετο· "Ὦ δείλαιος, τί μοι ταύτης τῆς
πίστιος; τί δέ μοι ὁδοῦ, τῆς τέλος ἤδη δέρκομαι;
νέος μὲν ἐγὼ καὶ γυναικὶ καλῇ ἕψομαι. τὸ δέ
μοι μεγάλη συμφορὴ ἔσσεται, εἰ μὴ ἔγωγε πᾶσαν

---

[1] The name Kombabos, which does not occur elsewhere in
Greek, has been identified as that of the opponent of
Gilgamesh in the Gilgamesh-Epic, Ḫu(m)-ba-ba (Schrader-
Zimmern, p. 570, and note 2). Clay has shown (pp. 49–53)
that this name is not Elamite, but Amorite or West Semitic;
he holds that it was borne by a historical personage who
lived in a cedar district of the West and humiliated Babylonia at the time of Gilgamesh, about 4000 B.C. However
that may be, Kombabos is Ḫumbaba, and in this story,
which is the temple-legend, the name of Kombabos is the

that highte Combabe,[1] and seyde : " For thou art
noble, Daun Combabe, I love thee most of alle mine
frendes, and I preyse thee gretli for thy coninge and
for thy gode wille to me, that thou hast discovered
beforn. And now me nedeth of grete feyth,
wherfore I wole that thou folwe my wyf, for to
acomplisshe the werke in my name, and to perfourme the sacrifises, and to reule the hoost ; and
whan thou retornest thou schalt gete highe worschipe
fro me."

Therwith anon Combabe gan preye and beseche
him ful besily that he scholde not send him forth ne
betaken him nouther that tresor, that was moche to *entrust*
gret for him, ne his wyf, ne the holy werk.   For he
was adrad lest that ialousie scholde assayle him
afterwardes as touching to Stratonice, that he moste
lede forthe allone.   But sithe the kyng wolde not
herknen in no kynde, he assayde an other requeste,
for to graunte him seven dayes space, and than sende
him forth, whan he hadde don a thing thereof he
hadde most nede.   And whan he obteyned this
bone lightely, he wente to his owne house and caste
himself adoun and pleyned right so : "Allas wrecche,
what have I to don with this feythe, what have I to
don with this viage, whereof I seighe now the ende ?
I am yong, and schal folwen a fayre womman.   This
schalle be gret meschief to me, but if I putte awey

significant part ; Stratonice has taken the place of an earlier
female. I believe her immediate predecessor was Semiramis,
from Ammianus Marcellinus, 14, 6, 17, and her general
connection with this site ; she in her turn probably ousted an
earlier Sima or Ata, with whom Kombabos may have been
brought into connection through building or rebuilding the
temple (cf. Clay, p. 51, note 22).

αἰτίην κακοῦ ἀποθήσομαι· τῷ με χρῆν μέγα
ἔργον ἀποτελέσαι, τό μοι πάντα φόβον ἰήσεται."

Τάδε εἰπὼν ἀτελέα ἑωυτὸν ἐποίεεν, καὶ ταμὼν
τὰ αἰδοῖα ἐς ἀγγήιον μικρὸν κατέθετο σμύρνῃ
τε ἅμα καὶ μέλιτι καὶ ἄλλοισι θυώμασι· καὶ
ἔπειτα σφρηγῖδι τὴν ἐφόρεε σημηνάμενος τὸ
τρῶμα ἰῆτο. μετὰ δέ, ὥς μιν ὁδοιπορέειν ἐδόκεεν,
ἀπικόμενος ἐς τὸν βασιλέα πολλῶν παρεόντων
διδοῖ τε ἅμα τὸ ἀγγήιον καὶ λέγει ὧδε· " Ὦ
δέσποτα, τόδε μοι μέγα κειμήλιον ἐν τοῖσι
οἰκείοισι ἀπεκέατο, τὸ ἐγὼ κάρτα ἐπόθεον· νῦν δὲ
ἐπεὶ μεγάλην ὁδὸν ἔρχομαι, παρὰ σοὶ τόδε θήσομαι.
σὺ δέ μοι ἀσφαλέως ἔχειν· τόδε γάρ μοι χρυσοῦ
βέλτερον, τόδε μοι ψυχῆς ἐμῆς ἀντάξιον. εὖτ'
ἂν δὲ ἀπίκωμαι, σόον αὖτις ἀποίσομαι." ὁ δὲ
δεξάμενος ἑτέρῃ σφρηγῖδι ἐσημαίνετο καὶ τοῖσι
ταμίῃσι φρουρέειν ἐνετείλατο.

21   Κομβάβος μέν νυν τὸ ἀπὸ τοῦδε ἀσφαλέα
ὁδὸν ἤνυεν· ἀπικόμενοι δὲ ἐς τὴν ἱρὴν πόλιν
σπουδῇ τὸν νηὸν οἰκοδόμεον καὶ σφίσι τρία ἔτεα
ἐν τῷ ἔργῳ ἐξεγένετο, ἐν τοῖσι ἀπέβαινε τάπερ
ὁ Κομβάβος ὀρρώδεεν. ἡ Στρατονίκη γὰρ χρόνον
ἐπὶ πολλὸν συνόντα μιν ποθέειν ἄρχετο, μετὰ δέ
οἱ καὶ κάρτα ἐπεμήνατο. καὶ λέγουσιν οἱ ἐν τῇ
ἱρῇ πόλει τὴν Ἥρην τουτέων αἰτίην ἐθέλουσαν
γενέσθαι, Κομβάβον ἐσθλὸν μὲν ἐόντα λαθέειν
μηδαμά, Στρατονίκην δὲ τίσασθαι, ὅτι οὐ ῥηιδίως
τὸν νηὸν ὑπέσχετο.

22   Ἡ δὲ τὰ μὲν πρῶτα ἐσωφρόνεεν καὶ τὴν νοῦσον
ἔκρυπτεν· ὡς δέ οἱ τὸ κακὸν μέζον ἡσυχίης ἐγένετο,
ἐς ἐμφανὲς ἐτρύχετο κλαίεσκέν τε δι᾽ ἡμέρης καὶ
Κομβάβον ἀνεκαλέετο καί οἱ πάντα Κομβάβος

al cause of evylle ; therfore most I perfourme a gret
dede that schal hele me of alle fere."

Thus he seyde, and thanne he marrede him self ;
and whan he hadde kutte offe his genitours he put
hem into a lityl pot, and bawme with alle, and hony
and othere thinges of swete smelle. Thanne he
selede it with a signet that he bar, and helede his
wounde. And after, whan him wel semede for to
don iorneye, goynge to the kyng, beforn manye men
that ther weren he toke him the pot, seyinge thus : *gave*
" O sire, this grete tresor I was wont for to kepe
prevely, and I lovede it wel ; but now, for als moche
as I schal gon a fer weye, I wole betaken it to you.
Kepeth it sikkerly ; for this to me is bettre than
gold, this to me is als dereworth as my lyf. Whan
I retorne, I schal bere it home ayen saf and sound."
So the kyng resceyved it and seelede it with an
other signet and bad his stywardes for to kepen it
curyously.

Than Combabe mad his weye safly ; and whan thei
were comen to the Holy Cytee thei gan bylde the
temple besily, and thei spenten 3 yeres in the werk,
and in tho yeres that Combabe dredde befel. For
in companyinge with him a gret whyl Stratonice
began for to love him, and thanne sche wex right
wode over him. Men of the Holy Cytee seyn that
Iuno was voluntarie cause thereof, to the entente
that Combabes godeness scholde not lye hidde and
Stratonice scholde ben punissched be cause that
sche ne behight not the temple buxomly. *readily*

Atte firste sche was mesurable and hyd hir
maladye ; but whan as hir miseyse becam to gret
for pees, sche sorwede openly and wepte everyche
day, and cryde on the name of Combabe, and Com-

ἦν. τέλος δὲ ἀμηχανέουσα τῇ συμφορῇ εὐπρεπέα
ἱκεσίην ἐδίζητο. ἄλλῳ μὲν ὦν τὸν ἔρωτα ὁμο-
λογέειν ἐφυλάσσετο, αὐτὴ δὲ ἐπιχειρέειν αἰδέετο.[1]
ἐπινοέει ὦν τοιάδε, οἴνῳ ἑωυτὴν μεθύσασα ἐς
λόγους οἱ ἐλθεῖν. ἄμα δὲ οἴνῳ ἐσιόντι παρρησίη
τε ἐσέρχεται καὶ ἡ ἀποτυχίη οὐ κάρτα αἰσχρή,
ἀλλὰ τῶν πρησσομένων ἔκαστα ἐς ἀγνοίην
ἀναχωρέει.

Ὡς δέ οἱ ἐδόκεε, καὶ ἐποίεε ταῦτα. καὶ ἐπεὶ
ἐκ δείπνου ἐγένοντο, ἀπικομένη ἐς τὰ οἰκεῖα ἐν
τοῖσι Κομβάβος αὐλίζετο, λίσσετό τε καὶ γούνων
ἅπτετο καὶ τὸν ἔρωτα ὡμολόγεεν. ὁ δὲ τόν τε
λόγον ἀπηνέως ἀπεδέκετο καὶ τὸ ἔργον ἀναίνετο
καὶ οἱ τὴν μέθην ἐπεκάλεεν. ἀπειλούσης δὲ
μέγα τι κακὸν ἑωυτὴν ἐργάσασθαι, δείσας πάντα
οἱ λόγον ἔφηνεν καὶ πᾶσαν τὴν ἑωυτοῦ πάθην
ἀπηγήσατο καὶ τὸ ἔργον ἐς ἐμφανὲς ἤνεικεν.
ἰδοῦσα δὲ ἡ Στρατονίκη τὰ οὔποτε ἔλπετο, μανίης
μὲν ἐκείνης ἔσχετο, ἔρωτος δὲ οὐδαμὰ ἐλήθετο,
ἀλλὰ πάντα οἱ συνεοῦσα ταύτην παραμυθίην
ἐποιέετο ἔρωτος ἀπρήκτοιο. ἔστιν ὁ ἔρως οὗτος
ἐν τῇ ἱρῇ πόλει καὶ ἔτι νῦν γίγνεται· γυναῖκες
Γάλλων ἐπιθυμέουσι καὶ γυναιξὶ Γάλλοι ἐπιμαί-
νονται, ζηλοτυπέει δὲ οὐδείς, ἀλλὰ σφίσι τὸ
χρῆμα κάρτα ἱρὸν νομίζουσιν.

23   Τὰ δ' ὦν ἐν τῇ ἱρῇ πόλει ἀμφὶ τὴν Στρατονίκην οὐδαμὰ τὸν βασιλέα λέληθεν, ἀλλὰ
πολλοὶ ἀπικνεόμενοι κατηγόρεον καὶ τὰ γιγνόμενα ἀπηγέοντο. ἐπὶ τοῖσι περιαλγέων ἐξ
ἀτελέος τοῦ ἔργου Κομβάβον μετεκάλεεν. ἄλλοι

---

[1] αἰδέετο Lehmann : ἐδέετο Γ, ἠδέετο N.

babe was alle the worlde to hir. And fynally, for
sche ne mighte not susteyne suche adversitee, sche
soughte a wel semynge peticioun. Now sche was
war for to avowen hir love to ony other, yit sche
hadde scham for to assayen ought hirself. Therfore
sche bethoghte hir of this devys, that sche scholde
make hirself dronke with wyn and thanne speke
with him; for what tyme wyn cometh inne, boldness
of speche cometh inne with alle, and disconfiture
nys not over schamful, but all that is don passeth
into foryetynge. *forget-*
fulness

Right as hir thoghte, right so sche didde. For
aftre mete sche wente to the house wherin Combabe
was logged, and besoghte him and embraced his
knees and avowed hir love. But he resceyved hir
wordes rudeliche, and wolde not assente to the dede,
and reprevede hir of dronkenesse. But whan sche
made manace to don hirself som gret harm, thanne
for fere he told hir alle the storie and descryved al
his owne cas and discovered his doynge. And
whan Stratonice saughe that hir ne thoghte never
to seen, sche stente of hir wodenesse, yit sche forgat *desisted*
not at alle of hir love, but companyed with him *from*
alle weyes and in that gyse solacede the love, therin
sche mighte not speden. That maner love abydeth
yit in the Holy Cytee, and is mad now a dayes;
wommen coveyten Galles and Galles wexen wode
for love of wommen; natheles is no man ialous, but
hem thenketh this thing right holy.

Now that that had happened in the Holy Cytee
touching Stratonice scaped not the kyng in no
kynde, but manye that retorneden acuseden hem
and reherceden here doynges; wherfore the kyng
was grevously troubled and sompnede Combabe fro

δὲ λέγουσι λόγον οὔτι ἀληθέα, τὴν Στρατονίκην,
ἐπειδὴ ἀπέτυχε τῶν ἐδέετο, αὐτὴν γράψασαν ἐς
τὸν ἄνδρα τοῦ Κομβάβου κατηγορέειν πείρην οἱ ἐπι-
καλέουσαν, καὶ τὸ Ἕλληνες Σθενεβοίης πέρι λέγουσι καὶ Φαίδρης τῆς Κνωσσίης, ταυτὶ καὶ
Ἀσσύριοι ἐς Στρατονίκην μυθολογέουσιν. ἐγὼ
μέν νυν οὐδὲ Σθενεβοίην πείθομαι οὐδὲ Φαίδρην
τοιάδε ἐπιτελέσαι, εἰ τὸν Ἱππόλυτον ἀτρεκέως
ἐπόθεε Φαίδρη. ἀλλὰ τὰ μὲν ἐχέτω ὅκως καὶ
ἐγένετο.

24   Ὡς δὲ ἡ ἀγγελίη ἐς τὴν ἱρὴν πόλιν ἀπίκετο
ἔγνω τε ὁ Κομβάβος τὴν αἰτίην, θαρσέων τε
ἦεν, ὅτι οἱ ἡ ἀπολογίη οἴκοι ἐλείπετο, καί μιν
ἐλθόντα ὁ βασιλεὺς αὐτίκα μὲν ἔδησέν τε καὶ
ἐν φρουρῇ εἶχεν· μετὰ δέ, παρεόντων οἱ τῶν
φίλων οἳ καὶ τότε πεμπομένῳ τῷ Κομβάβῳ
παρεγένοντο, παραγαγὼν ἐς μέσον κατηγορέειν
ἄρχετο καί οἱ μοιχείην τε καὶ ἀκολασίην προΰ-
φερεν· κάρτα δὲ δεινοπαθέων πίστιν τε καὶ
φιλίην ἀνεκαλέετο, λέγων τρισσὰ Κομβάβον
ἀδικέειν μοιχόν τε ἐόντα καὶ ἐς πίστιν ὑβρίσαντα
καὶ ἐς θεὸν ἀσεβέοντα, τῆς ἐν τῷ ἔργῳ τοιάδε
ἔπρηξεν. πολλοὶ δὲ παρεστεῶτες ἤλεγχον ὅτι
ἀναφανδὸν σφέας ἀλλήλοισι συνεόντας εἶδον.
πᾶσιν δὲ τέλος ἐδόκεεν αὐτίκα θνήσκειν Κομβάβον θανάτου ἄξια ἐργασμένον.

25   Ὁ δὲ τέως μὲν ἑστήκεεν λέγων οὐδέν· ἐπεὶ δὲ
ἤδη ἐς τὸν φόνον ἤγετο, φθέγξατό τε καὶ τὸ

the werk or it was finissched.   Othere men seyn not
sooth, that whan Stratonice fayled of hir purpos,
sche hir self wroot lettres to hir housbond and
acused Combabe, blamynge him of assayinge hir.
Right as men of Grece seyn of Steneboye and of
Fedre Cnossien, right so seyn Assuriens of Stratonice.[1]   Now to me, I ne beleve not that Steneboye
dide no suche thing, ne Fedre nouther, if Fedre
trewely lovede Ypolite.   But lat tho thinges worth *go*
right as thei weren.[2]

Whan the tidinges were come to the Holy Cytee,
and Combabe lernede the acusaccioun, he wente
boldely, for because he had laft his answere at home.
And at arryvinge, anon the kyng bond him and
kepte him in prisoun ; and after, whan his frendes
there weren that there weren beforn, whan Combabe
was sent forth, he ladde him in presence and began
for to blamen him, reprevinge him of avowtrie and
vileinye ; and in sore bitternesse of herte he putte
him in remembraunce of feythe and frendschipe,
seyinge that Combabe didde 3 fold wrong be cause
he was avowtrer and brak feyth and synned ayeyns
the goddesse in whoos servys that he so wroughte.
And manye stode forth and made witnessing that
thei saughen hem companye togider openly.   And
atte laste alle demeden that Combabe scholde dye
right anon, for his dedis disserveden dethe.

In this tyme he stondynge seyde noght.   But
whan thei wolde leden him to his dethe, he spak,

[1] The story of Joseph and his master's wife (Genesis 39)
would be in this instance a parallel more apt.   And with
both compare the scorning of Ishtar by Gilgamesh in the
Epic (Schrader-Zimmern, p. 571 *sq.*).

[2] This sentence parodies Herodotus 2, 28 : ταῦτα μέν νυν
ἔστω ὡς ἔστι τε καὶ ὡς ἀρχὴν ἐγένετο, and similar transitions.

κειμήλιον αἴτεε,[1] λέγων ὡς ἀναιρέει μιν οὐχ
ὕβριος οὐδὲ γάμων εἵνεκα, ἀλλὰ ἐκείνων ἐπιθυ-
μέων τά οἱ ἀπιὼν παρεθήκατο. πρὸς τάδε ὁ
βασιλεὺς καλέσας τὸν ταμίην ἐκέλευεν ἐνεῖκαι
τά οἱ φρουρέειν ἔδωκε· ὡς δὲ ἤνεικεν, λύσας
τὴν σφρηγῖδα ὁ Κομβάβος τά τε ἐνεόντα ἐπέ-
δειξεν καὶ ἑωυτὸν ὁκοῖα ἐπεπόνθεεν, ἔλεξέ τε,
"Ὦ βασιλεῦ, τάδε τοι ἐγὼ ὀρρωδέων, εὖτέ με
ταύτην ὁδὸν ἔπεμπες, ἀέκων ἦον· καὶ ἐπεί με
ἀναγκαίη μεγάλη ἐκ σέο κατέλαβεν, τοιάδε
ἐπετέλεσα, ἐσθλὰ μὲν ἐς δεσπότεα, ἐμοὶ δὲ οὐκ
εὐτυχέα. τοιόσδε μέντοι ἐὼν ἀνδρὸς ἐπ' ἀδικίην
ἐγκαλέομαι."

26 Ὁ δὲ πρὸς τάδε ἀμβώσας[2] περιέβαλέν τέ μιν
καὶ δακρύων ἅμα ἔλεγεν, "Ὦ Κομβάβε, τί μέγα
κακὸν εἰργάσαο; τί δὲ σεωυτὸν οὕτως ἀεικέλιον
ἔργον μοῦνος ἀνδρῶν[3] ἔπρηξας; τὰ οὐ πάμπαν
ἐπαινέω. ὦ σχέτλιε, ὃς τοιάδε ἔτλης, οἷα μήτε
σὲ παθέειν μήτ' ἐμὲ ἰδέσθαι ὤφελεν· οὐ γάρ
μοι ταύτης ἀπολογίης ἔδεεν. ἀλλ' ἐπεὶ δαίμων
τοιάδε ἤθελεν, πρῶτα μέν σοι τίσις ἐξ ἡμέων
ἔσσεται, αὐτέων συκοφαντέων ὁ θάνατος, μετὰ
δὲ μεγάλη δωρεὴ ἀπίξεται χρυσός τε πολλὸς
καὶ ἄργυρος ἄπλετος καὶ ἐσθῆτες Ἀσσύριαι καὶ
ἵπποι βασιλήιοι. ἀπίξεαι δὲ παρ' ἡμέας ἄνευ
ἐσαγγελέος οὐδέ τις ἀπέρξει σε ἡμετέρης ὄψιος,
οὐδ' ἢν γυναικὶ ἅμα εὐνάζωμαι." τάδε εἶπέν τε
ἅμα καὶ ἐποίεεν· καὶ οἱ μὲν αὐτίκα ἐς φόνον
ἤγοντο, τῷ δὲ τὰ δῶρα ἐδέδοτο καὶ ἡ φιλίη

---

[1] αἴτεε Koene: ἀὐτεε ΓΕ, ἄτεε Ν.
[2] ἀμβώσας Valckenaer: θαμβώσας MSS.
[3] οὕτως—ἀνδρων Ν: lacuna in ΓΕ, in which the supplement
(a conjecture) has been entered by a late hand.

and requered that tresor, seyinge, he wolde sleen him, not for no vileinye ne avowtrie, but coveytinge tho thinges that in goynge he hadde betoken him. Thanne the kyng called his styward and bad him brynge what hadde ben goven him for to kepe ; and whan he broght it, Combabe brak the seel and schewed what was with inne and what he himself hadde soffred. And he seyde : " O Kyng, for I was adrad of this whan ye wolde sende me on this weye, therfore me was loth to gon ; and whan ye gretly con-streyned me, I wroghte this maner dede, that is gode for my maistre but not wel for me. Natheles, I that am such as ye seen am reprevede of a mannes synne."

At this seyinge that other youled and toke him in armes and wepynge seyde : " O Combabe, wherfore hastow wrought gret mescheef ? Wherfore hastow don thiself suche a despyt that never yit no man ne sayde ? I preyse this not at alle. O herde herte, that wast hardy for to don suche thinges, that I wolde thou hadde neer soffred ne I neer seen ! Me wantede not this answere. But for als moche as it was goddes wille, first shaltow han vengeaunce of oure grace, the dethe of thi false chalengeres hem self, and after schal comen a gret yifte, moche gold and gret plentee silver and Assuriene clothes and rialle destreres. And thou shalt come before me withouten that ony man presente thee, and noon schalle lette thee fro sight of me, thoghe I be abedde with my wyf." [1] Right as he seyde, right so he didde. Tho weren ladde to dethe anon, but to him the yiftes were goven and grettere frendschipe

royal chargers

---

[1] A plain reminiscence of Herodotus 3, 84 and 118, with the significant change of ἢν μὴ γυναικί to οὐδ' ἢν γυναικί (Allinson).

μέζων ἐγεγόνεεν. ἐδόκεεν δὲ οὐδεὶς ἔτι Ἀσσυρίων
Κομβάβῳ σοφίην καὶ εὐδαιμονίην εἴκελος.

Μετὰ δὲ αἰτησάμενος ἐκτελέσαι τὰ λείποντα
τῷ νηῷ—ἀτελέα γάρ μιν ἀπολελοίπεεν—αὖτις
ἐπέμπετο, καὶ τόν τε νηὸν ἐξετέλεσε καὶ τὸ
λοιπὸν αὐτοῦ ἔμενεν. ἔδωκεν δέ οἱ βασιλεὺς
ἀρετῆς τε καὶ εὐεργεσίης εἵνεκα ἐν τῷ ἱρῷ ἑστάναι
χάλκεον· καὶ ἔτι ἐς τιμὴν ἐν τῷ ἱρῷ Κομβάβος
χάλκεος, Ἑρμοκλέος τοῦ Ῥοδίου ποίημα, μορφὴν
μὲν ὁκοίη γυνή, ἐσθῆτα δὲ ἀνδρηίην ἔχει.

Λέγεται δὲ τῶν φίλων τοὺς μάλιστά οἱ εὐνο-
έοντας ἐς παραμυθίην τοῦ πάθεος κοινωνίην
ἑλέσθαι τῆς συμφορῆς· ἔτεμον γὰρ ἑωυτοὺς καὶ
δίαιταν τὴν αὐτὴν ἐκείνῳ διαιτέοντο. ἄλλοι δὲ
ἱρολογέουσιν ἐπὶ τῷ πρήγματι, λέγοντες ὡς ἡ
Ἥρη φιλέουσα Κομβάβον πολλοῖσι τὴν τομὴν
ἐπὶ νόον ἔβαλλεν, ὅκως μὴ μοῦνος ἐπὶ τῇ ἀνδρηίῃ
27 λυπέοιτο. τὸ δὲ ἔθος τοῦτο ἐπειδὴ ἅπαξ ἐγένετο,
ἔτι νῦν μένει· καὶ πολλοὶ ἑκάστου ἔτεος ἐν τῷ
ἱρῷ τάμνονται καὶ θηλύνονται, εἴτε Κομβάβον
παραμυθεόμενοι εἴτε καὶ Ἥρῃ χαρίζονται· τάμνονται δ' ὦν. ἐσθῆτα δὲ οἴδε οὐκέτι ἀνδρηίην
ἔχουσιν, ἀλλὰ εἵματά τε γυναικήια φορέουσιν
καὶ ἔργα γυναικῶν ἐπιτελέουσιν. ὡς δὲ ἐγὼ
ἤκουον, ἀνακέαται καὶ τουτέων ἐς Κομβάβον ἡ
αἰτίη· συνενείχθη γάρ οἱ καὶ τάδε. ξείνη γυνὴ
ἐς πανήγυριν ἀπικομένη, ἰδοῦσα καλόν τε ἐόντα
καὶ ἐσθῆτα ἔτι ἀνδρηίην ἔχοντα, ἔρωτι μεγάλῳ
ἔσχετο, μετὰ δὲ μαθοῦσα ἀτελέα ἐόντα ἑωυτὴν

---

[1] Hermocles of Rhodes is known only from this passage;
his name must have been preserved by an inscription on the
statue, which we may be sure was the restoration of an

was graunted. And it semede that Combabe hadde
not his pere in Assurye for wisdom and for blisse.

And after, ther as he besoghte to finissche the
remenant of the temple, for he hadde laft it un-
finissched, he was sent eftsones and broght it to an
ende, and abood there fro thens fromward. And be
cause of his vertue and wel doynge, the kyng vouchede
saf that his ymage in brasse scholde ben set in the
seyntuarye. And so for gerdon Combabe dwelleth yit
in the close, formed of brasse be crafte of Ermocle
the Rodien, lyk a womman in schappe, but clothed
as a man.[1]

The storie telleth that his beste frendes, for solas
of his wo, chosen to parte his lot; for thei gelten
hem and ladde that same manere lyf. But othere
men rehercen prestes lore to this matere, how that
Iuno lovynge Combabe putte it in the thoghtes of
manye to gelden hem, in the entente that he
scholde not mourne allone for manhode. But ever-
more sithen that this custom was first establissched,
it abydeth yit, and everyche yeer manye men
gelden hem in the close and becomen as wommen,
wher it be that thei solacen Combabe or reioysen
Iuno. Algates thei gelden hem. And thise no
lenger clothen hem as men, but weren wommenes
wedes and don wommenes werkes. And as I herde,
the blame of this also is leyde on Combabe; for a
thyng befel him in this wyse. A straunge womman
that cam thider on pilgrimage saughe him whyl
he was fayre and clad yit as a man, and sche was
seysed of gret love. But after, whan sche lernede

older statue of the putative originator of the Galli and
possibly real founder of the temple, installed in connection
with the Seleucid restoration of the temple itself.

διειργάσατο. ἐπὶ τοῖσι Κομβάβος, ἀθυμέων ὅτι
οἱ ἀτυχέως τὰ ἐς ᾿Αφροδίτην ἔχει, ἐσθῆτα
γυναικηίην ἐνεδύσατο, ὅκως μηκέτι ἑτέρη γυνὴ
ἴσα ἐξαπατέοιτο. ἥδε αἰτίη Γάλλοισι στολῆς
θηλέης.

Κομβάβου μέν μοι τοσάδε εἰρήσθω, Γάλλων
δὲ αὖτις ἐγὼ λόγῳ ὑστέρῳ μεμνήσομαι, τομῆς
τε αὐτέων, ὅκως τάμνονται, καὶ ταφῆς ὁκοίην
θάπτονται, καὶ ὅτευ εἵνεκα ἐς τὸ ἱρὸν οὐκ ἐσέρ-
χονται· πρότερον δέ μοι θυμὸς εἰπεῖν θέσιός
τε πέρι τοῦ νηοῦ καὶ μεγάθεος, καὶ δῆτα
ἐρέω.

28 Ὁ μὲν χῶρος αὐτός, ἐν τῷ τὸ ἱρὸν ἵδρυται,
λόφος ἐστίν, κέαται δὲ κατὰ μέσον μάλιστα τῆς
πόλιος, καὶ οἱ τείχεα δοιὰ περικέαται. τῶν δὲ
τειχέων τὸ μὲν ἀρχαῖον, τὸ δὲ οὐ πολλὸν ἡμέων
πρεσβύτερον. τὰ δὲ προπύλαια τοῦ ἱροῦ ἐς
ἄνεμον βορέην ἀποκέκρινται, μέγαθος ὅσον τε
ἑκατὸν ὀργυιέων. ἐν τούτοισι τοῖσι προπυλαίοισι
καὶ οἱ φαλλοὶ ἑστᾶσι τοὺς Διόνυσος ἐστήσατο,
ἡλικίην καὶ οἵδε τριηκοσίων ὀργυιέων. ἐς τουτέων

---

[1] Since Kombabos bears a very ancient name, since the
temple-story ascribes the origin of the Galli to him, not to
Attis, and since Attis does not figure at all in the worship as
described by Lucian, the Galli can hardly be a Seleucid
importation from Phrygia (Cumont); in that case Attis
would have been imported also. Meyer, who believes the
cult ancient here, but Hittite-Anatolian in its origin, finds
evidence of Attis-worship in the name Atargatis (Atar-Ata),
which he interprets as the Astarte of Attis; *i.e.*, the goddess
that is characterized by the worship of Attis (*Gesch.*, p. 650).
This view not only leaves Kombabos out of account, but
does not reckon with the fact that the deity Ata was often,
if not always, thought of as feminine (cf. Baudissin, p. 158, 1).

that he was marred, sche slowe hirself. Thanne for despeyr that Combabe hadde be cause he was acurst in love, he didde on femele clothinge to the ende that never non other womman scholde ben so begyled. That is whi Galles weren femele aparayl.[1]

Of Combabe have I seyd ynow, and of Galles I schalle make mencioun sone in another partie of my boke,[2] how that they ben gelded, and in what manere that thei ben buryed, and wherfore thei entren not into the temple. But first it listeth me to telle of the site of the temple and his gretnesse, and therfore I schalle don right so.

The place therinne the temple sytt is a hille; and it liggeth wel in the myddes of the cytee, and two walles enviroune it. Oon of tho walles is auncien, but the tother is not mocheles elder than oure tyme. The entree of the holy place maketh out toward the Septemtryon, wel a 100 fadmes of largenesse; and in that entree stont tho yerdes that Bachus leet set, on heighte a 300 fadmes.[3] A man goth up the oon

The connection, however, between Attis and Ata is indubitable; and I believe that there is an analogous connection between Kombabos (Assyr. Ḥum-ba-ba, Babyl. Ḫu-wa-wa, with characteristic w for b) and Κύβηβος (Gallus), Κυβήβη (the goddess Cybele). It cannot be mere coincidence that in Syria Ku(m)baba serves Ata, while in Phrygia Cybebe is served by Attis. That the transfer in which man and goddess exchanged names was from Semitic to non-Semitic soil is, it seems to me, likely from the antiquity of the name Ku(m)baba. Other arguments are not wanting.

[2] C. 50–53.

[3] Some reduce these 300-fathom emblems to 30 by conjecture, but it is in unimportant details like this that Lucian gives rein to his inclination to parody. Mandeville gives the Tower of Babel the modest height of 64 furlongs—eight miles.

τὸν ἕνα φαλλὸν¹ ἀνὴρ ἑκάστου ἔτεος δὶς ἀνέρχεται
οἰκέει τε ἐν ἄκρῳ τῷ φαλλῷ χρόνον ἑπτὰ ἡμερέων.
αἰτίη δέ οἱ τῆς ἀνόδου ἥδε λέγεται. οἱ μὲν
πολλοὶ νομίζουσιν ὅτι ὑψοῦ τοῖσι θεοῖσιν ὁμιλέει
καὶ ἀγαθὰ ξυναπάσῃ Συρίῃ αἰτέει, οἱ δὲ τῶν
εὐχωλέων ἀγχόθεν ἐπαΐουσιν. ἄλλοισιν δὲ δοκέει
καὶ τάδε Δευκαλίωνος εἵνεκα ποιέεσθαι, ἐκείνης
ξυμφορῆς μνήματα, ὁκότε οἱ ἄνθρωποι ἐς τὰ
οὔρεα καὶ ἐς τὰ περιμήκεα τῶν δενδρέων ᾖσαν
τὸ πολλὸν ὕδωρ ὀρρωδέοντες. ἐμοὶ μέν νυν καὶ
τάδε ἀπίθανα. δοκέω γε μὲν Διονύσῳ σφέας
καὶ τάδε ποιέειν, συμβάλλομαι δὲ τουτέοισι.
φαλλοὺς ὅσοι Διονύσῳ ἐγείρουσι, ἐν τοῖσι φαλ-
λοῖσι καὶ ἄνδρας ξυλίνους κατίζουσιν, ὅτευ μὲν
εἵνεκα ἐγὼ οὐκ ἐρέω. δοκέει δ᾽ ὦν μοι, καὶ ὅδε
ἐς ἐκείνου μίμησιν τοῦ ξυλίνου ἀνδρὸς ἀνέρχεται.
29 Ἡ δέ οἱ ἄνοδος τοιήδε· σειρῇ μικρῇ² ἑωυτόν
τε ἅμα καὶ τὸν φαλλὸν περιβάλλει, μετὰ δὲ
ἐπιβαίνει ξύλων προσφυῶν τῷ φαλλῷ ὁκόσον
ἐς χώρην ἄκρου ποδός· ἀνιὼν δὲ ἅμα ἀναβάλλει
τὴν σειρὴν ἀμφοτέρωθεν ὅκωσπερ ἡνιοχέων. εἰ
δέ τις τόδε μὲν οὐκ ὄπωπεν, ὄπωπεν δὲ φοινικο-
βατέοντας ἢ ἐν Ἀραβίῃ ἢ ἐν Αἰγύπτῳ ἢ ἄλλοθί
κου, οἶδε τὸ λέγω.

---

¹ ἕνα φαλλόν N: lacuna in ΓΕ, in which these words are
entered in a late hand.
² μικρῇ Kuster: μακρῇ MSS.

---

¹ This is evidently the true reason, and not either of the
two that follow. That the gods can hear better from near
at hand is good Semitic psychology ; but the use of a pillar
instead of a mountain-top, or a ziggurat, or the roof of a
house, appears otherwise unevidenced in early Syria. "It
was perhaps the memory of this strange rite (not however

of thise yerdes twyes in the yeer and woneth at the
cop of the yerde for the space of 7 dayes.   And the
cause of his goynge up, as men seyn, is this.   Lewed
folk trowen that he speketh with the goddes on highe
and axeth bones for alle Surrye, and the goddes
heren his preyeres fro there nyghe.[1]   But othere
wenen that this also is don be cause of Deucalioun,
in tokene and mynde of that tribulacioun, whan
men wenten into montaynes and into the gret highe
trees for fere of the flode.   Now to me, that is not
to beleven.   I suppose wel that thei don this for
worschipe of Bachus, and I conclude it thus.   Yerdes
that thei maken for worschipe of Bachus, on tho yerdes
thei setten alle weyes wodene men; but I schalle
not seye whi.[2]   Therfore me thenketh, in goynge
up, that oon countrefeteth that other woden man.

The manere of his goynge up is this.   He putteth
a schort corde abouten himself and the yerde, and
thanne he climbeth on peces of wode ynaylled on
the yerde, bigge ynow for to lette setten on his *set his toes on*
toon; and ther as he climbeth he throweth up the
corde with bothe hondes right as he mighte schake
the reynes of a charre.   If ony ther be that hath
not seen this thing, but hath seen men that climben
trees of palme in Arabye or in Egypte, or elles
where, he undirstondeth wherof I speke.[3]

peculiar to Syria, but known also in India) which led
Simeon the Stylite to ascend his column four centuries later
at a site not very far west of the old temple of the Dea
Syria" (C. R. Conder, *Palestine*, p. 206).

[2] Compare Herodotus 2, 48, and the ἱερὸς λόγος.   The
explanation that Lucian has in mind is probably the
Prosymnos story (Clement of Alexandria, *Protrept.* 2,
p. 30 P.).

[3] This method of climbing palms is alluded to by Pliny,
13, 29.

Ἐπεὰν δὲ ἐς τέλος ἵκηται τῆς ὁδοῦ, σειρὴν ἑτέρην ἀφεὶς τὴν αὐτὸς ἔχει, μακρὴν ταύτην, ἀνέλκει τῶν οἱ θυμός, ξύλα καὶ εἵματα καὶ σκεύεα, ἀπὸ τῶν ἔδρην συνδέων ὁκοίην καλιὴν ἱζάνει, μίμνει τε χρόνον τῶν εἶπον ἡμερέων. πολλοὶ δὲ ἀπικνεόμενοι χρυσόν τε καὶ ἄργυρον, οἱ δὲ χαλκόν, τὰ νομίζουσιν, ἐς ἐχῖνον[1] πρόσθε κεί-μενον κατιᾶσιν, λέγοντες τὰ οὐνόματα ἕκαστος. παρεστεὼς δὲ ἄλλος ἄνω ἀγγέλλει· ὁ δὲ δεξά-μενος τοὔνομα εὐχωλὴν ἐς ἕκαστον ποιέεται, ἅμα δὲ εὐχόμενος κροτέει ποίημα χάλκεον, τὸ ἀείδει μέγα καὶ τρηχὺ κινεόμενον. εὕδει δὲ οὐδαμά· ἢν γάρ μιν ὕπνος ἕλῃ ποτέ, σκορπίος ἀνιὼν ἀνεγείρει τε καὶ ἀεικέα ἐργάζεται, καί οἱ ἥδε ἡ ζημίη τοῦ ὕπνου ἐπικέαται. τὰ μὲν ὦν ἐς τὸν σκορπίον μυθέονται ἱρά τε καὶ θεοπρεπέα· εἰ δὲ ἀτρεκέα ἐστίν, οὐκ ἔχω ἐρέειν. δοκέει δέ μοι, μέγα ἐς ἀγρυπνίην συμβάλλεται καὶ τῆς πτώσιος ἡ ὀρρωδίη.

Φαλλοβατέων μὲν δὴ πέρι τοσάδε ἀρκέει. ὁ
30 δὲ νηὸς ὁρέει μὲν ἐς ἥλιον ἀνιόντα, εἶδος δὲ καὶ ἐργασίην ἐστὶν ὁκοίους νηοὺς ἐν Ἰωνίῃ ποιέουσιν. ἔδρη μεγάλη ἀνέχει ἐκ γῆς[2] μέγαθος ὀργυιέων δυοῖν, ἐπὶ τῆς ὁ νηὸς ἐπικέαται. ἄνοδος ἐς αὐτὸν

---

[1] ἐχῖνον *A.M.H.* : ἐκεῖνον ΓΕ. N reads: οἱ δὲ χαλκὸν κομίζουσιν, εἶτ᾽ ἀφέντες ἐκεῖνον πρόσθε κείμενα ἀπιᾶσι, etc. This Byzantine correction has been followed in all editions since the *princeps*, which reads as ΓΕ.

[2] γῆς Longolius : τῆς MSS.

---

[1] Very likely the bronze sistrum ; fragments of these have been found in Phoenicia (Cook 45). The object was to scare

Whan he is comen to the ende of his weye, he letteth falle an other corde that he hath, that is long, and draweth uppe what him list, wode and clothes and purveyaunce, of the whiche he frameth a sete lyk as a nest, theron he sytteth and abydeth for the space of the before seyde dayes. And manye comynge putten gold or silver or peraunter brasse, that thei usen for here moneyes, in to a vesselle that lyeth there neer, seyinge everychon his name. Thann oon that stondeth there beside calleth it uppe; and whan that other resceyveth the name of eech, he preyeth for him, and in preyinge schaketh a thyng of brasse that souneth gret and schrille whan it is stered.[1] And he ne slepeth never. For if that ever he falle on slepe, a scorpioun goynge up awaketh him and doth him pitous harm; and that is the peyne that is leyde on him for slepynge.[2] Now this tale that is told of the scorpioun is a holy tale and wel semyng, but wher it be trewe or non, I wot neer. Natheles, me semeth that drede of fallynge avayleth moch to wakfulnesse.

Now thanne, of yerde-climberes have I seyd y now. But as touching the temple, it loketh ayenst the sonnes rysynge, and the form and makyng therof is right as thei bylden temples in Ionye. A gret platte forme ryseth fro the erthe 2 fadmes of highte, where on the temple sytt. The weye up to

---

[1] away evil spirits, which as Lucian says elsewhere (vol. iii, p. 343), take flight if they hear a chink of bronze or iron.

[2] There is probably special significance in the scorpion. Not only does it occur frequently on Babylonian seals, and later become the sign of the Zodiac, but in the Gilgamesh Epic (Frazer, *Folklore*, i, 112), the mountain, where the sun goes down (*i.e.* Antilian on; Schrader-Zimmern, p. 573), is guarded by a scorpion man and woman.

λίθου πεποίηται, οὐ κάρτα μακρή. ἀνελθόντι
δὲ θῶυμα μὲν καὶ ὁ πρόνηος μέγα παρέχεται
θύρῃσί τε ἤσκηται χρυσέῃσιν· ἔνδοθεν δὲ ὁ νηὸς
χρυσοῦ τε πολλοῦ ἀπολάμπεται καὶ ἡ ὀροφὴ
πᾶσα χρυσέη. ἀπόζει δὲ αὐτοῦ ὀδμὴ ἀμβροσίη
ὁκοίη λέγεται τῆς χώρης τῆς Ἀραβίης, καί
σοι τηλόθεν ἀνιόντι προσβάλλει πνοιὴν κάρτα
ἀγαθήν· καὶ ἢν αὖτις ἀπίῃς, οὐδαμὰ λείπεται,
ἀλλά σευ τά τε εἵματα ἐς πολλὸν ἔχει τὴν πνοιὴν
καὶ σὺ ἐς πάμπαν αὐτῆς μνήσεαι.

31 Ἔνδοθεν δὲ ὁ νηὸς οὐκ ἀπλόος ἐστίν, ἀλλὰ ἐν
αὐτῷ θάλαμος ἄλλος πεποίηται. ἄνοδος καὶ ἐς
τοῦτον ὀλίγη· θύρῃσι δὲ οὐκ ἤσκηται, ἀλλὰ
ἐς ἀντίον ἅπας ἀναπέπταται. ἐς μὲν ὦν τὸν
μέγαν νηὸν πάντες ἐσέρχονται, ἐς δὲ τὸν θάλαμον
οἱ ἱρέες μοῦνον, οὐ μέντοι πάντες οἱ ἱρέες, ἀλλὰ
οἳ μάλιστα ἀγχίθεοί τέ εἰσιν καὶ οἷσι πᾶσα ἐς
τὸ ἱρὸν μέλεται θεραπηίη. ἐν δὲ τῷδε εἵαται τὰ
ἔδεα, ἥ τε Ἥρη καὶ τὸν αὐτοὶ Δία ἐόντα ἑτέρῳ
οὐνόματι κληίζουσιν. ἄμφω δὲ χρύσεοί τέ εἰσιν
καὶ ἄμφω ἕζονται· ἀλλὰ τὴν μὲν Ἥρην λέοντες
φέρουσιν, ὁ δὲ ταύροισιν ἐφέζεται.

---

[1] The other name, the right one, is Hadad, or Ramman,
god of the lightning and of the waters (rains and floods),
known from very early times to the Semites, to the Mitani
folk under the name of Teshub, and to the Hittites, upon
whose monuments he is conspicuous, with the axe and the
thunderbolt for attributes. He underlies not only Jupiter
Heliopolitanus but Jupiter Dolichenus. Consequently his
identification here also with Jupiter was inevitable, and it
is chiefly in virtue of this that his spouse was identified
with Juno (cf. Dussaud, Pauly-Wissowa, s.v., and Schrader-
Zimmern, p. 447).

[2] Lucian's statement is borne out by the coins; see Head,
Hist. Numm., 2nd ed., p. 777. Atargatis is seen sometimes

it is mad of stone, that is not over long. **And**
whan thou art aboven, the parvys of the temple
scheweth thee a thing of grete merveylle, for it is
dight with dores of gold. And with inne, the temple
schyneth with mocheles gold, and the ceylours ben
alle goldene. And a hevenlyche savour cometh out
of it, lyk as cometh, men seyn, out of the londe of
Arabye. In goynge up, fro fer it sendeth toward
thee a wondur swete brethe ; and ther as thou gost
thy weye, it fayleth never, but thi clothes kepen
that brethe ful longe tyme, and thou schalt ever-
more ben in remembraunce ther of.

And with inne, the temple is not oon, but in it is
mad an other chambre, to the which is an other weye
up, that is but schort. That chambre is not dight
with dores but liggeth alle open ayens thee. In to
the grete temple comen alle men, but in to the
litylle chambre the prestes only, and not alle the
prestes, but only thei that ben most nyghe to
the Goddes and han in governaunce alle the servys
of the temple. And in that chambre arn throned
the ydoles, that oon Iuno and that other that is
Iove, algates thei clepen him be another name.[1]
And both ben of gold, and both sytten, but lyouns
beren Iuno, and that other sytt on boles.[2]

riding on a lion, sometimes enthroned between two of them ;
Hadad (not Baal Kevan) is seated between two oxen. " On
an inscription from North Syria (eighth century) Hadad has
horns, and with this agrees the association of the bull with
the god . . . we may conjecture that the small heads of
bulls unearthed by the excavations are connected with his
worship" (Cook, 90 ; cf. Schrader-Zimmern, p. 778). Compare Tobit, 1, 5. The lion appears also in connection with
Ata, with "Kadesh," who stands upon a lion in an Egyptian
representation of her, and with several Babylonian deities,
as well as with Cybele.

Καὶ δῆτα τὸ μὲν τοῦ Διὸς ἄγαλμα ἐς Δία
πάντα ὁρῇ καὶ κεφαλὴν καὶ εἵματα καὶ ἕδρην,
32 καί μιν οὐδὲ ἐθέλων ἄλλως εἰκάσεις. ἡ δὲ Ἥρη
σκοπέοντί τοι πολυειδέα μορφὴν ἐκφανέει· καὶ
τὰ μὲν ξύμπαντα ἀτρεκέϊ λόγῳ Ἥρη ἐστίν, ἔχει
δέ τι καὶ Ἀθηναίης καὶ Ἀφροδίτης καὶ Σεληναίης
καὶ Ῥέης καὶ Ἀρτέμιδος καὶ Νεμέσιος καὶ
Μοιρέων. χειρὶ δὲ τῇ μὲν ἑτέρῃ σκῆπτρον ἔχει,
τῇ ἑτέρῃ δὲ ἄτρακτον, καὶ ἐπὶ τῇ κεφαλῇ ἀκτῖνάς
τε φορέει καὶ πύργον καὶ κεστὸν τῷ μούνην τὴν
Οὐρανίην κοσμέουσιν. ἔκτοσθεν δέ οἱ χρυσός τε
ἄλλος περικέαται καὶ λίθοι κάρτα πολυτελέες,
τῶν οἱ μὲν λευκοί, οἱ δὲ ὑδατώδεες, πολλοὶ δὲ
οἰνώδεες, πολλοὶ δὲ πυρώδεες, ἔτι δὲ ὄνυχες οἱ
Σαρδῷοι πολλοὶ καὶ ὑάκινθοι καὶ σμάραγδοι, τὰ
φέρουσιν Αἰγύπτιοι καὶ Ἰνδοὶ καὶ Αἰθίοπες καὶ
Μῆδοι καὶ Ἀρμένιοι καὶ Βαβυλώνιοι. τὸ δὲ δὴ
μέζονος λόγου ἄξιον, τοῦτο ἀπηγήσομαι· λίθον
ἐπὶ τῇ κεφαλῇ φορέει· λυχνὶς καλέεται, οὔνομα
δέ οἱ τοῦ ἔργου ἡ συντυχίη. ἀπὸ τούτου ἐν
νυκτὶ σέλας πολλὸν ἀπολάμπεται, ὑπὸ δέ οἱ
καὶ ὁ νηὸς ἅπας οἷον ὑπὸ λύχνοισι φαείνεται.
ἐν ἡμέρῃ δὲ τὸ μὲν φέγγος ἀσθενέει, ἰδέην δὲ ἔχει

---

[1] Compare Plutarch, *Crassus*, 17, 6: "And the first
warning sign came to him from this very goddess, whom
some call Venus, others Juno, while others (cf. Cornutus 6)
still regard her as the natural cause which supplies from
moisture the beginnings and seeds of everything, and points
out to mankind the source of all blessings. For as they

THE GODDESSE OF SURRYE

And certeynely the symulacre of Ioue ressembleth
Ioue in alle pointes, as heed and garnements and
throne; and thou mightest not lyknen him unto
no thing elles, and thou wolde.   But whan thou
lokest on Iuno, sche wil schewe thee grete dyver-
sitee of semblauntz; for al be it that the hool, trewely
considered, be Iuno, natheles it conteyneth some
dele of Minerve and Venus and Luna and Cibella
and Deane and Fortune and Parcas.[1]   And in that
oon hond sche holt a troncheon, and in that
other a distaf; and on hir hede sche bereth rayes,
and a tour, and that ceynt that men arayen with *cestus*
Venus Celestial allone.   And abouten hir sche hath
mo gold and precious stones right costlewe, some
whyte and some watry, and manye lyk wyn and
manye lyk fuyr; and therto sardoynes withouten
nombre and berylles and emeraudes.   Thise stones
bryngen men of Egypte and Inde and Ethyope and
Medye and Ermonye and Babyloyne.   But I schal
devyse you a thyng that is yit mo to speke of.
Sche bereth on hir hede a ston that hight Lampe
and hath his name after that that it doth.   That ston
schyneth in the nyght with grete claretee and
serveth all the temple with light, right as it were
of lampes.   In the daye his schyninge is feble but

---

were leaving her temple (where, Plutarch says, he had been
taking an inventory of the treasures), first the younger
Crassus stumbled and fell at the gate, and then his father
fell over him" (Perrin's translation).   The identification
with Aphrodite, which occurs on inscriptions from Delos, is
due to her Astarte side ; to Lucian in this case it is of course
particularly suggested by the famous cestus.   What suggested the other goddesses is not clear to me in the case of
Athena or of Nemesis ; the rays indicate Selene, the distaff
Artemis, and the sceptre the Parcae, or Moirai (Fates).

κάρτα πυρώδεα. καὶ ἄλλο θωυμαστόν ἐστιν ἐν
τῷ ξοάνῳ. ἢν ἑστεὼς ἀντίος ἐσορέῃς, ἐς σὲ ὁρῇ
καὶ μεταβαίνοντι τὸ βλέμμα ἀκολουθέει· καὶ
ἢν ἄλλος ἑτέρωθεν ἱστορέῃ,[1] ἴσα καὶ ἐς ἐκεῖνον
ἐκτελέει.

33 Ἐν μέσῳ δὲ ἀμφοτέρων ἕστηκεν ξόανον ἄλλο
χρύσεον, οὐδαμὰ τοῖσι ἄλλοισι ξοάνοισι εἴκελον.
τὸ δὲ μορφὴν μὲν ἰδίην οὐκ ἔχει, φορέει δὲ τῶν
ἄλλων θεῶν εἴδεα. καλέεται δὲ σημήιον καὶ ὑπ᾽
αὐτῶν Ἀσσυρίων, οὐδέ τι οὔνομα ἴδιον αὐτῷ
ἔθεντο, ἀλλ᾽ οὐδὲ γενέσιος αὐτοῦ καὶ εἴδεος
λέγουσιν. καί μιν οἱ μὲν ἐς Διόνυσον, ἄλλοι δὲ
ἐς Δευκαλίωνα, οἱ δὲ ἐς Σεμίραμιν ἄγουσιν· καὶ
γὰρ δὴ ὦν ἐπὶ τῇ κορυφῇ αὐτοῦ περιστερὴ
χρυσέη ἐφέστηκεν, τοὔνεκα δὴ μυθέονται Σεμιράμιος ἔμμεναι τόδε σημήιον. ἀποδημέει δὲ δὶς
ἑκάστου ἔτεος ἐς θάλασσαν ἐς κομιδὴν τοῦ εἶπον
ὕδατος.

34 Ἐν αὐτῷ δὲ τῷ νηῷ ἐσιόντων ἐν ἀριστερῇ κέαται πρῶτα μὲν θρόνος Ἡελίου, αὐτοῦ δὲ ἕδος[2]
οὐκ ἔνι· μούνου γὰρ Ἡελίου καὶ Σεληναίης
ξόανα οὐ δεικνύουσιν. ὅτευ δὲ εἵνεκα ὧδε νομίζουσιν, ἐγὼ καὶ τόδε ἔμαθον. λέγουσι τοῖσι μὲν
ἄλλοισι θεοῖσιν ὅσιον ἔμμεναι ξόανα ποιέεσθαι,

---

[1] ἐσορέῃ du Soul, Edd.
[2] ἕδος Schaefer: εἶδος MSS.

---

[1] Compare Herodotus 2, 44, on the great emerald pillar in
the temple of Melkart at Tyre ; also Mandeville, pp. 239,
276, ed. Halliwell, on luminous stones in the possession of
the Emperor of Cathay and of Prester John. Diodorus (3, 39,
8) credits the topaz with this power.

[2] It is clear from the passage in Melito quoted above that
Lucian's "token" (semeion) rests upon a misunderstanding

it hath a right fuyry aspect.[1] And ther is an other merveylle in that ydole. Gif thou loke on hir stondynge ayenst hir, sche loketh on thee, and if thou remeve thee, hir regard folweth thee; natheles if an other beholde hir fro the tothere syde, sche doth right so to him also.

And betwene hem stont a symulacre of gold, not lyk the othere symulacres in no kynde, that hath no propre schap but bereth the qualitees of the other goddes. And the Assuriens hem selve clepen it Tokene, for thei han not goven him no propre name; in sothe thei mowe not seyn whens it cam ne what maner thyng it is. But some beleven, it is of Bachus, and othere that it is of Deucalioun, and othere that it is of Semiramys. And for sothe a dowve of gold stont on his hede, and so thei devisen that it is Semiramys Tokene. And it doth iorney twyes eech yeer to the See, for to fecchen that water aforseyde.[2]

In the temple himself on the left syde in entrynge is first a thron of Elye the sonne, but noon ymage of him sytt there on. For of Sonne and Mone only schewen thei non symulacres, and I lernede wherfore thei folwen this usaunce. Thei seyn that of othere goddes it is leful to lete make symulacres, for that

---

of the name of a goddess, Simi, Simia, Semea (Nöldeke; cf. Hoefer, s.v. Semea in Roscher). The name also figures in the Semiramis-Derceto myth, for the royal overseer is called Simmas. Note also that the figure has a dove on its head. A Talmudic gloss cited by Drusius says: " Samaritanus circumcidit in nomine imaginis columbam referentis quam inventam in vertice montis Garizim certo quodam ritu colunt" (Selden, *de Dis Syris*, p. 275). See Montgomery, *Samaritans*, p. 320.

THE WORKS OF LUCIAN

οὐ γὰρ σφέων ἐμφανέα πάντεσι τὰ εἴδεα· Ἥλιος
δὲ καὶ Σεληναίη πάμπαν ἐναργέες καὶ σφέας πάντες ὁρέουσι. κοίη ὦν αἰτίη ξοανουργίης τοῖσι ἐν
τῷ ἠέρι φαινομένοισι ;

35 Μετὰ δὲ τὸν θρόνον τοῦτον κέαται ξόανον
Ἀπόλλωνος, οὐκ οἷον ἐώθεε ποιέεσθαι· οἱ μὲν
γὰρ ἄλλοι πάντες Ἀπόλλωνα νέον τε ἥγηνται
καὶ πρωθήβην ποιέουσιν, μοῦνοι δὲ οὗτοι Ἀπόλλωνος γενειήτεω ξόανον δεικνύουσιν. καὶ τάδε
ποιέοντες ἑωυτοὺς μὲν ἐπαινέουσιν, Ἑλλήνων δὲ
κατηγορέουσιν καὶ ἄλλων ὁκόσοι Ἀπόλλωνα
παῖδα θέμενοι ἱλάσκονται. αἰτίη δὲ ἥδε. δοκέει
αὐτέοισι ἀσοφίη μεγάλη ἔμμεναι ἀτελέα ποιέεσθαι τοῖσι θεοῖσι τὰ εἴδεα, τὸ δὲ νέον ἀτελὲς ἔτι
νομίζουσιν. ἐν δὲ καὶ ἄλλο τῷ σφετέρῳ Ἀπόλλωνι καινουργέουσι· μοῦνοι Ἀπόλλωνα εἵμασι
κοσμέουσιν.

36 Ἔργων δὲ αὐτοῦ πέρι πολλὰ μὲν ἔχω εἰπεῖν,
ἐρέω δὲ τὸ μάλιστα θωυμάζειν ἄξιον. πρῶτα δὲ
τοῦ μαντηίου ἐπιμνήσομαι. μαντήια πολλὰ μὲν
παρ' Ἕλλησι, πολλὰ δὲ καὶ παρ' Αἰγυπτίοισι,
τὰ δὲ καὶ ἐν Λιβύῃ, καὶ ἐν τῇ δὲ Ἀσίῃ πολλά
ἐστιν. ἀλλὰ τὰ μὲν οὔτε ἱρέων ἄνευ οὔτε προφη-

---

[1] Compare Meyer, *Gesch.*, p. 192, on the lack of images and
temples in the Egyptian worship of Ra.

[2] Apollo is Nebo, whose statue, bearded and clothed,
erected at Kelach by Adad-Nirari III, son of Semiramis,
may be seen at the British Museum (illustrated in Roscher,
Lexikon, I, p. 49). The inscription that it bears implores
long life for Adad-Nirari, king of Assyria, and for Sam-
muramat, the Lady of the Palace. Nebo was highly favoured

here schappes ben not seen of alle men. But Sonne and Mone ben wel visible and alle men beholden hem. Whi thanne make symulacres of thynges that aperen in the eyr? [1]

And ther nyghe this throne is sett a symulacre of Apollo, not lyk as he is wont to ben formed. For alle othere leven Apollo yong and formen him as a stripling, but thise allone schewen a symulacre of Apollo berded. And doynge this thei preisen hem selve and repreven Grekes and alle othere men that worschippen Apollo in lyknesse of a child. And the resoun is, for it semeth hem gret folye to maken schappes of Goddes inperfyt, and al that is yong thei demen yit inperfyt. And here Apollo hath other novelrye; for thei allone arayen him with clothynges. [2]

Now of the wondres that he doth I can speke largely, but I wol telle only that that is most marveyllous; and first I schalle make mencioun of the oracle. Ther ben manye oracles amonges Grekes and manye amonges Egyptyens, and some in Libye, and also manye in Asye. But thise oracles speken not withouten prestes or prophetes; but

by Semiramis, and also, in later days, by Antiochus Soter, who rebuilt his temple at Borsippa in 268 B.C. At Edessa, near Hieropolis, his worship continued until the coming of Christianity (Cureton, *Ancient Syriac Documents*, pp. 14, 22, 41). Contemporary testimony to its existence at Hieropolis is furnished by Melito; see above, p. 353, note 3. The statue at Hieropolis that we find described in Macrobius seems to be a later one; for though it was bearded and clothed, as in Lucian's day, there was a calathus on the head, a spear topped with a little figure of Victory in the right hand, a flower in the left, a breastplate on his body, and over it a snaky aegis; also, two eagles near by (*Saturn*, 1, 17, 67–70).

τέων φθέγγονται, ὅδε δὲ αὐτός τε κινέεται καὶ τὴν
μαντηίην ἐς τέλος αὐτουργέει. τρόπος δὲ αὐτῆς
τοιόσδε. εὖτ' ἂν ἐθέλῃ χρησμηγορέειν, ἐν τῇ
ἕδρῃ πρῶτα κινέεται, οἱ δέ μιν ἱρέες αὐτίκα
ἀείρουσιν· ἢν δὲ μὴ ἀείρωσιν, ὁ δὲ ἱδρώει καὶ ἐς
μέζον ἔτι κινέεται. εὖτ' ἂν δὲ ὑποδύντες φέρωσιν,
ἄγει σφέας πάντη περιδινέων καὶ ἐς ἄλλον ἐξ
ἑτέρου μεταπηδέων. τέλος ὁ ἀρχιερεὺς ἀντιάσας
ἐπερέεταί μιν περὶ ἁπάντων πρηγμάτων· ὁ δὲ ἤν
τι μὴ ἐθέλῃ ποιέεσθαι, ὀπίσω ἀναχωρέει, ἢν δέ
τι ἐπαινέῃ, ἄγει ἐς τὸ πρόσω τοὺς προφέροντας
ὅκωσπερ ἡνιοχέων. οὕτως μὲν συναγείρουσι τὰ
θέσφατα, καὶ οὔτε ἱρὸν πρῆγμα οὐδὲν οὔτε ἴδιον
τούτου ἄνευ ποιέουσιν. λέγει δὲ καὶ τοῦ ἔτεος
πέρι καὶ τῶν ὡρέων αὐτοῦ πασέων, καὶ ὁκότε οὐκ
ἔρονται.[1] λέγει δὲ καὶ τοῦ σημηίου πέρι, κότε
37 χρή μιν ἀποδημέειν τὴν εἶπον ἀποδημίην. ἐρέω
δὲ καὶ ἄλλο, τὸ ἐμεῦ παρεόντος ἔπρηξεν. οἱ μέν
μιν ἱρέες ἀείροντες ἔφερον, ὁ δὲ τοὺς μὲν ἐν γῇ
κάτω ἔλιπεν, αὐτὸς δὲ ἐν τῷ ἠέρι μοῦνος ἐφορέετο.
38 Μετὰ δὲ τὸν Ἀπόλλωνα ξόανόν ἐστιν Ἄτλαν-
τος, μετὰ δὲ Ἑρμέω καὶ Εἰλειθυίης.

---

[1] ἔρονται Fritzsche : ἔσονται MSS.

---

[1] At Heliopolis, Jupiter Heliopolitanus, who had absorbed
"Apollo," gave oracles in much the same way (Macrobius,
Saturn, 1, 23. 13 *sqq.*). So also did Ammon at his great
Libyan shrine (Siwa); the description of the procedure when
Alexander consulted it (Diodorus, 17, 50–51), somewhat blind
in itself, is clear in the light of these parallels. The ikon of
the Virgin at Phaneromene, Salamis, is credited with similar
powers to-day (Capps), and for a parallel in modern Sierra
Leone, see Frazer, *Folklore*, iii, p. 323.

[2] This is very likely the same triad of Semitic deities
under another set of names, and in slightly different mani-

that oon meveth be himself and be himself acom-
plischeth his fercastinge, wher of the maner is right
so. Whan he is in wille for to make predicatioun, atte
firste he meveth on his thron, and thanne anon the
prestes beren him up; but if thei ne beren him
not up, he sweteth and meveth ever the more. And
whyls thei carryen him on here scholdres, he dryveth
hem, tornynge hem in alle weyes and lepynge fro
that oon to that other. And atte last the Chefe
Preste meteth him and axeth him of alle manere
thinges; and gif he wole not that a thyng ben don,
he draweth him backwardes; but if he commende a
thyng, he dryveth his bereres forwardes right as he
were dryvinge a charre.[1] So assemblen thei the
predicatiounes, and withouten this don thei no
thing, ne solempne ne lewede. And he speketh of
the yeer and the sesouns ther of, ye, whan thei
ne axe not; and he speketh of the Tokene, whan
it schal gon that iorney aforseyde. And I schalle
seye you an other wonder that he wroghte in min
owene presence. Whan the prestes wolde beren
him up and carryen him, he lafte hem doun on the
erthe and fleighe in the eyr al be him self.

There beside Apollo is a symulacre of Atlas, and
there neer, of Mercure and of Lucine.[2]

---

festations. For Atlas I would suggest Hadaranes, who
according to Melito was worshipped here; a sign of the
Zodiac would have sufficed to suggest the supporter of the
heavens. Hermes (Mercury) should be Nebo at bottom, because that planet is the planet of Nebo; but the Helio-
politan Mercury who took the place of the Hieropolitan
Apollo-Nebo in the triad is thought to have been called
Simios (Dussaud). Eileithyia (Lucina), the helper in child-
birth, is Mylitta, though here they may not have called her
by that name (cf. Schrader-Zimmern, 423, note 7).

39 Τὰ μὲν ὦν ἐντὸς τοῦ νηοῦ ὧδε κεκοσμέαται·
ἔξω δὲ βωμός τε κέαται μέγας χάλκεος, ἐν δὲ καὶ
ἄλλα ξόανα μυρία χάλκεα βασιλέων τε καὶ ἱρέων·
καταλέξω δὲ τῶν μάλιστα ἄξιον μνήσασθαι. ἐν
ἀριστερῇ τοῦ νεὼ Σεμιράμιος ξόανον ἔστηκεν ἐν
δεξιῇ τὸν νηὸν ἐπιδεικνύουσα. ἀνέστη δὲ δι᾽
αἰτίην τοιήνδε. ἀνθρώποισιν ὁκόσοι Συρίην
οἰκέουσιν νόμον ἐποιέετο ἑαυτὴν μὲν ὅκως θεὸν
ἱλάσκεσθαι, θεῶν δὲ τῶν ἄλλων καὶ αὐτῆς Ἥρης
ἀλογέειν. καὶ ὧδε ἐποίεον. μετὰ δὲ ὥς οἱ θεό-
θεν ἀπίκοντο νοῦσοί τε καὶ συμφοραὶ[1] καὶ
ἄλγεα, μανίης μὲν ἐκείνης ἀπεπαύσατο καὶ
θνητὴν ἑωυτὴν ὁμολόγεεν καὶ τοῖσιν ὑπηκόοισιν
αὖτις ἐκέλευεν ἐς Ἥρην τρέπεσθαι. τούνεκα δὴ
ἔτι τοιήδε ἀνέστηκεν, τοῖσιν ἀπικνεομένοισι τὴν
Ἥρην ἱλάσκεσθαι δεικνύουσα, καὶ θεὸν οὐκέτι
ἑωυτὴν ἀλλ᾽ ἐκείνην ὁμολογέουσα.

40 Εἶδον δὲ καὶ αὐτόθι Ἑλένης ἄγαλμα καὶ
Ἑκάβης καὶ Ἀνδρομάχης καὶ Πάριδος καὶ Ἕκ-
τορος καὶ Ἀχιλλέος. εἶδον δὲ καὶ Νειρέος εἶδος
τοῦ Ἀγλαΐης, καὶ Φιλομήλην καὶ Πρόκνην ἔτι
γυναῖκας, καὶ αὐτὸν Τηρέα ὄρνιθα, καὶ ἄλλο
ἄγαλμα Σεμιράμιος, καὶ Κομβάβου τὸ κατέλεξα,
καὶ Στρατονίκης κάρτα καλόν, καὶ Ἀλεξάνδρου
αὐτῷ ἐκείνῳ εἴκελον, παρὰ δέ οἱ Σαρδανά-
παλλος ἔστηκεν ἄλλῃ μορφῇ καὶ ἄλλῃ στολῇ.

---

[1] συμφοραὶ N, du Soul : συμφορή ΓΕ.

THE GODDESSE OF SURRYE

Now have I devysed you how that the temple
is aparaylled with innen. Withouten is set a gret
awtere of brasse, and there nyghe ben othere symulacres of kynges and prestes withouten nombre; and
I schalle telle you tho that ben moste worthy of
mencioun. At the lefte syde of the temple stont a
symulacre of Semiramys schewinge the temple with
hir righte hond, the whiche was sett up for this
resoun. Sche made ordeynaunce unto alle that
duelleden in Surrye that thei scholde worschippe hir
as here goddesse, recchynge nought of the othere
goddes and Iuno hirself. And thei didde right
so. But after, for als moche as syknesses and tribu-
laciouns and peynes weren leyde on hir by the
goddes, sche cessed of that folye and knouleched that
sche was mortalle and commaunded alle hir subgettes
to tornen hem ayen un to Iuno. Wherfore sche
stont yit in suche gyse, devysing to alle that comen
that thei schulle worschippe Iuno, and knoulechynge
that sche is not goddesse no more, but that other.[1]

And in that place saughe I also ymages of Eleyne
and Ecube and Andromacha and Parys and Ector
and Achilles. And I saughe Nireos ymage, that
was sone of Aglaye, and Philomele and Progne, that
weren yit wommen, and Tereus himself, that was a
brid, and an other ymage of Semiramys, and of
Combabe that that I spak of, and a right fayr of
Stratonice, and oon of Alexaundre lyk as it were the
verray man, and there beside him stont Sardanapalle
in other schappe and other aparayl.[2]

[1] There may be some truth in this legend, for Semiramis
actually received worship in Carchemish, just north of
Hieropolis.
[2] That is, with the figure and clothing of a woman.

41 Ἐν δὲ τῇ αὐλῇ ἄφετοι νέμονται βόες μεγάλοι
καὶ ἵπποι καὶ ἀετοὶ καὶ ἄρκτοι καὶ λέοντες, καὶ
ἀνθρώπους οὐδαμὰ σίνονται, ἀλλὰ πάντες ἱροί τέ
εἰσι καὶ χειροήθεες.

42 Ἱρέες δὲ αὐτοῖσι πολλοὶ ἀποδεδέχαται, τῶν οἱ
μὲν τὰ ἱρήια σφάζουσιν, οἱ δὲ σπονδηφορέουσιν,
ἄλλοι δὲ πυρφόροι καλέονται καὶ ἄλλοι παρα-
βώμιοι. ἐπ' ἐμεῦ δὲ πλείονες καὶ τριηκοσίων ἐς
τὴν θυσίην ἀπικνέοντο. ἐσθὴς δὲ αὐτέοισι πᾶσι
λευκή, καὶ πῖλον ἐπὶ τῇ κεφαλῇ ἔχουσιν. ἀρχιερεὺς δὲ ἄλλος ἑκάστου ἔτεος ἐπιγίγνεται, πορφυ-
ρέην τε μοῦνος οὗτος φορέει καὶ τιάρῃ χρυσέῃ

43 ἀναδέεται. ἔστι δὲ καὶ ἄλλο πλῆθος ἀνθρώπων
ἱρῶν αὐλητέων τε καὶ συριστέων καὶ Γάλλων,
καὶ γυναῖκες ἐπιμανέες τε καὶ φρενοβλαβέες.

44 Θυσίη δὲ δὶς ἑκάστης ἡμέρης ἐπιτελέεται, ἐς
τὴν πάντες ἀπικνέονται. Διὶ μὲν ὦν κατ' ἡσυχίην θύουσιν οὔτε ἀείδοντες οὔτε αὐλέοντες· εὖτ'
ἂν δὲ τῇ Ἥρῃ κατάρχωνται, ἀείδουσίν τε καὶ
αὐλέουσιν καὶ κρόταλα ἐπικροτέουσιν. καί μοι
τούτου πέρι σαφὲς οὐδὲν εἰπεῖν ἐδύναντο.

45 Ἔστι δὲ καὶ λίμνη αὐτόθι, οὐ πολλὸν ἑκὰς τοῦ
ἱροῦ, ἐν τῇ ἰχθύες ἱροὶ τρέφονται πολλοὶ καὶ
πολυειδέες. γίγνονται δὲ αὐτῶν ἔνιοι κάρτα
μεγάλοι· οὗτοι δὲ καὶ οὐνόματα ἔχουσιν καὶ

---

¹ Sacred animals were a common feature of temple-closes
in Greece (Gardner-Jevons, *Manual*, p. 188). Plato intro-
duces sacred bulls into his utopian Atlantis, *Critias*, 119 D.

And in the clos at large pasturen grete boles and hors and egles and beres and lyouns; and thei don no manere harm to men but ben everyche of hem holy and tame.[1]

Prestes thei apoynten withouten nombre, of the whiche some sleen the victimes and some beren the offrynges of licours and some ben cleped Fuyrbereres and some Awtere Prestes. Whan I was there, mo than a 300 weren wont to assemblen hem for sacrifise. Thei ben clothed in whyte robes alle, and thei han a poynted cappe on here hedes.[2] And everyche yeer a newe chefe preste is sett over hem, that allone wereth a robe of purpre and is crouned with a coronale of gold.[3] And therto is other gret multy-tude of religious men, of floyteres and piperes and Galles, and also wommen that ben wode and out of here witte.

Twyes each day sacrifise is perfourned, to the which alle comen. To Iove thei sacrificen withouten ony noys, ne syngynge not ne floytynge; but whan thei presenten offrynges to Iuno, thanne thei syngen and floyten and sounen cymbales. And as to this thei mighte not telle me no thing certeyn.

Ther is also a lak, a lityl fro the temple, in the whiche holy fissches ben norysscht, withouten nombre and of dyverse kyndes. Some of hem ben ful grete, and thise han names and comen whan thei ben

[2] For the pointed cap, see Cumont in Daremberg-Saglio, *Dict. des Ant.*, *s.v.* Syria Dea, fig. 6698, and the reference in the next note (Abd-Hadad).

[3] Coins of Hieropolis, of the fourth century, B.C. (Babelon, *Perses achéménides*, No. 315), show the high priest Abd-Hadad in the dress here described. Compare Herodian 5, 3, 6 (costume of Elagabalus; cf. Dio Cassius 79, 11); Cureton, *Ancient Syriac Documents*, p. 41 (Sharbil, priest of Nebo); Athenaeus 5, 215 B.C. (priest of Sandan at Tarsus).

ἔρχονται καλεόμενοι· ἐπ᾽ ἐμέο δέ τις ἦν ἐν
αὐτοῖσι χρυσοφορέων. ἐν τῇ πτέρυγι ποίημα
χρύσεον αὐτέῳ ἀνακέατο, καί μιν ἐγὼ πολλάκις
ἐθησάμην, καὶ εἶχεν τὸ ποίημα.

46 Βάθος δὲ τῆς λίμνης πολλόν. ἐγὼ μὲν οὐκ
ἐπειρήθην, λέγουσι δ᾽ ὧν καὶ διηκοσίων ὀργυιέων
πλέον ἔμμεναι. κατὰ μέσον δὲ αὐτῆς βωμὸς
λίθου ἀνέστηκεν. δοκέοις ἂν ἄφνω ἰδὼν πλώειν
τέ μιν καὶ τῷ ὕδατι ἐποχέεσθαι, καὶ πολλοὶ ὧδε
νομίζουσιν· ἐμοὶ δὲ δοκέει στῦλος ὑφεστεὼς¹
μέγας ἀνέχειν τὸν βωμόν. ἔστεπται δὲ ἀεὶ καὶ
θυώματα ἔχει, πολλοὶ δὲ καὶ ἑκάστης ἡμέρης
κατ᾽ εὐχὴν ἐς αὐτὸν νηχόμενοι στεφανηφορέουσιν.

47 Γίγνονται δὲ αὐτόθι καὶ πανηγύριές τε μέγισται, καλέονται δὲ ἐς τὴν λίμνην καταβάσιες, ὅτι
ἐν αὐτῇσι ἐς τὴν λίμνην τὰ ἱρὰ πάντα κατέρχε-
ται. ἐν τοῖσιν ἡ Ἥρη πρώτη ἀπικνέεται, τῶν
ἰχθύων εἵνεκα, μὴ σφέας ὁ Ζεὺς πρῶτος ἴδηται·
ἢν γὰρ τόδε γένηται, λέγουσιν ὅτι πάντες ἀπόλ-
λυνται. καὶ δῆτα ὁ μὲν ἔρχεται ὀψόμενος, ἡ δὲ

---

¹ ὑφεστεὼς Gesner : ἐφεστεὼς MSS.

---

¹ " At Hierapolis in Syria, in the lake of Venus, they (the
fish) obey the spoken commands of the *aeditui ;* when called,
they come with their golden ornaments ; they show affection
and let themselves be tickled (adulantes scalpuntur), and
they open their mouths for people to put in their hands"
(Pliny, *Nat. Hist.* 32, 17). According to Aelian (*Nat. Hist.*
12, 2) they swam in regular formation, and had leaders.
The pond still exists, but the fish are no more (Cumont,
Études Syriennes, p. 36 *sq.*). There were similar ponds at

cleped. And whan I was there, amonges hem was
oon that werde gold. On his fynne was festned a
ioyelle of gold; and often tymes I saughe him, and
he hadde that ioyelle.[1]

That lak is passynge depe. I assayde it not, but
men seyn that it hath wel mo than a 200 fadmes;
and in the myd place ther of stont an awtere of
stone. Seeynge it on a sodeyne, thou woldest
trowen that it fleyted and rode upon the water, and
manye men wenen thus; but I suppose that a gret
piler pight undernethe bereth up the awtere. And
it is ever more dressed with gerlondes and hath
encens brennynge, and manye swymmen overthwart
to it eech day for a vowe that thei han, and bryngen
gerlondes.[2]

At that place ben wondur grete festes, the which
highte Desceyntes unto the Lak, be cause that in
tho festes alle the ydoles gon doun to the lak.
Amonges hem Iuno cometh first, be cause of the
fissches, to the entente that Iove schalle not seen
hem first; for if so be that this happeth, thei dyen
alle, as men seyn. And for sothe he cometh to

Ascalon, Edessa, and Smyrna: see the interesting inscription
from Smyrna in Dittenberger, *Sylloge Inscr. Graec.*[2], No. 584.
The custom was transmitted to modern times (Baudissin,
Studien, ii, pp. 159 and 165; Hogarth, *l.c.*, p. 189).
On the fish tabu in Syria, see Xenophon, *Anab.* 1, 4, 9;
Menander, fragment 544 Kock; Cicero, *de Nat. Deor.* 3, 39;
Diodorus 2, 4, 3; Plutarch, *Moral.* 170 D, 730 D; Ovid,
Fasti 2, 461 *sqq.*; Athenaeus 4, 157 B; 8, 346 C *sqq.*;
Clement Alex., *Protrept.* 2, 39, p. 35 P; Hyginus, *Fab.* 197;
Astron. 2, 30.

[2] Gruppe (*Gr. Myth. u. Religionsgesch.*, p. 813) connects this
"Floating" island with the holy island of Tyre, the floating
island of Chemmis in the swamps of Buto, and with the
Greek stories of Delos and Patmos.

πρόσω ἱσταμένη ἀπείργει τέ μιν καὶ πολλὰ
λιπαρέουσα ἀποπέμπει.

48 Μέγισται δὲ αὐτοῖσι πανηγύριες αἳ ἐς θάλασσαν
νομίζονται. ἀλλ᾽ ἐγὼ τούτων πέρι σαφὲς οὐδὲν
ἔχω εἰπεῖν· οὐ γὰρ ἦλθον αὐτὸς οὐδὲ ἐπειρήθην
ταύτης τῆς ὁδοιπορίης. τὰ δὲ ἐλθόντες ποιέουσιν, εἶδον καὶ ἀπηγήσομαι. ἀγγήιον ἕκαστος ὕδατι
σεσαγμένον φέρουσιν, κηρῷ δὲ τάδε σεσήμανται.
καί μιν οὐκ αὐτοὶ λυσάμενοι χέονται, ἀλλ᾽ ἔστιν
ἀλεκτρυὼν ἱρός, οἰκέει δὲ ἐπὶ τῇ λίμνῃ, ὃς ἐπεὶ
σφέων δέξηται τὰ ἀγγήια, τήν τε σφρηγῖδα ὁρῇ
καὶ μισθὸν ἀρνύμενος ἀνά τε λύει τὸν δεσμὸν καὶ
τὸν κηρὸν ἀπαιρέεται· καὶ πολλαὶ μνέες ἐκ του-
τέου τοῦ ἔργου τῷ ἀλεκτρυόνι ἀγείρονται. ἔνθεν
δὲ ἐς τὸν νηὸν αὐτοὶ ἐνείκαντες σπένδουσί τε καὶ
θύσαντες ὀπίσω ἀπονοστέουσιν.

49 Ὁρτέων δὲ πασέων τῶν οἶδα μεγίστην τοῦ
εἴαρος ἀρχομένου ἐπιτελέουσιν, καί μιν οἱ μὲν
πυρήν, οἱ δὲ λαμπάδα καλέουσιν. θυσίην δὲ ἐν
αὐτῇ τοιήνδε ποιέουσιν. δένδρεα μεγάλα ἐκκόψαν-
τες τῇ αὐλῇ ἑστᾶσι, μετὰ δὲ ἀγινέοντες αἶγάς τε
καὶ ὄιας καὶ ἄλλα κτήνεα ζωὰ ἐκ τῶν δενδρέων
ἀπαρτέουσιν· ἐν δὲ καὶ ὄρνιθες καὶ εἵματα καὶ
χρύσεα καὶ ἀργύρεα ποιήματα. ἐπεὰν δὲ ἐντελέα
πάντα ποιήσωνται, περιενείκαντες τὰ ἱρὰ περὶ
τὰ δένδρεα πυρὴν ἐνιᾶσιν, τὰ δὲ αὐτίκα πάντα

---

¹ " The rite of descending to the water (κατάβασις, Semitic
yerid) was common all over Syria. . . . Its purpose was to
revive the water-sources and bring rain " (Dussaud, Pauly-
Wissowa s.v. Hadad). Why the fish should need protection

seen hem, but sche, stondynge beforn him, letteth him, and with manye supplicatiouns sendeth him his weye.[1]

Wondur grete ben also the festes that thei ben wont to make in goynge to the see. Of tho festes ne can I not seye no thing certeyn, be cause that I ne wente not myself ne assayde not that pilgrimage. But what thei don whan thei retornen, that I saughe and schalle devyse you. Thei beren everychon a pot fulle of water, and thise pottes ben seeled with waxe. And of hem self thei ne breke not the seel for to schede it out; but ther is a holy Cokke,[2] that woneth nyghe to the lak, that whan *dwells* he resceyveth the vesseles he loketh to the seel, and getteth him a fee for to undon the bond and remeve the waxe; and the Cokke gadereth moche silver thorghe this werk. And fro thens thei hem self bryngen it in to the temple, and scheden it out; and after this thei perfourmen sacrifise, and than thei wenden hoom ayen.

But the grettest of alle festes wherof I knowe is kepte in the firste somer sesoun, and some men clepen it Fuyr Feste and some Torche Feste. Ther inne thei don sacrifise in this wyse. Thei kutten grete trees and setten hem in the clos, and after, brynginge gotes and schepe and othere bestes, thei hangen hem fro the trees, alle on lyve, and eke briddes and clothes and ioyelles of gold and of silver. *birds* And whan thei han mad everyche thing complet and perfyt, thei beren the ydoles aboute the trees, and thanne thei casten inne fuyr and als swythe alle tho *instant'y*

from Hadad is a mystery to me, unless here too Hadad had begun to be identified with the sun.

[2] Not, according to Dussaud, a Gallus, but an overseer.

καίονται. ἐς ταύτην τὴν ὁρτὴν πολλοὶ ἄνθρωποι
ἀπικνέονται ἔκ τε Συρίης καὶ τῶν πέριξ χωρέων
πασέων, φέρουσίν τε τὰ ἑωυτῶν ἱρὰ ἕκαστοι καὶ
τὰ σημήια ἕκαστοι ἔχουσιν ἐς τάδε μεμιμημένα.

50 Ἐν ῥητῇσι δὲ ἡμέρῃσι τὸ μὲν πλῆθος ἐς τὸ
ἱρὸν ἀγείρονται, Γάλλοι δὲ πολλοὶ καὶ τοὺς
ἔλεξα, οἱ ἱροὶ ἄνθρωποι, τελέουσι τὰ ὄργια, τάμ-
νονταί τε τοὺς πήχεας καὶ τοῖσι νώτοισι πρὸς
ἀλλήλους τύπτονται. πολλοὶ δὲ σφίσι παρεστεῶτες ἐπαυλέουσι, πολλοὶ δὲ τύμπανα πατα-
γέουσιν, ἄλλοι δὲ ἀείδουσιν ἔνθεα καὶ ἱρὰ ᾄσματα.
τὸ δὲ ἔργον ἐκτὸς τοῦ νηοῦ τόδε γίγνεται, οὐδὲ
ἐσέρχονται ἐς τὸν νηὸν ὁκόσοι τόδε ποιέουσιν.

51 Ἐν ταύτῃσι τῇσι ἡμέρῃσι καὶ Γάλλοι γίγνονται. ἐπεὰν γὰρ οἱ ἄλλοι αὐλέωσί τε καὶ
ὄργια[1] ποιέωνται, ἐς πολλοὺς ἤδη ἡ μανίη
ἀπικνέεται, καὶ πολλοὶ ἐς θέην ἀπικόμενοι μετὰ
δὲ τοιάδε ἔπρηξαν. καταλέξω δὲ καὶ τὰ ποιέουσιν. ὁ νεηνίης ὅτῳ τάδε ἀποκέαται ῥίψας τὰ
εἵματα μεγάλη βοῇ ἐς μέσον ἔρχεται καὶ ξίφος
ἀναιρέεται· τὸ[2] δὲ πολλὰ ἔτη, ἐμοὶ δοκέει, καὶ
τοῦτο ἕστηκε. λαβὼν δὲ αὐτίκα τάμνει ἑωυτὸν
θέει τε διὰ τῆς πόλιος καὶ τῇσι χερσὶ φέρει τὰ
ἔταμεν. ἐς ὁκοίην δὲ οἰκίην τάδε ἀπορρίψει, ἐκ

[1] ὄργια du Soul : ὄρκια MSS.
[2] τὸ A.M.H.: τὰ MSS.

---

[1] Baudissin (176, 3) knows no closer parallel than the
Continental *Mai-feste*, and thinks that, if the Syrian custom
came down from the North, a community of origin is possible.
Somewhat similar is the practice at Tarsos of erecting a
pyre, setting on it an image of the god Sandan, and then
burning it up. Frazer (i, 126, 146) associates the two
customs and ascribes their origin to the immolation of a

thinges brennen.[1]   To this feste comen manye bothe
fro Surrye and from alle the marches there aboute ;
and alle bryngen here owne holy thinges and han
alle here Tokenes made in lyknesse of that on.

And upon sette dayes the multytude assemblen
hem in the clos, and manye Galles and tho religious
men that I spak of perfourmen here cerimonyes ;
and thei kutten here owne armes and beten that oon
that other upon the bak.[2]   And manye that stont
ther neer floyten, and manye beten timbres, and
othere syngen wode songes and holy.   This is don
withouten the temple, and thei that don it comen
not in to the temple.

And in thise dayes Galles ben made.   For whan
tho floyten and perfourmen here rytes, that folye
sone entreth into manye, and manye ther ben that
camen for to seen and thanne wroghten in thilke
manere.   And I shal descryve what thei don.   The
yong man to whom Fortune hath goven this adversitee, he casteth offe his clothinge and cometh in to
the myddes, cryinge in a grete voyce, and taketh
up a swerd that hath stode there thise manye
yeeres, I wene.   Thanne he geldeth him right anon
and renneth throghe the Cytee berynge in his
hondes tho parties therof he gelt him.   And that
house into the whiche he schalle casten thise, he

human victim, the priest-king. For myself, I should like
to know what became of the tree in the Attis-cult, that was
cut down and brought into the temple, that the image of
Attis might be tied to it (Frazer, i, 267). In the Gilgamesh
Epic, Humbaba is posted by Bel as *watcher of the cedars*
(Schrader-Zimmern, 570) ; and sacred trees still have offerings
hung on them (Robertson Smith, *Rel. of the Semites*, pp.
185–6).

[2] See 1 Kings, 18, 26–28.

ταύτης ἐσθῆτά τε θηλέην καὶ κόσμον τὸν γυναι-
κήιον λαμβάνει. τάδε μὲν ἐν τῇσι τομῇσι ποιέουσιν.

52 Ἀποθανόντες δὲ Γάλλοι οὐκ ὁμοίην ταφὴν
τοῖσιν ἄλλοισι θάπτονται, ἀλλ' ἐὰν ἀποθάνῃ
Γάλλος, ἑταῖροί μιν ἀείραντες ἐς τὰ προάστεια
φέρουσιν, θέμενοι δὲ αὐτὸν καὶ τὸ φέρτρον τῷ
ἐκόμισαν, ὕπερθε λίθοις βάλλουσιν, καὶ τάδε
πρήξαντες ὀπίσω ἀπονοστέουσιν. φυλάξαντες
δὲ ἑπτὰ ἡμερέων ἀριθμὸν οὕτως ἐς τὸ ἱρὸν
ἐσέρχονται· πρὸ δὲ τουτέων ἢν ἐσέλθωσιν, οὐκ
53 ὅσια ποιέουσιν. νόμοισι δὲ ἐς ταῦτα χρέωνται
τουτέοισι. ἢν μέν τις αὐτέων νέκυν ἴδηται,
ἐκείνην τὴν ἡμέρην ἐς τὸ ἱρὸν οὐκ ἀπικνέεται, τῇ
ἑτέρῃ δὲ καθήρας ἑωυτὸν ἐσέρχεται. αὐτῶν δὲ
τῶν οἰκείων τοῦ νέκυος ἕκαστοι φυλάξαντες
ἀριθμὸν ἡμερέων τριήκοντα καὶ τὰς κεφαλὰς
ξυράμενοι ἐσέρχονται· πρὶν δὲ τάδε ποιῆσαι, οὐ
σφίσι ἐσιέναι ὅσιον.

54 Θύουσιν δὲ βόας ἄρσενάς τε καὶ θήλεας καὶ
αἶγας καὶ ὄϊας. σύας δὲ μοῦνον ἐναγέας νομί-
ζοντες οὔτε θύουσιν οὔτε σιτέονται. ἄλλοι δ'
οὐ σφέας ἐναγέας, ἀλλὰ ἱροὺς νομίζουσιν. ὀρνί-
θων τε αὐτέοισι περιστερὴ δοκέει χρῆμα ἱρότατον

---

[1] Compare Joshua 8, 29, and for the modern practice,
Baldensperger, 16, 1. Perhaps originally the Gallus was
stoned to death at the expiration of a certain time.

[2] On the pollution of death, see Leviticus 21, 1–3 ; Ezekiel
44, 25. Cf. Frazer, ii, 227 *sqq.* On shaving the head, Levit.
21, 5 ; Ezekiel 44, 20.

[3] Elagabalus, by way of *sportula*, gave away all manner
of animals except pigs ; "for he abstained from them by the
law of the Phoenicians" (Herodian 5, 6, 9 ; cf. Dio Cassius

getteth thens femele wedes and wommanlyche aparayles. Thus don thei whan thei gelden hem.

And Galles at here dyenge ben not enterred in lyk manere as other men, but gif a Galle dye, his felawes liften him up and carryen him in to the skirtes of the Cytee and sette doun the man himself and the fertre on the whiche thei broghte him, and casten stones aboven;[1] and whan this is don, thei wenden hoom ayen. And thei wayten for the nombre of 7 dayes or that thei entren in to the temple; for if thei entren before, thei misdon. And the custmes that thei folwen therto ben thise. If so be that ony of hem seeth a dede man, he cometh not in to the temple that day; but on the nexte daye, aftre that he hath pured him, thanne he entreth. And tho that ben of the dede mannes kyn wayten for the space of 30 dayes and lette schaven here hedes or thei entren; but before that this hath ben don, it is not leful for to entren.[2]

Thei sacrificen boles and kyn and gotes and schepe. Swyn only thei ne sacrificen not nouther eten be cause that thei demen hem unclene.[3] But othere men demen hem not unclene but holy. And amonges briddes the dowve semeth hem wondur holy thing,

79, 11). Suidas *s.v.* Δομνῖνος alludes to the custom as Syrian, and Sophronius (Migne 87, 3, p. 3624) in the case of a girl from Damascus ascribes it to the worship of Adonis. See Baudissin, p. 142 *sqq.* "In Palestine and Syria the animal was used in certain exceptional sacrifices which were recognised as idolatrous (Isaiah 65, 4 ; 66, 17) and it was an open question whether it was really polluted or holy" (Cook, 48). There was similar uncertainty in Egypt; see Herodotus 2, 47, and Plutarch, *Isis and Osiris*, 8. Lucian is perhaps thinking of the pig as holy in connection with the Eleusinian mysteries, and Demeter worship generally. It was holy also in Crete, and apparently in Babylon (Ninib).

καὶ οὐδὲ ψαύειν αὐτέων δικαιέουσιν· καὶ ἢν
ἀέκοντες ἅψωνται, ἐναγέες ἐκείνην τὴν ἡμέρην
εἰσί. τούνεκα δὲ αὐτέοισι σύννομοί τέ εἰσι καὶ
ἐς τὰ οἰκεῖα ἐσέρχονται καὶ τὰ πολλὰ ἐν γῇ
νέμονται.

55 Λέξω δὲ καὶ τῶν πανηγυριστέων τὰ ἕκαστοι
ποιέουσιν. ἀνὴρ εὖτ᾽ ἂν ἐς τὴν ἱρὴν πόλιν πρῶτον
ἀπικνέηται,[1] κεφαλὴν μὲν ὅδε καὶ ὀφρύας ἐξύ-
ρατο, μετὰ δὲ ἱρεύσας ὄιν τὰ μὲν ἄλλα κρεουργέει
τε καὶ εὐωχέεται, τὸ δὲ νάκος χαμαὶ θέμενος ἐπὶ
τούτου ἐς γόνυ ἕζεται, πόδας δὲ καὶ κεφαλὴν
τοῦ κτήνεος ἐπὶ τὴν ἑωυτοῦ κεφαλὴν ἀναλαμβά-
νει· ἅμα δὲ εὐχόμενος αἰτέει τὴν μὲν παρεοῦσαν
θυσίην δέκεσθαι, μέζω δὲ ἐσαῦτις ὑπισχνέεται.
τελέσας δὲ ταῦτα, τὴν κεφαλὴν αὐτοῦ τε στέφεται
καὶ τῶν ἄλλων ὁκόσοι τὴν αὐτὴν ὁδὸν ἀπικνέονται,
ἄρας δὲ ἀπὸ τῆς ἑωυτοῦ ὁδοιπορέει, ὕδασί τε
ψυχροῖσι χρεόμενος λουτρῶν τε καὶ πόσιος
εἵνεκα καὶ ἐς πάμπαν χαμοκοιτέων· οὐ γάρ οἱ
εὐνῆς ἐπιβῆναι ὅσιον πρὶν τήν τε ὁδὸν ἐκτελέσαι
56 καὶ ἐς τὴν ἑωυτοῦ αὖτις ἀπικέσθαι. ἐν δὲ τῇ

---

[1] ἀπικνέηται Werfer : ἀπικνέεται MSS.

---

[1] "In Syria by the sea is a city named Ascalon. . . . I
saw there an impossible number of doves at the crossways
and about every house. When I asked the reason, they said
it was not permissible to catch them; for the inhabitants,
from a remote period, had been forbidden to enjoy them.
So tame is the creature through security that it always lives
not only under the same roof with man but at the same
table, and abuses its immunity" (Philo Judaeus, quoted by
Eusebius, *Praep. Evang.* 8, 14, 50). See Hehn, *Kulturpflanzen
und Haustiere,*⁶ p. 329 *sqq.* ; Baudissin, *Studien,* ii, p. 191.

[2] Shaving the head and brows was probably purificatory
in this connection. See Plutarch, *Isis and Osiris,* 4.

and thei ben not wont so moche as to touchen hem;
and gif thei touchen hem maugree hem selven, thei
ben unclene that day. Therfore dowves lyven
amonges hem and entren here houses and gadren
here mete for the moste part atte erthe.[1]

And I schal telle you what the pilgrimes alle don.
Whan that a man wole faren for the firste sythe to *time*
the Holy Cytee, he schaveth his heed and his browes,[2]
and after that, he sacrificeth a schep; and than he
kerveth it and eteth it alle, saf only the flees that
he leyeth on the erthe and kneleth ther on, and
taketh the bestes feet and heed and putteth upon
his owne heed. Ther with alle he preyeth, askynge
that this present sacrifise be resceyved and behotynge *promis-*
a grettere that nexte sythe.[3] And whan alle this is *ing*
atte ende, he putteth a gerlond on his owne heed
and on the hedes of his felawes that wolle gon that
ilke pilgrimage. Thanne levynge his owne contree
he doth iorney; and he useth cold watre bothe for
to wasschen with and to drynken, and slepeth
alle weyes on the erthe; for he ne may not liggen
in no maner bedde un to tyme that his pilgrimage
be fulfilled and he be comen ayen to his owne
contree.[4] And in the Holy Cytee he is resceyved

---

[3] By this procedure the worshipper seems clearly to
indicate that the sacrificed sheep is a substitute for himself;
it is so understood by Frazer, *Folklore,* i, 414, 425–428.
What the worshipper says and does is equivalent to: "Take
this poor offering in my stead, part for part; myself I will
offer next time." In Schrader-Zimmern, p. 597, a cuneiform
inscription is cited that concerns such a vicarious sacrifice:
"The lamb, the substitute for a man, the lamb he gives for
the man's life; the head of the lamb he gives for the head of
the man," etc. For another view, see Robertson Smith, *Rel.
of the Semites,* p. 438.

[4] Psalm 132, 3; cf. Robertson Smith, *Rel. of the Semites,*
481 *sqq.*

ἱρῇ πόλει ἐκδέκεταί μιν ἀνὴρ ξεινοδόκος ἀγ-
νοέοντα· ῥητοὶ γὰρ δὴ ὧν ἑκάστης πόλιος αὐτόθι
ξεινοδόκοι εἰσίν, καὶ τόδε πατρόθεν οἴκοι δέκονται.
καλέονται δὲ ὑπὸ Ἀσσυρίων οἵδε διδάσκαλοι,
ὅτι σφίσι πάντα ὑπηγέονται.

57 Θύουσι δὲ οὐκ ἐν αὐτῷ τῷ ἱρῷ, ἀλλ᾽ ἐπεὰν
παραστήσῃ τῷ βωμῷ τὸ ἱρήιον, ἐπισπείσας
αὖτις ἄγει ζωὸν ἐς τὰ οἰκεῖα, ἐλθὼν δὲ κατ᾽
ἑωυτὸν θύει τε καὶ εὔχεται.

58 Ἔστιν δὲ καὶ ἄλλης θυσίης τρόπος τοιόσδε.
στέψαντες τὰ ἱρήια, ζῷα ἐκ τῶν προπυλαίων
ἀπιᾶσιν, τὰ δὲ κατενεχθέντα θνήσκουσιν. ἔνιοι
δὲ καὶ παῖδας ἑωυτῶν ἐντεῦθεν ἀπιᾶσιν, οὐκ
ὁμοίως τοῖς κτήνεσιν, ἀλλ᾽ ἐς πήρην ἐνθέμενοι
χειρὶ κατάγουσιν, ἅμα δὲ αὐτέοισιν ἐπικερ-
τομέοντες λέγουσιν ὅτι οὐ παῖδες, ἀλλὰ βόες
εἰσίν.

59 Στίζονται δὲ πάντες, οἱ μὲν ἐς καρπούς, οἱ δὲ ἐς
αὐχένας· καὶ ἀπὸ τοῦδε ἅπαντες Ἀσσύριοι
στιγματηφορέουσιν.

---

[1] A relic of child-sacrifice. "Shall I give my first-born
for my transgression, the fruit of my body for the sin of my
soul?" (Micah 6, 7). On traces of infant sacrifice discovered
in the excavations in Palestine, see Cook, pp. 36, 38, 43 ;
Frazer, *Folklore* i, 418 and note. From recent excavations in
a sanctuary of Tanit at Carthage, it is apparent that first-
born children were offered to that goddess during the whole
period of Punic occupation (*Am. Journal of Archaeol.*, 1923,
p. 107). "Jephthah's daughter had many successors before
Hadrian tried to stamp out the practice. At Laodicea a
virgin was annually sacrificed to 'Athena' until a deer took
her place ; Elagabalus was accused of offering children in his
sun-temple at Rome ; . . . an Arabian tribe annually sacrificed a child, which they buried beneath the altar that served

of an hoste that he knoweth not propurly. For certeyne men in that place ben apoynted unto everyche cytee as hostes, and dyverse kynredes han this office of linage. And Assuryens clepen tho men Maistres be cause thei techen hem everyche thing.

And the sacrifises ben not perfourmed in the temple, but whan he hath presented his victime beforn the awtere, he schedeth offrynge of wyn there on, and thanne he ayen ledeth him on lyve to his logging, and whan he is comen there he sacrificeth and preyeth be him self.

Ther is also this other maner sacrifise. Thei dressen here victimes with gerlondes and hurlen hem doun the degrees of the entree on lyve, and in fallynge doun thei dyen. And some men hurlen here owne children thens, but not in lyke manere as the bestes. Thei putten hem in a walet and beren hem doun in hond, and thei scornen hem with alle, seyinge that thei ben not children but oxen.[1]

And alle leten marke hem, some on the wriste and some on the nekke; and for that skylle alle Assuryens beren markes.[2]

them as an idol. In many parts, too, bodies of slain victims were used for purposes of divination" (Bouchier, *Syria as a Roman Province*, p. 247 *sq.*).

[2] Lucian probably means tattooing, although actual branding was practised on occasion. "Some are afflicted with such an extravagancy of madness that, leaving themselves no room for a change of mind, they embrace slavery to the works of human hands, admitting it in writing, not upon sheets of papyrus as the custom is in the case of human chattels, but by branding it upon their bodies with a heated iron with a view to its indelible permanency ; for even time does not fade these letters" (Philo Judaeus, *de Monarchia* 1, 8 fin.). The view that this was the "mark of Cain" is

60 Ποιέουσι δὲ καὶ ἄλλο μούνοισι Ἑλλήνων
Τροιζηνίοισι ὁμολογέοντες. λέξω δὲ καὶ τὰ
ἐκεῖνοι ποιέουσιν. Τροιζήνιοι τῇσι παρθένοισι
καὶ τοῖσιν ἠιθέοισι νόμον ἐποιήσαντο μή μιν
ἄλλως γάμον ἰέναι, πρὶν Ἱππολύτῳ κόμας
κείρασθαι· καὶ ὧδε ποιέουσιν. τοῦτο καὶ ἐν τῇ
ἱρῇ πόλει γίγνεται. οἱ μὲν νεηνίαι τῶν γενείων
ἀπάρχονται, τοῖς δὲ νέοισι πλοκάμους ἱροὺς ἐκ
γενετῆς ἀπιᾶσιν, τοὺς ἐπεὰν ἐν τῷ ἱρῷ γένωνται,
τάμνουσίν τε καὶ ἐς ἄγγεα καταθέντες οἱ μὲν
ἀργύρεα, πολλοὶ δὲ χρύσεα ἐν τῷ νηῷ προση-
λώσαντες ἀπίασιν ἐπιγράψαντες ἕκαστοι τὰ
οὐνόματα. τοῦτο καὶ ἐγὼ νέος ἔτι ὢν ἐπετέλεσα,
καὶ ἔτι μευ ἐν τῷ ἱρῷ καὶ ὁ πλόκαμος καὶ τὸ
οὔνομα.

---

forever being advanced anew, only to be anew denied. The
practice was forbidden to the Jews (Levit. 19, 28, where
the Septuagint reads: καὶ γράμματα στικτὰ οὐ ποιήσετε ἐν
ὑμῖν). Among the Moslem population it still survives, but
apparently without any religious significance. "A Syrian
custom: the workers in tattoo are generally Syrian, and the
decoration is seen mainly in Syria and North Palestine";
(H. Rix, *Tent and Testament*, p. 103). In du Soul's time all
Christians who visited the Holy Land came back tattooed,
he tells us (Lucian, ed. Hemsterhuys-Reitz, iii, p. 489).

THE GODDESSE OF SURRYE

And thei don another thing, in the whiche thei
acorden to men of Trosen allone of Grekes, and I
schalle telle you what tho don. Men of Trosen han
made ordeynaunce as touchinge the maydens and
the bachelers, that thei schulle not maryen or thei
lette scheren here lokkes for worschipe of Ypolite;
and so thei don. That thing is don also in the
Holy Cytee. The bacheleres offren of here berdes,
and the children from here birthe leten holy crulles
growe, the which thei scheren whan thei ben presented in the temple and putten in boystes outher
of silver or often tymes of gold, that thei naylen
faste in the temple, and than gon here weye; but
first thei wryten there on here names everychon.
Whan I was yong, I fulfilled that ryte; and bothe
my crulle and my name ben yit in the seyntuarye.[1]

[1] For the custom at Troezen see Pausanias 2, 32, 1; but
he speaks only of girls. Its general prevalence is shown in
Frazer's note on that passage, in which the item of chief
interest in connection with Lucian is that in Caria, at the
temple of Zeus Panamaros, it was customary for a man to
dedicate a lock of hair in a stone receptacle on which was
carved his name and that of the priest or priestess in charge;
the receptacle was preserved in the temple.

INDEX

Abonoteichus, city on the coast of Paphlagonia, now Ineboli, 175, 187, 189, 217, 251

Abradatas, king of Susiana, contemporary with Cyrus the Great, according to Xenophon in the *Cyropaedia*, 275, 291

Achaeans, 129

Acheron, Lake, in Hades, 89, 115

Acherusian Plain, beside Acheron, 97

Achilles, 323, 331, 395

Acropolis, of Athens, 25, 265

Adonis, 343, 345, 347

Adonis River, in Phoenicia, 347

Aeacus, nephew of Pluto, son of Zeus and Europa, brother of Minos and Rhadamanthus, gate-keeper of Hades, 87, 103, 115, 123

Aegeus, king of Athens, father of Theseus, 117

Aegiali, village on the coast of Paphlagonia, about half-way between Abonoteichus and Amastris, 249

Aeginetan (obol), 119

Aeschines, Attic orator, opponent of Demosthenes, 149

Aeschines, the Socratic, 287

Aëtion, famous painter, 271

Agamemnon, 99, 101, 331

Agathon, Athenian tragedian, whose effeminate manners were ridiculed by Aristophanes in the *Thesmophoriazusae*, 149

Agenor, of Sidon, 341

Aglaïa (Aglaye), 395

Aïdoneus (Pluto), 89, 123

Alastores, *see* Avengers

Alcamenes, sculptor, 261, 263, 265, 267

Alcestis, wife of Admetus of Thessaly, who gave her life in exchange for his, and was brought back from Hades by Heracles, 117

Alcmene, mother of Heracles, 323

ALEXANDER, THE FALSE PROPHET, 173–253

Alexander of Abonoteichus, 175 *sqq.*

Alexander the Great, 139, 141, 149, 175, 185, 199, 305, 307, 395

Alexandria, 231

Alibantis, name of "tribe" in Hades, coined from *alibas*, corpse, 107

Amalthea, the goat that nursed Zeus, whose horn became the Horn of Plenty, 141

Amastris (*see* p. 210, *note* 1), 209, 211, 247, 249

Amazons, 55, 265, 267

Amphiaraus, of Argos, a seer, one of the Seven who led the Argives against Thebes, worshipped as a god after his translation at Oropus in Boeotia, where he gave oracles to those who slept in the temple, 201

Amphilochus, son of Amphiaraus, who also had an oracular shrine at Mallus in Cilicia, 201, 215

Amphion, who, with the aid of a lyre given him by Hermes, built the wall of Thebes by making the stones move of their own accord, 281

ANACHARSIS, OR ATHLETICS, 1–69

Anacharsis, the Scythian, visited Athens in quest of Greek learning and was introduced to Solon by his countryman Toxaris (Lucian, *Scytha*), 3 *sqq.*

Andromache, wife of Hector, 395

Anonymus (poet), 159, 325, (Pindar ?) 333, (Epicharmus) 143

Antenor, one of the elders of Troy, 289

Aornus, in India, 143 (*see note* 1)

Apelles, famous painter, contemporary of Alexander the Great, 261, 271, 295

413

INDEX

INDEX

INDEX

INDEX

Evagoras, king of Cyprus, *fl. ca.* 400 B.C., extolled in the *Evagoras* of Isocrates, 333

Fame personified, 141, 143
Fates (Moerae), 387
Fedre Cnossien, *see* Phaedra of Cnossus
Fortune, *see* Tyche and Nemesis
FUNERALS, ON, 111–131
Furies, *see* Erinyes

Galatia, 187, 199, 215, 231
Galli (Galles), emasculated devotees of Atargatis, 359, 371, 379, 397, 403, 405
Germany, 235
Glaucus of Carystus, victor in boxing at Olympia (*ca.* 520 B.C.), Delphi (twice), Nemea, and the Isthmus (eight times each), 321, 323
Glycera, a name commonly adopted by courtesans, borne by the mistress of Menander, and by the leading character in his *Perikeiromene*, 151
Glycon, 201, 225, 227, 229, 231, 247, 251, *cf.* 173
Gorgon (Medusa), 257, 281
Graces, the, 149, 179, 273, 333
Great Mother, the (Rhea-Cybele), 193
Greece, Greeks, 7, 17, 61, 63, 109, 127, 135, 323, 341, 351, 353, 359, 361, 373, 391, 411

Hades (Pluto), 73, 75, 87, 209, 221, (lower world) 113, 125, (ambiguous) 83
Hebrew, 193
Hecate, 89
Hector, 395
Hecuba, wife of Priam of Troy, 395
Hegesias, sculptor, 147
Helen of Troy, 293, 387, 395
Helicon, mountain of Boeotia, haunt of the Muses, 139, 285
Heliopolis, city in Lower Egypt, just N. of Cairo, 343
Helios, the sun, 389–391
Hellanodicae, the ten officials in charge of the Olympic games, 307
Hellespont, bridged, and so "crossed afoot," by Xerxes, 159
Hephaestion, as a man's name, 333
Hera, 271, 303, 305, 309, 311, 319,

333; (Atargatis), 339, 353, 355, 359, 361, 365, 369, °77, 385, 387, 395, 397, 399
Heraclea (Pontica), coastal city of Bithynia, 249
Heraclean stone (*i.e.* either from Heraclea, or of Heracles), the magnet, 258
Heracles, 87, 91, 97, 143, 179, 323, 341
Heraclids, name of a company of young men in Sparta, 63
Hermes, 117, 285 (a giver of eloquence), 393 (a Syrian god)
Hermes, as man's name, 333
Hermocles of Rhodes, sculptor, 377
Hesiod, 35, 79, 81, 113, 139, 143
Hieropolis, in Syria, 339, 349, 353, 355, 365, 369, 371, 373, 407, 411
Himera, city in Sicily near Termini, 313
Hippolyta, Queen of the Amazons, invaded Attica to punish Theseus for carrying off Antiope, 55
Hippolytus (*see* Phaedra), 373, 411
Homer, 35, 75, 79, 87, 97, 99, 113, 117, 129, 145, 151, 183, 219, 243, 249, 271, 273, 279, 283, 291, 295, 325, 329, 331, 333, 335
Hydra, 59
Hymettus, mountain E. of Athens, famous for honey, 149

Icarius, father of Penelope, 289
Icarus, nephew of Daedalus, who flew too high on his artificial wings, so that the sun melted the wax, 293
Ida, Mount, 177
India, Indian, 127, 159, 231, 237, 359, 387
Ionia, Ionian, 215, 259, 261, 287, 383
Ionopolis, later name of Abonoteichus, 251
Irus, 99
Isocrates, 157
Ister (Danube), 235, 237
Isthmian games, held every other year near the sanctuary of Poseidon, on the Isthmus of Corinth, 9, 13, 59
Isthmus (of Corinth), 13, 21
Italy, 215, 221, 223, 243
Ixion, punished in Hades for his endeavour to seduce Hera by being bound to a revolving wheel, 97

Jove, *see* Zeus (Hadad)
Juno, *see* Hera (Atargatis)

417

INDEX

INDEX

Olympias, wife of Philip of Macedon, and mother of Alexander the Great, 185

Olympic games, 9, 13, 59, 307

Orpheus, 87, 281

Osiris, 345

Osroes (Chosroes), Parthian general, 213

Othryades, a Spartan, who, left for dead on the field of Thyrea by two surviving Argives, erected a trophy and inscribed it in his own blood, 159

Otus, and Ephialtes, sons of Aloeus, nine years old, nine ells broad, and nine fathoms high, who tried to scale heaven and were slain by Apollo, 153

Pacate, 271

Paetus, physician, 253

Palamedes, Greek hero at Troy, famous for wisdom and inventions, unjustly put to death on a charge of treason, hence Socrates (*Apology*, 41 B) wished to compare experiences with him in Hades, 103

Panathenaea, festival held at Athens, the "Lesser" every year, the "Greater" every four years, 9, 13

Pandion, father of Philomela and Procne, legendary king of Athens, whose daughters were turned into the swallow and the nightingale, 281

Panthea, mistress of Verus, *see* p. 255

Panthea, wife of Abradatas (*see* p. 274, *note*), 275, 291

Paphlagonia, Paphlagonians, 187, 189, 191, 197, 199, 215, 227, 231, 233

Parcas (Moerae), the Fates, 387

Paris, 331, 395

Parrhasius, celebrated painter, rival of Zeuxis, 261, 295

Parthi, 213

Patroclus, 329

Peleus, father of Achilles, 221, 331

Pelias, usurping ruler of Iolcus, uncle of Jason, who was dismembered and boiled by his daughters at the suggestion of Medea in order to restore his youth, 301

Pella, city of Macedonia, which Philip made its capital instead of Aegae, 185, 193, 197

Penelope, wife of Odysseus, 289, 291, 303

Pericles, 287, *see* Olympian

Persephone, 89, 113, 117

Perseus, son of Danae, slayer of the Medusa, 189, 251

Persia, Persians, 127, 139, 141

Phaeacians, king of (Alcinous, in the *Odyssey*), 99

Phaedra, daughter of Minos, King of Crete, and wife of Theseus, who brought about the death of her stepson Hippolytus by falsely accusing him of attempting her honour, 373

Phaon, mythical boatman of Mytilene, who received youth and beauty from Aphrodite for carrying her across the water without pay, 299

Phidias, 261, 265, 267, 311, 329

Philip of Macedon, 103, 149, 175

Philomele, and Procne, daughters of Pandion, 281, 395; Philomele was ravished and maimed by Tereus of Thrace, husband of Procne, who in revenge slew Itys, her son and his. She was changed into a nightingale, Philomele into a swallow, and Tereus into a hoopoe.

Phineus, blind king of Salmydessus in Thrace, 325

Phobi, pluralization of the earlier Phobos, son of Ares, spirit of panic, 117

Phoebus (Apollo), 189, 223

Phoenicia, Phoenician, 193, 341, 343, 349, 355

Phrygian, 97, 105, 357, (Paris) 331

Phrynondas, "notorious among the Athenians for rascality, no less than Eurybatus" (Harpocration; *see* Suidas, and Blaydes on Aristoph. *Thesm.* 861), 179

Pindar, 271, 321, 325, 333

Plataea, battle of, 159

Plato, 145, 151, 157, 171, 209

Plenty, Horn of, *see* Amalthea

Pluto (*see* p. 115, *note*), 89, 113, 115, 117, 123, 127

Pnyx, where the Athenians assembled, on the slope of the hill adjoining the Areopagus, 25

Podaleirius, the Healer (*see* p. 190, *note*), 189, 191, 225, 251

419

INDEX

Poenae (Tormentors), personifications of retaliation in Hades, 89, 91, 117

Pollux, see p. 133

Polus of Sunium, son of Charicles, actor, 101

Polycrates of Samos, tyrant renowned for the brilliancy of his court, sixth century B.C., 99, 103

Polydamas, of Scotussa in Thessaly, Olympic victor in the pancratium, 408 B.C., renowned for feats such as killing a lion without arms, 321

Polydeuces (Pollux, Castor's twin), famous as a boxer before he achieved immortality, 323

Polygnotus of Thasos, 5th-century painter, active at Athens, 271, 295

Polymnia, Muse of Sacred Poetry, 285

Polystratus, interlocutor, 257 sqq., 299 sqq.

Pontus, Roman province on the Black Sea, E. of Bithynia, 189, 199, 209, 227, 233, 249

Poseidon, 331

Posidonius, man's name, 333

Potheinus, 331

Praxiteles, Attic sculptor, 4th century B.C., best known by his Cnidian Aphrodite (copy in Vatican) and his Hermes (original at Olympia), 263, 267, 269, 329

Priam, 101; son of (Paris), 331

Procne (see Pandion and Philomele), 281, 395

PROFESSOR OF PUBLIC SPEAKING, THE, 133-171

Protesilaus, of Thessaly, first of the Greeks to fall at Troy, who was allowed to revisit earth and see his bride Laodamia, 117

Protogenes, slave name, 239

Pylos, old man from, Nestor, 279

Pyriphlegethon, River of Burning Fire in Hades, 89, 115

Pyrrha, wife of Deucalion, 161

Pyrrhias, a cook, probably fictitious, 99

Pythagoras, 179, 181, 209, 219, 227

Pythian Apollo, 151

Pythian games, held at Delphi ("rocky Pytho") every four years, 9, 59

Quadi, a German people, 235

Rhadamanthus, son of Zeus and Europa, brother of Minos and Aeacus, viceroy of Hades, 77, 89, 107, 117

Rhetoric personified, 131-171, esp. 141 sqq.

Rhodian, 377

Rome, Roman, Roman Empire, 177, 191, 213, 215, 217, 223, 237, 287

Roxana, daughter of a Bactrian chief, wife of Alexander, 271

Rutilia, wife of an Imperial steward, 225

Rutilianus, prominent Roman, commemorated in two inscriptions (C.I.L. xiv, 3601, 4244; see note, p. 214), 179, 215, 217, 219, 221, 225, 235, 245, 247, 249, 251, 253

Sacerdos, of Tius, otherwise unknown, 229, 231

Salamis, 159

Samothracians, 357

Sappho, 289

Sardanapalus, Assurbanipal, King of Assyria, 7th century B.C., to the Greeks a byword for luxury and effeminacy, 103, 149, 395

Satyrus, of Marathon, son of Theogiton, actor, 101

Scythia, Scythian, 7, 13, 17, 25, 69, 127, 241, 351

Selene, 221, 225, 341, 387

Seleucus, 303, 361-373

Semeion (see p. 388, note 2), 389, 393, 403

Semele, daughter of Cadmus, mother, by Zeus, of Dionysus, 359

Semiramis (see p. 354, note 1), 355, 357, 389, 395

Severianus, 213

Sibyl, 191

Sicily, 95

Sicyonian, 155

Sidon, Sidonian, 139, 341, 343

Simonides, 323

Sinope, 191

Sipylus, Mount, near Magnesia on the Maeander, 257

Sirens, 283

Sisyphus, who, for telling Asopus, father of Aegina, that her abductor was Zeus, was compelled in Hades to roll uphill a huge stone which kept rolling down again, 97

420

INDEX

Skeletion, 107

Smyrna, 259, 261

Socrates, 103, 151, 287, 289

Solon, as an interlocutor in the *Anacharsis*, 1–69

Sosandra, statue by Calamis, 265, 267, 269

Sostratus, possibly the effeminate Athenian whom Aristophanes dubs Sostrate, 179

Sparta, Spartan, 63, 65, 67

Steneboye (Stheneboea), of Tiryns, who falsely accused Bellerophon to her husband Proetus of attempting her honour, 373

Stentor, a Greek at Troy " who used to shout as loud as fifty men " (*Iliad*, 5, 783), 121

Stesichorus of Himera, lyric poet, 313

Stratonice, wife of Seleucus Nicator, 303, 361–373, 395

Sunium, an Attic deme on the promontory of that name, 101

SURRYE, THE GODDESSE OF, 337–411

Syria, Syrian (*see also* Assyrian), 241, 339, 341, 349, 353, 357, 359, 381, 395, 403

Tantalus, father of Niobe, 97, 117, 257

Tarentine, 155

Teiresias, Theban prophet, consulted in Hades by Odysseus in Homer and by Menippus in Lucian, 75, 85, 107

Tereus (*see* Philomele), 395

Terpsichore, Muse of choral dance and song, 283

Terrors, *see* Phobi

Thais, not the historical courtesan, but " Thais pretiosa Menandri," a character created by Menander in his lost comedy *Thais*, 151

Theano, wife of Antenor of Troy, 289, 303 (?)

Theano, the Pythagorean, 289, 303 (?)

Theban, 75, (Theban poet, Pindar) 271; Thebes, 201

Theogiton, father of the actor Satyrus, 101

Thersites, ugliest of the Greeks at Troy, 99, 323

Theseus, went to Hades to help Peirithous to carry off Persephone,

was imprisoned there, and at last brought back by Heracles, 117

Thessaly, 117

Thmuis, town in Egypt, 167

Thon, king in Egypt, 183

Thrace, Thracians, 55, 187, 199, 281

Thucydides, 185

Tiber, 213

Tigris, 85

Tillorobus, 177

Timocrates of Heraclea, philosopher, otherwise unknown, 249

Tisiphone, one of the Erinyes, or Furies, 127

Tityus, 97 (*see note*), 153

Tius, coastal city of Bithynia, 229

Token, *see* Semeion

Tormentors, *see* Poenae

Tricca, town in Thessaly, 191

Trophonius, legendary builder, with Agamedes, of early temple at Delphi, worshipped as a hero at Lebadeia in Boeotia, in a cave deemed to be an entrance to Hades and much visited by seekers after oracles, 109

Trosen (Troezen), birthplace of Theseus, city near S. shore of Saronic Gulf, approximately opposite Athens, 411

Troy, 161, 323

Twin Brethren, the Dioscuri, Castor and Pollux, 179

Tyana, city in Cappadocia, near the Cilician Gates, 183

Tyre, 341

Venus, *see* Aphrodite

Verus, Lucius, Emperor, 161–169 A.D., (255), 275, 293, 295

Wealth personified, 141, 143

Xenophon, of Athens, 275

Xenophon, unknown companion of Lucian, 247

Xerxes, 103, (his flight from Greece after Salamis) 159

Xoïs, town in Egypt, 167

Ynde, *see* India

Ypolite (Hippolytus, *see* Phaedra) 373

Zeno, man's name, 333

421

INDEX